Marion Nelson
118 Falcon St
Freeneburg NJ

Other novels by Eugenia Price

LIGHTHOUSE

NEW MOON RISING

BELOVED INVADER

DON JUAN MCQUEEN

MARIA

MARGARET'S STORY

SAVANNAH

TO SEE YOUR FACE AGAIN

Eugenia Price

BEFORE THE DARKNESS FALLS

The third volume in
the bestselling Savannah Quartet

Doubleday New York
1987

Library of Congress Cataloging-in-Publication Data

Price, Eugenia.
Before the darkness falls.

"The third volume in the best selling Savannah quartet."
I. Title.
PS3566.R47B3 1987 813'.54 87-556
ISBN 0-385-23068-0

FOR BARBARA BENNETT

PART I

April 1842-Autumn 1843

Chapter 1

Branches barely clouded with late April green, the sourwood, beech, maple and oak trees across her upcountry valley seemed to Natalie to be arranging the lavender morning around their trunks as though they had fingers and could lift mist and drape it to their liking.

Natalie's own body, slender and lithe the first time she stood in this enchanted spot behind her cabin home nearly three years ago, today leaned heavily against the old pignut hickory which stood guard over her iron soap kettle. She'd managed late yesterday to finish making the soap, in spite of a strange, dizzying weakness; in spite of the added weight within her, the oddly quiet, still weight of the child she would give to Burke in a little over six weeks.

Today, she meant to fill and store her cleaned, dried gourds with the lovely soap—gourds she'd proudly grown herself from seed. She loved living in this exact spot in the Georgia upcountry, beside the winding Etowah River. There was new life within her and her own life became new each time the sun rose from behind the nearest mountain. Every single thing she'd done in the years before she began to love Burke Latimer now seemed frivolous and without meaning. How had she endured the boredom of her girlhood years without hard work to do? One of her happiest memories from last fall was the evening spent with Burke scraping and cleaning the green-and-yellow-striped gourds. How they'd laughed and how proud he was of those gourds. He'd be proud of the new soap too. She could count on that.

"Burke," she breathed, and felt comforted by speaking his name into the early-morning chill of their own backyard. Burke, her heart cried, you should be close by me now . . . but it's all right that you're not here. I always mean it when I tell you that. Day after tomorrow you will be here and Indian Mary will be back sleeping in her own cabin with her moon-eyed brother, Ben. I don't really need Mary to stay with me anyway. I agreed just to humor you, Burke. You can't help it because the church you and Ben are building is too far away for you to ride home at night. I'd be fine in our cabin alone. I'd be a lot better, in fact, than having Mary tipping around being so kind she gives me the creeps!

Natalie shivered in the crisp, new day, but found the lightly greening hills in the distance so familiar and safe—so hers and Burke's—that she couldn't bring herself to go inside.

The low, cloud-strewn sky moved above her in a way she'd learned meant rain. She'd never noticed sky signs back in Savannah, where her family still lived—dear, worrywart Papa and Mama and her brother, Jonathan. On a deep sigh, she felt momentary pity for all three, having to suffer through the heat-choked, wet coastal summers, the snowless winters and quick, hot springs. Savannah's seasons didn't even know one another apart! Upcountry seasons knew. The high branches of the hickory against which she leaned, the masses of tall trees that covered the circling hills recognized themselves because they could feel each weather change suddenly and sharply. Burke laughed at her for thinking that trees felt snow in winter and warm sun in April, but he really believed it too.

I know him, she thought. I know how to make him laugh and exactly what will force him to grab me in those hard arms and groan because even he can't think of a new, better way to—love me. I can also tell when he's edging toward being like Papa, a worrywart. She frowned. And that's when I have to be awfully smart. I always know how to handle Papa because he only looks hurt and frets. Burke doesn't fret. He scowls. He orders. She laid both hands across her distended body, feeling, as she'd done for weeks now, for a tiny kick, a response to her touch. A response from Little Burke, as she'd begun to call the baby for whom they both waited, their love mounting, straining toward the proud day when she could give the child to Burke. "Kick," she commanded the weight inside her. "How is it you're so quiet this morning? You were quiet yesterday too—and all last night."

"He rest," Indian Mary had said as she spread an extra comforter over Natalie at bedtime. "The baby, he need to rest some. He has a big battle up ahead—getting born."

Seeing that there could be rain today, Natalie was reminded that she'd better cover the beautiful soap lying thick and amber in its iron kettle, like apple jelly. Mary had kept the fire burning under the kettle during the long hours Natalie had stood stirring the mixture yesterday, back aching, shoulders stiff, arms stubborn. But no one else was going to stir *her* soap! And as though some inner voice had urged her to make it during this full moon and not next month, Natalie had somehow managed to stand and stir until Mary finally said, "Now, lift the stick. See? It flake off—just right! You make the most beautiful kettle of soap ever made."

Smiling to herself now, proud, because, after all, Indian Mary knew all about making soap, she moved heavily over to Burke's new toolhouse and dragged out the canvas cover for the pot. No rainwater is going to spoil my perfect soap, she thought, and struggled to pull the cover into place.

Feeling nausea and more dizziness, she peered at the path to her cabin. It was suddenly endless, but she steeled herself for the effort of the walk which usually seemed so short. Partway along the pine-straw path, she remembered with sudden painful clarity how she had forced herself to stay awake, to stay conscious time and time again during the nightmare five days and nights she and Burke had spent on their makeshift raft in the Atlantic Ocean. Burke had rescued her from the ghastly wreck of the steam packet *Pulaski,* now nearly four years ago. Ever since then, steeling herself for anything had never been all bad. Even suffering had turned to near-ecstasy during those five days because Burke had been there with her.

"You afraid of pain at childbirth, Miss Natalie?" Mary sometimes asked.

"Never! Not with Burke beside me." And not once had she been able to resist reminding Indian Mary that Burke Latimer belonged to *her.* Not Mary. "You'll find another man to love, Mary. Just wait patiently."

Each time Mary would smile and say, "I wait. But if I find no one, I go on loving good Mister Burke by helping you." And each time Natalie bit her tongue to keep from saying, "Well, don't bother!"

Any minute, Mary would be running back across the field this side of the old Indian cabin she shared on weekends with her brother, Ben. Mary would be running, as she always ran, to "love Mister Burke by helping" her. She and Mary had used the last of Mary's wild blackberry preserves at breakfast yesterday. While biscuits baked now on the open hearth in Natalie's cabin, Mary had hurried for more preserves, ordering Natalie to stay in bed.

"Foot," Natalie said aloud as she fought her way along the path, fought hard because Burke had cleared away the scrub trees and there was nothing to hold on to for a hundred yards or so. "Foot," she repeated. "No one orders me around but Burke."

"Foot" was her mother's favorite word. Poor Mama, poor Papa, she thought as she reached her porch at last and shuffled inside. I can just feel them both trying to restrain their real feelings when they write to me. They're worried sick just because I'm going to have a baby. But what else could I expect? As elegant and upper-class and *Browning* as they both are, they're just plain silly, even ignorant, where I'm concerned.

Inside the cabin, she sank awkwardly into the rocking chair Ben had made just for her. How Indian Ben bored her! Mama worries that he might be dangerous simply because he allowed himself to fall in love with me. "Foot," she said aloud again. "He's perfectly harmless. Burke and I know how to handle Ben. Burke needs him at work and I intend to go right on ignoring him."

Having a baby is a terribly uncomfortable, peculiar ordeal, she thought, but at least I did the right thing to convince Miss Lib Stiles to do all the writing back to Savannah. I certainly wasn't going to put myself through that too. Miss Lib's mother can handle Papa and Mama. They're both very dear, but oh, so—helpless! I hope they don't decide to visit us anytime soon. They'd be lost on the frontier and I'd just have to use energy I don't have now to keep them calm and occupied.

Chapter 2

BRACING herself against one upholstered side of Mark Browning's normally comfortable carriage, Eliza Mackay held on to Mark's arm for dear life. Jupiter Taylor, the Brownings' free man of color, was driving the blooded team as carefully as horses could be driven in such a downpour of rain, but she sensed Mark's anxiety for their safety even before he cautioned Jupiter for the third time to watch out for those deep, muddy ruts in the street.

"I'm doin' the best I can, sir," Jupiter shouted from his high, exposed seat up front. "Trouble is, they's so much water, I can't see the holes till we pitch into 'em!"

If her daily visit to the grieving young widow Sarah Gordon had not seemed so necessary today, Eliza certainly would not have permitted Mark to come for her in such weather. But here they were, lurching along from her house on East Broughton to the Gordon mansion at the corner of Bull Street and South Broad because young Sarah Gordon had come to depend upon her. Mark had helped overrule both her daughters, Kate and Sarah, who begged them not to go—at least until the rain stopped. "Being almost sixty-four is making you more stubborn than ever, Mama," Sarah had snapped, but Kate, the conciliator, had finally agreed.

"We can't know, sister, how poor Mrs. Gordon feels," Kate had argued. "We've never been married. Mama remembers how she felt when Papa died up in New York. Even if it was way back when William and Jack were so young—just starting school up there. You remember like it was yesterday, don't you, Mama?"

Indeed Eliza Mackay did remember. She had felt lost and young at thirty-eight. At thirty-six, Sarah Gordon, this morning of all times, must be feeling utterly hopeless. She had lost her William one month ago to the day. The carriage was rocking a bit less now, bumping a bit less. She relaxed her grip on Mark's arm and patted it briefly. Mark remembered Eliza's grief of so long ago too. He remembered his own. He'd been with her Robert on that trip North to put the boys in school. For nearly thirty long years she and Mark had been close, easy friends. She loved him as she loved her own sons, William and Jack. She cared deeply for his lovely wife, Caroline, too, and for their son, Jonathan, and their startlingly beautiful daughter, Natalie. Natalie, actually living now on the north Georgia frontier in a log cabin on land purchased from Eliza Mackay's own son-in-law, William Henry Stiles. It had been far from easy to see her daughter Eliza Anne move away from Savannah with her husband and three children to the primitive Cass County upcountry, but independent as Eliza Anne had always been, she was not pampered and indulged as Mark had indulged his remarkable Natalie. A spoiled child in all ways, but remarkable because the morning after her wedding night, Natalie had faithfully kept her promise to her parents. The child had recognized her helplessness to keep house on the frontier and after that one precious night with her adored Burke Latimer, had left him to return to Savannah in order to learn how. The hastily arranged wedding had taken place in tiny Cassville nearly three years ago, but Savannah tongues still wagged that the only daughter of Savannah's rich and prominent Mark Browning was actually cooking and sewing and washing clothes and scrubbing floors in an abandoned Cherokee cabin on the Etowah River. And today, haunting her poor father, Eliza knew, was the still unbelievable fact that in a few weeks Natalie would be giving birth to her first child.

Jerked from her thoughts when one set of carriage wheels slammed into a deep rut, Eliza escaped being thrown to the floor only because Mark grabbed her.

"Oh, Miss Eliza," he gasped. "Are you hurt?"

"No, no, no." She tried to laugh. "I know I'll be sixty-four on Saturday, but I don't feel sixty-four. And I don't break. Oh, Mark, I'm so sorry to be such a nuisance. You have enough on your mind these days without having to transport an old woman through the rain. No, I take that back. I'm shaken up, but I don't feel *old*. Dear boy, what about you?"

He smiled down at her. "I'm all right."

She studied the lean, taut, still handsome face and thought Mark seemed almost withdrawn this morning, even from her. Oh, he was attentive, careful of her every need, but worried half sick, she knew, over Natalie. I could shake her for neglecting her parents as she does. That girl knows perfectly well that her father, especially, suffers over her. Oh, Mark doesn't love her any more than he loves his son, Jonathan, but Jonathan's a helper. A peace-maker by his very nature. Natalie, attractive and spirited as she is, makes *unpeace*, even in what everyone is calling her new maturity. Not that she means to, but she *is* Natalie and I don't care if she did learn how to handle life on the frontier without a single servant, just by being Natalie, by not writing, she keeps her father in turmoil. She sighed heavily.

"That was an enormous sigh," Mark said, smiling again.

"It was?"

"I'm sure you dread this visit to Mrs. Gordon."

On a deeper sigh, she said, almost to herself, "I do, but Sarah will need me today, inadequate as I feel. I can't imagine what I'll say to her, but I'll be there, thanks to your kindness. Oh, Mark, you're still my 'dear boy' in spite of our advanced ages."

"Will you go on calling me 'dear boy' next year when I'm fifty?"

"You'll be my 'dear boy' long after I'm gone."

His deep-set gray eyes clouded. "Don't even mention such a thing again! I couldn't face waking up one single morning without you in my life."

She patted his knee. "Caroline said something like that to me the other day, but refusing to face a thing never does away with it. Today, I feel just fine. Although not up to comforting Sarah Gordon. Only God can do that anyway, but He can." They jostled and lurched through the rutted, puddled street in silence for a time, then she said, "Mark, God is enough for you too while we wait for Natalie's baby to come. Don't keep it all to yourself. I'm living through every uneasy minute with both you and Caroline."

"As usual, Caroline's far steadier than I about Natalie. I try not to show how worried I am, but I don't fool my wife." His short laugh held no humor. "I'm sure I don't fool my business associates or our friends. Other merchants congratulate me on becoming a grandfather, slap me on the back—I just swallow hard and—"

"Mark, listen to me. We don't actually know that anything is wrong at all! Eliza Anne and W.H. live almost within earshot of Natalie's cabin. W.H. was here in Savannah only a month ago. He thought she was doing fine. My daughter would tell us if the girl wasn't all right. You simply have to remember that even when she was away at school at the North, Natalie didn't write to you and Caroline as she should have. You also need to remember that Natalie works hard now. You've never been around any women but those in your own class. Some of them work, yes, but not all day at scrubbing and cleaning and cooking, as Natalie does now."

"I know, and I'm proud of her, but— Miss Eliza, you do think Eliza Anne would tell us if Natalie isn't doing well, don't you?"

"She wrote last month that your daughter is so beautiful now that she's going to give her beloved Burke a child—is glowing so—she dazzles the eyes."

"But we've had two letters since without a word of Natalie's actual condition."

"Eliza Anne has a busy life up there too, even with three house servants. And obviously, Natalie has persuaded her to do all the correspondence."

Mark laughed a little. "Caroline and I certainly know about our daughter's persuasive power. Three years ago up in Cassville she turned us both around in less than ten minutes when she made up her mind to marry Burke before we all came back to Savannah. Your son William and Eliza Anne helped save the day. I was dumbfounded—still am—that quiet William managed to persuade Caroline, especially, that Natalie should get married in that plain little Cassville chapel. For years, Caroline had dreamed of Natalie's storybook wedding right here at Christ Church."

"You hadn't dreamed of a fashionable wedding for her, Mark?"

"I guess I dreaded losing her so much I hadn't given a wedding any thought." He turned to look at her. "Oh, Miss Eliza, the whole idea of Natalie in the throes of—giving birth—is more than I'm man enough to face. I'm ashamed of myself, but I can't seem to face it."

For a time, Eliza said nothing. Finally, holding his hand tightly, she said, "You still haven't faced what she went through with her young man out there in the Atlantic Ocean after the *Pulaski* blew up, have you? You need to remember how she conducted herself on that raft with Burke for five whole days and nights. Your lovely daughter is tough. Giving birth isn't easy for a woman, but it's natural. Natalie will be fine. She's proven herself to be a survivor." When he didn't respond, she asked, "Have you really let your daughter go?"

Instead of answering directly as he usually did, he asked, searching her eyes, "Miss Eliza, am I wrong to feel that Eliza Anne's letters are somehow— too cheerful? That for love of us all, she might be trying to—"

"To fool us, dear boy?"

After a moment, he said slowly, "No. Eliza Anne wouldn't do that—unless she thought, for some reason, it was the right thing. It's just that at times your kind, intelligent daughter has—well, has tended to take things into her own hands . . . always for what she feels are good reasons."

Eliza smiled. "You know her pretty well, don't you? And you're right. She has always held the reins a bit tightly, though, as you say, with the best motives. She's just so perceptive and so often correct it's hard now and then for her to realize when she's overstepping. I understand your question. But no. Eliza Anne has just been a bit sketchy in her letters. She's right there with Natalie. She knows the girl's all right, so lately she's written mostly about her husband's political duties, about how much she and W.H. like the first four-roomed wing of their house Burke built and how successful Burke's future looks up there. Maybe it isn't terribly important to you and Caroline that Burke's now building the new Presbyterian church near Mr. Arnold Milner's place, but—"

"Oh, it is important to us! I'm downright fond of Burke, proud of him. But the church he's working on is too far away for him to ride home at night. Natalie's alone in that cabin except for little Cherokee Mary McDonald. What could Mary do to help if—"

"Wait just a minute, Mark," she interrupted. "Mary's a native of the up-country. I'd say she'd be able to do far more than Eliza Anne if Natalie needed help."

"You may be right. It's just that if I don't find out firsthand exactly how Natalie is, I—I feel I'll smother."

Jupiter had managed to get them safely along Bull Street when, less than a block from the Gordon house, rounding Wright Square, the carriage jerked abruptly to the left—this time knocking Mark's head against the roof. "Jupiter, watch out!" he shouted.

"He's headin' right for us!" Jupiter cried. "Hold on!"

Out of the pouring rain, Eliza could make out an empty wagon careening toward them, hogging their side of the deeply mired street. When it struck the carriage a sharp, glancing blow she was thrown all the way to the floor and lay there stunned, unable even to answer Mark's questions, too startled to move as he tried to lift her. She could see nothing that was happening outside and all she seemed able to hear were a man's crude, furious, abusive shouts and the rattle of harness as Mark's frightened horses bucked and reared.

"Mark," she gasped, "what on earth? I'm all right. Just get me up where I can see something! Who hit us?"

"I can't tell," Mark said, easing her back onto the carriage seat. "I just know his wagon turned over. Are you sure you're all right?" he demanded, seeming to ignore the wildly angry, still swearing man who, Eliza could now see, was crawling from under the tilted wagon. On his feet, he kicked his fallen, struggling horse, then headed straight for poor Jupiter, still glued to his high driver's perch.

"Get out, Mark, and help Jupiter," Eliza ordered. "Whoever it is, is going after Jupiter!"

"It's you I'm worried about," Mark said.

"Don't mind me! But do be careful. That cursing man out there is Obijah Biddle!"

"Dear Lord" Mark gasped. "It is? For sure, he'll take it all out on Jupiter."

"Of course he will. Bije hates poor Jupiter because he's free."

Even in the downpour, a handful of men were collecting in the street. Eliza shuddered at the sight of Bije Biddle, a trickle of blood running down his unshaven face, as he slogged through the mud until he was close enough to reach up and jerk Jupiter from his high driver's seat. The frightened servant fell to his knees in a puddle of water.

"Ain't no rotten free nigger gonna run into me an' live," Bije bawled as he yanked off Jupiter's beaver top hat and stomped it into the mud. Then, out of control, Bije turned on Mark. "You'll pay for this, Mr. High-and-mighty Browning—too good to own a nigger, too good to do like the rest of us! You'll pay for what your *free* person of color done to my wagon!"

"Indeed I will, sir," Mark said, jumping from the carriage. "I'll gladly pay any damages to your wagon wheel and your horse, *if* these witnesses say the accident was our fault."

Bije spit. "If these witnesses say? *I say!* I say your nigger was driving down my side of Bull Street an'—" His anger exploded and Eliza saw Bije strike Mark squarely on the chin so that he reeled and fell backward against the side of the carriage.

"Jupiter! Get on your feet," she called, pulling herself over to the open door. "Hold on to Bije, Jupiter—until I can get out there!"

Plainly paralyzed with terror, Jupiter was powerless to move, let alone stand up.

Someone from the knot of onlookers helped Eliza Mackay down from the carriage and, one foot in a mudhole above her ankle, she began pummeling Bije Biddle across the face with her reticule. Over and over she whacked him until, ashamed to be disadvantaged in public by a mere woman, he half fell over Jupiter and vanished into an alley, shouting over his shoulder something about "fixin' that nigger some dark night when he was out walkin' the streets like only a white man has a right to do!"

One side of her long skirt heavy with mud, Eliza hurried to Mark.

"I'm all right, Miss Eliza," he said. "Bije didn't draw blood when he hit me. He just hurt my dignity."

She forced a nervous laugh as he took her arm. "Then we'll just put the entire episode behind us and be on our way. I know Sarah Gordon is worried about why I'm later than usual."

Mark helped her back into the carriage while Jupiter, shaken with fright and humiliation, hurried to rescue his trampled, muddy hat and climb onto the high seat again.

"Sorry this had to happen today," Mark said after he closed the carriage door and settled again beside her as Jupiter carefully started the team. "Something like that has only happened once before in all the years I've been here. Most Savannahians appear, at least, to accept that I won't—can't—own my servants. I'm sorry, so sorry."

"Oh, Mark, it isn't your fault. More and more people are making an ugly issue of—slavery. It seems only a few years ago that just about everybody contended it was a *necessary evil*. Lately, they're trying to say more and more that it isn't an evil at all. I'm sure I don't know how we'd plant without our Negroes, but I'm also sure it's *wrong* for one human being to own another. And I'm dead certain it should not be allowed to spread to the new territories —never, never."

He smiled down at her, holding out his chin so that she could wipe off a smear of mud. "Thank you, ma'am, for making me presentable, but most of all, thank you for being such a fair-minded, great lady."

They had slowed to a halt now at the entrance to the Gordon house, and Jupiter, looking bald and exposed without his cherished top hat, stood outside waiting for Mark's sign to open the carriage door. The rain, Eliza noticed gratefully, was now only a shower.

"I'll take you up those steep steps in a minute," he said in a voice that held her where she sat. "I know Mrs. Gordon needs you."

"Yes. I must go to her—mud and all."

"Not until I ask an enormous favor!" Mark grasped both her shoulders, so that they faced each other. "Deep inside, I'm *sure*, absolutely sure that things are not right with Natalie. Caroline is apprehensive too, although not over Natalie having a baby with only one doctor sixteen miles away in Cassville. Her uneasiness is far more vague—something about poor Indian Ben McDonald being in love with Natalie, but she *is* frightened about that."

Eliza frowned. "I remember hearing something about the Cherokee boy over three years ago when you all got back from up there. But, Mark, three years? Could Caroline be imagining things after all this time?"

"I wish Ben were all I had to worry about." He released her and looked away. "It could be Bije Biddle knocked some sense into me just now. At least, I've made up my mind since we got back in the carriage. I'm going to find out! I'm going up to Cass County just as soon as possible. It's the only way to ease Caroline's distress and mine. Besides, Jonathan hasn't seen his only sister since she left Savannah. He's finished the term at Reverend White's school. The boy will be going to Yale College in the fall. This is the time to take him to the upcountry with us." He paused, but did not look at her. "Miss Eliza, I want you to go too. Will you? Please?"

She was on the verge of saying, "For heaven's sake, Mark, I can't just decide here in the rain with Jupiter getting wet and Sarah Gordon expecting me! I can't just up and decide to make that long, hard trip on the spur of the moment." Instead, she bit her lip, then whispered, "Yes. Yes, if William gets home from up there in a day or so and tells us the roads aren't too bad—I'll go with you."

He hugged her. "Oh, thank you! You know William isn't going to miss his mother's birthday party this Saturday. And don't forget, we can go in style on the Central of Georgia almost to Macon."

In response, because he had caught her so by surprise, she gave him only a tight smile.

"Thank you again," he went on, his voice unsteady with emotion. "I wish I could go right home and tell Caroline that you'll go with us."

"Why can't you?"

"I promised Jonathan I'd come by Sheftall's house while you're with Mrs. Gordon. Jonathan's there now reading to the old gentleman. I can tell my son, though, that we're going to see his sister and—"

"Don't," she interrupted. "Whatever you do, don't tell him in front of Mr. Sheftall! Not yet. We're not leaving today. It will break the old fellow's heart to have you take Jonathan away. He lives for the boy's daily reading sessions."

Mark gave her another hug. "Do you ever have an uncharitable thought, ma'am?"

"Yes. I had one toward you when you sprang that long, exhausting trip on me a minute ago."

His smile was more like Mark now. "But I'm forgiven?"

She nodded. "That is, if you'll get me out of this carriage and up to Sarah's front door."

As he helped her mount the steep steps to the entrance of the Gordon mansion, Mark chatted about Godfrey Barnsley's report on the roads from the end of the rail line twenty miles this side of Macon. "Godfrey bought a wagon in Macon, and you know if he and his Julia and the children made it by wagon to their new house site, we'll do fine by stage. After all, the Barnsleys are real comfort lovers and their new log house is only twenty-some miles from the Stileses' on the Etowah River, so I'm sure we'll make it just fine and—"

"Hush, Mark. You don't need to convince me further. I said I'd go and I meant it. As long as I'm able, I'll be on hand when you need me. I think you need me now."

Smiling down at her, he twisted the brass doorbell. "Yes, I need you. And I won't mention our trip to old Sheftall yet. You're right, of course."

Through the glass front door, they could see the Gordon children. Could hear their voices, plainly subdued.

"I'm so glad your son still has his father," she whispered. "Four children in this house—one barely two—left for poor, dear Sarah to rear alone. Oh, Mark, I do dread facing her sorrow. Today especially. Will you pray for me? And will you ask Mr. Sheftall to pray for me too?"

Chapter 3

AFTER Mark squeezed her hand and ran back down the steps to his waiting carriage, Eliza Mackay was breathing a prayer for herself when one of the big double doors opened. In a row inside the high-ceilinged entrance hall stood three of Sarah Gordon's four children. The youngest member of the welcoming party, five-year-old Eliza Clifford—called Cliffie—smiled tentatively up at her. Willie, about eight, bowed from the waist and announced, "Our father died exactly one month ago tonight, Mrs. Mackay."

"I know, Willie," she said. "I've come to be with your mother."

Tears streamed down the thin, pale face of the elder son, George, who bowed also, but said nothing. He's old enough, Eliza thought, to understand the loss. George must be almost twelve.

"I wish you'd brought Henry with you," the little girl said. "He knows I like to laugh."

Eliza bent down to hug the child. "My grandson doesn't live in Savannah anymore, remember? Henry lives way up north on the Etowah River."

"Could you take me up there to see him?"

"No, Cliffie," Willie said. "Mrs. Mackay can't do that!" Trying to smile at Eliza, the boy explained, "She's awful young, Mrs. Mackay. Henry always did make her laugh a lot, though. She was even littler last year when he moved away, but she still talks about him."

"Our papa isn't here anymore either." The pretty child face was distorted with perplexity at trying to solve the puzzle. "He was here all that night after Mama told us he was dead. But not anymore. Papa's—gone—too."

"She knows that," George said in a voice stern enough to hide at least some of his grief. "After all, Mrs. Mackay's been here every day since."

"But does she know Papa just laid there—without saying a word? That even his fingers wouldn't move?"

"Yes, sister, she knows that." Willie, the charmer, took their guest's bonnet and mud-spattered cloak and hung them on a hall tree. Then he bowed again and gestured toward the rear parlor on the left. "Our mama's in there, Mrs. Mackay. She told us to bring you in the minute you got here."

"I tickled my papa under his chin," Cliffie went on, twisting the ruffle on her tiny apron, "and he didn't even smile. He always laughed out loud when I tickled him under his chin!"

"That's enough," George said, reaching for his sister's hand. "You come on with me, Cliffie. Willie can take Mrs. Mackay into where Mama's waiting. You and I'll go upstairs and try to fix that broken spindle on your doll bed."

The little girl waved and George bowed again before the two began to trudge up the wide, curving stair.

"Thank you both," Eliza called to them, her own eyes brimming because the children were all trying so hard. "And thank you, Willie," she said, taking the eight-year-old's proffered arm, allowing him to escort her properly into the informal family parlor where slender, pretty Sarah Gordon sat ramrod straight on the edge of a tapestry-covered armchair, a hand clasping her newly made mourning brooch.

"Mrs. Mackay," she whispered, forcing herself to stand. "Oh, Mrs. Mackay, I've been waiting for you! It seemed such a long time before you got here—today. And your skirt's covered with mud!"

For a moment, the women embraced, Eliza murmuring, "I know it is. We —Mark and I—had a little accident on the way."

"What happened?" Willie asked.

"A—a man in a speeding wagon struck us. He broke a wheel, I think. We're all—all right, though. It was Bije Biddle, Sarah."

"Oh, dear. Everyone knows he—despises Mark Browning. Was there any trouble?"

"Some. Bije was furious, even though he plainly struck us on purpose. Most people accept, or at least ignore, Mark's views on—slavery. Some don't. Bije among them."

Sarah Gordon tried to smile. "My husband always said that Savannahians accepted Mark Browning because of his charm, his kindness, but also—his wealth. My William didn't see eye to eye with him either, but he respected him highly."

"I know," Eliza said, hoping to move away from the touchy subject. "I also know about your—heart today, Sarah. I don't have any idea what else to say, but I'm here—and I do know about your heart."

When Willie led her rather ceremoniously to a chair, Eliza sat down facing her friend. "You're quite a gentleman, Willie," Eliza said. "And I'm sure a great comfort to your mother."

"I'm named for Papa. I'm the only one named William Washington Gordon now." The boy's chin quivered, but he managed to control his voice. "It's—kind of up to me. I know George is older, but I'm the one named for Papa." His brave words were causing his mother to break down again. "I guess I'd better excuse myself," he said, the expressive young face solemn with concern. "Mama will have me around after you've gone home, Mrs. Mackay. You're awfully kind to come every day."

Sarah's whole body was tense with the struggle not to sob for her son's sake. "It would be very nice if you'd ask for our tea, Willie," she managed.

"Your children are beautiful little people, Sarah," Eliza said after the boy had left the room. "I'm also aware that even the tender comfort they give isn't much help—today."

"Mrs. Mackay, one month ago this morning, William—was still here! He was so ill with a high fever . . . I know he'd slept on the wet ground the week before when he insisted upon staying at trackside—somewhere this side of Macon. Nothing would do but that he, the president of the company, be there to make sure the laborers kept everlastingly at that Central of Georgia railroad. He was—oh, so ill just one month ago this morning, but he was still here. I could still put my fingers in his thick, dark, curly hair . . ." Her voice turned harsh with the effort to steady it. "Forgive me, but there have been so many callers today already. I—I'm trying. I'm *trying*. But somehow I just can't believe that—he isn't here to—stand by me in all this! I need to tell *William* how hard it is . . ."

"Oh, my dear!"

"Every caller has meant well." Sarah's words tumbled on. "They all wanted to help. They didn't. Mr. Andrew Low, for example, just left before you got here. He was kind—praising my William's enormous contributions to the city, the state—but he didn't help me. Somehow his brisk Scottish manner and speech were very hard for me. Mr. Low was just elected to the board of directors of William's railroad, you know. He made the proper speeches about how pleased my husband would be knowing that his own brother-in-law, Richard Cuyler, has been elected to—take his place as president of the Central of Georgia." Fresh tears streaked her face. "Richard's a dear person. He'll be most capable, but—oh, Mrs. Mackay—how can *anyone* even intimate that another man could take my William's place?"

"Mr. Andrew Low did mean well," Eliza said. "He spoke only of the future of your husband's railroad, I'm sure. Not of Mr. Cuyler's taking Mr. Gordon's place personally."

What she had just said meant nothing whatever, Eliza knew. Sarah's tearful sigh came from so deep within that Eliza begged God silently for some helpful insight. "Sarah, his place will never be filled. Not for you, not for your sons and probably not for Eliza Clifford. Most likely, your infant daughter, Guilielma, won't remember him too well."

"Guilie won't be two until August, but don't you think there's a chance that I could help her remember—his face? His laughter?"

Eliza nodded. "Oh, my friend, I can't find the words, but I can promise you that because God is God, you will learn how to live this half-life and live it fully."

"I don't want a half-life!"

"Neither did I. I still don't. But that's what I have without Robert, and because of what God is like, because of the way He will attend you through *every minute* of the rest of your life, you will somehow be—all right."

"I've managed to get through only one month!"

Without a word, a house servant brought tea, curtsied and left the room.

Sarah tried to compose herself, then poured the steaming amber brew into hand-painted cups.

"It finally came to me one day," Eliza heard herself breaking the heavy silence, "a long time after Robert left me, that even my most private, personal life without him—had a real purpose I hadn't seen before."

Sarah set down her untouched cup of tea. "Your children?"

"Even more personal than my children. More personal to me as Robert's wife. No stars shot across the sky when it came to me, but the hope did come that, for Robert's sake, by some means I would be able to live successfully what had become suddenly—at that moment—the second part of my married life."

For the first time, Sarah looked directly at her. Eliza felt at last that she had her friend's full attention. "Mrs. Mackay—did you say the second part of your—*married life?*"

"Yes. You see, I always knew that if I lost Robert, I'd never be able to marry anyone else. I faltered often while I still had him to share the marriage adventure, but I tried. I tried with all my might to make the first part of that adventure creative and strong. It did help me, Sarah, when I saw even the possibility of doing the same with the second part of my adventure as his wife. In my heart, he was still my husband. He wouldn't be with me in that second part—not where I could touch him, hear his voice—but for his sake, for love of him, I could work at making it a success."

For what seemed a long time, Sarah Gordon looked at her. Finally Eliza saw a hint of something resembling hope in the red, swollen eyes. "And— God helped you do that? God will help *me?*"

"Yes. God will help you and so will your William."

"William will help me?" The sound she made was not really a laugh, but Eliza heard lessened tension in it. "How can William help me?"

"Your husband and God are together now. He sees clearly this minute all that he was too busy, too human to see on earth. Oh, Sarah, your William sees so much more—understands so much more than you and I could bear to see or understand. He and God together. They both know what you're enduring now."

After a time, Sarah whispered, "I'll—give that a lot of thought. It—it could help. The Bible does say that when we are with God, we are like Him. But if William does know about *my* broken heart, don't you think he's still shattered not to have lived long enough to see the children grow up? To see the completion of the last twenty miles of his precious railroad? He had so set his heart on the tracks being finished all the way to Macon this year. He must be grieving to miss seeing it!"

"No, I don't think he's grieving, because there's no time and no distance to worry Mr. Gordon where he is now."

When Sarah spoke again, her voice was calmer. "I suppose not. Oh, I will try. I do want to become a part of the life of the city again—sometime. I want to be interested in other people's lives again." She leaned forward. "Could

you talk to me about your family? About your dear son, William? I've
thought of him so often all through this—empty month. How did he survive
losing not only his lovely wife, Virginia, but both his children in that steamboat explosion? And Eliza Anne and W. H. Stiles—are they faring well in the
upcountry? Is her health better? Does she still have asthma attacks? Talk to
me about your family. I don't want to add the burden of selfishness to my—
load of grief!"

"They all seem to be doing fine. William will know more when he gets
back from a visit to the upcountry in time for my birthday Saturday. He's
suffered a lot, but his heart is healing. I expect my Army engineer son, Jack,
tomorrow from Tybee Island, where he's working on that government survey. Eliza Anne is ever so much stronger in the pure upcountry air and she
writes that it's much cheaper living in Cass County than here. They not only
save their Savannah house rent; she needs no new dresses at all and their
garden supplies all they can eat and more. They make their own butter, have
their own beef and milk cows, their own pigs and chickens. Mary Cowper
and Robert and Henry love it. Etowah Cliffs is a haven for active children.
With W.H. in Savannah so often tending his law practice, I do think Eliza
Anne gets lonely for adult conversation, but once the Barnsleys are settled up
there, she'll be fine. She and young Julia have been friends forever."

"I've been surprised that my Cliffie still talks about Eliza Anne's older son,
Henry." Sarah sighed. "William used to prophesy that Cliffie and Henry
Stiles would marry someday."

"Stranger things have happened. Our families have been close for a long,
long time. My husband thought so highly of your uncle, Judge James Moore
Wayne." Eliza smiled a bit proudly. "Over and over again, two or three years
before Robert died, he predicted a swift, important rise for young James
Wayne because he was such a brilliant, fair-minded lawyer. I doubt, though,
that even Robert would have guessed he'd become a United States Supreme
Court Justice."

"Odd that you should bring up Uncle James. I had such a tender letter
from him a few days ago, telling me of his own heartache that there wasn't
time for him to get here from Washington City for William's funeral." Sarah
made a brave attempt to smile. "There, you see? We were talking of your
family and I've brought the subject straight back to my William!" She took a
deep breath. "I'm sure the Stiles children adore having Natalie so close by.
The girl's so pretty, my brood all loved just being able to look at her."

"Our latest letter from up there declares that Natalie's even more radiant
now that she's going to be a mother in a few weeks."

Staring blankly at the far wall where her harp stood, Sarah said, "I know
how Natalie feels—so deeply in love with her husband and longing to give
him a child of that love. All my children, even the two who died in infancy
and our little Mary Stites, who left us before her second birthday, fulfilled me
because I could—give them to William. Oh, dear friend, it's too early for me
to—accept that I'll never be able to make such a gift to him again!"

Eliza resisted the temptation to tell Sarah that she had, only moments ago, promised Mark to go with him to Etowah Cliffs. Her mind still whirled from the sudden decision, not yet discussed even with her own two daughters at home. She would have liked Sarah's opinion of Mark's anxiety, but she had come to the Gordon home today to comfort her young friend. She could not allow herself to tell her yet that probably within a fortnight their daily visits would end.

On the edge of her chair again, once more ramrod straight, Sarah asked, "Whatever would I do these terrible days—without you?"

"Please give your children every chance to help," Eliza urged. "Willie, in particular, seems to need the responsibility of—bearing his father's name. Let the boy help all he can."

Sarah nodded agreement. "I'll try. I'll try to remember all you've told me, Miss Eliza, but you're the only friend who comes here with whom I don't have to pretend I'm bearing up. I know I'm being selfish, but I hope Mark Browning visits a long time with Mr. Sheftall today."

Chapter 4

HEAVIER traffic in the streets had made the carriage trip to the unpainted frame Sheftall house on West Broughton seem endless. A wind had risen and the rain, falling hard again, blew across the rickety porch where Mark finally stood alone, coat collar up against the wet chill, waiting for Sheftall Sheftall's ancient servant, Mordecai, to answer his knock. Everyone, Mark knew, expected to wait because Mordecai was surely almost as old as his master, and Sheftall Sheftall, Savannah's last living Revolutionary War veteran, was now past eighty.

In spite of age and skeletal thinness, the frail servant was somehow able to care for Sheftall, the only surviving son of once prominent Mordecai Sheftall, donor of the land where Savannah's Jews were buried. Where Sheftall Sheftall would lie, Mark thought, in the not too distant future. The thought saddened him. Just being with his valued friend had always given him strength in spite of the old gentleman's eccentricities and quirks. Mark had never been able to call Sheftall by his demeaning nickname, Cocked Hat Sheftall. It was true, of course, that to this day, in the year 1842, the short, shrunken, homely man did still wear his old colonial cocked hat, his blue-and-buff long-waisted military coat and knee breeches. Sheftall seldom got out for a walk these days, but when he did, he most certainly still wore his silver-buckled slippers. Especially the town's children thought him fascinating and on patriotic occasions gaped and snickered when the feisty old patriot ceremoniously exchanged dips of snuff with every prominent visitor to Savannah. After all, he was the one remaining citizen who had actually fought for liberty against the British. Mark could never laugh at his friend. There was too much stored knowledge under that rusty leather cocked hat.

For more than two years, Mark's only son, Jonathan, soon to be seventeen, had come daily to read aloud to Sheftall because the failing eyes could no longer make out fine newsprint. Few other Savannahians bothered to visit the house on West Broughton except Mark's wife, Caroline, and Miss Eliza Mackay. For that matter, Mark supposed, few ever had, but for all the years since Mark had chosen Savannah as his permanent home, he had stopped often, more, he was sure, for his own sake than for Sheftall's. Always keenly interested in current events, the venerable Jew had somehow helped keep Mark's perspective sharp. Sheftall's wisdom dispelled vagueness from the past and linked the state of Georgia today under a modern governor elected by the people to the days of colonial Governor Wright, appointed by a British king. The old gentleman seemed to live agreeably with the fact of slavery in the South, but he had fought for the freedom of a *united* country, and Mark, concerned over the growing unease between North and South, encouraged Jonathan's friendship with Sheftall. Jonathan was a native Georgian, but believing in the Union as Mark did, he wanted his son to understand its sacrificial beginnings.

Carefully holding the loose side of the grimy brass knocker, its screws missing for years, Mark banged again, aware that unless Jonathan answered, he could easily stand there a quarter of an hour before Mordecai finished whatever he might be doing.

He would wait until later, when he and Jonathan were alone in the carriage en route to get Miss Eliza, to tell the boy that they were definitely going to visit Natalie, that a departure date would be set as soon as William Mackay returned with a firsthand report on the roads. Some of the nagging anxiety lessened with the decision—especially since Miss Eliza had promised to go too. His anxiety would lessen still more once William was back in town. Mark felt unlimited admiration for William, who had managed, after the loss of his entire family, to go on living. During the four years past, Mark had watched William become more and more the head of the Mackay clan. There was no question but that Miss Eliza's older son, Captain Jack, was the appealing one of the brothers—socially. Most Savannahians brightened at the mere mention of Jack Mackay's name, but William was the steady one on whom Miss Eliza depended.

He knocked again, then tried the curved colonial latch handle. As usual, in spite of Savannah's improved security, Sheftall's house was locked against burglars. Mark was damp through, but there was nothing to do but wait and hope that Mordecai was out of the rain inside the new washhouse which Sheftall had finally agreed to permit Mark to build in deference to Mordecai's age. Clothing and linens could now be washed and hung inside the shed out back on a day such as this.

The picture of trembly, parchment-thin Mordecai lifting heavy, hot sheets from one boiling tub to another merged with the thought of Natalie's pretty, rounded arms trying to heave about heavy, steaming laundry—and not in a tightly built washhouse, but out of doors in all kinds of upcountry weather. Oh, she was equal to it. Horrified, but proud, he'd watched at Knightsford, the Browning plantation, as she gritted her teeth while learning to do an entire laundry herself. At least there, she'd been under the watchful eyes of the Knightsford people, who could rush to her rescue if the backbreaking work grew too hard for her. Twice, she had scalded her hands, but remained undaunted. "This is the measure of my love for Burke," she'd call over her shoulder as her nervous parents stood watching—in silence and awe.

Forgetting to hold its loose side, he banged the knocker again. A glance at his watch showed that he'd waited over ten minutes. Then he heard the unhurried scrape of heavy boots along the bare front hall and Mordecai's thin voice calling, "Comin', comin'. Don't pound no more, whoever 'tis. Our knocker's 'bout to come loose!"

Eventually Mordecai unlocked, then dragged open the rain-swollen, heavy door. When he recognized Mark, his dark scowl changed to a toothless grin. Mark was smiling too as he held out his hand. "Good morning, Mordecai. Sorry if I banged too hard. It's chilly out here."

Pulling Mark inside the shadowy hall, the old man chuckled. "Don't you think I knows it's chilly? Been out in my washhouse more'n two hours. 'Bout froze even with all that steam spurmin' up roun' me." Once, then twice, he shook Mark's hand. "You know, Mister Mark, you the only visitor ever shakes my hand besides your fine son?" The smile gone, he added sadly, "Course, ain't much of nobody comes 'ceptin' you an' him an' Miss Caroline." A finger to his lips, the smile back, Mordecai whispered, "Step over here to the foot of the stairs an' listen to the two of 'em up there!"

Handing Mordecai his damp cloak and top hat, Mark obeyed. He could hear Jonathan's soft, musical voice reading, reading, with only an occasional grunt or comment from Sheftall.

"We're eavesdropping, Mordecai. I've taught Jonathan never to do exactly what we're doing this minute."

The grizzled servant tapped his lips, indicating that just the same, they would go right on listening.

"I think I need to speak to Jonathan about respect for his elders too," Mark whispered. "He's not very courteous leaving his father out in that weather all this time. He knew I was coming by. I'm sure he heard me banging at the door."

"Oh, he hear," Mordecai agreed calmly. "The boy figure you could stand gettin' a little wet easier than Mausa Sheftall could stand bein' disturbed when they're up there readin'. This be the happiest time of the old gent'man's day, sir." Shaking his clipped gray head, Mordecai mumbled, "It be bad, bad if you ever take that boy away from ol' mausa."

"Jonathan has to go North to school next fall, you know."

"Oh, Jesus . . . I knowed you'd take him off someday! Lord have mercy, you take that boy away from him an' I gonna 'bout lose my senses, he be so lonesome—all day long, day in an' day out. Lonesome, Jesus, lonesome . . ."

"But this is today. They're together today. You're borrowing trouble, Mordecai," Mark said, and began to climb the worn, uncarpeted steps.

In the upstairs hall, he could see that Sheftall's bedroom door was open. Sheftall's hearing was almost as bad as his eyesight, but even he had undoubtedly heard the banging. From where Mark stood, he could see his son, although not Sheftall. The reading went on. Mark took a step or two toward the bedroom, then waited until Jonathan, without missing a word, glanced up at him, winked and continued reading about the seemingly endless number of Georgia's splinter political parties, most of them floundering. " 'What is at present called the Democratic or Democratic-Republican Party,' " Jonathan read, " 'is made up mainly of farmers and frontiersmen, while the Whig Party, whose strength still lies in the wealthy planter-merchant class, may eventually—' "

"Enough!" Sheftall interrupted. "Hogwash, Jonathan. That's all redundant hogwash! You've read it a dozen times in one form or another. It's evident those editors write for idiots, not informed gentlemen like us. You must be sick and tired of political drivel."

"Oh, no, sir," Jonathan said brightly, glancing again at his father, who still stood in the hallway out of Sheftall's sight. "I need to learn all I can about Georgia politics now that Uncle W. H. Stiles is going to be a United States congressman in Washington City."

Mark heard Sheftall's scoffing snort. "He's not your real blood uncle and William Henry Stiles only *hopes* to become a congressman. He's a splendid, even brilliant young lawyer, is Stiles, but he'll have to find a way to make up his mind whether he agrees with his own social class or those upcountry Cass County farmers."

"Well," Jonathan said thoughtfully, "he's a farmer too now and lives right in Cass County. Most voters in Cass are farmers and Democrats, even though I'd have to place Uncle W.H. in the upper privileged class—I guess more like the Whigs."

"I understand why you call him Uncle W.H., since the Mackays and Stileses and Brownings are close, but the gentleman does tend to straddle, it seems to me. No mistake about it—I like William Henry Stiles. He's an outstanding, extravagant, cultivated gentleman, with excellent literary taste— knows the law—but he needs to come down on one side or another. He may find that those Democrat farmers on the frontier don't succumb to his superior oratory as did Chatham County folk. Campaigning in Savannah and Chatham County among equals, as he did when he won his seat in the state legislature two years ago, is one thing. Running a campaign on the frontier is another." After a dry cough, Sheftall asked, "Who in tarnation are you looking at out there in the hall, boy?"

"My father, sir," Jonathan said with a broad smile. "Papa's here to visit with you."

"Then what's he doing out there? Come in, Browning!"

Inside the large, shabby bedroom, Mark greeted Sheftall warmly, shaking the gnarled, stubby-fingered hand. "I was merely waiting for a break in the discussion. I know how deeply you two concentrate when you're together. How are you today, sir?"

"As disgusted with political parties as ever. Just stopped your boy reading about them, in fact. There was a time in my youth when a man's patriotism was ruled by principle—not by catering to this or that party. Even the enlightened editor of *Niles' Register* declares that in this year of 1842 no one—*no one* can possibly make sense of Georgia politics. He declared, in fact, as I'm sure

Jonathan remembers since we read it only yesterday, that no one should even try."

"W.H. feels, though, that he's found his rightful party," Mark said. "Now that he's a resident of Cass County, he seems to be comfortable with the Democrats."

"He'd better be if he expects to be elected from up there." Sheftall thought a moment. "Of course, he has to be nominated by the all-powerful state committee first. I have no doubt he will be. The most influential man on the selection committee is his old Savannah law partner, Levi De Lyon. Stiles has no peers when it comes to flowery oration, although I'n not sure how his new cracker neighbors will accept such erudition. Still, he'll have far less political competition up there on the frontier. Not many men of learning and brains in Cherokee Georgia right now." He raised a hand. "Enough politics. Put the paper away, Jonathan. Except for the one vital paragraph from our city council records, you're through reading for today. Time for good conversation now that your father's here."

Mark and his son exchanged amused, warm glances. Jonathan loves the old fellow as I do, Mark thought. Loves him and understands him. That city council resolution of last year may be what's keeping Sheftall alive.

"You see, the boy reads that resolution to me daily, Browning," Sheftall went on, with no hint of embarrassment. "Hearing it tides me over until Jonathan gets back the next day. Chirks up the spirits. Makes me feel appreciated. I'm probably not appreciated any longer. Few remember what I did for my country so long ago, but any man likes to believe he's well regarded."

Mark, of course, knew the council resolution by which the old man had been forgiven all his back taxes and all future taxes for the remaining years of his life. Almost everyone seemed glad for him, although many joked that since he couldn't pay anyway, he might just as well be relieved of the debt. In spite of that, Mark felt that the council had intended to honor Sheftall. Never in the town's history had the city fathers forgiven taxes to anyone else. That alone was a tribute.

"I'm glad I'll be present to hear the resolution again, sir," Mark said.

"Are you ready for it, Mr. Sheftall?" Jonathan asked. "Shall I read it now?"

"Not yet, if you and your father have time for a small visit." He reached a hand to Jonathan, who helped him to his feet. "Sit down, Browning. I have to relieve myself, then we'll have a good talk."

While Sheftall hobbled on his cane across the room to where a large lusterware thunder mug stood in one corner, Mark said, "I have plenty of time, sir. I took Miss Eliza Mackay to see W. W. Gordon's widow on my way here. She won't be expecting me before noon. Miss Eliza needs our prayers, undoubtedly, right at this minute. Mrs. Gordon lost her husband, you know, one month ago today."

Mark glanced at Jonathan. The boy was studying his father's face, a puzzled look on his own. Obviously he'd noticed the bruise on Mark's chin. Still, knowing how well his stocky, broad-shouldered son understood him, he would have sworn that Jonathan suspected that something new was afoot since they'd seen each other at breakfast. He would tell the boy of the planned trip later and of the run-in with Bije Biddle, but not until they were alone.

Father and son exchanged smiles as Jonathan got up to help their feeble friend, now making his way slowly back to the worn chair by the window.

Hands folded across his small, round stomach, Sheftall said nothing for a time, then, looking out the window, his mind obviously still on Eliza Mackay's difficult visit to the Gordon house, repeated her name in a soft tone, almost savoring it. "Eliza McQueen Mackay. There is no one anywhere who might be able to help Sarah Stites Gordon today but the gentle-spirited, wise, steady Eliza McQueen Mackay. I knew her father, the colorful, widely discussed—even gossiped about—gentleman called, in his later life, Don Juan McQueen. Used to be plain John McQueen of Thunderbolt, of course, until he fled Georgia debtor's prison to make his fortune in Spanish East Florida—St. Augustine and environs. Caused his wife, Miss Eliza's mother, Ann Smith McQueen, much pain by the long separation, but Ann Smith McQueen loved the man. Many did, in spite of his impetuous nature, the squandering of his vast Spanish Florida holdings. Especially did his daughter, our Miss Eliza, love him. Oh, her heart has known many kinds of pain. Part of it the same pain Sarah Gordon feels today. Twenty-six years since she lost her laughing, ebullient husband, Robert Mackay. I remember it as though it were yesterday. I still think often, Browning, of how hard it must have been for you to be forced to tell her that Mackay had died on your trip to New York to place their boys, William and Jack, in school . . . that you'd had to bury Mackay up there. That she was to be deprived even of a nearby grave to visit."

Jonathan moved quietly to sit on the arm of Mark's chair and laid a hand on his father's shoulder.

Still staring out the window that overlooked West Broughton, Sheftall added, "Too bad you missed knowing Mr. Robert Mackay, son."

"I guess I'm just glad I can know Miss Eliza."

"Yes." Sheftall spoke the word as though to close a door, then turned slightly toward Mark. "Now, what of that heart-stoppingly beautiful daughter of yours, Browning? Are you still borrowing trouble by fretting? And have you come to a decision about when you and Caroline will leave for the upcountry to hover over your girl child?"

The unexpected question stunned Mark to silence for a moment. Finally, he tried to laugh. "Where did you get the idea that we might be going to Cass County, sir?"

"From your wife, of course."

"Caroline told you that?"

"She told me you weren't about to rest until you do go. And why act so surprised? You know perfectly well that Caroline still visits me. That girl and

I have been confidential friends for all the years since I used to visit my client, her grandfather, Jonathan Cameron, at Knightsford when she was a child." Of course Mark knew. He and Caroline had talked often of her happy girlhood hours shared with Sheftall as they sat together swinging their legs off the Cameron dock. But he certainly hadn't guessed that Caroline still confided quite so freely in the man. Had she really told him? Or was the canny old gentleman attempting a bit of sleuthing in order to find out if Jonathan might be going too?

"Your wife is prepared to make the trip when you say the word, Browning," Sheftall went on. "You've always fidgeted over that daughter of yours, so the journey might well be in order. It could give you and Caroline some peace of mind." He looked as directly at Mark as his weakening eyes would permit and added, "Just so you don't rob me of your son."

For an awkward moment, no one spoke, then Jonathan said, "I don't know anything about a trip north, sir."

As though the boy had not spoken, Sheftall went on addressing Mark. "You miss Natalie, I'm sure. And I'm certain that you are convinced that no other woman on earth ever before carried a baby. Naturally, that's foolish. I have no doubt that the girl lives in perfect bliss with her husband, where she belongs, and that she's carrying that baby with aplomb. I'm not at all surprised that, as Caroline says, she leaves the letter writing to Eliza Anne Mackay Stiles. Your flame-haired daughter always did know how to get other people to obey her wishes. Especially her distinguished father."

Determined to keep his voice casual, pleasant, Mark said, "I have no argument there, sir."

"There is none. But quite evidently Natalie Browning Latimer has grown up, almost overnight, for love of her young man. It's understandable that you worry over the hard life she leads up there on the frontier. Except for Andrew Low, you're the richest man in Savannah. You fully expected Natalie to live out her days in luxury right here, married to a man of her own social class. Ridiculous expectation, since you knew from the day she was born that she is unlike any other young woman. She's where she wants to be, with that strong-willed, brawny buck who rescued her from the sea. I know of your painful concern, but I say that Natalie Browning Latimer is living in bliss and faring well."

Again, the room filled with an uncomfortable silence, until, abruptly, Sheftall held out both hands toward Mark and said in a husky voice, "I—I do know you miss her, Browning, but I beg you—don't take Jonathan away from me. Not yet!"

Obviously trying to lighten the old man's mood, Jonathan said, "My brother-in-law, Burke, whom I haven't even met, is building my sister a new five-roomed cottage up there. But I'm sure I told you about that."

"You did not, but your mother did."

Undeterred, Jonathan went right on. "Burke and his Cherokee helper, Ben McDonald, work on the cottage a little on Saturdays and Sundays. You see, during the week they're building a new Presbyterian church near Mr. Arnold Milner's place at Sallie Hughes's ford on the Etowah River—too far for them to ride home every day. It's taking longer that way, of course, but I guess Natalie's going to have a fine cottage. Burke rescued Ben and his younger sister, Mary, from where they were living in a cave after their Cherokee people had to go West."

Sheftall grunted. "Don't have any use for Cherokees. They fought with the British during our revolution."

"I know, sir, but the way Burke found Mary and Ben is an awfully interesting story," Jonathan went on. "The sister and brother lived with Burke in a deserted Cherokee cabin until Natalie moved up there. Mary and Ben have their own remodeled cabin now not far from Natalie and Burke—on land Burke bought adjoining the Stileses' property."

In an effort to stop Jonathan, Sheftall raised one hand, a warning flag. "I repeat, Jonathan, your mother has told me all that. All of it. Told me the same afternoon, as I recall, when she informed me that Cherokee Ben is smitten with Natalie and the pretty Indian girl, Mary, is smitten with Natalie's husband."

Mark stared at his old friend, but decided to say nothing. His son laughed. "Aw, Mr. Sheftall, that's just what Natalie thinks. She's so smitten with Burke herself she imagines all other women are too!"

"Your mother appears to believe it," Sheftall said firmly. "In my opinion, she is quite nervous about both relationships. The Indian's fascination with Natalie, in particular. She intends, I believe, to draw her own conclusions once your parents make their visit."

Mark glanced at his watch, then stood.

"I know you have to leave, Browning," Sheftall said, pouting a bit. "I'll let you both go gracefully—*after* Jonathan reads the all-important city council resolution." The filmy old eyes filled abruptly. "You see, Browning, Mordecai never learned to read."

"Of course," Mark said. "Jonathan will be glad to oblige and I'll be happy to sit back down and listen. I enjoy it each time it's read to me."

"My nephew, Dr. Moses Sheftall, is forever in a rush when he stops by to display his medical skills on his decrepit uncle. Too rushed to read anything to me. I depend only upon Jonathan." Leaning his head back against the chair, he took a deep breath and closed his eyes. "The glorious, heartening resolution, please, Jonathan?"

"Is it all right if I recite it from memory, sir? Will it be the same to you?"

"Very well, but I'll know, of course, if you miss a single word."

Jonathan's good laughter brought a smile to Mark's face.

"Stand, please, son, as you always do when you deliver the resolution," Sheftall requested.

"Certainly," the boy said, getting quickly to his feet. Then, with proper solemnity, he cleared his throat and began: " 'Be it resolved that Sheftall Sheftall, Esquire, one of the oldest citizens of Savannah and a relic of the

Revolution, a pensioner of the United States Government for services rendered in the War of the Revolution, is in arrears for taxes due the city. Resolved, that all back taxes be remitted and treasurer directed not to require any returns of taxes during his life, and resolved further that Sheftall Sheftall—' "

"Slow just a bit for this part, son," the old gentleman interrupted. "Speak this part with feeling, please."

"Yes, sir. '. . . and resolved further that Sheftall Sheftall be and hereby is entitled to all the privileges of a citizen in every respect the same as if his taxes had been returned and paid into the city treasury.' " After a moment, Jonathan asked, "Did I get it all right, Mr. Sheftall?"

"All. Every word." From his worn colonial jacket, the old man took out a crumpled handkerchief and blew his nose loudly. "Now go, both of you. In spite of my honored state as a hero of the American Revolution and the city's regard for same, I'm—not up to lengthy farewells."

Grasping Sheftall's hand, Jonathan said, "This isn't a farewell. I'll be back tomorrow!"

Sheftall only nodded. "You're a busy, prosperous merchant, Browning, but I—dare to beg that, before you—leave the city to flutter about poor, pampered Natalie, you too will once more pay your respects."

"You've been telling me how foolish I am to worry about her, sir," Mark said with a grin, "now I'm calling you foolish even to think we won't be back often. And there certainly are no definite departure plans. If they've had this kind of weather to the northwest, the roads aren't passable yet by stage from the end of the railroad line to—"

"Enough," Sheftall broke in. "I suggest only that you talk this all out first with Eliza McQueen Mackay. You will never go wrong to follow Miss Eliza's advice—on anything. I've watched you depend upon her since you came to Savannah as a sprout of a boy." Almost to himself, he added, "God help you, Browning, on the day you lose Eliza McQueen Mackay to death. Now go, please! Go *now*. And—God go with you."

Arm in arm, Mark and Jonathan left the house. Neither spoke until they'd settled themselves in the carriage and Jupiter had headed the team toward the Gordon house.

"I have two questions, Papa," Jonathan said.

"I'm sure this bruised chin is one of them. There was an accident after I picked Miss Eliza up this morning."

"Was she hurt?"

"No, thank heaven, but she might have been. Bije Biddle's wagon sideswiped our carriage. The wagon tilted from a broken wheel, but Bije wasn't really hurt. Nor the horse, although he fell. That's about all I can tell you except that I got Miss Eliza away as soon as I could."

"Mr. Biddle isn't too fond of you, is he?"

"That's putting it mildly."

"Papa, I think he could have hit our carriage on purpose. Most people seem reconciled to your not owning slaves, except the Knightsford people Mama inherited, but I know more than you think, Papa. I hear my friends repeat some of what their fathers say." Jonathan grinned. "I guess it all boils down to the fact that you're rich enough and prominent enough in town to make you—acceptable, regardless."

"You have the picture about right, I'd say."

"Did Mr. Biddle hit you on the chin?"

He nodded. "I hope it doesn't show too much. I'd hate it to start up another discussion with your mother. Do you think she'll notice?"

"Maybe not on such a cloudy, dark day. Papa, I know Mama doesn't understand the way you feel about owning people, but she'll just be glad you're all right. She thinks Bije Biddle is white trash anyway."

"You said you had two questions, son. What was the other one?"

"It's about Sister. You're really worried, I know. Does Miss Eliza think there's a reason to be worried about her?"

"No, she doesn't. In fact, I'm sure she's agreed to go with us to see Natalie just to humor me." Mark glanced at the boy. A big smile was spreading across his face.

"So, we're really going! Miss Eliza—and me too?"

"Why not? You've a lot of time on your hands between now and fall when you start Yale College. Besides, I need you to help me look after your mother and Miss Eliza on the way."

Up on the edge of the carriage seat now, Jonathan exclaimed, "If I weren't almost seventeen, I'd hug you right here in the middle of Bull Street!" Abruptly, he leaned back. "There surely is a lot to be said for—becoming a man, isn't there? Oh, I know grown men have many things to be responsible for, but because you really need me to go too, I—I suddenly feel like I've been let out of a cage of some kind!"

"Son," Mark said, giving him a quizzical look, "do you honestly feel that way?"

"Yes, sir. Shouldn't I?"

"Well, of course," Mark answered, not exactly sure what he meant. "It's just that—because I've always considered you as being so mature, you took me by surprise. I've never thought of you having felt caged up in boyhood. Almost all your life, your mother and I have depended upon you, maybe too much. Have we leaned on you too heavily?"

"Not that I know of. Jiminy crickets! We're really going to Etowah Cliffs— Miss Eliza too. Does Mama know?"

"Not yet. I just made up my mind on the way to the Gordon house with Miss Eliza this morning."

"When do you think we'll get started?"

"I hope sometime the first part of May. I thought you and I would try meeting the train from up that way tonight. William Mackay could be on it. He'll know about the condition of the roads on north of Macon."

"He's trying to get back for Miss Eliza's birthday on Saturday, I know."

"If he made it on the stage as far as Gordon, the end of the Central of Georgia line, it's just possible that he caught the six A.M. train this morning for Savannah. With luck he could be here sometime tonight. I've heard of the train reaching Savannah only three or four times before midnight." Mark grinned. "But that shouldn't be too late for you now that you've shucked your boyhood."

"Aw, midnight hasn't been too late for me for a long time. You and Mama just felt it was."

"I see."

Jonathan thought a minute. "The first part of May will give me two weeks or so to go on visiting Mr. Sheftall." Then, with no arrogance whatever, simply stating a fact, he added, "It's going to be awfully hard on him without my daily visits."

"I know," Mark said. "He made that plain. The old gentleman seemed so intent upon my discussing the possibility of our trip with Miss Eliza first, I felt sorry for him. I'm sure he expects her to talk me out of it. I couldn't bring myself to tell him she'd already agreed to go too."

"You're always kind, Papa. I'm glad. A lot of my friends' fathers expect everybody to jump when they say jump, no matter what."

Mark laughed a little. "Does it ever strike you as odd—unparental—that your approval means so much to me, son?"

"No, sir." He fell silent for a time. "*Are* you terribly worried about Natalie, Papa? Are you and Mama sure something is wrong up there?"

"No, we're not sure. You've read all the letters too. We know nothing you don't know. Eliza Anne—Miss Lib, as you and Natalie call her—wouldn't try to fool us, but somehow I just have to find out firsthand that your sister's really all right. I may be only imagining trouble. I've never been very sensible where Natalie's concerned."

"Sister has always bothered you a lot, I know, but that's because you love her so much."

"You know your mother and I don't love her one bit more than we love you, son."

"Of course I know that," Jonathan said evenly. "But Natalie's a—girl. And she's so beautiful, a man just about has to worry some about her."

"You are growing up, aren't you?"

"I'm relieved you know I am," the boy said matter-of-factly. "Do you think that maybe Natalie's not doing well with the new baby coming and all? Or that she's not happy with Burke?"

"It's hard for me to remember that you've never even met Burke. No. I don't think I'm concerned about her—happiness. Natalie loves her husband with all her little heart and mind and being. I'm—embarrassed to say that I don't know why I'm so anxious."

"You and Mother don't feel you know Natalie very well, do you?"

Mark waited to respond. "How long have you realized that?"

"Quite a while," the boy said. "But I understand."

"You do?"

All Jonathan said was "Yes, sir."

"Do you understand your sister, son?"

His laugh was easy. "Not always, but I just let her be Natalie, because no matter how much of a ruckus she causes, she loves us all a lot. When I don't know what she's up to, I just tease her about something. Brothers can do that, though, when parents can't."

Mark made no comment. He was suddenly too filled with gratitude that in his own old age, when so many he held dear today might be gone, there would be his real friend, Jonathan.

"Sometimes I think my sister gets sort of lost inside herself," Jonathan mused as they drove up to the entrance of the Gordon house. "Maybe she even gets scared. Not because she's a girl—not that kind of scared. But scared, mainly when things don't turn out the way she's always sure they will."

"And do you think that fear makes her so secretive? Or do I just imagine your sister works sometimes at shutting her mother and me out of the part of her life that really matters to her?"

Jonathan seemed to be thinking through his answer. Finally, while Jupiter waited in the muddy street, the carriage door open, he said, "I guess you mean the way she ignores Mama's worry over Indian Ben McDonald. At least, Mama thinks Natalie ignores it."

Mark stared at his son. "Has your mother talked much to you about her odd conviction that poor Ben is in love with Natalie?"

"Mama and I do talk. She's sure Burke's Cherokee helper is 'unhealthily obsessed'—as Mama puts it—with my sister. It troubles Mama a lot. It seems to me she's as nervous about Ben as you are about Natalie having a baby. From what you've told me about him, though, I can't see why she is."

Shaking his head—marveling at the boy—Mark said, "Are you sure you're young enough to be—my son, Jonathan?"

The quick smile came. "Come on, we'd better go in for Miss Eliza. She'll be wondering what happened to us." About to jump out of the carriage, he turned back to his father. "I wouldn't worry if I were you—or Mama. Miss Eliza will be with us when we go and whatever happens, you know she always knows what to do."

Chapter 5

FROM eight until nearly ten o'clock on Friday night, Caroline Browning, alone in the family drawing room of her home on Reynolds Square, tried to begin one and then another of four new books purchased that day at Mr. Williams's Book Shop on the Bay. All four volumes lay discarded on the piecrust table which held the room's one lighted candelabrum. Dressed comfortably in an ice-blue satin peignoir, she had counted on reading in order to quiet her nerves during the long wait while Mark and Jonathan were meeting William Mackay over at the Central of Georgia station on West Broad.

Her husband and son had waited in vain for the past three nights, but knowing William, he would surely be there tonight when the train eventually pulled in. Miss Eliza's other son, Captain Jack, had arrived that afternoon from Tybee Island, where he'd been heading an important government survey of the Savannah River. No one would have been too surprised had Jack not come in time for his mother's birthday tomorrow, but everyone fully expected William. The only doubts involved the train itself, the numberless stops along the way of the 170-mile journey from Gordon to Savannah—and the heavy rains of the past week.

"If only the sun would come out," Mrs. Gordon had moaned today when Caroline had gone with Eliza Mackay to visit. "I know this must sound ridiculous, but freshets caused my William so much trouble during the construction of his railroad that I find I still anticipate the worst."

Caroline's thoughts raced to the grief-distorted face of Sarah Gordon, still deeply mourning. Serious, overburdened Sarah Gordon, who, even when her famous husband was still alive, seemed to carry the weight of the world on her slender shoulders.

"My husband was away so much for so many years," she'd said today. "He was a wonderful provider, an important man, but he entrusted almost full responsibility for our home and children to me." Shaking her head in disbelief, Sarah Gordon had added, "I—I somehow feel that after all that time and all that responsibility, I should be—doing better without him. I'm—not doing well. Not able really to help my children at all!"

On her feet, Caroline crossed the spacious, tastefully furnished room and tried to pour herself more tea. The pot was empty. She banged the teapot onto its heavy silver stand and plopped herself down on the couch.

"When I think of poor Mrs. Gordon, I'm—ashamed of myself," she said aloud into the empty room. "I have Mark—Mark isn't dead. My children still have their father."

Jamming a cushion behind her head, she leaned against it and sighed. Still, her own nagging uneasiness over an almost anonymous Indian young man who had the unmitigated audacity to be infatuated with *her* daughter was just as real as Sarah Gordon's grief. Different, not as desperate—not as hopeless or final, but wasn't it just as *real?* Of course, Mark didn't think so. All he could worry about was Natalie giving birth. I have the normal amount of motherly concern over that. Nothing would do Natalie but that she marry Burke Latimer, and when a woman married, she bore children—if she were blessed. Natalie had always been blessed! Blessed by beauty, by wealth, by the instant gratification of her every smallest desire—thanks to Mark. Thanks to me too, I suppose, she admitted grudgingly. But my daughter *is married* now and I'm almost relieved to be rid of the awesome burden of being her mother. There, she thought, I've let the truth cross my mind, so I might just as well say it.

She did say it, speaking aloud again into the empty room, "I'm glad—I'm relieved to be rid of the awesome burden of being Natalie's mother!"

Once more, she picked up one of the new books, then, without opening it, slammed it down again. The truth is, I'm not burdenless, she thought. I simply have a strange burden I can't talk about, and, of course, it has to do with Natalie!

No matter how Mark tried to belittle her anxiety over poor, sullen Ben McDonald, after three years the fear lurked—darkening sunny days, filling Caroline's nights with dread. Each time Eliza Anne Stiles mentioned Ben in a letter, she mentioned how he moped around, how no one ever had even an inkling of what the half-breed young man was really thinking. No matter how she tried, she could not forget what Eliza Anne had told her of Ben's stricken face the night before Natalie's wedding in the ugly little church in Cassville. Never mind that the wedding was so long ago, Caroline still remembered Eliza Anne declaring that Ben looked—dark and tragic—as though he were capable of some dark, drastic deed! Both of Burke's Indian friends had refused to attend the wedding, and although the accident to her eye was Cherokee Mary's excuse for staying away, Ben had none beyond the obsession for Natalie which only she, Caroline, seemed to have sense enough to take seriously to this day.

To this day, only old Sheftall Sheftall had believed she had any justification for worrying over Indian Ben. Oh, Caroline admitted freely that her son-in-law, Burke Latimer, would not be moving ahead as a builder at such a rate without Ben's skilled help, but that was another matter altogether. Thank heaven, Miss Eliza Mackay will be making the trip up there with us, she thought. When Miss Eliza sees for herself how strangely Ben still behaves, she'll know I'm not exaggerating.

"What dreadful thing do you expect the poor fellow to do?" Mark had asked again and again. "Tell me, Caroline, exactly what?"

She couldn't tell him or anyone, because she didn't know, but the nagging unease had grown as though it had a life of its own. Certainly, she'd tried reason: If the unfortunate, tragic Ben did love Natalie, would he want to harm her in any way? Still, who could tell about an Indian? Up to a point, Caroline had come to agree with Mark and Miss Eliza that both the federal government and the state of Georgia had treated the Cherokees unfairly, but that in no way lessened her fear or her anger. At times, it *was* more anger than fear that Indian Ben *dared* to harbor what could, under the circumstances, only be called an irrational, shocking attachment to *her* daughter!

On her feet again, this time at the drawing-room window, she peered out into the dark, empty square. There was no movement beyond the trees, swaying moss shadows stirring in a rising breeze. The oil lamps allotted to each square did little more than turn Reynolds Square ghostly, causing her to wish fervently that the city would hurry with its much-discussed gaslights. Northerners undoubtedly have reason to call us slow in the South, she admitted, and felt irritated by her own admission. She also felt an unreasonable annoyance with Mark for not being back yet. The tall, graceful clock in the front hall struck half after ten. Should William Mackay indeed bring word of trouble with Indian Ben when the train finally puffed into the new frame station at Liberty and West Broad, would Mark even tell her?

Allowing the heavy drapery to drop back in place so that it covered the window again, she sat down very straight and scolded herself for, of all things, being annoyed with her gentle, thoughtful husband. She had been, though. And with Natalie, for falling in love with a young man who insisted upon settling in the wildest, most primitive part of Georgia. Only Natalie would marry someone who actually made social friends with half-breed Indians!

In a moment, her better nature took over and she smiled at herself. What's to be gained, she thought, by blaming either Mark or Natalie? And I'm certainly not going to take any blame for worrying. I'm *not* being merely an anxious mother. This uneasiness over that Cherokee and my daughter has been with me too long. There's a reason for it, but unless William knows, I'll just have to endure not finding out until we get up there. After all this time, I suppose a bit more than two weeks isn't long to wait.

At the train station, Mark had lost count of how many times he'd figured that at a speed of seventeen miles per hour the Central of Georgia should have reached Savannah almost two hours ago. His watch read ten-fifteen.

"Long wait, eh, sir?" a strange young Army lieutenant said as he paced the narrow room for the fourth or fifth time.

Mark merely nodded, not at all interested in small talk.

Overcome by sleep in the hot, stuffy air of the long, narrow waiting room, Jonathan dozed while sitting straight up on a wooden bench beside his father. The young can sleep through their troubles, Mark thought as he got up to stretch his own stiff legs. Only a handful of Savannahians were scattered here and there along the hard benches, none more inclined to talk than he, thank goodness. He yawned and stretched both arms over his head in an ungentlemanly fashion.

"You've been here three nights in a row too, haven't you, Mr. Browning?" The young lieutenant strode back again to where Mark stood and extended his hand. "I'm Lieutenant Robert Williams. Ordered to meet another Army engineer due sometime this week. I hope tonight."

Mark shook his hand, but again, only nodded.

"Of course, I've known your name, Mr. Browning, ever since I hit town. You were pointed out to me on my first day here." Glancing at the sleeping Jonathan, the talkative soldier asked, "Your son?"

Again Mark merely nodded. Then, feeling a bit rude, he said, "At least you and your arriving passenger won't have far to go to your bed once the iron horse puffs into the station. Aren't some of you Army men housed in the adjoining long room of this building?"

"That's right. Housed most inelegantly, I might add. I hear you're hoping to meet Mr. William Mackay."

Curious as to how the strange young officer knew, Mark said with a grin, "You must be trained as a spy. You seem to have all the answers about me and my foggy night mission to this lonely place."

"I'm a friend of Captain Jack Mackay's, brother of the gentleman you're meeting." With a somewhat sly smile, the young lieutenant added, "It's rather like Captain Jack to maneuver you here in his stead. The man undoubtedly charmed you into this long wait for his brother."

"No," Mark answered curtly, irked at the carefree familiarity. "No, I'm here because I want to be. Captain Jack Mackay's brother, William, has been my close friend for years."

"I hear the Mackay brothers are nothing alike."

They weren't, as Mark knew, if anyone did, but worried as he was over Natalie, the shallow chatter annoyed him. He excused himself abruptly and went out into the low-hanging, damp night. A stack of crates had been piled on the one platform bench. Exhausted, he leaned against the board-and-batten siding of the station. Outside air did nothing to buoy his spirits. It was no cooler than inside and now hung thick with fog. He removed his top hat so that he could rest his head against the building. He hadn't been exactly courteous to Jack's friend, the Army lieutenant, but all he could think of now, in his weariness, was seeing William, hoping that his friend would allay some of his fears over Natalie. William must have seen her at some point before he left the Etowah River by stage to handle his business in Marietta. Everyone loved Jack Mackay and no one was fonder of him than Mark, but Jack's very charm and good looks and sophistication somehow precluded the kind of confidence he'd always had in plain, kind William.

He peered again through the rolling mist for sight or sound of the approaching train. He saw no glimmer of the engine's headlamp. He heard nothing but an occasional foghorn from the river and a dog barking nearby. He wouldn't badger William with too many questions tonight. Just enough to settle some of his apprehensions. If only Jonathan would wake up and join him, the wait wouldn't seem quite so endless. "Dear God," he breathed, "don't let me turn out to be as foolish as I sometimes feel for getting in such a state over Natalie!"

A good thing, he thought, that the Lord evidently isn't insulted by such stupid prayers.

Actually, he'd rather hoped that Jack Mackay might join him and Jonathan tonight for the long wait. Tomorrow was Miss Eliza's birthday. William would surely be on the train.

The station door opened and Jonathan hurried up to him. "Sorry, Papa. I didn't mean to fall asleep," the boy said sheepishly. "You'd have been better off to have insisted that Jack come with you this time."

Mark hooked his arm with his son's. "I prefer my present company, thank you—to anyone else. Even good old entertaining Jack Mackay."

"He could have recited long passages of poetry to keep you occupied," Jonathan said. "Mama says in his spare time Jack's becoming a real Shakespearean scholar."

"She's right, he is. Actually, if I remember correctly, I read Jack his first passage from *King Lear* when I lived at the Mackay house right after I moved to Savannah."

"Papa, listen!"

They were both out on the tracks, straining for a sign of the train.

"I hear it—I'm sure I hear it," Jonathan exclaimed. "Yes! Look—isn't that the headlamp through the fog?"

The steady chug of the steam engine was unmistakable now, and flickering misty yellow, but visible, Mark could see the oil light moving slowly closer.

"In no time, we'll be able to hear the wheels clicking over Mr. Gordon's beloved wrought-iron splicing plates," Jonathan said. "Wouldn't he love to be standing right here with us watching his engine roaring down the track?"

Mark hugged his son briefly. "You'll have a good, meaningful life, Jonathan." In the dim lantern above the station platform, he saw the boy look at him, puzzled. "I mean that," he said. "You care about people and you don't miss any of the—basic, important things."

"Aw, I don't know about that. I just know how Mr. Gordon used to tell you by the hour at our house, when he and Miss Sarah came to dinner, what it would mean to him the day he could actually come here to the station night after night if he wanted to and—watch the iron horse thunder in."

"We should be able to see the whole train in just a minute now," Mark said.

When the engine, slowing its spurts of steam, finally inched into sight, Mark and Jonathan hurried to be right outside the door of the one passenger coach so that William would see them at once. They could tell he did when they saw him raise his arm in greeting while waiting his turn among the dozen or so other passengers, all of whom would get off in Savannah, the end of the line.

After handshakes and then bear hugs, Jonathan wasted no time: "Could you tell us about my sister?" he asked. "Papa's just got to know about how she is with the new baby and all. Is Natalie all right?"

"I do need to know, William. When did you last see her?"

William set down his satchel, stamped his feet on the wooden platform to get the blood going again after the long, cramped ride and thought a minute. "Let's see, I saw Natalie the evening before I left on the stage from Cassville."

"Was she all right?"

"Well, Mark, the girl's pretty big with child by now, but yes, I'd guess she's all right."

"Can't you do better than that?" Mark demanded.

"She sent her love to everybody, told me to be sure to tell you not to be a fussbudget about her." William fumbled slightly. "But I thought—well, I thought—"

"*What* did you think?" Mark demanded.

"It seemed to me that, for Natalie, she didn't quite have her old spizzerinctum, her usual get-up-and-go, but as I said, she is pretty big and awkward with the baby so far along."

"I think the very thought of that being true of Natalie is—pretty hard on Papa," Jonathan said.

Squinting wearily, William answered, "I'm sure you're right, son. So it has always been with your papa where that girl's concerned."

"I know you're exhausted," Mark said, "and I promise no more questions after this one—but if she were your daughter, would you be half out of your head with worry?"

"Is that what you are, Mark?"

"I'm ashamed to admit it, but yes."

William thought for what seemed to Mark an eternity, then keeping his voice steady with effort, he said, "If my little Delia were alive and grown up like Natalie and going to have a baby, yes. I'd be worried. Not out of my head, though." Looking directly into Mark's eyes, he added, "Far worse things can happen to your daughter than giving birth."

For a long, painful moment, Mark felt so ashamed, so sorry for the insensitive question he'd asked his old friend, he could think of nothing to say except "Oh, William, can you—forgive me?"

"Sure I can," William said with no expression whatever.

"Papa didn't mean to put the question quite that way," Jonathan offered. "You know that, don't you?"

"If anybody knows it, I do, Jonathan. Your father and I go back a long way." Looking around toward the one tiny baggage and freight cart piled with barrels, crates and trunks, William asked, "How long have you two been waiting here in this palatial station?"

"We came over about seven o'clock," Mark said, his voice still subdued.

"Then why don't we just go. I've got all I need tonight in this satchel. Easy to send for my other stuff tomorrow."

"Papa brought the carriage so we'd have room for all your luggage, sir."

For another moment, William looked steadily at Mark. "I wouldn't fret too much about Natalie. I always figured both times Virginia was carrying one of our children that it's mostly up to the Lord anyway. Sounds just like you, Mark, to bring the carriage. Where's Jupiter?"

"Papa did the driving," Jonathan said.

"I'm sending Jupiter to Knightsford with some supplies at dawn tomorrow," Mark explained. "He needed his sleep."

"William, we're going to Etowah Cliffs early in May," the boy announced to Mark's relief.

William didn't respond at once, but after studying Mark's face, he said, "I should have guessed that. Just hadn't thought about it. They've had torrents of rain, but the roads are passable. Not good. There's a new stretch this side of Marietta that's pretty bad, actually. You know, up there no one bothers to make a road. They just cut down trees and let the wagons and stagecoaches wear them into a roadbed."

"Miss Eliza's going with us," Jonathan said.

"*Mama's* making that hard trip, Mark?"

"Yes. Outside my family and you, William, she's the best friend I have. Do you mind that your mother's going too?"

"Oh, it could be risky, I guess. But if she's decided to go, that settles it." William picked up his satchel. "Well, it looks like the rest of my stuff's finally been unloaded."

On the way to the Mackay house on East Broughton, because William insisted upon driving the team from the high front seat, Mark and Jonathan sat inside surrounded by William's boxes and crates.

"Did William make you feel any better about Natalie, Papa?"

Mark sighed. "I don't know, son. I know he tried, but when a man fails as I do to conquer his fears, people—even good friends like William—tend to try not to add to it. They tend to say as little as possible, to be careful of you."

When Jonathan didn't comment at all, Mark knew his son was also doing just that.

While Captain Jack, William and Jonathan collected the luggage, Mark stood on the porch of the fully lighted Mackay house with Miss Eliza and her daughters, Kate and Sarah.

"Mama says you're terribly worried about Natalie," Kate said in her soft, urgent way. "Tell us, Mark, had William seen her lately?"

"About ten days ago, I guess."

"Well, for goodness' sakes," Sarah scolded, "what did he say about her? That is, if William managed enough energy to make a sentence."

"None of that tonight, Sarah," Miss Eliza ordered. "William's bound to be tired. Just leave him alone, do you hear me?"

"I want to know, Mark," Sarah urged, ignoring her mother.

"William did his best to calm me down," Mark said. "He seemed to feel Natalie's probably all right." He changed the subject. "Jonathan told him you were going up there with us, Miss Eliza."

"Good. That much is behind me," she said. "I had a time with these two daughters of mine, but I'm going. Oh, here come the boys. And thank you so much, Mark, for waiting at that train station for three long nights in a row."

"Well, here I am, Mama," William called, coming up the front walk empty-handed. "Jack and Jonathan refused to let me carry anything. Just pile it there by the front door," William instructed, embracing his mother. Then, turning to Mark, he said with a sly smile, "There is one other message from Natalie. Almost forgot."

Mark grabbed William's arm. "What? What, William?"

"Oh, simmer down, man. She took time in the pouring rain just to make me promise to tell you and Caroline that she and Burke are more in love than ever now that the baby's on the way."

From the corner of his eye, Mark saw Jack clutch at his heart. *"Thank heaven."* Jack gasped theatrically. "Then 'tis true—'tis really true that 'many waters cannot quench love, neither can the floods drown it' . . ."

"Jack! Be serious for once," Miss Eliza said. "Mark's *worried* over Natalie."

"Was that Shakespeare, Captain Jack?" Jonathan wanted to know.

"No, my good fellow," Jack said. "That was the Old Testament. The Song of Solomon, to be exact. You see, few know, actually, of my unfathomable spiritual depths."

"Hush, Jack!" his mother scolded. "But, Mark, isn't it good to know first-hand that there's no trouble between Natalie and Burke?"

"I know he's a worrywart," William chided, "but I can't believe even Mark would worry that those two might not still be head over heels in love."

Unable to enter into the affectionate banter, Mark murmured, "I guess I worry about everything that concerns Natalie. I must get awfully boring in the process."

"Well, there is that," Jack teased.

"It's past everyone's bedtime," Eliza Mackay declared, taking William's arm. "I'm sure poor Caroline's waiting up for Mark and Jonathan."

"I suppose you know, Jack," Mark ventured, "that your mother has agreed to go north with us."

"We all know," Sarah said in disgust.

"And it's a good thing we love all you Brownings so much," Kate added. "Otherwise, we'd never let her make that long, hard trip. Never!"

"Rubbish," her mother said.

"I think Mr. Sheftall expects you to talk Papa out of going, Miss Eliza," Jonathan said.

"I feel sorry for the old gentleman losing you, Jonathan, but you're going and so am I. I've already written Eliza Anne about when we might arrive. We'll get my birthday party out of the way tomorrow, gather our belongings, buy our tickets on Mr. Gordon's railroad and head north." Miss Eliza turned to Mark and pulled him down so she could plant a kiss on his forehead. "I want you, dear boy, to regain your peace of mind. There's only one way to do that, so we'll go and stay for as long as it takes. As a bonus, I'll get to visit my own daughter and grandchildren and see their house Burke and Ben built on those beautiful river cliffs. Right now, though, it's time to say good night."

Jack made a deep, exaggerated bow. "Our mother has spoken, so—Jonathan, Mark—'Fare thee well! And if forever, Still forever, fare thee well.' " He mussed Jonathan's hair. "No, my boy, that was neither Shakespeare nor the Song of Solomon."

Jonathan gave Jack a big grin. "What, then?"

"Lord Byron—Lord George Gordon Byron, sixth baron, English poet, born in London, the son of Captain 'Mad Jack' Byron, a notorious libertine. The dissoluteness and recklessness of Lord Byron's own life may be due in part to the *immoral* influence of his—"

"Enough!" Miss Eliza put her fingers over Jack's mouth. "William's tired, I'm tired, and you will wait, Captain Jack Mackay, at least until Jonathan's a little older for further enlightenment concerning your 'dissolute' English poet!"

Winking at Jack, Jonathan said, "Good night, Captain 'Mad Jack' Mackay. I guess I'd better take my father home now."

Chapter 6

As Tuesday, May 3, wore into late afternoon, Caroline sat on the window side of the scratchy maroon plush train seat beside her sleeping son and tried not to think. With eight other passengers, they had boarded the wooden coach before six that morning, unseasonable heat gripping the city. At least with the sun going down, the air might cool a little. Her legs cramped, her back hurt, but throughout the long, stifling day, she had not once caught anything in her eye from the wood-burning engine up ahead. Miss Eliza had not been so lucky. Something had blown in her eye that morning just seconds before she'd finished polishing the lenses of her new glasses.

The sun was streaking the sky with rose and gold now, as it moved slowly, steadily down behind the low hills rising along the Ogeechee River, whose path the tracks followed away from Savannah. Normally Caroline would have enjoyed the beauty, would have roused Jonathan to share it with her. Not today. The journey was so long and tiring even someone Jonathan's age needed every nap possible. For the past hour or so, the steady engine, its tall, thin stack spewing black smoke into the windless air, had pulled them along rather smoothly, almost as though on one of those straight clouds stretching across the sunset. She figured they'd come nearly eighty miles and would be turning away from the river soon and that meant slower progress because of the continuing heavy freshets that for almost a year had been eroding the track to the north. On its early runs back in 1840, the Central of Georgia had moved at the fast clip of twenty-two miles an hour until the unusual rainfall forced the decision to slow to seventeen miles. Plenty fast enough certainly, at least compared with the slow, back-wrenching stagecoach ride still ahead.

For the hundredth time she closed her eyes, then opened them to check on Mark across the narrow aisle beside Miss Eliza. His head was back against the seat, but his eyes were wide open, staring at nothing. Caroline longed over him. Even in profile, stress lines creased the still striking patrician face. A muscle in his lean jawline flicked steadily and she knew he was grinding his teeth again. The belching engine and clattering wheels made so much noise she could sigh heavily without anyone hearing. Involuntarily, over and over, they came—almost angry sighs. Natalie had obviously changed for the better, was far more amenable than in her younger days, but Natalie's father's obses-

sion over her was the same. Once more, this minute, as she'd had to do all
through her willful daughter's lifetime, Caroline stopped herself just short of
resenting the beautiful girl outright—deeply though she loved her.

She glanced again at her husband, who was now remoistening the soft
cloth from Miss Eliza's vial of weak salt water, brought along for the comfort
of anyone who might catch a speck in the eye through an open window. He
and Miss Eliza exchanged a few words as he gave her the freshened compress.
She patted Mark's hand and both again rested their heads back against the
dusty seats.

Caroline and Mark had started the trip side by side, but although one seat
was as hard as another, back three or four stops he had switched with Jonathan. If only the train didn't have to stop so often to take on passengers or
produce; if only the split wood didn't burn up so fast under the steam boiler
so that extra stops were needed; if only she knew what Miss Eliza was really
thinking this minute about the whole fuss and bother of such a long trip . . .
if only the stagecoach portion of the journey didn't have to be made at the
end when they would all be exhausted. She sighed again. Of course, Eliza
Mackay wanted to visit the Stileses at Etowah Cliffs, but surely a lady of her
age wouldn't be making such a trip merely for a visit until the roads had time
to dry a little after all the upcountry rains. Caroline had no doubt that Eliza
Mackay was along mainly to help Mark, who, years back, before he knew he
loved Caroline, had fancied himself in love with the young widow, Eliza
Mackay. The years had been kind, though. They were all still friends, close,
essential friends. Closer than some family members. Eliza Mackay had contained her own grief rather well, Caroline thought, when she'd lost her other
two grandchildren, little Delia and William Mackay, Jr., on the *Pulaski.* Undoubtedly she yearned to be with her Stiles grandchildren now, but Miss
Eliza was here, Caroline knew, in the rocking train on this hot afternoon, for
Mark's sake. Did the softly lovely, aging lady really think her "dear boy"
foolish to make the journey when they had no idea that anything at all was
wrong with Natalie? Or did she secretly agree that Mark might—just might
have reason for his foreboding?

Caroline frowned. Maybe I'm the peculiar one, she thought. And I admit
it's odd that I haven't even mentioned my own nameless fear of the Indian
boy to Miss Eliza. Only to Sheftall Sheftall and to Jonathan, other than Mark.
I don't understand myself at all. I covet Miss Eliza's opinion as much as Mark
does. I do wish I knew what she's thinking at this minute.

Eliza Mackay, still holding Mark's compress over her eye, leaned forward
just far enough to exchange smiles with Caroline. Her eye smarted far less
now, but Mark had insisted upon replacing the compress. She'd be firm in
refusing him the next time. Her arm ached from holding the cloth in place.
Young Jonathan had been able to see and remove the tiny black speck of
charred wood. Eyes heal quickly. She meant to humor Mark with only this

one last compress. He appeared to be dozing, but he'd surely rouse if she took the wet cloth away now.

Funny, she thought, how we endure irritation—and this patch does irritate me when I no longer need it—simply because we don't want to trouble someone we love. Mark is worried enough, heaven knows, and I saw no other way to lighten his burden than to make this trip, to give him a chance to see for himself that Natalie is carrying her baby well, that she's all right. The baby was due, Natalie had assured William, in less than six weeks. Will Mark insist upon staying until the child is born? I hope he does and I hope he doesn't, she thought.

Oh, I'll be so happy to see my own grandchildren again after all this time—nearly a year. In her mind's eye, she pictured them each one—pretty, dark-haired, dark-eyed Mary Cowper, now past nine; handsome, slender, somewhat hot-tempered eight-year-old Henry, as blond as his father, W.H.; and dear Robert, named for Eliza's own husband, who didn't live to see him—six now, chunky and muscular and cheerful, the picture of his grandfather Robert.

I long to see my grands, but I'm here trying not to fidget on this prickly, dusty train seat because Mark needs me to be here. Oh, I'm almost sorry William told me last night that Mark is ashamed of himself for being so unaccountably upset over Natalie. "He's ashamed," William had said, "especially with me, Mama, because both my babies drowned in the shipwreck and Natalie didn't. He still has his daughter and his son and it makes him ashamed, embarrassed, to be so torn up over Natalie. He feels weak. Mark's adding foolish embarrassment to his already overloaded heart. I wish he wouldn't do that."

Dear William. Even after nearly four years, her mother's heart went on breaking over William's loss.

Straightening her back, she felt a much-needed bit of strength rise in her as though God had noticed the necessity for it. Glancing at Mark, she longed to say, "Dear boy, everyone—*everyone*—has a weakness. You must not be ashamed of yours." She knew he was not asleep, although his eyes were still closed. Then, as though her thoughts had roused him, he lifted his head and looked at her.

"Shall I fix your eye patch again?" he asked.

"No. N-o," she spelled it out. "My eye is all right now." She felt sudden drops of water and stuck her hand out the open window. "Mark, it's starting to rain!"

"Oh, dear," he moaned, "that means another stop to get the canvas rolled down."

"Maybe not," she said. "Maybe it's just a refreshing shower. We could run out of it, couldn't we?"

"We could, I guess, but the engineer sitting out there in the open with a view of the sky may think otherwise."

Mark's words were scarcely out when she felt the train begin to slow, the brakes jerking them so that their backs bumped the seats. The fireman and the engineer and the few men passengers would be getting out to let down the side canvases.

When Mark and Jonathan left the coach to help, Caroline got up from her seat to stand in the aisle beside Eliza.

"What do you say, Caroline, we thank the Lord for this sudden shower? At least it should cool the air some. It felt good to me with the canvas rolled up."

"Me too," Caroline said, rubbing the back of her neck. "They'll get it down in no time, though, and the train noise will start up again, so let me ask you a blunt question. I want you to tell me the truth. Is Mark still fretting?"

"Actually, he hasn't said much about Natalie at all. What about you? Aside from being worn out—how are you, Caroline?"

Caroline laughed drily. "Me? Miss Eliza, I can't face telling even you about my—peculiar worries. They're stupid, I'm told, so don't insist. I do feel sure Natalie and her baby are all right. I don't agitate about the baby the way Mark does."

"Wouldn't you like to change seats and ride with me for a time once we start again?"

"No, thank you. I don't trust myself not to tell you what's on my mind and I'm determined not to dwell on it."

"You be the judge of that," Eliza said. "You know I understand."

After a while, when the train had puffed and pulled its way back to normal speed, Eliza, Jonathan beside her again in the stifling heat of the canvas-enclosed car, fell to thinking about Jonathan himself. How excited he must be with what lay ahead, not only to be entering Yale College this fall, but this trip to the upcountry. It would be the boy's first sight of the old Cherokee Nation where his sister now lived. He hadn't seen Natalie in almost three years, had never met either Ben or Mary McDonald, not even his own brother-in-law. She herself hadn't met any of the three either, for that matter. Eliza fell to marveling that the Cherokee brother and sister and Natalie's adored Burke had all come to seem such an integral part of her own life. Of Jonathan's too, she was sure, since he went on staying so lovingly involved with them all. She found herself enjoying the young man's very presence beside her. From the first, Jonathan Browning had, just by being Jonathan, blessed everyone.

With the canvas rolled down, she could still tell it was getting dark outside. They'd have to stop yet another time to raise the canvas and light the three oil lamps that hung from the tongue-and-groove ceiling of the darkening wooden coach. Jonathan's eyes were closed. The young slip quickly in and out of sleep. A good thing, she thought, since stopping would rouse him again.

After a time, although the train was still rolling, Jonathan sat up and took out the engraved gold watch his parents had given him for his sixteenth birthday, and for the first time, she noticed his strong, mature hands. Jonathan Browning was no longer a grubby-knuckled boy! Even sitting down, he towered above her almost as tall as his father, although heavier-shouldered and stocky. Knowing he'd be pleased to have her notice his watch, she asked, "What time is it, Jonathan?"

"Exactly five thirty-seven," he said. "We're late. We're due to pull in at the Gordon station sometime around eight, I think. That's if we're still only two hours behind schedule."

Eliza knew, of course, that the Central of Georgia line ended at Gordon, but boys turning into men enjoy being asked grown-up questions, so she pursued the matter: "They haven't finished the tracks beyond Gordon, have they?"

"No, ma'am, they haven't, but they expect to finish all the way to this side of the Ocmulgee River at Macon by next summer, I think. Papa said the freshets and the fever didn't hold up work quite so much this year as last year." The sunny smile broke on his young, open face. "I hope you're not terribly tired, Miss Eliza, because I guess our accommodations at Gordon won't be very nice. You and Mama will have to share a bed at what passes for an inn there. Mostly it's full of rough railroad workers. I hope you won't mind too much and that there won't be a lot of bedbugs."

"I'll be all right, son," she said, patting his knee. "After this fine stretch of railroad, it's that stagecoach trip up through White Hall and Marietta to the Etowah River I dread. But don't tell your parents I said that. They're both worried enough as it is."

Chapter 7

LYING beside him in their bed at Etowah Cliffs, Eliza Anne Stiles, after her beloved W.H. had made his singular kind of fiery, gentle love to her, waited for just the right moment to tell him that she certainly meant to go as far as Cassville with him tomorrow. He'd object, of course, hating the thought of her riding a horse alone the fifteen or sixteen miles back to their home by the Etowah River. Never mind, she fully intended to keep him in sight as long as possible. Her blond-haired, poetic-looking husband's political ambition was as much a part of him as his heart-piercing lovemaking, as much a part of him as his exquisite taste in china and crystal and furniture and paintings and literature. Long ago she'd accepted that ambition and vowed to match it in every way she could, being a woman. More than merely encouraging him in his campaign to win a seat in the United States Congress, she would find ways to become involved, even with his often perplexing political theories.

W.H.'s slender, strong hand pulled her head onto his chest, so that against her cheek, she could feel the patch of silky, sun-colored hair that grew there. She moved closer.

"How I love you, Lib," he breathed. "Right now—this minute—I wish to God I didn't have to leave on that infernal campaign trip. . . . How can I possibly bear trying to sleep at night so far from your—warmth and fragrance and—"

"—and you would have an equally hard time staying here so far from all those potential voters." She read his thoughts. "All those upcountry men who will flock to listen while you convince them with your magnificent oratory."

"You're beautiful, but you're also a witch." He laughed softly, the special laugh reserved for intimate times. "Just think," he whispered, "you know me as well as you do and you go right on loving me. Isn't that a miracle?"

"No. It's the most natural thing in my life." She took a deep breath, still seeking the exact right moment to inform him that, whether he liked it or not, she was riding as far as Cassville with him tomorrow morning. Then, openly teasing, flattering, she murmured, "I'm even in love with your stand in opposition to a national bank, to the tariff—W.H., I'm especially in love with your opposition to internal improvements sponsored by the federal government. And, oh, I'm smitten with your love of the Union *and* your strong states' rights stand!"

To stop the teasing, he pretended to be about to spank her, but kissed her mouth instead.

"In view of my romantic approval of your views, sir," she said firmly when he'd finally released her, "I feel you should know that this dark-eyed witch who adores you is riding her own horse alongside yours as far as Cassville tomorrow."

"You'll do no such thing! I forbid it."

In response, she kissed his elegant, almost delicate nose. "And I forbid you to forbid me, my love," she whispered.

"You know perfectly well, Lib, that no well-bred Savannah lady forbids her husband anything—but, as a compromise, I propose a compromise. If you'll accept without rancor or argument that I just might not get back home until after the Democratic State Convention in Milledgeville in June, there is a small chance that I might not forbid you to ride with me to—"

"Oh-h," she moaned. "I should have known you'd insist upon that stuffy State Convention! You're going to be nominated. Levi De Lyon will see to it. You waited purposely to spring that on me now, didn't you?"

"That's odd, I have the distinct feeling that you waited for just the right moment to inform me of your foolhardy ride as far as Cassville tomorrow."

She sighed. "I suppose we're even. But you'll miss most of our visit from the Brownings and my mother if you go to Milledgeville in June. Natalie's baby's due early that month too."

"Lib, Natalie's going to give birth as expertly as she's become a frontier wife. Wait and see." He rolled over on his back, thought a minute, then said, "You will be careful every minute I'm gone, won't you? I don't like the idea of Burke's not being nearby on weeknights. You must take special care in all ways."

"Shame on you! I not only have a grown-up nine-year-old daughter to help me, I have an eight-year-old protector named Henry, the very image of his handsome father, and a six-year-old named Robert, who's far less bad-tempered than his brother and who not only brings me flowers but has learned from his adored Natalie to brew all sorts of healing teas."

Abruptly he turned toward her and looked straight into her eyes. "I still say I'd be a lot easier if Burke's current building job wasn't too far away for him to sleep here in his own cabin at night."

"Dearest husband mine, Mother and Mark and Jonathan and Caroline will all be here in just two or three days! This is Thursday. The stage ride from the end of the Central of Georgia line can't take them more than—"

"Lib, no one can count on any stagecoach arrival at this time of year. I know you're eager to see your mother, but what do you suppose possessed Mark to decide to come before the roads dry out a little?"

"I've told you half a dozen times what Mother wrote. You don't listen.

Mark is worried sick over Natalie. Evidently I have simply *not* been reassuring enough in my letters to Savannah. Mark is obsessed with the idea that Natalie is not doing well at all."

"Her condition is perfectly normal with a baby due so soon."

"It seems to be, but have you ever known Mark Browning to act like a normal father where Natalie is concerned?"

"She's his weak spot, all right. The only weak spot so far as I can see in an otherwise rather flawless character—except, of course, his radical abolitionist ideas."

"Mark is *not* a radical abolitionist. He simply grew up in Philadelphia where—where our so-called peculiar institution was never a part of his life."

She said nothing more for a time, then asked, "Do you suppose Mark realizes that Indian Ben is still madly infatuated with his precious daughter? It could be that he and Caroline are worried about that."

"You're beyond me now," he mumbled inattentively. "I don't have time to keep up with such things."

"You do admit, don't you, that Ben never takes his eyes off Natalie? I'll never forget the look on his face the night before her wedding, and three years later he has that same stricken, hopeless look. Only worse."

"Well, he's an Indian."

"Indians are people too. Ben McDonald is in pain every minute over Natalie."

"A man can make no sane comment whatever about such an insane idea!"

"Insane or not, it's true. You know it is," she insisted.

"I suppose so. What rotten luck! I pity both little Mary and Ben. I pity Ben more, though."

"You do? Why? I'm convinced Mary's sun rises and sets in Burke, which compounds the irony."

"But in spite of the scar on her face and her half-blinded eye, Mary's a pretty little thing. She doesn't look at all Indian—her Scottish father, I guess. I have no doubt she'll marry some young man one day. Still, if you're right about Ben, that could be a different matter. A tragically different matter. He looks like a full-blood. Only white scum would marry a Cherokee now."

"Ben will never marry anyone," she said grimly, "because he worships Natalie."

"I must say she handles it rather well."

"By ignoring him. Natalie has always ignored anyone who might rock her little boat."

"I suppose the arrival of her baby—hers and Burke's—could cause the Cherokee still more anguish."

"You please me very much, sir, by understanding such a bizarre situation."

"And why wouldn't I understand it?"

"There's so much on your mind always. Few men would even notice. But you know, as much as they both help Burke and Natalie, I confess I wish almost daily that neither Ben nor Mary were in any of our lives." She reached for him. "What an utterly selfish wife you have, Congressman Stiles . . ."

"Selfish, irresistible and stubborn. You really mean to ride with me as far as Cassville tomorrow, don't you? Don't answer. I know you do, but will you agree that Indian Mary ride along on her pony, so she can come back with you?"

She arranged his arm under her head as she did every night and snuggled close. "Breakfast is time enough to discuss travel plans. Right now, I'm interested only in sleeping beside you while you're still here . . . but will you kiss me again, please? I need to stop thinking about poor Ben and Mary—*and* my aging mother enduring that ghastly stagecoach ride . . ."

Thursday evening, at the end of their third day on the road, Eliza Mackay stretched her weary body in the bed beside Caroline at White Hall and felt she'd never experienced such luxury. The bed was not as good as her own back home, but compared to their first night in Gordon after the long train ride and last night in Forsyth, where bedbugs raced over the lumps in the beds, White Hall Tavern was heaven. Mark had repeatedly told them that once they reached White Hall, all would be well. He was right.

When their stage had passed through Macon, Eliza longed to be able to stop for an hour or so. It was such a pretty little town, set in waves of low hills, and the stage rolling smoothly across the Ocmulgee River on the splendid bridge had been so exciting to them all they'd discussed it for miles afterwards. But here in White Hall, just south of Marthasville, except for Mark's continuing anxiety, she would have settled gladly for a few days' rest. It still seemed odd for the rough, uncouth, new town of Terminus to be called Marthasville—recently named for the governor's daughter, Martha Lumpkin—but everyone predicted its present minor building boom would continue and the governor would get full credit.

She breathed deeply of the clean upcountry air and was glad she'd taken the side of the bed near an open window. If she were unable to sleep, at least she could enjoy the fresh breeze and listen to the spring peepers in the trees outside their second-story room. The large, columned White Hall Tavern was indeed a rarity in north Georgia and Eliza made a mental note to write about it to Sarah and Kate once she was settled in with Eliza Anne and her family at Etowah Cliffs. The air up there on W.H.'s picturesque Etowah River, Eliza Anne vowed, was even better than at White Hall, where she and her children had spent a night last year when they first moved to Cass County. "All aside from the good, clean beds," her daughter had written then, "I was impressed with Mr. and Mrs. Charner Humphries, who own White Hall Tavern. She's shy and kind and quite aptly named Mary. Her husband is as nearly a typical Dutchman as anyone could imagine—solid, practical, smooth of face and gracious. Their establishment is so successful it has been an election precinct for De Kalb County for years. When you come up to visit us, White Hall Tavern will be the remembered stop en route."

I wonder, Eliza thought, if I'm lying awake just to enjoy this nice place longer. Not altogether true. I'm too tired and still too concerned over Mark for sleep. I've pieced together from talking to all three Brownings along our way that Mark and Caroline are not necessarily worried about the same thing. Natalie is the focus of their uneasiness, of course, but Caroline isn't fretting unduly over Natalie's baby. She is oddly—almost darkly—worried over that young Indian helper of Burke Latimer's. It wasn't until yesterday right after our stage almost turned over on that rough stretch of new road out of Forsyth that she admitted it to me, although she said she'd told Mr. Sheftall weeks ago.

Caroline stirred in the bed beside her and gave a muffled, sleep-flattened cry, then fell silent and turned over. Eliza decided not to try to rouse her and breathed a prayer that the nightmare—if it was a nightmare—would be forgotten by morning. Caroline needed her rest. They all needed rest because tomorrow would be the longest, most exhausting travel day yet. From White Hall, Mark had told them at dinner, they would pass through a primitive place aptly named Slabtown, in which railroad gangs, mostly Irish, lived and worked, then on through Marthasville, where they'd cross the Chattahoochee River on Mr. James Montgomery's ferry not far from old Fort Gilmer and the abandoned Indian settlement called Standing Peachtree.

At the mere thought of the old Cherokee town of Standing Peachtree, Eliza shuddered. Why? she wondered. Were their spirits still near? Quietly, keeping it to herself when it might have caused comment or a quarrel, she had felt deeply sorry over the Cherokees, had agreed with her son Jack, whose Army duty had stationed him in the midst of their suffering and grief; had agreed that they were victims of the white man's greed. The long, forced march west for the Cherokees was now being called, ironically, the Trail of Tears. She had not shuddered just now, though, only from sympathy for the Indians. Her deep dread had to do with what Caroline feared about poor Indian Ben McDonald. Eliza had tried to reason a little with Caroline. Perhaps Ben did almost worship Natalie from afar. It wouldn't be at all surprising if, from the ugly tragedy of his own young life, Natalie now symbolized all beauty to Ben. The boy was human. As with everyone else in the world, he needed a bright object for his dreams.

Against her pillow, she shook her head. How incredibly perplexing! It just wasn't like Caroline, always optimistic, to become obsessed with the idea that trouble lay ahead. As she'd continued to do for almost twenty-six years, Eliza found herself wondering what her husband, Robert, might have thought of Caroline's notion that somehow it meant danger or trouble if the half-blood Ben did indeed love Natalie.

No man was more sensitive, kinder than my Robert, she thought, but as with us all, he had his blind spots. I wish I felt sure he'd understand, but he might be outraged if it turns out that Caroline is right. Still, I wonder . . . Somehow, I think Robert might just say, "How in tarnation can anyone really *know* about what an Indian will do?"

Well, they could reach Sallie Hughes's ford at the Etowah River by tomorrow evening. Eliza prayed for the strength to endure what would surely be an eight- or nine-hour day in that jolting, bucking stagecoach.

When one of her children couldn't sleep during their early years—Robert too, for that matter—she'd always urged, "Take several deep breaths and you'll be able to doze off." Eliza tried it now, but she was so exhausted that only one thing seemed to steady her: Mark had promised that if she wasn't up to the long trip, they'd travel only thirty-some miles to the thriving town of Marietta tomorrow, where there was also a splendid new hotel with fifteen well-furnished rooms.

She longed to see the Brownings reach Natalie as soon as possible. For that matter, she longed to see her own daughter and her precious grandchildren, but she was making this hard trip at the muddy time of year because of Mark and Caroline. If she could just hold out, they'd be there late tomorrow evening.

Oh, dear, she thought, I won't hold out if I don't get some sleep! I know my poor old jolted, battered body is resting, but my mind is in a stir over so many things . . .

Still holding her beside him in their bed at Etowah Cliffs, W.H. could tell by her slow, even breathing that Lib had fallen soundly asleep. His own eyes were wide open, his mind racing. "Tangling" might be a better participle, he thought, editing even his thoughts because to him words were treasures, deserving of the utmost care. He hadn't, he knew, been altogether honest with Lib when he'd said there was only a probability that he would stay away for the State Nominating Convention in Milledgeville. He fully intended to be there, even if it meant canceling that last campaign speech in Paulding County. The current trip was, of course, merely a preparatory swing about the district. Until the Milledgeville convention, he was not yet a candidate, but surely he could count on his longtime Savannah friend and law partner, Levi De Lyon, so prominent on the committee. The actual nomination of William Henry Stiles of Cass County, he felt, was a formality. Once he'd written his acceptance letter, probably in July, serious campaigning for votes could begin. He simply meant to be already known because of this trip through Cass, Floyd, Cherokee and Paulding counties.

He could speak freely to the settlers in the upcountry now as one of them. He was. This early campaign swing would help him acquaint himself with the wide variety of men who lived in his district. He meant not to overdress, even to be folksy where expedient. Many of his own farming problems would be those of his constituents. His land purchases and the move to Etowah Cliffs had certainly drained his resources. He would find the simple, straightforward words to let them know that he was, in spite of his Savannah background and the erudition that came naturally to him, one of them. He would be speaking against several Whig candidates who were old family friends—R. W. Habersham of Habersham County, A. R. Wright of Floyd, A. H.

Kenan of Baldwin—but as with any important speech, W.H. would carefully write out his thoughts ahead of time. In fact, his saddlebags, when he rode out of Etowah Cliffs tomorrow morning, would contain a sheaf of detailed notes which could be switched around to fit this or that locale. In order not to make enemies socially, he hoped the Cherokee subject had worn thin enough by now so that there would be no need to involve himself in either agreeing or disagreeing with the way Georgia had disposed of the Indians. The entire issue was no longer relevant. Right or wrong, the Cherokees were gone.

Well, not all of them of course, his mind running crazily back to Lib's conviction that the two half-breeds still in their midst were in love with his longtime law client Mark Browning's son-in-law and daughter. What if they are? he asked himself. Little Mary is gentle as a lamb and her brother, Ben, while morose at times and silent, seems harmless. Heaven knows, he's devoted to Burke Latimer, who rescued both Indians from a cave and gave Ben his chance to become a skilled carpenter. Any futile feelings Ben might have toward Burke's wife, Natalie, could do no possible harm. Ben *is* half Scottish. He's not a savage.

He scooted down in the bed to find a more comfortable position, careful not to rouse Lib. She stirred a little, then turned over. Good. He liked sleeping spoon fashion with her, an arm around her slender waist.

I'm glad her mother is coming, he thought, hard as the trip over these muddy spring roads must be on the old lady. Compared to the mothers-in-law of some of my gentleman friends, I'm fortunate to have Mrs. Mackay. She's a remarkably reasonable lady. My Lib adores her. Having her here while I'm away is splendid, although I admit freely that I am already hoping they're all back in Savannah by the time I return in a few weeks. He tightened his arm lightly about Lib. This four-roomed wing of our house is so inadequate for guests, Caroline Browning will have to room here with Lib, I imagine. What I can't imagine is either Caroline or Mark sleeping in the Latimer log cabin!

He took a deep breath, feeling drowsy at last. That's Lib's problem, where they all sleep. Lib . . . his face buried in the back of her neck, he breathed deeply of the familiar fragrance of her skin.

The last conscious thought before he drifted off was his own heart's cry: "Lib, Lib . . . how I'll miss you!"

His first plunge into sleep was so deep, Lib had sprung from their bed and was struggling into her old blue silk dressing gown, calling his name in such panic that W.H. had to fight his way to consciousness before he could even ask what she was doing up thrashing about.

"There's some kind of trouble," she gasped. "Indian Mary's down in our yard! She galloped over from Natalie's cabin on her pony. Get up and come downstairs with me—now!"

By the time he found his own robe and slippers and stumbled after her, she was out of the house shouting Mary's name. From the open upstairs window, he could see Mary's shadowy figure—astride her white pony bareback. He could hear her pleading with Lib: "Come quick! It's Natalie—I'm so afraid! Something is wrong. It's Miss Natalie's—baby!"

Still groggy, W.H. hurried downstairs and reached the front door just as his agile wife leaped up behind Mary.

"Get Solomon out of bed in the stable, W.H.," she called out, "and have him saddle your horse! Ride as fast as you can to Natalie's cabin!"

Mary and Lib were galloping away at such a clip he couldn't make out the remainder of what else his wife might be ordering. Up the stairs to the second floor—two steps at a stride—he hunted around for his trousers and shirt and a pair of boots.

Never mind getting his horse saddled. He would reach the Latimer cabin faster if he ran all the way on foot.

Chapter 8

As soon as she and Mary were in sight of the dimly lit cabin, Eliza Anne could hear Natalie's screams.

"Faster, Mary! We've got to—ride faster."

"Little Star go fast as he can, Miss Lib. Hold on to me!"

"When did Natalie go into labor? Was she screaming when you left her?"

"Yes, yes," Mary gasped. "Excuse me. I—no talk—good now. I try for Little Star to—go faster!"

"All right. Hurry—do hurry!"

By the time she and Mary reached Burke's new front porch, the screams had stopped. No sound came from inside the cabin. Eliza Anne's heart almost stopped too.

"Bring a candle, Mary," she ordered as she ran through the large front room toward the back of the house where Burke had added a bedroom. Holding the hot, limp hand in both her own, Eliza Anne spoke Natalie's name desperately—over and over. There was no response. No movement whatever. In the flickering yellow light of the single candle which Mary now held above the motionless figure on the rumpled bed, Eliza Anne thought her heart would break at the irrelevant sight of Natalie's shining red hair spread over the white pillow. Even now, unconscious, crosswise on the bed, stomach distended, one leg drawn up, arms fallen spread-eagled—Natalie was *beautiful.*

"She—not dead," Mary whispered.

"No. No, Mary, she's breathing."

With the births of her own three babies, Eliza Anne had had loving, skilled help from her mother, from two Savannah doctors and three family servants. The pain and the wrenching, soul-emptying agony of trying to rid herself of each child were still sharp in Eliza Anne's memory, but she remembered almost nothing of what anyone did to help her.

"Where *is* W.H.?" She asked the question more of God than of Mary.

"I hear him run! He coming."

"Thank heaven." Then, instinctively, Eliza Anne leaned down to lay her ear against Natalie's bulging stomach.

"Lib! Lib . . . ! Where are you?" She heard W.H.'s frantic call from the lane along which Natalie and Burke had planted osage orange trees early last spring.

"Go to the door, Mary! Tell Mr. Stiles to wait. I'm trying to find some— movement." Not looking to see if Mary obeyed her or even if W.H. had entered the cabin, she spread her own body across the empty side of the bed so as better to sense what she already feared could not be sensed—or felt. There was no motion. Not even the weakest movement . . .

"Oh, God," Eliza Anne breathed. "Don't let it be true—not this, not this!" From the main room of the cabin, she heard Mary trying to stop W.H. from coming inside.

"It's all right, Mary," she called. "W.H.! Come here. I—I'm so afraid Natalie's baby—is dead."

He rushed into the small, tumbled bedroom and knelt on the floor beside her. "I'm sure you're wrong, Lib," he said. "Natalie's been doing so well. She's been doing very well. You said so yourself and—"

"It doesn't matter what I said! I know I've had three children, but, W.H., I really don't know how to handle a thing like this! Why aren't you riding as hard as you can to Cassville for a doctor? No, that's too far! Why didn't you bring Sinai? Sinai must know something about birthing!"

"Lib, she's a seamstress!"

"I don't care if she is a seamstress. Go get her—now!"

"Maybe I should run to the river and shout across for Elizabeth Holder," he offered. "She's lived on the frontier all her life—the hills of North Carolina. Her husband, David, can get her over here in less than half an hour."

For a panic-filled instant, Eliza Anne threw herself into his arms and clung to him. "Get someone, please, please get someone to help!"

"Then you'll have to let me go, Lib. Look here—this isn't like you! Natalie needs you to be calm now."

She dropped her arms and pushed him toward the door. "Get both Sinai and Elizabeth Holder. Even if the baby's dead, Natalie still has to be delivered of it!"

For a long time, Mary stood at the foot of the bed, staring at Miss Lib leaning over Natalie, who still had not stirred. The beautiful face Mister Burke loved was as pale as the moon in a high sky. I make Miss Lib some tea, she decided, and slipped soundlessly into the kitchen. When she returned, kind Miss Lib still refused to leave the bedside, or even to look away from the quiet, pale face, no matter how Mary tried to persuade her to take even one sip of hot tea to strengthen her for whatever lay ahead in this night of trouble.

"Thank you anyway, Mary," Miss Lib said finally, not looking at her. "Put the cup down and press your ear against her stomach. You're young. Maybe you can hear better than I. Please?"

The swollen belly felt hard as Mary bent to listen—to listen, to hope, to

pray. There was no sound beyond what might be Natalie's hunger causing
her stomach to growl, but only a little. Just the barest, faraway sound.

"There isn't a—sign of the tiniest kick or movement, is there, Mary?"

Miss Lib's voice was so empty and sad, tears began to roll down Mary's
cheeks. Her own voice, no matter how hard she tried, would make no sound.
She could only shake her head no.

"Did you notice what time it was when Mr. Stiles went for help?"

"Yes. Almost an hour has passed, but soon, I think, he will be here."

The heavy, helpless noise Miss Lib made was bigger, more desperate, more
filled with sorrow than a sigh could ever be. The sweet lady loved Natalie.
She loves Mister Burke too, Mary thought, her own heart twisting with pain
—for everybody. Even those coming to visit from Savannah—Natalie's parents, Miss Lib's mother and Natalie's brother, Jonathan. Her heart twisted for
Mister Burke, who might now not be a father as he so longed to be. Her
pain, though, was deepest for her brother. She stifled a sob. Poor, hopeless
Ben, who loved Natalie more than anyone loved her on this whole earth. For
Ben, who would be forced as always to stand alone outside—even of Natalie's pain.

Mister Burke and Ben were to meet the Savannah family—maybe tonight,
at Sallie Hughes's ford. She was sure Miss Lib's mother would know what to
do about Natalie, but even tonight could be too late. Mary would willingly
have tried to help, but as always, she, like Ben, stood—outside the lives of
their white friends—as long and as silently as possible.

By the time robust, red-cheeked Elizabeth Holder, still in her twenties and
six months pregnant herself, rushed into the room, Natalie was coming to.
Eliza Anne had watched the lovely face begin to swell. Now it glistened with
perspiration and drops of the cool water which Mary had brought from the
well outside.

"You've done the right thing, Mrs. Stiles," Elizabeth Holder said, grabbing both of Natalie's bare feet in order to straighten her bloated body on
the bed. "You brought her around with that cold water. I never delivered but
one baby and mostly I just watched that time, but up here we do what we've
got to do—right or wrong."

"What do you mean, Elizabeth?" Eliza Anne demanded. "We've got to do
this right!"

"Won't be done right with them two standin' in the doorway gapin' at us.
Men bring bad luck at a time like this."

Eliza Anne noticed for the first time that both W.H. and his overseer,
young David Holder, were standing just inside the room—both staring at
every move Elizabeth made with Natalie. "Please, W.H.," she said as gently
as possible, "take David and go outside! This is women's work."

"But where's Sinai?" W.H. asked.

"How would I know? You're the one who went for her." Eliza Anne tried
to soften the edge in her voice. "Did she promise to come?"

"Yes, yes, she did. Said she hated to deliver a baby, but that she certainly could. She promised to hurry over just as soon as she collected her supplies." Eliza Anne groaned. "That could take Sinai half the night! What on earth is she collecting? Natalie has kettles to boil water and clean cloths and—" At that moment, she heard Sinai's quick steps on the cabin porch and the thin, birdlike black woman whipped into the room, pushing everyone aside as she rushed to Natalie.

"Thank you, Sinai," Eliza Anne whispered. "What took you so long?"

"Had to get me a knife sharpened. Effen there's already trouble like Mausa Stiles say, need a good sharp knife."

"What on earth for?" Elizabeth Holder gasped.

"To throw in under her bed, whatcha reckon?" Sinai growled. "Birthin' is bad enough when it's natcheral. But nobody with sense has a mind to forget a sharp knife. Cuts the pain. Got water boilin', girl?" she demanded of Mary.

"Yes," Mary said, and hurried toward the kitchen, almost bumping into W.H. and Holder as they backed out the door.

With another sigh, Eliza Anne said to no one in particular, "Maybe it took that to get both men out of here."

"Mrs. Stiles?"

"What is it, Mrs. Holder?"

"Who's deliverin'—me or this nigger woman?"

"Well, I thought—I thought you'd both need some help and—"

"My granny was the most respected midwife in the whole state of North Carolina," Elizabeth Holder declared. "I used to ride with her. Helped her only that once, but I've seen a hundred babies brought out. Make up your mind which one."

"Mausa Stiles done axe *me,*" Sinai said, hands on hips.

The moan that came from Natalie brought both Sinai and Elizabeth Holder to their full height—Elizabeth towering above the wrinkled, older Sinai.

"Turn her over," Sinai ordered. "We gotta get her on her knees."

"No! First turn her to one side. She ain't ready yet!" Elizabeth Holder snapped.

For a terrifying moment, the two pulled at Natalie, each trying to turn her an opposite way. Eliza Anne stood it as long as she could, then, because Sinai had belonged to the Mackays for years and now belonged to her and W.H., she jerked the servant to one side and went to Natalie herself. "Don't try to be quiet, Natalie dear," she said, as comfortingly as her own panic would allow. "Scream if you need to, but you—you do have to be on your knees, I'm sure."

The pitiful moans and whimpers tore at Eliza Anne as Natalie began to writhe and throw her body in a desperate, frantic need to rid herself of the cause of her pain.

"Wait. I see 'tain't time yet," Sinai grumbled. " 'Tain't time to git nobody on no side—or knees!"

"Oh, yes, it is," Elizabeth said firmly. "Ain't no doubt about that!" When

Sinai refused to budge, Elizabeth stepped back and glared at Eliza Anne. "She's a nigger and I'm not, so who's going to win, Mrs. Stiles?"

"Well, is it time? Is she—having the baby prematurely?" Eliza Anne asked.

"Yes!" the Holder woman said.

"Not yit." Sinai appeared to have put herself in complete charge.

"Who's gonna win?" Elizabeth demanded again.

"I done won," the older woman mumbled, rummaging in a croker sack she'd brought with her.

"There'll be no argument," Eliza Anne said as firmly as she could manage. "It does look as though one of you would know whether or not she's—ready!"

Out of the sack Sinai jerked a long, sharp knife and a bottle. With one hand, she tossed the knife under Natalie's bed, then worked the cork out of the bottle.

Natalie's writhing became more frantic and her cries of "Help me! Miss Lib! Please—help me . . ." sickened Eliza Anne so that she ran from the room and vomited on the kitchen hearth. "Dear God," she breathed, "forgive me for—being—so helpless! Do something, Lord—do something for Natalie! Lord, that's—*Natalie* in there!"

Somewhat composed after splashing her face with cool water handed her by Mary, she looked around for W.H. He was nowhere in sight.

"You feel better, Miss Lib?" Mary asked.

"Yes. I'm sorry—for the mess I made. I'm all right, but I must go back to Natalie. You'll have to clean up the fireplace, Mary. I couldn't make it to the porch. I am sorry."

When Eliza Anne returned to the bedroom, Natalie was still on her back, still whimpering, struggling on the rumpled bed, but not as much, it seemed, and then she saw why. Sinai was slowly, gently massaging the distended stomach with oil of camphor. Fumes permeated the room, but Natalie *was* quieting some as the bony brown hands, softened by the oil, moved over her stomach, between her breasts, up and around her shoulders and neck.

Amazed that Sinai alone appeared to be in charge, Eliza Anne looked around the shadowy room for Elizabeth Holder. She stood clutching her own stomach, leaning against the cabin wall, pain distorting her face.

"Elizabeth?" Eliza Anne asked hesitantly. "Are you—not feeling well either?"

"I'm all right, ma'am," the younger woman croaked hoarsely. "I need to say I'm sorry I flew off the handle at—your nigger there. I—I see she knows a lot more than I know about birthin'. I—got dizzy myself—seein' Miss Natalie's issue of blood. I walked off over here out of the way. But I'll help—if I'm needed."

Eliza Anne stared more closely at Natalie. There *was* blood! Not spreading, but on the crumpled sheet beneath her was a dark stain. "Sinai! Sinai—did you know she's—bleeding? How can you be so—calm?"

"Sh! Rest is what she need now. An' *quiet*. The baby's gonna come. I see to that. But—it be dead. I—kin smell it."

"You—you what?"

When Natalie sprang upright in the bed and began to scream Burke's name, Sinai pushed her roughly down again and held her there.

"Why wouldn't she be screaming for her husband?" Eliza Anne demanded, grabbing both of Sinai's oily hands. Natalie was trying now to crawl out of the bed and would surely have fallen to the floor had not Elizabeth Holder rushed across the room to restrain her.

"*Mary,*" Eliza Anne cried wildly. "Mary, bring more light! In the name of heaven, Mary—come in here and help us!"

Carrying another candle, Mary McDonald slipped into the room, handed the light to Eliza Anne and took charge. Now they could all see how swollen Natalie's face was. And struck by throw after throw, her equally swollen body and legs thrashed about while she screamed for Burke.

Even when Mary managed to get her on her knees, Natalie was still crying Burke's name.

Eliza Anne and the two other women stood back, gaping at the Indian girl, whose hand, bathed in oil, was inserted now into Natalie's body.

"Mary—Mary," Eliza Anne could only whisper. "Mary, you—you knew—what to do all the time . . . Why didn't you tell me?"

Too busy to answer, Indian Mary was turning the baby, so that within minutes she brought down two discolored, swollen little feet, and then the blotched, lifeless body of Natalie's child.

Chapter 9

JUST before dawn the next morning, Friday, Eliza Anne and W.H. stood with David and Elizabeth Holder on Natalie's porch, thanking them for having crossed the river last night to help.

"Don't know that we helped much," Elizabeth said, holding her young husband's hand. "But I swan, I never saw a lady like you, Mrs. Stiles!"

Eliza Anne stared at her in surprise. "Like me? You found me out, Elizabeth. That's what really happened. You found out what a helpless city woman I am. You helped enormously by being here."

"Indeed you did," W.H. said, shaking hands with them both. "My wife and I—the Latimers too—will be forever grateful."

"Don't try to tell my wife you're a helpless city woman, Mrs. Stiles," David said. "She's already told me that if our baby is a girl, its name's going to be Eliza—after you."

"That's right," Elizabeth said. "You were so calm and full of God's grace in the midst of such a—a—" Her lips trembled and her eyes filled with the tears she'd been trying to hold back, Eliza Anne knew, since the moment they all realized Natalie's baby was dead. "Your nigger was fine too. I'm sorry I yelled at her. But—we'da been lost without Indian Mary. Even seein' good out of only one eye, she put us all in her shadow. Mary McDonald coulda done it all by herself without a one of us bein' there."

"Is it really true," David asked, "that Miss Natalie won't let you bury the baby till her husband gets home?"

"My wife and I will think of a way to dissuade her of that," W.H. said, slipping his arm around Eliza Anne's waist. "As you know, Mary's washed and dressed the baby. It's all laid out in the front room of the cabin. I think if I ride into Cassville this morning for a preacher, Natalie will agree to—burying the little fellow."

"I wouldn't be too sure of that," Elizabeth Holder said. "I never saw such a will as Miss Natalie's got—sick as she is."

Eliza Anne tried to smile. "You know her better than my husband does, Elizabeth. But—if our Savannah house guests and Burke don't reach here this afternoon or early evening, we'll have to bury Natalie's son, no matter what its mother says."

Chapter 10

For a reason he could certainly not explain, Mark's desperation over Natalie had mounted with every weary mile of the long journey from Savannah. The more he tried to hide it from the others, the more it gnawed at him. As the muddy stagecoach pulled within sight of the town square in Marietta at noon on Friday, it was all he could do to be responsive to Jonathan's pleasant talk of how much more civilized Marietta was than Sheftall Sheftall had led him to expect.

"They still don't seem to take much care of their horse lots," the boy was saying, "but Mr. Sheftall's going to be dumbfounded when I tell him about all these new stores and houses. Look, Mama, you and Miss Eliza could do a lot of shopping right here! We just passed Human and Irwin, Boots and Shoes, and over there across the square there's another new sign—J. H. Wiley and Company, Merchandise."

"There's a good hotel up ahead too, son," Mark said, his distressed thoughts more on the weariness and pallor of Miss Eliza's face now than on the new stores. "But maybe we should take pity on our exhausted ladies and not chatter so much."

"We're all right, Mark," Miss Eliza said, forcing a smile. "And I want you to take heart—we'll get to the Etowah River yet tonight."

"If you can hold out," Caroline said to the older woman, "then so can I. Gritting my teeth, but I'm all right."

Studying Eliza Mackay's drawn face, Mark stopped fighting the inevitable. He could not permit his own anxiety to make his old friend ill. He reached across to touch his wife's hand and then Eliza's. "We're going to stop this grim endurance," he said. "I've just made up my mind. If they have rooms for us up ahead at the Marietta Hotel, we're spending the remainder of the day and all night tonight right here."

"But, Mark," Miss Eliza said, "I'm sure someone will be meeting us this evening up there at Sallie Hughes's ford. And I know how worried you are about Natalie, so—"

"Oh, darling, *could* we stop here?" Caroline interrupted. "I'm not as brave as Miss Eliza and I really can't pretend any longer. Isn't it still thirty miles or so to the Etowah River?"

"I said I'd made up my mind, Caroline," he answered firmly. "Whoever Eliza Anne and Natalie have meeting us knows stagecoach arrivals can't be counted on. They'll have made arrangements for either tonight or tomorrow. We'll reach the Etowah on the New Echota Road Saturday afternoon while it's still day, if we do the sensible thing and rest in Marietta tonight."

Helpful as usual, Jonathan beamed at his father. "And you and I can scout around Marietta some after dinner. I'll really be able to dumbfound Mr. Sheftall if we have a good look at the place."

"What about you, Mark?" Miss Eliza asked. "Will you be able to sleep here tonight, worried as you are?"

"Oh, we're both worn to a frazzle already with worry over that girl," Caroline said. "One more night can't matter, can it, darling? A good, long rest might help us handle our embarrassment when we find out tomorrow that, after all, Natalie's just fine. We simply can't allow our obsessions to make Miss Eliza ill."

"I don't intend to," Mark said grimly as he jumped out into the rutted street in front of the Marietta Hotel even before the coach had come to a full stop. "Stay here with the ladies, son," he called up to Jonathan. "I'll see to our accommodations for the night."

After a remarkably well-prepared meal, Caroline agreed readily to Mark's suggestion that she and Miss Eliza lie down in their separate rooms in the new, well-furnished hotel while he and Jonathan inspected the town. Bathed and dressed in her nightgown, Caroline climbed—and it was a climb—onto the mountainous feather bed and collapsed. This far north, cool and cloudy outside, the quilt felt good.

Shifting her aching body between the fresh sheets, she breathed a prayer of thanks for the many kindnesses already shown them by Mr. and Mrs. Benson Roberts, managers of the hotel. In fact, everyone—from the clerk at the registration counter to the waiters in the dining room—had shown them every attention. The people of Marietta, Georgia, certainly appeared to welcome visitors and were truly proud of their town, which now covered three-quarters of a mile of land. The W & A Railroad had reached Marietta, the Cherokees were gone, the town was booming.

Pulling the quilt up over her shoulders, Caroline tried to dismiss any thought of a Cherokee. They *were* gone. Why did people have to go on mentioning them? Truthfully, she couldn't say she felt nothing for those poor people, struggling, she supposed, to make new homes in the faraway, strange newly formed state of Arkansas. She genuinely liked little half-blood Mary McDonald. She didn't actually dislike her brother, Ben.

"I fear him!" She spoke aloud into the quiet room. "I don't know why, but I—fear Ben McDonald . . ."

Quiet, morose, dark-skinned Ben had never done or said one thing to cause her to fear him. Her son-in-law, Burke Latimer, simply would not be on his way to what appeared genuine success as a builder without Ben's expert help. Indians, she was sure, except for their strange culture, were at least similar to other people. Curly-haired, pretty little Mary was even rather lovable. Oh, her English was broken. Evidently as a child she'd spent more time with their full-blood Cherokee mother than had Ben, who'd worked as a carpenter with his Scottish father. But Mary was sweet-natured and seemed unable to do enough for Natalie or for Burke. Of course, Caroline knew the girl fancied herself in love with Burke, but somehow that didn't alarm her—probably, if she were honest, because Mary was *not* Indian-looking. Oh, her eyes were dark, but with that light curly hair and round, attractive face, not Indian-looking at all. Unlike Ben, whose high cheekbones and straight, proud nose, direct, burning eyes and sullen manner—she stopped the thought. Since when do I judge another human being by the way he or she appears to me?

Since right now, she admitted, not admiring the trait. Caroline was, if nothing else, brutally honest with herself.

"I don't think Ben is going to harm my daughter," she spoke aloud. "I just don't know what to do with this haunting uneasiness! I simply know he's going to do *something* dark and terrible that could hurt all of us."

Too bone-weary to sleep, she pummeled, then stacked, the two feather bolsters so that she could sit up. The Marietta Hotel had fifteen rooms, all furnished extremely well for a frontier town. She and Mark and Jonathan would be more than comfortable in this room tonight—if Jonathan's parents were able to sleep. Miss Eliza's room—heavenly private—was quite like this one. In each room, apparently, were two beds with bolsters, quilts, high feather mattresses, even foot balances. Across the room stood a large, sturdy bureau with a huge looking glass. On a table between the windows, a washstand held a bowl and pitcher. There were—she counted—one, two, three tin candlesticks and three chairs. Caroline sighed deeply. They were dead right to have decided to stop in Marietta. More uneasy even than she, dear, kind Mark had, as almost always, made the right decision.

She tossed one bolster aside, stretched herself flat on the bed again and turned over. Dear Lord, she breathed, bring all this nameless fretting and anxiety to an end—tomorrow! Free Mark of his bondage to our daughter . . . free me of my fear of that Indian boy. She sighed again from the depths of her being, then said aloud, "God must be weary, weary of hearing the same monotonous prayer!"

From the steep roof of the tiny clapboard church where he was hard at work nailing down the molding at the base of the small steeple they'd just managed to set in place, Burke looked down at his helper, Ben, and gave him their accustomed thumbs-up sign. All was going well and inside half an hour, since it was Friday and early quitting time, they would be stowing their tools in the shed and riding to Milner's place on the Etowah River about a mile and a quarter from the church site.

"You can begin to gather things up, Ben," he called down. "Our favorite time of week's here. Don't you wish we didn't have to meet our Savannah visitors at Milner's? I'd like to ride hard toward home like any other Friday, wouldn't you?"

When Ben didn't answer, Burke laid down his hammer, balancing himself with his back against the steep rise in the church roof. "Ben?"

The only sound he heard was the clatter of tools as Ben evidently dumped an armload inside the shed.

"Hey, down there!"

Ben appeared from behind the church and stood looking up at Burke unsmiling, his face a dark mask. "You want something, Burke?"

Deciding not to make anything of Ben's oddly tortured expression, although it would have been natural to ask if Ben felt all right, Burke called down, "No. You've already put the tools away. You're ahead of me, as usual, partner. I'll be through here in less than five minutes, unless I split this molding trying to hurry." He set and drove one nail. "Go wash up, Ben. I expect we'd better not count on time for that at Milner's today. No way of knowing when a stage arrives. I'll lose my happy home if I'm not there waiting when Natalie's family and Mrs. Mackay reach this side of the ford. I'm too close to being a father to lose my happy home."

He knew at once that he'd said the wrong thing by mentioning either his happy home or the new baby. All week long, he and Ben did just fine together. Alone, working with Burke, Ben seemed secure. Burke needed him and he knew it. From Monday to late Thursday, Ben acted almost contented. At least, Burke wanted to believe he was. His affection and regard for his helper went deep. Natalie had finally convinced him that indeed Ben was in love with her. She'd also convinced him in her offhand manner that such things were inevitable. "Men have always fallen in love with me," she reminded him often. "But that's all right. I can manage it. I always have. I love *you*, Burke. I love no one else in all the world the way I love you."

Not for a minute would Burke have tolerated any other man being in love with his wife. But Ben was his friend. Back when Natalie first came to the rough upcountry to live, with the Cherokee brother and sister so nearby, Burke had thought about finding another helper. He'd even talked with a few master carpenters in Augusta, but found he didn't want to work without Ben. He simply cared about Ben McDonald as he would have cared about the brother he never had. He'd count on time to erase Ben's now obvious agony over Natalie. The subject never came up during the long days he and Ben worked side by side, alone in the Cass County wilderness, at one job site or another. Natalie, of course, believed that Ben's sister, Mary, was in love with Burke too. Talk about a mix-up! Of course, Ben and Mary were both partial to him. He'd been the one fortunate enough to have found them, right after the Cherokee removal, hiding like scared animals in their cave home. But that was years ago. He knew there was no problem where Mary was concerned. Somehow Ben was another matter. Why, he didn't know, except that Ben *was* more Indian than Mary. He was pleasant enough on the job alone with Burke. Otherwise, around anyone else—Ben was silent. Much of the time, darkly silent.

Burke ran his fingers over the joint he'd just finished. It felt smooth enough. The familiar, comforting rush of pride in his work swept over him. From below, out of sight, he heard Ben saddling their horses for the short ride to Arnold Milner's place at Sallie Hughes's ford on the Etowah, where they'd eat and wait for Natalie's family and Mrs. Mackay. Ben's going to hate that wait, he thought, frowning. More than the wait—Ben would undoubtedly swim or fish through that—he would hate the actual meeting. When other people were around, Ben seemed remote from Burke too, as though the fact that his own skin was not the same color made the two friends strangers.

"Comin' down, Ben," he called, easing his big, agile body toward the edge of the church roof where the ladder leaned.

On the ground, he hoisted the heavy ladder and started toward the toolshed. In no time, his load lightened. Ben had grabbed one end and was helping.

"You're the best burden sharer a man ever had," Burke laughed over his shoulder. The ladder laid carefully on the ground by the shed, he held out his hand. "Thanks once more, partner, for a fine week's work." Then he added, "Hey, you don't need to dread our Savannah visitors! They're nice folks."

Ben returned the handshake, looked him straight in the eye, but said nothing. He didn't even smile.

"I guess the horses are saddled."

Ben only nodded.

"Then let's head for Milner's and dinner. I'm starved, and if the travelers are going to make it today, they could already be there."

The light knock on Eliza Mackay's hotel-room door startled her from a sleep so deep she lost her way stumbling about in the darkness searching for what she took to be the door to her own upstairs hall on Broughton Street. But there was always light there; a tiny ruby glass oil lamp burned all night in the hall at home.

I can't be home, she thought, remembering with a jerk that she wasn't or there wouldn't have been a knock. Her children, Sarah or Kate—William or Jack, when Jack happened to be at home—would never knock. They'd just call to her. "Goodness gracious," she muttered, awake now. At least awake enough to remember where they were, that it must be Saturday and that Mark and Caroline had both reminded her that there was a box of sulphur matches in the small table beside her bed, a candle on the table. "Hold on," she called out. "I'll open the door in just a minute." Then, slowly, carefully, a hand out in front of her to prevent the fall all aging people dread, she worked her way back to the foot of the bed, felt up along the puffy mattress until she came to the bolsters where she'd been sleeping and found the table and the matches.

The single candle burning at last, she pulled on her dressing gown and went barefoot to the door.

"It's Caroline, Miss Eliza. I'm so sorry, but I need to talk to you."

When Caroline pulled up a chair, her face looked ashen in the candlelight.

"What on earth's the matter?" Eliza asked, back in bed under the covers, because the air was chilly. "You look—"

"I know. I must look dreadful."

"Frantic is the word, my dear."

"It's Mark."

"Is he ill?"

"Well, no, except in his mind!"

"Caroline!"

"Honestly, sometimes I worry that he might be—losing his balance. He had a dream—a ghastly dream about Natalie."

"Well, could he remember it to tell you?"

"Not in any detail. I tried for over an hour to—calm him, to quiet his fears." Caroline shivered. "He's still just lying there in our bed, staring up at the ceiling. He—he cried out in his sleep—scared me out of my wits. All I could think of to do was—to hold him."

"That's exactly what he needed. Dreams, especially if it's still dark outside, can seem more real than—"

"Miss Eliza, I'm so sorry I woke you! I—I hurried over here because I was —desperate. I didn't know what else to do but run to you!"

"I'm glad you did, but can you tell me what he said about the nightmare?"

"Nothing definite. He just clung to me so hard he hurt my shoulders. I didn't know what to do for him." Tears began to course down her stricken face. "I—I'm ashamed to say I finally woke our son sleeping in the other bed, then rushed out the door and over here to you. Mark and I both dump our burdens on poor, good Jonathan. We always have."

"You're shaking like a leaf, Caroline. Why not crawl into bed with me for a few minutes and get warm? It's cold in here."

On her feet suddenly, Caroline said, "No, no, thank you. I—I feel foolish even being here. I've never run away from Mark's fears over Natalie before. There's nothing you can do about any of it. Forgive me for—barging in like this."

"My dear, there's nothing to forgive—wait—don't go!"

Without another word, Caroline hurried across the shadowy room and out the door, almost banging it behind her.

Wide awake now, Eliza Mackay sank back against her pillows. Daylight will help, she told herself. The sun rising always wipes out groundless fears that come in the dark. But what if Mark's dream is prophetic? So far as Eliza knew, Caroline's forbearance with him had never crumbled this way before. Poor girl. Poor Caroline and oh, my poor dear boy, Mark.

She leaned to blow out the candle on the night table, then changed her mind. She put on her spectacles and picked up her pendant watch. They'd planned to get up in an hour anyway. She might as well bathe and dress and read some in the Scriptures while she waited for Jonathan's knock. She was sure the boy would come straight to her just as soon as he could leave his parents.

Sometimes Jonathan seems older and wiser than us all, and more and more freely, the boy talks to me. Maybe when I hear his version of his father's dreadful dream, I'll be able to think of something to do or say that might help.

Jonathan's heart was pounding when he tapped lightly on Miss Eliza's door at first light. Nothing had ever made his heart pound as had the misery in his father's face. His mother's face too.

He had only a few precious minutes to be alone with Miss Eliza now, but he had to see her.

"Come in, son," she said, closing the door softly.

"You're all dressed," he whispered.

"I've been waiting for you. Your mother told me. I felt you'd be here first thing."

He gave her a hug, then sat down on the edge of a chair, trying to smile so as not to alarm her. "Papa seems a little more like himself," he said.

"Oh, I'm glad to hear that. Did he tell you anything at all about his nightmare?"

"He swears he can't remember it, but, Miss Eliza, I never saw Papa cry before. It scared my mother too. How did she seem when she came over here?"

"Distraught. She didn't stay but a minute. Son, your father is a strong man. He's truly afraid or he—"

"I know that. I guess I'm afraid too."

"For your sister? Are you afraid something has happened to Natalie?"

"Mainly I'm scared over the look on Papa's face when I tried to comfort him. Miss Eliza—I never saw him like this before and I'm almost seventeen. I was—I was hoping you might have an idea of what I could do to help."

The still pretty, aging face was so full of tenderness and love Jonathan thought he might cry. For a moment, they just sat looking at each other.

"My parents are both—so fine," he said finally. "Why did Natalie have to marry a man who bullheadedly refused to live in a civilized town?"

He saw her fleeting smile. "We both know the answer to that question, don't we?"

Jonathan tried to return the smile. "Yes, ma'am. But I guess even you don't know how helpless I feel. It's not knowing about Sister that makes it so hard for them both. I think I do understand why she married Burke."

"She loves him with all her heart. Natalie isn't easy to figure out. She's never been, but no one doubts the depth of her love for Burke Latimer."

"I'm supposed to be downstairs seeing to an early breakfast so we can be

ready when the stage heads north. Papa said he was so troubled last night he
didn't arrange for breakfast."

"That isn't a bit like him."

"I have to go in a minute, but could I ask you something?"

"Oh, son, anything! I only pray I can give you an answer to hold on to
today while we travel."

"Well," he said, his forehead creased with hard thought, "I guess you do
know I feel pretty bad about being so helpless right now."

"But you're not helpless. You're helping them by being here. By being
Jonathan."

"Thank you, but—well, I was thinking, my sister probably won't change
much in the way she upsets Papa, especially. I mean—she doesn't mean to
upset him, but she is going to spend the rest of her life with Burke, out of
Papa's sight mostly. What I keep wondering is—Miss Eliza, I'm not a young
boy anymore. Do you suppose that when I find someone to love, I'll be able
to help Papa understand better how Natalie feels about loving Burke so
much? I honestly think Papa feels shut away from her now. If he knew I
loved a young lady the way she loves Burke, might it help him to—well, to
think of Natalie as just being like the rest of us? Maybe sort of like me? Just a
regular person? I mean—will I be able to help Papa more when I'm—also in
love?"

When Miss Eliza jumped up and hurried to him, both arms out, he held her
close for a long time, trying to think what any of the Brownings would have
done without her all these years. She hadn't said a word, she was just hugging
him, patting his shoulder over and over, somehow agreeing with what he so
hoped for in his heart—that yes, once he loved someone, he'd be stronger,
wiser, more useful to both the wonderful people who were his parents. Only
Miss Eliza could get such a thing across to him without a single word. She was
just there, being Miss Eliza, as she'd been through all the years of his life and
again it was enough. When he found the one girl to love with every fiber of
his mind and body, new strength and wisdom, beyond his understanding
today, would come. He had no idea what that one girl might be like. His
friends seemed to know, but Jonathan didn't. For a long time, he had hoped
he'd find her, though, and now, on this troubled morning, he was hoping
harder than ever. Something in Miss Eliza's hug reassured him.

"Thank you," he said, his arms still around her.

"What on earth are you thanking me for, son? I'm the one who should
thank you." She stepped back to look up into his eyes, but kept a hand on
each of his shoulders. "Would you believe that my joints and muscles *and*
heart don't ache quite so much as when you first slipped into this room?
Carry your special gift from God carefully, Jonathan. You do have a special
gift, you know. Your parents lean on you, depend upon you because they *can.*
You're the one who pulled my William out of his locked-up grief when his
family died. Your daily visits to our house helped heal William's heart and
mine too. Just by being with you, because you're Jonathan, got your parents

through those terrible days when we didn't know whether Natalie had survived the wreck." She was silent for a moment. "Yes, you'll find your heart's love, and when you do find her, I predict that your already great gift of understanding will grow. We'll all be blessed by it." She let her hands drop and gave him a little push toward the door. "Now, do you suppose while you're downstairs you could find this old lady a cup of hot coffee or tea? This is our last day on the road. We'll reach our loved ones before dark tonight." She straightened her shoulders. "And when we do, whatever we find, I want to be up to it."

Chapter 11

FULL daylight streaming into the Latimer cabin found Eliza Anne still sitting before the fire with W.H., while Mary stayed in the bedroom with Natalie—silent for most of the night, staring, her grief locked inside. Wrapped loosely in the soft blue blanket Caroline and Mark had sent, the body of the dead baby lay on a small table in the front corner of the main room. The sweet, sickening smell of death mingled heavily with the pungency of the camphor oil with which Mary had bathed the little body.

Ever since the sun began to sweep away the protective shadows, Eliza Anne had kept her eyes averted. W.H., sitting opposite her, stared at the tiny, discolored corpse. She could not. Nothing was the way it was supposed to be. Obviously, since Burke and Ben had not brought them, her mother and the Brownings hadn't even reached the Etowah River at Milner's place yesterday.

Dear W.H. just keeps talking all around his departure this morning, she thought now, her heart reaching toward the graceful, weary figure of her husband slumped in a wooden rocker. With all her might, she'd tried to say what she knew he needed her to say—that he must go ahead and leave as planned to begin his campaign for Congress. That with Mary's loyal help and the help of their servants and children, she would be all right. Also, that her mother and Natalie's parents and Jonathan would surely arrive before dark today. Burke and Ben were obviously staying over at Mr. Milner's in order to meet the afternoon stagecoach. Of course, she longed for W.H. to stay with her, to help her with Natalie's grief, with the baby's burial, but she knew him too well to suggest it. A dearer, tenderer man lived nowhere on the face of the earth, but in his mind, this long swing about the district was all-important to future political plans. Besides, in a way, Natalie was a part of Eliza Anne's own family, not her husband's. W.H. was too sensitive, too courteous ever to make an issue of it, but as close as they were, she guarded against burdening him with her own family troubles—with anything that might hamper his personal dreams for the years ahead. Without question, he would have stayed had she or one of their children fallen ill, but she'd known for a long time that the only way to keep their marriage whole, nearly perfect, was to follow

—blindly, if need be—where W.H. felt his career, his ambition, his dreams were leading him.

When she heard the first anguished sob break from the crumpled, stricken form on the bed in the back room, Eliza Anne felt some relief. Natalie had, after all the dark, silent hours, finally begun to weep. The irresistible, totally unpredictable girl had never responded to either life's blows or joys as anyone expected. She had shed no tear at the moment last night when she realized that her baby had been born early and—dead. As Natalie's sobbing went on now unabated, in spite of Mary's gentle efforts to comfort her, Eliza Anne found herself reliving the heart-shattering moment when, in her weakness and exhaustion, Natalie had grasped the truth. For an hour or so, Eliza Anne and Elizabeth Holder and Mary had managed, they felt sure, to keep it from her, to give Natalie at least a small rest before the ugly truth struck.

Sinai told them otherwise. "You ain't fool her," the birdlike woman said in her always superior fashion. "Miss Natalie done give me one look that tol' me she know her baby didn't cry none. That look tol' me. I can read looks. I knew right then that black grief done fill her down inside where her baby tried to live! Anytime now, she be demandin' to see it herself. You mark my word."

Natalie had waited, though, until the Holders had gone back across the river to their own home, until Mary had bathed and laid out the small, still body. It must have been nearly four in the morning when Natalie sent for Eliza Anne.

"Bring the baby to me, Miss Lib," her voice was oddly old and quite firm. "I want to see my baby—now."

A fresh wave of weakness flooded Eliza Anne just remembering her own helplessness at the mere thought of touching the cold, motionless little body. Mary had come to her rescue. Without a word, she had slipped from the bedroom and returned carrying the baby in the soft blue blanket.

Eyes wide, Natalie raised herself in the bed as Mary held the baby down for her to look. Here in broad daylight, in Eliza Anne's chaotic, weary mind, the heart-shattering moment was taking place again.

For a long time, Natalie studied the even, quite pretty features of the child's splotched face. No one spoke as the agonized young woman held out her arms. Mary placed the bundle beside her and stepped back.

After another wait, Natalie looked up at Eliza Anne, almost no expression in her enigmatic pale blue eyes. "Was my baby a boy—or a girl, Miss Lib?"

"A boy," she whispered. "Your baby was a—little boy."

Slowly—it seemed to take a full minute for Natalie's hand to move to the infant's head—she touched the silky, golden hair, already showing curl. "Burke," she whispered. Addressing no one, she repeated, "Burke . . . his name is Little Burke."

Then, abruptly, with more strength than Eliza Anne could conceive, Natalie clutched the tiny body in her arms and only her weakness from the ghastly ordeal of the night made it possible for Mary and Eliza Anne finally to get the baby away from her. Natalie made no cry of protest as she held the child against her. She merely clung to the boy, whispering her husband's name over and over.

When Mary finally carried the infant back into the main room, Natalie screamed Burke's name once, collapsed against the rumpled pillows, said not one more word, seemed almost not to move until, just minutes ago, when the sobbing had begun.

After bringing them some food from the Stiles house, Mary now waited and watched at the new cabin window Mister Burke and Ben had just finished putting in to give the main room more light for Natalie to sew by. Miss Lib and Mister W.H. were saying goodbye on the front porch. Mary wasn't looking at them, she was obeying Miss Lib, who had asked her to watch for David Holder, coming soon to tell them that the grave had been dug and the tiny coffin built. Mary's heart ached so she felt she might choke. She ached for the dead baby, who would never see his mother or his father, for Natalie, lying alone and silent now in her bed—and for Mister Burke, who might never even see the face of his dead son because it had to be buried today. Mister Burke and Ben could not reach the cabin until late afternoon since the stagecoach wasn't due at Sallie Hughes's ford until at least three o'clock.

She breathed a prayer that her brother, Ben, wouldn't find it too painful meeting the Savannah visitors. Her heart ached most of all, still, for Ben, who had told her once that he could—would—never face seeing his beloved Natalie suffer for any reason. "I can't help her," he'd said, his voice flat like wood. "I can't help her—I can never even try to comfort her, so I *would not* face seeing deep hurt in her!" Ben loved Natalie in some deep, mysterious way Mary didn't understand, though she kept trying.

A sudden, terrifying fear gripped her as she stood at the window. A nameless fear so heavy she just had to move—had to do something or be smothered by it. Hurrying across the cabin to the fireplace, she grabbed the poker and began stirring the half-burned oak logs. The day was warm now. There was really no need for a fire, but she had been told not to disturb Natalie, who just might sleep for a time, and Miss Lib was busy with her husband, going away when she needed him there with her so much.

Back at the window, Mary took up her watch again. Mister Holder was nowhere in sight. There was no sound of his horse and wagon. She heard only lusty birdsong outside in the spring sunlight and the low, soft talk of Miss Lib and her husband saying goodbye. The nameless, heavy nervousness over Ben still shadowed her thoughts and she tried concentrating on Miss Lib, who would, she knew, reassure her husband that once her mother came, all would be well. Mary longed to know Miss Eliza Mackay, kind Mister William's mother—Miss Lib's mother. Needing her own dead parents as Mary still did so often, she knew Natalie's mother and father would be able to comfort her and was struck by the realization that this was the first time she'd ever known Natalie to need comforting from anyone for any reason.

Mary had been sure, everyone had been so sure that nothing bad would ever happen to Natalie. Especially Natalie had been sure of that. She'd told Mary many times, always adding that one day Mary too would meet another man and learn how to love Mister Burke as a friend and only a friend. Natalie was always absolutely sure about everything she said and did.

Tears came that burned Mary's eyes because there had been so many tears during the long night and morning. She was weeping again now because for the first time the thought had struck that poor Mister Burke wouldn't even be able to build his own son's coffin! "God," she whispered, "give Mister Holder the skill to make it pretty and smooth and perfect!"

God had surely been with Mary through the long, sad night and morning. She must cling to the fact that He would stay with them all—with Miss Lib after Mister W.H. had ridden away, with Natalie, with sweet Mister Burke when he learned the cruel truth—with Ben. Her body grew so heavy with the burden of worry over her brother that she was relieved when at last Miss Lib came back into the room.

"Well," Miss Lib said, wiping her eyes, "he's gone, Mary. I actually felt sorrier for my husband riding off alone than for myself. He hated so to leave me. I thought he also seemed quite embarrassed to be away when my mother and the others finally get here."

"But his trip was planned long ago," Mary said, hoping the reminder would help Miss Lib. "I'm sure Mister W.H. would have stayed if he could. He has such important speeches to make in many places."

Miss Lib almost smiled. "Thank you, Mary. Yes. Yes, he would have stayed if he could. We all have—driving forces within us. Sometimes even—death can't slow them." After a pause, she asked, "Is Natalie asleep?"

Mary shook her head. "I haven't looked at her for a while because I was watching for Mister Holder to come with the coffin. I didn't want her to—to see it."

"You're most thoughtful, Mary. And have I told you lately how well you're speaking these days?"

"Ben prods me to speak right for Mister Burke's sake. Yours too. After a moment, she asked, "Will we—bury the baby before Mister Burke and the visitors from Savannah—and Ben—get here, Miss Lib?"

Sinking wearily into a chair, Eliza Anne groaned. "Oh, I—don't know what to do! My husband thinks we should—thinks we *must* bury the little fellow right away. He thinks we dare not wait. It could be late afternoon or evening before they finally come. The sun is getting warm and—"

"I will be right there with you at the burying," Mary said.

"Oh, I know, I know. I shouldn't put this burden on you, but—what do you think? Should we go ahead as soon as the minister gets here from Cassville? My husband is stopping to tell him. Would Burke and my mother and the Brownings be hurt if we—just went ahead?"

Mary weighed her answer. "No. Not because we went ahead." She felt tears burn her eyes again. "They will be—hurt, though. Oh, so bad."

"Should we ask Natalie?"

"Yes."

"Now?"

Mary nodded.

Inside the bedroom, they waited until Natalie opened her eyes.
"I'm—going to the—service, Miss Lib," she said. "I know it has to be today. Is the little grave ready? I hope it's in the right place. I—hope—Burke will think so."

After a glance at Mary, Eliza Anne said, "I told Mr. Holder to put it in the grove between our house and yours. But, darling Natalie, you're not strong enough to get out of bed yet!"

"Mary will help me if you won't. Mary, I want my yellow dress, please. And I'll need to bathe."

"But, Natalie," Miss Lib argued, "you mustn't put yourself through anything so—hard!"

Even in Natalie's weakened condition, Mary saw the pale eyes glare at Miss Lib. "You don't think I'm going to lie here—alone—with only Sinai staring at me, do you? Mary, hitch up your pony to the cart. I'll ride in that, please. And I do want the yellow dress on in case—Burke comes home—in time. It's his favorite."

Eliza Anne and her elder son, Henry, supported Natalie through the brief graveside service. Mary stood across the open grave with young Robert and Mary Cowper Stiles. Except for clumsy condolences from the minister and sniffles from Elizabeth Holder, great with her own child, no one spoke until David Holder had lifted Natalie back into Mary's cart. So far as Eliza Anne knew, Natalie shed not one tear. Swaying a little at first, she simply stood beside the tiny hole in the red earth and watched intently, much as any mother might oversee someone else tending her child.

As Henry drove the creaking cart back through the tree-shaded grove toward the Latimer cabin, Eliza Anne, beside her on the single seat, noticed that only once did Natalie look back.

"I think everything is in good order, Miss Lib. Even if he didn't get here in time, I think Burke will be satisfied, don't you?"

"Yes. Yes, I do, dear heart."

Alongside the slowly moving cart, the Holders, Mary Cowper and Robert walked in silence except that Elizabeth Holder was unable to control her weeping.

"I wish you wouldn't cry anymore, Elizabeth," Natalie said. "I'm sure your baby will be just fine. I'm sure you're going to be far more—successful than I."

Back at Natalie's cabin, Eliza Anne held a brief conference with her three children while Mary helped Natalie to her bed.

"Shouldn't Natalie be crying, Mama?" six-year-old Robert asked as they stood on the front porch.

"Yes, I suppose she should, Bobby. It would be a release if she could, I'm sure."

"Then why isn't she?" Henry wanted to know.

"I've thought about Natalie all the way back here," Mary Cowper said, her great, dark eyes tender with concern. "Maybe it happened so fast she hasn't quite taken it all in yet. But then, I also thought about how really different Natalie is."

"Yes, Mary Cowper, you're quite right. In fact, that's mature of you to have thought of Natalie's—difference."

"Well," the girl said, "she and I have come to be quite close lately. Oh, Mama, I want so much to help her! What can I do?"

"There's plenty for you to do—all three of you. I can't bring myself to leave her, so, Mary C., I expect you to check our whole house—linens for your grandmother Mackay in the bedroom downstairs, for the three Brownings in the upstairs room with two beds. You'll have to sleep with me while they're here. At least, until your father gets back several weeks from now—or longer."

"What about us?" Henry demanded. "I guess we have to give up our room and sleep on the floor."

"That's exactly right, son. And cheerfully, I might add, without that scowl on your face. Be sure, both of you boys, that all guns and slingshots and balls and tops and other male accouterments are out of sight."

"Where do we sleep?"

"You can make pallets on the parlor floor."

"Where do we find sheets and blankets and pillows and things?" Robert asked.

"Sinai or Rose will get them for you before they go to their quarters this evening. In the meantime, I want you boys to pick up any trash or limbs fallen in our yard. Is that clear?"

"I thought Mr. Holder was supposed to see that Solomon did everything like that," Henry complained.

"This is an unusual time," she said firmly. "And I want no more discussion."

Still scowling, Henry twisted his heel into Burke's new pine porch floor. "It seems to me like Solomon hasn't done much but garden since he got here from Savannah. He's lazy!"

"And so are you," his mother said. "Solomon has plenty to do in the garden this time of year. Now, no more complaints. Scoot. All three of you head for home and do as I've told you."

"Come on," Mary Cowper said in her most grown-up fashion. "Mama's got a hard job ahead of her—comforting Natalie. Other people cry and you can just put your arms around them. Natalie's a different story. We hope you'll be all right, Mama."

"Thank you, darling, I will be. Now, boys—don't get all dirty this afternoon while we're waiting for our visitors to arrive."

"Will Ben be with Burke and Grandma and them?" Henry called back.

"Yes. Burke and Ben will drive them here in Mr. Milner's wagon. It's all arranged."

"We'd be going to meet them in our carriage," Henry grumbled as he sauntered off, "if Papa hadn't gone away."

Chapter 12

THE SUN had just begun to color the early-evening sky when Eliza Anne, after sitting all afternoon with Natalie, walked out onto the front porch of the cabin. With the Brownings and her mother surely on their way over the last mile or so to Etowah Cliffs, her heart normally would be thumping with joy. If anything were normal, she would also be waiting for them at her own house. Nothing was. Her heart thumped all right, but with a mixture of dread and grief and anxiety. Natalie had spoken so little through the long hours after the funeral that Eliza Anne had no idea what the girl might be like when at last she faced her anxious parents. That Mark and Caroline were anxious, she had no doubt. Their recent letters informing her of their visit left no room for doubt. Out of her own exhaustion, Eliza Anne's troubling, self-questioning began again.

What did I do wrong in my letters to Savannah? she asked herself for the hundredth time since learning of the Brownings' distress over Natalie. Until the baby's death—so sudden, so unexpected—she'd honestly written all she felt needed to be told. She'd chalked up their worry, Mark's in particular, to his lifelong doting nature where Natalie was concerned. The latest letter from her mother had almost seemed to blame her for having been careless: "You know, Eliza Anne, that Mark isn't always so jumpy, except over Natalie. He just can't help it. He loves her so much."

Well, Mama, I love Mary Cowper too, she thought, but I'd hope never to burden other people because I do.

That wasn't fair and she knew it. She simply hadn't taken time to reassure Mark sufficiently—even in the long, newsy letters. She'd babbled on about her own house, what fun the children were having on the cliffs above the river, how successful Burke Latimer was. Natalie had seemed so fine! *How could such a thing have happened*—seemingly overnight?

Think back, she ordered herself. Think back to the week before last, to last week—and then she remembered that Natalie had sent Indian Mary over to beg off coming to dinner on Wednesday.

"No, she isn't in bed sick, Miss Lib," Mary had said. "She has a kind of stomachache. She and your sons ate some sassafras leaves, little new, tender red ones—in the woods."

Was that the beginning of Natalie's tragedy? Oh, not the sassafras leaves. They never hurt anyone. But Burke had told W.H. last weekend that for the first time Natalie turned down a ride through the woods with him. Well, after all, she was nearing her time. Who would pay any attention to the fact that she didn't feel up to a horseback ride? Still, on Tuesday of this week, when Eliza Anne had stopped by her cabin to remind Natalie that their loved ones were leaving Savannah that very day, Natalie had struck her as quiet. For the first time since Eliza Anne could remember, she hadn't fussed once because the baby had kicked half the night.

Dear God! Had the infant died during that week?

"Natalie was kind of—funny today, Mama," she remembered Mary Cowper saying yesterday at breakfast. "So quiet—for Natalie, who always has so many funny things to tell me when I stop by."

"Women are often moody when a baby's on the way, dear . . ."

The questioning got Eliza Anne nowhere.

"Oh, Mama," she spoke aloud into the quiet, cool evening. "Hurry! Hurry and get here. I need you. Poor Mama. She's lost a child of her own—suffered through William's grief over the death of both his babies—now this."

The unmistakable sound of a wagon and team got her to her feet. She ran out into Burke's front yard for a clearer view down the road they'd be traveling from Milner's place at Sallie Hughes's ford. They were coming!

"Why aren't you here, W.H.—to help me? Didn't you realize that—I'm going to have to tell them all by myself?"

Her own back ached so from jostling, Caroline marveled that Miss Eliza could still smile when Milner's overseer stopped the rattly wagon in front of Natalie's pitiful log cabin. To her, the last four miles or so from where the stage had forded the Etowah River had only added insult to injury. Six miles in a wagon bed over what would pass as a road only in the upcountry was an insult to any lady—and probably an injury if she lived long enough to escape from the wagon and try to walk again. No one in her right mind would live in such a primitive place, implying, she realized—but didn't care—that both her daughter and Eliza Anne Stiles were not quite sane. Beyond that, they certainly didn't mind putting their guests through torture. Well, at least they were there and, of course, nothing would do Mark but that they stop first to see Natalie.

He had already helped Miss Eliza down from the high wagon seat, and Jonathan, who had ridden beside Caroline and Mark in the wagon bed, was smiling up at his mother from the ground, hands out to help her.

Standing in the dusty road, Caroline tried to straighten her knotted muscles while Eliza Anne gave her mother a long embrace, hugged Mark and Jonathan, then hurried to throw both arms around Caroline in what seemed an unusually emotional greeting.

"You'll stay at my house, of course," Eliza Anne said, "but I knew you'd be stopping here first."

"Where are the children?" Miss Eliza wanted to know.

"At home, Mama. I hope following my instructions," Eliza Anne said, her voice plainly nervous and unsteady. "Your rooms will be ready or they and the servants will have to account to me. W.H. sends deep regrets to all of you. He begged me to tell you how sorry he is that you didn't get here before an important trip took him away. He simply had to leave—only a few hours ago, actually." Then abruptly, as though in her nervousness she'd just noticed, Eliza Anne asked, "Where's Burke? Ben? Didn't they meet your stage?"

"No," Mark said, giving her only half his attention, his eyes on Natalie's cabin. "Mr. Milner met us himself. Burke was there yesterday, but when we didn't come, it seems his helper, Ben, disappeared. Burke's still out hunting for him."

"It's all very strange, Eliza Anne," Caroline couldn't help saying. "I must say I didn't appreciate Burke's putting his missing Indian above meeting us. Mr. Milner's overseer drove that wagon like a madman!"

"I don't understand," Eliza Anne said, clasping and unclasping her hands. "I assumed Ben would be right with Burke when you crossed the river. He's never ten feet away from that man."

"Eliza Anne," Mark asked anxiously, "where's my daughter? Why isn't Natalie here too?"

For what to Caroline seemed an interminable moment, they all just stood there—Eliza Anne biting her lips, saying nothing.

Flashing his good smile, Jonathan asked, "Is my sister playing one of her tricks on us, Miss Lib?"

"Yes." Caroline reiterated Mark's question. "Where is our hearty frontier daughter?"

"Please don't keep Mark and Caroline in suspense, dear," Eliza Anne's mother said. "They're both in an agony of worry over Natalie!"

"I know," Eliza Anne said, just above a whisper. "Mama, *I know!*"

"Where *is* Natalie?" Miss Eliza pressed. "Is she in the cabin?"

Caroline saw Eliza Anne nod yes, and like a shot, Mark ran up the front walk toward the open cabin door.

"Please, Mark—wait!" Eliza Anne called after him. Then, leaving Caroline and the others standing there, she hurried to stop Mark. Caroline watched in horror as Eliza Anne told him something that caused Mark to stare at her, then, without a word, to race through the open door into the cabin.

With more energy than Caroline herself had left, Miss Eliza cut briskly up the path toward where her daughter still stood, head down, hands covering her face. Caroline's body felt as heavy as her heart and she might have gone on just standing there had not Jonathan begun to lead her toward where Eliza Anne and her mother stood.

Not looking at any of them, Eliza Anne sobbed, "Oh, Mama—Caroline—Natalie's baby was born—dead! We—buried the little fellow today. We had to! Burke should be here—he doesn't even know . . ."

Too stunned, too weary to embrace Eliza Anne as she longed to do, Caroline whispered hoarsely, "Is—my daughter all right?"

Eliza Anne nodded. "She—she's been—unbelievably strong. Ill and weak as she still is, she insisted upon—attending the graveside service."

Leaning heavily now on her son, Caroline could think only that Mark had been right! Mark had *known* that something dreadful was wrong with Natalie. He and their daughter had always been linked by some cord of knowing—of affection that she, Caroline, had almost resisted. Adoring their daughter as Mark did took more energy and more patience than she, Natalie's own mother, possessed.

Still, I love her too, she thought as she felt Miss Eliza's strong little arm slip around her, knew the lady was saying something to her, but couldn't have told what. I love Natalie too. I'd like it if I could just—lie down and—die this minute, so I wouldn't have to face any of what's happened! Her tormented thoughts rushed on: God forgive me . . . it's that I hate so seeing Mark hurt like this. In a way, my own pain doesn't count. I—I just want her to—stop hurting *him.* I want her to stop hurting us both!

"Don't you think I'm right, Caroline?" Miss Eliza was asking her, evidently for the second time.

"What, Miss Eliza? What—did you say?"

"Don't you think we should just give Mark a few minutes alone with Natalie?"

"Yes, yes, I'm sure we should. I try always to—defer to Mark and his daughter." Caroline's words sounded so stiff and formal she longed to take them back. They even sounded self-pitying.

"What mama means," Jonathan explained, "is that Natalie and Papa have a kind of bond between them."

For once, Jonathan hadn't helped matters, Caroline thought, her heart reaching in sudden, surprising sympathy toward both Eliza Mackay and Natalie's beloved Miss Lib, always so deeply fond of Natalie too. Caroline longed to thank Eliza Anne for having been with Natalie when she needed someone to mother her, when her own mother had been too far away to help.

"This must have been dreadful for you, Eliza Anne," she murmured. "Thank you. Mark and I—thank you from our hearts for all you've done."

"Excuse me, ma'am," Mr. Duffy, Milner's overseer, said, coming up the path toward them, hat in hand. "I'm mighty sorry about whatever's happened here. I've not been eavesdropping. I don't know what's wrong, but I figure something is. I best be getting on back if you don't need me anymore. I promised Mr. Latimer I'd help him hunt his Indian. It's gettin' late."

For the first time, Caroline noticed their driver, who had been standing back by the wagon. "Oh, Mr. Duffy, I'm so sorry," she said. "Can you wait until I—ask my husband?"

"Please forgive us all, sir," Eliza Anne said. "Where exactly *is* Mr. Latimer? Will he be here soon?"

"Burke doesn't even *know,*" Caroline said to no one in particular. "Burke's
—child is—dead—and he doesn't even know!"

"Burke will be here, Miss Lib," Jonathan said, "just as soon as he finds Ben
McDonald. Mr. Milner and Papa and I decided to take Mr. Duffy's kind offer
to drive us here. You see, Burke and Ben stayed at Milner's house last night.
This morning when Burke looked for Ben, he couldn't find him anywhere, so
he rode off into the woods to hunt for him. Mr. Milner told us Burke's very
upset over Ben."

"What a way to live," Caroline moaned. "What a dreadful way for my
daughter to live! She *needs* her husband and he's off in the wilderness hunting
some Indian! I knew, I just *knew* Ben McDonald was going to cause—terrible, terrible trouble!"

"You—you knew what?" Eliza Anne asked.

"Mark and I were both right. Mark knew something tragic was going to
happen to Natalie and I knew Ben McDonald was going to—"

"Now, Caroline, we don't know that Ben has caused any real trouble,"
Miss Eliza broke in. "Of course Natalie needs Burke, but there has to be an
explanation of some kind for why Ben—"

"Never mind, Miss Eliza," Caroline interrupted. "I want to know more
about how my daughter's taking all this!" She heard the sharp edge in her
voice, but could do nothing about it. "Natalie's mother seems to be the last
person to know exactly how she is—this minute."

"She's remarkable, Caroline," Eliza Anne said in her direct way. "Your
daughter is still terribly weak. She went right back to bed—after we buried—
her baby, but believe me, I'm not trying to keep anything from you. Natalie
just doesn't talk to *anyone.* She won't, I'm sure, until Burke gets here. She
hasn't said two words since we all got back from the—little grave. She's—
she's just waiting for Burke . . ."

"Burke or Papa," Jonathan said. "She's awfully close to Papa."

"I don't want to worry any of you, but somehow I don't think Natalie's
talking much to Mark either," Eliza Anne said.

"But you're her closest friend up here, Eliza Anne."

"I know, Mama. But no one anywhere is as close to Natalie as Burke. She
needs *him.* I'd give anything if I could tell you exactly how she's taking all this
—inside. I can't. I don't know Natalie that well." She spread her hands in a
helpless gesture. "I'll—never know her that well."

Without another word, Caroline pushed past them all and went straight
inside to find out for herself, remembering, but not caring at this point, that
Mr. Milner's overseer was still waiting instructions.

At the open door of the bedroom, she stopped and listened. When her
eyes grew accustomed to the sunset gloom, she saw them—Natalie pale and
quiet on the bed, Mark beside her holding both her hands. Neither spoke to
her, even though she waited as long as her troubled heart allowed before
approaching the bed.

Finally, Caroline whispered, "Natalie, darling—it's your mother."

With no change at all on the lovely white face, Natalie opened her eyes. "Hello, Mama," she said, "I guess you—know."

Mark stood aside so that Caroline could embrace her. "Yes, I know. And oh, my heart—breaks for you!"

Natalie nodded, the bright hair loosed and spread on her pillow. "Papa told me—Burke didn't come with you."

"But, dearest girl, he'd be right here," Mark said, "if he knew!"

Natalie closed her eyes again. "You've already said that twice, Papa. Burke needs Ben. Ben's his right hand."

"Natalie, we know!" Again, Caroline's voice was sharper than she intended. "We know he needs Ben. But you, dear one, what about you? What about you—inside where it must hurt so?"

Slowly, Natalie's eyes opened and she looked from one to the other for what to Caroline seemed an eternity. Then, her voice weak, trembly for the first time, she said, "I'm a—failure. I—failed Burke."

"No, Natalie!" Mark's voice broke. "Darling, don't ever say that!"

"What else is there to say? I—failed to give—Burke his son."

Caroline tried to imagine how she might have felt had she not been able to give Mark either Natalie or Jonathan. She couldn't. "But *you* didn't fail, darling. It was—God's will."

Natalie's short snorting sound was almost normal. "Miss Eliza will say that too, but it isn't true. There's no point in—belittling God, Mama. Just because *I*—failed."

"I'm not belittling God!"

"You are. God was—trying to give us—a son." Abruptly Natalie turned her head away. "He—tried so hard to give us—Little Burke."

"Did—you see your baby?" Caroline heard herself ask.

"Yes. He—had hair just like Burke's. Gold and shiny, curly. Only not springy—soft." After a time, during which neither parent could think of anything to say, Natalie turned her pale, unreadable eyes back to them. "Did —Mr. Milner have any idea when—Burke is coming home?"

"Tonight," Caroline said. "He left word for us to tell you he'd ride in sometime late this evening, I believe, whether or not he found—Ben." Her own voice speaking Ben's name caused Caroline to shudder. *What was it* she so feared about the quiet, hardworking young Cherokee? Mark was holding one of Natalie's hands again by the time Caroline found courage enough to ask Natalie the one question that had haunted her. "Has—has Ben McDonald have been causing any trouble for you, Natalie? Has he been—acting strangely?"

What she meant by "strangely," Caroline herself had no idea.

Natalie flipped her free hand. "No more so than usual, Mama. Ben's in love with me. But he's no trouble. Burke needs him."

"Darling," Mark asked, genuinely puzzled, "how can you just say so lightly—that Ben's in love with you? You're married to Burke. You're Burke's wife. What does Ben do—to keep you convinced that—"

"Mark, no. She doesn't need to be asked questions like that now," Caroline said, wanting desperately herself to hear Natalie's answer.

"He—doesn't *do* anything," Natalie said on a sigh. "He just—eats and sleeps and works—and looks at me with those black, moony eyes. We all know he's hopelessly in love with me. He has been from the beginning."

"Burke knows too?" Caroline asked.

"Of course he does, Mama. Burke knows everything there is to know about me."

Caroline's eyes were on Mark, who returned her searching look. Neither knew what to say.

"You and Mama can stop trying to—understand me," Natalie said at last, her eyes shut again. "Burke takes care of—understanding all about me now. Now and—always."

After another long, clumsy silence, Caroline asked, "Where's Indian Mary?"

"At their cabin down the road. She's washing our clothes and linens today. Miss Lib will whistle when you're leaving. Mary knows that means I'm alone. She'll come over to sit here till Burke comes."

The thought of elegant Eliza Anne Stiles giving a whistle loud enough for someone to hear in a cabin down the road startled Caroline. "Miss Lib will—*whistle?*"

"She's got a good, loud whistle. She didn't even know she had one until last month. Mary will hear and come." Natalie sighed. "I wish she wouldn't. I'd really like to be—by myself until Burke gets home."

"But you need someone with you, darling," Caroline said, feeling more helpless with her own daughter than ever before in her life. "Perhaps, though, we should let Mr. Milner's overseer take us to the Stiles house now, Mark," she said. "I know Miss Eliza is exhausted and Mr. Duffy is waiting to drive back."

"I'm not leaving Natalie," Mark said.

"Oh, yes, you are, Papa. I—I want to sleep. Mary can wash my face and comb my hair for when Burke gets here. He'll be here. Ben's run away before. He always comes back. Please go, both of you. But—I'm—I'm glad to see you."

Without opening her eyes again, Natalie turned her face away, plainly dismissing them.

Caroline and Mark said nothing until they were back on the porch, where Miss Eliza and her daughter were resting in wooden rockers.

"Should I go in and speak to Natalie?" Miss Eliza asked.

"I think not now," Mark answered. "She just—dismissed her parents."

"Where's Jonathan?" Caroline asked.

"He thought Mr. Duffy had waited long enough, so went with him to haul your baggage to my house," Eliza Anne explained.

"Will Jonathan come back for us in a wagon or carriage?" Mark wanted to know.

"We can walk that far, Mark," Eliza Mackay said.

Eliza Anne's sharp whistle caused them all to jump.

"That will bring Mary," Eliza Anne explained. "She and I agreed she'd come over to be with Natalie soon after I whistled. How did Natalie seem to you, Mark—Caroline?"

They exchanged helpless looks. "She—broke my heart," he said shakily.

"And to you, Caroline?"

"She—feels a failure. I've heard other women say they felt they'd failed not being able to carry a baby to term." She shook her head. "I certainly never, never expected to hear Natalie say she'd failed, though, at anything."

"Caroline," Mark said, "is that quite fair?"

"It's neither fair nor unfair. To me Natalie seemed brave—strong, really—but more a stranger than ever."

Chapter 13

STARING up at the freshly varnished tongue-and-groove ceiling Burke had put up in their bedroom just before they knew the baby was on the way, Natalie tried to concentrate on what had become her favorite pine knot—a dark brown splotch—rounded and with a sharply curved tail at one end. It reminded her of a comet. She'd seen a painting once of a comet streaking across a night sky. "Look, Burke," she'd said only a month or so ago, "we have a comet in our ceiling! Isn't that just like us to have a comet? A shooting star right above our bed where you love me? Where the miracle of our baby happened!"

Burke had laughed. Would he ever laugh again?

Had it been only last month—last week—that they were still expecting the miracle? She laid both hands on her stomach. Flat, empty—no movement of any kind.

"I won't have it this way!"

The shrill, rebellious cry almost frightened her. She had worked so hard not to rebel at anything now that she was married to Burke. But nothing had been this hard—nothing had ever hurt this much. The tiny, living body that had been a part of her every breath for all those months lay now in a shoddily built wooden box under the ground in Miss Lib's grove of trees and Burke didn't even know his son was dead! Didn't even know there had almost been a son with golden hair like his. Curling, silky hair she'd actually touched—and could never touch again.

She squeezed into a fist the hand that had smoothed the well-shaped, soft little head.

Why doesn't Burke come home? Where could Ben be? Ben, who never, never did anything to make her unhappy except to love her, and she'd grown accustomed to ignoring that.

From the front of the house, she heard the subdued voices of her family complaining about leaving her before Mary got there. Poor Mama and Papa, she thought, and wished with all her heart that they hadn't come. Having them there only added to her burden of grief because they were grieving too.

Tears stung her eyes and she fought them back, swiped at them with the back of her hand. The tears did not stop and suddenly every dream she and

Burke had ever had for their child unrolled before some inner eye so that swiping at her real eyes did no good. Deep down, pain-filled, tearing sobs wracked her flat, empty body.

"If our baby's a girl," Burke had said, "I want her to be the image of you, Natalie. With your free, wild spirit, your mind and heart and—beauty. Only she'll be my daughter too, so she could never match her mother in the kind of beauty that stops a man's heart . . ."

Burke had always talked about how she could stop a man's heart . . . Well, *she'd* wanted a son, who would be the image of Burke—a skilled, golden-haired builder like his father. "I want him to love the Cherokee land just the way you love it, Burke," she'd told him. "I don't want to give birth to a Savannah gentleman!"

Now they would never know what their son might have been. The soft, tender little head lay cold and still on Miss Lib's own baby pillow in that shoddy box Mr. Holder had built because Burke wasn't there to make their baby's coffin pretty and smooth and perfect.

A few minutes ago, she had heard Miss Lib's whistle. Mary would be coming. Both fists hit the bed hard. If only they'd all leave her alone until Burke got home!

The soft click of the latch on her front door was like a stab of pain. Good, sweet Mary was the last person she wanted to see, even though it would all have been harder, much harder, without Mary, who seemed to know exactly what to do. It took her long enough to begin to do it, though, and stop waiting for Miss Lib and the others, she thought. Miss Lib had been wonderful too, but no one was really any help now . . . no one could be until Burke's arms were around her.

She lay motionless in the bed, willing Mary to stop in the front room, willing her not to force her to talk, to pretend that she was doing all right. The willing did no good. Soft, quick steps crossed the cabin floor and stopped just outside the closed bedroom door. Thank heaven, her father had closed the door when he left. Maybe Mary would wait to be called—later, much later.

A chill crept up from her already cold feet to engulf Natalie's entire body. She shivered and pulled the quilt over her shoulders. There had been no further sound of footfalls from the front of the cabin. The steps had come right up to the bedroom door and stopped, without another single sound of any kind. More than feeling cold, she was suddenly *terrified.*

"Mary?" She waited, her breath quick, the terror mounting. "Mary!"

Not once had she called out to Mary that the eager, warmhearted girl had not run to her side.

"Mary!"

She could feel the hairs rise on her forearms as she lay utterly still—helpless on the bed. Whoever stood on the other side of the door was as silent as a tree. No hand had been placed on the knob. No sound of any kind.

"Is that you, Mary?"

"No," a man's husky voice said through the closed door.

Natalie's head swam so that she felt she might faint. Then, slowly, still creaking a little on its new hinges, Burke's door began to open. Someone was slipping up on her! "Who is it?" she demanded.

And then she saw Ben in the doorway, his head wrapped in the red-and-green Indian turban he hadn't worn in years, his face darker than ever.

"Ben!" she gasped. "Who told you to barge into my house this way?"

"Nobody, Natalie," he answered hoarsely.

"Then what are you doing here? Don't you know Burke is riding around the woods over at the church site hunting for you? He doesn't even know our baby's dead! Burke would be with me now except for you!" Her voice was not her voice at all. "What do you want? Did you see Mary coming over from your cabin?"

"Mary will be here. I told her to fix my supper, that I would watch over you."

"What do you want?"

"To—tell you something—important." He faltered, then after two long, quick steps, knelt beside her bed.

"Well, it had better be important!"

"The most important thing I will ever say—until I die." Ben's voice was now almost angry and so intense that terror prickled her whole body. "I went to the place where—they buried your baby. I was there, at the setting of the sun."

She stared at him. "How—did you know? How did you know—my baby was dead? Does Burke know?"

"He does not know."

Irrelevantly, she wondered at the way Ben was talking—almost brokenly—the way Mary talked.

"I was there—hiding in the grove. I saw the burial."

"Ben, Burke is somewhere hunting for you—right now! That's why he isn't here yet."

As though she had said nothing, Ben went on, "I prayed there a long time—beside the grave. I left dogwood blossoms."

She was bolt upright in the bed now, not daring to take her eyes off his drawn, tragic face. "Thank you, Ben. But couldn't you have told Mary to tell me? Did you have to come plunging into my bedroom like this?"

"Yes. Only God knows how I struggled—every day, every night, all these years—to stay away. Natalie? Could I—touch your hand?"

"*What?*"

"Forgive me, please! Just once—could I touch your hand with mine? Only your—hand, Natalie."

"Burke has asked you to call me *Miss* Natalie. So have I!"

"I know, I know—Natalie. I promise never again to call you—Natalie. That will be an easy promise to keep, but could I please touch your hand?"

Puzzled, and in spite of her growing anger, Natalie nodded yes and barely lifted one hand. Ben clasped it eagerly in both his own. Then, for a few seconds, he closed his eyes and smiled. She'd almost never seen Ben smile.

"What is it you have to tell me?" she asked. "Is it about Burke?"

"No."

"Then what is it about?"

The dark, pain-filled eyes open now, he said, "I am—going soon—to be there—waiting for you, Natalie."

"Where?"

As though he hadn't heard her question, he went on, the words coming gently now, measured, from somewhere deep inside—a place in Ben she had never even thought of as existing. "I cannot stay here—waiting for *nothing*. I am a man, Natalie. I love you."

"Oh, I know that, Ben!"

"No, you do not know truly. Burke doesn't love you more than I love you. I have stayed because Burke is like a—brother. I have stayed too for glimpses of you. At last, I have faced the truth. A man cannot live long enough on this earth—to wait as I would have to wait—without hope." He lifted her hand to his mouth and kissed it tenderly. "I will—take your love to—your little son. To Burke's son."

Before Natalie could think of anything at all to say, Ben had sprung up and was gone. She heard his light, running steps cross her kitchen, her front porch, and she was sitting straight up in bed when the swift footfalls died away into the gathering darkness outside.

After a minute, two minutes . . . three, just as Mary called Ben's name from the cabin porch, a single gunshot split the soft, evening silence . . .

Chapter 14

WITH THE dark beginning to fall, Burke spurred Major to a gallop and headed toward home. Maybe Ben had just ridden back to his own cabin early so as not to have to face greeting Natalie's family and Mrs. Mackay. "Come on, Major," he urged the steady mount. "We've been fools to waste time hunting for shy old Ben."

The sun was gone behind the hills north of the tiny settlement they now called Cartersville, but the upcountry sky, making its magic with colors that never failed to fill Burke with a sense of belonging, hung protectingly above, its evening green washing out from streaks of red-gold and pink and gray. Red-gold, like Natalie's hair. Ben had surely gone on ahead, in order to avoid even meeting their aristocratic visitors from Savannah. "Why did you let me get so worried about him, Major? Huh? Why didn't you just start home instead?" He patted the plunging chestnut neck of the horse he'd bought some four years ago when he'd first returned to north Georgia—before he'd even seen Natalie again after they'd begun to love each other on their makeshift raft in the Atlantic. "You know me, Major, and you know the way home. Why did you let me make a fool of myself worrying because Ben just vanished while I was still asleep at Milner's place this morning?"

He had always talked to Major. Major never talked back. That was a relief. He and the horse were barely acquainted the day they entered the deep woods near the old Cherokee capital of New Echota back in 1839 and accidentally came upon Ben and Mary McDonald hiding in a low, wide cave, afraid to be seen by a white man. Brother and sister had been a part of Burke's life ever since. Even when Natalie let him know in no uncertain terms that, after their marriage, she considered Ben and Mary a burden, Burke had stuck to his friends. God only knew what he would have done without Ben working beside him on the Cummings place, his first house in Cassville, then on the Stiles home at Etowah Cliffs, two stores and now the Presbyterian church near Milner's. Steadily, he was working his long-held dreams into reality and by now Ben was even more important to all future plans.

When Major dashed over the slick, round rocks through the shoals of a mountain river that emptied into the Etowah and carried him triumphantly up the opposite bank, Burke looked around at the bright green spring woods and smiled. This was his land, and Ben, one of the few Cherokees who had managed to escape the federal stockades into which his people—Ben and Mary among them—had been herded, was as close as a brother. Maybe closer. Oh, because they were half-breeds, it was never going to be possible, with the Stiles family so nearby, for Mary and Ben McDonald to be an easy part of Burke's social life. Not that Miss Lib and Mr. Stiles were haughty folk. They weren't. It would simply never cross their minds that Burke and Natalie might want to invite Ben and Mary to dinner now and then. Just as well, he thought. Poor Ben still believes he's in love with Natalie. Actually, Burke believed it too, although not one jealous or resentful thought had ever crossed his mind. Not one. He'd pondered it a lot too, but always with only pity for kind, intelligent, hardworking Ben. Actually it had been nearly a year since Ben had mentioned Natalie's name except in passing. He'd never really spoken of his love for her. But neither had he denied it. It was common knowledge. Burke frowned. He'd give anything if Ben could find someone else. He hated the idea of his friend without hope.

Within a mile or so of the cabin he'd remodeled for himself and Natalie, he wondered, for the first time, how Ben would take the actual sight of Natalie with Burke's baby in her arms. That's a crazy thought, he chided himself. Ben's feelings for me are as real as mine for him. In his way, he'll be glad for us both. He did give one veiled hint sometime last week, though, about how he hated the thought of Natalie suffering in childbirth. Ben had mentioned something about maybe staying in the woods if he and Burke happened to be at home when the baby came. Poor Ben couldn't bear the thought of hearing Natalie scream.

Burke shuddered. Neither could he, but in the three years of their married life, Natalie hadn't shown many signs of being like other young women. It would be just like her to bear the agony in silence. It would be just like her to surprise them all. He was smiling again now, proudly. When she'd first tried to prove that she could, no matter how he argued, keep house on the Georgia frontier, she'd managed to burn his old cabin to the ground. He'd married her only a few days later because neither of them could bear for her to return to Savannah to learn *how* to cook and sew and scrub floors without at least one night to—make their love whole. Well, *she had learned.* In six months' time, she was back in the upcountry as his wife, surprising everyone with her domestic skills. In less than a year he'd finish the good cottage he and Ben were building for Natalie. He honestly doubted that she'd be any happier in a well-built frame house than she was now in their patched-up old Cherokee cabin. He'd be prouder to give her a good house to keep and care for, but he wouldn't be any happier either. He couldn't be.

He could see the Etowah River up ahead, a touch of sunset color still lighting it. He was almost home. He and Major had crossed the jut of land that extended out into the sharply curving little river—the five or six miles of land that separated Milner's place and Etowah Cliffs, where they all lived, almost within hailing distance of one another. Still not one to ask God for every little thing, Burke thanked Him often these days that Miss Lib and Mary lived so near the Latimers' cabin. Mary spent every night now with Natalie and he knew Miss Lib kept close tabs on her. He hated every moment away, but he hadn't worried too much because the church building site was too far for him and Ben to ride home each night.

Ben . . . this wasn't the first time Ben had just vanished. Burke's mind raced back over the other two times, both, he now knew, because of his friend's love for Natalie. Still, none of it had raised a single barrier between him and Ben. Certainly not on Burke's side and he'd long ago learned to accept Ben's occasional dark moods. Not only had he learned to accept them —in a way he couldn't explain even to himself, he understood Ben and never stopped counting on his loyalty.

Up ahead, he could see smoke curling from the tall chimney of the Stiles house. The company from Savannah had evidently arrived. The first frame wing of the house he and Ben had built some time back was probably ringing with family talk and laughter. He and Ben would be starting work on the remainder of the big house—a mansion by the time they finished—just as soon as they were through with the Presbyterian church. The additional wings of the Stiles place would be made of brick, the first brick building he'd tried.

"Come on, Major—let 'er rip, boy. I need my wife in my arms!"

Major had just pounded around the curve in the river lane when Burke saw the wavering yellow light of pine-knot flares in Miss Lib's favorite little grove between his cabin and the Stiles place. He frowned, puzzled at what could be going on outside at this hour. Surely, the travelers were too exhausted for a picnic. Besides, now that it was almost dark, the air was cool. A stiffening wind had caused him to hold his wide-brimmed hat in place for the past mile or so. Something must have happened, but what on earth could it be? That little grove of trees held no danger of any kind. For him and Natalie, it had always been their place to go for privacy—"their cozy," she called it, because the scrub oaks and hickories and pines stood so close and sheltering.

Burke kicked Major to a faster gallop. Suddenly, he was more than curious —he was afraid.

They had all heard the gunshot at supper in Eliza Anne's parlor, where, until a dining room could be added, W.H. had set up the good oak table Ben made last year. At first, Eliza Anne had assured them the shot was only one of their hands out hunting coons—and then a chill had settled over the room. No one, including Eliza Anne, believed that. The Stiles people were all unarmed.

Insisting that Miss Eliza stay in the house with the children, she and Caroline hurried outside with Mark and Jonathan to the woodshed for one or two good pine knots for light. Excited by the adventure, Jonathan had run back in the house to light the knots at the parlor fire.

They stood now, in a motionless half-circle around the little grave in the sheltering grove of scrub trees, a brisk wind off the river moving the pine flames so that young scrub tree shadows tossed and jerked and made the night unreal. This night is not unreal, Eliza Anne kept telling herself as they stood staring down at Ben McDonald's body sprawled across the tiny grave.

Eliza Anne and Caroline clung to each other as Mark and Jonathan knelt to examine the body.

"He's dead," Mark said, feeling about him on the ground. "And here's— his pistol."

Jumping to his feet, Jonathan ran to the women and turned them both away. "Don't look, Mama—Miss Lib," he gasped. "Ben nearly blew his head off! Papa's right. His gun's there beside him."

"Dear God," Eliza Anne breathed, "I—need my husband!"

Mark, still on his knees beside Ben's corpse, looked up at them, his stricken face white in the wavering light. "Caroline," he asked tonelessly, "what else is going to happen?"

When his mother said nothing, Jonathan asked, "You—did think Ben would—do something—bad, didn't you, Mama?"

"I knew he would," she murmured. "Just as your father knew—about Natalie."

"I'll tell you what else will happen." Eliza Anne heard the sudden hardness in her voice when she spoke. "Burke is going to ride in here any minute and one of us is going to have to tell him—about Ben *and* his dead son . . ." Eliza Anne felt herself taking charge. Taking charge had always been her way of shielding herself. "Mark, I think you're the one who should tell Burke!"

"Why?" Caroline demanded, protecting her husband as plainly as though she'd rushed to throw her arms about him. "Why should poor Mark be the one?"

"Because he's Burke's father-in-law! Jonathan and Burke haven't even met. *I can't tell him.* I've already had more than I can bear . . ."

Eliza Anne looked at Mark. His face was drawn. He looked old in the yellow torchlight, but she saw him lift his head.

"I'll tell Burke, of course," Mark said.

At that moment, Eliza Anne felt Jonathan's hand on her shoulder. "No," the boy said firmly. "I'm a man now and Papa's already had enough."

"Son," Mark said, his voice breaking, "you know I won't let you do that. It's my place."

"Listen!" Jonathan whispered. "Burke's coming! I hear—a horse galloping this way."

"Yes," Eliza Anne whispered. "That must be Burke . . ."

"God help him," Mark breathed, still kneeling beside Ben. "The man's lost his son—*and* his best friend!"

"Mark," Caroline asked sharply, "how can you call that violent Indian Burke's best friend?"

"Because he was, Caroline."

Horse and rider headed straight for the little grove and reined up beside where they all stood. Without a word, Eliza Anne watched Burke dismount hurriedly and stride to Ben's sprawled, still body. For a long moment, he stared down at the bleeding head, the Indian turban half torn away by the gun blast. Then Burke removed his hat, tossed it on the ground and knelt beside Mark, who got slowly to his feet finally and stepped back.

Mark knows, Eliza Anne thought. He knows how close Burke and Ben were. Thank God he does. Poor Burke . . . oh, poor, poor Burke!

For an endless moment, as no one spoke, Burke smoothed and smoothed Ben's blood-soaked black hair. At last, Eliza Anne took a few steps toward him, her hand out. He seemed not even to notice her.

"Burke," she said softly, "you must ride straight to Natalie. She—she needs you far more than Ben now."

Still kneeling, the big, yellow-haired young man turned slowly to look up at her, his open, stricken face wet with tears. "Natalie?" he asked just above a whisper. "Natalie—needs me?"

"She—needs you," Mark choked out, "because, because—"

Eliza Anne saw Caroline stumble over the rough ground to embrace her husband, who had broken into hard, tearing sobs. Almost at once, Jonathan moved quickly toward Burke.

"I'm Jonathan, Burke. Natalie's brother. We—we have more bad news for you than any man should have to hear," he said. "It's hard to see in this flickering light, but—Ben shot himself beside a—fresh grave. Your—son is buried in that grave. My—sister lost her baby. He was buried today, this afternoon, just before we got here, I guess. Miss Lib's right. Natalie needs you."

Burke, still on his knees, could only stare up at Jonathan, who was giving him the kindest, tenderest look Eliza Anne had ever seen on a human face.

His eyes blank, still searching the boy's face, Burke asked, "Ben—shot *himself?*"

"Yes," the boy said. "I hope it—helps some that we're here. You can count on us, Burke. All of us. It might help a little. I—hope so."

Burke touched the tiny mound of freshly turned earth, fingered one of Ben's wilting dogwood blossoms, then got stiffly to his feet and picked up his hat. "Thank you, Jonathan," he said, and headed for his horse. But before he mounted again, he buried his head against Major's sweating side and shattered the night silence with wrenching sobs.

When Burke had ridden off in the direction of his own cabin, Eliza Anne asked woodenly, "We—we can't just leave Ben out here all night like this, do you think?"

"I—can't think," Caroline said. "I believe I'm—glad I can't."

"I guess Papa and I could get Ben's body up onto a wagon, Miss Lib,"

Jonathan offered. "Could one of your people bring a wagon? We can take Ben to—his own cabin."

"Is his sister there?" Mark asked. "Where is Indian Mary?"

"Where *is* Indian Mary?" Caroline repeated.

"With Natalie, I'm sure," Eliza Anne said. "She never leaves her except when told to go. Jonathan?"

"What can I do, Miss Lib? I'll do whatever you say."

"Take a flare and go to the river, run down along the bank fifty yards or so —then call across to Mr. David Holder. He's our overseer. He and his wife live in a cottage just on the other side of the river. David Holder will know what to do—only, dear God, never in my life have I wished for W.H. the way I wish for him now!"

At last, David Holder's voice, shouting that he'd come right over, reached Jonathan on the rising wind. Miss Lib had said it would take half an hour for Holder to reach their side of the river and Jonathan figured that would give him time to do the one thing he suddenly had to do. Burke would be in his own cabin by now, with Natalie, trying to comfort her, trying to contain his own grief, but who would be with Ben's sister, Mary? And where was she? Burke and Natalie would have each other and, up against black tragedy like this, would not be likely to think about Mary at all.

He certainly didn't blame them. Jonathan had never even been in love, so how could he possibly understand the pain they must both feel that their baby was dead? But he *was* a brother. He had a sister and he would never forget his own pain during the long days and nights when they were waiting to learn if Natalie was dead or alive after the *Pulaski* went down. Even though he didn't know Indian Mary, he could understand something, at least, of her feelings when she learned that Ben was dead too.

Still carrying a pine torch, he hurried, stumbling through the woods along the river cliffs. When he reached the road, he began to run . . . all the way to the dimly lighted cabin where his sister lived, where Miss Lib had said Mary would be. His legs were so heavy he prayed for strength to run faster, because for a reason he didn't try to figure out, nothing was as important as getting to Indian Mary.

To take his mind off stumbling over the rutted road, he tried to remember what he'd been told about the accident to Mary McDonald's eye when his parents and Natalie had made their first trip to the upcountry. His mother had said something about Natalie and a runaway horse and a catamount that screamed and scared the horse—but all he remembered for sure now was that a flying stirrup had struck Mary in the face and almost blinded her in one eye.

"She's still quite pretty, though," Papa had said, "and such a cheerful, pleasant girl, she's taken the partial loss of sight extremely well."

His mother thought rather highly of Mary too. In fact, it seemed important to Mama, he recalled, as he ran up the path to the cabin, that Mary, unlike poor Ben, didn't look very Indian. She and Ben had had a Scottish father, but a full-blood Cherokee mother who was a member of the Willow family. Ben's Indian name was Bending Willow. Mary's Indian name was Merry Willow. "Fitting," Papa had mused. "She is a merry little thing."

The pine-knot flare was burning down some as Jonathan reached the cabin porch, but there was light enough for him to see someone sitting in a dark, small, crumpled heap on the top step. A girl. *Mary.* It must be Indian Mary. And she must have heard his running footsteps on the hard-packed path, but she said nothing, did not even lift her face from her hands.

Did she know her brother was dead? Had Burke told her the horrible news that Ben had shot himself?

At the bottom step, Jonathan stopped and waited. He cleared his throat. The girl remained silent, motionless.

He spoke softly. "Miss Mary?"

Before she lifted her head, he heard Burke and Natalie from the rear of the cabin, heard Burke's sobs, Natalie's sobs, heard Burke's voice saying something comforting, he hoped, to his sister, then Natalie's. He couldn't understand their words at all, but his sister's response was in a helpless tone so unlike any he'd ever heard from Natalie that he just stood there before Mary's huddled form and tried to imagine what the sorrowing parents could possibly be saying to each other. Of course, his sister's heart was broken, but for all the years of his life, he had expected some measure of resilience from Natalie; some reasonably firm comment—cross, angry or otherwise—to any bad situation. She had always been either cocky or even smart-aleck—or had found a reason to joke. You're dumb, he scolded himself. How could the poor little thing be any of those ways tonight? Mama said she feels a failure. I don't think that can last with Natalie, but she wouldn't have told Mama she'd failed Burke if she didn't really feel she had. Two words he had never even thought of hooking together in his mind were "Natalie" and "failure."

He longed to run straight to his sister, but Mama had explained that being married meant that husband and wife became as one person and that they were to cleave to each other—not to a kid brother.

He lifted the flickering pine torch for a better look at the crumpled girl still on the top step and wondered if she was in such shock that she hadn't even heard him.

"Miss Mary?" he said again. "Miss Mary McDonald? My name is Jonathan Browning. I'm Natalie's brother and I'm here to—to—" He broke off speaking. Why *was* he there? For one reason only, so far as he knew—because he had to be. What he said to her was "I'm here, Miss Mary, in case you need me . . ."

As though she had indeed just heard him, Mary sprang to her feet and made a pathetic, small curtsy. "You—are Miss Natalie's brother?"

"Yes, ma'am. I—I don't have very long to stay. I'm waiting for Mr. David Holder to get here from across the river, but I—"

"Why Mister Holder come across the river tonight?"

Jonathan's heart sank. He could tell she didn't know about Ben! Burke had evidently run straight past her to Natalie.

I'll have to tell her, he thought. I'm the one who will have to tell her . . .

"You here to see your sister?" Mary asked. "She with Mister Burke—in the cabin." She curtsied again self-consciously. "Excuse me. I not talk very good tonight. It is a sad night." Keeping her head down a little, she asked, abruptly, "You know Ben, my brother, and I are Cherokee half-blood?"

Trying to keep his voice calm, although she'd stunned him with her question, Jonathan said quickly, "Oh, yes. Of course I know that. I find it—very interesting too."

"Not bad?"

"Bad?"

"You no find Cherokee bad?"

He tried to keep his shaky voice merely pleasant. "Why should I? I have English blood in me and a little German, I think."

Lifting the flare a bit higher, he looked straight into her face. She was—truly beautiful. She was looking straight up at him too now, the scar from the accident in the woods showing plainly. The iron stirrup had slashed her tender, rounded cheek from the corner of one eye almost to her mouth. Without the scar, though, he felt sure her beauty would be more than he could endure. Even with the jagged scar, his body, his heart—his whole being was shaken with a kind of emotion he'd never before experienced. Not in all his nearly seventeen years.

If only I could take her in my arms, he thought wildly, she'd be all right. Somehow, she'd even be all right when I have to tell her about Ben . . .

"My brother, Ben, he work side by side with Mister Burke," she said. "Mister Burke, he teach Ben skills. They are friends."

"I—I know," Jonathan answered, struggling to pull together his own warring emotions and also to find the best way to tell this unassuming, disarmingly honest girl that her only brother had shot himself. "May I sit down beside you?" he asked.

"Yes, please."

Slowly, Jonathan sat down on the step beside her and wondered what to say next.

"Not to be impolite to you, but since Mister Burke is with Natalie, Ben is eating his supper alone in our cabin. I must go," she said. Then: "Oh, I pray Mister Burke comfort Miss Natalie! I pray hard for that."

"Me too," he said. "Miss Mary? Do you have to go?"

"My brother was hungry. Ben is bashful with strange people." She brightened. "But maybe when he eats I bring him here to meet you."

"Miss Mary, wait . . . There's something you have to know and—I wish I didn't have to tell you, but—I hope my being here will help."

"Help *me?*"

"Uh, yes. You see, there's no need for you to hurry back to your cabin. Ben—isn't there."

"But he tell me he was hungry. I fix supper for him!"

He reached for her hand. She made no effort to stop him when he clasped it in one of his own, holding the pine flare in the other. "Miss Mary, sometimes people hate the bearer of—bad news. I—surely hope you won't—hate me, but—"

She jumped to her feet and stood on the porch staring down at him where he still sat on the top step. There was fear in her face, but she said nothing.

"Mary—oh, Mary, your brother, Ben, is—dead."

She still stood staring down at him, unbelieving. Slowly, from side to side, she began to shake her curly head. On his feet beside her now, Jonathan touched her forearm with his free hand.

"No! *No!*" she cried. Then, screaming Ben's name, Mary leaped down the three steps and raced off through the darkness toward where her cabin stood.

Still clutching the pine torch, Jonathan ran after her.

Chapter 15

"WHAT WAS that cry, Burke? Burke! It sounded like Mary!"

"Natalie, wait . . . don't try to get out of bed, *please.*" He struggled to restrain her, but she slipped away and by the time Burke reached the front porch, she was running around the front yard in the dark, calling out for Mary, her voice a weak, hopeless wail. Not Natalie's voice at all.

Burke caught up with her and held her, bodily stopping her from running around to the back in the direction of Mary's cabin.

"Burke, let me go! I know that was Mary—I know something dreadful has happened to Mary too! Let go of me!"

"Somebody probably just told Mary that—that—"

"Told her what?"

His deep breath was nearer a sob. "About—Ben."

"*What* about Ben?" She tried to jerk free of his arms, the dim light from inside their cabin barely enough for Burke to see the horror in her face. "*What happened to Ben?*"

"He—he killed himself."

Burke felt her body go limp, and before he could catch her, she slipped like a rag doll to the ground.

"Natalie! The ground's cold—don't do this." Picking her up, he begged, "In the name of God, darling, don't do this to me! Haven't we got enough without this? You're weak as a little kitten. You'll get sick out here in this cold night air!"

She made no sound at all, not even a whimper as he carried her back toward their cabin. Her voice was so flat, so tiny, he could scarcely hear her when finally she spoke his name. There was nothing to say, so he just held her and climbed the steps. Once inside the house, he whispered, "I don't know how, but things are—going to be—all right. Somehow, Natalie, things are going to be—all right for us again someday. You'll see . . ."

"No, they won't be. Not ever—not ever again! And everything—our baby, what Ben did—everything that hurts you is—my fault!"

Carrying her through the main room and in to their bed, he could feel her shivering and yet her skin was so hot. She must be burning up with fever, he thought wildly as he laid her on the bed and hurried for an extra quilt.

"Burke, no," she cried. "Don't leave me!"

With the extra quilt tucked around her, he stretched out beside her and lay there for minute after minute after minute—willing warmth from his own body into hers. Willing Natalie to feel warm and safe again, to stop chilling, to stop blaming herself. Twice, he tried to slip outside to whistle for Mary. Both times Natalie's pathetic cries brought him running back. As long as he lay beside her, holding her in his arms, she was fairly quiet, except for an occasional hard shudder, so pronounced that he longed to know if the shuddering came from chills or from hard jerks of realization in her fevered mind.

The sound of the front-door latch at last was such a welcome relief that he could only lie there silently thanking God that someone was coming who might be able to help him with Natalie. She needed warm bricks to her feet, more covers to hold out the chill night air. Long ago, he'd given up any notion of leaving her long enough to find Mary. The long, futile search for Ben, the hard ride home—the ghastly double tragedies once he got there— had exhausted him, had wrung from his strong body the last ounce of energy. He had none left to fight Natalie's need of him. He needed her too.

He could hear footsteps crossing the main room now, coming closer to the bedroom door, barely ajar. Dear God, he breathed, let it be Mary! Mary would know what to do for them both.

"Mr. Latimer? Mr. Latimer—you in there?"

It was a woman's voice, but not Mary's. He'd heard the pain-filled cries that Natalie had been so sure were Mary's, but until now, when he needed her so much, he hadn't even remembered. Where could Mary be? Had anyone told her about Ben?

"Mr. Latimer?"

He groaned, but did not answer.

"It's Elizabeth Holder, Mr. Latimer," the voice called again, nearby now— just outside the bedroom door. "I thought you'd want to know that my husband's helping haul Indian Ben's dead body to his cabin. How's Miss Natalie?"

"Sick," he gasped weakly. "My wife's having terrible chills. Will you— help us, please? Would you build up the fire—find more covers? Maybe she'll let you stay with her while I hunt some bricks to warm for her little feet."

This time, when he tried to ease himself up off the bed, Natalie made no sound, no move to stop him. She just lay there.

"My God, Mrs. Holder! Is—is my wife dead too?"

"No, no, no," the woman said comfortingly, her hand on Natalie's fore- head. "She's just tuckered out. Her skin's too hot for her to be dead. Go for the bricks, Mr. Latimer. I'll get more quilts. Your wife's got a high fever. Most likely it came from the little dead body she carried."

In the backyard, Burke set his lantern on the woodpile and began picking up bricks he'd asked the Stiles hands to start making for the day he and Ben could lay the foundation for the second wing of Miss Lib's house. Gathering bricks made from the good Cass County clay, he struggled to gather his own torn emotions, his crazily scattered thoughts. The way he counted on the sun rising in the morning, he'd counted on Ben to help him with everything he would ever build. He'd also dreamed of leading his own child from room to room of Miss Lib's big house as it progressed during the child's growing years. Secretly, he'd hoped for a little girl who might be even half as beautiful as her mother, but somehow there had also been the dream of leading a small son through what would surely be his proudest achievement—the William Henry Stiles mansion gracing the high cliffs above the winding Etowah River.

Having a man's dreams all ripped away at once is like ripping off his arm, he thought, dropping a brick and then stooping to pick it up. His head ached. His hands shook. His world had shaken apart; would never, no matter how he'd tried to reassure Natalie, be safe and sure again as long as he lived. As long as he might live, he would never—could never forget this tragic spring of the year 1842 . . .

Back in the cabin, he knelt before his fireplace to heat the bricks and wished for Mary, who would know where to find an extra blanket in which to wrap the hot bricks to warm Natalie's feet. Those perfectly formed little feet had once before caused him worry and concern. On his knees, waiting for the bricks to warm, he thought of the tiny white scar on the top of Natalie's right foot, the only physical reminder of their five days and nights spent on a fragment of the *Pulaski*'s deck—a sunburn scar. Her feet had been so blistered from the sun, the memory still pained him.

Where, he wondered, is Mary—this minute? He knew David Holder was helping Mr. Browning and Jonathan take Ben's body to her cabin, but who had told Mary that Ben was dead?

"I certainly didn't tell her," he said aloud, and felt a hot wave of shame. Who's with Mary now? he wondered frantically. Will they just carry Ben into the cabin and let that be the first she knows?

He shuddered. Ben was the only person in all the world on whom Mary could depend. The poor, trusting girl thought she could depend on me! She'll know better now. When push comes to shove, when a man has to make a choice, the first loyalty of his heart shows. He would always choose—only Natalie. If either of her parents or Miss Lib had been with her earlier, he might have taken time to tell Mary about Ben as he raced into his own cabin to be with Natalie. No one had been there but Mary, though, because Natalie had sent them all away and he'd just let Mary slip silently past him and out onto the front steps alone. After that, holding Natalie, struggling to take some of her grief and pain into himself, he hadn't given Mary another thought until he needed her!

Still on his knees by the fireplace waiting for the bricks, he tried hard to pray for Mary. It seemed as though God had forgotten them all.

After he helped carry Ben's body into Mary's cabin, Jonathan did not leave her side. Both parents, he knew—and certainly Miss Lib, who'd been up all the night before with Natalie—were exhausted. Still, they'd insisted upon staying while Mary herself cleaned her dead brother's face, washed his body and dressed him, with Jonathan's help, in his one pair of buckskin Indian trousers and jacket. Around Ben's shattered head, Mary, with trembling hands, skillfully wrapped a fresh, blue-and-yellow Cherokee turban.

"His real name is Bending Willow," she whispered, glancing only at Jonathan, as though it were important that he know. "We bury him as—our mother's son, Bending Willow. It not be bad in heaven to be—Indian."

Finally everyone but Jonathan left. Ben's body lay at the front of the cabin on Ben's own bed. Beside Mary, who was stretched on her bed near the fireplace, Jonathan sat in a straight chair, almost never taking his eyes from her pale, drawn face—expressionless except for moments of sweeping grief.

So much had happened since they'd reached Etowah Cliffs, Jonathan couldn't sort out anything beyond the sure knowledge that he was exactly where he should be—beside Mary. Her Cherokee name, Merry Willow, kept moving in and out of his mind. In her shock and grief, she looked almost as Indian as Ben. Oh, the brown, soft curls were those of a white girl. The small, perfect nose might have been the nose of one of her father's Scottish forebears, but he could think only Cherokee as he looked now at the lovely, vulnerable, scarred face of the one person he had ever loved as a man loves a woman. At least, it seemed to him that the way his heart was reaching toward Mary must be the way a man's heart reaches toward his beloved.

Had he really taken Miss Lib off alone on the tiny cabin porch to tell her that he loved Mary? He felt so confused by the tangle of his own emotions that he couldn't be sure. Nothing was too clear beyond the new, unfamiliar, suddenly essential longing toward Mary. He was tired too—all the way to the marrow of his bones—but he remembered Miss Lib trying to reason with him. He remembered the look on her face and the strict tone in her voice warning him to be sensible, not to confuse deep pity with love—especially at such a tragic time.

He couldn't have just imagined Miss Lib had said all that. She must have said it, which meant he had told her what he knew to be true—that he would never love anyone else now that he had found Mary McDonald.

He reached for Mary's hand. She clasped his fingers in quick response. Slowly, her swollen eyes opened and she looked squarely into his face. "Thank you, Mister Jonathan," she whispered. "Thank you. Ben thank you too. You take care of me."

He covered her hand with both of his and leaned eagerly toward her. "Oh, Mary—I'll take care you for as long as I live!"

"No!" She frowned and turned her head away.

"Mary! What's the matter?" His head felt about to burst. "Tell me what I said that was so—wrong?"

Her face still turned away, she whispered, "You say nothing—wrong."

"Then what's the matter? Why are you frowning like that?"

For a long, long time, she was silent, her hand still clasping his, then, slowly, he felt her fingers loosen. "Mary, can't you think of anything to say to me?"

After another frightening silence, she turned her face back to him. "Ben is dead," she murmured, "because he was foolish enough to love—white woman. Your sister. I am as—Cherokee—as Ben."

"No!"

"I am."

"Mary, that isn't what I meant. I know you're half Cherokee. I don't care about that."

"Other people care."

"But this is different. I'm—pretty sure I love you."

"Promise you never say that again!"

Jonathan waited for only a second or two, then he said in a soft, firm voice, "I'd promise anything I could, but I can't promise that. A man can't help what happens—in his heart. I—I love you exactly the way—my sister loves Burke Latimer. I know I do. I always thought she was—a little crazy to be so determined to find Burke again after the shipwreck, but—"

"Miss Natalie not crazy one bit!"

What, he wondered, did Mary mean by that? Was Jonathan's mother right to think Mary also loved Burke? He'd only known Mary for a little while, but somehow, he knew that if he questioned her further this minute, she'd tell him the truth. He opened his mouth to speak, then decided against it.

If Mama's right, he told himself, I don't want to know it! Maybe Mary does think she's in love with Burke, but I'm going to change that. I don't care what Miss Lib says. I don't even care what Mary thinks about Cherokee blood being—bad. I love her. I love Mary McDonald. I love *Merry Willow*. I mean to win her love. I'll do it too. I'm almost seventeen!

Chapter 16

NEARLY a month after they buried Ben behind his cabin in the good oak coffin Burke himself built, Eliza Mackay, with her two grandsons and granddaughter in tow, set out for the Stiles garden early one morning to pick new green onions and young, tender turnip greens. She had darned and mended every sock and shirt she could find, had, at Mark's insistence, rested and rested from the long trip until she was ready to run at the sight of a rocking chair or a bed. Mostly, she had tried to make herself useful. In spite of the tragedies and her own sorrow, she meant to do her level best to be content, to enjoy to the fullest the hours spent with her grandchildren.

Kate and Sarah wrote often from Savannah, urging her to come home before the weather grew too hot. She should be getting back for her own garden's sake, she knew, even though Emphie would have planted seeds after a fashion. So would Kate and Sarah, but her backyard—both flower and vegetable—was Eliza's pride and pleasure. The latest letter from William assured her that Jack, home from Tybee for a few days, had merely been tired, not ill, and that he was back at work on the river survey. William's letter had mentioned not one word about his sister Sarah, though, and that troubled Eliza. It could mean only one thing—Sarah was using her sharp tongue on William again.

Keeping the children in sight up ahead as the two boys showed off by jumping fallen logs and riding pine saplings, she realized that she couldn't remember a time when Sarah and William had really hit it off for long. Oh, they curbed their mutual irritations before her, but Sarah, who wanted to do everything yesterday, and William, who tended toward tomorrow, had rubbed each other the wrong way—even when Sarah was just a child Cliffie Gordon's age.

Swinging her basket as she took her time along the sandy road to the garden, Eliza breathed a prayer for Sarah Gordon and her fatherless children, glad that her grandson Henry seemed to remember little Cliffie so well. In a letter she planned to write to Sarah Gordon yet today, she would be sure to say that Henry had asked about the girl and said to tell her he hoped she'd be her happy self again soon. Eliza had counted on Henry's saying something that would let Cliffie know he remembered her too. She smiled. Young Robert Stiles was certainly closer to five-year-old Cliffie's age, but it was Henry whom Cliffie adored—had always adored. And Henry still seemed to thrive on it.

As she told the children to run on ahead to play in the big oak grove while she picked in the garden, a rush of the now familiar sadness swept over her. Minute by minute, her heart ached for Mark and Caroline and Natalie and Burke. The Lord had wisely said that "the kingdom is within." Eliza Mackay definitely did not feel sixty-four years old, but deep inside, each thought of the Browning family's tragedy seemed to add years to the way she felt. They'd been in the upcountry almost a month and the usually lively Natalie still spent nearly all of every day in bed, sick and grieving. Burke had sent a letter by the Stileses' Solomon to Mr. Arnold Milner, telling him that since Burke's helper, Ben, had killed himself and his wife had lost their child, he would not be able to finish the church any time soon.

Mark and Caroline kept trying to dissuade Burke from sitting all day by Natalie's bed, but neither she nor her daughter, Eliza Anne, had tried even once to change Burke's mind. Nothing could have pried Eliza from her Robert's side all those long years ago when he'd had his first heart attack. Burke wasn't being stubborn. As much as his work meant to him, Natalie came first. Eliza Anne certainly agreed. "I die a little every night, Mama, because W.H. isn't here. I'm sure he's all right riding about the district making speeches, but believe me, if he were ill and I could get to him, I'd be there and nothing in the wide world could stop me!"

The sun was climbing the late spring sky. Eliza had a basketful of vegetables and knew she should be heading home before they wilted. Instead, she put down her basket and sat on a moss-covered log to try once more to think of a way to help Natalie. If she brightened even a little, it would do wonders for Mark and Caroline and Burke. The girl felt a total failure and nothing anyone—even Burke—could say or do seemed to change that. Of course, the fever didn't help, but Eliza was as sure as that she sat there on the fallen log that until at least a shred of Natalie's old buoyancy returned, the fever would linger.

" 'The kingdom *is* within,' " she said aloud. "Dear Lord, how true! I beg You, for her sake, for all our sakes, to set things right again in the dark, gloomy kingdom within our beloved Natalie . . ."

How long she sat there, Eliza had no idea, but she became aware that the children's voices had been silent for some time. Getting to her feet, she looked around and was startled to see Mary Cowper, Henry and young Bobby standing only a few feet away staring at her.

"Are you sick, Grandma?" Mary C. asked. "Henry thinks you must be. We're worried about you."

Tender, cheerful Robert hurried up to lay his grubby hand on Eliza's shoulder. "Even I got kind of worried when we saw you sitting on that log for such a long time."

"Are you just thinking hard about something?" Henry asked in his most grown-up manner. "I know people do think a lot when they get older. Of course, Bob wouldn't know about that yet—at his age."

"I do so know," Robert said.

"Grandma, were you just thinking?" Mary Cowper asked. "And were your thoughts troubled? Every time Natalie thinks, she cries. Are you going to cry?"

"No, no, child. I'm not going to cry at all. I—I was thinking fairly hard, though. And praying. I—I'm just so concerned about Natalie—and her parents."

"And Burke," Henry said. "Burke's the one I worry about. He not only lost his son born dead, but Indian Ben, his right hand."

"Mama says she wonders if Burke will ever finish the church so he can get started on the best part of our house," Bobby said, his high forehead furrowed. "I feel sorry for ol' Burke. He's scared to leave Natalie and he sure needs Ben or somebody to help him build our house. Mama says Papa has his heart set on a real mansion!"

Tears on her face, Mary Cowper threw both arms around her grandmother. "I—do love Natalie so much! We always had so much fun with her. Do—do you think Natalie might die too?"

"Oh, child, child," Eliza soothed, holding the girl close. "No. Nothing more is going to happen any time soon, I'm sure. We all just have to get through this bad period."

"But couldn't Natalie die too? The way her baby did?"

"No," Eliza said firmly. "We're going to think of a way to help her so she'll be more like herself again. You'll see, Mary Cowper, you'll see," she repeated, smoothing the girl's dark hair back from her sweaty forehead. "I don't know what it's going to be, but God does know and He does hear our prayers. I've asked Him to make it all bright and shiny again—down inside Natalie's heart. He will, He will."

"But when?"

"I don't know when. These things take time. I do know that when Natalie's more like Natalie again, Burke will be all right too. You'll see."

"I'm trying awfully hard, Grandma," Henry said, his face solemn, "to think of something that might make Natalie laugh."

"That's kind of you, son," Eliza said, "but maybe this just isn't quite the time for laughter. It will be again, though. God stays busy every minute arranging and rearranging life for us all."

"Look, Grandma," Bobby said, pointing toward the path they'd left when they entered the oak grove. "Mrs. Holder's comin' this way! She's gonna' have a baby too. Do you think her baby might die?"

"No, I do not," Eliza said.

"She sure is all out of shape," Bobby marveled.

"But she's fine. Look at the way she's cutting through those woods. Good morning, Mrs. Holder," Eliza called. "Are you here to pick some of our fresh things?"

"No, Mrs. Mackay," Elizabeth said, puffing up to them.

"Nothing's wrong with Mama, is it?" Bobby asked.

"Not a thing. I just saw her a few minutes ago on her way to the Latimer cabin. She's the one told me you were all out here pickin', Mrs. Mackay. So I come straight here as fast as I could."

Eliza studied the woman's young, flushed face, then said, "Well, it's nice to see you, Mrs. Holder, but did you have a special reason for tracking us down this morning?"

"Yes, ma'am, I did. David and I never worked for nicer folks than the Stileses and we're both mighty partial to Mrs. Latimer. We don't always know exactly how to take Miss Natalie, but we can see plain as the nose on your face that help is needed. You know that poor little heartbroken Cherokee girl, Mary, does her best to help out, but she's grievin' something terrible over her brother shootin' himself." She stopped to catch her breath. "I heard in a letter from my mama up near Ellijay, Georgia, where she's livin' now, of a woman named Lorah Plemmons that might help a lot. She's even got a boy that's a carpenter to work with Mr. Latimer."

"Why, that's awfully kind of you to think about us all," Eliza said carefully, "but I can't help wondering why you didn't mention this to my daughter, Eliza Anne, since you said you just saw her."

"Oh, I can tell you're the one of all of 'em to keep a level head, Mrs. Mackay. David and me, we talked it over at breakfast. We thought to tell you first to see what you think 'bout tryin' to get Mrs. Plemmons to come here to look after Miss Natalie till she's over her fever an' up and around again. Lorah Plemmons and the boy she took in need a home bad. She's a widow woman an' she's white. She's smart as she can be an'—if you get my meanin' —she just could make Miss Natalie sit up an' take notice."

"Well, you are thoughtful, Mrs. Holder, but I'd have to talk to both the Brownings and Burke Latimer."

"Yes, ma'am, I know that. I just thought it best for you to do the talkin'— not me. You see, I'm real partial to Lorah Plemmons. She and her boy would have a good home here, but since my husband's Mr. Stiles's overseer, I hate to stick in my two cents."

"Can the lady cook good food?" Robert asked.

"Best you ever tasted, Bobby," Elizabeth Holder said. "That woman can make corn bread that's so good it makes a body tremble just thinkin' about it. She's a hard worker, too, but—" She broke off.

"But what, Mrs. Holder?" Henry asked.

"I reckon her cookin' and housework is the least of it. It's Miss Lorah herself that could make the big difference. I swan, there just ain't nobody anywhere like her! Oh, I know Miss Natalie's parents and Mrs. Stiles an' you, along with Cherokee Mary, sees to all Miss Natalie needs now, but—"

"We try, but the Brownings and I have to be getting back to Savannah one of these days. It would make such a difference to know that a responsible woman lived right here whose only duty was to see to Natalie."

Elizabeth Holder smiled a little. "Excuse me, but doin' that ain't no small job."

"We know that," Eliza said. "But the girl's a lot more amenable than she once was. Mostly right now, I'd say she needs her spirits bucked up. She needs someone to convince her that she isn't a complete failure."

"Yeah," Henry said, deep in thought. "Natalie's changed a lot. Oh, I don't think she's any less stubborn, but—"

"If anything," Robert interjected, "she's even harder to handle."

"You've found Natalie harder to handle, Bobby?" Eliza asked, masking her own amusement that the two boys had even noticed.

"A lot harder," he said. "Oh, she always got her way and we didn't care since she was so pretty and so much fun. But Natalie's no fun anymore, is she, Henry?"

"Naw, not really. And that's sad because we all used to love to be with her. These days, though, she's a lot more likely to bust out cryin' than bust out laughin' the way she used to."

"The Bible says, 'A merry heart doeth good like a medicine,' " Elizabeth Holder said. "Lorah Plemmons has had a hard time of it all her life, but she's got the merriest heart of anybody I ever seen!"

Eliza held out her hand to Mrs. Holder. "I wish I could express my own gratitude to you for making the effort to tell us about her."

"I hope Mrs. Stiles won't be offended that I didn't tell her first."

"Do you find my daughter easily offended?"

"No, ma'am. But she *is* the mistress of Etowah Cliffs. I guess I didn't want to take a chance on her thinking I was buttin' in." A shy smile pulled at one corner of Elizabeth's mouth. "I'd just be so tickled to have Lorah Plemmons livin' close to me again, I feared I might sound too pushy to Mrs. Stiles. I think the world of your daughter, but I also know she likes to come by her own ideas herself."

"That's Mama all right," Henry said. "She's always sure she's right."

"And isn't she, most of the time?" Eliza asked.

"I dunno. I guess so. It would take a big load off of Mama if this lady did come to work for Natalie and Burke, wouldn't it, Grandma?"

"Yes, indeed," Eliza said. "Especially after we're back in Savannah."

"You don't have to go any time soon, do you?" Henry wanted to know.

"Oh, not this week or next, I guess. How long might it take for Mrs. Plemmons to get here—to settle her affairs at Ellijay?"

Elizabeth Holder laughed. "She ain't got many affairs, Mrs. Mackay. No property, very few clothes. The lady she used to work for died a month ago. She's got her boy, Sam, to help her get ready. Sam's got a mule and an old wagon to bring her in—her and the few belongings she might have. Miss Lorah and my mother, they're good friends. Lifelong friends. Grew up together. Mama does want Miss Lorah to have a good place to work."

"Is she an old lady?" Henry asked.

"I don't reckon you'd call her old exactly," Elizabeth said. "Mama's nearly fifty. Miss Lorah may be fifty. Got a lot of good working years left. Strong as a mule too. Mama always says she can do so much because she never lets life settle on top of her."

Eliza Mackay had been trying to smile often lately in what had seemed to her a subtle effort to lift all their spirits. Now she smiled because she felt like it. "Here, Mrs. Holder," she said, gesturing toward the flourishing garden. "Pick yourself anything you want. These new onions and turnip greens seem to be all I can think of in the way of gratitude. You've given me the first ray of hope I've had since we got here."

"Grandma?"

"What is it, Mary Cowper?"

"Does this mean everything's going to be happy again?"

In response, Eliza gave the girl another hug.

"Does it mean we'll all begin to laugh a lot again around here?" Bobby asked.

"Maybe not overnight, honey. But if Mrs. Plemmons can come to take charge of Natalie, in time all these long faces just might be gone."

Chapter 17

ON THE tenth day after Elizabeth Holder sent her letter to her mother in Ellijay, Mark rode with Burke toward Cassville hoping against hope that they would find a reply. There had been not one dissenting voice when Miss Eliza had told them of the possibility that Lorah Plemmons might come to take care of Natalie.

Actually, Mark thought now, riding abreast of Burke on Eliza Anne's good mare, they hadn't risked disapproval from Natalie, the one person who was likely to say no. Everyone, including Jonathan, agreed not to say a word about it to her. At first, Burke had been unsure of the wisdom of keeping it from Natalie, knowing better than anyone how insistent she had always been that the two of them live absolutely alone in their cabin. In spite of Elizabeth Holder's high opinion of Lorah Plemmons, Mark saw Burke's point. The whole idea of a strange woman coming to live and take over Natalie's housekeeping could easily infuriate her. But, as Eliza Anne argued, how could things be much worse than they were now? What other choice did they have but to believe Elizabeth Holder when she vowed that her mother's friend, Lorah Plemmons, was one of a kind—a mountain woman who'd never before been far from the isolated community of Ellijay—but who possessed a rare buoyancy of spirit so desperately needed by them all right now?

"Even if Natalie flares up at me for hiring the lady," Burke had said as they'd mounted their horses today, "at least she'll be flaring up at something! Mr. Browning, I can't face many more days of watching her wilt on the vine. Maybe I'm not the man I thought I was, but my strength is about gone. I'm— empty. As empty as a rain barrel in a long drought."

Mark knew Burke hadn't done a single day's work. The little church stood unfinished, exactly as he and Ben had left it the day before Ben shot himself. The stacks of newly made bricks grew and grew in Burke's yard, but not a tap of work had been done on the Stileses' foundation.

After several minutes on the Cassville road, Mark's mare had dropped a few steps behind Burke astride his horse, Major. A glance at the sagging, normally broad, strong back of the blond young man increased the weight in Mark's heart. Like Burke, he'd give all he owned if Natalie would flare up again over something—anything. He'd welcome even anger toward him in

Natalie's pale, haunting eyes, the eyes that for weeks now had been only dull and listless and full of pain.

In sight of the brick courthouse on the Cassville town square, Burke slowed his horse and walked it past the square and the newly laid brick sidewalks to the tiny post office across the street. Dismounting and hitching the mare alongside Burke, Mark asked, "Shall I go in and inquire about our mail?"

A fleeting, sheepish smile crossed Burke's drawn face. "Would you mind, sir? I—I'm not up to conversation today. The post office is usually full of nosy people. Cassville folks don't know you. I'm past the place where sympathy helps."

"I thought as much," Mark said, and strode into the tiny frame building, where a rail-thin woman and four men customers fell into dead silence the minute he entered.

"Any mail in care of Stiles for Browning, Mackay—or especially Mrs. David Holder?" he asked the bespectacled postmaster.

The small cluster of people remained silent, listening intently, he knew.

"Got quite a bundle," the postmaster said, his face lighting up in the process of thumbing through an already sorted stack of letters.

"Those are all in care of W. H. Stiles?" Mark asked nervously.

"Every single one of 'em. Four for you, Mr. Browning. You are Mark Browning, Esquire, from Savannah?"

"That's right. Could I just have the lot?" Mark asked.

"You'll get the lot—one at a time, sir. It's my job to make sure they're sorted right. Now, lemme see. Here's your four—all but one from your own countinghouse. The one's from Mr. William Thorne Williams!" He handed Mark the four letters.

"Thank you."

"*Mr. Williams's* the mayor of Savannah, ain't he?"

"That's right. The remaining letters, please, sir?"

In absolutely no hurry, glancing often at the others still standing in attentive silence, the postmaster said, "Only prominent gentlemen receive personal letters from the mayor of a city the size of Savannah, Georgia, I'd say." He pushed his glasses up to his forehead and swept a hand around the room. "We've all heard how prominent *you* are, Mr. Browning. Mighty proud to have you visitin' us up here in Cass."

"That's kind of you. The other letters, please? Is there a letter for Mrs. David Holder?"

Flicking his spectacles back into place, the man thumbed slowly through the remaining mail. "Yes siree! Here 'tis. Mrs. David Holder, care of W. H. Stiles, Cass County, Georgia." Handing Mark that one letter only, he added, "We aim to please, Mr. Browning."

"So I see," Mark said, hoping not to have sounded too unneighborly in his eagerness to get back to Burke. "Now, if I could have the others too?"

"Three more here, I believe. Ah-ha. I thought I remembered seeing this one from William Henry Stiles, Esquire, for his wife. I'd wager, Mr. Browning, that W. H. Stiles has got himself five solid votes to be our congressman in Washington City right here in this post office today! He's a mighty highfalutin gentleman, but he's got the pulse of our people around here. We're all Democrats and I, for one, heard him make his speech the night he hit Cassville a month or so ago. His first stop on this early campaign swing, I believe it was. Course, the man ain't nominated yet, but he will be and he'll be elected too, mark my word."

Everyone standing around the room agreed warmly.

"Say," the woman asked, "did we hear right, sir, that some Indian shot hisself just after Mr. Stiles left last month?"

Mark frowned. "Yes, I'm sorry to say. The young man was a great loss to everyone. He was my son-in-law's skilled helper."

"Oh, we know all about your son-in-law, Mr. Browning," the postmaster said. "Burke Latimer's considered the finest builder in these parts. Our smartest lawyer, Fred Bentley, thinks the sun rises and sets in him. And, sir? We all extend our sympathies for the death of Latimer's infant son too. Of course, we know his pretty red-haired wife is your daughter."

"Thank you. The other two letters now, please?"

"Yes, sir. One for a Mr. Jonathan Browning—and will ya just look! It's from Yale College way up in New Haven, Connecticut! What do you know about that!"

"Jonathan Browning's my son," Mark said. "That will be his acceptance to school for this fall. I asked to have it forwarded from my office in Savannah."

"I'd say it costs a pretty penny to send a boy to Yale College," the rail-thin woman gasped, stepping toward Mark. "My name's Phoebe Turner, sir. I'm proud to make your acquaintance."

Mark bowed politely, then held out his hand for the last letter in the stack. It was for Miss Eliza from her daughter Sarah.

"We're just real proud to have you among us," an elderly gentleman wearing a string tie announced as he too stepped toward Mark, his hand out.

Mark shook the bony hand, bowed to them all and fled out the front door into the early June sunshine.

"Here it is, Burke," Mark said, holding up the letter from Elizabeth Holder's mother in Ellijay. "But I guess we'll have to wait a little longer. It *is* addressed to Mrs. Holder."

He saw Burke's shoulders sag. "Of course."

"Will it take us long to pick up those supplies Eliza Anne ordered?" Mark asked. "If we can make short work of our shopping, we'll know Mrs. Plemmons's answer in less than two hours—providing we ride hard all the way back. I did have sense enough to make sure before we left that Mrs. Holder would be at the Stiles house waiting—in case the letter came."

Burke sighed heavily. "Shouldn't take long, but it was a lot better in the old days when the post office was right in Hawke's Store."

"Sorry it took me so long," Mark said as he remounted. "There was a whole handful of people in there, each one bursting with curiosity about all of us. A lot has happened at Etowah Cliffs, I guess, to cause talk here in Cassville."

"Let's ride straight home, sir. I don't think we should wait to do Miss Lib's shopping. The only way Natalie would let me leave her was to promise I'd be back before noon. I'll come back to town first thing tomorrow. I've got to know what's in Mrs. Holder's letter." He clicked his tongue at Major. Over his shoulder, Burke called, "Do you suppose I'm counting too much on Elizabeth Holder's idea of bringing that woman here to help out?"

Starting the brown mare too, Mark called back that they would all just have to wait to find out. To himself, trotting after Burke past the courthouse square, he tried to control his own high hopes that somehow Lorah Plemmons just *might* do what no one, including Eliza Mackay, had been able to do —bring Natalie out of her sickness and grief and sense of failure.

Of course, until they heard what was in the letter, there was no way even to know that Miss Lorah would come. And no one on earth knew how Natalie might react to her if she did. For that matter, no one knew how she might react to the fact that they'd all just sent for Miss Lorah without a word to her.

Chapter 18

As EAGER as Burke was to know the contents of the letter, he hurried first to Natalie, while Mr. Browning rode on with the mail to the Stiles place, where Elizabeth Holder would be waiting.

Evidently Mary had heard their horses, because by the time Burke hitched Major at the front steps, she was on the cabin porch, a finger to her lips.

"What's wrong?" he asked. "Is she—worse?"

"No, Mister Burke. Natalie sleep now. To me that's good."

"Good, why? She does almost nothing but sleep or stare up at the ceiling."

"This time, today, she talk some to me."

"What do you mean, she talked some? Did she really talk? Did she actually say something that—sounded like Natalie?"

Mary nodded, smiling a little, in spite of the tears that abruptly filled her eyes. "Today, Mister Burke, for the first time, she told me how sorry she is that—Ben is dead."

"Well, what did she say?"

"She still blame herself until I put my fingers over her mouth and swore I'd never, never come back to her cabin again if she say that once more! And blame herself."

He frowned. "You actually told her that? Mary, unless that woman from Ellijay comes here to live, there'll be no one but you to take care of Natalie after her family and Miss Eliza leave for Savannah. You know I've got to get back to work sometime." His frown deepened and he looked away. "Although, I'll be honest with you, I—I can't face ever picking up another hammer—without Ben."

"Ben feel sorry enough that—he leave you, Mister Burke. He would not be glad to hear you say that."

He looked at her briefly, then turned his eyes away again. "Are you going to tell me more about your talk with Natalie?"

"I tell you. She—she take my hand—"

"Natalie took *your* hand?"

Mary nodded. "Yes. I know someone else always first to take her hand, to try to make her to talk, to smile. But that is wrong even if all of you mean to be right with her. Miss Natalie is not any longer a child. She need to talk of what is inside her, but only *she* knows the right time to do it. I—not say this too good—" Tears were flowing now. "It too deep and heavy for me to talk good English the way Ben still wants me to talk . . ."

"I know, Little One," he said, looking down at her. "You do believe that I understand, don't you? I've been rotten to you since Natalie—lost our son, since she isn't getting well the way she should be. Mary—" His eyes pleaded with her. "Mary, I haven't meant to be neglecting you. If anyone in the whole wide world knows how broken your heart is, I know it. You and I loved Ben more than anyone else anywhere. I—I'm just not the man I thought I was. I can't seem to help Natalie *or* you—certainly not myself. Can you forgive me for not being with you through your own heartache over Ben —the way I should have been?"

For an instant, he felt her fingers touch his forearm. "Do not say such things of yourself! A few minutes ago, you called me 'Little One' again. That be enough, Mister Burke. Remember?" She tried to smile. "Remember the happy days when we all live together in the old cabin Natalie burn down near Cassville? Remember you called me 'Little One'?"

Just in case Natalie had been right in her notion that Mary was in love with him, Burke had tried hard never to give Mary any false reason to hope. Deliberately, he had stopped calling her "Little One."

"It be good that you once more call me that," she went on, her voice stronger now. "But there is a new good now."

He smiled at her. "A new good?"

"I already explain I no talk right when my—heart is full! Do not tease! But, yes. However you say it, there is new good. Miss Natalie's brother, *he is good.* Mister Jonathan so good to me. I do not feel any pain now when you only think of Natalie."

Burke put a hand on each of her shoulders and made her look straight at him. "Am I understanding you correctly? You—you haven't noticed my neglect because—you're seeing a lot of Jonathan Browning?"

Blushing so hard the scar turned white on her cheek, she could only nod fast and smile.

Burke's first impulse was one of joy for her and then dismay. Mary must not allow herself to care too deeply for Natalie's brother! A half-breed Cherokee girl had no right to care for the only son of Savannah's wealthiest gentleman . . .

"Mister Burke?"

"Hm?"

"Do not frown. Do not worry. There is truly only today. Do not worry. Jonathan still here today. After he is gone away, there will still be God with me. Do not worry. I not think of—tomorrow. Only today. And Jonathan does not think to be Cherokee is bad." She took a small step toward him and smiled. "I maybe have to teach him about that. What else for right now, today, is Natalie. She sleep in better way. Natural. Her fists not clenched. Also she talk to *me.*"

"Tell me what she said to you when she took your hand."

"She say she knows of my heavy heart. That she is sorry I grieve. That she is sorry you grieve for Ben too. That she worry much for you to try to build without him. That—that—" She broke off.

"That what, Mary? What else?"

"She—also say never again will she want to—die too. Until today, like Ben, she want to *die.*"

He could only stare at her. No words came.

"Mister Burke, I understand that you cannot believe Miss Natalie—so loved by you—would want to die. But ever since she fail you with the baby son, she lay there on her bed, day after day, wanting to die too."

Abruptly, he turned away, walked to the end of the cabin porch and looked unseeing out into the woods toward the little grove where they had buried his son. Natalie *die?* Natalie—*wanting* to—die?

"Mister Burke, we must not wake Natalie by loud talk. Her sleep is good. Not bad sleep. She had to tell—somebody. Forever, I am happy that she—pick me. She still very sick—with fever. I can come to stand beside you so she not hear our talk and wake up?"

He motioned for her to join him at the far end of the porch.

"There is more to tell you, Mister Burke . . ."

"What?" he asked in a hoarse whisper.

"Jonathan, he say they must go soon home to Savannah. He ask me to go too—to visit his house and see city doctor for my—bad eye. I say to him: No. I cannot leave Miss Natalie and you." She clasped her hands with joy. "But he want me to go!"

"Mary! Oh, Mary—I'd be scared half out of my wits for you to show your —pretty face in Savannah. The people there are—well, they aren't like us!"

"Miss Natalie's family, I love them."

"Yes, but—you and Ben were—my family. I'm the Brownings' son-in-law. They just about had to—to—"

"To—be nice to Cherokee brother and sister because of you, Mister Burke?"

"Well, something like that, I guess."

"Not true!"

"What?"

"They be kind, good people—Miss Caroline, Mister Mark and Jonathan! But why does Jonathan just smile at me and look secret when I say I cannot go home with him because I must care for Natalie? He knows the Ellijay woman is coming?"

"Mary"—he spoke carefully—"you're sure Natalie's really sleeping? Should we slip in and find out? If she is, I can hurry to the Stiles place and get a missing piece of information. Then I can talk to you more about going to Savannah."

He caught her half-smiling, suspicious look. "You know why Jonathan act secret with me? You know, Mister Burke?"

"I have an idea. Come on, let's go look in on Natalie."

They tiptoed through the main room and, satisfied that indeed she was sleeping soundly, he felt enormous relief. The tiny frown between Natalie's eyes, for the first time since she'd lost the baby, was no longer there.

On the porch again, Burke promised Mary to tell her all he might find out after a quick trip to the Etowah Cliffs house, and so as not to rouse Natalie by riding Major, he struck out running to learn the news of Lorah Plemmons.

Before he reached the simple, sturdy two-storied wing of Etowah Cliffs which he and Ben had built so proudly not quite a year ago, he saw Jonathan break away from the family group on the narrow front porch and race toward him, waving a letter.

"She's coming," Jonathan called. "Miss Lorah Plemmons is leaving Ellijay tomorrow with her boy, Sam, in a mule-drawn wagon! She's coming, Burke. The road's pretty crooked and bad, I guess, but the lady will be here in two or three days to live and take care of Natalie!" Panting, he handed Burke the letter. "Here, read for yourself. Mrs. Holder's mother doesn't spell too well, but it's all right there!"

Without a word, Burke grabbed the single sheet and began to read:

> 6 June 1842
> Ellijay, Georgia
>
> Dear Lizbeth,
> I thot to right rite back to tell you that Lorah Plemmons took but a hour or two to say she'd come. Sam, the boy she took in to raise some years back, is near 22 now and as slow as ever in his head, but a fair carpinter. Sam will drive her mule and bring her in there ol' broke down wagon. You know Lorah's twinkle. Well, she pert near twinkled herself to peeces when I red her what you rote to me. She don't wear her religion on her dress sleeve, as you know, but she said for me to keep on thankun the good Lord in her behaf. Her and Sam has slep on my sister's parlor floor for more'n 3 weeks. They need a home bad. Neether one is putikular where. Lorah is just so glad to be earnin' her keep agane. So, look for them in 3 or 4 days from today. Sooner if Sam can git the wagon grease and rolling. The mule is as ready as he'll ever be. So is Lorah. Count from date on this letter.
>
> Yr loving mother
> Edna Holder
>
> P.S. The sick, funny-turned young woman she's to keer for don't bother Lorah none at all.

Burke rechecked the date on which the letter was written. June 6. "Today is June 9," he said, more to himself than to Jonathan.

"Miss Lib says Ellijay's between fifty-five and sixty miles," Jonathan said.

"Miss Eliza Mackay says mules are slow. They figure Miss Lorah and Sam could get here sometime late today or by noon tomorrow, with luck."

Burke whistled softly. "I'd say they'll need some luck traveling over those hills behind a mule." With a broad smile—the first smile he'd actually *felt* in a long, long time—he added, "Run back to the Stiles place, will you? And tell them how happy I am. Take my regrets for not coming in. I promised Mary I'd get right back."

"Burke, wait!" The boy was smiling too.

Fully suspecting the reason Jonathan was so happy, he asked, "Something else to tell me, son?"

"Yes, sir! Now that Miss Lorah's coming for sure, we'll be heading back to Savannah in a couple of weeks maybe and I've asked Mary to come along. We have quite good doctors there—for her eye, you know."

"Yes, I know. I also know you'd already asked Mary to go back to Savannah, even before we knew Miss Lorah was on her way."

Jonathan blinked and then smiled. "Did Mary tell you herself?"

"That's right."

"Well, what did you say to her?"

"Do you really want to know?"

"Yes, sir."

"I said I'd be scared half out of my wits to have her show her pretty face in Savannah."

The smile faded from Jonathan's face. "Because she's half Cherokee?"

Burke nodded. "Because she's half Cherokee and also because Savannah people—are Savannah people. Mary's my friend. She's closer than if she'd been my real sister. With Ben gone, I'm responsible for her now. You may be too young to understand what I mean, but I do mean it."

Jonathan bit his lower lip, stood looking at the ground. Finally, he gave Burke his direct, honest attention. "I understand every word you've said, Burke. I also know why you felt you had to say it all to me. I am a lot younger than you, but I love Mary McDonald—Merry Willow—as much as you love my sister."

"How do you know how much I love Natalie?"

"You've proven it to me, to my parents. To all of us. Natalie, in spite of her almost terrible beauty, is not easy to love right now. In fact, because she thinks she failed you by not bearing your son alive, she's not even like Natalie. But I know her. I've known her all my life. My sister will come back to her old self someday."

"You seem very sure of that."

"I am and the reason is because I do know her. I've watched you with her since we've been up here too. What I'm trying to say, sir, is that I know you better than you know me."

"We've seen very little of each other, Jonathan."

"And that's the only reason you're scared to have me take Mary back home with me. If you knew me better, you wouldn't be scared at all."

"You—really believe that, don't you?"

"Yes, sir. And don't think I'm offended that you haven't had time to spend with me. Far from it. My sister means the world to me and she needed you with her—every minute." The half-smile returned. "You see, I know Natalie doesn't like having you out of her sight even long enough to go to work."

"You're right about that."

"And that doesn't make you feel smothered?"

Burke laughed a little. "With Natalie? She's far too elusive ever to make a man feel—smothered. In fact, as a rule, I have to hop to keep up with her. Even in the old days, when she was in my arms, only now and then did I really feel as though—I'd captured her."

"I expect that's true. I'm not like Natalie, though. I'm more like Mary," the boy said simply.

Burke returned Jonathan's straightforward gaze, then said, "I always know where I stand with Mary."

"You can always know that with me too, sir. I tease Natalie about playing games, but I don't play them myself." The smile was full now. "Mary's promised to teach me how to play Cherokee stickball, but you know the kind of games I'm talking about."

"Jonathan, to tell you the truth, I never thought Natalie was playing games with me. Maybe right at first, when we met each other on shipboard—but never after the explosion. Never since we've both known how deeply we love each other."

He could see Jonathan pondering that. "I doubt that she ever tried one of her games with you. You see, I never—not in my almost seventeen years— ever, ever saw Natalie feel about anyone the way she feels about you. Are you a lot like Mary too, Burke? Maybe a lot like me?"

Burke laughed softly. "After this little talk, son, I can only say I hope I'm a lot like you."

"You can trust me with Mary in Savannah. I'll look after her." The sturdy shoulders squared. "Since the minute I saw her, the night Ben shot himself, the one thing I've wanted is to protect her."

"Do you know what I mean about—Savannah people, Jonathan? Do you know why it scares me to let her go down there with all those social-minded, critical, high-toned citizens of the Georgia coast?"

"Oh, yes, sir. I certainly do know. And if Mary really looked Indian, I might worry some too. I would still want to take her, though, because I love her."

"What about the way she talks? Ben worked every day with their Scottish father, but Mary stayed at home with their Cherokee mother. The little thing tries so hard to speak good English, but— What about her speech, Jonathan?"

"I've thought about that too. I love the way Mary says things. It's—awfully romantic to me. But I can help her. And I will. I'll spend lots of time with her. She isn't a bit touchy about being taught."

"Mary isn't touchy about anything."

"I guess I never thought much about this, but there *is* a lot of difference between being touchy and being sensitive, isn't there? Mary's awfully sensitive. She seems even to know what I'm thinking most of the time!"

"She's always seemed almost able to read my thoughts."

"Burke . . ."

"Hm?"

"Natalie thinks Mary's in love with you. Did you know that?"

Burke nodded.

"Well, you can stop worrying about it now. Mary loves me. And now that Miss Lorah is coming to hire on as Natalie's housekeeper, you can also stop worrying about Mary leaving."

"It's those Savannah people who bother me. They'll never, never accept Mary! Not even as a house guest of the all-powerful Brownings."

"Savannahians aren't all like that, Burke. Look at Miss Eliza Mackay and Miss Lib and Uncle W.H. Anyway, is anything ever—really just right? Isn't there always something to, well, to kind of work around?"

After he left Jonathan, Burke hurried back to Natalie, his own heart somehow lifted by the brief talk. He loved Jonathan's sister more than anyone in the world, but no brother and sister could be more unlike. Natalie was everything else to him, but even Burke couldn't call her wise. As he headed up his own front path, he realized he'd give almost anything if Mary *could* have a young man like Jonathan to protect her always. If any two people ever deserved each other, it seemed to be Jonathan and Mary. Of course, he knew Mary better, far better, but Jonathan Browning had a kind of openness about him—a transparency—that gave a person a clear, revealing look right off. Even on such short acquaintance, he felt he could trust Jonathan, would almost swear that the boy *could* be trusted.

Don't I trust Natalie? Yes. Oh, yes. I have trouble at times figuring her out, but I've always been able to trust her. It would just make things a lot easier, right now especially, if she'd really say exactly what she's thinking—to me. As Jonathan just did.

Still, he thought, tossing his hat onto a peg on the wall of the main cabin room, the boy's too young to have lived through what Natalie has faced. Jonathan had never been near death as had Burke and Natalie when the *Pulaski* exploded, killing far more passengers and crew than were saved. Jonathan had never known grief, had never, so far as Burke knew, been ill or felt he'd failed anyone. He'd never forget that only a few weeks ago, Natalie —ill, filled with grief and loss—had stood alone at the tiny open grave. Burke hadn't been there, but he could picture the same courage and determination to see it through that he'd watched on that lovely face through five miserable, terrifying days on the open sea. He had watched her live through that ordeal, pulling strength from somewhere deep inside herself. His own heart still ached that he had been off hunting Ben and not beside her at the grave of their dead son, but he didn't have to imagine how she looked, didn't have to wonder how she'd managed. He knew. He would always trust that strength in Natalie, no matter how unpredictably she behaved.

"She's not being unpredictable right now," Miss Eliza Mackay had told him yesterday when they'd met on the road between his cabin and the Stiles place. "Make no mistake about it, Burke, Natalie does feel as though she failed you. Don't try to talk her out of it. Trust her to find her own way. Trust God to send us a way to help her right herself in all this. It must be hard for a man to understand exactly how a woman feels when she gives birth to a—dead child. It may be impossible for you ever to understand. With all her heart, Natalie longed to give you a healthy son. Still, the baby died in *her* body. I guess as long as we're on this earth, we'll all go on judging ourselves by what our bodies can or cannot do. I can't walk as fast or as far as I once could. At times, I *blame* myself that I can't. I didn't will the years of my life to stack up as they've done. I know better. Natalie knows better too, but she's still carrying a fever and she isn't yet able to find her way back. She will, though. She will."

No wonder Mark Browning leaned on Miss Eliza Mackay as he did, Burke thought, easing open the door to the bedroom. I could come to depend on the lady too, if I had half a chance. She gave me my first flimsy hope.

As always, he found Mary right beside Natalie, sponging her face and forehead with a damp cloth. Both of them looked up and smiled.

"Afternoon, ladies," he said as Mary got up quickly so that he could take Natalie into his arms. As usual, her arms circled his neck. "How's my girl? Here, let me have a good look at you."

"We talk together some more," Mary said happily, from the doorway, then left the room.

"Gossiping?" Burke teased. "Have you and Mary been—"

"No. Mary's been talking to me mostly," Natalie answered, still clinging to him. "And, Burke, I'm pretty sure she's shifted her affections from you to my brother. *She's been talking about Jonathan* all the while she brushed my hair."

Burke kissed the shining hair. "So that's what hurt my eyes the minute I walked into this room! My beautiful one's bright, bright hair. Oh, Natalie—even sick with a fever and still so weak, you're stopping my heart again."

"Do I—look too sick and—gloomy for you to kiss me?"

"Dear Lord, never," he breathed, and kissed her hot, dry mouth gently, but over and over. "You know something?" he asked finally.

"What?"

"That's the first time you've asked me to kiss you in over a month!" Clasping her close to him, he whispered, "Is it all right, ma'am, if I thank you for asking me to kiss you? You're such a kissy-mouth girl, I—I feel hopeful again now that you really *asked* me. Let me feel hopeful, Natalie. Please let me! And you kissed me back too."

With surprising strength, she pushed him away. "I've never stopped kissing you back! Never!"

"I know, darling. I know that."

"Maybe my lips felt all parched and rough, but—Burke, I'm always kissing you. Every minute of my life and—" Abruptly, she was crying, clinging to him, trying to press herself closer. "If—if only I—could be—strong enough to love you back, maybe—maybe we could make the—miracle again."

"Natalie, Natalie, we will, but give yourself time! We're going to find a way to get you well again, darling. You'll see."

"No, I won't see! That stupid doctor from Cassville just stands by my bed and shakes his empty head. Maybe I'll never be better. Maybe I'll never be strong enough to—love you back, Burke and—I couldn't bear that! Even if we never have a child, I have to be strong enough to let you love me, to love you back!" She was sobbing, out of control now. "Don't you—know that I don't—want to live if we can't—love?"

"Natalie, dearest, we do love—we never stop loving."

She hit the bed with her fist. "I'm not talking about the kind of—old-age devotion my parents have for each other. I'm talking about passion! Even on our raft, burned to a crisp by the sun, we—kissed with—all of us, Burke!"

"I know and we will again. I promise. Natalie, did you hear me? I—promise you we will!"

She turned her head away. "I don't know how even you can promise that."

He turned her face back to him and held her close against his shoulder. The sobbing had stopped almost as suddenly as it had begun. Dear God, he thought, am I putting too much stock in what a stranger named Lorah Plemmons can do for her? We're all going on Elizabeth Holder's word that somehow this woman can weave a kind of cheerful magic that will bring Natalie back to herself again. Miss Lorah could very well be just an ignorant old lady whose every clumsy effort will rub Natalie the wrong way. If that's true, we'd all be worse off than now.

"Burke?"

"What is it, darling?" he asked, still holding her.

"I want to ask you something."

Trying to give her a bright smile, he released her and looked into her eyes. "Shoot. What is it you want to know?"

"I'm—I'm kind of tired from talking so much, so I won't waste my breath trying to say how much I love them, but is there some way you can get my mother and father and Jonathan to leave?"

She had startled him so, he could only stare back at her. "Why, darling, I don't—know about that. I think they'll be going home in a week or two."

She sighed and turned her face away again.

"I'm sorry, Natalie, but—I've grown too fond of your parents—and certainly of Jonathan, too—"

"I might have known. They're dear and sweet, all of them. Everyone always loves my brother especially."

"He's a wise young man. Wise beyond his years."

"Oh, I've heard that all my life! Mary's worn off both my ears spewing about how wonderful Jonathan is. Well, he is a dear brother. Never causes anyone an ounce of trouble—unlike me. And I'm rather pleased that Mary's fallen in love with him," she went on, "although she didn't make me a bit jealous loving you. That just annoyed me. Do you think Jonathan is in love with Mary? Do you think my goody-goody little brother is that gullible, that kindhearted?"

"Since when is it kindhearted to fall in love?" He grinned at her. "Is it your kind heart that makes you love me so much?"

"That's ridiculous and you know it. We're different from any other people on earth."

He smoothed back her hair. "You exaggerate, but I like for you to try to convince me."

"It would be like Jonathan to fall in love with a half-breed girl just to make her feel good."

Burke took his time in answering. "If I didn't know what your heart is really like, I'd dislike you a little for saying a thing like that about either your brother or Mary."

She gave him a long look. "I'm going to ignore that, because if anybody knows what's in my heart, you do. Will you promise me you'll at least think about finding a way to get my family to go home?"

"You've talked enough, I think. More, in fact, than for a long time and—almost like yourself too. Do you realize that?"

"Don't dodge my question, Burke. Having my family here makes me work too hard. I'm always having to try to act cheerful, pretend I feel better to keep them from looking so worried. Especially Papa. He's always worn me out with kindness, dear as he is." She grabbed his hand. "Burke, what happened to us—to our son—is only between us. Why can't Miss Lib and Mama and Papa and Miss Eliza just *leave us alone?*"

Sensing how really exhausted she was, Burke urged her to try to sleep while he fed, watered and rubbed Major down after the ride from Cassville. After he kissed her again, she agreed, and on his way through the cabin, he motioned for Mary to follow him outside to where Major was hitched.

"Not far," she warned, when they reached the front porch. "I stay where Natalie can call to me."

"And I thank you for that," he said, "but I do need to tell you what is going to happen around here, probably tomorrow. Could be even later today, since it doesn't get dark so early now."

Mary listened without a word while, briskly rubbing down the horse, Burke told her about the impending arrival of Lorah Plemmons and her young man, Sam, who needed a home as much as they all needed help from them both.

When he'd finished, for the first time he noticed the troubled look on Mary's face. "What is it, Mary? Is something bothering you?"

"I not take good care of Natalie, Mister Burke?"

"The best! I hope you don't, but what if you do go back to Savannah with the Brownings? Anyway, as long as Natalie can't work at all, there's too much for you to do alone. I can afford to hire a housekeeper now. You have your own house to look after. Anyway, you're far more to us all than a housekeeper. Now, does that make you feel better?"

She nodded, then smiled up at him. "Jonathan, he know this woman is coming?"

"He does. To his mind, it frees you to go to Savannah. That's why he looked secretive and—"

"Yes," she interrupted, her smile gone. "But where this Miss Lorah Plemmons live here? I sleep on pallet on your floor when you and Ben were gone all week to build the church. Only one bed in your cabin. Miss Lorah live with me and sleep in Ben's bed? Where her boy, Sam, sleep?"

He dropped the damp croker sack with which he'd been rubbing Major and gave Mary a long look. "You know, Little One, I hadn't given any of that a thought. I suppose Miss Lib has, though. There's surely no room in her four-roomed house. I can add an extra bedroom onto the new cottage I'm building for Natalie and me, but without Ben, I don't know when I'll get to our place. Could Miss Lorah and Sam stay in your cabin for now? He can sleep on the floor. She'll be with Natalie all day, of course."

"I can visit Natalie, though?"

"Yes, yes, yes. I want you to. She'll want you to."

"She not much want her parents to visit so long," Mary ventured.

"She told you too, eh? First things first, though. How about Miss Lorah staying with you for now?"

Mary gave her small curtsy. "I be most cordial for her to sleep in my bed, Mister Burke. Sam in Ben's bed." A shy smile barely showed her even white teeth. "Jonathan teach me that new word—cordial. I say it right?"

He laughed softly. "Well, almost. Knowing you, you will be most cordial to Miss Lorah. And, Mary—maybe it will help just a little bit to have someone else, the boy, Sam, sleeping in that other, empty bed at night."

"Maybe. Thank you for our talk. You come right back after you take Major to the stable? I must visit—Ben."

"Do you go every day to Ben's grave?"

She nodded. "Today, I pick mountain laurel. I see some yesterday behind Miss Lib's house. I take a bunch to Ben."

"I see."

"Miss Lorah's boy, Sam, is her son?"

"I don't think so. He's an orphan she took in years ago, Mrs. Holder says. He's supposed to be a carpenter. God knows, I need him."

"I hope he is good carpenter. He not Ben."

"No. No one will ever be Ben—again. Not for you. Not for me."

Chapter 19

As SOON as she'd spent time with her house guests on the front porch, discussing the arrival of Lorah Plemmons, Eliza Anne excused herself for a few minutes and went to her room in order to scan her husband's personal note to her—always on a separate page.

"The trip is being more than successful, beloved Lib, but oh, I ache all over to be with you again," he wrote. "I'm weary to the bone but am, in spite of primitive accommodations, planning to spend a week here at Brown's Crossing before riding on to Milledgeville for the convention. There, I will need my head clear and every ounce of energy I can muster. Could I but hold you in my arms again, my strength would return without so much as one night's sleep. Still, before this endless month is over, I will again be beside you in our very own bed and whether or not I am nominated (my hopes rise daily, however) I will once again be my own energetic, charming self. Until then, I love you, Lib, I love you."

There were two more pages, all written so that she would feel free to read them aloud to the children and their visitors. These she folded and took with her back downstairs where Mark and Caroline, her children and mother waited. It was no secret to anyone, even the children, that when a letter came from W.H., she needed at least a few minutes alone.

"We're out here waiting, Mama," Robert called from the yard.

"And we're not waiting very patiently either," Mary Cowper said as Eliza Anne appeared again on the narrow porch.

"Did Papa get the letters you've been sending him about how well behaved we've all been?" Henry wanted to know.

"No," she answered, exchanging a look with the adults. "He got none saying that, Henry, because I always tell your father the absolute truth about all three of you."

"Aw, you're making that up," Robert teased.

"No, she isn't," Mary C. said. "Mama tells Papa when you two fight or argue, especially when Henry has a temper tantrum, because she doesn't want Papa to be surprised when he finally gets home."

"I suppose *you've* been Little Miss Perfect," Henry scowled. "I haven't seen you doing much to help around—"

"That's enough, children," their grandmother interrupted. "We aren't waiting very patiently, Eliza Anne, to hear all about how W.H.'s faring on his hard trip. Mark was just telling us, though, that in his letter from Mayor Williams back home, he learned that people in Savannah are talking about how effective your husband is up here when he makes a speech."

"Savannahians expect W.H. to be nominated and elected," Mark said.

"And," Caroline added, "that news came straight to Mayor Williams from W.H.'s friend and law partner, Levi De Lyon. Isn't he one of the most powerful members of the nominating committee?"

"He most certainly is," Eliza Anne said proudly. "And Levi thinks almost as highly of my husband as my husband deserves." She unfolded the remaining two pages of her letter, sat down on the front step beside Caroline and Mark and began to read aloud:

> "Brown's Crossing
> 3 June 1842
>
> My dear Lib and Children,
> For a few days I am here in what are laughably called 'adequate accommodations' resting from the long rides and the pressures of the large crowds I have drawn almost everywhere I've spoken. I could rest much faster, were I there with all of you atop our beloved Etowah Cliffs, but I am en route in a week to Milledgeville and so must manage with present circumstances. I pray you to remind your dear mother and the Brownings that I am truly sorry my important journey precluded my being there during their visit. I must also thank them since my own peace of mind has been vastly increased by the knowledge that they are with my sweet wife and children. I beg you also to send my warmest regards to Burke and Natalie and my deepest sympathy in their sorrow and loss. You and I, Lib, have been so blessed that all three of our children are with us and that we have escaped such devastation as the Latimers must now be experiencing. I sincerely hope that by now Burke and Natalie have sufficiently recovered, so that he and Ben have gone back to work on the Presbyterian church."

"Say, that's right!" Henry interrupted. "Papa doesn't even know—what Ben did, does he?"

"No, son, he doesn't know," Eliza Mackay said sadly. "Your father rode off to Cassville earlier the same day poor Ben died."

"Your papa will learn about everything that's happened," Eliza Anne said, "once he reaches Milledgeville. His stops en route were not definite enough for me to send mail anywhere else. In fact, he should have several letters at the capital when he gets there."

"I certainly hope he doesn't let the trouble back here worry him too much," Mark said. "He's got enough on his mind. He'll have to manage to see and talk with every key man at that convention before the list of candidates is whittled down to the actual nominations. I believe they select eight from a list of twenty-five or more."

"You do feel W.H. stands an excellent chance, don't you, Mark?" Caroline said.

"Indeed I do. Not only because he's so close to De Lyon either. Because W.H. is the best man for the Democrats to nominate."

"Even though you're not exactly a Democrat, Mark?" Eliza Anne's mother asked.

"That's right, Miss Eliza."

"Our papa's pretty smart, I guess," Robert said. "He's also the handsomest and makes by far the best speeches."

Eliza Anne was hunting her place in the letter to continue reading when they all heard the rattle and rumble of a wagon moving slowly along the road that skirted the cliffs.

"Listen," Mary Cowper whispered. "I hear a wagon—coming this way! It's not Mr. Holder. He's riding the fields with our hands. I saw him an hour ago —on his way to the new cotton field."

"I saw him too," Henry said. "It can't be Mr. Holder. Who do you think it is, Mama?"

On her feet, still holding the letter, Eliza Anne said, "I can't imagine— unless—Mark, do you suppose it could be Elizabeth Holder's woman from Ellijay? Isn't that nearly sixty miles?"

"I thought so," Mark said, joining Eliza Anne as she walked slowly toward the road to look. "That's a long, bumpy trip with only a mule and wagon."

All three children went too, the boys running ahead in order to get the first sighting of whoever might be jouncing along the road toward their house.

"I didn't see how Mrs. Plemmons could possibly make it before tomorrow," Eliza Mackay said to Caroline, who stayed back on the porch with her. "The woman's in a big hurry to get here, I'd say."

"She must be," Caroline answered, frowning. "I think I almost dread to find out what she's really like. If she's even half as fine as Mrs. Holder claims, I'll still worry leaving Natalie in her sole care."

"Eliza Anne will keep the path slick between here and Natalie's cabin, Caroline. You know that. And up to now, Mary hasn't left Natalie alone for a single minute unless one of us has been there right with her."

"Miss Eliza, I might as well tell you. Jonathan is worrying Mark and me half sick wanting to take Mary McDonald back to Savannah with us!"

Eliza Mackay stared at her. "Jonathan wants to take Mary home with you?"

"Yes! Never in my wildest dreams did I ever expect Jonathan to—set his heart on such a shocking thing. He seems convinced that one of our Savannah doctors could do something to help the damaged sight in her eye."

"Why, I can't imagine what any doctor could do, can you? When part of a person's sight is gone, it's gone."

"Of course it is. And for us to bring a half-breed Cherokee into our home as a house guest is— Oh, Mark and I don't feel that way about little Mary at all, but—"

"Savannah's full of wagging tongues."

"*Sharp* wagging tongues. I don't want that girl hurt any more than she's already been hurt. It seems to me in every way that—she's so much better off up here. Jonathan, in my opinion, is taking real advantage of us, but how on earth can we refuse at least to offer her medical help?"

Chapter 20

"IT'S Lorah Plemmons, all right," Eliza Anne gasped as she, Mark and the children stood watching the old mule plod toward them pulling a wagon with wheels so loose and crooked they made half-circles as they somehow kept rolling in and out of the ruts in the hard-packed road. On the backless wagon seat, bolt upright, sat a bonneted woman in a print dress. Beside her, a stringy young man in a straw hat was driving the mule.

When the boys started to run toward the newcomers, Eliza Anne called them back sharply. Henry just might make some tactless remark about the back wheels of her old wagon and Eliza Anne had no intention of getting off on the wrong foot with the woman on whom they had all gambled their hopes. Perhaps foolishly, she thought, but Natalie's need for help right now is too desperate not to take chances.

"Whoo-hoo! We're a-comin'," the woman called cheerily.

Eliza Anne and Mark exchanged looks—puzzled, curious. She knew mountain people were informal, to say the least, but Lorah Plemmons had whooped a greeting even before the old mule had made it abreast of where they stood and in a voice that indicated they'd all known one another for years.

"Mama! Look, Mama, that lady's got a grown chicken on her lap," Mary Cowper cried. "I never saw anyone hold a chicken on her lap before, did you?"

"I sure never did," Robert piped. "Mr. Holder said he once had a pet pig, but—a *chicken?*"

"What dumbfounds me," Mark said, "is why that one back wagon wheel keeps on rolling. The right one—look!"

A startled whoop came from the wagon as the right rear corner of the wagon bed hit the ground, sending boxes and flour-sack bundles sliding onto the road down which the lost wheel went rolling. Lorah Plemmons was no longer in sight, and Sam, hat knocked off, was just sitting there aslant, holding on to the seat, long hair gently blowing in the breeze. Stopped in his tracks, the ancient mule calmly flicked his tail and waited. For a hilarious instant, a kind of happy mood seemed to envelop them all.

No one did anything. No one said anything until from somewhere toward the rear of the half-tipped-over wagon bed, Eliza Anne saw both Lorah Plemmons's feet go straight up in the air, her long, full-flowered skirt flounced back, covering her face and head.

"Dear Lord," Mark whispered, "she could be hurt!"

As he hurried past Eliza Anne and around to the back of the tilted wagon, he called out, "Mrs. Plemmons—are you hurt? Don't try to move, ma'am. You may be badly injured!"

"I hear her chicken squawking, Mama!" Henry yelled. "Look, it just flew out from under her skirts!"

"You'd better come, Eliza Anne," Mark called, leaning helplessly over the skirt-covered bundle that was Miss Lorah, still wedged in the rear corner of the wagon bed, both feet kicking.

Almost tripping over the chicken, Eliza Anne ran to the wagon. Quickly, she lifted the flowered skirt to uncover Miss Lorah's face. Far from weeping in shock or pain, Lorah Plemmons was convulsed with laughter—at herself.

"Easter? *Easter*," the woman yelled.

"Mama," Mary C. whispered, "she's calling somebody named Easter!"

Everyone knew the young man's name wasn't Easter. Plainly having no idea what else to do, he was still glued to the steeply sloping driver's seat, his thin, scrawny face turned away in what appeared to be humiliation or, Eliza Anne thought, stupidity.

Then, in a thin, shrill voice still half choked with laughter, the woman called, "Sam? Git yourself down offa that seat an' lend me a hand!"

Not waiting for Sam to collect himself, Eliza Anne and Mark began to pull and haul at Lorah Plemmons until, at last, they had her out of the sloping wagon bed and upright, both feet on the ground.

Fringes of graying hair, which had been neatly pinned in a hard, round knot on top of her head, were blowing in the rising breeze, and using the hem of her long skirt, she wiped away tears. The merry woman—neither homely nor handsome—had laughed until she cried at her own entrance into the lives of those who lived at Etowah Cliffs, her new home.

Bowing, Mark said, "Welcome, Mrs. Plemmons. We're awfully glad you're not—hurt."

The children merely stared, and after Eliza Anne also greeted her warmly, Lorah Plemmons, still chuckling, said, "This is what you might call dumping myself at your doorstep!"

By now, Eliza Mackay and Caroline had joined the welcoming party and were shaking hands with the new hired lady. To each one, Lorah said, "Pleased to meetcha" or "Pleased to make your acquaintance." Then, abruptly, she shouted for Easter again. "Now, where did that chicken wander off to? Easter?"

"Your chicken's over there, ma'am," Henry said in his most adult manner. "She's made herself right at home. Your hen likes it here just fine, I think."

"She ain't the only one," Miss Lorah said pleasantly. "Me an' Sam, we like it fine too, don't we, Sam?" The cheery voice became abruptly stern. "Sam! Climb down from there an' act civil! You hear me?"

"Yes, ma'am, I'm comin' down," Sam mumbled, forced to jump because of the steep slant of the wrecked wagon.

Mark stepped forward to shake Sam's hand.

"We—uh, we didn't really expect you to be able to make it all the way from Ellijay today," Eliza Anne said. "Sam, you're a good driver."

"That must be a pretty good mule too," Robert offered, stroking the mule's long, graying nose.

"Oh, we did fine," Miss Lorah said, totally collected already and sounding as contented as though she were settled in a comfortable rocker. "I knew we'd get here today." Chuckling at the little joke she hadn't yet made, she said, "After all, from up Ellijay, it was mostly downhill."

Eliza Anne noticed that her mother, especially, enjoyed that lightly delivered, brief account of what must have been a terribly hard and tiring journey and to fill the somewhat awkward silence said how good it was to hear her mother laugh again.

"No good not laughin' long as yer able to," Lorah Plemmons said directly to Eliza Mackay. "Now, is there?"

"None at all, Miss Lorah," Eliza responded. "We're happier to see you than even you suspect."

"Had some trouble come down on all of you, I hear," Mrs. Plemmons said, her voice tender now. "Sorry to hear it. I sure hope I can be of help. Sam too." Turning to Mark, she asked, "You the builder, sir?"

"Uh—no, ma'am," he said. "My son-in-law's the builder. And he's in dire need of a skilled carpenter to help him."

Miss Lorah chuckled from somewhere so deep inside that her stomach, which wasn't really large at all, seemed to jiggle. "Well, now, you skilled, are ya', Sam?"

In response, Sam dug his old boot heel into the hard-packed road.

"Mostly log cabins where we come from," Miss Lorah explained, "but Sam's good at fittin' logs. None better. Now, don't you turn red an' drop your head, boy," she said to Sam. "Might not learn too fast, but once Sam learns, he's got it for keeps. An' he's a good, hard worker."

The warmth and encouragement in her voice seemed to buoy Sam, Eliza Anne thought, almost as by magic, because, for the first time, she noticed that he looked directly at them all, his head lifted from what had seemed a steady examination of every pine cone and pebble in the road.

"Got a sick young mother too, I hear," Lorah said. "Where's she now?"

"You passed her cabin on your way here," Mark said. "She's my daughter, Natalie Latimer." Including Caroline in his always loving way, he added, "Natalie's—our daughter. Our only daughter."

"Married to the master builder, eh?"

"Yes," Caroline said. "Her father and I hear that our son-in-law is considered the best builder in this entire area."

"He at work now?" Mrs. Plemmons asked.

"No," Eliza Anne answered. "He's where he's been ever since the terrible day they lost their baby—with his wife. The Latimers are devoted to each other. I'm sure you'll learn all about that from Natalie herself before too long."

"We are, oh, so relieved that you're here," Eliza Mackay offered. "I, for one, am relieved that you're—the kind of lady you so plainly are. Sensible, but just as Elizabeth Holder told us, with a truly merry heart."

Her blue, blue eyes twinkling, Miss Lorah quoted, " 'A merry heart doeth good like a medicine,' the Bible says. I go it one further. I say: A merry heart doeth *better* than any medicine!"

Eliza Anne thought they laughed a little too much—all except the children, who, in their separate ways, still seemed to be trying to figure out this somehow unique woman.

"Well, I reckon you'd better let me go straight to Miss Natalie," the woman said. "It could take a while for her and me to get acquainted enough to trust one another." Surveying her flowered skirt, she grinned. "Guess I've got myself together all right. At least, I promise to be upright when me an' her first meet."

"Should one of the children run on ahead to tell Burke Mrs. Plemmons is here?" Eliza Anne asked. "He might prefer to meet their new housekeeper first, then introduce her to Natalie. Mama, what do you think?"

Eliza Mackay thought a minute, then said, "You know, that might be best. You see, Mrs. Plemmons, we—well, we just never know what—frame of mind Natalie will be in these days." To Henry, she suggested, "Son, your legs are young. Why don't you run over to Natalie's place and call Burke outside to meet Mrs. Plemmons. Tell him she'll need a cool drink too. We'll give Sam one here."

"Thank you, ma'am." Sam spoke softly, barely glancing at Eliza. "I sure am thirsty, but we hope not to be trouble."

After Henry hurried off up the road, Lorah Plemmons caught her chicken, spurning Mark's offer of assistance, smoothed her skirt again, repinned the knot on top of her head and laughed softly. "We'll all do fine," she said, glancing at everyone still standing around the wagon. "Ain't often Sam just up and says something on his own like that. Yes siree. Might run into a bramble patch here and there, but, in time, we're gonna do just fine. I take Sam's speech as a good sign. I thank you too for your kindness to us." Chuckling, she added, "I'm already at home. Your kindness even made Sam talk, so why wouldn't I be at home?"

Henry saw the scary scene on the cabin porch before he turned in at Burke's path. Burke was on his knees leaning over Natalie, calling her name, smacking her cheeks, then splashing water from a well bucket on the steps on her face. Henry raced up to the porch. "Burke! Burke, what's wrong? Did she get sicker? Is she—dead too?"

"No, no, Henry," Burke said without taking his eyes from Natalie. "Nothing would do her but I help her outside and she fainted. Run to Mary's cabin, will you? I need Mary!"

"She's not there. I saw Mary and Jonathan heading toward Termination Rock with a picnic basket. But that woman from Ellijay's here. Her boy Sam's fixing the wagon. They lost a wheel. She'll have to walk, but she's comin' on over. My grandmother and Mama said for you to get her a cool drink and introduce her to Natalie, but—whew! She's out cold!"

"Is that woman I see coming up the road now the new housekeeper?"

"It sure is and I'll eat my new straw hat if she can't think of a way to get Natalie awake! She's—she's a real side-wheeler!"

Burke turned just long enough to let Henry see how such a comparison had surprised him, but he said nothing, just kept trying to bring Natalie around.

"I like her fine," Henry went on. "She laughs a lot and when she does, her stomach kind of shakes. She's not fat, though. But she sure is funny."

"Funny isn't what we need. I need help!"

"Are you sure Natalie isn't dead?"

"Don't even say that again, do you hear me? Run for the Ellijay woman and tell her to stop plodding along!"

"I guess she's comin' about as fast as she can. She's carrying her pet chicken named Easter."

"Well, tell her to drop the chicken and get on up here. I need help now!"

In no time at all, Lorah Plemmons puffed up to Burke's front steps, said "How do, sir," and pushed him firmly out of her way. Then Lorah's strong arms lifted Natalie to a sitting position, pushed her head over so that it hung between her knees and held it there.

"Ma'am, what are you doing to her?" Burke demanded. "My wife's been very ill—she's still very ill. She's weak, she—"

"That's it exactly," Lorah said, her attention riveted on Natalie. "She's so weak she fainted dead away."

"But shouldn't I carry her back to her bed and—"

"Not yet," the woman said sharply, still holding Natalie's head down. "And I'd be much obliged if you'd hush, sir. Just give her a little time. Give the blood a little time to get back to her head." After a pause during which Burke and Henry only stared at her, she said tenderly to Natalie, "There now, Missy, can you hear me?"

Natalie moaned, then whimpered.

"I believe you can hear," Lorah said, still addressing Natalie as though they were alone. "There, ya see? We're doin' just fine. We got that good, warm red blood back where it belongs."

Burke mumbled, "Thank God!" when he heard Natalie whimper again and saw her struggle against the woman's strong, work-worn hands.

"Not yet! We don't lift up that pretty red head just yet, little girl. Not quite yet. Just lemme hold it down for ya."

"No! Let go of me! Who—are you? Burke? *Burke?*"

"I'm right here, Natalie, and this smart lady's the one who brought you around. I tried. I couldn't do it. You fainted, darling."

"I did not."

"Well, now, that depends on the way you look at it," Lorah Plemmons said, still holding her. "Funny, I always thought a person stretched out flat on her back might just have fainted." She gave her easy chuckle. "Course, this little lady might be as different from common folks as she is pretty."

Slowly, Lorah allowed Natalie to raise her head. The two peered intently at each other.

"How did you know I'm so pretty," Natalie asked finally, "when you kept holding my head down between my knees?"

Still smiling at her, Lorah answered evenly, "I'll tell you what—I'll give that a little thought when I have time. Right now, your mister and this young feller here can carry you back to bed, then I'll get you to swallow a sip or two of buckeye tea so's you won't faint again—*if* it turns out that's what you did." She turned to Burke. "Got any buckeyes in the house, sir?"

"Why, I don't know, ma'am."

"Got to be red buckeyes."

"Our neighbor Mary McDonald's part Cherokee," Burke said. "She takes care of such things."

"Want me to find her, Burke?"

"Would you do that, Henry? Tell her we need some red buckeyes right away."

"The nuts need to be ground up. Bring me two good flat stones too, sonny."

"What if I don't want to go back to bed?" Natalie asked when Henry had run toward the river to hunt for Mary.

"I expect you'll go anyway," Lorah said firmly. "Unless the Mary we're after has got some red buckeyes already ground, that'll take some time. Got to let 'em steep on top of that."

"I'm sick of that bed!"

"I expect you are sick half to death of it." Lorah's voice was sympathetic. "Would you rather faint again than have your husband carry you back to bed, though? By the look of you, I reckon you kin carry her by yourself," she said to Burke with an easy smile.

"Oh, yes, ma'am!"

"Stop saying 'yes, ma'am' as though this woman is in charge," Natalie ordered sharply. "Burke, I demand to know who she is! How did she get here? And what right does she have to boss us around?"

Still gathered in chairs and on the steps of the Stileses' porch, they all waited impatiently for some word from Henry or Burke as to how Natalie and Lorah Plemmons were getting along. As always, Mark's mind was on Natalie.

"I just hope," he said, addressing no one in particular, "that we did the right thing to let the lady go in on Natalie with no advance notice that she was even coming."

"Not one more word about our daughter, Mark," Caroline said crossly. "We all agreed and we've done the only thing that could be done with Burke having to go back to work any day now." Then she smiled. "I—I sound forbidding, don't I?"

"In a way, yes," he said, not showing irritation, but not returning her smile either.

"Surely Henry will be back soon," Eliza Mackay said, "and we won't gain anything by hashing our decision back and forth, now will we? Why don't you finish reading W.H.'s letter to us, Eliza Anne."

"Yes," Mark agreed. "Burke's with our newcomer and Natalie. There's nothing we can do but wait. I plan to write to Mayor Williams before the day is over. I'd like to be able to tell him how W.H.'s prospects look from up here."

"There isn't any chance my papa won't get nominated and then go to Washington City, is there?" Robert wanted to know.

"Of course not," Mary Cowper assured him from the wisdom of her advanced age of nine. "There isn't anyone anywhere to equal Papa!"

"He did write about how things looked to him politically just before the Milledgeville convention, didn't he, Eliza Anne?"

"Yes, Mark." Eliza Anne found the page in W.H.'s letter where she'd been so surprisingly interrupted by the arrival of Lorah Plemmons and her pet chicken, smoothed the pages over her knee and began again to read aloud: " 'I should be home no later than mid-July, providing I am chosen by the nominating committee on an early ballot, but from what I hear so far in my travels, my ultimate election seems most promising. I plan to reach Milledgeville a day or two before the convention is called to order, in an effort to contact each man of the 33-member committee. I'm sure Mark knows, if he is still there, that 3 members from each of the 11 judicial circuits comprise the nominating committee. Of course, only 8 of us will be chosen now and when reapportionment is finally settled upon, 11. Perhaps the additional three, should reapportionment succeed, will be held in abeyance. My hope is to be selected as one of the first eight. I am counting heavily on the influence of Levi De Lyon. My next letter will be written from the flurry of the convention itself, a brief letter I'm sure, but in it should be more definite news of my return. Pray, beloveds, for my nomination on the first ballot. You know, Lib, your husband does not wait easily or with much grace.' "

"Is that it?" Mark asked.

"Yes," Eliza Anne answered. "Except for my personal page."

"Of course. Well, ladies and children," Mark said, "I feel sure we'll have a United States congressman in our family soon."

"I'm going to have one dejected, heartbroken husband if not," Eliza Anne said, refolding the letter. "His hopes are so high!"

Mark turned to Miss Eliza. "What do you think, Miss Eliza, about our lady from Ellijay?"

"That she's one of the most remarkable women I've ever met and needs none of our help."

"But she doesn't know Natalie at all," Caroline protested.

"She will. Just give her time."

"You don't think I should walk over there?" Mark asked.

"No, dear boy, I don't."

"Not even to let her and Burke know we're interested in how Natalie accepted the idea of a new housekeeper?"

"He knows, I'm sure," Eliza Mackay said. "I'm also sure that our Ellijay friend—if not today or even tomorrow—will eventually manage to get things under control so we can start back to Savannah. Maybe in time for me to have a little say over my own garden."

Chapter 21

MARY Cowper, considered by her father, even before her tenth birthday, to be a splendid horsewoman and an excellent shot, let no one forget Papa's promise to her when she turned ten, on June 29, even though he was still away on his political business. "When you reach your tenth birthday," he had said, "you may ride your own horse with an adult beside you all the way to Cassville for the mail."

When her birthday finally arrived, she reminded Mama of the promise, and in spite of a light drizzle when it was time to go, her mother allowed her to ride with Burke. "Your father should be here to keep his own promise," Mama had said, "especially since it's raining, but go, Mary C. And for heaven's sake, bring back a letter from Papa!"

Mary Cowper and Burke had made the trip just fine. After about five miles or so the rain stopped, and even though there was no letter from Papa, she tried hard to feel ten. About halfway back to Etowah Cliffs, the sun came out and Mary Cowper was glad when the two of them stopped to rest and eat some fresh cheese Burke had bought in town at Hawke's Store, with two red apples from Papa's fruit cellar and a sack of Little Sinai's biscuits.

"You and I haven't had much chance before to talk, have we?" Burke asked after they'd hitched their horses to a tree and were strolling toward a shaded clearing by the side of the Cassville Road. "It isn't much like me to have missed out on conversation with such a pretty young lady."

Burke laughed when he said that, but it wasn't, she thought, the kind of making-fun laugh grown people gave children.

"Do you think I'm a good horsewoman?" she asked.

"Oh, yes. You ride as though you were born on a horse. Your mount likes you too. I can tell."

"How can you tell?"

"Years of experience with horses, I guess."

Sitting side by side under a huge white oak, Burke, evidently not as hungry as she, took off his straw hat, leaned against the tree trunk and thought for a time. Then, looking down at her, he asked, "Tell me, Mary C., do you feel ten years old today? A whole decade?"

She shrugged. "I suppose I do. I'm trying. I think there is a kind of new feeling. I like it. Were you ever in love with anyone else before Natalie?"

She thought he looked somewhat surprised, but he answered quite seriously: "I'd say no. Oh, I've always had an eye for beautiful women, but—"

"You didn't hope, I'm sure, ever to see one as beautiful as Natalie, did you?"

Slowly, Burke unwrapped, then broke off a piece of yellow cheese and handed it to her. "Did you bring the biscuits?" he asked.

"Oh, yes," she said, jumping up, "but I'm so excited about our long ride I left them right where Little Sinai tied the bundle onto my saddle! Here, hold my cheese." Over her shoulder, running back to her horse, she called, "Don't move, Burke. I'll be right back."

Seated again under the big oak, she watched him cut the string with which Little Sinai had tied the four biscuits in a piece of soft cloth and waited for him to answer her question. Then, thinking maybe he'd forgotten, she asked again: "Did you ever even expect to see anyone as beautiful as Natalie, Burke?"

He laughed a little. "How does a ten-year-old girl know a thing like that? I'll bet you think a lot of surprising things, don't you?"

Not knowing exactly how to answer that, she waited.

"Your question about Natalie took me off guard," he said.

"Why?"

"Well, you seem so quiet usually, you obey your parents so well, you—"

"I what?"

"You always struck me as being contented to think only—little-girl thoughts. Thoughts about pretty dresses, ribbons for your hair. Oh, I know you're a crack shot, a good swimmer, a lucky fisherman, and you certainly sit a horse magnificently, but—"

"But what, Burke? What's so surprising about seeing how beautiful Natalie is?"

"Nothing," he said. "Only a blind person could miss that!"

"The truth is, I'm going to fall in love any time now," she announced, tearing open a biscuit so she could make a cheese sandwich. "Do you want me to make a sandwich for you?"

"That would be nice." He handed her his slab of cheese. "Now, what's this about falling in love some time soon? I haven't seen any eligible young men around lately."

"Oh, there aren't any, but it's something I just know. Could you give me any pointers on what happens when you fall in love?" she asked, handing him his biscuit and cheese.

This time Burke grew serious. "You won't need any pointers, young lady. There will just come a time when you're only—half there without one certain person. When everything you do or think or feel whirls around only one— face."

"Whirls? Did you say things whirl?"

He laughed. "That's what I said and believe me, my wife still keeps things whirling for me. Sick as she's been, subdued and defeated as she still seems most days, my heart skips around like an awkward young colt sometimes when I just look at her."

"Do you like that?"

"Doesn't really matter whether you like it or not. It's the way things are when you're in love. You—well, you only feel complete when you're close to that one person."

"When you are—hugging each other?"

"That's right. Either with your arms or when you're both thinking such close thoughts it's almost the same as hugging."

"Do you suppose Mama and Papa still feel that way at their age? Did they ever feel that way about each other? Will Mama be—maybe on the verge of tears when we tell her there's no letter from Papa?"

"I know she'll be disappointed."

"Do you think Papa is the only man Mama ever truly loved?"

Burke smiled down at her. "Oh, don't forget, you've known your mother a lot longer than I have. Natalie did tell me once that the gossip around Savannah a long time ago was that your mother and Captain Jack Mackay's best friend from West Point, another Army officer named Robert Lee, I think it was, were pretty close. It didn't work out, though. Probably just more of that stupid Savannah gossip. The important thing is that she married your father. Otherwise you and I wouldn't be here having this good talk. Don't you want your apple?"

"I don't think so, thank you."

"Ready to ride for home?"

She sighed, longing to go on talking because she felt so free with Burke. "I suppose we should leave," she said, but made no move to get to her feet. As Burke rewrapped the leftover cheese, she thought how much she liked being with him and wondered how Natalie, beautiful as she was, had been so lucky. Mary Cowper felt warm and safe and very pleased when Burke took her hand for the short walk back to their horses.

"Do you like Miss Lorah Plemmons, Burke?"

"Oh, I certainly do," he said. "She's one fine lady. I wonder what on earth I did without her. For that matter, I wonder how Natalie got along before she came."

"Well, you had Mary McDonald and before Natalie was so sick, Mama says she'd learned how to be an excellent housekeeper and cook."

Holding the stirrup as she mounted, he said, "That girl of mine can do anything she sets that lovely head to do. There. Are you all set to ride?"

"Oh, yes. But not till after I ask one more question." How she wished they could just go on talking! Still, being ten now, she mustn't act like a child.

Erect and balanced in the saddle, she watched the golden-haired, broad-shouldered man unhitch their mounts and swing easily onto Major's back.

"What's the one last thing you want to ask me, young lady?"

"It's about Jonathan Browning and Indian Mary. Why were Mama and Uncle Mark and Aunt Caroline so dead set against Mary going home with them to Savannah to see a doctor about her half-blind eye?"

Looking off down the road, Burke frowned, and she felt ever so sorry if she'd somehow spoiled things, because they'd been having such a happy time and she hadn't seen Burke enjoy himself much since his baby son had been born dead.

He pushed his wide-brimmed straw hat back on his head and sat his horse in silence for a time. "You did save one *big*, tough question till last, didn't you?"

"Was I wrong to ask that?"

"No. No, not wrong. I just need more time than we have to give you an answer, I guess." He turned in his saddle to face her. "Mary C., Savannah people aren't like people here in the upcountry. Do you know at all what I mean?"

She thought a minute, then said, "Well, maybe. I'm not sure. Which class of people do you mean, Burke?"

"I hate that word 'class,'" he said. "But your question is right on the mark. You see, I wish people were valued or not valued only by what they do with their lives. By what they are—down inside—honest or dishonest, responsible or irresponsible. Not by whether or not they're rich or poor, upper-class or lower-class. I'd say your family and the Brownings are very, very upper-class."

Thinking as hard as she could, Mary Cowper answered, "I think you're right. At least, that's always what I've heard we are. Is that good or bad, Burke?"

"Neither," he said. "But from what I know of most Savannah people, those who consider themselves upper-class tend to be snobs. Tend to feel as though, because of their family or property or money, they're better than poor people—better than Negroes or Indians, say."

"Are you upper-class?"

He laughed again, but this time it didn't seem to be because he was enjoying himself. "If anything," he said, "I guess my family was middle-class. I don't feel *any* class. Never have. Never intend to."

"Are you rich?"

"No, ma'am! I aim to be well-off one day, but I also intend to work for every dollar of it with my two hands." He thought for a time, then asked, "Do you know how I met up with Ben and Mary McDonald the first time?"

"The white people drove the Cherokees away and you found Mary and Ben hiding in a cave—like foxes. You rescued them and gave them a home. Mama and Papa think it's really good what you did. So does our grandmother and so do the Brownings."

"But everyone in Savannah isn't like them. I had a bad time of it even up here back in the days when there were almost no upper-class people settling yet. Just because Mary and Ben were part Indian, white folks—even scum—

looked down on them. Ben even got himself beaten to a pulp at New Echota the first day he found the nerve to show his dark Indian skin outside that cave, in fact." He glanced at the sun. "We've got to be riding. Will this answer your question? The Brownings and Miss Eliza worry about how some other Savannahians might treat Mary when they get her down there. They care about her. They don't want her hurt. And neither do I."

"But Jonathan cares about her too. I've watched very closely and I've come to the decision," she said in her most mature manner, "that Jonathan Browning is in love with Indian Mary!"

Burke walked his horse over close to her and gave her sunbonnet an affectionate jerk. "You're smarter than a girl ought to be at ten," he said. "Now, let's go!"

Galloping behind him toward home, she thought of a lot of other questions she needed to ask Burke. He was going back to work on Mr. Milner's Presbyterian church tomorrow and heaven only knew when she'd get another chance to ride to Cassville with him so they could have a further talk. One of her questions was about his new helper, Sam. Sam and Burke had already done some work on the foundation of her family's house. She'd surely meant to ask if Sam was going to be half as good as Ben was. She'd also meant to find out if Burke had any idea why Ben had shot himself right on top of the baby's grave.

She wondered also if no letter from Papa today could mean that he wasn't going to become a United States congressman after all. She loved her parents so much, the very thought scared her, a lot, even though she really didn't want to leave Etowah Cliffs and the river and the woods and move to Washington City, or maybe be sent off to school by herself.

The thought crossed Mary Cowper's mind, as she rode along behind Burke, that he'd surely stop for more talk if she said she was tired. She wasn't tired, though, and Grandma Mackay said part of growing up meant you began to consider other people. What Burke wanted most right now, she knew, was to get home to Natalie, who did seem better, but who still didn't like the idea of having Miss Lorah there "bossing" her. Miss Lorah just went about her work, taking Natalie in stride, as she did most things. Mary Cowper liked her in a way she thought she should be able to understand now that she'd turned ten, but didn't really. She'd meant to ask Burke why he liked the woman from Ellijay so much.

We'd better keep riding, though, she thought. I might even get back in time to help Miss Lorah arrange the fresh bouquet of flowers she fixes every day for Natalie's room. Mary C. had learned quite a lot already from Miss Lorah about how to go about making a pretty bouquet. She might someday get up enough nerve to ask her how it was that a lady who had never lived in a fine house knew so well about so many things.

*   *   *

Lorah Plemmons pushed Natalie's bedroom door open with her foot and carried the vase filled with freshly cut black-eyed Susans across to the bedside table.

"There," she said in her slightly ragged, but cheerful voice, "is a little splash of yellow to brighten up this dark room. You sure you don't want me to help you outside to sit awhile in that good chair your husband made just for you?"

Without turning over in the bed, Natalie murmured, "No, thank you. If I wanted to be outside, I'd have told you."

"You don't sound too chipper, Missy. It's stopped raining, but on a gray, cloudy day like this, we can use all the brightening up we can get, don't you think so?"

Hands on hips, Lorah stood looking down at her, the pretty, pale face still turned away, and wondered exactly what to do next. Oh, there was plenty of work to be done. After fixing breakfast for Sam and Mr. Latimer and Natalie, she'd slipped outside between showers to pick the flowers, convinced as always that if she didn't get another thing done, she'd see to fresh blossoms of some kind to lift Missy's spirits. Somehow, when Lorah thought of her new charge, and she thought a lot about her, she thought of her as Missy. It had been a long time since she'd been so challenged by anything or anybody. Daily, her determination to bring the sorrowful, still grieving young woman out of her down-in-the-mouth attitude seemed to grow stronger. As Lorah perfectly well knew, Missy *was* growing stronger, although she seemed not to want to admit it. Lorah's warm, reaching heart ached for this girl who'd failed to bring her baby to term and who went on clinging to her failure no matter how hard her fine, strong, loving husband tried to help her, to assure her that she had not failed, that there just was no way to explain what had happened to the child they both wanted so much—that they could try again.

Lorah herself hadn't used any of these arguments with her. She knew her place in more ways than one. If Missy was to be convinced by any of those reasons that she hadn't failed, it would have to be her husband's doing. Nobody, including Mr. Latimer, knew from one minute to the next what Missy might do or say, but sooner or later, Lorah meant to find a way to bring her to her senses. Heartbreak was heartbreak. A dark cloud hanging over any human mind and heart was the same, no matter what caused it. Only the person who felt the darkness could lift it. To Lorah's mind, Missy had just latched on to the notion of failure as a reason not to battle her way out of plain old destructive grief.

Looking down at Natalie now, she thought, I tried the same thing myself all those years ago when my Luke left me. I must have been every bit as worrisome as Missy when I blathered to anybody who'd listen about how I blamed myself for Luke's death. Nobody believed me when I'd say that if I'd gone down to the river with him that day he might not have been drowned. Nobody believed me because they knew, as well as I know now, that I couldn't have gone with him—that somebody had to fix supper. But sayin' I'd failed him because I stayed at home that day to cook gave me an excuse to go on wrappin' myself in gloom. Missy's baby's been dead less than two months. She's sorry for herself but she's still not as sorry for herself as I was. I badgered folks by blamin' myself for more'n a year. Might still be gloomin' around if old Aunt Essie hadn't come to visit me.

Lorah remembered, would never forget Aunt Essie's exact words spoken in a firm voice on just the right morning. She remembered the morning too. How the autumn sun slanted off the mountain back of her log cabin, firing up the dark green pines, the bright, fall-colored oak and maple and sumac and beech and sassafras leaves so they near hurt Lorah's eyes as she stared out into them while Aunt Essie talked. She refused for a long time even to act like she'd heard what Aunt Essie had said about the danger, the mortal danger of crossing that line from natural grief over into feeling only sorrow for yourself. Lorah had no intention of allowing Missy to step too far over that line. Mr. Latimer was too good a man, loved her too much, didn't deserve a wife who wallowed in self-pity from morning to night.

The question was *when* to bring it up. Only the good Lord knew whether Missy was ready or not. With all her heart, Lorah Plemmons wished for Missy's release. Oh, she hadn't had but a handful of kind words from her in the whole time she'd been there, but there had to be another reason beyond her beauty why Mr. Latimer loved her so deeply. Missy's parents were fine, genteel folks too and heaven knew they all but worshipped the ground she walked on, especially her soft-spoken, warmhearted father. They deserved better.

"Miss Lorah, are you still just standing there peering down at me?" Natalie asked. "You know I don't like it when you do that."

"Oh, I know you don't like me bein' here at all," Lorah answered pleasantly. "But I'm here and we're both going to make the best of it. Don't you want to turn over and at least take a peek at these pretty yellow flowers I brought you?"

Instead of the polite, cold "No, thank you" Lorah had expected, Natalie turned her head slowly in the direction of the flowers.

"Black-eyed Susans?" she asked.

"That's just what they are," Lorah answered, as though Missy had said something special. "I thought not to mix 'em in with any other colors. We need yellow today."

Allowing her pale, pale eyes to stay briefly on Lorah's eager face, Natalie smiled weakly. "I hope Burke didn't get wet riding to Cassville for the mail. Did you say it's stopped raining?"

"Yes, but I doubt a little drizzle could hurt such a big, rugged man like Mr. Latimer. You don't reckon he'd melt, do you?"

"Did anyone ride with him?"

"Yes, ma'am. That pretty, well-mannered little Stiles girl went, proud as a peacock. You know she had her tenth birthday yesterday, didn't you?"

"Of course I know! Why do you always end everything you say with a question? I'll be courteous, but I don't intend to bother answering your questions unless I feel like it."

Chuckling, Lorah said, "That's the longest and best speech you've made today!"

"I don't consider that remark a bit funny."

Deciding to let that go, Lorah went on. "Yes siree, I expect the two of them will be ridin' in now just about any time."

"I certainly hope so," Natalie said, turning away again, so that her voice was barely audible. "Please leave me alone now."

"You don't want anything?"

"No, thank you."

"All right. I've got a panful of breakfast dishes to wash up before I start to cook again."

Natalie mumbled, "Good. I wish you'd do that now."

"Sure you don't want a cup of peppermint tea or some milk and cookies?"

"I'm sure I want you to wash those breakfast dishes! And"—in a somewhat less sullen voice—she added, "I do thank you for the flowers. I suppose you'll bring more tomorrow."

"That's my plan."

When Natalie lapsed into the now familiar silence, Lorah waited for a few seconds, then left the room, feeling a tiny, but definite ray of hope. The two of them hadn't had such a long talk since she'd come to Etowah Cliffs.

From the kitchen window, she could see the pale, lemon-yellow sun trying to push its way past a low, thick bank of clouds. Scraping and stacking the breakfast dishes in her big dishpan before she poured boiling water over them, she breathed a prayer that Sam wasn't making a botch of the bricklaying Mr. Latimer had left in his care this morning. The big second wing of the Stiles house would take far fancier work than Sam had ever tackled. She meant to pray a lot that Sam would learn how to please Mr. Latimer, who was giving him the chance of a lifetime to work along with him on the Presbyterian church and the Stiles mansion.

There was nothing in the world she wouldn't do for fine-looking, burdened young Mr. Latimer, because he'd already done so much for her and Sam.

Lorah Plemmons was no stranger to hard work. Her big challenge here was Missy. Washing and scrubbing and cooking and ironing were second nature to her. The hardest job was going to be to bring Missy around to the place where she began to think about how she was making other people feel —not only what life had done to her. The job was twice as hard because she understood and felt the dark, heavy pain in Missy's heart.

Chapter 22

WHEN the second week in July came and went, still with no letter from her husband, Eliza Anne agreed to accompany her mother on a walk along the cliffs above the river—alone, just the two—something she'd been obviously avoiding.

"I admit it, Mama," Eliza Anne said as they strolled in the clear morning air after family breakfast, "I've been unsubtle, to say the least, about dodging time alone with you."

"And do you know why, dear?" her mother asked in her careful, gentle manner.

"Yes. It's going to sound disgustingly noble, but you're leaving so soon with Indian Mary, I—I hated to add my worries to—to—"

"To what?"

"Heaven only knows, Mama—and I do hear the irritation in my voice— but only heaven does know what burdens the Brownings may heap on you once you're home! Taking Mary back there is madness. Everyone knows Mark and Caroline have always given in to Natalie, but I certainly didn't realize they'd begun to spoil Jonathan too!"

Her mother didn't respond at once, a familiar habit which had always made Eliza Anne feel ill at ease and, with or without reason, somehow guilty.

"I'm not ignoring the problems that certainly may lie ahead for all the Brownings once we're back in town," her mother said finally, "but their problems aren't my reason for maneuvering you to take a walk with me now. I'm really concerned over your anxiety for W.H."

"Oh, I know I'm cross and not hiding my worry a bit well, but every time someone rides for the mail and there's no word—no word at all from him, I —I—" She broke off, leaving her mother to wait. "I try to hide my feelings from Mark and Caroline, because they've already had so much heartache, but I'm not trying to hide anything from you. I'm not!"

"Are you afraid W.H. might be ill?"

"I always worry that he won't take care of himself when he's away, but no." She stopped walking to face her mother. "Mama, what if they didn't nominate him on the first ballot? He had his heart so set on being selected among the first eight gentlemen—on that first ballot!"

"Would it make all that much difference if he made it on the second?"

"To him, it would. He's always a bit shaky about the impression he makes on the average frontier voter, but I'm sure he fully expects his social equals on the committee to select him right away, especially with Mr. De Lyon such a powerful member. W.H. expects to be thought—different by many of the lower-classed settlers, although he tries so hard to meet them on their ground, but it could crush him to be rejected by his peers."

"I see, but we're not at that ford in the river yet, Eliza Anne. We simply don't know that any of what you fear is true. Miss Lorah's Sam is riding for the mail today. Can't we hope, at least, for a letter from W.H.? Sam will be here soon—I'd think within a couple of hours or so anyway."

"But, Mama, I have to plan ahead! I need to have thought of what I can say to W.H. to restore his self-esteem if the worst is true. He'd already begun to compose his acceptance letter! I found some of his preliminary notes after he left. What if the—worst is true?"

"Would the worst be a nomination on the second or third ballot or no chance at all to run in the election? Eliza Anne, do you really want to move to Washington City?"

"I want to be wherever W.H. is," she said without hesitation. "Of course, he'll have to go ahead alone—if he's elected. The children and I will stay here until he finds a place for us to live. I wouldn't have to leave this wonderful place at once. The election isn't until fall and his Congress won't convene for months after that."

"Then you *aren't* too eager to move to Washington, are you?"

They began to walk slowly again. "Don't be clever with me, Mama, by trying to change the subject. Wherever W.H. goes for as long as we both live, I go with him because I live only a piece of life without him. Right now, I'm worried about what to do to help him—if he fails. It will be all up to me somehow to make things right for him again, should this one dream of his not come true." She took a deep breath. "Don't you see? *It will be all up to me!*"

Once more, her mother lapsed into what she always insisted was merely a "thinking time" and Eliza Anne felt like shaking her. The river lapped around the small stones below at the foot of Termination Rock. A jar fly in a tree seemed to be buzzing inside her head. Unable to endure the silence another second, Eliza Anne said in a sharper voice than she meant, "Now, aren't you sorry you—had this idea to get me off alone? Even you can't think of a single answer!"

"No, I can't," her mother said slowly, quietly. "In fact, I wouldn't even try. No one knows your husband the way you know him, daughter, and what you say and do to help him is up to you."

"But you were lapsing into one of your 'thinking times.' "

"Yes. I was thinking about how little you've changed since you were Mary Cowper's age or younger."

"I'd be grateful if you wouldn't try to turn me back into a child. I have a— woman's problem!"

"I wasn't even thinking about your problem," the older woman said evenly. "I was thinking about *you*. You, my dear, were the one of all my children who always, always struggled to take charge—to fix a problem— even before it happened. You also have always tried to take charge of other people's thoughts, much as you tried a minute ago to take charge of mine."

Again, Eliza Anne stopped walking to study her mother's face. "I'm not at all sure I like any of what you just said, Mama. You certainly can't say I've butted into Natalie's affairs lately. Not even when Burke came to me to ask my opinion on how to bring her around to liking Miss Lorah!"

"You're right. You haven't taken charge there at all, even though I'm sure Natalie expected you to be on her side. And I'm proud of you for staying out of it."

"Well." Eliza Anne tried a little laugh. "At least, this isn't turning entirely into a parental scolding."

"You're old enough for us to be friends now. Friends don't scold, but they do have the obligation to be honest."

"I know and this isn't the first time you've told me I'm a worrywart, that I tend to grab the reins too tightly, too fast." They strolled on. "It's no virtue on my part that I've left poor Burke to fend for himself. I—I honestly didn't know what to tell him when he asked me to talk to Natalie about how really helpful it's being to him to know she's in Miss Lorah's good, strong hands."

"What *did* you say to Burke?"

"That perhaps only time would bring Natalie to see her need of a house-keeper. A friend. Do you feel Mrs. Plemmons is a real friend? I do—to us all. I'm not quite sure why I think that, but then, she's so different from anyone we've ever known, I'm not sure why I feel drawn to her. I've never had anyone but Negroes working for me. I find it difficult to be a friend to—hired help. Still, I admit to you that before you asked me to take this walk, I thought how I'd love to be able to pour out my worries over W.H.'s odd silence to Miss Lorah. Not that I'm on the verge of preferring her to my own mother." She smiled at Eliza. "Did you take it that way?"

Eliza Mackay laughed. "No, I did not take it that way, because I've wanted so much to ask her advice too about the predicament we all face when we take little Indian Mary back to Savannah. I know the woman's never even been to Savannah, but she seems to be able to see us all exactly as we are. She seems to know just where we all fit into the world around us. I haven't talked to Miss Lorah about Mary having to face Savannah people because her hands are more than full with Natalie."

Eliza Anne sighed heavily. "You're every bit as wise as Lorah Plemmons, Mama, and we've all always leaned on your wisdom. I actually think I hoped you'd have a neat, pat solution ready to hand me today. Something to whisk away my worry over W.H."

"I wish I had, my dear," her mother said a bit wistfully, "but you see I didn't. Perhaps Lorah Plemmons has something other than wisdom—an instinct. An instinct I lack."

"It's time we began walking back," Eliza Anne said, taking her mother's arm. "You're all I could ever ask in a mother and with all my heart I wish you weren't facing the Indian Mary trouble when you get home. You know Mark will be turning to you night and day, expecting you to tell him what to do when those razor tongues go after poor little Mary."

"I don't want you to worry," her mother said. "I want you to pray."

"Oh, I will, I will."

"The Lord already knows how the Mary McDonald visit will turn out and, Eliza Anne, He knows all about W.H.'s future too—and his pride."

Chapter 23

BY August, the Brownings, Mary McDonald and Eliza Mackay were back in Savannah, everyone feeling fairly secure in the knowledge that Lorah Plemmons was in charge of Natalie.

"As much in charge of Natalie as anyone will ever be," Mark said when Eliza greeted him on her porch just before noon on August 18. "I brought your mail and a copy of today's *Georgian*, Miss Eliza. I came early because there's a letter for you from Eliza Anne."

"Sit down, Mark," she urged. "We might as well stay out here. It's just as hot inside today. After our visit to the upcountry, this Savannah heat smothers me—in the house or out."

Handing her the mail Mark asked, "Will you scan Eliza Anne's letter while I'm here and read me anything—anything she might say about my daughter?"

"You know I will, dear boy, and I have a strong feeling that Eliza Anne will, from now on, write all there is to tell about Natalie." She broke the seal and glanced at the first page. "Here, read for yourself and you'll see I'm right."

"Want me to read it aloud?"

"Please. My new spectacles don't seem to help much with Eliza Anne's fast scrawl."

Anxiously, Mark began to read the letter dated August 12, 1842. " 'Dear Mama and Everyone . . . Because I'm sure Mark and Caroline will be eager to know, I'll begin with Natalie, although I have much to write about my own beloved husband, who is due home tomorrow, we hope and pray, before dark. With all of you back in Savannah, I find myself forced to be disciplined or I'll interfere too much with what Miss Lorah and Burke seem to be trying to achieve with Natalie, much of the time still in her dark, unfamiliar state of mind. To ease Mark's fear some, I will say it seems to me they are making a little progress with her. Oh, she still snaps at Miss Lorah and lapses into a mood each time Burke has to leave for work, but he's about finished now with the Presbyterian church and thinks that after another week or ten days, he'll be able to stay at home while he puts all his efforts and those of poor, clumsy, well-intentioned Sam into the new wing of our house. In case I forget to add this later, I must mention here that Sam is definitely *not* Ben, according to Burke's reports of his work, but he tries hard and Burke shows a kind of patience which amazes us all—even my children, who, by the way, are fine. The boys, especially Henry, are sassy without their father.' "

"Mark, I'm going to stop you only long enough to say how glad I am that you and Caroline both seem to admire Burke as much as the boy deserves," Eliza interrupted.

"We do. He's so shattered over the loss of their son, but he hasn't burdened Natalie with his grief."

"He seemed to me to know the fine art of merely sharing hers," she said. "Now, read on. I know how eager you are to learn about everything."

Mark smiled his thanks. "Eliza Anne starts a new paragraph. 'I continue to marvel at the patience of both Burke and Miss Lorah because, loving Natalie so deeply myself, I still want to shake her almost daily for the oddly unfeeling way she treats us all. Oh, she's invariably polite, but her silences, especially with a warm, outgoing woman like Lorah Plemmons, must hurt. Still, fresh bouquets appear each day, the attention to Natalie's every need and to most of her wants goes on. I simply feel that Mrs. Plemmons is so grateful that she and Sam have a roof over their heads, plenty to eat and work to do, that she shows her gratitude both to God and to Burke by her continuing patience. Oh, Miss Lorah is very human. I sense the times when she'd also like to shake Natalie, but the woman's sense of humor is not only her own salvation, it's ours too—and ultimately, perhaps it will save Natalie. Lorah Plemmons is one of the most secretive, private persons I've ever encountered. I've come right out and asked her about her early life, her parents, if she had ever married, etc. All I've found out is that at some period her father owned an orchard near Ellijay. She is never rude over my nosiness. She just doesn't tell anything—whether she has ever borne a child, if Sam is legally adopted, if her husband is dead or if he deserted her—nothing. I'm sure it's no secret to any of you there that Natalie acts, at least, as though she is the only person who ever knew true grief. Mark and Caroline, I am not being critical of your daughter. I simply know her. Of course, I also know that since I have experienced only the deep grief of losing my father, I cannot possibly understand the singular pain at the loss of a child. Should I lose either of my sons or Mary Cowper, I might well be worse than Natalie, who does appear stronger and much less pale now than when you left us.' "

Eliza Mackay noticed Mark leafing ahead in the long letter. "Is that all about Natalie?" she asked.

"Yes," he said. "It seems to be. Perhaps you'd rather read the remainder yourself. I see W.H. mentioned often on this page."

"Go ahead," she urged. "I know how interested you are in W.H.'s political doings."

"I am indeed," he said, glancing at the *Georgian* on the floor beside his chair. "In fact, I brought the paper in case something about him appears in it. We know he is a nominee, but that's about all."

Eliza smiled. "Yes, but nothing of why it all took so long."

"Well, here's what Eliza Anne has to say: 'After W.H. arrives tomorrow, I'll have more detailed information about the Democratic Convention in Milledgeville, his nomination, etc., but for now, I can report only that for some reason he stayed over to compose his acceptance letter on the spot, an act which any man less learned than my husband would surely have done en route. At any rate, he sent me no copy of it, but feels it will appear at least in part in many Georgia papers. Living in your huge city of more than 11,000 souls, I feel sure you may see his acceptance in print before I can copy it for you in a letter. *He is a nominee,* though, and I rejoice for him and swell with pride in his eloquence and talent.' "

"Why not look in the paper you brought, Mark? This is August 18. There could be something about W.H. in today's *Georgian.*"

She watched Mark search the tightly packed columns of what to her had become incredibly fine print in the *Georgian* and let her mind jump to little Indian Mary's visit and the sticky problem of *how* to introduce the girl to Savannah society. They'd been home only a bit more than two weeks and so far Jonathan had merely been showing Mary the city—Commerce Row and Factor's Walk, the older mansions, the numbers of new houses and stores—especially the new Georgia Historical Society building at 30 East Bryan Street and the extent to which Savannah was growing. They, of course, were all proud that the city limits now extended from Liberty to Jones—but Mary? She smiled to herself. Such a fact, she felt sure, had little or no relevance for her, whose Cherokee world had known no property boundaries of any kind.

"Here it is, Miss Eliza! I found an announcement of W.H.'s acceptance letter and a short quotation from it. Listen: 'In reply to your notification, sirs, I have to state that duly sensible of the honor conferred, I accept the nomination, and should the result of the election show a majority of the people of Georgia to be favorable to the political principles which I profess, I will endeavor to represent them in the national councils.' " Mark took a deep breath. "Well, it's official now. And I, for one, will be watching closely to find out just how the people of Georgia respond to W.H.'s 'political principles,' won't you?"

"Yes, indeed, I'll be watching. And, Mark, even after all these years, I still try to imagine what my Robert might be thinking about politics now were he alive. I don't always feel I've guessed rightly. For example, I'm not at all certain he'd agree that W.H. is right in opposing a national bank."

Mark laughed a little. "That's because you yourself aren't sure W.H. is correct when he blames our money problems on overbanking and overtrading. Frankly, neither am I. He charges that the Bank of the United States has been corrupt and unconstitutional. That may be, but we do live in the *United* States—no longer a loose confederation of states each going its own way. Oh, even as a Whig, I'll do all I can to support him, but the issue of states' rights over federal rights and obligations still bothers me. I suppose I mean by that I haven't made up my mind about which should take precedence." He grinned. "That could, of course, be my northern background showing."

"Women aren't supposed to have political ideas, but one thing I know, and I'll shout it from the housetops when I dare, is that our country *is* the *United States of America!* Each state has its own beauty and advantages, but they'd be mighty helpless trying to go it alone."

She liked Mark's teasing smile. "You're not, by any chance, a secret Whig, are you, Miss Eliza Mackay?"

"No, I'm not. Being a woman, I'm not anything. In my heart, I'm a Democrat, but I don't like divisions—not in a family, not in a country. I think the northern abolitionists, while some of them—maybe most of them—mean well, are going to make trouble just by putting us in two boxes—North and South. Mark, why can't we just live our lives according to our own needs and our own backgrounds and upbringing? Not once, so far as I know, did God make a single person exactly like any other. He *created*—He didn't pour plaster casts!"

Still smiling, Mark asked, "Do you talk to your son-in-law, W. H. Stiles, in this manner, dear lady?"

"I do not. What a woman thinks about politics and government makes no difference anyway."

"What you think about everything makes a difference to me," he said.

She reached to pat his arm. "Well, then, I do think we have lots of reasons to hope for Natalie's improvement. Grief takes time." For a moment, she studied the brown spots on the backs of both her hands, then said, "I need to make a confession." His surprised look didn't stop her at all. "I need to confess to you that much of the time we were at Etowah Cliffs, I felt humiliated."

"You?" he asked. "Why on earth did you feel humiliated?"

"Because I went so I'd be there to help you and we found so much tragedy and heartbreak I felt helpless as a new puppy every day! That means only one thing, Mark."

"What?"

"That I had come to put too much stock in what you all say about—about being able to lean on me. I think I'd begun to believe your opinion of me as a strong, wise woman. Oh, I didn't know any of this—we seldom do until we come up against the real thing in someone else. We did come up against the real thing in Lorah Plemmons, you know. I went to sleep last night wishing she were right here in Savannah now! She'd know exactly what you and Caroline should do about introducing Indian Mary to Savannah society. Miss Lorah would know by instinct, whether you should do it or just go on letting things slide by until it's time for Jonathan to leave for Yale and Mary to go back to the upcountry where she's at home and—comfortable."

For what seemed to Eliza to be the longest time, Mark looked at her, then his deep-set gray eyes moved away. Staring out over her tree-shaded side yard, he said not one word.

"You were counting on me to have just the right sage advice, weren't you, dear boy? Well, I don't have it."

Finally, he looked at her. "You're my—rock, Miss Eliza," he said. "I don't have another close friend in the world but you!"

Tears smarted her eyes, but she gave him a tender smile, then heard her unsteady voice say only, "Oh, dear boy . . . dear boy."

"Don't ever diminish yourself again, please," he said, with surprising firmness. "Even if you gave me—bad advice—you'd be the one I'd turn to when it didn't work. That will always be true." For a few seconds, they just sat there, then Mark said, "You think we *must* introduce Mary to—our friends, don't you?"

"Yes, I do. Prominent people like you and Caroline introduce their house guests. Savannahians—right or wrong—feel they have a right to know who's visiting. And the first thing they want to know about any newcomer is— family. What on earth are you going to tell them about Mary's family?"

"I don't know! I honestly don't know." He gave her a solemn look, then a weak smile. "Yes, I do. If Caroline will agree, I think we should tell them the truth, and soon. You see, I believe my son is serious about Mary."

"Serious enough to—marry her someday? Mark, he's so young!"

"Don't forget that his mother knew she loved me just after her seventeenth birthday."

"And she certainly hasn't stopped for all these years."

"That's right. Miss Eliza, could Jonathan and Mary ever live in Savannah— among our friends and acquaintances—as man and wife if people knew she's a half-blood Cherokee?"

She shook her head. "Oh, don't expect me to answer that! I—I suppose they could—after time. But how do you feel? Caroline? Could you both accept Mary as your daughter-in-law? The mother of your—quarter-blood Cherokee grandchildren?"

Mark waited, then said, "You don't mince words, do you?"

"Should I?"

"No. I could accept all that," he said in his direct way. "I could accept Mary if I knew she was the one person Jonathan loved. I can't speak for Caroline."

"You can't? Or you won't?"

"You know Caroline and I don't agree, don't see eye to eye at all about owning servants. We've rather learned to live to one side of that issue. I suppose this would be vastly different, though."

"It certainly would be! I've told you over and over that I understand both you and Caroline where owning people is concerned. But yes, a half-breed Indian becoming a part of the Browning family is nothing like that. You'd be asking Savannahians to accept a Cherokee socially because of the standing you and Caroline enjoy. Even some of our kinder folk who feel we mistreated Mary's people look down on Indians, consider them inferior savages.

I've prayed and prayed to be able to help you, Mark, but I don't know which
way you should turn."

Neither spoke for a time, then Mark took a deep breath. "Miss Eliza, my
feeling is that we should meet it head-on. Once Mary's seen Dr. Bulloch,
once we know if anything at all can be done to restore some sight in that eye,
I'm in favor of our giving a dinner party right away, with a well-planned list
of guests, and introduce her as she is, telling the whole truth."

"Will Caroline agree?"

"Your opinion will affect how she feels, I know."

"Do you think that's quite fair to me?"

"No, but wouldn't blunt honesty be fairer to Mary in the long run? When
people know the truth, isn't some of the temptation to gossip and fabricate
eliminated?"

"Some, yes. And I'm proud of you for thinking so straight." She thought
for a moment. "Of course, the fact that she had a Scottish father will help.
What did he do for a living?"

"Like Burke, he was a carpenter."

Eliza sighed. "The same people who will look down on Mary for being half
Cherokee will look down on her for having a father who worked with his
hands."

"I suppose tongues still wag because Natalie's husband works with his
hands too, even though no one here even knows Burke."

"Now and then tongues still wag about him, yes," she said, "but everyone
looks up to Natalie's parents—both her father and her mother."

Mark's laugh was ironic. "In spite of the fact that most must know by now
that Caroline's grandfather, Jonathan Cameron, fathered my own mother and
poor old Osmund Kott out of wedlock by his own indentured servant!"

"But you're one of the two wealthiest men in town," Eliza said. "Savannah
does its judging by nonsensical standards."

Mark stood to go. "Thank you for talking to me. There's no doubt life
would be far simpler had Jonathan fallen in love with a pretty, wellborn
Savannah belle, but I can promise you this—I intend to stand by those two
young people, come what may. You see, I find I genuinely care about little
Indian Mary."

"Oh, so do I." Crossing the porch with him, she added, "Will you promise
me not to push Caroline too fast? She knows Mary's true worth too, I'm sure,
but give her time, plenty of time. The Lord had something just like this in
mind when He warned us: 'Sufficient unto the day is the evil thereof.' Whatever you do, dear boy, don't borrow what might turn out to be tomorrow's
trouble. Jonathan hasn't married her yet."

Chapter 24

ELIZA Anne had never learned how to ready herself for bed at night in what she called a casual, routine way—alone. Never mind that W.H. had been gone a lot even in the first year of their marriage, when, at twenty-two, he'd been solicitor general of the whole eastern district of Georgia. The time spent away campaigning for the Georgia legislature later on helped her not at all now that he would be leaving again.

Tonight, unusually chilly for mid-September, was, even after eleven years of marriage, little different, in spite of the fact that W.H. was just downstairs at his desk in the corner of their parlor working and reworking speeches he would make after he rode away tomorrow. Less than three weeks remained before the election on October 3. As she slipped a flannel nightgown over her head, the thought struck that this could well be his last night at home before election day! Once he was traveling, she knew that another and then another opportunity to speak would surely come, and he would take them all.

Climbing into the cold bed, she tried to smile at herself as the inevitable wave of pride swept over her because her husband was, even by his opponents, considered a magnificent public speaker. His reputation for oratory had begun, actually, during his college days at Yale and later, because of his pronounced successes while still so young, had grown and grown so that, even before their marriage, he had been recommended to Chatham County as a nominee for the state legislature. W.H. refused the honor, not from fear of losing, but because even then he was a wily politician who knew he would, in the long run, gain from still wider public exposure to his talents.

She settled herself into a comfortable spot in the bed and wished her mind would settle with her body, but W.H.'s chances for success this time were too much in her thoughts. She would not sleep tonight until he climbed into the bed beside her, near enough for her to nestle her head on his shoulder.

Even then, would she be able to sleep if, once more, she put off demanding an answer to the still troubling question of exactly what had happened at the Milledgeville convention?

Oh, she knew generalities. W.H. had given her what at the time had seemed a fairly detailed account—even to the names of the final eight nominees: From Screven County, E. J. Black; from Muscogee County, M. A.

Cooper; H. A. Haralson from Troup; J. B. Lamar from Bibb; John Millen from Chatham County, which, of course, included Savannah; J. H. Lumpkin from Floyd; Howell Cobb of Clarke—and W. H. Stiles from Cass. Everyone seemed to think the list not only electable but distinguished. Of course, no one could have convinced her that any one of the nominees was a match for W.H. when it came to brains or oratory. The newspapers, especially one article which appeared in the Milledgeville *Federal Union* on September 13, 1842, declared that W.H. had made "a masterly refutation of everything his adversary had adduced." She sensed, though, that something was still troubling him.

Over and over, Eliza Anne—even the children—had listened to speech after speech, Eliza Anne often for the third or fourth time, following, as he spoke, W.H.'s careful, meticulous revisions. Even her younger son, Bobby, knew perfectly well that Georgia Democrats, and especially his father, strongly opposed the national bank and high tariffs and absolutely did not believe that sale of public lands, such as those acquired from the Indians, should be distributed to all the states. The children may not have remembered just why their father objected to a federal bank, but Eliza Anne certainly knew. As he'd campaigned that summer and early fall, W.H. had kept a scrapbook of each news account of his own appearances. She could have recited most of those clippings by heart. Often, he'd spoken against the brilliant, short-statured Alexander Stephens and against Mr. A. H. Kenan of Baldwin County. It was W.H.'s pride and joy that his criticism of Kenan's argument in favor of a federal bank had gained wide acclaim. How, Eliza Anne still wondered, could anyone have believed Whig candidate Kenan when he contended that the mere act of chartering a national bank made it constitutional, when her husband declared such an argument not only belittled the Constitution but "made it nonsense, because if constitutionality could be conferred by a mere bank charter, then it followed logically that it could be terminated by revocation of the charter."

Burke, of course, supported W.H., although Eliza Anne found Natalie's strong, patient husband less interested in politics than she'd hoped. She needed an adult with whom to discuss W.H.'s every victory and obstacle. She missed her mother terribly after her return to Savannah and longed for the day when her closest girlhood friend, Julia Barnsley, finally settled in the upcountry next year. "Now and then," she wrote to her mother, "I'd give almost anything for just one hour with you or Mark or Julia—with any of you who care and remotely understand what's going on in Georgia politics. You see, Mama, I'm still worried that something happened to hurt W.H. at the Milledgeville convention. In my heart, I know that W.H. tells me the truth, but I also *know him.* He is a proud, sensitive man and wants especially his wife to think highly of him on all accounts. Soon after he got back from Milledgeville last month, I felt—still feel—that he simply did not tell me everything. I sense somehow that in a part of the procedure there, W.H. was deeply hurt. I do not know why. I may never know, but there is something he hasn't told me and it has to do with his all-important self-esteem."

Of course, her mother wrote back with advice: "If it truly bothers you, I hope you'll make a point of asking W.H. outright. If, as you say, it seems at times to make him moody with you and the children, why not get to the bottom of it?"

Why not, indeed? she thought. I really need to find out before he leaves me tomorrow . . .

She lay listening for a footstep downstairs, a creak on the stair that would mean that in a matter of minutes he'd be coming up to bed. There was no sound beyond an owl hooting down by the river and the soft scrape of a breeze-tossed gum branch against her window, a sound that had come to be like the soothing visit of a friend during the long nights while W.H. had been gone. It was not friendly tonight. Uneasy, she tossed and wondered what on earth he could be doing downstairs that was keeping him so long. Mama would say I'm worrywarting, she told herself, and I am.

Would there always be these dreaded last nights to make love, to hold, to try to get everything said that needed to be said before he rode away again the next day? Would W.H. ever want to let go of his political ambition and actually become a gentleman planter as he kept insisting he meant to do? Here they were in the wilds of Georgia's frontier in a crowded, four-roomed frame house with only two sets of neighbors closer than the Holders across the river—with acres and acres of half-cleared and only partially planted land around them and W.H. leaving to campaign again! She thanked God that in their cabin just down the river road Natalie and Burke lay together in their bed and that behind their house Lorah Plemmons and her son, Sam, slept in beds where Mary and Ben once slept—all nearby. She would not be entirely alone when W.H. left. There was always the bright comfort of her three children, but for an instant, as she heard his steps on the stair, she felt she could *not* let him go again. W.H. was coming up the stairs carefully, wanting, she knew, not to rouse her if she was sleeping. Of course, the stairs creaked so, particularly near the top, she could picture exactly where he was, second by second. The doorknob turned slowly, slowly. He was trying so hard to be quiet that she would have laughed at him had not her heart been so heavy.

She shuddered as he began to undress, because even victory, for which she prayed, would take him away from her again—this time for months and months—all the way to Washington City! They had already decided that he would go alone at first to make all the necessary living arrangements. Someone had to remain at home in charge of the servants and the half-planted lands.

"W.H.? I'm not asleep. You know I'm not. I'm waiting for you."

"Oh, Lib," he groaned as he crawled into the bed beside her, his weary body seeming to welcome the warm place under the covers she had waiting for him. "Lib, Lib," he whispered, enfolding her in his arms, holding her so close it almost frightened her. Certainly it brought back the rush of worry over him.

But until—hands caressing, arms insisting, mouths meeting, bodies melding—their love reached and eased beyond the crescendo that almost always seemed more ecstatic than each could endure, neither spoke an intelligible word—both gasping to choke back the joy-filled pain so as not to wake the children sleeping nearby.

At last, head on his shoulder, a calm like a quiet pool in the river stilled her body, but not her mind. In her mind, she still reached toward him, still yearned to hear him tell her whatever it was that he was keeping from her.

"Not tonight, W.H.," she heard herself say in a voice she might have used with young Robert. "You're not going to avoid telling me tonight!"

"What are you talking about, Lib?" His breath was still labored, his voice husky. "What, my darling? What?"

"Something happened at the State Convention at Milledgeville last July that still bothers you. Before you leave me again tomorrow, *I have to know about it.* It's too hard being away from you to carry this worry too. Will you tell me? Will you please tell me—now?"

His sigh was so heavy, so helpless, she felt guilty. But she had asked and now surprised herself by repeating the question: "Will you please tell me what happened?"

"Yes," he said after a long silence. "Yes, Lib, I'll tell you. I've been longing to tell you, but—"

"Why didn't you?"

"I—well, I thought it would all—vanish once I'm actually elected by the people."

"What is it that would vanish after the election? What if—what if you aren't elected?"

He groaned. "I can't face even the thought of that, so don't say it again!"

"All right, I won't, but, W.H., I'm waiting to hear what happened at Milledgeville that so obviously damaged your self-respect. Do you hear me? I'm waiting!"

"I thought I was hiding it pretty well."

"You weren't." Raised on her elbow, she smoothed his forehead. "Darling, it must have been something fairly—bad. You're not the world's humblest man, nor should you be, but you've acted, especially when we've been alone for our precious few hours this summer between trips, like a—hurt little boy."

"I'm sorry."

"Don't be sorry! Just tell me what's wrong."

"I—I guess I'd better and have done with it. And now that I'm about to tell you, it may sound pretty silly."

"Nothing that hurts you could ever be silly to me."

He took a deep breath. "Well, although none of it got in the newspapers, six of the needed eight men—Black, Cooper, Haralson, Lamar, Millen and

Lumpkin—were all chosen by the committee on the first ballot." He paused. "Howell Cobb and I weren't chosen until—"

"The second ballot?"

"No. The *third.* Why, Lib? Why did my peers on that nominating committee take so long to decide on me? Especially with my old law partner and close friend Levi Da Lyon on the committee? It nearly humiliated me to death. Howell Cobb and I weren't chosen until the third ballot! And if you say it makes no difference, I'll—I'll—" He broke off. "Lib, you're not laughing at me in the dark, are you?"

"I certainly am not, but, W.H., only the most sensitive of men could possibly be insulted to have been chosen on the same ballot with a distinguished man like Mr. Howell Cobb! Doesn't that help some? Did you talk to Mr. Cobb about it at all?"

"Yes. I did."

"And what did he say?"

"Cobb paid me a great honor," he answered solemnly, so solemnly that, for the first time, Eliza Anne did smile in the dark. "Cobb said he didn't care at all, just so he had been chosen along with a gentleman of my stature. Lib, are you ashamed of me for minding so?"

"Come here," she whispered, turning and pulling him into the curve of her body. "If I didn't know how late it is and how long your ride tomorrow, I'd entice you into making love to me again just to prove that you are the handsomest, most exciting, most brilliant, most desirable gentleman on the face of the earth and that because you're so sensitive, you probably should be either a poet or a writer—or, oh, W.H., if you could be satisfied with writing and planting, you'd be here with me all the time!" She pressed close to him. "Then I'd never, never have to try to sleep at night without you. I'd have you right here to make the difficult decisions with the children, with handling our people, with planting the fields. Burke and Sam will be making lots of headway with the second wing of our house from now on. How can I take the responsibility of the problems that always come with building? I need you here!" When he lay silent, motionless, she begged, "Oh, darling, forgive me! I vowed I wouldn't complain—ever again. But I get so frightened . . ."

"So do I," he whispered. "I'm frightened too, Lib."

"You are? Why?"

"I'm so frightened I won't be—elected. God knows, I've tried to become a part of Cass County. No man up here loves his land more than I love mine, but someone is always reminding me that I should learn to drop my *g*'s, to speak in a north Georgia dialect—to act and express myself more like a farmer Democrat than a well-to-do Whig from the coast!"

"If you're even half as brilliant as I think you are," she said firmly, "or half as wise, you'll go on being William Henry Stiles. The most self-doubting, frightened W. H. Stiles is superior to any other man on the entire Democratic ticket! You'll see. Once the election results are announced and *you're* the United States congressman from Cass, all that magnificent Stiles self-confidence will rush back."

He kissed her. "You're very convincing. I beg *you* not to be—frightened at my going, though, because *I have to go,* Lib. There's no way to explain it, even to you, but I—*have* to win this election. You'll be fine here without me. Your husband's opinion of you is high too, don't forget. Burke is nearby all the time now, working right here on our home. I'm aware Natalie takes all his time otherwise, but if you need him, he'll—"

"I know, I know. And I don't mean to grumble. I did, but I didn't mean to. Everyone will try to help me, I'm sure of that. And Natalie's better company now that she's stronger. Do forgive me for feeling sorry for myself. I'm not, really. I'll be—all right, but always, always lonely for my beautiful husband, my brilliant, handsome husband, the United States congressman!" She burrowed her head into his shoulder. "And I promise to pray for Sam to be of more real help to Burke. Poor Burke does miss Ben so much. And no matter how busy you are on this trip, you must pray about that too. Promise?"

Settling himself for sleep, W.H. mumbled, "If I think of it, yes, of course, I will."

"I know I sound preachy, darling, but prayer can give you all the strength you need in these last hard weeks before the election."

"I know, I know."

"Do you—do you really?"

He laughed softly. "Yes, Eliza Mackay's daughter, I know."

Because W.H. would probably not be back at Etowah Cliffs until well after the election on October 3, he had given permission for all their people to gather along the river road in front of the house to say goodbye. He needed ninety-five or more field hands to plant the six hundred acres he'd accumulated so far, but could not afford them. As it was, the ten on loan from William Mackay, the twenty from Knightsford sold to him on delayed payment by Caroline Browning, the thirty left by Cousin Margaret in her will and twelve inherited from his own father, were all there waiting—seventy-two strong. As were the house and yard servants.

His people were standing in a half-circle when W.H., Lib and the children came out of the house. W.H. shook every hand, hugged his children, ignored the tittering and whispering as he kissed his wife as lovingly as he dared in public. Then he walked with his family toward his favorite horse, which Burke had ridden from the almost finished stable some distance downriver from the house.

"Is Natalie here yet?" Burke asked as he dismounted and handed the reins to Sam, who until then had been hanging back a little.

The Stileses all looked surprised. "Is Natalie coming too?" Lib asked.

"So she said at breakfast," Burke answered, with a noticeably proud smile. "I wanted to bring her myself, but she won, as usual."

The words were barely spoken when young Robert shouted, "Here comes

Natalie and Miss Lorah in Mary's pony cart! Look, Papa—Mama! Natalie's sitting up on that narrow little old seat just like old times."

"And she's waving," Mary Cowper gasped. "Smiling! And all dressed up in her yellow dress—look, Mama! Her first time away from her cabin!"

"I see, I see," Lib said. "W.H., she hasn't worn that yellow dress since—her baby's funeral!"

"Good sign, I'd think," he replied, interested, but obviously eager to be on the road. "Should you ride my horse to meet her, Burke?"

"I'd hate to insult Miss Lorah," Burke said, beaming. "That lady can drive a mule, don't forget. Mary's pony, Little Star, is nothing to her."

"Oh, Burke," Lib whispered. "This is a—triumphant moment, isn't it?"

He laughed softly. "More triumphant than even we realize, I'd think. Let's just wait—let them plod along by themselves. They'll be here in a minute, Mr. Stiles. Sorry to keep you, but I know this means a lot to Natalie."

The small pony cart moved toward them, over the narrow lane along the river, close enough now so that they all saw the plume of goldenrod Miss Lorah had stuck in Little Star's halter—yellow, to match Natalie's yellow dress.

Smiles were on every face as they waited and even in his eagerness to be off, W.H. was pleased with his people when they struck up a happy, quickened version of "Ham Bone, Ham Bone," livelier than north Georgia Negroes would have sung it, he knew, because most of the Stiles people came from the coast where God's pantry, the ocean, had always kept them fed. The people sang in a lively tempo too, he felt, from sheer joy that, for the first time since she lost her baby, pretty Miss Natalie was coming closer and closer in that little pony cart. W.H. smiled broadly when Miss Lorah stopped the cart nearby and Natalie jumped down, with no help, and all the young servants leaped into a ring dance.

Even before Burke got to her, W.H. hugged Natalie and thanked her for making the effort to see him off. She still looked pale, he thought, but felt only relief that she'd made the short trip. Natalie might yet be good company for Lib during his absence.

"Looky here," Lorah Plemmons shouted, beaming from the driver's side of the pony cart. "Will you all just take a look at who's here?"

"Oh, we see, we see," Lib called, her face glowing exactly as W.H. had hoped it would on his last sight of her.

"Why shouldn't I be here?" Natalie asked, her manner almost as pert as they all remembered. After she'd stopped the people dancing, hugged the Stiles children briefly, she turned to Burke, both arms out. "Hold me a minute," she ordered. "I've got quite a bit to say before Uncle W.H. goes and I need courage. Everyone else has hugged me but you, Burke. Hug me!"

W.H., resigned now to the delay in view of the happy reason for it, watched the tall, muscular young man take his wife in his arms and embrace her as unselfconsciously as though they were alone.

"That's enough," Natalie said, pushing Burke away. Then, turning to face

them all, the smile gone from her incredibly lovely face, she announced, "I'm
—back. I want every Stiles and every one of you people and Sam and Burke
to know I'm—back." A round of cheering went up, but she silenced it and
turned to face Lorah Plemmons, still beaming from the seat of the pony cart.
"Mostly, I want you to know, Miss Lorah, that I'm back because you—*let* me
come back."

The woman's good chuckle warmed W.H.'s heart, as it always had when
he took time to notice. "Well, that's my job, takin' care of you, Missy," Miss
Lorah said.

"Do you like not having to work so hard anymore, Natalie?" Mary Cowper asked.

W.H. saw Natalie's frown and wondered if his daughter had spoken out of
turn, an easy thing to do with Mark Browning's girl since she lost her baby.
"Do I like having Miss Lorah do all the hard work?" Natalie asked directly
of Mary C. as though the question had surprised her. "It's a big help, yes,
Mary Cowper, but that's not the main thing. I also liked proving I could keep
my own house."

"What is the main thing, then?" W.H. asked.

"Miss Lorah lets me be—myself and doesn't get her feelings hurt when I
am the nasty way I—sometimes am."

A murmur of amazed half-laughter moved through the crowd. W.H. and
Lib exchanged looks. W.H. and Burke exchanged looks, but almost at once,
Burke took Natalie in his arms again.

"I love you exactly the way you are," he said, "and so does Miss Lorah."

"Oh, Burke, I know you do! You'd better." Abruptly, tears began to
course down her pale cheeks. "Our—baby was your son too. We're one and
the same person."

"You are?" Henry asked, genuinely puzzled. "How could you be?"

"You're too young to understand that, Henry, and don't interrupt." Her
voice trembly, but determined, facing the others now, Natalie went on. "I'm
back, but I'll never be the same again, because I—lost our son." When Burke
tried to take her once more in his arms, she pushed him away. "No, can't you
see I'm having a hard time not crying? But I just had to say it right out—in
front of everyone that—"

"You've already done it, Natalie," Lib said tenderly. "Don't tire yourself."

"Hush, Miss Lib. I'm not finished." After wiping tears with the back of her
hand, she brushed at a wisp of shining red hair and lifted her chin. "I thought
I'd grown up all the way. I hadn't. But"—she smiled a little—"I think I'm
pretty far along. I want you all to know, though, that none of this means I'll
ever stop—being me!"

"I sure hope not," Robert interrupted. "You wouldn't be any fun if you
weren't you, Natalie."

"The big change in me is that—" Suddenly she was controlling her voice
with great difficulty. Burke slipped his arm around her waist to steady her.
"You see, the big change in me is that once I thought just because I'm me,

everything would always be the way I wanted it. Without scolding or preaching a sermon, Miss Lorah, just by telling me finally—about all she's had to bear in her own life, convinced me that—I've been wasting time grieving for Little Burke."

W.H. glanced again at Lib, who was looking at him, both wondering, he knew, what Lorah Plemmons had really told Natalie.

"Oh, I'll—never stop wanting my baby, but—after I made those sugar cookies yesterday—"

"What sugar cookies?" Robert asked.

"I wish you boys would stop interrupting me," she said, only a little cross. "I got tired listening to Miss Lorah tell me so cheerfully that if I'd just busy myself at something, I'd feel better! So I made sugar cookies and yes, you may have some. And—I do feel better. Anyway, what I decided was, once you say a thing in the presence of just about everyone you know, you—well, you think twice before you forget it yourself. For that reason, I'm telling all of you right now that, from this day on, I'll try hard to remember that Natalie Latimer isn't as special as she thought she was. Oh, I'm pretty special because you love me, Burke," she said, looking up at him. "But—terrible as it is to accept, I also know bad things happen to me too. I know that because—I—don't have my son anymore. I also hope to be able—to obey Burke by never, never blaming myself again—for our baby's death."

Lib rushed to embrace Natalie. "Dear girl, I've never been so proud of anyone as I am of you this minute!"

"Thank you, Miss Lib," she said, pulling away to look straight at W.H. "And, Uncle W.H.?"

"What is it, Natalie?"

"I hope you've listened to what I just said. Bad things do happen to everyone. You just might *lose* the election!"

W.H. stared at her in surprise, but he didn't say a word.

"Well, now, Natalie dear," Lib said quickly, "I don't think you need to—"

"Oh, yes, I do, Miss Lib," she answered. "Uncle W.H. is terribly smart and surely more qualified to be a congressman than anyone else, but he certainly can lose through no fault of his own. I think he should face that, so he won't get sick and difficult the way I did. You see, giving in to your own feelings of gloom only hurts those who love you, Uncle W.H. Isn't that right, Miss Lorah?"

Without a word, while swiping at a tear on her own cheek, Lorah Plemmons gave her a proud nod.

"Now, I know you have to ride to Cassville, Uncle W.H., so that's the end of what I had to say. I sincerely hope it helped prepare you for whatever may lie ahead."

"From what Mr. Holder says," Lorah Plemmons put in, "I don't think Mr. Stiles is gonna lose, though. Good things happen lots more often than bad things, Missy."

Some waving, others walking along slowly as though deep in thought over what they'd just heard, the people moved back toward the fields and the house. Again, W.H. hugged the children, then Natalie. He bowed to Miss Lorah, shook Burke's hand and took Lib in his arms once more.

Finally, after a silence more meaningful than words, he smiled down at her. "Wonders never cease, do they, Lib?"

"No, my darling," she whispered. "And since Natalie just gave you a small, pointed lecture, I feel you have every right to request of her that she, not I, write to her worried parents, giving them the same speech we've just heard."

In his most eloquent, gallant manner, W.H. made his request of Natalie, who startled them all by casually promising to do exactly as he'd asked.

When he mounted his horse and galloped away toward Cassville, W.H. was smiling to himself as the chorus of four voices—Lib's, Robert's, Henry's and Mary Cowper's—shouted for as long as he could hear: "You're going to win! You're going to win!"

Chapter 25

"IF IT'S possible," Caroline said to Mark at dinner in late October, "I feel both happy for Eliza Anne and so, so sorry for her!"

"How can you feel sorry for her? W.H. would have been hard to live with if he *hadn't* won the election."

"I agree, but nothing is as hard as being away from the man you love." She reached to touch his hand. They were having midafternoon dinner alone today because Jonathan, for the first time on his daily visit to Sheftall Sheftall, had taken Mary along. "I'm glad you aren't interested in politics, dearest," she said. "I am blessed. Except for your very occasional trips North and that one long-ago voyage to the Liverpool market, you're always here—with me."

"The Twenty-eighth Congress doesn't convene until early December of 1843. Eliza Anne and W.H. will be together for over a year. And she plans to take the children and live in Washington City, doesn't she?"

"Eventually, yes," Caroline said, "but who knows how long it will take for him to find suitable rooms, to handle all his mysterious congressional affairs. I just hope Eliza Anne and the children don't have to travel to Washington alone."

Maureen served their dessert and when she returned to the kitchen, Mark asked, "Do you wonder how Jonathan and Mary are getting along with old Sheftall?"

"All right, I'm sure," she said, knowing full well she didn't sound convincing.

Caroline had known Mark would bring up Indian Mary sooner or later. And yes, to Caroline's mind, the girl was still *Indian* Mary. She'd broken herself of the habit of actually speaking of her that way because she'd honestly been ashamed of herself—as she was ashamed now for not having introduced Mary after all these weeks to Savannah society. Oh, Dr. Bulloch had allowed a month's plausible respite during which time he was examining and diagnosing Mary's bad eye. That excuse no longer held. The diagnosis had been given. Mary would never have improved eyesight. Caroline had stalled as long as possible. The dinner party must be given soon, next week, because Jonathan was due at Yale College in a little over a fortnight and Mary would go back to Cass County.

"I've jotted down a partial guest list for Mary's dinner party," Mark said, as though he'd read her every thought. "We simply must give the party, darling," he went on, reaching into an inside pocket for the list.

"I know, I know," she said, her nervousness plainly showing.

"And don't berate yourself—even to yourself—for worrying," Mark said. "No amount of gossip can really hurt us, can it? We know who we are. What harm can a few wagging tongues possibly do?"

"Mark, Jonathan hasn't said one word to us about ever *marrying* her!"

Caroline could no more help the sharp edge in her voice than she could help cringing at the thought of actually telling Savannahians that their son was in love with a half-breed Cherokee. Her eyes were on the compote of custard in front of her, but she felt Mark studying her and looked up.

"Darling, I know our son hasn't said he means to get married any time soon and you know I'm perfectly aware of what people might—will say about Mary's lack of education, family background, her odd way of speaking. I know your dread of that." He paused. "I also know something of what Tocqueville meant by the 'tyranny of public opinion' in America. I live day in and day out doing my best to avoid that 'tyranny' right here in Savannah because I refuse to own slaves, yet love the city with all my heart."

A deep frown creased Caroline's forehead. "Do we have to go into that?" she demanded.

"Of course not. I know too, as do you, of Mary McDonald's intrinsic worth —the fineness of her nature. You're not married to a dunce, Caroline. You're married to me."

Slowly, a real smile replaced her frown. She held out her hand. "Let me see your guest list, dear. Please? And—forgive me for being afraid of your Monsieur Alexis de Tocqueville's 'tyranny.' Just forgive me, Mark, and go on trying to be patient."

Carefully, she began to run down the list of names. The Mackays were all there, of course, and the John Millens. Mr. Millen, she knew, had just been elected to Congress from Chatham County on the same slate with W.H. Mark had also included their kind, intellectual friend William Thorne Williams, the much-beloved mayor of Savannah, but His Honor was away. Too bad, she thought. Mayor Williams would be generous about Mary's Cherokee blood and odd speech. There also, leaping from the page like danger signs, were the names of Mr. and Mrs. Samuel Potter. Bertha Potter's tongue was the original two-edged sword!

"I can see you're objecting to the Potters," Mark said. "Don't you agree, though, that they'll be the ultimate test? If she can charm Bertha Potter, we have nothing to worry about."

"I don't worry about Mary's charm or lack of it! I'm fond of her too. It's just the terrible strangeness. Most of these guests haven't even been in the old Cherokee Nation! They have no idea how different it is up there where Mary grew up."

When he made no comment, she scanned the remainder of the list. The

Mercers were there. All right, she thought. They're warm and most civil and certainly prominent. "I think Mrs. W. W. Gordon a good choice," she said. "She and Miss Eliza are so close, I don't worry about her acceptance of Mary. At least, Sarah Gordon's too much a lady to gossip, no matter how shocked she may be at Jonathan's—taste."

Mark remained silent for what, to her, seemed an unbearably long time. When he spoke finally, his words were measured. "Caroline, would you have married me anyway even if the true story of my mother's illegitimate birth by Jonathan Cameron and his indentured servant, Mary Cotting, had been common Savannah gossip?"

"Of course I'd have married you! Jonathan Cameron was my grandfather too, even if we didn't know it when we fell in love."

"But *my* lovely young mother was illegitimate. Your father was the legitimate son of old Jonathan Cameron by his legal wife, Ethel."

"That's enough," she said shortly. "You're twisting things all out of proportion. You and I *were* both educated young people—and from well-bred Anglo-Saxon families!"

Again, he looked at her for a long time. His gaze made her squirm until Mark's irresistible smile softened his face.

"What's so funny?" she asked.

"I was just thinking how mysterious, how unexplainable real love is. How its arrival on any scene can change things."

"Can cause trouble?"

"Yes, it can and often does. But at my advanced age, I think I'm finally beginning to learn that there are a few areas where people have to bow—to mystery. Our son loves a half-breed Indian girl. You and I don't have to understand it. We do have to accept it." He folded his linen napkin. "Wouldn't you give almost anything to know exactly how things are going at Sheftall's house right now? Jonathan's spent time with him every day since we got back from Cass. It must have taken a lot of self-discipline not to take Mary along weeks ago."

"Well, he took her today," she said drily.

"The old gentleman does *not* care for Indians. They fought with the British during our revolution. How I'd love to be a mouse in the corner of Sheftall's bedroom this minute!"

"That's funnier than you intended," she said. "Mr. Sheftall does have mice! He told me last week when I stopped by."

On a straight chair near Sheftall's familiar armchair by the window that looked out onto West Broughton Street, Jonathan had been reading from the *Georgian,* dated October 26, for over an hour. As usual, Sheftall Sheftall listened, but with few comments today, and Jonathan fully expected the old gentleman to object because he was reading faster than usual. He felt certain Sheftall had detected his apprehension, and why not? His elderly friend didn't know it, but Mary was waiting downstairs in the musty old parlor where Sheftall's servant, Mordecai, had seated her. Of course, it would take Sheftall time to digest and discuss what Jonathan had read of the recent general election, in which "the entire Democratic slate was victorious by an average margin of 2,314 votes," and he honestly wondered if he would be able to wait today for Mr. Sheftall's ponderous commentary.

Finished at last with the long account of the election, Jonathan began his wait, while Sheftall thought for a time.

Finally, he spoke: "Well, I see that Uncle W. H. Stiles, as you call him, came in fifth in the voting results. The man is soundly elected from Cass County to represent the people in the Twenty-eighth Congress. Being neither a rabid Democrat nor a rabid Whig, I'm unconcerned, but if my memory serves, this is the first time one party, namely the Democrats, has elected an entire congressional ticket since 1834—eight years. And that is all I have to say by way of analysis today, because something is different in you, boy. I sense it. Are you ready to tell me what it is?"

Dumbfounded, though half expecting the old fellow to know, Jonathan gave him a weak smile. "Wouldn't you like me to read the city council resolution honoring you—before I tell you?"

"Before you leave, of course. Not yet. The cause of your uneasiness first, please."

"Well, sir, there's someone here with me. She's—waiting downstairs in your parlor."

Sheftall rubbed the gray stubble on his chin. "She? Did your mother come with you? Miss Eliza Mackay?"

"No, sir. I brought the young lady I hope to marry someday, once I've finished my four years at Yale College. I don't mind telling you that—four years seems an awfully long time to wait too."

"Such a long time that I could well be dead."

"I certainly hope not!"

"You brought your young intended today expecting my approval, I take it, just in case I am dead in four years."

Determined, as always, not to permit his friend to edge over into a dark mood because of his advancing age, Jonathan laughed. "Oh, no. I brought her because I wanted to give you a treat! Mary too. I'm proud of your friendship and I enjoy impressing Mary."

"Mary, eh? Mary what?"

"McDonald," Jonathan said.

For a few seconds, Sheftall toyed in his mind with the name. "McDonald . . . can't think of a single prominent McDonald in town."

"She isn't from Savannah. I met her when my parents and I were visiting Natalie in the upcountry."

"Then that would make her the daughter of a settler from another part of Georgia or another state, most likely. Perhaps a wealthy planter, as your Uncle W.H. considers himself, cash or no cash in his pocket. Or perhaps a plain North Carolina or Virginia farmer."

"No, sir."

"No, sir—what, son? Who was her father, McDonald?"

"A Scottish carpenter. A pretty good one, I'd guess, considering how skilled Mary's brother, Ben, was. He was Burke Latimer's right-hand helper. They built a cottage in Cassville first, then two stores, a new church, and were just about ready to start the second wing of the Stiles house when Ben died."

"Sorry to hear. Her brother must have been young to die."

"He was. Somewhere in his middle twenties, I think."

"Sickly family, eh?"

Jonathan frowned, but answered evenly. "No, sir. Ben McDonald shot himself the same day they buried Natalie's little son."

"Suicide, to my knowledge, is not characteristic of the Scots," Sheftall said. "Scots tend toward courage."

Jonathan weighed his response this time. Of course, he meant to tell Mr. Sheftall that Mary was a half-blood but actually saying the words was harder than he'd expected. "You see, sir, Ben wasn't entirely of Scottish blood. His mother was a full-blood Cherokee. I'm sure that has nothing to do with why poor Ben did what he did, though."

Sheftall removed his spectacles, exhaled deliberately on each lens, smeared at them a little with a soiled handkerchief, took a long time stuffing the handkerchief back into his jacket sleeve, then said, "Never cared much for Indians. They fought with the British during my war."

"So you've told me," Jonathan said. "But from what I know of the Cherokees, they were intelligent, courageous people. I know my Mary is. For years before they were driven off their land, their chieftains tried bravely to reason with our federal government—right up to the last minute. They published their own bilingual newspaper called *The Phoenix*. They even went so far as to pattern their government along similar lines to ours."

"More along the lines of the British than ours," the old man corrected him, his face showing Jonathan almost nothing. "The fact that Mary's half-Indian brother shot himself shows cowardice."

"I'm not sure about that. I think it was hopelessness. Mama believed Ben was really in love with my sister. Mary now says she knew it too. If ever there was a hopeless situation, that was!"

"Where is Miss Mary Cherokee? Did you say she's in my parlor?"

"Yes, sir. Shall I call her?"

"By all means. Haven't seen my parlor in months. Last year's dust covers every inch of it, so far as I know."

At the bedroom door, Jonathan called back pleasantly, "Mary and I signal each other with a special whistle she used after the removal, when she and her brother, Ben, were living in a cave. It's a winter sparrow's whistle."

He waited briefly to see if mention of a cave might bring a change of expression on his friend's face. It didn't. Sheftall merely nodded and kept his eyes fixed on the sunny street outside.

From the hallway, Jonathan gave the high, shrill three-toned whistle, and before he was halfway down the stairs to meet her, he heard Mary's soft, quick steps in the hall below. Smiling down at her, he whispered, "He's waiting for you."

Hand in hand, he reclimbed the stairs with her and gave her the smile he couldn't help giving Mary. "Don't worry."

"I should be scared?" she asked softly.

"No." He laughed. "Not of Mr. Sheftall. Just expect him to say exactly what he's thinking and also to tell you the whole truth."

"As Miss Lorah says, 'he does not palaver?'"

"Nor does he mince words. If he likes you, he likes you all the way and he'll make it plain."

"He will like me?"

"He'd better. Just in case he fools me, which he certainly does at times, I'll just make up for it by liking you all the more."

Her smile of confidence made his knees feel weak. "Besides like, you also *love* me, Jonathan."

Outside Sheftall's door, he gave her a quick squeeze. "That's right. I love you with all my heart."

"That be so good!"

"That *is* so good," he corrected her.

"That *is so* good," she repeated after him. "I remember. I try hard to remember."

When Jonathan introduced her to Sheftall, he waited for the small curtsy he knew she'd make. This time, Mary's curtsy was unusually pretty, deeper than usual, and when the old man extended his gnarled hand, she leaned to kiss it lightly, something Jonathan had never seen a woman do.

"Well, good day to you, Miss Mary," Sheftall said, surprise plain even in his dim old eyes. "I've kissed a few ladies' hands in my day. No lady ever kissed mine before."

"I am wrong to do that?" she asked in her guileless way, and then added quickly, "I am glad to be meeting Mr. Sheftall Sheftall, a gentleman of great honor."

"Well! I believe you are, little lady, and I thank you! Could I but stand without Jonathan's help, I should bow from the waist."

"I help you to stand," she offered brightly.

He silenced her with his hand. "Thank you, no. But speaking, as you did, of honor, perhaps you'd care to listen while Jonathan reads aloud, as he does daily, the splendid resolution from the city council concerning me."

Relieved that he had explained all about Sheftall's lifted spirits each time he heard the resolution excusing him of all future and back taxes, Jonathan cleared his throat, about to begin, when Mary clapped her hands.

"Oh, please, Mr. Sheftall! Please to let me hear him read it!" she cried.

Reciting from memory, but with the paper in his hand, Jonathan felt he performed rather better than usual. Even the well-worn resolution sounded fresh and new with Mary listening. When he'd finished, Sheftall waited cannily for her comment. She looked uneasily first at Jonathan and then at the old man.

"Except for Chief John Ross," she whispered in awe, "I never know—*knew* —such an honored man before you, sir."

"And who, pray tell, is John Ross?" Sheftall asked, only a bit insulted that anyone else had come to her mind.

"He was a great man," Mary explained. "Eighth-blood Cherokee only, but with a full-blood wife, Quatie. She die on long march from our homeland."

A little clumsily, Jonathan felt, the old gentleman cleared his throat, coughed, then said only, "I see."

Plainly Sheftall was trying hard to readjust his long-held opinion of Indians. "Struggling" might be a better word, Jonathan thought. He longed for these two—both so dear to him—really to like each other, so he decided to trust them together with no help from him.

Abruptly, Mary knelt beside Sheftall's worn chair and looked up at him. "To be Cherokee—is bad to you? You will tell me the truth?"

Using both hands, Sheftall crossed and uncrossed his short, stiff legs. "Uh —to be Indian is bad?" he repeated her question.

"I do not speak so good," she said, as always, showing no embarrassment, just stating a fact.

Jonathan had noticed, especially since they'd been together in Savannah, that her English became more halting when something made her uncertain.

"You have a superb teacher in Jonathan Browning," Sheftall assured her. "Tell me, Miss Mary, how many people in Savannah know you are a Cherokee half-blood?"

Jonathan swallowed hard. He'd hoped his old friend might be a bit less harsh, a bit more helpful to Mary. Still, he meant to leave the two of them to work their ways out of the difficult predicament.

Mary gave Jonathan a questioning look, then turned her gaze back to Mr. Sheftall. "You think I am ugly because of my scarred cheek, sir? Because I squint some in my bad eye to look straight into your face?"

Jonathan and his father had said often that neither of them had ever seen Sheftall at a loss for words. Jonathan suppressed a smile. Mary had come very close to besting him this minute with a question which must have been almost as disconcerting to the old patriot as his had been to her.

"Uh—you *ugly?*" Sheftall asked, his voice suddenly unsteady. Then gathering his wits rather quickly, he asked, "Do you honestly think, young lady, that my fine friend here would fall in love with any but a beautiful woman?" As though surrendering to her already, Sheftall took a deep breath and slumped down a little in his chair, palms upward and open on his knees.

"I admit I don't see too well anymore," Sheftall went on. "But well enough, I assure you, to recognize a beautiful face! I noticed only a quite becoming scar and no squint whatever."

Bless him, Jonathan thought. Bless them both. He'd been right to trust them to each other.

"But you have ignored my question to you," Sheftall went on. "Who in this city of money-grubbing, self-appointed aristocrats knows you're a Cherokee half-blood?"

Mary countered by repeating her earlier question which Sheftall had ignored. "To be Indian is so bad? I will work later to say that better, sir," she promised. "But you will answer first?"

Actually squirming in his chair now, the old man repeated the evasive procedure of repolishing his spectacles.

Eyeglasses back in place, he said slowly. "Miss Mary, listen and do not interrupt, please."

Still kneeling beside his chair, she nodded eagerly. "You talk," she said.

"Jonathan here knows that I am a fair-minded man. That I am a man who believes wholeheartedly in not making judgments upon any group of persons —be it by race, religion, politics, wealth or lack of it. Jonathan and his father both know that I make a sincere effort to judge each man, each lady, on his or her own merits. *Individual* merits. I fought for liberty for each and every person. I think only in terms of—individuals. So you see, my dear, there is no way I can answer your surprising question."

Mary was waiting in apparent rapt attention for him to go on. Jonathan knew he'd finished. He also felt that Sheftall had quite successfully wormed his way out of that one. The old man was sitting up a little straighter now, not quite so totally surrendered to Mary's charms and somewhat picked up by his own artful dodging. So picked up, in fact, that he pursued his own unanswered question with her.

"You have not yet told me who else in this city of finely honed tongues knows you're part Cherokee and, more important, that the only male heir of prominent, wealthy Mark Browning finds you attractive." In case Mary was ready to respond, he lifted a hand to halt her momentarily. "I might insert here, for your edification and for your vanity, young lady, that in all the seventeen years in which I've known and revered young Jonathan Browning, I've never observed that he has even looked sidewise at another girl. Now, who else knows and don't circumvent this time!"

Once more, she looked at Jonathan, almost begging for help. Perhaps it was time he stepped in. "No one else knows, sir, except my parents and the Mackays," he said firmly. "But the happy times Mary and I have had roaming the city alone are about to end. You see, I feel sure my parents have decided to give a dinner party in Mary's honor, to present her to certain people in Savannah society. Does that answer your question, sir?"

After some thought, Sheftall nodded. "Yes. Yes, it does. Of course, I've known a bit of your father's conflict with your mother, Jonathan, over this very dinner party. I've understood them both in the conflict. Your father's direct way of doing things is one of his most admirable traits. Your mother's family background, in particular the haughty influence of her grandmother, Ethel Cameron, causes her to worry, far more than even she thinks she should, over what people might say."

Mary, Jonathan could tell, was lost in Sheftall's convoluted speech. He, Jonathan, could only stare at his friend in both surprise and amusement. Sly old fox, he thought. His short legs may be stiff, but not his brain. Both parents had confided the dilemma to Sheftall without telling Jonathan! Well, why not? They'd both known him for years and among the three there was strong respect. Perhaps Sheftall, with his seemingly straightforward questions today, was testing Jonathan. Undoubtedly, he was testing Mary. For just an instant, Jonathan felt annoyed at that. The annoyance vanished almost as quickly as it came.

"I'm a Jew," Sheftall was saying to Mary. "You're a Cherokee and I'm a Jew. You find me honorable. I find you pretty and I also find you almost entirely guileless. Good. Your forebears were dead wrong to fight with the British during the War for Independence, but you and Jonathan and I are living today in these modern times. I say we let bygones be bygones and as long as the Lord God sees fit to keep me on this earth in this city, you both have in me a staunch supporter and friend."

With all his heart, Jonathan believed the old man, and his relief was enormous. Savannahians—some, certainly—*would* be cruel to Mary. It was enough for his own need now, though, that Sheftall Sheftall had surrendered his prejudice against Indians. At least where one sweet Cherokee girl was concerned.

Chapter 26

ENSCONCED on the porch of the Mackay house, Kate Mackay, sewing basket on a table beside her, rocked impatiently as she waited for her sister Sarah to return from shopping at Price and Mallery's. As usual, Sarah was late and after promising faithfully to be back by ten this morning with the new pale blue ruching Kate wanted to sew inside the brim of her navy-blue winter bonnet. She rocked faster. Sarah was also to bring material for a new collar and cuffs to brighten Kate's blue silk dress and a length of gray velvet to line her new shoulder mantle she intended to wear to the Brownings' dinner party—if they gave it.

I should have gone myself, Kate thought, still rocking, but with Mama not feeling too well, I'd hoped to be able to trust Sister with at least that much shopping.

To pass the time, Kate rummaged in her sewing basket and, for once, found just a pair of William's socks, a hole in the toe of only one. Kate so loved her younger brother that even darning for him was pleasant. Most people adored Captain Jack Mackay, handsome and always so lighthearted, people invariably mentioned him before William, but somewhere down inside Kate, there had always run a deep river of love and concern for quiet, thoughtful William. Here, she and Sarah certainly differed. She knew her sister respected William, but even as a child, Sarah had picked at him for every little thing, her reason being only that she was sure William's face would crack if he allowed himself to laugh. Oh, Sarah had been kind and quite sympathetic when William had lost his family at sea, but once he'd sold Causton's Bluff and moved back home to live, it was Sarah who'd decided exactly when it was time for William to "stop moping around."

The mended sock rolled neatly into its mate, Kate tucked the pair back into her sewing basket and checked her pendant watch. Nearly eleven o'clock! What on earth was Sarah doing all this time? Had she disobeyed their mother and stopped by the Browning house, unable to wait another day to find out if they were entertaining for Indian Mary in town at a formal dinner party or, as Jonathan had urged, at the Brownings' Knightsford plantation out on the Savannah River? Naturally, all the Mackays were invited either place and, of course, they did need to know how to dress, but if everyone else on the guest list had to wait to find out, surely Sarah could hold her horses too.

Trying to calm herself by folding her hands in her lap and resting her head on the high-backed wooden rocker, Kate thought about the poor Brownings, especially Caroline, who desperately wanted to do the right, loving thing by Indian Mary, but whose upbringing had caused her to put the whole affair off all fall. So long after Dr. Bulloch had given his hopeless diagnosis, that there was nothing to be done for Mary's half-blind eye. Mama was right to believe that Caroline's procrastination had only made the town more curious, had started tongues wagging, even more than they might have had people found out the truth about Mary's Cherokee blood right off. When people were kept in the dark about something, they simply made up what they didn't know. With her own ears, at the market last week, Kate had heard someone say that in spite of her brown curly hair and quite fair skin, little Mary McDonald was part Negro—a light, light-skinned mulatto from New Orleans! She shook her head, wondering which would stir up the town more—thinking Mary was a mulatto or finding out that she was really a half-blood Cherokee.

She pitied poor, gentle Jonathan too, who begged that a picnic be held at Knightsford because "Mary feels so much more at home outside." Young as he was, Kate had no doubt at all that Jonathan knew the danger, sensed the trouble that could lie ahead for them all should he actually marry the girl and bring her to Savannah to live. She felt for Mark too, who had wanted to present Mary to Savannah society soon after she arrived. But one thing and then another had provided Caroline with excuses for putting it off. First Mary's appointment with Dr. Bulloch, then the need to buy her a wardrobe of proper city clothes, then the damaging gale in early October which had literally inundated Hutchinson Island just across the river from Factor's Walk and caused cancellation of numerous other city events. The Ogeechee River plantations had been far more damaged by the heavy rains and gale winds than had those on the Savannah River, but a picnic at the Browning planta-tion would have been out of the question earlier. Now, though, Caroline's stalling time was over. Jonathan would take a boat north to Yale College next week and Mary a train back to the upcountry.

Kate herself certainly felt warmly toward Indian Mary and marveled at her ongoing cheerfulness amidst such upsetting changes in her young life. Partic-ularly disturbing was the suicide death of the last member of her family only last spring, since every other family friend and relative had either died on the long march west or lived now far west of the Mississippi. Here Mary was in the eye of what could build into a storm of Savannah gossip, having to learn how to walk in dress slippers, to sit down in the elegant, extended skirts of the two new silk gowns William had insisted upon buying for Mary because she and her brother, Ben, had once saved William's life when he'd been robbed in the wilds of the old Cherokee Nation back in 1838. Now, just after Mary had found Jonathan, he'd be leaving for Yale College and the lonely girl would have to go back to life in an old log cabin.

Probably, Kate thought, Mary might even be relieved to escape Savannah, but she'd never known anyone to be jerked around from what amounted to one whole strange world to another so fast. Mary might be scared to death, she thought, but she certainly doesn't show it. Of course, she makes mistakes —curtsies too often, mixes up her English when she speaks—but she keeps smiling. And she tries. Oh, how she tries.

Kate was checking her watch again at the very moment she saw Sarah, arms loaded with bundles, appear around the corner by the tall stand of palmettos. "It's about time," Kate called.

"Never mind the scolding," Sarah called back. "I found out! Wait till you hear. The Brownings are giving a dinner party *in town*. I think they'll be sorry," she said, hurrying up the front walk. "Mary will have a far harder time knowing how to conduct herself shut up in those elegant rooms, but they're afraid of more bad weather at Knightsford and Jonathan finally relented."

Kate jumped up to help with the bundles as her sister climbed the front steps. "Did you see Jonathan and Mary today? Mama told you not to go by the Brownings'! Did you get my velvet? Is it a warm gray?"

"I got it and it's a *good* gray and no, I didn't see either Mary or Jonathan. Caroline says Jonathan keeps her outside a lot." Dumping the remaining bundles on a chair, she asked, "Kate, do you suppose Indian Mary knows which fork to use—when?"

"She's as smart as she is pretty, if you ask me, scar and all," Kate said firmly. "And she's beeen eating at the Brownings' table all summer and fall. Stop stewing!"

"Well, I'll tell you one thing, I'm *not* stewing half as much as Caroline! Kate, it must be awful to be so honestly humiliated by someone you care about as deeply as Caroline Browning obviously cares about Indian Mary. She does care about her. Caroline has come to love Mary!"

"Have they set a date for the dinner party?"

"Next Wednesday, November 2, and poor Jonathan has to take a boat north to Yale the very next day! And, Sister, maybe worst of all, Mark insists upon inviting the Potters—something about meeting the enemy head-on. He knows, of course, that Bertha Potter will do all she can to make Mary stick out like a sore thumb. I almost wish we didn't have to go."

Busily opening the package of gray velvet, Kate scoffed, "You know you can't wait. Oh, thank you so much—the velvet is exactly the gray I wanted!"

"I'm glad," Sarah said, her mind no longer on her shopping. "William and I both think Mary could fool everybody by doing just fine."

"William doesn't know Bertha Potter as well as I do!"

"She'll try to fuss Mary, of course. Don't forget I know Bertha too, but I also know Jonathan. There's a depth of strength in his Mary that doesn't always meet the eye or he wouldn't be so taken with her."

"Being strong doesn't help one bit where lack of breeding is concerned.

I've come to be as fond of Mary as you, Kate, but Indians are—Mary is—at least part savage. How's this blue ruching?"

"Fine, thank you. Mary's *not* a savage. Her father was a Scot, don't forget."

"Well, I know a few Scots in this town who wouldn't know one fork or spoon from another, believe me." On the edge of her chair abruptly, Sarah gasped, "Kate! What if the word has gotten around town that Mary's brother shot himself?"

"How could it? No one knows but our family and the Brownings."

"But we've discussed it at dinner lots of times. You know how nigras are. What if one of ours heard us and put it out on their grapevine?"

"Put what out on what grapevine?" William asked, slipping up on them from the front walk.

"William, do you have to creep around like that?" Sarah demanded.

"Not creeping," William said mildly as he climbed the steps to the porch. "What's got you so riled up this time, Sarah?"

"Nothing for you to worry about, William," Kate said. "Sister's just borrowing trouble for the Brownings and Indian Mary."

"Guess you heard about the dinner party at Mark's place next week," William said. "Does that have anything to do with your grapevine, Sarah?"

"It most certainly does! I feel so sorry for Indian Mary, I don't know what to do. That will be her last night with Jonathan before he leaves for school and only heaven knows what a dreadful mess that dinner party might turn out to be!"

"I always thought Maureen was a fine cook, even if she is white and Irish," William said from the doorway in the even, teasing voice that sharpened Sarah's tongue. "And if you're worried about little Mary McDonald not knowing how to conduct herself—just stop. Mary will make mistakes in English, no matter how hard she tries. She might even knock a long-stemmed goblet over, like I did at our table last week, but she'll be all right. Wait and see. She'll be Mary and that's more than enough."

"But how could she really know etiquette?" Sarah asked. "Burke found her living in a cave!"

From inside the entrance hall, William called, "That was just temporary housing. I'm more at home with Mary than most people I've known in my entire thirty-eight years."

"That, sir," Sarah called after him, "says very little for poor Mary. Your table manners, in spite of Mama's efforts, never matched Jack's!"

Chapter 27

O N THE night before the dinner party, Mary lay awake a long time, trying to sort things out, feeling happy in her heart because Jonathan loved her, but struggling with all her might not to be afraid or too sad. There had been so much to feel sad and afraid about this year. The worst sorrow she had ever imagined had actually happened. More than five years ago, in the weeks and months after she and Ben had escaped from the stockade at Spring Place, Mary had known many bad dreams from fear that her brother might meet with danger—might drown swimming a river while hunting their food, or worse, that a white man could mistake him for a thief and shoot him. Now, Ben, for a reason she still could not understand, had killed himself!

She twisted her slender body in the big, soft bed, unable, for the life of her, to find a way to fix her arms and legs so that she would drop off to sleep. Asleep, the night would fly past here in faraway Savannah, but day after tomorrow, she would have to say goodbye to Jonathan. Jonathan . . .

I say to you, Jonathan, she spoke to him in her thoughts, I *not so afraid* to be sitting at that long, gleaming table before strangers who are friends of your parents. I am a little afraid I will not act right among all those spoons and goblets and forks and important people, but *not* afraid like seeing you go.

Why do they come to examine a nobody like me? she asked herself. Do not lie to yourself, Merry Willow, she scolded. You know they come because you live in a part of Georgia which to them is called "wild frontier."

In the dark, she frowned. What did they mean by "wild"? Her lifelong friends, the rabbits and deer and possums and coons, even snakes, were creatures of the wild to her, but even though her "wild" was the same word as theirs, her skin prickled when even Jonathan's kind parents used "wild" as Mary supposed with a strange Savannah meaning. Oh, she was nervous, all right, and again fighting sharp sorrow over Ben. Sorrow that could still almost stop her heart each time she let herself remember that good, loving, gentle Ben had caused a bullet to tear into his own head and he lay there, on this night, shriveling, she was sure, rotting inside the perfect box Mister Burke had made for his body. The beloved brown body which would never run again or leap even one more berry hoop. She shuddered at the thought of Ben's strong hands folded forever across his chest. She had so loved and depended on those hands, had so easily placed in them her very life—but one forefinger of Ben's right hand had pulled the trigger and he lay dead, first across Natalie's son's grave, now in his own.

Why? Why had Ben pulled that trigger? *Why?*

Mister Burke would be dear to her heart forever for all the goodness he'd given to her and Ben, but he belonged to Jonathan's sister, Natalie, and since the first time her own eyes met Jonathan's, from the depths of her being, Mary had given Mister Burke to Natalie forever.

Almost all of every day since she'd begun to love Jonathan, she had feared life without Ben a little less. But now—this minute—because Jonathan would have to leave her on the day after tomorrow, she was afraid again. Back in Cass once more without Jonathan beside her, Ben would somehow be more absent than before. Oh, Ben—*why?* Somehow she must smother the question. Ben could not answer.

Tears wet the fine, smooth pillow where her head lay. Tomorrow evening, when all those strangers—"Savannah's most prominent people"—would be watching her, was to be her very last evening with Jonathan before he boarded a big boat to leave for a school called Yale College. "This is our last full day alone together, sweet Mary," he'd said in the late afternoon today, just before darkness fell over Savannah's flat land and wide river and plain, rustling marshes. "I'm sorry, Mary, but sometimes things just don't work out right. I'm so sorry Mama and Papa couldn't agree to have their dinner party earlier, but I'll ask them to leave us alone in the family drawing room after the dinner guests leave."

A great sadness swept over her again as high and heavy as the Atlantic Ocean waves the day Jonathan took her in one of his father's boats out into the sea for her first look at so much water all at once. A vast stretch of rolling blue-gray water with no banks anywhere and almost angry waves pushing in to be sucked back across the sand where she and Jonathan sometimes stood. Mary had felt little and nearly lost beside the water. She had not been lost, though, because they stood holding hands. Jonathan's hand in hers right now would calm the sadness . . . the fresh fear.

Many moons ago, when she and Ben still lived happily with only Mister Burke, before Natalie found him, Mary remembered how in the dark night, she would long even for a touch from Mister Burke—even a glimpse of his strong forearm flung across the covers of his bed in the next room. She would leave her own bed to slip in to him, hoping he just might need her to do even one small thing to please him. Her heart raced. Jonathan lay this minute in his room just above where she lay in Natalie's girlhood bed! She knew how to take soundless steps. No one in the big Browning mansion would hear if she crept up the stairs and went to Jonathan for even one minute alone with him. Still, she had been in Savannah long enough by now to know that if she did that, somehow it would be *bad.* "Savannahians don't do this—Savannahians don't do that, Mary. Civilized society does this and this alone—never that." Miss Caroline, Jonathan's beautiful mother, always spoke in the kindest way while trying to teach her; appeared almost embarrassed to be trying. Why? Mary wondered. And felt afraid again because she had no idea how she would know what is right at the "civilized" dinner party so as not to make Miss Caroline ashamed of her.

"Well," she whispered, to console herself, "Jonathan won't be ashamed of me! Jonathan loves Mary McDonald. He also loves Merry Willow! He tell me so a hundred times. He will not make fun of me if I turn my head too far in order to see the person who will sit beside my bad eye." Her fingers touched one cheek. "Jonathan even loves my—scar. Tomorrow evening will end and he will kiss my scar when his parents leave us alone in the drawing room . . ."

Why, she wondered for the first time, did they call the room where people sat together a—drawing room? Ben drew pictures with flint on the walls of their cave on sunny days and they looked for all the world just like a horse or a cow or a squirrel when he finished, but they'd never thought of their cave as a place to draw. She'd remember to ask Jonathan when all the strangers had gone home tomorrow night.

Oh, they wouldn't all be strange to her. Even though Miss Eliza Mackay, so loved by everyone, did not feel well enough to come, gentle, kind Mr. William Mackay would be there and he and Mary had been friends for a long time. Mr. Mackay's two sisters, Miss Sarah and Miss Kate, were coming too and even though Mary didn't know them well, they must be kind to be Mister William's sisters. As was Miss Lib. Mary loved Jonathan's parents too. Not once since she'd been what they called their "honored house guest" had she failed to hug each good night. Mr. Browning hugged her back the most, but Miss Caroline sometimes even kissed Mary's hair lightly at bedtime.

For just a flicker of time, she had the small worry again, that maybe Jonathan's mother didn't really want her to be there. But the fleeting worry vanished almost as fast as a night sky blackened again after lightning flashed across it. Jonathan had said that he wished his mother had not waited so long to entertain for Mary and a few times she'd seen a kind of disappointed look on Jonathan's face when he glanced at his pretty mother, but putting off the party so that now it could be called a "departure party" for Jonathan too had certainly not bothered Mary. She could never live long enough to be with Jonathan all she wanted. If his mother had entertained more, they wouldn't have had all those days and evenings alone.

Sometime later, sitting straight up in the bed, Mary felt as though she must have slept for a long time, maybe through the whole night. But then, the big polished clock in the corner of the front hall downstairs struck just once. She'd slept, but only for a few minutes! Long enough, though, for this first waking moment to seem like sun shining right in her face. The instant of sleep had brought her the gift of a dream. She had, in her dream, just relived the evening in their old cabin near Cassville when Mister Burke, maybe four years ago, had called Mary from washing their supper dishes to tell her and

Ben, for the first time, that he loved the beautiful, flame-haired Natalie Browning—that he meant to marry her someday. Mary, who loved Mister Burke then, had felt her heart almost stop beating. Ben's face, when she'd looked at him standing alone in the door of the cabin, had been suddenly old. Miss Natalie Browning and her family from Savannah had been in Cassville only three days, but Mary knew, at that moment, that her brother was in love with Miss Natalie and that Ben's love, like hers for Mister Burke, was hopeless!

From the dream, which could have been so troubling, had now come a light—a clear, white light that suddenly made plain so much she had never understood! Not once since the instant at Etowah Cliffs when Jonathan had told her Ben was dead by his own hand had she understood *why* her beloved brother would have chosen to leave her. In the clear light shining inside her head this minute, as she still sat straight in the bed which had once been Natalie's, *she knew.* She knew and she understood: Ben had loved Natalie in the same way she, Mary, loved Jonathan! Until Jonathan, she had no way of understanding why Ben had left her.

"I would want to die too if Jonathan did not love me in return," she whispered into the dark room. "Maybe, to understand is to know the way to peace again someday—without Ben."

A little peace was coming even now as, lying down again, she slid slowly toward sleep. Jonathan would be right there tomorrow at the crystal-and-china-and-silver-laden Browning dinner table where she would sit with all the prominent Savannahians. She would be all right because she could be herself with Jonathan always. And in a way she could never explain, she knew now that Ben, in heaven, would also be helping her. Almost the same as always, she could again depend on Ben.

All night long, she slept.

Chapter 28

AFTER a final consultation with Maureen and her two Irish cousins she had brought to assist in serving, Caroline watched in her dressing-table looking glass as Gerta beamed with pride at her skill in dressing Madam's lightly graying black hair. One of the big adjustments Caroline had been forced to make because Mark refused to own Negroes was learning how to do without a personal maid. Her husband would never have forbidden her to bring black Nellie from Knightsford had she insisted, but although she thought Mark stubborn to go on year after year with hired help, she loved him too much to disobey or even attempt to manipulate him. "Try Gerta," he'd suggested way back when Jonathan was a little boy and Natalie still a Savannah schoolgirl. Stodgy, willing Gerta, the children's German nurse, had been all thumbs for over a year, so that dressing usually ended up with Caroline arranging her own hair. But Gerta had persisted, and tonight, pride showed in every aging angle of her square, flushed face as she drew a perfect middle part and formed even, becoming loops on either side to cover the ears.

"There, Miss Caroline," Gerta said, continuing to admire her handiwork, "look at yourself. We've managed to just about hide every gray hair at your temples!"

"You've done well, Gerta," she said, using a silver hand mirror to inspect the well-formed knot at the nape of her neck, "but I find I'm rather proud of my gray streaks. Perhaps I've even earned them."

Gerta laughed. "You'll earn them this evening," she said in her still noticeable accent, "with the high-and-mighty in town pushing their way inside to inspect little Miss Mary McDonald. Might end some of the talk I've heard, though."

"What have you heard? I do wish you'd tell me and stop being so mysterious about it. You, of all people, know how nervous I am. Just look—here I sit ready to have you help me into my new gown and I'm wearing only three petticoats! That green-striped taffeta skirt will hang like a damp sheet over just three petticoats. Will you hand me at least two more, please? Lace-trimmed, I think. Then we'll get me into the corset and bodice. Do you like these new exaggerated leg-o'-mutton sleeves?"

"I do, ma'am. You have the shoulders for them. They're rightly named too. Look just like a raw leg of mutton ready to bake!"

Caroline shuddered. "Do you have to be so graphic? My stomach's churning as it is. Churning far too much to have you squeeze me into that corset, actually, but the bodice would never fasten without it."

After spreading the extra petticoats on the bed, Gerta stood grunting from the effort of pulling the corset strings as tightly as she could.

"There," Caroline gasped. "No more! By the way, Gerta, do you think you should drop in on Sarah Mackay helping Mary dress down the hall? I can put the finishing touches on my own hair once you've gotten me into my gown. I'm so worried about whether Mary really likes the yellow dress I had made for her." She held up her arms while Gerta slipped the petticoats, then the damask skirt over her head. "Natalie always loved yellow. I do hope Mary likes it."

"Nonsense, Miss Caroline. She's a grateful, grateful child!"

"I know that. I don't want gratitude, I—oh, I'm just so nervous—partly, I think, because I do want Mary to have a happy evening. I really do. In spite of—everything, I am so—fond of her." She smoothed and arranged the full green-and-white-striped skirt. "I'd try hard to care for any young woman Jonathan picked out, but—I'm sure I'm as nervous for Mary as for myself at the prospects of this first introduction to such prominent people. Would you look in on Miss Sarah and Mary, then come back to finish me, please? I'll need the emerald necklace and—well, I'll think later about which bracelet."

"I'll go gladly," Gerta said, smoothing the back of the tight matching green bodice. *"Mein Gott,* you're a—picture, madam. A lovely picture!"

"Thank you. Remember, I want the exact truth when you come back concerning Mary's feelings about her yellow gown, do you understand?"

"Perfectly," Gerta said, bustling out of the room.

From her carved-ivory jewel box, Caroline decided against the necklace and chose instead the handsome ruby brooch Mark gave her on their twentieth wedding anniversary. It would be just right to hold the white gauzy silk shawl in place around her shoulders. Besides, Mark would be pleased. She touched the brooch to her lips, then laid it to one side on her dressing table. Pinning the shawl in place would be the last thing, after Gerta returned. Mark . . . how is he feeling right now? she wondered. Nervous too, she was sure, but, being Mark, acting poised in spite of how much he loathed the latest style in men's clothing—especially the corset, which he didn't need at all. And a tail coat, as difficult to handle, he declared, as any woman's bouffant skirt. Foppish, he called men's styles, but he wouldn't have shown his disapproval by wearing a frock coat instead. "Why give reason for further talk?" he'd always asked. "Don't people find enough without my rebelling?"

She sighed. Mark was always the handsomest gentleman anyway, always drawing attention to his still youthful figure, so needed these days for a man to be flawlessly dressed. At least men were no longer wearing what Mark called "torture trousers," as in the early days of their married life. Trousers had eased, but the old style of wearing straps under the instep was back and Mark hated them too.

Let's face it, she thought, I'm only thinking about Mark's gentle grumblings to keep from fidgeting still more at what our guests will think and may well say about poor little Mary. I must stop thinking of her as "poor little Mary." There's an unmistakable strength in the girl and often she's surprisingly wise. She has an innate wisdom. Mark certainly agrees and we must both count on that. If things are too awkward this evening, if she's just too out of place, maybe that innate wisdom will somehow win out.

For an instant, she permitted a return of yesterday's anxiety when they'd learned that Eliza Mackay was still too weak from a deep cold to attend the dinner party. Miss Eliza's presence invariably helped. The day would come when their old friend would be gone. Tonight, they could all practice acting as adults without her, she thought, loathing the idea.

Listening vainly for the clip-clop of Gerta's slippers in the hallway outside her room, she felt certain her lessons with Mary as to which fork to use with each course, which glass or goblet, had been well learned, but anyone can forget if she's shy or nervous. Caroline had seated William to Mary's right and Mr. Potter to her left. Bertha Potter, the most dangerous tongue at the table, was four chairs away between the Mercers, who could be counted on to be tactful, should tact be needed. Jonathan had asked to be seated straight across the table from Mary. "That way I can look at her every minute," he'd said. Jonathan, Jonathan, I don't blame you, and yet, I suppose I do. I've heard rumors that there are Savannahians with Cherokee blood, but I've never, *never* heard of anyone admitting it.

Caroline was so lost in her thoughts that she jumped when Gerta burst excitedly into the room, her broad face glowing. "She's a picture, madam," she gasped. "Miss Mary's a picture in that pretty gown you had made for her! You'll never believe it even with your own eyes beholding her. The three-tiered embroidered velvet skirt—golden as the sunrise on a summer day— makes her look so tall and regal. Regal like a queen, I say. Wait till you see her and wait, oh, wait till poor Master Jonathan sees her!"

"My son needs no more stimulation, I promise you, but I am relieved. Was she dressed when you went to her room? Had she and Sarah Mackay gotten on well?"

"Miss Sarah's putty in the girl's hands, madam! They were laughing together so hard I heard them down the hall."

Caroline sighed. It was not a wholly satisfied sigh. Justly or unjustly, their guests' opinion of Mary was critical. Still, what if most of them did fall under her simple, childlike, disarming spell? Oh, maybe, maybe it will somehow work out.

Sarah Mackay had powdered Mary's face in such a way that, until more than halfway through the first two courses—crab bisque, standing rib roast with squares of perfect Yorkshire pudding—Caroline thought Mary's scar didn't show too much at all. What is *too much?* she asked herself. After all, she has that scar because of my daughter's headstrong determination to see Burke Latimer that long ago afternoon in the woods behind the log cabin where he lived then with Mary and Ben—before Natalie married him.

She noticed that Jonathan had not stopped beaming once, and wonder of wonders, took two helpings of every vegetable. The boy was plainly enjoying himself, his mother thought, seemingly not at all worried about Mary, only watchful of her, sharing his bright smile each time he caught her eye. Mark appeared unruffled too, entering into the far more affable talk at his end of the table, where he and Mary and William Mackay and Jonathan and Mr. Potter laughed frequently.

Seated the length of the table away from Mark, Caroline ate less than usual because engaging the rather quiet Mercers, Bertha Potter and Kate Mackay in conversation was not easy. They covered the death in September of President Tyler's wife rather quickly, because, actually, there was little to be said about the poor woman who had never entered into Washington City society, and had entertained only when necessary for her husband's position. Mrs. Tyler had attended her daughter's wedding, Bertha Potter remembered, but so far as anyone else knew, that was the one big event in her social season. Caroline remarked that a trip to New York might be even more interesting now that a Philharmonic Orchestra had been formed and was to give its first concert in December. Society functions anywhere along the coast would undoubtedly be more interesting, Kate Mackay offered, now that the rather wild dance called the polka had invaded America from Europe.

"Can't you just see my husband dancing the polka?" Bertha Potter asked, her mind mainly on Mary, who, obviously feeling warm on the unseasonably hot fall evening, was casually wiping her entire face and neck with her dinner napkin. Caroline could see that Mark noticed too, but he acted as though nothing unusual was occurring. Jonathan merely beamed across at Mary.

Seated on the same side of the long, elegantly appointed table as Mary, Bertha Potter had to lean forward in her determination to bring Mary into their conversation. "My dear Miss McDonald," she asked, raising her voice, "do you dance the polka?"

Everyone, Caroline was sure, noticed Mary's quick, hopeful look at Jonathan, who answered for them both: "Mary and I haven't yet learned how," he said in his most charming manner. "We hear it's becoming very popular, though, at the North."

"We do, Jonathan?" Mary asked, loud enough for everyone to hear.

"I thought I'd told you," the boy said sweetly. "I'm sure I'll have to learn once I'm at Yale College. I promise to teach you the steps on my first visit to the upcountry, Mary."

As though they were alone at the table, Mary asked excitedly, "You visit me in Cass, Jonathan?"

"Of course I will! Even before Savannah, I'll be up in Cass to see you and —of course, all the Stileses and my sister and Burke."

Leaning forward again, Bertha Potter said, "Do tell us, Miss Mary McDonald, about your family. Do your parents live in Cass County? And is their home anywhere near Eliza Anne and W. H. Stiles?"

A desperate pang of longing for Miss Eliza struck Caroline. She was sure Eliza Mackay would have responded to Mrs. Potter's deliberate, pointed question in a way that would have ended the matter forthwith, without embarrassment to Mary. But she could tell that Mary, smiling only a little sadly, was about to answer herself. Everyone would hear her this time too, because abruptly there was silence around the entire table.

"Perhaps you didn't hear me in the midst of all the talk," Bertha Potter persisted. "Does your family live in Cass County near—?"

"Oh, I hear you," Mary said. "I hear you fine, lady. My family—my parents—live now in heaven."

Even Jonathan thought of nothing to say.

Bertha plunged ahead. "And have you no brothers or sisters or aunts or uncles?"

"Nobody is left to me," Mary said. "Uncle Running Deer once lived in our house. My brother and I, we afraid—we *were* afraid our uncle die when—when—" She broke off, and looked across at Jonathan for guidance.

Caroline could see that her son was not smiling, but listening intently to Mary. He gave Mary no inkling of any guidance except to go on if she wanted to.

"When—what, my dear?" Bertha pressed her.

"When—they drive, *drove* us from our cabin as we ate supper."

"Your—cabin?" Mrs. Potter was leaning on the table now in her effort not to miss a single change in Mary's expression. *"Who drove you?"*

Plainly, Mark had heard enough. "Mrs. Potter"—he spoke firmly—"our son's friend, Mary McDonald—*our* friend—is half Scottish, but she's also half Cherokee."

If one of Maureen's Irish cousins had dropped an entire tray of china and shattered every piece, the effect in the room would not have been more startling.

Why did Miss Eliza have to get a cold now of all times? Caroline thought wildly. She could think of nothing that might help, nothing at all! Of course, Mark had not exactly surprised her by doing what he wanted to do the first week or so of Mary's visit—"hit them all with the truth head-on"—but she felt almost faint.

After what seemed an interminable silence, Bertha Potter gasped, "My heavens! A real *Indian!*"

"Mary's mother was a real Indian, ma'am," Jonathan offered politely. "With the beautiful name of Green Willow."

In the brief stillness that followed Jonathan's disclosure, of which he seemed rather proud, Caroline thought, William Mackay cleared his throat and announced, "Our Mary here has a beautiful name too. Her real Cherokee name suits her to a T. It's Merry Willow. That's M-e-r-r-y Willow."

A hopeful look on her face, Mary said, "Since at Moravian school in Spring Place, where my brother and I were born, I learn that M-a-r-y was the name of Jesus' mother, I go now by M-a-r-y."

Several guests coughed nervously, no one really looking at anyone except Mary and Jonathan, both of whom smiled broadly at each other and at their friend William Mackay.

"So, our house guest is Miss Mary McDonald now," Mark said, then added with surprising clumsiness, "McDonald's a good old Scottish name, you know . . ."

"But someday, when I've graduated from Yale College and have begun to work in my father's business firm, her name will be Mary Browning—I hope. In fact, I hope so with all my heart." Jonathan flashed her his bright smile.

This so delighted Mary that in the ensuing silence her tinkling laughter was so much like a bell, Caroline blinked back quick tears.

One of Maureen's cousins saved them all by elbowing her way through the swinging door, triumphantly carrying a large silver tray on which reposed Maureen's perfect Lady Baltimore cake. The cake she'd taught Natalie to bake. Behind her came the other cousin bearing a crystal compote of fresh fruit.

Maureen followed, trying and failing to appear modest, with everyone overcomplimenting her—from nerves, Caroline was sure, in spite of the splendor of the cake. Exchanging a somewhat relieved glance with Sarah Mackay, seated to her right in the chair where her mother would have sat, Caroline breathed a prayer that perhaps the subject would now be changed.

Kate Mackay must have shared the same wish, because as Caroline sliced the cake, Kate proclaimed a bit loudly that P. T. Barnum's American Museum had either just opened in New York or would open soon and that General Tom Thumb would be exhibited.

"I saw that too, in the *Georgia Republican!*" William Mackay said with unnatural enthusiasm. "When the Twenty-eighth Congress convenes next year, it wouldn't surprise me if our own W. H. Stiles doesn't make a trip from Washington City just to see the General."

No one gave William any help, and while Caroline had handed only the sixth piece of cake down one side of the table, Bertha Potter, still holding on like a bulldog, asked, "What of your brother, Miss Mary? You mentioned having a brother, I believe, in reference to when your uncle somebody— lived with you at—was it Spring Valley?"

"No, ma'am," Mary said, frowning slightly. "Spring Place."

"Where is your brother now, my dear?"

Unsmiling, but with only true courtesy, Mary said, "He live also in heaven now. Ben. Indian name, Bending Willow."

Caroline went on slicing cake, passing each serving along on her prized gold-accented, green Spode china. Even Bertha was quiet. Caroline saw Jonathan flush, William Mackay frown and Mark lean forward as though to speak. Evidently, he thought of nothing to say.

After Mary's cake reached her, she murmured, "Thank you," then picked up the large dinner fork still on the table at her place. Caroline had not quite finished serving, and was sure that if she noticed, so did everyone else. Mary had eaten her entrée with her dessert fork!

The girl's laughter was a bit less bell-like now. "I—I forget and use wrong fork," she said. "So sorry. I hope to be forgiven." Her smile was at her own expense, but she was not at all embarrassed. "I did mean to—do right, Miss Caroline, as you taught me to do."

Caroline gave her the warmest smile she could. "Well, both forks work just fine, Mary," she said.

"And I did like small one best." Half rising, she asked quite unselfconsciously, "I go wash small fork for—cake?"

"Not on your life," Mark said, reaching across William to pat Mary's forearm. "Bring another dessert fork, Maureen, will you, please? Miss Mary likes a small one. I want her to have exactly what she likes."

Fresh fork in hand, Mary joined the others in tasting and exclaiming over the deliciously flavored, fluffy, custard-filled cake. Then, after a time, looking around the table, she asked in an earnest and only slightly shy voice, "All of you—it is *bad* to be—half Cherokee?"

Caroline could see that Mary had asked her jarring question, not of the family or of the Mackays, but of the other invited guests, whose stunned faces Mary was watching, her gaze moving intently from one to another. Caroline's heart ached for Jonathan, who said nothing. She could read the pain on his handsome young face, though, and longed to respond to Mary herself. Mark and William Mackay both looked stricken, both searching, as was she, for the right words to drop into the terrible silence.

Mary herself broke the tension with another question: "It is bad to be—half *Scottish?*"

"Oh, my dear, of course not," Mrs. Mercer said. "Some of our best people in town are Scots, members of our splendid St. Andrew's Society."

In response, Mary gave Mrs. Mercer her quick smile. "Sure," she said. "I try, from now on, to be—Scottish."

"Mary, no!" Jonathan seemed almost to be begging her.

"Sorry," Mary said, still smiling. "I understand." Her eyes moving again from one face to another, as though to reassure them all, she repeated, "I understand."

After another awkward silence, William Mackay said softly, "I honestly believe you do, Mary. Of course, that puts you quite a piece down the road ahead of the rest of us, but I honestly believe you do understand."

Chapter 29

IT WAS raining the next day when the Mackays and the Brownings and Mary were to meet at the Pulaski House for breakfast before seeing Jonathan off on the steamer that would take him north to Yale College. William overruled his sisters, who finally agreed that their mother could go with them. "She'll just fidget staying at home," he argued, "and it's only a step from Mark's carriage to the hotel door. Mark and I arranged it all last night, Mama. He'll be by for you and I'll take Kate and Sarah in my buggy."

Once they reached Captain Wiltberger's superbly run Pulaski House, William was glad he'd insisted, because his mother seemed more like herself this morning and he wished now he'd tried harder to get his sisters to let her attend the Brownings' dinner party last night.

Every thought of last night brought a smile to William's face. Yes, Mary had mixed up her forks, but she'd been so sweet and natural, he was still amused this morning recalling how pleasantly everyone had taken their leave once dinner was over. They'd actually seemed kind of stunned, he thought, as he winked slyly at Mary and Jonathan, who were, at William's suggestion, sharing a table across the room by the wall. Bertha Potter had certainly tried at dinner to fuss Mary, but in a way she'd fallen flat on her face doing it.

He'd seated his mother at the large, round table where everyone but Jonathan and Mary would eat breakfast, then, as usual, he just listened while Mark and Caroline and his sisters tried to tell Mama everything that had happened at the Brownings' dinner. He gave his mother a big smile of agreement when she said, "It seems to me we don't have too much to worry about Mary's life here in Savannah—*if* she and Jonathan do become man and wife someday." Then she turned to William. "I see you agree with me, son."

A half smile still playing at his mouth, William said in his cautious way, "You know, Mama, how much I've come to care about little Mary, but I guess this is all mainly up to Mark and Caroline."

"Caroline, I'm sure you're relieved the party's over, but you really haven't had much to say this morning."

"I know, Miss Eliza. And I don't think I quite understand why. I would give almost anything, though, to be able to agree with you that—Mary might be accepted here. There were some dreadful moments last night. I'm afraid it's all a risky, risky business."

"No one's denying that," William said, "but I think Mary does understand our Savannah highbrows, maybe better than we do. I think she had a better idea of what everyone around that table was thinking than I had!"

"And we're supposed to be of their class," Sarah said wonderingly. "I think William's right, though, for once. It seemed to me that Mary more or less took care of the whole awkward moment when Bertha Potter pinned her down on her—family background."

"Well," Mark said, "it's over. Caroline and I gave the two lovebirds an hour or so alone after everyone had gone last night. Jonathan told me when he came upstairs that they were both agreed to wait until he graduates. A lot can happen in four years."

"Will Mary be going right back to Etowah Cliffs now that Jonathan's leaving town?" Kate wanted to know.

"Caroline and I didn't sleep much last night," Mark said, "debating that very question. At first, Jonathan wanted her to stay on a while, so his mother could continue teaching her Savannah's ways. Mary wants to go back, I think, although she's careful, as always, not to hurt our feelings. The boy also told me last night that he really wants only what Mary wants." On a sad laugh, Mark added, "Personally, I wish she'd stay. I'm certainly going to miss Jonathan. That big house will be—so empty."

"What do you think, Caroline?" Eliza Mackay asked.

"I—I see no reason why Mary shouldn't do as she prefers."

"But surely no harm could be done by her staying a while," Mark argued. "You're remarkable with her, darling. The girl could be taught everything she needs to learn socially. Wouldn't that improve their chances for a happy marriage?"

"There's plenty of time for that!" Caroline spoke rather sharply, William thought, not at all surprised. "Both young people may have changed their minds by the time Jonathan's through Yale," she went on, pushing back her plate—almost untouched. "Frankly, I admit to being weary of the whole affair! I'm—not exactly proud to admit it, but I'm a nervous wreck. There's still *so much* Mary needs to learn!"

"Very little more than my own mother had to learn," Mark reminded her. "Aunt Nassie had to teach her almost everything about living in Philadelphia society—and my mother had been with a well-mannered Scottish lady right here in Savannah for years before she met my father."

"Your mother was *not* an Indian, Mark," Caroline flared. "She was, after all, the daughter of Jonathan Cameron! I don't care what our son seems to believe—you either, William—blood does matter. In the long run, it matters a lot."

"Maybe so, Caroline," William said in a quiet firm voice, "but all I have to say is that from somewhere, Mary McDonald got a lot of poise and all the sweetness and gentleness of spirit any woman ever needs."

"I am weary," Caroline said, trying to control her voice. "Could we—drop the subject, at least for now?"

"Yes, we should all just hush," William's mother said flatly, her eyes on the two engrossed young people at a small table just out of earshot. "Look at them and try to imagine—whatever happens in the future—how difficult this day is for Jonathan and Mary. They've only just found each other and in an hour or so now, they have to part. I doubt very seriously if either of them is giving one thought right now to Mary's manners or her faulty English. They've far more important things to think about."

For the first time in his life, Jonathan paid little or no attention to the hearty breakfast he'd ordered. His stomach felt as though it had been closed off— squeezed shut by the weight of his heart.

"You eat," Mary said. "I think your boat trip will maybe be very long. You be—you *will* be hungry, Jonathan. That hurts me. You eat."

"I can't." He tried to smile. "You haven't touched your food either. Oh, Mary, Mary . . ." He reached across the table to take her oddly fragile hand, fragile for a girl who'd worked so hard all her life. "You will remember that even though I probably will have to attend some social events at Yale, I won't really *see* any other girl, won't you? I'll just see *you* in my mind. I'll—hold you too and—"

"Yes! You hold me."

"Every night when you snuggle down in your bed, you can just be sure I'm thinking about you—hard. That I'm longing to hold you close to me, to see your face—oh, Mary, I do love your face so much!"

"Natalie once tell me she hate it when she and Mister Burke ride to Cassville—to be before people. She hate not keeping her eyes on Mister Burke's face—'in public.' We are 'in public' now?"

He laughed a little. "We're in public and I'd give anything if we weren't. My sister's right. This very minute, I'd like to put my arms around you and here we sit with this table between us and all these people around. Mary, I'll find a way to give you a long hug—before I get on that boat. I promise."

"Yes! I make a promise to you too."

"What?"

"To work hard to learn how to say—everything right. Natalie, Miss Lib, they teach me. Sure. Both will teach me."

"I'm glad now you're going back to the upcountry. You're welcome to stay on here, but—I found you up there. I want to think about you up there by the river, because you're at home there." He frowned. "I am worried about one thing, though. I don't want you to make that trip back to Cass alone. I've had my mind on so many things, I haven't made any arrangements for someone to go with you, but I'm going to before I—"

"No! Do not worry. And do not spoil Mister William's surprise to you."

"Surprise?"

Her smile was triumphant. "Mister William already get me ticket and he

will go with me! We go—tomorrow early on Central from Georgia train."
She grinned at her own mistake. "We go on Central *of* Georgia train, right?"
"Right," he said, relief in his voice. "Good old William! That's so like him.
I'll bet he hasn't even told my parents or Miss Eliza yet."
She shook her head. "No. And I keep our secret—even from you—but it
hurt me to see you worry, so now you know."
Jonathan laid down his fork and looked at her for a long time. "Dearest
Mary, I was *proud* of you last night. You were so calm and poised and—"
"I did not mean to use wrong fork."
His heart pounded so, for an instant he thought he might die of loving her.
"What's a fork? You just sat there shining like a bright candle in the dark.
You put them all—in the dark."
"That is good, Jonathan?"
"The way you did it, yes. Does the family know you're going back to Cass
tomorrow?"
"Only Mister William. I tell your parents after you are gone."
"Oh, Mary, look! They're all getting up from the table." He grabbed her
hand. "It must be time for me to get to the boat."
"I—I miss you *now!*"
"Me too," he said, helping her to her feet in his most gallant manner,
holding on to her arm far longer than necessary. "Don't forget, I'll find a way
for us to be alone before the boat sails—even if it's just for a few minutes."
"I not—I *won't* forget." She clung to his hand. "Jonathan, we walk to-
gether alone—to the boat? Not ride in carriage? There is time?"
He took out his watch. "Just barely," he whispered. "We might have to
walk kind of fast, but that's a fine idea. And it's just what we'll do."
"Your mother and father will let us?"
"I won't ask, I'll just tell them we're walking over to the wharf. After all,
we're in love, aren't we?"
"Sure. Sure, Jonathan."
Her face was so radiant, he scarcely noticed, once they were all outside,
that it was still raining. And for once, his mother didn't object to their walk-
ing or warn that he might catch cold from getting wet.

Sitting beside Mister William on the scratchy train seat the next morning,
Mary kept her head back, her eyes closed against the smoke and wood ash, as
Miss Eliza had urged, at least until the train had moved some distance away
from the wind off the river. Everyone had been so kind. Jonathan's parents
and Miss Eliza had come with her and Mister William in the Browning carriage to catch the six o'clock train back home. And Gerta and Maureen went
to the trouble of packing her pretty new gowns and daytime dresses the
Brownings and Mister William had bought her. She wouldn't have said so,
but Mary thought it useless to take the fancy gowns back to Cass, not knowing even where to put them in the cabin she shared with Miss Lorah and Sam.
She would never forget the visit to her bedroom last night by Miss Caro-

line, the beautiful lady who bore Jonathan. Her words had been so kind, so full of understanding that Mary hadn't been able to keep from crying fresh tears of joy on top of the tears of loneliness because Jonathan was no longer there in the big, elegant mansion that was his home. She had learned the word "elegant" soon after reaching Savannah. It was a word Savannah people must like, she decided, because they used it a lot.

"Who knows," Miss Caroline had said last night, sitting on the side of Mary's bed, "this may be your home someday too—if you and my son do get married."

"Oh, we marry," she'd answered quickly, then corrected herself to say, "We *will* marry, Miss Caroline. We are in love."

Jerking along on the fast-rolling, rattly train, she tried hard to obey Miss Eliza Mackay and keep her eyes closed, but found herself peeping at good Mister William beside her. He'd be sure to tell her to close her eyes for a few more miles if she said anything to him, but she had to let him know somehow that the pain in her heart because Jonathan was gone was far less because Mister William had insisted upon making the long trip with her.

Squeezing her eyelids shut, so even if she spoke, he'd know they were still closed, she said, "Thank you for being here. Thank you, thank you!"

"Why, Mary, I'm ashamed of you for thinking I'd ever let you make this trip by yourself! No one else was free to come. I'd rather be here beside you heading back for Cass than any other place on earth."

Still holding her eyes shut, she reached to pat his hand. "We friends," she said, then laughed at herself. "I am so happy to be with you, I not talk right! I know I must say, 'We *are* friends.' "

He laughed too and that was good, because Mister William didn't laugh very often.

She sighed, almost happily. Everything was as good as it could be away from Jonathan, she decided, and when Mister William patted her hand too and laid it gently back in her lap, she felt suddenly drowsy. She had worked at not crying much before Jonathan on the wharf yesterday, but through the long hours of the night, she wept for him, giving thanks, though, that she had once also loved Mister Burke so deeply. Otherwise, she would not now know how to love Jonathan from the deepest part of her heart.

Mary felt her head roll over onto Mister William's shoulder, but was too exhausted to straighten up in her seat.

She slept.

Chapter 30

A FTER HE and Caroline and Miss Eliza had seen Mary and William off on the morning train, Mark asked Jupiter and the ladies to wait on Bay Street in front of his countinghouse, just long enough for him to look through the mail he failed to check yesterday because of the dinner party.

As he hurried now across the wooden bridge to his own entrance, his eyes squinted against the rising sun off the river. As usual, Natalie hadn't written since they'd all left Cass last summer and it had been almost a month since anyone had heard from Eliza Anne.

Glad it was too early for his clerks to be there, Mark let himself in the front door and went straight to his private office. At his desk, he tossed all business mail aside for later and looked only for personal letters for either the Brownings or the Mackays. He certainly didn't want Miss Eliza's lingering cold to worsen by waiting for him in the chill of the morning. Perhaps, though, a few minutes alone with Miss Eliza might help Caroline. His wife had, he admitted, puzzled him a bit when they'd said goodbye to Mary. In spite of all her recent conflict, she'd seemed genuinely sorry to see the girl go. What did I expect? he asked himself, flipping through the mail. Somehow today, he admired Caroline even more than ever. Even when her head was in fierce conflict with her heart, nine times out of ten, he could count on her heart to win.

And then, ten or twelve letters into the stack, there it was! In his hand, he was actually holding a thick letter from Natalie herself. He felt a flash of anxiety because a letter in Natalie's own unmistakable script was so rare, but then he broke into a happy smile, and without waiting to break the seal on what certainly appeared to be a long letter, he scooped up the Mackay mail and raced along the corridor to the front door and ran all the way back to the carriage, waving Natalie's letter high above his head.

After she and Caroline and Mark had settled in the old Mackay parlor, Eliza was relieved when Hannah said that the two daughters had taken breakfast to an elderly, ill neighbor. "We need this time alone," she said. "Time to share this all-important letter without the interruption of too many questions."

"Thank you," Mark said, still smiling. "It is good to be alone with you."

Eliza Mackay ordered tea and studied the faces of her two guests. "Go on, Mark," she urged. "Break the seal at least. Hannah won't be long. She and Emphie always have hot tea waiting when I've been out on a chilly morning."

"Yes," he said, his face still glowing. "Yes, of course. It's just that I've waited such a long time, I—"

"It's been so shamefully long since she's written, her doting father wants to savor it just a little longer," Caroline said.

Knowing them both as she did, Eliza could feel the difference in their separate anticipation. Mark was deliriously excited, while Caroline's face showed a trace of dread. Once Jonathan reached New Haven, he would write regularly. No one doubted that. Mark and Caroline would read and reread each word the boy wrote, but without the apprehension that invariably accompanied any word from Natalie.

The tea came and Hannah went back to her kitchen. Filling Caroline's cup, Eliza urged again that Mark open the fat envelope.

A rather embarrassed look on his face, he apologized. "Miss Eliza, I'm sorry! You have a letter from Eliza Anne too. Please read yours first."

"Mine can wait, dear boy," she said impatiently. "I'm eager to know what on earth Natalie found to fill up so many pages!"

"If you go on sitting there keeping us in suspense, Mark," Caroline scolded, "I'll read it myself!"

"Uh—don't pour my tea yet, Miss Eliza," Mark said. "You two drink yours, get rid of the chill and—listen."

Eliza saw his hands tremble breaking the seal. She and Caroline gratefully sipped the steaming tea and watched him devour the first page silently.

The boyish smile lit his face again. "It's good! Oh, Caroline, dearest—it's wonderful news!"

"Thank heaven," Caroline breathed.

"The very best news we could possibly have," Mark went on, his voice choked now with emotion. "Listen: 'Dear Ones . . . Before you get impatient with me, Mama, or before you have a heart seizure, Papa, I want to say right off that *I'm back!* I know I should have written this long ago, but here is the whole story. I got out of bed early the day Uncle W.H. left on his last campaign trip, put on my yellow dress and rode in the pony cart with Miss Lorah to the Stiles house and made a speech. A good one. I told everybody, including the Stileses' people, who had gathered to tell Uncle W.H. good-bye, exactly what I've just told you—*I'm back.* Oh, I'll never be able to forget that I failed Burke, never forget our little son, but—' " Mark handed the letter to Caroline, his voice too choked with emotion to read more.

" '. . . I'll never forget our little son,' " Caroline picked up the unfinished sentence, " 'but Miss Lorah finally convinced me that dreadful things happen to everyone. I guess she didn't really convince me, she proved to me that no matter how tragic a thing is, we always have to pick up and go on. And she did this in the only way she could have done it. She told me a little of what had happened to her when she was only about two years older than I am. When Miss Lorah was twenty-three, and so happily married to Luke Plemmons, a young man she vows looked something like Burke, she had her first baby, a pretty little girl named Sarah. According to Miss Lorah, Sarah's hair was like her father's—like Burke's—golden and curly, and her eyes were blue and lively, I imagine like Miss Lorah's. As Miss Lorah said, "The sun rose and set in that child for me. I took care of her like she was the only little girl in the world, and, Missy, that's just what she was to me." Miss Lorah had the hardest kind of life in those days. I guess she's always had to work like a mule, as she says, because they were very poor. Right after her baby was born, she was back splitting rails with her husband within two weeks! She'd take tiny Sarah along in a basket and watch over her as they worked. Even now, Miss Lorah vows those were the happiest days of her whole life and she must be in her fifties. I believe her, even though I have no idea how she managed to cook and wash and sew and keep house and still split rails like a man all day. I believe her because she's just one person you can believe. She was happy because both her adored husband, Luke, and her baby were where she could see them all day long. Those two were her entire world. She swears that her devotion to them both grew every day. She smiles a bit when she speaks of it now, but in her words, "I got so every time I went to sleep at night, I'd pray for strength—for room to love them both more, since I knew as sure as gun's iron, I'd wake up the next day needin' to love them still more." I guess it was then I really began to listen to Miss Lorah. You both know how I tend to close my mind to any kind of lecture from anyone!' "

Caroline stopped reading and looked at Eliza, then at Mark. "Can either of you believe Natalie wrote that?" she asked, her voice filled with pure wonder.

"Our girl has suffered a lot, darling," Mark whispered. "She's learning from it. Please go on."

"Yes, Caroline, do," Eliza said, so flabbergasted by the letter she forgot her manners and poured only herself more tea.

"All right, let's see here," Caroline said, finding her place again. " 'You both know how I've only listened to what I wanted to hear. Miss Eliza knows it too. Anyone who's ever known me, knows that. But when Miss Lorah began to tell me that her whole world revolved around Sarah and Luke, I suddenly wanted to hear every word she had to say. My world has revolved around Burke for over four perfect years. And had he lived, I know Little Burke would have been right there with his wonderful father in the very center of my world—my universe. When Miss Lorah's child was nearly five years old, just one week before her birthday, Luke took her as usual to the river when he went to bathe at the end of a day's work. Miss Lorah usually took her river bath a little later because she always started supper while Sarah and Luke were in the water. That one evening, she peeled her potatoes, put them on to boil—Luke loved her mashed potatoes with red-eye gravy and ham and so did little Sarah. Miss Lorah says she remembers the hymn she was singing as she worked in her kitchen that evening. It was "On Jordan's Stormy Banks I Stand." I didn't even know the hymn and even when she sang some of it to me in her funny, cracked voice, I couldn't remember they ever sang it at Christ Church. I've just stopped writing to ask her to repeat the words she sang so I can copy them down. Here they are:

> *On Jordan's stormy banks I stand,*
> *And cast a wistful eye*
> *To Canaan's fair and happy land,*
> *Where my possessions lie.*

Now, just be patient and you'll understand why I bothered to copy that. Miss Lorah sang and sang that stanza (the only one she knew) and felt guiltier and guiltier because she knew in her heart that her possessions—the most important part of her world—did *not* lie in some distant "Canaan" but were splashing around that minute down at the river! I guess she felt guilty because she believed that she had, as she said, "put little Sarah and Luke ahead of the good Lord from the start."

Caroline lowered the pages. "Mark, can you believe this is actually a letter from our daughter?"

"I know what Miss Lorah meant, believe me," Eliza Mackay said, almost as to herself. "Many times I also put my Robert and the children in God's place."

"Aunt Nassie used to say there is no such thing, since we love God, or should, with a totally different kind of love," Mark mused.

"I think I agree with Aunt Nassie," Caroline said, "but that wasn't my point, Mark. I can't get over Natalie actually taking the time to write to us on such solemn subjects."

"Why not just finish the letter, Caroline?" Eliza interrupted.

"Yes, of course," Caroline said. " 'Miss Lorah told me she sang and puttered around her kitchen for what must have been a whole hour that evening, expecting any minute to hear Luke and Sarah chatting and laughing as they climbed up the riverbank to the house, but there wasn't a sound from the yard. The potatoes cooked tender, she mashed them with plenty of fresh butter she'd churned that morning before she went to split rails with Luke, and enough milk to make them creamy; put the ham slices in a frying pan to set over her fire and, in between things, stirred a pot of greens and began to worry more and more. Oh, Mama, Papa, what happened is almost too terrible to write! As darkness began to fall, Miss Lorah, her supper getting cold, left the house and began to look for them. She found them all right, the next day, some half mile downriver, lying side by side, their dear bodies floating right at the edge of the riverbank.' "

"Dear Lord in heaven," Eliza Mackay gasped. "Think what that poor woman went through alone during that long night—not knowing what had happened!"

"I can't think," Caroline whispered. "I can't *bear* to think!"

For a few seconds no one spoke, then Mark said, "I wonder what did happen. Miss Lorah's husband must have been a good swimmer or he'd never have taken the little girl to the river . . ."

"Caroline, as soon as you—can, read more," Eliza begged. "Maybe Natalie tells us."

"Let me find my place. Here. Natalie goes on, 'Miss Lorah's house was something like a mile and a half from the nearest neighbor. She managed to get only the little girl's body up onto the riverbank, but had to leave her there to run, sobbing her heart out, to get help. Tears were running down her face when she told me, even after more than thirty years! Tears are running down my face as I write, because I know how she felt when she saw the still, lifeless body of her child. I still can't imagine how she learned to live, though, without Luke. But she did—she did. That's what dawned on me as clear as sunlight, and right then, *I came back to life.* I didn't lose Burke! I might well do what Ben did if I lost Burke. Somehow, Lorah Plemmons managed to live, though, and she is the one who made it possible for me to come back. Burke vows no one ever gave him such a gift as Miss Lorah has given him. I guess he'd do anything humanly possible for her, but she seems to have reached the place where she really doesn't mind one way or another whether people make a fuss over her or not. She just goes about the business of living. In fact, she told me as much: "Missy, you can now just go on about the business of living—and living's as good *as we make it.*" Oh, she's pleased when Burke brings her a length of new calico or some other gift from Cartersville, but what seems to please her most is that I no longer go around moping and feeling sorry for myself (at least, most of the time, I don't). Miss Lorah not only lost her entire family (as did poor William), she had no parents to turn to and, in order to find work, had to leave her beloved North Carolina mountain home for Ellijay, Georgia, where she knew no one except the mean, stingy woman she went to work for.' "

Caroline stopped reading to dry her eyes. "That's the end of the letter, except for this: 'I'm a little tired and need to mind Miss Lorah and take a nap before Burke comes home with Sam for supper. Sam is an orphan Miss Lorah took in some eighteen years ago in Ellijay. He's "good as gold," as she says, just a "mite slow." But my husband is very patient with him, and although he will never be as skilled as Ben, Burke is too happy over me to complain. With all my heart, I hope this letter has made you both happy—you and all the dear Mackays. Your always affectionate, and now not quite so selfish, daughter, Natalie Browning Latimer.' "

Eliza Mackay looked from one to the other. Both were smiling and both had tears in their eyes. Tears of relief and joy. Able to think of nothing worthwhile to say, she poured tea all around, then lifted her own cup in a toast "to two great ladies, Lorah Plemmons and Natalie Browning Latimer."

* * *

Within ten days there was a letter from Jonathan, a happy letter. He'd reached New Haven, Connecticut, safely, liked Yale College, was ensconced in a fair room in Old North Middle with a New York classmate named Earl White. It was a fine letter, the boy was well, but it filled only one page. Being Jonathan, he explained the brevity in his straightforward way: "In my next, I'll write more details about everything, but even though I'm up a whole hour ahead of 5 A.M. chapel, I do still want to write as much as I have time for to Mary at Etowah Cliffs. When I first reached my room, I found a letter from her waiting for me! A man can't ask for more than that, now, can he? She writes quite well, I think, far better than I imagined she might. Her letter was really a note and printed instead of in script, but she arrived safely with good old William at Etowah and she loves me. That's what matters. I send love to all. Your son, Jonathan Browning."

When Mark and Caroline refolded Jonathan's note, they were both smiling. The house was painfully empty, but the children were *all right,* though far, far away. W.H. had won his seat in the U.S. Congress and was most likely already at home with Lib and their children. Mark and Caroline had each other, the Mackays were nearby and after Natalie's tragedy and the ordeal of Mary's dinner party, each admitted that the prospect of a cozy winter alone seemed anything but dismal.

"I do hope Jonathan's room isn't too cold," Caroline said as Mark slipped his arm around her where they sat side by side before the fire on the family drawing-room sofa. "New England can be bitter in winter."

Mark smiled down at her. "I know. I was born a Yankee, remember? And I lived in the very same dormitory at Yale. Only back when I was there, it wasn't called *Old* North Middle yet. If Jonathan looks, he should find his father's initials cut on the Fence, by now a Yale landmark, I'm sure. He'll be chilly, all right, especially getting up for that compulsory early-morning chapel, but I predict his first snowball fight will compensate. Remember the day five years or so ago when we had our historic Savannah snowfall?"

Caroline shuddered. "How could I forget? Eight inches! But it *was* quite beautiful. And yes, I can still see you and Jonathan outside in Reynolds Square—you teaching him how to make snowballs—the kind that hurt!"

Mark laughed. "I'm sure you also remember that our tenderhearted son liked building a snowman best. He refused to hit me with one of those hard snowballs."

"Oh, Mark, he *is* a tender boy, isn't he? I so hope he won't someday be too hurt by Savannahians who refuse to—to accept Mary. Some will refuse, you know. Maybe most, or at best, most will only pretend to accept her because she's your daughter-in-law."

"Mary and Jonathan aren't man and wife yet, or hadn't you heard?"

"I'm too happy and comfortable, sir, to be teased right now. She let her head rest on his shoulder. "Mark, I really hope Mary won't be hurt either by anything. What if Jonathan finds someone else at the North? He might, you know. He'll have all sorts of chances to meet other young ladies of his own class."

"And I trust my son to be his usual courteous self with all of them. I also believe he will live out his life—with Mary."

She sighed. "I finished an absolutely unbelievable novel the other night—everything in it highly improbable, but nothing—nothing happened on a single page as wild and—improbable as *our* son falling in love with a half-breed Cherokee! Even more amazing, I think, Jonathan's mother does care about Mary's good, guileless heart."

"His father too. Mrs. Browning?"

"I know what you're going to ask. 'Could we just be content with this fine, safe moment before our own blazing fire?' Answer—yes. Oh, yes, yes . . ."

PART II

June 1843-August 1844

Chapter 31

IN SPITE of three girlhood years in school at the North, Natalie still found the upcountry winter exciting. Waking up to a good snowfall invariably sent her running outside without a cloak to gather handfuls of the lovely white blanket that turned ordinary pine and oak trees and winter brown grass into what to her seemed an enchanted land of clean beauty.

The upcountry late fall and winter of 1842 and early 1843 had been fairly severe, causing complaints—especially from Uncle W.H.—because so much plantation work had been stopped by the snowstorms. But Natalie had no complaints. She loved it when the wind blew a blizzard of thick snowflakes, keeping Burke inside their cabin all day—with her. On dry days, though, with help from three fairly good carpenters from nearby Cartersville, Burke and Sam had made progress on the large addition to the Stiles house. She could tell, in spite of his impatience to get to Washington, how pleased Uncle W.H. was with Burke's work, even without Ben's skilled help. A hard wind and rain storm at the end of May 1843 had blown down a section of framing around Burke's sturdy, queen-post truss which would one day support a portion of the roof, but by early June, Burke, himself, had even repaired that.

"You'd never know anything had blown down to look at it now," Natalie boasted as she walked hand in hand with Burke down the road toward their cabin after he'd given her a careful inspection of the new building. "I can't believe how much you've done, dearest, in spite of our big storms last winter. Weather makes a lot of difference up here, doesn't it? I love it all, but do you think there's any more beautiful time than June?"

He smiled down at her. "Yes. When autumn comes, that will be still better. For you, at least, even winter's beautiful—and when it's spring? Nothing can equal spring!"

"Isn't it good that I'm so happy in your upcountry, Burke?"

"It's better than just good," he said. "I'm the luckiest man in the world."

"Poor Miss Lib."

"Is there a particular reason to pity her today?" he asked.

"She loves Etowah Cliffs as much as I do. She doesn't want to move to dirty old Washington City away from all this thick, green June beauty!"

"I know the congressman's leaving sometime in October, but has she given you any idea when she'll be joining him up there?"

"No, because the poor woman doesn't know. She'll be burdened down with all the responsibility of their plantation once he's gone. Her common sense tells her she shouldn't go at all, but you know how Uncle W.H. is about Miss Lib and the children. He won't be gone a month before he sends for her!"

Burke stopped walking, lifted her face and kissed her. "I'm glad I don't have to send for you. Building that church near Milner's place kept me away all I can stand—ever." He returned her eager embrace. "Oh, Natalie, you're not only *back,* as you say, you're closer than ever before." Grinning down at her, he whispered, "Not close enough. I'll never get you close enough—but we are like one person now, aren't we?"

"Except for our delicious differences." She reached to kiss him again on the nose. "Tell me the truth. Do you love me as much—maybe more now that I'm less infuriating?"

He laughed.

"Don't laugh! You fell in love with me when I was still a spoiled baby. I don't want you only to admire and respect me for growing up. Oh, respect me a little, maybe, but—Burke, I want you to stay madly, wildly, helplessly in love with me!"

In answer, his arms tightened around her and he kissed her so long, so deeply—holding her body so hard against his—that, her whole being open to him, she gasped, "Burke . . . we must never lose this good hurt! Never—not even when we're old and feeble."

After another penetrating kiss, she asked, "Do you think Jonathan and Mary—love each other this way?"

His breathing uneven from the passion she so loved to stir, Burke echoed, "Jonathan and Mary? Why, darling, I—I guess so, only I still think of Mary as —so young!"

"She isn't. She's a year older than Jonathan and my brother has always been sort of—old." She took his arm and they started walking again. "You know, I think I'll be glad to see Jonathan next week."

"You will?"

"I've always loved him a lot, but when he was young, he was underfoot. Having him away at Yale this year has made me quite eager to be with him, I think. And, oh, I know how Mary feels today! Back when I finally got Papa to bring me to find you when you vanished after our shipwreck, I thought I'd die of—of longing and joy and excitement the night before I only *hoped* to find you up here! Poor little Mary must be beside herself today. She knows Jonathan will actually be here early next week!"

"You really care about Mary now, don't you?"

"You know I only fought having her around as long as she was in love with you!"

"Now you see she really wasn't. She just confused gratitude with—being
in love."

"I've never believed that and I never will."

"Why? Mary's world revolves around your brother now."

She took a minute to answer. "Burke, I'm doing my best to stay—changed,
but you have to let me be right about some things. Mary *was* in love with you
even though I kept telling her that someday she'd find the one man just right
for her"—she pressed her arm tightly inside his—"the way you're just right
for me. But Mary *was* in love with you and I wasn't unreasonable when I
refused to let her live in the same house with us!" Before he could say
another word, she added, "And don't you dare laugh at me! You were going
to laugh, weren't you?"

"I guess so, but I'd much rather make love to you . . ."

"Now?"

He kissed her again. "Yes, now. Right here on this stretch of springy
summer grass . . . You want me to, don't you?"

"Yes, *yes*, but—"

"Why not? What law says an old married couple can't love—anywhere?"

"Somebody might come along—"

"Where's that derring-do spirit? The Stiles family won't be back from
Barnsley's until day after tomorrow. Not a living being around anywhere but
a few goldfinches and squirrels . . ."

She grabbed both his hands and began to pull him along a shortcut to their
cabin. "We can't be sure one of the Stiles people won't wander by. Even Miss
Lorah or Sam. Don't be bullheaded, Burke!"

"Sam's helping make bricks and Mary and Miss Lorah are making a new
dress for Jonathan's visit. Natalie, please?"

Still pulling him at a good clip, both half laughing, clinging to each other,
she said, "I don't even want the squirrels to interrupt. Burke, hurry! We're
making love at home, in our bed—but walk faster!"

Lorah heard Mary's footsteps pounding up the path to the cabin they
shared with Sam and looked up from the pink-striped cotton skirt she was
hemming. Why, she wondered, is that child running so hard? Her sewing
laid aside, she hurried toward the front window just as Mary rushed into the
room.

"Mary, what on earth?" she demanded when Mary just stood there, in the
middle of the floor, eyes wide. "Is something the matter?"

"I—I don't know!"

"You don't know? Well, did you go to Natalie's cabin for our thread?"

"Yes," Mary gasped. "I—go, I mean I *went*. But I did not go inside . . ."

Lorah frowned. "Was there a reason you didn't go on in?"

Nodding hard and fast, her face awestruck, Mary whispered, "Yes, ma'am.
I—could *hear* them. I got scared!"

"Scared, Mary? Look, girl, could you just stop nodding your head up and down and tell me why?"

"Mister Burke, he was groaning and—grabbing for his breath! Natalie, the same, only sometimes she—whimpered like a puppy. Finally, Mister Burke—he almost shout and she—cry out and—"

Lorah felt a chuckle start down inside, then curbed it. She hadn't been able to be sure, not living in their cabin, that Missy and her husband were trying—really trying to have another baby. Lord, how she'd prayed they would! Mary needed her attention now, though.

"You did the right thing to run on back here, Mary," she said in her gentlest voice. "But don't you have the slightest idea what Missy and her man were doing?"

She didn't answer. Lorah waited.

Finally, Mary asked in a husky, hopeful voice, "They—they make—another baby?"

Lorah chuckled now. "We'll have to wait and find out about that, but glory be, they're trying! It doesn't take an ounce of book learning to know those two are head over heels in love and Mr. Latimer's certainly been careful with her all this time." She stepped over to hug Mary. "What you heard, Mary, is just as natural for two who love one another as for the neddies to mate in the spring!"

"Neddies?"

"You don't know what neddies are? Just one of my words. A neddie is a redbird."

Mary managed a half smile. "You make up that word?"

"No, an old friend taught it to me a long time ago. I thought maybe you knew it too. Back when I was a little girl of six or seven, my best friend was one of your people—a Cherokee Indian."

Wide-eyed again, Mary asked, "Your best friend was—Cherokee?"

"Yes, indeedy. He always called me Sissy. We'd meet every day by a big, flat rock near the crick that ran past our place in North Carolina. He didn't miss a single day meeting me neither. Not in nearly four long years."

"What was his Indian name? What did you call him?"

"Oh, I never did know his real name. I just called him Friend. He was too. He was my best friend. Taught me everything I know about the woods and flowers and trees and what can and can't be made into medicines."

"Friend is dead now?"

"I s'pose so. He always told me that one day they would call him and he'd have to go. Told me that if I went to our flat rock and he wasn't anywhere to be seen, I'd know they'd called him and he had to go."

"Who call?"

Lorah shrugged. "We didn't press questions on one another. I guess we didn't need to. He never said who might call. But one day, he wasn't there. Never showed up again. *They* called him."

"Maybe from Indian's Spirit World?"

"Maybe. My ma and pa died shortly thereafter. I had to move in with some of my father's people more'n twenty mile away. Friend was gray-headed even then. He's likely long dead."

Mary followed when Lorah went back to her sewing in the rear of the cabin. "Miss Lorah?"

"Whatcha want, child?"

"Could I—like you even more now that I know about—Friend?"

Lorah smiled at her. "You sure can! Anybody likes to be liked. I'm no different. You can baste that bodice onto the skirt now, then we'll try it on you, Mary. We'll have plenty to do here till the coast is clear at the Latimer cabin so's you can get the spool of thread I need to finish the hem."

Out of the corner of her eye, Lorah could see Mary beginning to smile to herself now.

"You got a mighty pretty smile, Mary. But I'm sure Mister Jonathan's told you that often enough."

At the mention of Jonathan's name, the smile grew happier. "Oh, yes, he love—*loves* my smile. Miss Lorah?"

"Hm?"

"Jonathan and I—we do like Natalie and Mister Burke just now—when Jonathan come tomorrow?"

"Well, I certainly hope not!"

Lorah saw Mary's smile vanish. "It is bad?" she asked.

"No, no, no. Not bad, once you two get married to one another. Mister Burke and Missy are married folks. What they were doing together is right and good in the sight of God."

"You think Jonathan knows that?"

"With a mother and father like his, I'm sure he does. And he loves you, Mary, so he'll wait for the proper time. He wouldn't take advantage. Not for all the tea in China or I miss my guess about the boy."

On her feet abruptly, Mary whirled round and round the cabin. The child can hardly wait to see Jonathan, Lorah thought. And I know how she feels too. I can live to be a hundred and two and still remember dancing with joy as a girl if I knew Lucas was coming to see me. Hoping she'd been right in all she'd said about Mary catching Missy and her man together, she asked, "Didn't they teach you at the Moravian School at Spring Place that folks had to wait to be married—for certain things, Mary?"

"Yes, ma'am. To have a baby, but I—I stupid, I guess." The pretty face flushed so that the scar popped out white.

"Not stupid, Mary," she corrected. "Innocent. You were just too young to know."

"I one year older than Jonathan! Scuse me. I correct—I *am* one year older than Jonathan. But—" Her eyes filled with wonder. "I did not know until—today—about shouting and cries of pain and joy."

"Well, you know now, and when you're married to Jonathan someday, you'll understand all about it."

Suddenly, Lorah felt the young arms circle her shoulders and squeeze hard. She liked it when Mary hugged her. Lorah believed in hugging. A body needed lots of it. Anybody did, especially if the hug, like Mary's, came right up from the heart.

Twenty-some miles away, at the Barnsley place now called Woodlands, Eliza Anne and her lifelong friend Julia Barnsley were happily spending the morning alone bringing each other up to date, after such a long time apart, on the news of family and mutual friends back in Savannah and elsewhere. Eliza Anne's three children and five of Julia's seven were busily playing in the newly planted gardens. W.H. was off on horseback with Godfrey Barnsley inspecting the vast Woodlands acreage and wouldn't be back until dinnertime, two hours from now. Their husbands had been close business acquaintances long before either family thought of leaving Savannah to build new homes on the frontier. They had, with the Reverend Charles Howard, actually discovered the beauty and fertility of the upcountry land together and their mutual dreams of moving there had been almost simultaneous. Eliza Anne and Julia Scarbrough Barnsley, though, had been friends—close, intimate friends—all their lives. Only to Eliza Anne had Julia confided her agony during the months before she finally married Godfrey, because no one knew better than Eliza Anne that Julia Scarbrough, Sr., longtime friend of the Mackay family, had protested the marriage, seemingly without reason. Certainly, British Godfrey Barnsley was an enormously wealthy young man, with prosperous mercantile interests in Savannah and Liverpool, and certainly, he loved young Julia. Eliza Anne knew, from having shared some of Godfrey's letters, that handsome Julia Sr. had not been the only objector to the marriage. For a reason no one seemed to understand, Godfrey Barnsley's English friends did all in their power to discourage the wedding. There had never been any love lost between Godfrey and young Julia's socially prominent mother, but even Godfrey was puzzled at his friends' complaints, since the William Scarbrough family certainly passed anyone's social or economic muster. More than passed it. Until he'd lost most of his fortune investing in the SS *Savannah*, the first steamship built to cross the Atlantic, William Scarbrough had also been a well-to-do Savannah merchant, his magnificent home on West Broad, the social center of the city. The problem between Julia's mother and Godfrey had been purely personal, not helped along one bit, Eliza Anne was sure, by her friend Julia's brilliant older sister, Charlotte, whose prickly, domineering personality had always had a deep effect on their mother.

It had been a long, long time, though, since she and Julia had enjoyed time alone like this to talk, and Eliza Anne wasted little of this day in gossip about people outside their immediate families.

"Your husband has obviously won your mother's affections," she said, going straight to the point. "The last time Mama visited her in Savannah, she had nothing but praise for Godfrey. Did Godfrey do it with his singular British charm?"

"His charm and his endless kindness—and perseverance. Only Mother knew why she so disliked him from the start, but . . ." Julia laughed a little. "Only Mother ever needed to know—anything, you know. Her poor heart was so broken when Papa died, the family coffers so depleted, she—she had no one to whom to turn but Godfrey. By then, Charlotte had begun maneuvering in the courts to gain sole possession of the family home in Savannah and—none of us was welcome in it. She did tolerate an occasional visit from Mother. Mama's there now, in fact, but will be back up here as soon as Godfrey can go down to fetch her. God's miracles never cease, do they? The two are close now. Mother's mind is a bit quixotic these days, you know. So, I give thanks every day that she and Godfrey get along. He's infinitely patient with her."

Eliza Anne sighed. "Your mother has had far more than her share of grief for her dead children through the years and I know she'll never stop needing your father. As my mother hasn't stopped needing Papa." She smiled at Julia. "Remember how Papa adored dancing with your mother in the old days when you and I were girls?"

"Didn't he call her the Duchess?" Julia laughed. "Well, maybe not to her face. Your father's humor was right on the mark, though. She *was* a duchess. Not anymore, I'm afraid. Mama is dear, good with the children most of the time, but a broken woman without Papa. And she's aged terribly."

For a time, they sat in their rockers on Julia's wide cabin porch, both gazing out over Godfrey's newly planted formal gardens.

Then Julia smiled. "How do you like the artistic effect of my husband's elegant gardens spread around a log cabin?"

"I marvel at how his gardens have grown since W.H. and I rode over here last month. And don't apologize for a splendidly built, roomy cabin like this one! Your eight rooms make it seem like a palace compared to my four. Until Godfrey showed me the plans for the Italianate mansion he intends to build, I thought W.H. had extravagant ideas for our house. You'll live like royalty for the rest of your days, Julia! Do you have any idea how happy I am for you?"

"I think I do. But enough about the Barnsleys and the Scarbroughs. Talk to me about your family—the children, W.H.'s exciting election to Congress, your mother, sisters, brothers. And, oh, the Brownings and especially Natalie. Her handsome, blond husband was here overnight a year ago, you know. I wouldn't be at all surprised if Godfrey doesn't hope to have Mr. Latimer supervise the building of his—mansion, as he loves calling it."

"He wouldn't find a better builder anywhere, but if Godfrey Barnsley manages to pry Burke away from his own home and Natalie long enough to build a mansion twenty-some miles away, I'd be the most surprised of anyone! She hates every minute that man's out of her sight."

Julia shook her head. "Still the same Natalie, eh?"

"Actually, no, she isn't—quite," Eliza Anne said. "Losing her baby crushed her, but she's come out of her first dreadful period of sorrow remarkably well. I'm quite proud of her."

"I can't imagine even Natalie deterring a man like Burke Latimer if he really wanted to build our house. He struck me as knowing his own mind."

"Oh, he does indeed," Eliza Anne agreed, "but he's as deeply bound to Natalie as she to him. And along with their white housekeeper, Burke truly helped her work her way past that agonizing sense of having failed him because the baby was born dead."

"Godfrey tells me that both the Brownings were there right after the baby died. That must have helped Natalie too."

"Julia, Julia, one never knows about that girl! Anyone would think it would have helped, but I can't impress upon you too much how Natalie lives for her husband. She's devoted to her parents, but Mark, in particular, has spoiled her so."

"I think everyone in Savannah knows that. What of the Browning boy, Jonathan? He must be almost a man now."

Carefully, Eliza Anne began to tell her about Jonathan and Cherokee Mary. In passing, she mentioned Ben's suicide, but wanting to avoid the awkward subject, did not dwell on it, choosing instead to go into rather more detail than she'd intended by defending Jonathan's odd choice of Mary. Dwelling on Cherokee Ben's audacity at allowing himself to become infatuated with Natalie suddenly seemed too ridiculous—too obvious—even to try to explain.

Somewhat helplessly, her eyes averted from Julia's attentive face, she said, "Why I'm discussing all these—Indians, I'm sure I don't know."

"I do," Julia said, sitting up straight now. "No one would ever dream that a gentle, obedient boy like Jonathan would—" She stopped short. "No, I'm not going to say it. Godfrey and I literally bulled our way through my mother's thick wall of prejudice and objections. If Jonathan loves his Cherokee and if she can learn how to live in Savannah society, I wish them well."

"Julia, you do?"

"Yes. And that's all I'm going to say. I've—known my own tragedies, Eliza Anne," she said, her eyes seeming to follow the formal garden paths that led away into deep woods. "First Papa, then my own little Reginald, not quite two and a half when he died. I think I've learned what matters most. Love. The Brownings accepted Natalie's marrying a carpenter. They'll find a way with Cherokee Mary too, I'm sure. Now I want to know all about your three, Eliza Anne. They all look the picture of health, but talk to me about Mary Cowper. Such a strikingly beautiful girl! How old is she now?"

"She'll soon be twelve."

"My, my, just the age when a girl begins to think about romance."

"Oh, Julia! At twelve?"

"Don't you remember those love poems I used to pass for you to the Minis boy when you were only ten?"

Eliza Anne laughed, but it was forced. "What? Oh, yes, but that was silly business."

"Not to you then! How is Mary Cowper down inside? Surely you've given that some thought. I've probably not done too well, but I've tried to stay close to my Anna from the time she was ten. Can you believe she's thirteen now?"

"No, I can't, Julia. Well, I'm certainly close to Mary C. We've always been close. It shows, I think, in her marked, quick obedience—at least most of the time. She's a child yet, of course, but quite a docile little girl."

"She shows no signs whatever of rebelling—inside?"

"None!" Then less defensively, she asked, "Julia, does a mother ever really know the answer to that? She'll be enrolled at your Anna's school, Montpelier, in the fall, just before her father leaves for Washington City." Eliza Anne sighed. "I'm sure I'll know even less once she's away from me. I'm counting rather on Anna's good influence. One thing I do know is that Mary Cowper's father and I are agreed that she will not be permitted to marry someone—outside *our* choice for her!"

Eliza Anne could feel her friend's lovely, deep-set gray eyes boring into her. She felt oddly uncomfortable, puzzled by the unexpected silence.

Finally, Julia spoke. "I can't quite believe I heard that come from *you*. After such a brilliant defense of both Natalie and Jonathan's peculiar choice of mates, I frankly thought you'd somehow moved past our parents' bent toward what they consider 'good marriages into proper families.' I'm not at all sure I'm past it, but somehow I expected that you were. That perhaps I could learn from you. Tell me, is Mary Cowper attracted to someone you and W.H. disapprove?"

"No, no, no, dear Julia. I told you, she isn't quite twelve yet! I really don't know what made me say that. I did sound dreadfully old-fashioned, didn't I?"

"Frankly, yes, but I've noticed both here and in England that most parents still feel it their right to decide for their offspring. Do you intend to supervise the young ladies Henry and Robert choose?"

"Oh, dear, I haven't thought about them that way yet! Even though Bobby insists that he dreams of pretty girls every night."

"Well, I try to live day by day with my—brood of seven—reminded of something wise your mother, Miss Eliza, once said to me."

"What did she say? Maybe I need to hear it."

"Mrs. Mackay once told me that a truly good mother keeps ever in her mind that everything she does for any of her children, every sacrifice she makes, every lesson she teaches, moves *her* inexorably toward the day when she must stand by and freely watch that child leave home—go out on its own."

"Sounds like Mama," Eliza Anne said, unsmiling. "W.H. and I have one dream, though, and that is to work and plan and give our children such a comfortable and beautiful home at Etowah Cliffs that they will all choose to stay at least nearby."

"Speaking of your startlingly good-looking husband, will you be moving to Washington City when he goes this fall?"

"Not at first, because of the demands of our property up here. The thought that November's even coming—sickens me! How do you bear it when Godfrey stays away in Savannah—in Liverpool for such long periods of time, Julia? It's no wonder you're so frail and have so much trouble with your nerves, my dear!"

"I go with him when I feel equal to it. Otherwise, I do what all lonely women have to do. I manage, somehow. I hate it, but I muddle through the months until I have him back again. W.H. has to leave in November?"

Eliza Anne sighed heavily. "Yes. And although we talk and talk about his political future, neither of us ever actually mentions November. I can't allow myself even to admit the year 1843 has such a month!"

"You will go eventually, though, won't you? If he writes begging you and the children to come?"

She looked directly at Julia. "Wherever William Henry Stiles asks me to go, I'll go. I'm thirty-five years old and at times I startle myself at the way I just go on falling more and more in love with that man, but I do. There isn't a door anywhere in the whole wide world which I could bear to shut against him—if I thought he wanted me to step through it. Our new house and every foot of land can disintegrate before I'd refuse him. I won't like leaving my river, but I'll go. I'll always go where W.H. is, if at all possible." She smiled. "If it's impossible, I'll go anyway!"

Chapter 32

MORE THAN a year had passed since Sarah Gordon's husband died, but Eliza Mackay still called at the Gordon mansion every other week or so. She'd made herself walk this morning, in spite of rheumatism in her knees, because June was one of her favorite months in Savannah. Her heart felt leafed out, as new as the green on the trees and bushes beside which she walked. Even the live oaks, which dropped their dull winter green only when spring pushed in, were bright and cheerful today.

I hope Sarah is more cheerful this morning, Eliza thought, as she labored a bit up the steep front steps of the Gordon house. She hates so to leave Savannah and I'm not sure she's right to go. Coming back later to an empty house is almost like losing her husband all over again, but it's been a long time since she's seen her uncle, Judge Wayne, in Washington City, and her other northern relatives. Anyway, it's none of my business.

Cliffie Gordon, now nearly seven, opened the front door at Eliza's knock and, as always, wanted to know about her grandson Henry Stiles.

"Henry's just fine. Fine and sassy, according to his mother's latest letter, Cliffie," she said as the pretty child politely took her bonnet. "I believe Henry and his family are visiting the Barnsleys at Woodlands this week. They all rode horseback and I think it's more than twenty-five miles!"

"They didn't go in their carriage?"

"No, the roads shake a carriage to pieces! Anyway, Henry's mother is so full of energy up there where the air is clear and light, she seems to thrive on long rides. I think my daughter wanted to be able to brag about how well she held up over those miles. How's your mother today, Cliffie?"

"Smiling more at me," Cliffie said. "She wasn't a bit fussy at breakfast. We're taking a trip too."

"I know and I'll miss all of you."

"I miss Henry. I wish we could visit him, but we have to visit relatives, Mama says."

When Eliza and Sarah were seated a few minutes later in the family parlor, Sarah Gordon, seeming far more spirited, plunged straight into a subject Eliza hoped wouldn't be discussed at all today.

"I understand," Sarah said, "that the Browning boy is already en route to visit his little Cherokee up in Cass—without even coming here to see his poor parents first. Eliza, am I un-Christian to wish that boy had fallen in love with a —white girl? One of our own? I know Mary's sweet and pretty, but I can't help feeling sorry for Mark and Caroline. For both young people, actually. What chance do they have for real happiness here in Savannah? Tell me, do you pray that Jonathan might find someone else at school?"

"No, I don't. Those two love each other, Sarah. Mary and Jonathan just might do far better than we think, and you and I can do a lot to help. We've already agreed on that and I have nothing more to say on the subject. Cliffie asked still again about my grandson Henry just now. Wouldn't it be a happy event if, years from now, those two children—?"

"Oh, yes! A perfect match, I'd think. Same family backgrounds, our families already close all these years. Do you realize that Cliffie carries the buckeye Henry sent her for her sixth birthday right in her dress pocket every day?"

"She showed it to me last week." Eliza laughed. "And it could be that Henry is the true-blue kind of boy his mother thinks he is. She writes that young Bobby sees girls in his dreams all the time. Not Henry, though. Just listen to us, Sarah. Here we sit, two widows sounding like the romantics we most certainly are!"

Only recently had Sarah Gordon been able to endure the word "widow." Eliza was still careful not to overuse it, but sooner or later, its meaning had to be accepted.

"Did you even *hope*, Eliza," Sarah went on, *not* allowing the change of subject, "that Jonathan Browning might meet another, more acceptable young lady at New Haven? I know you said you didn't pray that he would, but—"

"I don't hope for it either," she said firmly. "I stay too busy trying to keep Mark and Caroline hoping for the best—whatever that turns out to be." Still determined to change the subject, she asked, "You will give all our deepest regards to your uncle, Judge Wayne, won't you, Sarah?"

"Of course I will. How long do you think Jonathan plans to stay in the upcountry? I can just imagine how his parents long for him to be here with them during his school holiday."

"Jonathan will do what's right, I'm sure. Mary McDonald is wise too, in her way, and Eliza Anne writes that with Natalie's help, the child is refining her English. Sarah, those two young people are going to be—all right."

"Perhaps. *If* Bertha Potter ever lets the gossip die down."

"That's one place you and I can help." Eliza was firm. "And we *must*. We must. I believe real love is planted in the human heart by God Himself. We dare not do anything but try to help those two young people."

On Monday, Lorah Plemmons tried, but even she couldn't convince Mary not to ride alone to meet Jonathan's stage at Sallie Hughes's ford over at Milner's place. Mrs. Stiles tried too, begged her to think about the danger for a young woman riding even five miles or so by herself, but Mary could be as stubborn as she was sweet, so they all gathered to wave her off on her pony just before noon.

"If he does not come today," Mary called to them from Little Star's sturdy back, "I will sleep tonight in the warm woods. I am not afraid of the night or animals."

"Good for you, Mary," Natalie called back. "Old Arnold Milner doesn't care for Cherokees. You'll be better off in the woods. They're far friendlier than he'd ever be!"

"Tell Jonathan he can get a horse from Milner, though," Burke said, "to ride back here with you."

"And one of my people can return it," W.H. added. "Milner's a good Democrat, Mary. He'll treat Jonathan right in all ways."

"Being a good Democrat makes him just about perfect with Papa," Henry joked.

"Absolutely, son." W.H. laughed, mussing Henry's blond hair. "Milner not only voted for me—he worked for me."

In response, unable to wait a minute longer to begin her ride to Jonathan, Mary laughed and waved, and Little Star's sudden, eager gallop left them all laughing too.

After a mile or so, Mary slowed the pony, to rest him a little and to give herself time for happy thoughts and talk of what lay ahead. Talking to Little Star was as natural as breathing, and she didn't have to worry about correcting her English when she discussed something with him because they'd belonged to each other for so long. "As someday Jonathan and I belong to each other, Star," she said. "Oh, we belong now too. Every step you take— every turn of his stage wheels—he comes closer to me. Every step, Star, is magic! Did you know you have magic hooves? And Jonathan's stagecoach has magic wheels?"

Once, over the five miles that separated Etowah Cliffs from the ford, she remembered to pray that she had not been too stubborn with everyone back home, because now, she felt almost like one of the family. Jonathan do that for me, she thought. Jonathan love me and so they all love me too. Mister Burke, he always love me—and Miss Lorah. Also, Natalie love me good now . . .

Riding again, she spoke aloud to Little Star. "I learn, Star. I learn so much every day. Something new every day! I learn to speak good, like Ben want me to speak." Every thought of Ben still shot pain through her heart. How he had tried to teach her to speak right! Ben, who lay dead under the ground in the grassy backyard of her cabin . . .

As though to cheer her, with no urging at all, Little Star broke into a joyful gallop along the narrow clay road. "Good!" she cried, drying her eyes on the back of her hand. "Good, Star! We hurry to Jonathan. When he is here and I am in his arms, I can only smile. Not cry."

The new pink-striped skirt Miss Lorah had helped her make billowed in the wind stirred by Star's gallop. From happiness, she cried out . . . and the cry sounded like the cry of Natalie she had overheard from inside Mister Burke's cabin last week.

Would loving her cause Jonathan to shout as Mister Burke shouted—helpless from both pain and joy?

Remembering Natalie's warning that Mr. Milner did not like Cherokees, Mary hid in the woods on the bank of the stream to wait for the first sight of the stagecoach. Before she saw it come from behind the thick growth on the far side of the Etowah, she heard its rattle and the horses' hooves pounding along the last stretch of flat road before the driver shouted "Whoa!" to ease the stage down the bank and into the shallow water.

Her heart pounded too and it was all she could do to stay out of sight until the long wait was over and the team forded the river and pulled the coach triumphantly up the very bank where she was hiding. There would be no need to sleep in the woods. She knew he could not yet see her, but she saw Jonathan leaning out the coach window, waving his arm—just in case she was there.

Out of her hiding place now, Mary curtsied as Jonathan saw her and raced up the path. People watched from the wet, muddy stage cab and from the bank, but smiling proudly at her curtsy, Jonathan threw both arms around her and leaned down to kiss her forehead. Even in her ecstasy, she thought he seemed almost angry to have to release her so quickly because they were not yet alone.

"Mary, *Mary,*" he said hoarsely, stepping back to look and look hungrily down into her face. "Oh, Mary, it's been—such a long time! It was dangerous, but you did come alone on Star, didn't you? You said you would in your last letter."

She could only nod fast and beam up at him. "You borrow a horse from Mr. Milner," she managed at last. "We ride home together—alone!"

Hiding in the bushes again, she tried to put together the tumbling thoughts in her brain while he hurried away to find a horse. He was—Jonathan, but a different Jonathan! He had let his sideburns grow, dark and thick—far down on both cheeks. His face was somehow older and a dark beard shadow spread across his fine, square chin and jaws. *Jonathan was now a man* and in a different, almost strange way, he was drawing her to him. He was a—man. Older, even more handsome, almost breaking her heart with love. Her love for him. His love for her. There had been no need to ask. Jonathan loved her more too.

The long, dragging months away in a place called Connecticut had not caused him to forget. True, she had not worried much that he might, because in every letter he had told her that even hard hours of study in books had not blotted her face, the scent of her skin, the feel of her mouth, from his memory.

Then the thud of a horse's hooves pounding along the hard-packed lane from Milner's stables exploded her thoughts wide open. He was galloping toward her—galloping fast, not walking the horse even over such a short stretch of road to where she waited with Little Star pawing the earth impatiently.

"Come on," Jonathan called without dismounting. "We're going to ride hard for a few minutes, Mary. I've got to get us out of sight. I've got to—hold you close to me—without anyone seeing us!"

Beating along right behind him on the road that led back to Etowah Cliffs, she couldn't help wondering how long they'd have to ride before Jonathan felt certain they would be far enough away from people to kiss and hold—to kiss and hold. The question had barely formed in her mind when, one hand lifted high in a signal to stop, Jonathan reined Milner's brown mare sharply. The lightest tug at Star's reins halted the pony, so that at the same moment Jonathan dismounted and started toward her, Mary was running into his arms . . . Arms that felt harder, stronger than she remembered were holding her so close, she grew almost faint with the struggle of trying to push closer.

"When do they expect us, Mary?" he asked finally. "Do they expect us at any—particular time?"

"No, Jonathan. No time. I mean—no *particular* time." He was holding her away from him just far enough now to look and look at her face, her body, even her feet. "My slippers are muddy. Excuse me," she said, unable to keep her face as serious as his. "They are new slippers for your visit. I stepped in the river a little—at my first sight of you."

"You're—beautiful, Mary! You're—even more beautiful than I remembered you."

His voice sounded hoarse again and solemn.

"You—you, Jonathan are—"

"What, Mary? What am I—to you?"

"You—oh, you are—*Jonathan!* To be Jonathan is—everything. You are also older."

"Yes," he said quickly, sounding pleased. "I'm older and I know myself still better. I know you better too. I don't know how to say this, but for the past few months I just *know so much!* I know I love you and that I will never, never love anyone but you. I—know you still better now, my love."

Smiling up at him, she said simply, "I *am* your love. And you are my love. I once longed to touch—just to touch Mister Burke's arm. Now, he comes toward me down the road or moves past me in a room and—he is only kind, good Mister Burke who help Ben and me to—live again."

She thought Jonathan's face looked younger now, because he was smiling too.

"You can't be anything but honest, can you, Mary?"

"I always tell you true, Jonathan. Your sister, Natalie, wants happiness for you and me also."

"My sister's really behaving, eh? Oh, I know what a hard time she's had, but if she's being kind to you, that really makes me happy. And it's a good sign for her."

"I speak better now?"

"You certainly do!"

"Natalie and Miss Lib, they help me with many things." She laughed. "I even use the right fork!"

"I suppose we'd better ride on a ways now," he said, one arm still tenderly around her waist. "But first, I want to know how it is with you—about Ben? You haven't mentioned him in a letter for over three months. Is it—better?"

"It is bad and also better," she said. "I cry once as Little Star brought me to meet you. I cry for Ben. Not for Ben, for me without him. But you give me —so much sweetness like honey—Ben is glad for me in heaven. I am always reminded of that."

Back in their saddles, she blew a kiss which Jonathan returned. "We'll talk some more when we let my mare and Star rest the next time," he called. "I want to know all about the Stileses and Miss Lorah and Burke's new helper, Sam—I want to know everything." Without even a nudge from Mary, Little Star pranced up beside Jonathan's horse. "I want to know everything about— your world," he said.

"You talk to me about Savannah too? How is your mother and father and Miss Eliza Mackay and"—her laughter bubbled up—"and all the—dinner guests at your house?"

Making Jonathan laugh was what she liked almost best. He was laughing when he wheeled his mount and called, "Savannah with all her dinner guests will be your world someday, Mary. And I'm not sure I can wait three more long years!"

Soon after they reached Etowah Cliffs, the Stileses and Natalie and Burke took Jonathan on an inspection tour of the still unfinished main house, whose exterior now gave a good idea of how grand a place it would one day become. Jonathan, though longing to be with Mary, showed keen interest in every carefully made joist, and took note that Burke had refused the use of even one two-by-four—all three-by-fives—thereby pleasing the particular architectural taste of Uncle W.H. to a T. He thought he'd never seen his sister look so beautiful, in spite of the past year's grief. Certainly, he thought Burke the happiest of men, and when the Latimers said goodbye at the end of the house tour and walked off arm in arm toward their own old Indian cabin, Jonathan felt real pride in Natalie. Anyone could see that his once spoiled sister's contentment had little or nothing to do with where she lived. Savannahians would surely be aghast—even the kind ones—at the primitive log-cabin residence of Mark Browning's daughter.

Seated on the porch of the old frame wing of Uncle W.H.'s house with him and Miss Lib, Jonathan couldn't help smiling in a kind of triumph that both he and Natalie had *not* been robbed by their parents' wealth or social standing of what *really mattered* in life and said as much to the Stileses.

His words produced a heavy silence, then an uncomfortable chill, when Miss Lib said, "I do hope being off at Yale hasn't instilled the wrong northern ideas in you, Jonathan! You and Natalie should feel only pride in your parents' social standing and wealth. You and Natalie are *Brownings!* Do you honestly believe your sister's lost any of her—good breeding living up here with us in the wilds?"

"Just a minute," Uncle W.H. joked. "I think I resent that, Lib! We've tamed the place."

Smiling a little, Jonathan said, "What I really believe, Miss Lib, is that Natalie has made her own choice and she's happy with it."

"And you, Jonathan?" she asked. "Have you truly, permanently made your choice?"

"Yes, ma'am," he answered quickly. "I'm going to spend the remainder of my life as close to Mary as—humanly possible."

"I'm sure it does seem that way now," Uncle W.H. said easily. "After all, Jack Mackay's great friend Captain Robert E. Lee might have made much the same answer in his youth about spending his days with my lovely wife!"

"W.H., don't tease."

"I'm not teasing, Lib. Merely stating a fact."

Miss Lib flared a little. "Lee's a happily married gentleman and the father of six children he adores!"

"*Now* he is, yes, my dear. But only because I came along and swept you off your feet."

"Only Robert Lee himself knew whether or not he was once in love with me and let that be the end of this ridiculous talk!"

She sounded quite cross, Jonathan thought, and he tried to change the subject a little. "Just before I left school, Mama wrote that Jack's planning to visit Captain Lee sometime this fall."

"Where is Lee stationed now, Jonathan?" Uncle W.H. asked.

"Fort Hamilton on Long Island, I believe, sir. It seems autumn's Captain Lee's favorite time up there, so he's urging Jack to visit during his present sick leave from the Army."

Miss Lib sat up, startled. "Sick leave, Jonathan? Mama hasn't written one word to me about Jack's being that ill!"

"Oh, I'm sorry," he said. "My mother wrote that he does look pretty pale, but with the same old feisty spirit and still quoting Ecclesiastes and Shakespeare by the yard."

"But the Army doesn't hand out sick leave for pleasure!"

"I guess it's that congestion in his lungs, but don't you think if they were purposely keeping something from you, Miss Lib, Mama would have warned me not to mention it? They all knew I was headed this way."

He thought she sighed with some relief. "I suppose so. You must forgive me, son, for being cross. Your congressman uncle here knows perfectly well that I get vexed when he brings up that long-ago girlish romance—so called —between Captain Lee and me."

"I've read some of Lee's old letters to you, Lib, don't forget," Uncle W.H. said slyly.

"And if you'd read some he wrote my sisters, you'd dredge up an equal amount of nonsense about them!"

"How could I possibly be jealous of your sisters? It's you I love."

"Pay him absolutely no mind, Jonathan," she said. "My husband's become quite cocky since his victory in last year's election." The frown that had formed a quite becoming furrow between her wide-spaced dark eyes gave way to the smile that Jonathan thought must still drain Uncle W.H. of all resistance. "A man as handsome as W.H. Stiles is free, I suppose, to be the cock of the walk when he pleases," Miss Lib went on. "Don't mind our well-worn exchanges about poor Lee. I always know your uncle is feeling proud and accomplished and sure of himself or he wouldn't dare bring up the subject."

Sitting on the top step, Jonathan leaned his head against a porch post and studied them both. What a handsome couple, he thought. Miss Lib's right when she insists he looks like a poet. And growing up, I don't think I realized how truly beautiful she is. "You two are still terribly in love—even after all these years, aren't you?" he asked.

"It's that evident?" Uncle W.H. wanted to know. "At our advanced ages?"

"Yes, sir! I'm glad too. The way I'm glad about my parents. I honestly think they're closer than ever now that Natalie and I have 'flown the coop,' as Miss Eliza says. You see, I'm old enough to recognize a lot of things I missed before."

"A year at Yale's made a big difference?" Uncle W.H. asked.

"Oh, yes, sir. Surely you found that it did for you. Do you know they still talk about the Bread and Butter Rebellion that got you and some of your classmates expelled from Yale way back there in—was it 1828?"

"That's right, Jonathan. All but four of us were allowed to apply, though, for readmission. I chose not to." He gave Miss Lib a devilish smile. "Good thing too. I'd have lost her to Captain Lee for certain had I gone back to Yale. You see, son, Lee spent half his time at the Mackay house in those days while he was ostensibly working so hard on the drainage system or some such at Fort Pulaski."

"W.H., that's more than enough! Lee did work hard. He only spent weekends at our house. He was the handsomest visitor Savannah had seen in those days and—"

"—and so a romance with the most beautiful belle in town was inevitable," Uncle W.H. finished for her.

"Jonathan," Miss Lib asked out of the blue, "why didn't Mary come along when we inspected our new house?"

He had tried to persuade her to come. Explaining Mary's gentle refusal, her excuse that she much preferred to wash and iron his travel clothes herself, seemed suddenly difficult. "She had some work to do in her own cabin, I believe," he said lamely.

"Nothing Miss Lorah wouldn't have done for her gladly, I'm sure. Don't you agree, W.H.?"

"I suppose so, yes," he said, not paying full attention.

"You'll have to excuse him, Jonathan," Miss Lib said. "His mind wanders to the Hall of Representatives in Washington City at the drop of a hat these days." She paused. "Mary just doesn't feel—one of us, does she?"

"I—I think she does, Miss Lib. I mean, in the short time I've been here, it seems to me she feels quite at home with all of you. She and Natalie are—"

"Oh, I know about Mary and Natalie," Miss Lib said a bit tartly. "Natalie is always on the side of anyone or anything that tends to break with—tradition."

"Lib!" Uncle W.H. was paying attention now, Jonathan thought, judging by the tone of his voice. "This is Jonathan's first evening here. He's been most charitable, in my opinion, to have spent it with us instead of Mary. Do you really think the boy needs a lecture about—proper consideration of his family background in choosing a wife? I tend to agree with you, naturally, but perhaps Jonathan would enjoy a discussion of when you plan to join your husband in Washington City this fall. I feel that's a far more pertinent subject."

"And I feel it's time I went upstairs," Miss Lib said, getting to her feet—both men with her—"to check on our sons, who should be getting ready for bed by now if you really intend to take them fishing at dawn."

When she'd gone in the house, the two men sat down again. "Miss Lib isn't too keen about living in Washington City, sir?"

Uncle W.H. gave his easy, charming laugh. "Don't take Lib too seriously, son. She and I enjoy our little fracases at times. We both know exactly when *not* to indulge in one." He frowned slightly. "But, to tell you the truth, I'm not sure actually just how she feels about leaving Etowah Cliffs. She'll have to stay on here for a time, at least, in order to look after the place. She also despises being away from me. I'm not too modest to know that for a certainty, nor to admit it. I somehow think my successful political career, at this point, is rather a nuisance to her."

"Oh, she's terribly proud of you!"

"I know that. She doesn't allow me to forget it for a minute. She—simply feels so well here in our upcountry air and so loves this beautiful spot on the cliffs above the river. Washington weather can be as bad as or worse than Savannah's. Don't you notice how invigorating our climate is here?"

Jonathan smiled. "Everything's better for me because Mary's here."

"You—do mean to marry her, don't you?"

"Oh, yes, sir! In fact, I haven't figured out how to live without her for three more years until I graduate from Yale."

"That bad, eh?" Uncle W.H. thought for a long time, then said, as though he'd just reached a decision, "Well, I believe you know your heart, so in that case I'll put in my own small two cents, if I may. Your question, I believe you said, is how to live without Mary until you graduate from Yale."

"That's right. I battled my way through every bit of the first term!"

"Very well, let me remind you then, especially in view of my recent success at the polls, that I chose *not* to graduate, Jonathan."

Jonathan stared at him, felt a surge of hope, but decided to wait for Uncle W.H. to say more.

"As I told you, after the Bread and Butter Rebellion up there, I could have reapplied, been readmitted and—graduated with my class. I didn't. I finished only my second year and quit to do what I'd always planned anyway. I read law in Savannah, went into private practice, was solicitor general of the eastern district in my early twenties, sat on the city council, served in the state legislature and now am about to begin my first term as a United States congressman!"

On his feet out of sheer excitement, sensing that he and Mary just *might* have a surprise ally in Uncle W.H., Jonathan said, "That's right! Maybe I—won't graduate either. Our plans, mine and Papa's, were for me to graduate, then learn his mercantile and factoring business straight from him anyway. What can a man learn at Yale or anywhere else beyond Latin, mathematics, grammar and composition? I guess my parents and I just always took it for granted that—well, that I'd graduate—because Papa did." He frowned. "I—I guess, though, my parents would be pretty disappointed in me if I didn't graduate. Uncle W.H.?"

"What is it, son?"

"You'll be in Savannah to catch your boat for Washington City in about three months, won't you?"

"I will be. It's far easier to take the stage and train to Savannah, then make the voyage north by water. Of course, I know what you're about to ask of me, but I'm not at all sure I should become involved in this."

"But you're such a convincing speaker, you have such a way with words—on any subject."

"*If* I believe in my subject."

"You're the one who gave me the idea!"

"I know I am, and if you press me to promise to try to talk your parents into agreeing with you—into allowing you to quit Yale—you may well be sorry."

"Why? Why would I be sorry? There's nothing I want to do as much as to marry my girl and work in his countinghouse with Papa."

"I know that's what you think now."

"Miss Lib's mother once told me that only getting older can enable a person to see both sides of an issue. You may not believe this, Uncle W.H., but I do see both sides of this." He paused while the truth slowly dawned on him. "*You* are on *both* sides, aren't you?"

"In a manner of speaking, son, I suppose I am."

During the awkward silence that followed, Jonathan remembered that Sheftall Sheftall once said, "W. H. Stiles has to stop fence straddling on political issues," or words to that effect. Maybe Uncle W.H. straddled more than just political issues, he thought, and felt a little sorry for the man he'd looked up to all his life. Jonathan had often seen both sides of things too, and knew there was absolutely nothing easy about it.

"I've kept you talking long enough," the boy said. "I do thank you for treating me like a man, though."

Uncle W.H. ran his slender fingers through his slightly thinning blond hair, as though struggling to be as definite as he felt obliged to be. "You are a young man now, Jonathan. As a young man, I rose quite rapidly in the world of law and politics, but I admit I didn't always think as—as fairly as you seem to already. You are not yet twenty-one, though. Even if I erred in putting the idea of leaving Yale early into your mind, you must consider your parents' wishes first—above your own *and* above Mary's."

"Oh, I'm sure Mary hasn't even thought there might be a chance for us to get married for at least three more years!"

"Quite probably she hasn't."

"I'm sure she hasn't. But, sir, will *you* think some about talking to my father when you go down to Savannah in November?"

"Yes, but I can only promise to *think* about it, Jonathan. Parents give enormously, if they're good parents, to their children for years and years. They do have a right to be heard and heeded in any matter as serious as higher education—and marriage."

"Do you and Miss Lib plan to choose marriage partners for Mary Cowper? For Henry? For young Bobby?"

"They are *our* children, Jonathan, and their children will be *our* grandchildren."

Deciding to ignore that, Jonathan said with his ready smile, "You're not leaving for the North until November, sir. I promised my parents I'd be back in Savannah in September. I only have about two months up here with Mary. If you do decide to talk to Father, I'll have already broken the news of what I want to do. You won't have to do that. And, Uncle W.H., I'm not planning to get married for at least a year. I'll do just what you did—finish two years at Yale. Captain Jack Mackay is going North to visit his friend Lee in October. I hope to make the voyage with him. I'll have had most of the month of September to ease the idea into my parents' minds before you get there. Somehow I think Jack will also help me a lot."

Uncle W.H. cleared his throat uneasily. "I have no doubt he will. Natalie too, I'm fairly certain."

"She seems to be awfully kind to Mary these days."

"Yes, I've noticed. Natalie also wields enormous power with your father."

Smiling again, Jonathan said, "Not with Mama, though."

"That's correct. Good night, son. Lib and I appreciate your sharing your first evening up here with us. Such respect and courtesy to your elders definitely becomes you."

Jonathan ran all the way to Mary's cabin, where she waited patiently for him on the front steps. Miss Lorah Plemmons, whom he liked so much, and her Sam were just inside, he knew. It was nearly dark. If he and Mary were to be truly alone, he guessed they'd have to find a lantern and walk along the river cliffs.

As it turned out, though, what they both seemed to prefer was just to sit there together on the cabin steps and hold each other. One of Mary's great charms for him was that silences didn't seem to bother her. Between the two of them, silence held more meaning at times than words.

Chapter 33

"ONE THING we have to hold on to, Caroline," Miss Eliza said, fanning with a well-worn, hand-painted Japanese fan, a cherished gift from her late husband, "is the fact that this dreadful, stifling heat will pass. It's the third of September, after all, and by the time W.H. gets here in November, we could be chilly enough to wish for a little heat."

Swatting mosquitoes and gnats while sipping iced lemonade with her friend on the shaded Mackay porch, Caroline pressed the cold glass against her forehead. "I know it's no worse for me than for anyone else," she said, forcing a smile. "And I didn't come here this morning to complain, Miss Eliza." She paused. "No, that's a lie. I think I did come to complain."

The older woman laughed. "That's a favorite Savannah summer pastime, isn't it? It's no wonder Natalie loves the upcountry. I remember how she used to throw herself across her bed on a smothering summer day and pound the mattress in sheer anger at our heat."

"Her mother would do the same thing if she weren't a hypocrite!"

"Whatever you are, you're not a hypocrite, Caroline Browning."

"Yes, I am. Even with Mark. I've wanted to pound him a dozen times through this wretched summer weather for not taking me to Newport—or at least to visit Natalie. I love Savannah too, but oh, that man does frustrate me at times. He actually prefers to stay here and swelter. What's the good of having as much money as Mark and I have if we smother in his beloved steaming city year after year?"

Knowing Eliza Mackay as she did, Caroline imagined the brief silence that followed her outburst was intended to give her time to get hold of herself, to *hear* her own self-pitying, cross voice.

I wish I hadn't managed all my life to end up seeing myself as I really am, she thought. I've spoiled everyone who knows me well. Good old Caroline may spout and scold but she'll wind up righting herself, using common sense, facing facts as they are. Maybe that's one reason I've come so close to resenting Natalie all these years. Maybe my daughter has been far more honest than her mother, who demands of herself—sheer nobility in the face of any maddening circumstance. It's too hot to be sensible today!

"According to what Mark's told me," Miss Eliza said carefully, "he's never been happier than during these few months alone with you."

Caroline gave her a quick, penetrating look, then a smile. "You do know me, don't you?"

"I would hope so. I've loved you a long time. I wish with all my heart I had just the right thing to say to you today, but the older I get, the more I dislike my lifetime habit of doling out advice. I must be dreadfully annoying."

"Oh, Miss Eliza, you? Mark and I both know we lean too heavily on you—for almost everything!" She thought a minute. "You—and until now—Jonathan."

"Jonathan will be home from Cass tomorrow. Surely that helps a lot."

"Oh, yes, yes. And please don't think I haven't loved every minute of the time Mark and I have had alone this summer. I have. You, of all people, know I have. You remember me as a lovesick young girl, Miss Eliza. I—I think I still am. Every evening when it's time for him to come home, I feel I can't wait a minute longer. And don't remind me that he has a good and valid reason for not leaving Savannah in the summer. If anyone knows of his love affair with this city, I do. When there isn't a breath of air stirring, Mark feels a 'nice, cool breeze'!"

Miss Eliza laughed. "To Mark, Savannah has no flaws, but I honestly think he'd have taken you North this year if he'd been able to find a responsible young man to run the business, don't you?"

"I suppose I do, but he's so particular. He's tried three different people since that dreadful Olin Wheeler attempted to abscond with the money old Osmund Kott left Natalie. No one's careful enough with those precious planter accounts to suit Mark. And yes, I'm proud of his integrity, and no, I wouldn't want him to be different. I just despise Savannah heat! Other men also have important businesses in this town. Other men take their wives away from it."

"Other men don't have Mark's conscience. You've managed through all but half a dozen or so Savannah summers, my dear. Somehow I think you'll make it through three more—until Jonathan graduates and can run the business. Three years is a very short time."

"I suppose so." She sighed. "I also know that if Jonathan were graduating this next year, I'd be stewing even more because he must still be determined to marry his little Cherokee or he wouldn't have spent the entire summer away from his parents up there with her."

"Caroline, I think they are going to get married. I wish you could stop fighting it."

She frowned. "I don't fight it, really. I'm more—afraid than rebellious. Maybe I've always been." Turning in her rocker to look straight at her friend, she said, "You may not believe this, but I feel I understand why my son loves Mary. She and Jonathan are—a great deal alike. Jonathan's always been so kind and sweet-tempered and agreeable. Still, he's seemed to live contentedly within himself in a way that, as the months go by, I see more and more clearly makes me think of—Mary. Until lately, I felt her odd, self-contained silences and sweetness had something to do with being an outsider, with feeling—different. I believe now she's really quite like my son."

"You're a remarkable woman, my dear. You—deserve Mark and you know I couldn't pay any woman a higher compliment."

"Mark and I believe you're right about most things," she said softly. "I wish I thought I did deserve him."

"Caroline, we can't control what strikes us as right or wrong. We *can* control how we react, though. I haven't once heard you mention Natalie's broken promise to you about coming back here for a proper wedding in Christ Church. I know how you longed for her to keep that promise. You've controlled that disappointment admirably."

She laughed. "I don't think I ever really counted on her keeping it."

"Adjustments like that are the measure of real intelligence, Caroline. You —do deserve Mark."

"Thank you, dear friend," she said, getting to her feet. "I feel better now that we've talked. You have a way of forcing me, however gently, to sort things out in my own head. Don't get up, please, but I must go. I want Jonathan's room to be exactly the way he likes it. After all, he'll only be here for a little over a month or six weeks."

Still seated, Eliza Mackay let her eyes wander out over her dry, summer-browned yard. "Yes," she mused, "a little over a month, and my Jack will be going with him on a steamer north. I suppose we'll go right on feeling uneasy after what happened to William's family when any of our loved ones travel on a steamer, won't we?"

"Yes, but the trip to Long Island to visit Captain Lee will do Jack a world of good."

"I hope so," Miss Eliza said when Caroline stooped to kiss her goodbye. "Come again soon, dear. Anytime," she murmured absently, her mind still obviously on her own heartache over Jack's continuing illness. "I know the trip will benefit Jack. It's been good having him and William with me all summer, but Jack's getting no better in this weather. Robert Lee takes very good care of him. I'll miss Jack, though. I miss all our loved ones who don't live here anymore."

From the steps, Caroline saw Miss Eliza shake her head slowly, almost sorrowfully. For an instant, Caroline waited.

"Here it is September of 1843," the older woman went on, as if to herself, "and I find it still hard to believe William's Virginia and the two children have been gone more than five long years!"

Feeling helpless and guilty for every single one of her own complaints, Caroline said, "I know. Please take care of yourself. Try to keep cool."

At that, Miss Eliza gave her a cheerful smile, and when Caroline reached the corner and looked back, her friend was on her feet, waving.

Chapter 34

BECAUSE Jack Mackay felt stronger than usual and seemed eager to go the first week in October, they all agreed that Jonathan would sail with him ten days earlier than planned. Once more, all the Mackays and Caroline and Mark met in the noisy, busy confusion of still another ship's departure from the Savannah waterfront. In spite of the early sailing date, everyone seemed in good spirits, and after the stately sailing ship was out of sight on its way downriver to the sea and the Mackays en route home in William's carriage, Mark and Caroline stood a while on the wharf and watched the gulls wheel above a little white fishing boat as it docked with its load of fish.

Saying goodbye to Jonathan had not been easy, but they'd managed to send him off on his Yale adventure with smiles and words of encouragement. Both were pleased that their son would make the eight- or nine-day voyage north with Jack Mackay. As Jupiter headed their carriage for home, Mark and Caroline exchanged smiles and reached at the same instant to grasp hands.

"Do you suppose we're learning at last how to be parents of adult children?" Mark asked.

"I did feel quite proud of us both," Caroline said. "And you're dear to agree to spend the rest of the day at home. The house will seem empty again."

"I'm not sure I relish what we're learning about our independent children, but aside from wanting him with us a few more days, we didn't have any logical reason to refuse Jonathan's leaving early. I know Miss Eliza feels easier having him on shipboard with Jack."

"And that they took a sailing brig instead of a steam packet," she said. "My heart ached to see them go, but I thought the *G. B. Lamar* quite handsome when the wind caught her square rigging and moved her away from our wharf. I've heard Captain Sanneman's a fine ship's master too. They should have a good voyage."

"Our son's first voyage on a sailing ship," Mark said.

"I thought he seemed quite excited about it too." After a moment, she asked, "Mark, aren't we working awfully hard at making conversation? Welcome back, darling, to being alone again with your adoring wife."

He smiled down at her. "A warm welcome to life again with only your adoring husband." They rode in silence for the time it took Jupiter to turn right on Congress, then left along the east side of Reynolds Square toward their house on Bryan. "Caroline," he asked, "did you find anything in Jonathan's manner this past month that—rather puzzled you?"

"Well, of course, he was—a bit absent. Much as I used to be when I had to leave you to go back to Knightsford all those years ago. Grandfather Cameron always knew, I think, that part of me had stayed in Savannah with handsome young Mark Browning, my reason for living—even in the months before you knew you loved me. Our son is in love, therefore—all of him did not leave Etowah Cliffs and Mary."

"Darling," he said intently, "I promise to try to take you North next summer just as soon as Jonathan's school term ends. Maybe he'd agree to see us first if we met him up there. Perhaps the three of us could go to Newport, even Philadelphia for a time. Jonathan's never even seen the city where his father was born. Don't you think he might like that?"

"If we don't stay too long, don't keep him away from Mary too long."

Neither spoke again until Jupiter had brought the carriage to a stop in front of their house. Mark was unlocking the front door, in fact, before Caroline said, "I suppose having him fall in love with—a girl from such a difficult background wouldn't be so hard if Jonathan hadn't always been such an otherwise trouble-free son."

Mark waited only until they were inside the spacious entrance hall to take her in his arms. "Right now, I know just one thing," he whispered. "You're beautiful in that dark green dress . . . and the smartest decision I've made in a long time is to stay here this afternoon with you." He kissed her. "Take off your bonnet and gloves, please, ma'am. I find I need to kiss you for a long, long time . . ."

She untied the ribbon beneath her chin, gave him her direct, searching look, then handed over the green-plumed hat. "If you'll help me unbutton these gloves, I'll kiss you gladly, sir. You know that never changes, my longing to kiss you. Even when I'm worried, kissing you has always helped more than—anything!"

He felt her hand tremble as he worked at the tiny jet buttons. "Don't worry, darling," he said. "We just have to—wait."

"For what?"

"For Jonathan. For the boy to grow up a bit more. He told us absolutely nothing about any plans he and Mary might have made. He confused me, actually, by acting so certain and quiet, as though he'd come to a secret decision and was—peaceful, but saying nothing. There," he said. "There's one row of buttons."

"Let me get the other one. You're all thumbs." Unbuttoning the other glove, she said nervously, "I suppose you're right. We just have to go on—waiting." She jerked off the second glove and tossed the pair on a hall table. Then, arms reaching to encircle his neck, she whispered, "But no waiting now. We're alone. I dismissed Gerta and Maureen until tonight. We're alone,

Mark. Today we can't do one thing about either of our children. Let's go upstairs. I need to be—only your wife!"

Under full sail, the *G. B. Lamar* plied the Atlantic between Savannah and Charleston, held steady by an even-tempered southeast wind. Jack Mackay, reading in a deck chair, laid aside his book and welcomed Jonathan to take a seat beside him.

"I couldn't ask for more pleasant, intelligent company, now, could I?" Jack asked, sitting up a little straighter.

"Are you sure you're warm enough, Jack?"

"With such a fine sun beaming down? How could you question it? And we'll have an even more enjoyable voyage, my man, if you'll forget that I'm said to be teetering on the edge of my grave. I had more than enough admonition at home. Moreover, I'm heading for a visit with a fussy, admonishing 'hen' named Lee, who'd rather hover over me than dance with a beautiful lady." Jack laughed. "Well, who would *almost* rather hover than dance."

Jonathan laughed too, and of course, Jack was delighted. He loved nothing more than a spontaneous, appreciative audience. Jack kept himself mostly free of worry over the worsening condition of his tubercular lungs by provoking others to laughter with him. He also read and read and read, memorizing long portions from plays and passages from the Bible, providing a certain passage of Scripture struck him as good literature.

"Was I cheerful enough back at the Savannah wharf when we left our families, Jack?" Jonathan added. "It wasn't easy saying goodbye to my parents. Harder than before, I think. But knowing you'd be along on the voyage really helped. You've always been a favorite of mine. Of Natalie's too. I guess you're used to being just about everybody's favorite, though."

"In a manner of speaking, yes. The same holds true with you, doesn't it?"

The almost shy smile on the boy's good-looking young face amused Jack. "I'm Mary's favorite and that's what matters," he said.

"You fully intend to marry her, don't you?" Jack asked.

"Oh, yes, sir. And if I won't be imposing, I'd like to tell you something I haven't told anyone. Not my parents, not even Mary."

"I've never felt imposed upon," Jack said airily, "except by the United States Congress, which prides itself in taking advantage of the poor Army and all who people it." Head back against the wooden rocker, Jack closed his eyes. "It takes a great man, 'tis said, to be a good listener. Fire away, son. I'm listening."

In his straightforward manner, Jonathan told him of a conversation last summer with his Uncle W.H. when Stiles—to Jack always a rather haughty aristocrat—had dropped a startling idea into the boy's mind: the idea that there was no law that said Jonathan had to graduate from Yale, since Stiles himself had not. Like Stiles, Jonathan could also drop out at the end of two years, thereby meeting his parents halfway. The boy had obviously given it a lot of thought and felt convinced that, also like Stiles, he could become a success anyway, without a college degree. Jack's own decision to sail early was Jonathan's excuse for not having told his parents. The right time to tell them just hadn't come.

When Jonathan ended his story just short of mentioning the word "marriage," Jack waited briefly, then asked, "So, you mean *not* to return to Yale at the end of this school term, eh?"

"Yes, sir. I'll begin at once to work with Papa, to learn his business. The way Uncle W.H. read law back in Savannah. Working with my father has always been my goal. Papa's too."

"But haven't you left out something? W.H.'s astounding suggestion fascinates me, coming from him, but the honorable congressman aside, I've heard no hint of just why you mean to quit school. Surely my esteemed brother-in-law's vanity because of his own success isn't the single reason. I've heard you're a superb student. Could it be you dislike school that much?"

"I like Yale just fine, but—"

"But?"

On the edge of his chair, his face alight, Jonathan said, "I now know, Jack, I can't wait three more long years to make Mary my wife!"

Jack sat up, grabbed his heart and exclaimed, " 'Oh, wonderful, wonderful . . . and yet again wonderful, and after that out of all whooping!' So, it's romance at the root of it! Few believe it, but true love, I *can* comprehend."

Jonathan whacked him on the arm. "I should have known you'd tease about it. Was that Shakespeare? Or did you make up 'out of all whooping'?"

"It was Shakespeare, *As You Like It,* and I'm only half teasing. Such a marriage could bring on a torrent of problems. Still, anyone looking at your face would believe you mean to do it. But tell me, my boy, is *she* ready to face the saber tongues of Savannah? Has your lovely Indian maid agreed to this wild and glorious plan?"

"Mary doesn't know anything about it yet, but she will. She loves me as much as I love her."

"That would seem to settle it, then, but you're sure she's not at all afraid of life in the '*upper clawss*' of the old hometown society?"

"Yes, sir, not as long as I'm with her. I don't know of anything now that really frightens Mary. She's been through a lot, you know."

"I certainly do know. Don't forget, I was stationed up there in the old Cherokee Nation right at the time the Georgia Guard and our noble Army drove her people out. Your lady love has endured great grief and punishment. I tried to tell her when she was in Savannah how sorry I felt that I'd had a part in it—under orders." Jack thought a minute. "Well, enough of that. Perhaps your lovely Mary won't be too afraid of Savannah's gossip and snobbery. But how will your parents feel about it? Your mother especially."

"Why Mama—especially?"

Jack shrugged. "Oh, her own background, I suppose. She's a southern lady through and through. Kind, warm of heart—usually generous in her attitudes toward those of a class other than her own, but when an event occurs in one's own family, people have been known to blow it all out of proportion. You remember what Lady Macbeth said when they told her Duncan had been murdered, don't you?"

Jonathan grinned at him. "No, tell me."

"The lady gasped, 'What, in *our house?'* "

Jonathan laughed a little, then grew solemn. "I can count on Mama, Jack. She'll be upset at first, but I can count on her. Papa's very fond of Mary and, maybe best of all, Natalie and Burke will help all they can. My sister's changed a lot and Burke's always cared about Mary. He cares about her as though she'd been born his own sister. Say, you haven't even met Burke, have you, Jack?"

"No, but I intend to one of these days, providing I manage to stay safely six feet aboveground."

"You should visit Etowah Cliffs. I'll bet your cough would get better in that air up there."

"I plan to someday when Latimer finishes the new Stiles house. I'm enough like my late father to despise discomfort." Taken by a sudden fit of coughing, Jack grabbed his chest, then struck the chair arm in anger at himself. "Sorry," he said, getting his voice back a little, "and thanks. If you pay no more attention to my infernal coughing than you just did, we're going to get along famously."

After waiting for Jack to breathe more comfortably again, Jonathan said brightly, "Say, I heard they have ice cream on board. Would you like some?"

"I would indeed. What a glorious invention—ice cream! Shall I go find a bowl for us?"

"Oh, no," Jonathan protested, already on his feet. "You stay right there. I'll be only a few minutes."

When the boy had gone, Jack eased back into the chair and tried to think through what Jonathan had just told him about quitting school at the end of two years to marry his Cherokee. Unable to resist the clean, crisp October air at sea, he breathed deeply. No coughing. The air felt good, cleared his head. He hoped Jonathan's head was as clear as the boy had made it seem when he'd confided his secret plans. In time, Jack supposed, even the most vicious Savannah gossip might die down. Mark's enormous wealth would curb it some, he was sure, but he had read quite recently that physical characteristics often skip a generation. Jonathan's Mary certainly did not look Indian. In fact, Jack had thought it somewhat foolish that the extremely pretty young lady didn't try to pass herself off as white.

From his own brief talk with Mary during her stay in Savannah, Jack could tell that the girl was well aware of the prejudice against her people. Early in their conversation, she'd asked a question he was sure she'd asked many times: "Is it bad to you to be Cherokee, Captain Jack?" The girl would not be walking blindly into a trap.

He sighed and coughed, but it was soon past. Jonathan is sure that Mary loves him as much as he loves her, he mused. I wonder if they both know how truly blessed they are to have found love. God above knows I've looked for it. All my life I've been capturing, then releasing lovely damsels like butterflies. Oh, well, so be it. I'd certainly be no prize these days. He smiled at the mere idea of consumptive Jack Mackay as a lover between fits of coughing.

"Here you are, Captain," Jonathan called, hurrying back along deck with two bowls heaped with vanilla ice cream. "The purser said this stuff won't last long after the ice they brought on board melts, so I got us big bowls."

As they sat relishing the treat, several Savannah acquaintances strolled by. Jack was relieved that the sight of the ice cream sent them rather quickly scurrying away after the same novelty for themselves.

"I despise shipboard chitter-chatter," he said. In no time he was scraping the last melting spoonful from the bowl.

"Shall I go for more?"

Jack set the empty bowl on the deck and rubbed his thin, flat stomach. "If you can hold it, son. I certainly can't. And not one word about how much stronger I'd be if I would only eat more!"

"Not a word," Jonathan promised. "But would you like to take a nap?"

"No, I would not like to take a nap."

"Good, because I've got a question for you."

"Shoot."

"Well, I guess this is none of my business," Jonathan began, "but sometime in November—next month—Uncle W.H. will be going to Washington City to be ready for the opening of the first session of the Twenty-eighth Congress on December third and I was wondering about something. Doesn't your friend Captain Robert Lee spend some time in the national capital?"

"He does. He and his wife, Mary Custis, and the children have a home in nearby Arlington, Virginia. And every successful and trusted Army captain unfortunate enough to be stationed near Washington City spends—wastes— valuable hours chained to a Department desk battling endless mounds of paper." He peered suspiciously at Jonathan. "I think I've guessed why you asked, but tell me."

"Well, I was just wondering if Captain Lee and Uncle W.H. are—friends."

"Friends? They know each other, certainly. Bob Lee lived at our house in Savannah in his youth—in my youth. As did your own father. Of course, the Mackays have known the Stileses forever, so Lee and W.H. met often."

"Miss Eliza still keeps Captain Lee's room pretty much as he left it."

"She does indeed. My mother loves the dirt under Lee's boots. It's mutual, I might add, but your question has to do with my lovely dark-haired sister, Eliza Anne, if I'm not mistaken."

Jonathan grinned. "Miss Lib won't be going with him at first, but judging from the way Uncle W.H. hates being away from her, I expect him to start begging her to come soon after Congress convenes."

"And, of course, she'll go. What you're wondering is if my sister will see

Bob Lee and how W.H. will cotton to it. Not at all, son, but my theory has always been that W.H. rather enjoys his periodic jealous sulks over old Bob and Eliza Anne. What's more, the bond between her and Captain Lee is so strong, a show of W.H.'s jealousy would not deter the continuing friendship in any way."

"Were they always—just good friends?"

"Or does W.H. have a real reason for jealousy?" Jack shrugged. "Perhaps only my sister and Lee know the answer to that. They were the subject of Savannah gossip years ago. Not unkind gossip, of course. Happy gossip, since they were both from 'acceptable stock.'" Jack sat up. "Say, an idea just struck! If Bob Lee brings it up during my visit, I promise to report back to you. His explanation might be most interesting—happily married though he is."

Jonathan smiled. "Wouldn't that be gossip?"

"Of course! I've never even pretended not to enjoy it."

Chapter 35

THE REMAINDER of their sea voyage was unusually pleasant, and a cooperative wind moved the *G. B. Lamar* into New York before noon on the ninth day, in time for Jonathan to make it to New Haven by steamer before dark. Jack thought the young man exceptional in all ways and was proud to have had the chance to introduce him, however briefly, to his beloved friend Captain Robert Lee, who met the boat.

"I wish young Browning could have had a little time to spend with you, Bob," Jack said as he and Lee rode together in a rented carriage toward Lee's garrison at Fort Hamilton on Long Island. "He's remarkably balanced in most ways, but at a somewhat risky time in his life. Jonathan's grown up hearing your praises from my family. I think he'd listen to you."

Lee threw back his dark, handsome head and laughed. "Dearest Jack, I needed you even more than I knew! I've missed your flattery. Tell me, is Jonathan's problem his career or a pretty young lady?"

"Oh, the boy's quite content to go into business with his father. His dilemma is the misfortune of having fallen in love with a half-blood Cherokee girl. He means to finish only his second year at Yale and then marry her. Does that shock you?"

Instead of the usual quick answer, Lee gave Jack a long, thoughtful look. "I was reared on a childhood adage that went like this: 'Never marry unless you can do so into a family which will enable your children to feel proud of both sides of the house.' Having said that, I rather envy young Browning his courage to have allowed himself the liberty of falling in love with his red squaw."

Jack frowned. "Young Browning would not like his Mary being called by such a name. She is not Indian-looking."

"I meant no insult. One of my best friends lives happily out of wedlock with a full-blood he calls his red squaw. They don't, of course, move in Savannah society. Should Jonathan go through with his marriage, your mother may be the only Savannahian to accept her. Does the Indian maid love young Jonathan enough to weather that storm?"

"Yes, she does."

After a brief silence, a twinkle in his bright, penetrating eyes, Lee said,

"Make no mistake, Jack, I still believe in high romance. Still pursue a good flirtation when possible, but that old childhood adage is valid too. You know I'm content with my own marriage, but you also know I took the plunge with great care the year before Eliza Anne married Stiles. There was no passionate romance involved, although my Mary loved me, heaven knows, or she'd never have agreed to the rootless, restless life of an Army officer. Her father did not approve me until the birth of our first child, Custis. Due to the stigma of my own father's reputation, I didn't have a very wide choice, actually—in spite of my many charms. Due to my father's reckless ways, I was poor to boot."

"You exaggerate your disadvantages," Jack said. "I've always believed my sister would have married you gladly. Our family would have continued to welcome you as one of us exactly as we did when you were working on Cockspur Island in the old days." When Lee said nothing, Jack added, "But you're speaking now of Mary Custis, whom you did marry."

"Yes." Lee glanced at Jack. "You see, my good, though eccentric wife, Mary Custis, related also to the Lees, shared, in a way, the stigma of my father. She also shared my roots in Virginia, my devotion to the state. When I thought it through, my choice of her as my wife lived up to the very letter of the old adage. Our six children can be proud of 'both sides of the house.' Mary and I shared another bond—my reverence for George Washington. My Mary's great-grandmother took Washington as her second husband. Marriage to my wife gave me a desirable spiritual tie with the great man. There is also the salient point that I was without fortune or lands—Mary Custis was not."

"So, you're telling me you're a happy man in spite of having married advantageously?"

"I find your question cold, Glorious Jack," Lee said in his joking, but still straightforward manner. "Mary and I are more than content. Oh, she dislikes my being ordered from pillar to post by the Army. Moving about is even harder on her since her roots are so eternally planted in the Custis home at Arlington, but she's loved me loyally and well for years and has given me six fine gifts in our children. Mary is as true and faithful and unmethodical and forgetful as ever, of course. She's as outspoken as ever too, and I rely on that. I always know where I stand with her."

"The woman loves you shamefully, but why not? You're looking as fit and manly as ever—the dashing 'picture of a cavalier.' "

"You haven't once mentioned my mustache."

"You have missed my flattery, haven't you? Would you have counseled young Browning not to marry below his social station? Is that what you've been saying in your roundabout fashion, Bob?"

"The older I become, the less I feel adequate to counsel. There wasn't time to talk with young Jonathan, so the entire matter is hypothetical. Tell me, how is your lovely, warmhearted mother, Miss Eliza?"

"Remarkably well for her sixty-six years," Jack said. "And deeply concerned for Jonathan because she's as devoted as ever to his father, Mark Browning."

Lee turned to face Jack on the carriage seat. "We're almost at the fort and we've talked and talked all around you, dear friend. You look a bit better than I'd expected, but that could be merely color from shipboard sun in your thin face. I want the truth. How are you, Jack?"

"For a diagnosed tubercular, faring rather well, except for the ghastly weakness." He forced a laugh. "Of necessity, I am *not* romantically involved at the moment with anyone."

"We'll fix that," Lee said firmly, "and without the help of any doctor. With my own wise and loving care while you're here. You will stroll under Long Island's autumn leaves, rest in a rocking chair, eat wisely and before our visit is ended, you'll—"

"—die of boredom."

"In my company?" Lee laughed. "I'm humble, Blessed Jack, but not that humble."

Keeping up their familiar bantering after they reached Lee's quarters at Fort Hamilton, Lee tenderly helped his friend into a fresh nightshirt and to bed at what Jack called a "preposterously early hour."

"Will you be comfortable in this room?" Lee asked, arranging a stack of pillows behind Jack's head. "My good Mary has done wonders with our quarters here, I think. Did I give you her regrets that she's staying this fall at her mansion in Arlington? The children's schooling keeps her happily there these days. The woman is still wedded to her family home. Of course, she goes on being grateful because you and your loved ones spoiled me in Savannah while I struggled with the beginnings of Fort Pulaski on muddy old Cockspur. Need another pillow?"

"That depends on whether or not we're going to talk. I feel strictly under orders and I'm not sure I like it."

"We'll talk for no more than a quarter hour," Lee said, adding another pillow to the stack, then seating himself on the foot of the bed. "Oh, Jack, I grieve at times that you have no wife and no children. Do you?"

"Grieve? Never. It's enough being a burden to my mother and sisters and poor, steady William."

"How are they—my dear friends in Savannah?"

"Kate and Sarah go along quite peaceably in their spinsterhood. William is turning into the family elder statesman. He'll never fully recover from his loss, I'm sure, but even though he's a little younger than I, it relieves me no end that he assumes the responsible role in the family."

For a time, they sat in silence, then Jack gave Lee a sly look. "It is now the appropriate moment, Robert, for my answer to the one question you've been longing to ask. Eliza Anne is doing splendidly in her expanding frontier mansion in the old Cherokee Nation by the river. Her health is much improved up there away from Savannah's damp and heat and she asks to be remembered to you."

Lee sighed. "Do you know there are times when I grow almost ill with longing to see Eliza Anne's children? Mine are my *raison d'être*, but not once have I laid eyes on hers. How handsome her boys must be! How lovely her daughter, Mary Cowper."

"Correct. After all, W. H. Stiles is one of the most attractive of men. The older son, Henry, favors him, even to blond hair. Young Bobby is the picture of my father, for whom he's named. This, of course, pleases Mama. Mary C. might just grow up to be even more beautiful than her mother."

"Impossible! Tell me, does Eliza Anne truly like living away from society on the frontier as much as she claims in what few letters she deigns to write?"

"She revels in all of it. Even horseback rides with no ill effects whatever over twenty-some miles to visit her girlhood friend Julia Barnsley, whose husband, by the way, has also moved his family up there."

Another silence fell between them, then Lee asked if Eliza Anne might be coming to Washington City when her newly elected husband arrives for the opening of Congress in December. When Jack only gave him a wicked grin, Lee added, "I've been waiting for you to volunteer the information. I hope you've enjoyed my suspense. Well, will she be with Stiles when he comes next month?"

"Not at first," Jack said. "But young Browning, who's been with my sister far more than I lately, seems sure she'll come if W.H. begs her. She loves her congressman, Bob. Hates him out of her sight."

Rather abruptly, Lee got to his feet. "Stiles is a splendid fellow in spite of being happy only when drowning in politics. Are you still as uninvolved with the stuff as I am, Jack?"

"Totally. As Southerners used to say of slavery, I find politics a necessary evil."

Lee thought for a moment. "I suppose we should be glad there are still a few moderate southerners like us, who at least admit to the 'evil' side of slavery, albeit necessary. W. H. Stiles is a strong pro-slavery, states' rights man, isn't he?"

"He is now, I believe, although he also claims to be a supporter of the Union. Brilliant as he is, W.H. has been known to sit a fence on some issues, but he was elected as a states' rights democrat and perhaps only time will tell."

At the door, Lee looked back with a half smile. "I wonder where he stands on the perpetual need of the Army for funds from Congress. Will we be able to count on his help?"

"If Eliza Anne's influence is as strong as I think it is, maybe—just maybe—we can extract at least a small bag of gold for Savannah River improvements from his compatriots. It's a congressional crime that the old river is still clogged by debris sunk during our revolution!"

"I agree, but 'maybe' sounds like a congressman's answer to any need of the poor old Army. Good night, dearest friend. You haven't given me one shred of hope for funds. But sleep as long as you can and I'll come home from duty tomorrow as early as possible."

"Do," Jack said. "Our time together will end soon enough."

Chapter 36

W HEN the Central of Georgia pulled into the Savannah station after dark on a rainy Tuesday, November 11, Mark stood waiting for his friend and former attorney, W. H. Stiles. He'd begged the Mackays to be allowed to meet W.H.'s train, and because they understood his eagerness for news of Natalie, they'd agreed. Best of all, to Mark, W.H. agreed readily to drive with him first for a brief personal visit together in Mark's office on Commerce Row.

"It's not only good to see you, W.H.," he said as they walked along the corridor of his countinghouse. "I'm grateful for this time alone, even though I know how you must long for a bath and a soft bed at the Mackays'."

"Wrong, old friend," W.H. said, taking an armchair in Mark's private office. "It's like old times to be here in this room with you again. As you know, the campaign kept me away during your visit to Cass. Anyway, by the time we get to Broughton Street, it will be too late for family talk there. I'm deeply fond of my wife's people, but I find this a pleasant respite." He smiled his pleasure as Mark clipped two cigars and provided a light with a newfangled sulphur match.

"Of course, I'm full of questions about Natalie," Mark said, sitting down behind his polished desk. "How is my girl? Is she still doing so much better? Still so fond of Miss Lorah Plemmons?"

"Natalie's doing extremely well, I'd say, and we're all fond of Miss Lorah. Natalie, actually, is quite involved, I believe, with Lib in teaching Indian Mary what the two of them feel she must learn before another visit here to the city. Lib swears she's never seen Natalie more determined than when teaching Mary proper table manners, how to dress, how to arrange her hair and so on. I'm sure Natalie has let you and Caroline know the extent of her support for Jonathan and the girl, Mary."

Mark's smile faded. "She has indeed. We've begun to scan every letter first to find the Jonathan-Mary portion." He took a deep drag on his cigar. "We're glad, of course. We've both come to care deeply about Mary McDonald. We —do go on hoping three more years at Yale might change some of Jonathan's ideas, though."

"At the risk of sounding provincial, and a man does grow a touch provincial living up there," W.H. said, "I must say I find myself cheering more and more for the two lovebirds. Naturally I know that such a marriage could bring much heartache. And, I admit, neither Lib nor I could face the thought of our Mary Cowper marrying out of her class, but—"

Mark laughed drily. "But you're not faced with such a dilemma yet, eh?"

"Oh, I doubt we will ever be. Our Mary C.'s always been such a well-behaved, submissive child. Strong in her spirit, but not at all rebellious."

"Answer me honestly, friend—was my son, Jonathan, ever before considered by anyone to be the least bit rebellious?"

W.H. knocked a long white ash from his cigar. "I see your point. One never knows, does one?"

Mark studied Stiles's patrician features. "Have you told me everything I need to know about Natalie?"

"Oh, I believe so. Her recovery, when it finally came, was quite remarkable. Lib gives full credit to her breeding and to Miss Lorah, who seems able to concentrate Natalie's attention when no one else can."

"And what of Miss Lorah's young man, Sam? Has he learned his trade yet?"

W.H. frowned as he blew smoke toward the ceiling. "That's one question I don't know how to answer, Mark. The fellow tries so hard, but he also tries Burke's patience. I—I wonder at times if Sam's quite sound in his head. Lib wonders too."

"Oh? No one has mentioned that to us in a letter."

"Let's face it, man, both Lib and Natalie try to shield you and Caroline since there's so much distance between us." He took a shallow puff of the cigar. "Strange, isn't it, Mark, that both your children made such—odd choices in affairs of the heart?"

"I suppose so," Mark said uncertainly, "but Caroline and I have long ago made peace with the fact that Natalie married a man who works with his hands. We've been fond of Burke almost from the start. But I see what you mean."

"And don't think your keen daughter doesn't know you both struggled at being forced to approve such a sudden marriage. Natalie may never tell you, but I can assure you she'll always protect Burke with you and Caroline. She isn't really defensive, though. Natalie knows Burke has won you over. As for the way your son-in-law and Sam work together, I'm not at all amused, though Lib seems to be, at poor Sam's clumsiness. He and Burke are hard at work on my new house now, of course, so it doesn't amuse me, because I'm the one who pays for Sam's blunders and mistakes."

"Can't Burke find another carpenter?"

"Part-time only. There are too many houses going up in Cass and adjoining counties these days. Barnsley's started his Italianate villa and he and I are not the only men who've chosen the upcountry. Burke's committed to me, thank heaven, or Godfrey would have him. As for tolerating Sam, Burke's

heart gets in the way. He's so infernally grateful to Miss Lorah for what she's
done for Natalie, I daresay he wouldn't think of letting Sam go."

Mark thought a moment. "You and Eliza Anne don't feel Sam's retardation
might be—dangerous, do you?"

"Oh, I think not. But then, I'd never have thought Ben McDonald capable
of shooting himself. It's always difficult, very difficult, Mark, when one attempts either to live or to work closely with those not born to privilege, to
culture."

"Have you seen anything untoward from Sam?"

"Not really. He's pleasant enough. Says very little. Is devoted to Burke—a
hangdog kind of devotion. To Miss Lorah too. He's just abominably slow in
his mind, it seems to me. Makes the same mistake over and over. Eventually,
he learns well enough, I guess. And he's most willing." W.H. put out his
cigar. "No reason to worry, I'm sure. We don't. It's just another example of
the awkwardness of living so close to—limited people. Of course, our nigras
are entirely different."

"How so?"

"We own them. They know better than to go on making the same mistake
again and again." W.H. smiled a bit wryly. "I suppose you're still an abolitionist?"

Mark laughed. "No, I was never an active abolitionist. My dear Aunt
Nassie was in the years before I came to Savannah, but more and more, I
sense abolitionist pamphlets and tirades against 'lords of the lash,' as they call
you and other slave owners, only weakens their cause. My aunt would have
seen through that too. Extremes have taken over. Bitterness in the South
grows because of abolitionist accusations. I think bitterness in the North
grows too. Miss Eliza deplores, as do I, the fact that Southerners are becoming so defensive many no longer call slavery a 'necessary evil.' These days it's
actually being called beneficial."

"Well, you know where I stand," W.H. said. "I would collapse financially
without my people. At times, I teeter on the edge of ruin anyway, thanks to
the stupid Whig insistence on a federal banking system and higher tariffs. But
these days, a wise politician, in both major parties, stays as clear of the slavery
issue as possible. It's incendiary." He studied Mark for a time. "You are still a
Whig?" When Mark nodded yes, W.H. added, "Well, with your wealth, I
suppose that's inevitable."

"I take citizenship far more seriously than any political party, though,"
Mark said quickly. "My grandfather was a Jeffersonian. I voted for Democrat
Van Buren in 1840."

"You did? Why?"

"I think mainly because the Whigs went crazy trying to capture the Jacksonian vote of the workers and frontiersmen by all that campaign hullabaloo,
noise and fakery. I agree with old John Quincy Adams, you know. To me, the
sight of a presidential candidate on the stump making speeches is degrading.

If I'd had any thought of voting for Whig William Henry Harrison, his bad-taste campaign ended it."

W.H. laughed. "Couldn't picture old Harrison in a log cabin, eh?"

"The man probably never saw one except as slave housing on his family's Virginia plantation. The fact that Harrison was a hero in our last war with the British had no influence on me at all." In response, W.H. merely smiled.

"I'm enjoying this," Mark went on, "but I'm sure you're worn to a frazzle. I should take you to Broughton Street for a good night's sleep."

"I'm in no hurry, but I suppose I shouldn't keep the Mackays up too long." Both men stood. "Mark, you have a remarkable son in Jonathan."

Beaming, Mark handed his friend his top hat and stick. "I think so, thank you. I take it you and he had some time together at Etowah Cliffs?"

"Indeed we did. One evening in particular stands out. The boy knows exactly what he wants from life."

"He seems to," Mark said as they walked together down the hallway. "Jonathan's always been quite satisfied with the idea of coming into the business with me when he graduates from Yale. I certainly look forward to that day. By then, I'll be well into my fifties and Caroline longs to travel."

During the carriage ride to the Mackay house, W.H. steered the talk back to politics, relieved that evidently Jonathan had not told his father about leaving Yale early. He spoke at length of the present occupant of the White House, widower John Tyler of Virginia—President only because Whig William Henry Harrison died after a month in office. Never before in the country's history had a Vice-President actually been sworn in as President. Both men thought it amusing that Whig Tyler was being called "His Accidency" by his enemies, and they had always been numerous in both parties. During his brief month in office, elected President Harrison had all but ignored Tyler, who had to be summoned from his Williamsburg, Virginia, home at Harrison's sudden death and who still resented what he felt was a lack of respect for him as President.

W.H., Mark thought, even as a strong Democrat, tilted toward Tyler, a fellow slaveholder. At least, he seemed to know a lot about the man and clarified Tyler's background as they rode along. Son of a Virginia governor, John Tyler had been reared in the aristocratic republicanism of tidewater Virginia and graduated from the College of William and Mary at the age of seventeen. Like W.H. in Georgia, Tyler had climbed the political ladder from the Virginia House of Delegates to the national House of Representatives, but later, Tyler had moved on to the Virginia governorship and the United States Senate. Along the way, he had shifted to the Whigs, but W.H. seemed fairly satisfied that Tyler remained a strong constitutional constructionist and an equally strong states' rights advocate. As most knew, Tyler had been chosen as a balance in the South for the Whig ticket, a fact which comforted W.H. in spite of the fact that the man was chosen only after several other, more noted politicians had turned down the vice-presidential nomination.

"Even if he is a Whig of sorts," W.H. said as Jupiter turned the carriage into Broughton, "I rather imagine Tyler's set a precedent by insisting upon being considered the new, constitutional President, rather than a mere Vice-President acting as President. He tried, you know, to keep Harrison's Cabinet, while complaining at being surrounded by 'Clay men, Webster men, anti-Masons, Old Whigs, New Whigs'—each jealous of the other and each struggling for power."

As the carriage came to a stop, Mark laughed. "But doesn't he still vow to reconcile them all?"

"I'll believe that when I see it happen," W.H. said. "The Whigs, my good man, have simply plastered over their factional splits with populist hokum. Congress will fight the White House even within the President's own party. Mark my word."

"I don't doubt you for a minute. I well remember the account of Henry Clay's half-drunken rage when he first learned of old William Henry Harrison's nomination. Do you think Clay will ever reach his own goal of the presidency?"

"Frankly, no. And I fully intend to do my bit to bring him down as present commander of the congressional wing of his party. Even with a Whig of sorts in the White House, this is the Democrats' big chance," W.H. predicted as he opened the door and jumped from Mark's carriage to the street in front of the Mackay house. "Actually, I believe Tyler has close ties with states' rights Democrats still."

Reaching down to shake his hand, Mark asked how long W.H. planned to stay in town.

"Just overnight. We may not meet again any time soon. Hard as it is already being away from Lib and the children, I find I can almost not wait to arrive in Washington City."

Chapter 37

A T NOON on a chilly November 27, Sam rode up to the frame house where Eliza Anne and the children still lived. He had brought her the first letter from W.H., actually postmarked Washington City. What might have been Eliza Anne's usual cursory greeting to Sam turned warm and so cordial, the shy, odd young man appeared almost frightened.

"Don't hurry off, Sam," she said, joyfully holding the unopened letter in both hands against her heart. "I'm going to read this most welcome letter you've brought—but do ride around back. Someone in the kitchen will give you a hot cup of tea or coffee. You must be cold from that ride back from Cassville. Look, the puddles in the road are still frozen!"

"Thank you, ma'am," Sam said, as usual, not looking directly at her, "but Miss Lorah will have dinner ready. I best be ridin' to our cabin."

"Please have a hot drink first!"

"No, ma'am," he said, shivering. "And you better get back inside. You'll ketch a cold out here."

Eliza Anne had never heard Sam say so much before, but what mattered now was her letter. When Sam rode off without another word, she glanced up at the second story of the handsome new addition where Burke was installing a wide window frame and shouted, "Burke! Burke, look what I have! My first letter from W.H.!"

She returned his cheery wave and hurried inside, thinking to see Burke later on to invite him and Natalie for tea. They'd both want to know what W.H. had to say.

Banging the front door to be sure it closed tightly against the cold wind off the river, she hurried to sit down before the roaring fire in their tiny parlor. She missed Mary Cowper dreadfully and felt real pity for herself that school had taken her only daughter away so soon after W.H. left for Washington City. The child should be here to share her father's letter. Well, at least she was relieved that the boys were out hunting with Solomon. She'd be spared their many questions and interruptions while she read.

Smiling at the first notice of his new seal—an artistic, simple intertwining of the initials W.H.S.—she thought: How like him to have bought a new one already. "Oh, my elegant darling," she whispered, breaking the wax and unfolding the thick, longed-for pages:

19 November 1843
Washington City

My Beloved Lib,
    After a pleasant visit with Mark, who met my train in Savannah—only an hour late in arriving—I spent a good night with your family and here I am settled in a quite comfortable boardinghouse owned by a Mrs. Hewitt. It is located on 3rd between Pennsylvania and C. I spent my first night in Gadsby's Hotel and was most fortunate in finding this boardinghouse on my first day of searching. I occupy two rooms, a rather well-furnished parlor and a bedroom and if last night's rest indicates my satisfaction with the accommodation, I should be well fixed. I am not so confident of the wearing nature of Mrs. Hewitt's personality: The world appears in her eyes to revolve entirely around her, but the place is clean and the food acceptable. Along with his pleasant wife, Senator Walter T. Colquitt of Georgia also lives here. He is in his middle forties, I'd think, virile, active and strong of body—a former Whig turned Democrat. But best of all and conducive to our friendship, he is and has always been a firm supporter of states' rights. Walter Colquitt took me yesterday on a splendid tour of government buildings and I already feel somewhat acquainted with the city which has rightly been called "an ill-contrived, ill-arranged, rumbling, scrambling village." It is all that and yet, as our nation's capital, there is, if one looks discerningly, an aura of excitement, almost of grandeur.
    Pennsylvania Avenue was macadamized a decade ago, but now, alas, is potholed and mudholed. In spite of this, there is a parade along it of some description every day. I will take time here only to say that the view from the portico of the Capitol, where my office is located in Room 43 on the second floor, is remarkable as one looks out over the distant shore of the Potomac and down Capitol Hill into the surrounding woods and cleared vistas. Of course, we visited both the Senate and the Hall of Representatives, and I can now tell you that I will be in Seat Number 189, the back row, and will find myself next to Charles M. Reed of Pennsylvania. Colquitt claims Reed is most personable and quick of intellect, so we should have many stimulating exchanges since he is definitely a northern Whig and, as usually follows, is quite rich, the owner with his father of a prospering ship company. The Hall of Representatives is arranged in a semicircle and is also on the second floor of the Capitol building. As we knew by mail before I left, I have been assigned to the Post Office and Post Roads committees, which will undoubtedly entail much detailed paperwork and regular reports.
    My old nemesis, Alexander H. Stephens, has rooms at Mrs. Carter's on Capitol Hill. John H. Lumpkin, also of Georgia, as you well know, is at Mrs. Rumner's, as is Howell Cobb. Hugh A. Haral-

son and his wife are, for now, on C near the corner of 4½ at Mrs. Fletcher's. General Duncan L. Clinch stays where your friend Captain Robert E. Lee abides when he is in Washington, at Mr. Julian's on Pennsylvania Avenue between 17 and 18.

I look forward with extreme pleasure to attending the debut of the Italian Opera Company on 18 December, at the National Theater. Since the opera will be Bellini's *Norma,* the town is buzzing, and if the weather is fine, everyone of note should be there. Oh, but I will be lonely without my beautiful wife! I both anticipate and dread the start of Washington's social activities, with you so far away, but I fully intend to join the Union Literary and Debating Society and attempt to revive some of my old Yale talents for debate. Wherever possible, I mean to take part in such pursuits as a lone gentleman can with his heart only reasonably intact.

I paid my respects at the White House as soon as I was settled here at Mrs. Hewitt's and found the President's abode impressive. President Tyler received several congressmen in company with his courteous daughter-in-law, Mrs. Robert Tyler, acting hostess for most of his tenure due to the paralysis and death last year of his wife. As we discussed before I left you, protocol has it that members of the House must call on the President immediately. I longed for you on my arm, beloved Lib. Young Mrs. Robert Tyler is plain beside you (as are all ladies) but most agreeable in what I'm sure is a tiresome duty. The White House itself rather awed me. We entered under the portico whose Ionic columns ornament the northern front of the house. Our entrance opened upon a plain but spacious vestibule or hall. Immediately opposite the front door is the reception room with walls covered by rich and beautiful paper. The chimney pieces are magnificently wrought of marble. The tabletops are also of marble and the curtains of deep crimson.

Enough of my descriptions for now, dearest Lib, for I am weary and the time stands late. We will never live in such grandeur as the President, I daresay, but seeing that lovely marble gave me the brilliant idea that one day I mean to build in marble windowsills for the main section of our mansion by the river. I know you are smiling at the extravagance of my dreams. I love your smile, but rest assured I am being as frugal as conditions permit. I walk most places —on rainy days I slog. But hackney carriage fares are rather reasonable. Between daybreak and 8 P.M. one can ride a mile and half for 25¢, twice that for over a mile and a half, etc. I plan to walk to Trinity Episcopal Church come Sunday. I tell you that to reassure you of my excellent intentions and behavior and to quiet your longings over my soul. My regards to Natalie and Burke, to Miss Lorah and Sam, my love to our children and, as always, my entire heart to you, blessed Lib.

Think of me always as your slavishly devoted and lonely husband,

W. H. Stiles

Eliza Anne sat for a long time, watching but not really seeing the fire burn down to lightly spitting embers. This was the first time in all their years of married life that W.H. had not written his separate page of love words just for her eyes. The momentary twinge vanished. He's weary, she thought, and so excited over his new life as a congressman, I doubt that he even noticed that all his declarations of affection for me were scribbled right into the body of the letter for all to share. She would share it, of course, and maybe this was his way of showing that his love for her was an integral part of even his professional life in Washington City.

Marble windowsills indeed, she thought, pleased that he had at least mentioned their house on the cliffs, but not one word of counsel or advice to her about operating this big place without him!

A rapid knock on the front door startled her. She was even more startled when she opened the door to see Mary standing there.

"What on earth, Mary? I thought you'd be having dinner with Miss Lorah and Sam by now."

"I need to talk," Mary gasped, her face contorted as though she might cry. "Sam and Miss Lorah, they are eating, but I run here."

She motioned Mary into the parlor, where they both sat down—Eliza Anne feeling both curiosity and irritation at the unexpected visit. She disliked it in herself, but Mary did seem to annoy her these days, as fond of her as she had grown. It isn't Mary herself, she thought, so much as her audacity at loving Mark Browning's son. Hoping to cover her feelings, she leaned toward Mary and asked urgently, "Is something wrong? You—you look so troubled!"

From her bodice, Mary took out a letter. "Sam bring—*brought* this to me." She handed over the crumpled pages. "From Jonathan."

"How nice. I also got a letter from my husband."

"Mr. Stiles—he is fine?"

"Yes, yes. Busy settling into Washington City. Mary, you look upset."

Mary only nodded, biting her lower lip.

"Why on earth would a letter from Jonathan bother you?"

"I am—afraid. You read, please, Miss Lib. You read his letter. You see why he—make me afraid."

"All right," Eliza Anne said reluctantly, "but could you wait just one minute while I run outside and speak with Burke? I'm so afraid he'll climb down his ladder and disappear and I—I need to talk to him."

"You go," Mary said quickly. "I wait here."

Grabbing a cloak, Eliza Anne ran outside and around the end of the porch, climbed up and over an evenly stacked pile of new bricks, calling to Burke to come down.

"I think I just had a streak of good luck framing that troublesome second-story window, Miss Lib," he called, coming nimbly down the ladder, wool cap in hand, cheeks rosy from the wind, yellow hair blowing. "Poor old Sam did his best, but the wind really beats against that window. No cracks allowed."

"Oh, dear," she said when Burke reached the ground, "is Sam doing any better at all? He is so slow and clumsy!"

"I know he is, but he can't help it. His mind isn't weak, just slow. Don't worry about Sam."

"How can I not worry when the entire responsibility of this house rests on me now that W.H. is gone for heaven knows how long? Oh, Burke, I worry more without him about everything. He's never been any help with our house servants, but as soon as he's out of sight, they give me still more problems. Little Sinai has been downright impudent today."

Burke laughed.

"I fail to see anything funny about her."

"I'm sorry, Miss Lib, but it strikes me funny every time you call old Sinai's daughter *Little* Sinai. She must weigh a hundred pounds more than her mother!"

"That amuses Natalie too, but neither of you has to put up with fat Little Sinai. By the way, can you two come to tea today? You'll want to read my letter from W.H. and I need some intelligent conversation—some adult conversation. Please say you'll come."

"Why, yes, ma'am. We'd like to. Is Mary invited too?"

"No, Burke. This time, she's not."

He gave her a guarded look. "I see."

"You know I didn't mean that to sound so—snooty."

"I hadn't thought you sounded—that way, exactly," he said.

"Well, what did you think?"

"Haven't quite decided, I guess. Not much like you, though."

"I'm not—very like me some of the time. I'm devoted to Mary, Burke, but —I do want to share my letter, and what would Mary know about our nation's capital?"

"Only a little, I guess," he said, looking out over the cliffs to the winding Etowah River. "Except that a President named Andrew Jackson once lived there."

"The Indian trouble's all in the past now," she said sharply. "Anyway, W.H. says President Jackson can't be expected to take all the blame for— removing the Cherokees."

"He's right, but Mary knows it *was* Jackson who looked at Cherokee Chief John Ross and said, 'It's too d——— late.' "

"I think you might watch your language a little."

"That's Jackson's language, not mine." He laid his hand on her shoulder. "Sorry, Miss Lib. I lived through a little of the horror with Mary and Ben. You know our treatment of the Cherokees still rankles in me. That doesn't give me a right, though, to be rude with you."

"Burke, forget it. That Indian business is past and gone."

"But Mary's still here." He paused, looking her straight in the eye. "I sincerely hope you'll—accept what I'm about to say, Miss Lib."

Eliza Anne took a step back. "Somehow I'm not sure I'll like it."

"Neither am I, but it's the truth. Natalie and I have both noticed how your attitude toward Mary has changed since Jonathan let us all know how much he loves her. That he means to marry her."

"I've never heard him say that in so many words!"

"But you know it. We all do and I'm uneasy about—" He broke off. "Didn't I see Mary run up and pound on your door just now?"

"Yes, she's waiting to talk to me—something about a letter from Jonathan she wants me to read. I know I need to get back to her." Eliza Anne heard the edge in her voice and hated it. "It's just that I'd so hoped you and Natalie and I could just talk about—civilized, pleasant things today. I know Natalie once spent a month in Washington City visiting with her boarding school roommate—some ambassador's daughter. I'd hoped she could tell me more about the social life there and—"

Burke laughed. "That's a Natalie I don't know much about. She visited in an—ambassador's house?"

"She most certainly did and that's a Natalie you'd better learn to know, if you ask my advice—which, of course, you didn't, did you?"

"No, ma'am," he said pleasantly. "I know Natalie used to be a society belle. I also know my wife now and she's happy right where she is. In those society days," he added with a grin, "she hadn't met me yet."

"It's a wonder you two don't annihilate each other," Eliza Anne said, returning his smile in spite of herself. "Underneath your rough, sturdy frontiersmanship, you're as arrogant as she is, aren't you?"

"That probably did sound that way," he said easily. "And while I don't expect Natalie to live in our log cabin one day longer than it takes me to finish your house, then ours, I do know she's found herself there. We're happy, Miss Lib. And we're planning to have another child too. In fact, Natalie's almost sure it's on the way."

Eliza Anne stared at him. "Burke, how wonderful! She hasn't said one word to me about it."

"Oh, but she's told Miss Lorah, I guess it was almost two weeks ago. Even before she told me."

Undoubtedly, Eliza Anne thought, I climbed out on the wrong side of the bed this morning. I simply can't be jealous of Lorah Plemmons! "I—I suppose Natalie told Miss Lorah because nothing ever seems to—upset or worry her," she said lamely.

"I think Miss Lorah worries. She loves Natalie so much by now, she worries a lot about her doing too much, not bothering to take care of herself. Miss Lorah just doesn't spread her worry around."

"But I do. Is that what you're saying?"

"We're all different. Miss Lorah's been through so much, she sorts things out in her mind before she talks."

"Burke, I simply have to go find out what Jonathan wrote that Mary insists I read. I've been out here so long, I'll be embarrassed to face her."

"Don't change toward Mary, Miss Lib. Try to be patient with her. Natalie and I both understand how you feel about her marrying Jonathan."

"I haven't changed toward Mary at all! I—I just think Jonathan has no right to—to do what you say he's going to do."

"Any young man has the right to marry."

"But a boy with Jonathan's breeding needs to consider his parents too! He can't just act on the love he *thinks* he feels for Mary. He must consider Mark and Caroline."

Burke smiled broadly. "Jonathan's sister didn't consider them too much, as I remember."

"Well, Natalie was just unusually fortunate that you—that you—"

"That I didn't turn out to be a hopeless misfit?" he finished for her.

"That is not what I said, and I'm going in to Mary, who must be wondering what on earth's happened. Besides, I'm cold!" She laughed weakly. "I'll see you two at teatime. *Fat* Sinai's made fresh bread . . ."

Back in her parlor, Eliza Anne found Mary huddled in W.H.'s big wing chair by the fireplace, her pretty, scarred face pinched and pale even in the heat from the roaring blaze she'd evidently just rebuilt. In her hands she still held Jonathan's letter.

Taking her own chair directly across from Mary, Eliza Anne apologized and reached for the letter. "Now, then, what did that young man write that so frightened you?" she asked, glancing at the warm, beautifully worded endearments with which Jonathan began. She looked up, "Oh, Mary, isn't this awfully personal to be—sharing with me? Are you quite sure?"

"Yes, ma'am, I'm sure," Mary said, looking surprised. "You already know Jonathan love me, Miss Lib. You know I love him from all my heart. Please read it all and help me!"

"Very well, but I can't promise any help."

"You and Natalie help me so much already. You help me again now."

Eliza Anne scanned page after page, only now and then glancing up at Mary, who kept her own dark Indian eyes riveted on the crackling fire. Jonathan, after the opening endearments, was merely telling Mary in detail of a weekend he'd spent as a house guest in the palatial home of a New Haven, Connecticut, girl, considered to be the "best catch in town." The beautiful young lady with golden hair, it seemed, had personally invited Jonathan to be her escort to a fancy-dress ball on a certain Saturday night. Eliza Anne skimmed the clear, strong script when Jonathan began to go into too much detail to interest her. Evidently it had been a glorious affair, which must have cost enough to keep them all fed, dressed and schooled at Etowah Cliffs for a year. The mansion's own ballroom had been festooned with fresh flowers and evergreens and a ten-piece orchestra played for the latest dances until the wee hours of the morning. Wine and food were epicurean and abundant and so on and on and on. At the close of his letter, Jonathan announced to Mary in his simple, guileless way that one day she, Mary, would live every bit as well as the New Haven belle and once she learned to dance would be the most graceful young lady on the floor as other handsomely dressed couples waltzed around her in Jonathan's arms.

Eliza Anne had stopped merely skimming about halfway through the boy's endless descriptions of the fashionable festivity. She had grown up attending similarly elaborate balls, so they were certainly not novel to her, but partway through the letter she could almost *feel* Mary's fear.

"I love you with all my heart, beautiful Merry Willow," Jonathan's letter ended, "and sooner than you expect, my dearest girl, I will be twirling you in a lovely gown across polished dance floors in Savannah, in New York, in Newport—in London and Paris, or wherever you show the least interest in going. Be secure in my love, sweet Merry. Our bright day will come—I repeat, *sooner than you expect.* Be patient in my love for you and wait for me. Oh, please wait for me."

The letter finished, Eliza Anne looked at Mary, who was clumsily examining her own work-worn hands. Staring down at the woods dirt under her fingernails from having planted ferns for Eliza Anne that morning, Mary asked, "You read it all, Miss Lib? You see now why Jonathan scare me?"

"Yes, I read it all, Mary. But you tell me what it is I'm supposed to see."

Mary leaped to her feet. "That I no can marry—Jonathan! Scuse me. That I *cannot* marry Jonathan and—Miss Lib, *I love him!*" Tears welled in the dark eyes. "I love him so much it—hurt—*hurts* me! I can be happy here at Etowah Cliffs with him, walking beside him in the woods, climbing up into trees, laughing with him, telling him about wildflowers and how to read clouds and blowing leaves before a rain comes." Through the still standing tears, her eyes brightened a little. "I—I plan to show Jonathan how to build a fish trap of rocks to catch fish down in our river when he comes again, but—"

"But the idea of fancy-dress balls and having to learn the latest dances frightens you."

"*Tells* me!"

"Tells you—what, Mary?"

"That—that"—she shook her head—"I can never be for always—with Jonathan."

Eliza Anne thought a moment, then asked, "And did you think you would be with Jonathan for always?"

"Oh, yes! We love each other."

"I know you both believe that now," Eliza Anne said carefully. "But tell me, Mary, has Jonathan actually proposed to you?" When Mary looked puzzled, she explained: "Has Jonathan actually asked you to become his wife?"

"Yes, ma'am."

"And what did you say?"

"Nothing."

"You said—nothing?"

"No words. Jonathan already know—*knew*—when I bury my face in his shoulder and hug him hard."

"He took that to mean yes, you would marry him?"

Mary nodded.

"And now you realize the—distance between your two backgrounds is too great, is that it?"

Eliza Anne could honestly not tell from Mary's look whether the girl really understood her meaning, but the troubled, scarred face was plainly still full of terror.

"I—I am all alone in the world," she said just above a whisper. "Ben is gone. Natalie and Mister Burke do not—need me. Miss Lorah be old. Sam looks funny at me often. Only—Jonathan is left to me and—"

Mary broke off in a flood of tears. Eliza Anne could only put her arms around her and try to bring some form of comfort. Mary felt like a child in her arms, sturdy and strong of body, but at this minute, as helpless as a child. Dear God, Eliza Anne asked, what can I say to her? What *is* there to say? She can't marry Jonathan. She mustn't, but—what else does she have to cling to? What else, who else is there for Mary—anywhere? Then Sam flashed into her mind.

"What did you mean, Mary, when you said Sam looks at you in a funny way? Did you mean a strange way? Does Sam scare you?"

"Not scare. Always he is smiling at me, but—oh, Miss Lib, in all the world, only Jonathan—is Jonathan. I can only ever belong to Jonathan . . ."

"And you're afraid you'll never be able to live up to being Mrs. Jonathan Browning?"

Her face still buried in Eliza Anne's shoulder, the girl only nodded.

"You're very wise, Mary," she said, knowing full well that her words hurt. "I think it is asking far too much of yourself even to try."

She felt Mary's body stiffen. Slowly, and Mary was courteous even in the act of pulling away, the young woman stepped back to give Eliza Anne her direct, clear look. Amazing, Eliza Anne thought irrelevantly, that both her eyes seem so clear, even when I know she's almost blind in one of them.

Seconds passed and, unaccountably, Eliza Anne began to feel afraid too. Mary was, at this moment, somehow seeing *her*—all the way down inside.

"You do try to teach me, Miss Lib," Mary said firmly. "But to be Cherokee —is—bad. To be Cherokee and—*wise*—is worse. Just now, your arms around me, I—understand still more why Ben needed to die."

Eliza Anne's mouth opened, but she could say nothing.

Her face a mask, Mary said, "When he die, I did not see how Ben could bear to miss—all spring flowers, all changing moons forever." Turning her eyes away, she added, "I understand his—terrible deed now. So, goodbye. I go."

Chapter 38

AFTER tea was over, Eliza Anne and her two neighbors sat before the fire and waited with casual small talk until Little Sinai, her enormous stomach barely permitting her to squeeze past the furnishings in the crowded parlor, had cleared the tea service and left for the kitchen.

Unfolding W.H.'s long letter, Eliza Anne said, "Well, finally! Now, you're in for a treat, but do break into my reading anytime, Natalie, if you remember something I might need to know about Washington City. Something my excited husband forgot to tell me."

Side by side on the sofa, Natalie and Burke settled closer together to listen, and Eliza Anne read aloud every word—endearments and all. Not once did Natalie interrupt except to sigh happily over the romantic portions. When she finished the very last page, Natalie sighed again.

"Burke," she demanded, "why don't you ever call yourself my 'slavishly devoted and lonely husband'?"

He kissed the top of her head, luminous in the last brilliant shafts of the late-afternoon sun. "I could have sworn you knew how slavish I am," he teased, "and I'm not at all lonely. You're right here. You didn't interrupt once. Not one word to give Miss Lib a better idea of what kind of mischief her husband may get into up there in Washington society?"

"Washington is just another city," she said, not very interested. "Oh, because it's the national capital, Washingtonians feel dreadfully important, as I remember, but a dance is a dance and a dinner party is a dinner party. Savannah society is far more sophisticated. After all, every kind of peculiar person gets elected to national office. I think Uncle W.H. will enjoy himself, though. His rooms are probably quite nice—in an acceptable part of the city. Anyway, Miss Lib, you're going to be there with him in no time. I predict a few weeks after the new year begins."

"Don't bring that up. I'm trying to keep my mind off dates and distances between W.H. and me."

"I don't believe in lovers being apart," Natalie said.

All through their visit, Eliza Anne had tried as well to keep her mind off the disturbing episode with Mary. Natalie, with her remark about lovers being apart, had brought that rushing back too.

"Don't even intimate that you and Uncle W.H. aren't still true lovers, Miss Lib," Natalie went on, "because I wouldn't believe it. With Jonathan and me both out from underfoot, I even think Mama and Papa might well be lovers again."

"What makes you think they've ever stopped being?" Eliza Anne asked.

"Oh, I haven't really thought much about it. Loving has to do with feelings, not thinking. At their age, romance would improve both my parents quite a lot." She laughed. "Heaven knows, Jonathan and I are both doing our best to set them examples about being in love." She leaned to kiss Burke on his new, thick blond sideburns. "I'm sure every letter they get from my brother is full of how much he loves Mary." Natalie shook her head in disgust. "Isn't it dreary that Jonathan has almost three more years at Yale before he and Mary can even begin to live? I don't know how she stands being so far away from him. All I can say is that she must trust Jonathan. He's really gotten to be quite handsome and New Haven is swarming with popular society belles teeming to marry even dull, slow-witted boys with pimples, so long as there's a modicum of family money. My brother must be in constant demand."

"I think he is in demand, Natalie," Eliza heard herself say, facing at last that she was going to tell them both about her visit from Mary. As well as she could remember the troubling moments, she recounted the whole story, including Mary's final remark about Ben's suicide just before she left the house so abruptly.

When she finished, Burke and Natalie were both sitting up, listening intently, and Eliza Anne sensed a warning signal even before Burke jumped to his feet.

"Where is Mary now?" he demanded. "Did she go straight home?"

Natalie was up too. "We'd better go find her, Burke! I don't like any of this."

"Neither do I," he said with obvious alarm. "Did you try to reason with her, Miss Lib? Did you tell her you'd been wrong to try to discourage her? We all know Jonathan isn't going to let wagging tongues or different background hurt Mary. He loves her too much."

"If Jonathan insists upon kowtowing to Papa's wishes for him to sit in that stuffy countinghouse in Savannah all his life, it's going to be harder for Mary, but she can do it. We're making a lot of progress teaching her, Miss Lib."

"I suppose so," Eliza Anne said uncertainly. "But I'm not sure of anything right now except that Mary's afraid! That letter from Jonathan really scared her. I think it made her see things as they are, not the way she imagines them to be."

"Nonsense," Natalie said, "but I'll persuade you later. Come on, Burke. We have to find Mary and talk some sense into her."

"Natalie, they're both—so young," Eliza Anne said, feeling as helpless as she sounded.

"Young, foot," Natalie said over her shoulder as Burke helped her into her warm cape. "They're both older than I was when I knew I had to be with Burke forever. For goodness' sake, Miss Lib, don't *you* turn into an old woman right under my nose!"

When they didn't find Mary in her own cabin, Burke grabbed Natalie's hand and headed her toward Miss Lib's little grove of trees where their baby was buried. Since they were almost sure Natalie was carrying another child, he guided her carefully to avoid tripping over wild berry hoops and vines, mostly bare now as the woods waited for winter.

"Why don't we go back to Ben's grave, Burke?" she demanded while hurrying along with him willingly. "Don't you think Mary might be there?"

"Ben shot himself on our baby's grave. We'll go there first," he said grimly.

"I'm not going to let myself think Mary has any such crazy idea," Natalie gasped, stepping over a fallen log. "We're not going to let Mary stay frightened. I intend to convince her once and for all there's nothing to be scared about. I'm not going to let Mary break my brother's heart!"

In sight of the tiny grave, Burke almost jerked her to a stop. "Sh! There she is, on her knees just about where Ben fell that night . . ."

"Let me go to her," Natalie whispered. "Mary pays attention to me. Miss Lib's acting—so ancient! I don't intend to let her exert her influence on my friend Mary."

For a brief moment, Burke smiled down at her.

"Stop laughing at me!"

"I'm not laughing at you—only at the way you've changed now that you're sure Mary doesn't love me."

"You certainly are conceited," she said.

"With reason. You love me. That's enough to make any man conceited."

There was no more reason to hurry. Burke could still see Mary. She was all right. At least, she hadn't done anything crazy and he didn't want Natalie to get overtired.

"You stay right here," Natalie ordered. "No—over there, behind that stand of scrub oak where Mary can't see you. This is the time for Mary and me to have a good talk alone."

"Darling, do you think so?"

"I know so. Now, do as I say. Go behind those trees and let me walk up to where Mary is by myself. I know best how to handle this situation. I'll do it just right. You'll see. Jonathan is *my* brother."

"Darling," he argued, "are you sure you should?"

"Which one of us lived and endured so long in Savannah society—you or I?"

He was smiling down at her again. "Did you really 'endure'? Or did you revel in it as much as you seemed to when I first found you?"

"You didn't find me. I found you," she said, reaching up to kiss him on the mouth before she turned and began to walk slowly, steadily, toward where Mary knelt, her face buried in her hands.

The closer Natalie came to Mary, the more convinced she was that Miss Lib had somehow twisted whatever Jonathan had written in his letter. Jonathan loved Mary! He had some other reason for telling her all he did about that social affair. He would never, never mean to scare her. Maybe Mary had just not understood what he wrote. Heaven knew, she did have a lot to learn yet, but Jonathan believed in the love he and Mary had for each other. He'd told Natalie himself, and Jonathan always meant everything he said.

No one can ever convince me love is too weak to triumph over fancy-dress balls and gossip, she thought, coming close now to the tiny grave where Mary still knelt, both hands covering her face.

Softly, so as not to startle her, Natalie spoke her name.

Mary raised her head and looked around. Natalie had never seen such sadness or so much pulsating, deep-down sorrow and beauty. The scar on Mary's cheek stood out white and ragged. Like a torn heart, she thought, and quickly put aside the truth that her own passionate, headstrong desire to get to Burke that day so long ago had caused Mary's scarred face, her half-blinded eye.

I can't help any of that now, she thought as she dropped to her knees beside Mary. One arm about her shoulders, Natalie whispered, "Will you let me read for myself what my brother wrote to you?"

Merely nodding, the girl took Jonathan's letter from the bodice of her flowered challis dress and handed it to Natalie, who began to read in the fast-fading light before she allowed herself to say another word.

Finishing the very last lines of the letter, she refolded it and announced, "Just as I thought. Jonathan's a victim of your misreading and Miss Lib's provincial viewpoint!"

Frowning, Mary asked, "Miss Lib's—what?"

"Oh, never mind. 'Provincial' isn't a word we need to worry about now except to know that it means Miss Lib is twisting what my brother wrote in his innocent, trusting way because she can't get it through her head that *love is all that matters in life!*"

"Yes," Mary said, nodding her head again. "It is all that matters for you and me, Natalie, because of Mister Burke and Jonathan. But Miss Lib, she stand in her own moccasins."

From habit, she almost reminded Mary that with the singular pronoun "she," the verb "stand" needed an *s,* but decided against it. "Jonathan wrote this letter without the slightest notion that you'd read it as meaning that life with him would be in any way scary. You jumped to that conclusion on your own, and while I see why you did, you have to jump right back—*now.* Do you understand me?"

For a time, Mary pulled at a few weeds growing in the dried grass on the little grave, smoothing the loose dirt, patting the weeded spots.

"Answer me, Mary! Say something. I know where we are. I saw those weeds on my baby's grave, but there's a time and a place for everything. This is *your* time. I can come back out here tomorrow and—take care of the weeds. What we both have to do now is put some sense back into your head about marrying Jonathan. We have to get rid of your foolish fear that you'll never learn to dance properly, speak properly, pick up the right fork at dinner—all that unimportant nonsense. Mary, compared to love, it *is* unimportant!"

Fresh tears began to flow down Mary's cheeks, over her scar, onto the loose dirt. But she said nothing.

"We have to take action this minute," Natalie went on. "You've been to Savannah. You got through that boring dinner party my parents thought they had to give in your honor. Jonathan told me he was proud of you—all evening. Even the way you carried it off when you used the wrong fork for your entrée. Real love lifts people above all that. Do you think I wasn't scared of having to learn how to cook and sew and dig sassafras and wash clothes and darn the holes in Burke's socks? Do you think I wasn't terrified even of becoming a mother? I was! If it turns out I'll be a mother again, I'll still be terrified. But nothing to compare with how frightened I was during that long year before I got Papa to bring me up here to find Burke when I thought he had left me forever. Mary, do you know what it means to get things in their right perspective?"

"I think yes. It means to put one thing beside another and *see.*"

Natalie beamed at her. "That's brilliant! Well, put learning how to move your feet on a dance floor and proper table manners alongside losing the feel of Jonathan's arms around you forever and *see* how things look." When Mary kept her eyes averted and said nothing, Natalie asked, "Are you jealous of that New Haven girl Jonathan had to take to that fancy-dress ball? Are you really afraid that he might fall in love with someone else at Yale? I want an answer, Mary, and I want the truth!"

Shaking her head and finally looking straight at Natalie, she said, "I could not lie to you or Mister Burke. Until you say 'jealous,' I have no thought of it."

"All right, I believe you. I have to believe you when you look at me like that." Natalie sighed a bit helplessly. "Funny how much of the time you seem *so much* younger than you are."

Natalie unfolded Jonathan's letter. "Listen. Listen to what my brother actually wrote—the way he ended his letter: 'I love you with all my heart, beautiful Merry Willow, and sooner than you expect, my dearest girl, I will be twirling you in a lovely gown across polished dance floors in Savannah, in New York, in Newport—in London and Paris, or wherever you show the least interest in going.' Mary? Are you listening?"

The girl nodded, her eyes fixed on one mountain peak which rose in the distance behind the Etowah Cliffs land.

"Then don't you see that Jonathan only wants to spread the whole world at your feet, because he loves you so much?"

"I see, Natalie," she said softly, her voice still hopeless.

"Well, if you do, why are you suddenly so far away? What are you thinking, Mary?"

"I can—be bare truthful with you?"

"I said I wanted you to be, didn't I?"

"I do not doubt Jonathan's love for me. It is bad, though, to be Cherokee. I cannot change my mother's blood in me."

Natalie worked at controlling her patience. Somehow, by some means, she would have to learn patience, certainly if she had another baby. People have to be patient with children, and in so, so many ways, Mary is a child, she reminded herself. In the softest possible voice, she asked, "Do you mean you didn't notice that Jonathan called you—right here in this letter—by your Cherokee name, *Merry Willow?* How could you miss that? Jonathan actually told me before he left the last time that he loves everything Indian about you! He loves the way you know about the sky at night and the woods and the habits of every kind of bird, the deer and rabbits and coons, where all the different wildflowers and ferns and herbs grow. Being half Cherokee is part of you, Mary, and my brother is hopelessly and forever in love with *you.* With all of you."

"I will have to lose Cherokee in—New York, in London, in Savannah. I am foreigner to those cities because I am Cherokee. Cherokee people believe they are one with the land we live on. I am still one with this land." She pointed toward the distant, hazy mountain range. "I am one with the mountains and hills. They are my *backbone.* The gullies and creeks between the hills are my heart veins. I can never breathe in the world where Jonathan is at home. That is my fear."

Natalie thought for a minute, then asked, "Mary, how do you know the mountains and hills are your backbone? How do you know the gullies and creeks are your veins?"

"I learn it," she said quickly. "I learn it many years ago."

"And do you plan only to love Jonathan for a matter of a few weeks or months and then stop loving him—stop wanting to be with him?"

Mary's eyes darted to Natalie's. They were black, grave. "I love Jonathan until my last breath!"

"And can't you learn anything more? Have you stopped your brain at your backbone, so that it can never learn one other new thing as long as you live?"

Mary was still looking at her, the intensity in her Cherokee eyes almost severe. Natalie didn't even risk batting her own eyes for fear their interlocked gaze would be broken. There had been a time—there had been more than one time—when Natalie had suddenly begun to *see* the way a person sees coming out of a dark room into the sunlight. No amount of talk could cause Mary to see the truth. Mary would have to begin to see *for herself.* Natalie meant to find the patience to wait until Mary herself began to see the truth of *everything* that had to do with Jonathan's love for her. But until then she needed some small sign that Mary was with her in all this and so she kept their eyes locked for fear of missing even the first tiny glimmer that Mary *was* beginning to see through love's eyes. To see more than just Jonathan, to see herself with him and all she would be capable of learning and doing.

If I can change, Mary can change, she told herself, conveniently pushing aside the fact that once, before Mary had met Jonathan, and was still in love with Burke, the Cherokee girl hadn't mattered to Natalie at all—had been only a sort of semi-savage, a too sweet nuisance.

At last, Natalie broke the long, heavy silence by speaking Mary's name. There was no response beyond what might be the barest beginning of a smile, a slow, almost imperceptible softening in the black Indian eyes.

Still Mary said nothing.

After another silence, so long that only a Cherokee could endure it, Natalie, her own nature forcing her to action, began to reread aloud the very last lines of Jonathan's letter: " 'Be secure in my love, sweet Merry. Our bright day will come—I repeat, *sooner than you expect*. Be patient in my love for you and wait for me. Oh, please wait for me.' "

Jumping to her feet, Natalie reread one line, pointing to it with her finger —showing it as proof to Mary: " '. . . *sooner than you expect.*' Did you hear that, Mary? Did you even notice that when you first read Jonathan's letter? What do you think he means by 'sooner than you expect'? Do you know what I think? I think my brother has a secret plan! Something he means to do about marrying you that he probably hasn't told a living soul!" When Mary still said nothing, Natalie prodded: "Don't you think he must have a secret plan?"

Mary only looked at her.

"You can be so exasperating! Well, tell me this much anyway. A minute ago, did I see the start of a smile on your face? Proof that you're finally beginning to see what Jonathan really meant in that letter? What really matters after all?"

The way the sun begins to edge up over the hills ever so gradually, Natalie saw a kind of light begin to spread over Mary's upturned face.

Then, unmistakably, the smile told Jonathan's sister all she needed to know. Natalie was smiling too and not a bit annoyed when Mary said, "Poor Mister Burke can stop hiding behind the scrub oaks now."

As Natalie and Burke walked back to their cabin, arm in arm, she tried to tell him of her time with Mary.

"I'm not doing very well letting you know exactly what happened," she said, "because most of everything took place inside Mary. Really, all I did was remind her that nothing—absolutely nothing in the whole wide world should keep her away from Jonathan."

"What had Jonathan written? I saw you reading his letter."

Natalie giggled. "Mary saw *you* too. You just thought you were hiding."

"I'm not surprised," he said. "Mary and Ben were both born with eyes in the back of their heads. Are you going to tell me what your brother wrote?"

"Nothing that would scare *anyone* but Mary! Poor honest Jonathan only meant to be giving her something to look forward to by describing some fancy-dress ball he had to attend in New Haven."

"Uh-oh. If he even mentioned that Mary might have to go to one of those shindigs with him, she'd be scared half to death."

"She was." Natalie stopped walking to look up at him. "Burke, I don't care a fig if I ever go to another ball. I'd much rather be right here on our path with you, but Mary's going to live in Savannah someday and Savannah would crumble and fall into the river without fancy-dress balls! I didn't try to fool her into thinking he wouldn't have to attend some of them."

"Well, what *did* you do?"

"I reminded her that if I could learn how to keep your house and cook and scrub, she could learn to waltz. She went on at some length about how our hills up here are her backbone and the rivers and creeks her life's blood and—"

"That's all true," he interrupted. "For me too now. Also for you."

"You and I are beside the point, Burke! Mary is the point. When I asked her how she knew the mountains were her backbone, and the streams her blood, she said she'd *learned* it. That was my coup de grace! After that, I mostly just waited for the truth to sink in on her." She thought a moment. "Burke?"

"Hm?"

"Do you remember the time right after I burned down your old cabin near Cassville when—out in the yard by the rubble with Mary and Miss Lib and poor old Ben—I began to see me as I really was? *Seeing* is just terribly important. I guess I have to go on having those revelations about myself. Miss Lorah made me see how I was keeping myself sick, after we lost our baby, by clutching on to my grief and being stubborn about insisting that I'd failed you. I may not act as though I do sometimes, but I remember those moments when I began to *see*. Plainly, Mary needed to *see* too."

"And did she? Did she lose her fear of being Jonathan Browning's wife who might well have to learn to waltz?"

"Oh, maybe not forever. I'm sure she'll be petrified by society manners over and over again, but I also reminded her that she could *learn*. She really speaks much more fluently now, don't you think?"

They were walking up the cabin path, Burke smiling down at her. "I'm proud of you, darling," he said. "Proud that you're my girl."

"I'm proud of myself. Now, if I can only control Miss Lib until she goes to live in Washington City, Mary will be all right. She doesn't mean to, but I think Miss Lib terrifies Mary sometimes. She can act quite old and rigid, you know. Sometimes just plain chilly toward Mary since it's common knowledge that Jonathan means to marry her."

"What makes you think Miss Lib is really going to live in Washington City?"

"Because she loves Uncle W.H. He'll begin to beg soon. She'll go. She vows she doesn't want to leave Etowah Cliffs, but I think part of her really longs for the whirl of Washington City social life. Even though his wife hasn't been dead long, the papers say President John Tyler entertains a lot at that drafty, damp White House."

Burke laughed briefly. "You've been in the White House, have you, Mrs. Latimer?" he teased.

"Yes, I had to go to something there once because my roommate's father was the French ambassador. I like our cabin better."

"Could you give me even one small reason why?"

"You're in our cabin with me. Uncle W.H. will adore being invited to the White House, though. He's a Savannah gentleman."

Burke laughed again. "Unlike me."

"That's right. Unlike you."

"I'll bet it's true old Tyler is making the most of 'His Accidency.' Socially and otherwise. The Whigs only put him on the ticket to pull southern votes to Ohio and William Henry Harrison. No one in a Whig high council ever dreamed Tyler, a slave-owning Virginian, would end up as host in the White House. Tyler's a Whig President, but somehow I think Democratic Congressman Stiles will be dancing there—with or without Miss Lib. My hunch is, since Tyler's such a rabid states' rights man, our illustrious congressman from Cass will support him in Congress now and then. The Cassville paper vows Tyler is secretly pleased that so many southern Democrats were elected—to the horror, of course, of his Secretary of State, Daniel Webster, who wants no slavery at all."

As they climbed the cabin steps, she said, half joking, "That, sir, was quite a speech! I never heard you talk politics before. I do remember—you voted, didn't you?"

"I did, but I'm not much interested except as a citizen of what your Uncle W.H. calls 'our troubled, expansion-crazed country.' "

" 'Expansion-crazed' sounds just like Uncle W.H." Inside the cabin, she hugged Burke. "Well, let the droves move west. You and I are staying right here and that's all I care about."

He helped her out of her cape and hung it on a peg. "That's all you need to care about, darling."

"Burke?"

He came back from barring the door to take her in his arms. "What, my beautiful?"

"Uncle W.H. said this is a troubled country. Is he just being flowery or is there really trouble?"

"There can always be trouble because of the 'expansion craze,' I suppose." He held her close to him. "But, oh, beautiful Natalie, we're safe and soon—I promise—*soon* I'll be free to finish our very own cottage. You've been so—great about living in this place!"

"Hush! I've been happier here than ever in my long twenty-two years and you know it."

"Sure you wouldn't rather be trekking west with me in a Conestoga wagon?"

She kissed him. "West would be too far from Savannah."

"Do you miss Savannah?"

"Not at all," she said. "But my family and Miss Eliza and William love coming up here to visit us. You see? I do consider other people. But I never really *miss* anything or anyone but you! How Miss Lib goes on living with Uncle W.H. so far away, I simply don't know."

"Someone has to be here to run this place or she'd be with him now. Managing their hundreds of acres is no easy job."

"You don't think you and I could do it?"

"I certainly don't want the responsibility. I know nothing about handling slaves."

She thought a minute. "The—'trouble' you and Uncle W.H. talk about is over—owning slaves, isn't it?"

"In large part, yes."

"Burke, I want you to stay out of the whole messy thing, do you hear me?"

"I plan to, but all those years ago old Tom Jefferson was already hearing a 'firebell in the night.' Today's politicians try to avoid the subject, but slavery divides us North and South, Natalie. Even you may have to face up to that. Could be sooner than you think."

"I'll simply refuse." She pulled away. "Sorry, love, but I promised to make my famous Lady Baltimore cake for Miss Lib this evening. The Barnsleys are stopping with her tomorrow night on their way to Savannah for Christmas."

Burke watched as she began to bustle about the kitchen, getting out flour, sugar, butter and milk . . . separating the egg whites . . . and being too lovely for a man to bear. He had longed to have their cottage finished for Christmas, but with Sam so clumsy, finishing would be months away. Last week, from a peddler he'd met at the courthouse in Cassville, he'd bought Natalie a fine gold bracelet as a Christmas gift. That and his love would have to do for this year.

Watching her struggle to blend hard, cold butter into sugar, he hurried to work the butter for her. "Would you like to be with your parents in Savannah over the holidays?" he asked, rather surprising himself. "I'm sure Jonathan can't make it home this year."

"Burke! Would you really be willing to spend Christmas in Savannah?"

He took a deep breath. "If that's what you want, yes."

Plainly smothering a laugh, she said, "That's the ultimate sacrifice! But no, no, *no*. I don't want to go to Savannah. I only want to be right here in our cabin—with you." Her laughter faded as she looked straight at him. "Besides, I'm absolutely certain we have made the miracle again!"

There was butter on his hands, but he grabbed her to him. "Natalie, you're —sure?"

"Yes, and after what happened before, I'm not taking any chances in a rough old stagecoach—or even a train! We're staying right here for Christmas!"

Chapter 39

O N Friday evening, February 10, of the new year, 1844, again Mark sat in the Central of Georgia station, wondering if he'd done the right thing in deciding not to bring little Cliffie Gordon along to meet Eliza Anne and her two boys. The train was due in less than half an hour, but no one remembered a single night when it had reached Savannah on time. William Mackay would be joining him any minute. He always welcomed time alone with William, but he'd honestly felt the wait could be too long for a seven-year-old girl.

Mark was impatient for Eliza Anne to arrive, eager, as usual, for word of Natalie, now carrying another child. In her latest letter, giving them all her Savannah arrival date and her reasons for the quick decision to join W.H. in Washington City, Eliza Anne had seemed sure that Natalie was doing well so far. The familiar pain squeezed Mark's heart. Natalie had seemed to be doing well with her first child too.

Come on, William, he thought nervously. I need your calm, solid company. Being with William always helped curb his own agitation over both his children. His friend not only gave him strength but kept Mark's own sorrow at the loss of his first grandchild in perspective . . . reminded him that in one ghastly blast of an overheated steamship boiler, William had lost his entire family. One of W. H. Stiles's goals in the United States Congress, Mark knew, was to do all he could to introduce and pass a bill to enforce better regulation of steamship boilers.

He sighed. Nothing to increase steam-travel safety had been done in all the years since people had begun to travel on steamboats. What made W.H. think that he, as a freshman congressman, could bring off such a thing? Knowing W.H.'s ambition, Mark predicted frustration ahead for his friend, who always wanted to accomplish everything yesterday.

It was a difficult time to have been elected to Congress, with President John Tyler in almost constant battle with both houses. Still, Mark knew that W.H., a Democrat, and Tyler, a Whig, saw eye to eye on the always divisive states' rights issue *and* on slavery. It was common knowledge that, off the record, Tyler had been pleased at the recent Democratic victory. Mark and W.H. disagreed on the "peculiar institution"—could not be farther apart on slavery—but he felt proud of W.H. and relished the idea of receiving letters now straight from the seat of power in Washington City. Mark considered himself a Whig, although he'd voted for W. H. Stiles. Splitting his ticket, he'd also voted for the Whig William Henry Harrison for President, mainly because Daniel Webster of Massachusetts was almost certain to be the Secretary of State. But now, with Harrison dead and Tyler in the highest office, Webster had resigned from the Cabinet. Mark felt a little at sea about the whole national picture. Tyler's pro-slavery opinions, his staunch belief in spreading slavery into the new territories, made the loss of Webster loom large in Mark's mind. Daniel Webster and Henry Clay were, to him, the brainiest men in Washington. He would, he supposed, have to include John C. Calhoun, in spite of his total disagreement with most of Calhoun's thinking, all the way from his frightening nullification policy to his strong adherence to slavery. Daniel Webster was Mark's ideal statesman. Webster not only opposed slavery; he favored centralized government and a national bank. Mark smiled again. He and W.H. had enjoyed some of their most rousing arguments on those very issues. Mark made no bones about his vote for W.H. He had voted his affection for the man last year and not his political convictions. With Daniel Webster, Mark opposed the annexation of Texas too, fearing the addition of still another slave state. W.H. embraced it. Mark had always been lukewarm on old Andrew Jackson and, so far as he knew, W.H. was a Jacksonian. He'd voted his friendship, for certain.

Mark marveled at Miss Eliza Mackay's strong stand against permitting slavery in any new territory. Women didn't vote, and, like Caroline, Eliza Mackay had grown up with slavery as an accepted part of life. Still, she was Miss Eliza, and more than able to do her own thinking.

Jumping to his feet, hand out, Mark welcomed the sight of William ambling through the entrance of the train station.

"I saw you from outside on the platform," William said, a grin on his pleasant, thin face. "You looked mighty deep in thought."

"I confess I was," he replied with a laugh. "Actually, I was thinking about your mother's opposition to the extension of slavery."

William sat down. "She and I have gone around the barn more than once lately on that subject. Sometimes I think you're more Mama's son than either Jack or me. She sees no reason *ever* for war either. Oh, she'd have been on our side during the Revolution, if she'd been old enough to take sides. I think Mama was only about two when our Declaration was signed. But even agreeing to Jack's going to West Point was hard for her. You're a lot like her, Mark. Probably why you've always been her favorite."

"You couldn't pay me a higher compliment." He looked at his watch. "Train's already an hour and ten minutes late."

"Well, that isn't bad," William said in his easy way. "She'll come chugging down the track soon. I thought little Cliffie Gordon might have convinced you to bring her along so she wouldn't have to wait till tomorrow to see young Henry."

"She tried. Maybe I should have agreed. Mrs. Gordon says not a day goes by that Cliffie doesn't say something about Henry. I just hope he remembers her half as clearly."

William crossed his long legs. "I guess you and Caroline read our latest letter from Eliza Anne. She hated to leave Mary Cowper behind in school, still nothing would do W.H. but that my sister head for Washington City—now."

Mark laughed. "You're not surprised, are you? At him or at Eliza Anne for agreeing to go on such short notice."

"Not a bit. Especially after W.H. wrote that the fashionable ladies in the Hall of Representatives gallery stand and applaud his every golden utterance —and cry for more. No doubt W.H. needs his wife with him. Being in Washington is about fifty percent social, I'd think." William frowned. "Mark, I'm worried about Jack."

"So am I. He seemed so much improved when he got back from visiting Captain Lee, but I didn't like the way he looked at all the last time he came home from Tybee Island. I don't like that sallow color. Will he be in town for Eliza Anne's two-day visit?"

"My guess is that he'll come, if he feels up to it. For overnight, anyway. Jack's got good men working under him on that survey out there. He could get away all right. I think he uses his heavy work assignment as a ready alibi in case he isn't up to making even the short boat trip to town. Jack can lie so charmingly, you know, even Mama believes him most of the time."

"Your brother's got to be a lonely man," Mark said after a time. "Have you ever known Jack to fall in love? He's always been the most popular bachelor in Savannah, but—have I missed something? Has Jack ever been serious about anyone?"

William shook his head. "Not that I know of. Oh, back when Eliza Anne and Robert Lee were close, Jack saw my sister's friend young Julia Scarbrough some. I think Mama actually prayed they might marry, but along came Godfrey Barnsley and off went Jack. As I remember, Jack was easing out of things even before young Barnsley got here from London. My brother puzzles me too. The Bible's right, you know: 'A merry heart doeth good like a medicine,' but I wonder if that doesn't mean a *happy* heart. Jack's merry enough. Always has been. There's no way a man can be happy, though, can he, being lonely?"

"I can't imagine it," Mark said. "But then, I stop short of even trying to imagine what I'd do without Caroline."

"You'd have to make do," William said. "I'll always be glad I—loved the way I loved Virginia. In a way, it goes on sustaining me. What do you say we change the subject? How about politics? Do you think your godlike Daniel Webster will try to become President this year?"

"I doubt it. There aren't enough of us who swear by him," Mark said. "It seems to me you Democrats have your golden chance. You have the knack of appealing to ordinary Americans. Old Jackson's spoils system still works.

We've got a Whig President of sorts now in Tyler, but he is *accidentally* the President. The Whigs go on appealing mainly to the elite in the industrial North and big slave owners in the South. Not all of them, but many. I honestly don't know what to think these days. With Webster resigned from the Cabinet and Clay out of the Senate to run for the presidency, it seems to me almost too much is changed in Washington."

"I'm certainly not an expert," William said, "but as I see it, the age of the 'political gentleman' is over and it's being replaced, as fast as water rushes over Niagara, by economic men—men bent first and foremost on making more money. Look at the way they're pouring west these days."

Mark smiled. " 'Manifest destiny'?"

" 'Manifest destiny,' " William said. "This westward push is changing everything. Maybe for the best, maybe not. I only know I don't try to decide on anything anymore unless I know how it's going to affect *my* pocketbook! I make no bones about it. I also know you and other folks think those of us who want to annex Texas want to extend slavery. Well, that may be true in part, but annexing Texas has to do with *economic man* too. No longer political man only. Boosterism is in the saddle now. Making money is all mixed in with so-called morality, if you believe the papers—with liberty, commercialism, expansion—and, Mama insists, with military opportunity."

Mark tapped his friend on the arm. "You're far more politically informed than you admit, aren't you? And for my money, Miss Eliza is too."

The first faint clang of the train bell brought them both to their feet.

"They're coming," William said, heading for the door that led to the platform outside. "We'll have to continue settling the country's problems another time."

"Oh, how I wish I thought we could do just that," Mark said, standing beside his friend as they watched the engine lantern break through the darkness. "What I'm interested in, now that she's actually almost here, is your sister's report on Natalie!"

After affectionate greetings all around in the Mackay front hall, Mark followed the family, at Miss Eliza's insistence, into the familiar parlor, and over the happy din of talk and laughter, tried to hear what young Henry Stiles seemed determined to whisper to him.

"We'll only be here two days, Uncle Mark," the boy said, "so I was hoping you'd bring Cliffie Gordon to the station tonight."

"I should have brought her," Mark whispered back, directing the boy out into the hall since it was plain that Henry did not want the family to hear. "I'm really sorry, son, because Mrs. Gordon's taking her North soon. I can drop you by their house, though, first thing tomorrow morning. I promise. If I can't get away, I'll send Jupiter."

Henry's smile, so like his father's, gave Mark the same uneasy feeling W.H. had so often given him over the years. There was just enough of a sense of superiority in the smile to make him feel he'd somehow said the wrong thing.

"You forget I'm an upcountry man now," Henry said, one eyebrow cocked. "I'm used to walking everywhere. Is Cliffie still so pretty? I haven't seen her, you know, for years. My sister got prettier as she got older."

"Cliffie Gordon's no exception," Mark said. "At least, I consider her quite beautiful."

"I guess you're satisfied now that Mama's told you how healthy and fine Natalie is," the boy said, giving Mark the smile again, "but wouldn't you like to know *my* opinion of Natalie?"

"I would indeed. From what your mother writes, she spends more time with you and Robert than almost anyone else, except maybe Mrs. Plemmons."

At the mention of Lorah Plemmons, Henry's eyes lit up. "Did you know Miss Lorah can play a Jew's harp?"

"No, I certainly didn't."

"Aw, I don't suppose Natalie writes much, but Miss Lorah can really whang that Jew's harp of hers like nothing you've ever heard, Mark."

Mark grinned, but said nothing when, for the first time, Henry left off the "Uncle" as though they were the same age.

"She's teaching me to play too. Natalie already knows how! Papa bought me a Jew's harp in Cassville before he left for Washington City. I aim to play it some for Cliffie tomorrow. Do you think she'd like that?"

"Oh, yes. In fact, she'll want to learn too, I'm sure."

"Naw, I'd rather she didn't," Henry said. "That would spoil my serenade."

"I see. Son, I should tell you that Cliffie really wanted to meet your train this evening. I talked her out of it, since the Central of Georgia has been known to be so late at times."

After a withering look, Henry said, "Mark, I'm too old to be put off by the kind of excuses grown-ups give children. And even though you didn't ask me, I can tell you to stop worrying about Natalie. She's even learned how to chop wood. You oughta see her splinter a fat pine stump! Miss Lorah handles an ax like a man. She taught her."

"Will you and Robert miss the woods and the river once you're settled in Washington City?"

Henry's big sigh registered on his face. "Yes, sir. Nothing would do Mama, though, but that we pick up and go when Papa started to get desperate in his letters. He's lost without Mama, I guess. What Bobby and I want doesn't matter to Mama if she thinks Papa's bent on his way."

"Oh, living in the nation's capital will be a fine experience, I'd think. And someday you'll understand how much your father needs your mother."

Henry's eyebrow shot up again. "Do you think I don't understand now? I'm as much in love with Cliffie Gordon as Papa is with Mama! I'm going to marry her too, just as soon as I'm old enough."

Mark struggled to keep his face straight. "Is that so?"

"Yes, sir, just as soon as we stop moving around. I'm almost ten and I've thought about her every day I've been gone." He sighed heavily. "I guess she needed me a lot when her father died. One day, though, I can stop trailing along wherever Papa says. Before I'm twenty, I plan to be married to Cliffie. I'm going to be in charge of my life then the way Jonathan is. I'd say by—eighteen."

Riding alone toward home a while later, in the back of his comfortable, damask-lined carriage, Mark felt older than he'd ever remembered. Older and yet suspended. Tonight, after Henry's amazing announcement, he felt suspended somewhere in the midst of his fifty-one years, Jonathan's eighteen and Henry's ten. In his own tenth year, Mark and Aunt Nassie were still living happily in the old Browning mansion in Philadelphia, having fun to-gether between his father's infrequent visits. In his own eighteenth year, Mark's father had paid his last visit and was off on his final sea voyage, heading for the storm off the Bahamas that drowned him in his stateroom.

Could Mark's son, Jonathan, at such an early age, really know that he wanted to marry a half-breed Cherokee girl whose life in Savannah as Mrs. Jonathan Browning would surely be much like that of a young trout heading innocently for a man-made fish trap in the Etowah River? Ten-year-old Henry was already rebelling against parental decisions. Jonathan had never once seemed rebellious. Mark himself had never had the chance to rebel against authority. Both his parents and then Aunt Nassie had died. There had been no one against whom to rebel.

The same was true of Caroline—except for her difficult, bitter grand-mother, Ethel Cameron. Had he and Caroline, orphaned at such an early age, been too lenient with both their children? Neither had forbidden Natalie to marry a then penniless carpenter and move to the Georgia frontier. Neither had been firm enough to forbid Jonathan his Indian girl. That most responsi-ble parents selected mates for their offspring seemed somehow not to have occurred to either of them. They both just worried, relented and then went on worrying.

He leaned his head against the tufted seat. At least he had good news for Caroline tonight. So far, Natalie was doing well carrying her second child. The remarkably wise Jew's-harp-playing Miss Lorah had helped, would go on helping Natalie in all ways. According to both Eliza Anne and Henry, Miss Lorah and their daughter were real friends. If anyone had told him or Caro-line but a few months ago that their haughty, spoiled, incredibly beautiful Natalie would—could ever be friends with her hired help, they would have laughed at the idea. Years, he mused . . . the years temper so much. Change a man's circumstances more than any man dares face. By the infinite kindness of God, as Miss Eliza said, we are spared knowing what of good and what of bad may lie ahead. "If we knew it all," she always added, "there'd be no need to make choices. And—we learn, Mark, from making choices."

At home, beside Caroline on the family drawing-room sofa, he asked a question he really hadn't intended to ask: "Do you and I really make choices where our children are concerned? Or do we just do our best to adjust to whatever happens to either of them?"

"Oh, Mark," she said, her head on his shoulder, "not tonight, please! For right now, we know Natalie's doing well. I'm as grateful as you are, but can't we concentrate on easy, possible subjects such as my need to be close to you tonight?"

"Yes, my darling. Forgive me."

"I do so love these months alone with you. I'm falling in love all over again with my gallant, tender husband, did you know? Honestly, I've never seen you so handsome as just a few minutes ago when you smiled at me from the doorway. I love your new sideburns and your hair is graying just right." She sighed. "Jonathan isn't even half finished at Yale yet. Anything could happen in the next two and a half years. Natalie is—fine, and we're alone in the whole house for a change! Even Maureen and Gerta are with their own families tonight . . ."

He traced the dear, familiar line of her cheek and mouth, allowing his finger to move down her still slim neck, marveling that a woman nearing fifty could be so desirable. The years had not changed that. Caroline would be Caroline—his absolutely essential Caroline—even if she lived to be far older than Miss Eliza. God, let her live, he prayed, kissing her lips ever so gently. *Someday I may learn to let go of my children, but, Lord, I could never, never get along without Caroline.*

As though he had been seeing them, his children's faces dimmed and were lost in the immediacy of Caroline in his arms . . . the scent of her hair and skin enlivening his body. The same sweet, painful enlivening that, nearly thirty years ago, had kept him tossing in his old room at the Mackay house, tormented and reaching for this beautiful woman he then didn't even know he loved enough to live beside for the remainder of his life . . .

Striding along the next morning past the familiar houses on East Broughton toward Abercorn, on his way to the Gordon mansion, young Henry Stiles felt both strange and puzzled that the city he'd grown up in to age eight had changed so much. Oh, he'd heard there were lots of new houses and stores, but the change seemed to have taken place inside him, even more than in the city. Of course, he was dressed up for his first visit to the Gordon house, where he'd surely have to greet Mrs. Sarah Gordon, but more than his stiff new shoes restricted him. The new long, dark trousers felt too tight around the waist, even though his mother had declared them loose and poorly styled. Men were wearing corsets in Savannah. Henry thought that stupid. Only women needed to torture themselves that way. Burke had gone with him to Cassville to buy this new outfit before they'd left the up-country and had risen in Henry's estimation because he'd sympathized with the boy's dread of having to spend who knew how many months in city clothes.

But more than what Mama had called "ill-fitting" new pants, a short coat and a somber black cravat bothered him this morning. It seemed as though clothing cut very like his congressman father's should have made him feel grown-up and powerful. Instead, he was all hands and feet and the ham and biscuits he'd had for breakfast less than an hour ago churned in his stomach. Would Cliffie Gordon think him handsome?

I'm supposed to look like Papa, he reassured himself. I'm sure he's the handsomest man in the United States Congress, but do I look enough like him to cause Cliffie Gordon to agree to marry me? Nearing the Gordon mansion, he felt of his straight, arrogant nose, the high forehead which he knew was his father's, and thought about how his light hair grew thick and long at the sides like Papa's, just slightly curled on his neck. Mama always says Papa looks like a poet. I hate poetry, but I guess poets are especially good-looking men or she wouldn't keep saying that. He longed for side-burns, but that couldn't be until he was old enough to shave.

His brother, Bobby, had still been sound asleep when Henry crawled out of bed in the room on the second floor of his grandmother's house where Mark Browning slept when he was young, right when he first came to Savan-nah. Of course, Henry wasn't even born then and Mama was just a little girl like Cliffie, but over and over until he was tired of it, he'd heard about the years when Mark lived in the old frame house on East Broughton. Once, during her last visit to Etowah Cliffs, he'd overheard his mother and Grand-mother Mackay talking about how young Mark Browning had once thought he was in love with Henry's grandmother! Even today, nervous and excited as he was now that he was nearing the Gordon house, the whole idea still made him laugh. Mark's pretty old now, he thought, but nothing like as old as Grandmother Mackay! He wished fleetingly that he'd asked Mark last night how he finally found out it was really Caroline Cameron he loved after all. Who could tell about grown-ups, anyway, due to their age?

Take his own mother, for example. Captain Jack Mackay's best friend from West Point, another Army captain, named Robert E. Lee, was supposed to have been sweet on her once years ago. Everybody in town knew it, he'd been told by some of his childhood friends in Savannah. Now, Captain Lee was married to a cousin and was the father of six children and he, Henry, and Mary Cowper and Bobby were the three children of Eliza Anne Mackay Stiles and William Henry Stiles. You surely could never tell what grown-ups might change their minds and do, and he, William Henry Stiles, Jr., meant *never* to be so peculiar. Of course, he realized that his parents, when they took him seriously at all, would think that he was too young to know for certain that he wanted to marry Eliza Clifford Gordon, but he did know. And even Mama and Papa, who thought it was so terrible for Jonathan Browning to love Mary McDonald, a half-blood, would never disapprove his marriage to the daughter of the founder of the Central of Georgia Railroad. Of that much he was certain. Henry had learned well about class, about what was considered good family.

Of course, it might not matter to him if Cliffie'd been part Indian or the daughter of a seamstress.

He felt superior, though, to both Jonathan and Natalie because he had shown the good sense to choose a prominent man's daughter. The Gordons and the Mackays and the Stileses had been family friends forever. Birds of a feather did flock together, he thought, and agreed with his mother that it really isn't natural for Jonathan to have fallen in love with a half-breed, much as Henry liked Indian Mary and always had.

Climbing the steep steps of the Gordon mansion—less steep, he noticed, now that his legs were longer—he tried to picture Cliffie as looking older than the last time he'd seen her. Oh, she'd still be wearing shorter skirts than women, also lace-trimmed pantalets, he was sure, since she was not nine yet, but her hair should be parted in the middle and pulled back into curls on her dear neck. It made a man feel superior, he decided, to have made his lifetime choice while still young. Now and then, Papa had told Henry he had quite a mature mind. He agreed with Papa on that, if not on the subject of moving the family to Washington City. Everyone, including Mark, thought his father could be making lots more money planting corn and keeping a hand in his old Savannah law practice.

He rang the bell three times and waited, his heart pounding with hope that Cliffie herself might open the door. Before he could ring again following a courteous wait, the door opened and there stood Cliffie Gordon smiling up into his face. Once he would have lunged to give her a hug, but that was before he knew he'd chosen her as his future wife. Today, he returned her smile, bowed and stepped inside the almost forgotten entrance hall of the impressive Gordon mansion.

For the first half hour or so of his long-awaited visit—he'd known for nearly a year, he figured, that Cliffie was to be his wife—her mother, Mrs. Sarah Gordon, sat talking with them in the family parlor, causing Henry to ask what he was sure his mother would consider an impertinent question: "Do you know, Mrs. Gordon, that my mother, Bobby and I have to leave for Washington City day after tomorrow? That our time here is awfully short?"

Henry felt sure he saw Cliffie's large, luminous eyes sadden. He cleared his throat quite loudly and took a fairly noisy sip of the hot chocolate served to him and Cliffie. It was barely warm and not half as good as chocolate made with the milk from their own cows up in Cass.

"This is quite good for city chocolate," he said.

"Thank you. And yes, we know you're leaving soon for Washington, Henry," Mrs. Gordon said. "We're so glad you could visit us before we have to leave Savannah too. I'm taking the children North next week."

Until now, Cliffie had mostly just looked at him, adoringly, and he thought she certainly had done well pouring her mother's tea and their chocolate.

"Now," Cliffie was saying, "I know it's awfully chilly outside, Henry, but we could take a walk together if you'd care to do that."

He jumped up so fast he clattered the thin china cup and saucer returning them to the huge serving tray. "Oh, I was hoping for a walk, Cliffie! To me, it isn't a bit cold. Savannah weather's nothing to me anymore after our ice and snow in the upcountry. It was snowing the day we left."

Sarah Gordon bundled her daughter into a warm coat, totally covering her pretty blue plaid dress, its full sleeves tied at the wrists with ribbons to match, and then tied a darker blue bonnet under Cliffie's chin.

"Now, walk briskly, you two," Mrs. Gordon warned at the front door. "I'm sure your mother wants no bad colds developing on the voyage North, Henry. And don't stay out too long. The wind's really whipping. I'll have hot soup when you get back—that is, if you have time for another visit, Henry."

Bowing to Mrs. Gordon, he assured her that for the next two days he had all the time in the world.

Taking Cliffie's arm, as he'd seen his father do, he led her down the steps into the street, and then, in broad daylight, without even looking one way or another, he touched her warm cheek with his fingers.

"I—I only came back to Savannah to see you," he said. "I don't think more than three days have gone by that I haven't thought of you, Cliffie." She was smiling up at him so sweetly he grew almost dizzy with the thought that someday he would be old enough to lean down and kiss her perfect lips.

"My—my papa died," she said, eyes brimming. "People don't even talk a lot about him anymore, but they did for quite a while. I—I'll always miss him. For as long as I live, I'll miss my papa's laughter. You and Papa were always making me laugh. Make me laugh now, Henry!"

His head was whirling and, for the life of him, he couldn't think of one funny thing to say, so he turned a cartwheel, and when he came upright, his hat was rolling in the dusty winter wind, so that he had to chase it. A quick glance at Cliffie as he settled the hat back on his head told him that what he'd done hadn't been a bit funny. She only looked concerned.

Hurrying her along Bull Street, he stopped directly in front of her and blurted: "Cliffie, I've come to ask you to marry me!"

A slow, adorable smile pulled at the corners of her mouth and soon it widened into one of sheer delight, then—finally, she began to jump up and down, clapping her hands and laughing.

"Did—did what I asked make you—laugh?" he wanted to know, so nervous inside he tried to smile and couldn't. "Cliffie Gordon! Don't just stand there jumping and—laughing at me! I don't like that one bit."

Her mittened hand slipped into his. "Have you forgotten that I always jump up and down and laugh when I'm—happy, Henry?"

His head didn't itch under his hat, but pretending it did, he scratched it, then asked, "Does that mean we will get married someday? And do you think you might be going to Washington City to visit your great-uncle, Judge Wayne, any time soon during your stay at the North? If you think you might, we'll see each other again, because my father's term as congressman just began in December."

"Oh, I think we'll surely visit Washington City sometime, but I don't know when. First, we visit just a plain uncle in New York State. I want most of all to see where you live in the upcountry. Is your house there very large and beautiful?"

Picturing the frame, four-roomed dog-trot wing where they still lived, Henry laughed. "Not now, but Papa says it will be grand if Burke and Sam ever finish the main part. Mama says Papa never dreams anything but big and expensive. There would be plenty of room for you and whoever might come with you once Burke gets through with the main house. There'll be the big middle part, then later on still another wing. We're building the two new parts out of brick made right on our own land with our own clay! The bricks are far superior to old, crumbly Savannah gray brick, Mama says."

Walking along Bull toward the river now, she said nothing for a while, then in the dreamiest voice Henry had ever heard, murmured, "Who knows? Someday I might be the mistress of Etowah Cliffs—when I'm married to William Henry Stiles, Jr."

As though someone had jerked him backward, Henry stopped walking and stared down into her pretty face—nose red now from the biting wind. "Cliffie, does that—does that mean you—plan to marry me too?"

Her smile vanished. Her gray-blue eyes locked with his. "Oh, yes, Henry! I've always planned to marry you. In all my life, I've never once thought of marrying anyone else . . ."

Chapter 40

"I WANT to know the whole truth, Mama," Eliza Anne said at breakfast the next morning in her mother's familiar dining room. "Jack must be too ill even to make that short boat trip from Tybee Island or he'd be here at least long enough to greet the children and me."

"Mama, I have something important to tell you—to tell all of you," young Henry said, his face glowing.

"Not now, son." Eliza Anne was firm. "When have you heard from Jack, Mother?"

"I tried to tell you last night," Henry went right on, "and it won't take a minute!"

"I had a short letter from Jack the day before you came," Eliza Mackay said, also ignoring the boy. "Your brother is certainly far from well, but evidently the Army believes he's well enough to sleep out there in that damp and cold and go on working. Jack's a soldier, he has to—"

"I know he's a soldier, Mama," Eliza Anne said, "but it isn't like him not to manage even a short leave while we're in town for only two days!"

Henry tried again. "What I have to tell everybody has to do with all the rest of my life!"

"I think Sister's right," William said. "Jack just isn't up to coming to town or he'd be here. I haven't the foggiest notion what we can do about it, though." To Henry, he said, "Want to whisper your big secret to me, son?"

"It's no secret," the boy sulked, "or I wouldn't be trying to tell it."

"Jack needs to be loved," Eliza Anne said as though thinking aloud. "He needs someone to love him and take better care of him. It's a tragedy that he never married!"

Out of the corner of her eye, Eliza Anne saw Henry brighten.

"What I have to announce," the boy proclaimed, "has to do with marriage."

"Your Uncle Jack's marriage, Henry?" she asked inattentively.

"No, not his! His marriage is his problem!"

"Is that any way to speak of your uncle while he's being forced to work when he's so ill?" Grandmother Mackay asked.

"Grandma, the Army isn't interested in seeing Uncle Jack get sicker and die," Henry sassed, pouting, his mother thought, exactly like W.H. "The Army wouldn't make him sick on purpose."

"Henry Stiles," Grandmother scolded, "that's a really silly thing to say! To a man—even to a boy like you—anything the Army does is perfect. Well, I can tell you it isn't."

"Who said it was?" Henry asked.

"Dear, dear Henry," Grandma Mackay said, soothingly now, "we only have tomorrow's breakfast together and then the house will be empty again of everyone but William and Kate and Sarah and me. Can't we just go on hoping Jack will get here, and talk about something more pleasant? Henry dear, you haven't touched your ham."

"I've been too busy trying to get a word in edgeways."

"Edgewise," his mother corrected.

"Well, may I have the floor now?" he asked.

"Just as soon as I have a small chance to discuss a really important problem with your Uncle William," Eliza Anne said.

Henry banged down his fork onto his breakfast plate.

"He's lost his temper again, Mama," Bobby said.

"This is no time for one of your tantrums, William Henry," Eliza Anne said, her voice very cross. "Pick up that fork and place it down softly. Do you hear me?"

"I hear you," he grumbled, obeying, "but *nobody* wants to hear what I have to say."

"When you boys and your aunts get back from your early shopping trip," Eliza Anne promised, "I'll spend the remainder of the morning with you children." She turned to her brother. "Now, William, please hear me out before you refuse what I must ask of you. Will you do that?"

"Everybody gets heard but me," Henry muttered.

"I told you I'd spend the entire morning with you and—"

"What I have to say isn't for young kids like Bobby!"

"Well, who is it for?" William asked.

"Grown-ups. Cliffie Gordon promised to marry me."

"William, you know I'd never ask such a big favor of you if there was any other way to manage, but—" She whirled on her son. *"Henry!* What did you say?"

"You heard me. Yesterday, Cliffie said she'd marry me."

"Oh," Eliza Anne said absently. "Well, that's nice, son. Cliffie's a sweet little girl and from an excellent family." Her attention back on William, she went on: "I can't *begin* to tell any of you how insistent W.H. was that the children and I join him right away in Washington City. Heaven knows, I was struggling at managing our plantation up there alone, but I was doing it after a fashion, considering the shortage of money. Oh, he didn't surprise me by begging, but W.H. did create a dreadful problem. I doubt I'd have agreed until he began to write that he wasn't well physically—that he was exhausted by social events, by having to do his own secretarial work, by being forced to escort other ladies to this ball or that dinner party. He hates the Washington climate and I know I'll hate it too after upcountry air. But I'm going to him. He's arranged for additional rooms at Mrs. Hewitt's boardinghouse, and hard as it was for the boys and me to say goodbye to Etowah Cliffs, we're going."

Without a word beyond a perfunctory "Excuse me," Henry left the table.

When the front door slammed, Eliza Anne said, "He's off to visit Cliffie Gordon, I'm sure. I hope he isn't being a nuisance to poor Mrs. Gordon."

"Well, I hope we didn't hurt Henry's feelings too much just now," her mother said.

"I do believe my stripling son's wedding plans can wait a few years, Mama. Listen to me, William. All our land up there is without anyone but the overseer, David Holder, to operate it. There hasn't been one move made toward preparing a single field for spring planting. And here I am on my way to Washington City!"

Seeing William methodically folding his napkin, she said sharply, "Don't you dare fold that napkin and leave the table, brother! I need you. I need you desperately to take over for me in Cass until W.H. and I can get back." When William said nothing, looked at no one, she began to plead: "Please say you'll go! If you get there by early March, the fields won't be too terribly far behind, and unless some special legislative business comes up, we'll be home in June. William, please, please—that's only a little over three months away from your Savannah business—whatever it consists of by now. I promised W.H. I'd see to it that you help us!"

Still not looking at her, William smiled a little and said softly, "I'm sure you have trouble keeping up with my assorted business interests these days, sister, but I do have my Causton's Bluff money invested fairly widely. W.H. knows all about what I'm doing. He, of all people, knows someone has to keep tabs on my investments. At least, he used to know until he put all his funds into Cass."

"William, don't change the subject!"

"I didn't plan to say much about Jack's tuberculosis, Eliza Anne, but this just isn't a good time for me to leave Mama and the girls. Holder's a good man, young and strong. I'd think he'd do a fine job running your place up there. Does W.H. think David Holder isn't equal to it?"

"W.H. has my promise that *you* will help us!"

Before William said another word, they all heard the front door open and Jack's cheery voice called out, "Anybody at home in this house?"

Eliza Anne saw her mother's face light up and then sadden, when the cheerful greeting sent Jack into a heavy fit of coughing. She began running to the front hall, then stopped, remembering how her brother hated to be caught in the midst of a spell.

Within a minute or so, the silence around the breakfast table gave way to happy voices and laughter when Jack entered in his dress uniform, the coughing under control.

Eliza Anne hugged and hugged him, saying she knew he'd come to town before she and the children left.

Jack embraced their mother, shook William's hand and congratulated Eliza Anne upon the wonderful news he'd just heard.

"What news, Jack?"

"Henry's victory with little Cliffie Gordon," Jack said, his voice now quite recovered. "The boy's riding the crest of romance. Cliffie's agreed to marry him!"

"Oh, that," Eliza Anne said distractedly. "Jack, I'm so glad you're here. I need you to help me convince William to help us at Etowah Cliffs. I *have* to join W.H. in Washington City. He's begged me to come—and someone has to supervise our spring planting and—"

"Who's better equipped to do that than the old farmer, William Mackay, eh?" Jack teased. "Brother mine, how could you possibly resist such an opportunity to breathe real air again? No man alive loves the sight of a field crying for seed as much as you—" Jack broke into another siege of coughing, but held up a hand to indicate he hadn't finished talking yet. "That dispensed with," he said after clearing his throat, "I conclude that you have no valid reason, William, with me so nearby to monitor your business interests, not to oblige this lovely damsel in distress."

William's slow smile caused Eliza Anne's heart to leap with hope. When he began to chuckle softly, she flew to give him a big hug.

"Doesn't take much to get hugged in this house, does it?" William asked drily.

Stepping back to glare at him, Eliza Anne said, "You meant to go all along, didn't you? You could see—anyone could see how desperate I was. I might expect Jack to tease at a time like this, but not you—"

"I haven't said I'd go, have I?" William asked.

"Mama, do something about both of them!"

"Of course, I'm considering it," William went on, "but instead of counting on Jack to look after things here in town for me, I was about to suggest he get a leave of absence and go with me to Cass."

"Oh, William," their mother cried, "that's the best idea yet! Jack dearest, you've never seen Etowah Cliffs, and oh, my darling boy, the weather up there could make you well! Couldn't it, Eliza Anne? Aren't you ever so much better for living up there in that clean, clear mountain air? Jack, you know your sister's asthma is almost gone. Try for a sick leave, son, please try!"

Jack grinned. "At the risk of permanently damaging the Savannah River? Besides, the Army doesn't parcel out sick leaves like candy at Christmas and you know it, Mother. But—I'll give it a try. When do you plan to leave, brother?"

"To tell the truth, I hadn't made any plans at all," William said, obviously teasing Eliza Anne again. "But, in case I do go, probably around the end of this month. No use if I don't make it by then. It takes a while to prepare that much land for planting."

"Could Robert Lee help with your sick leave, Jack?" Eliza Anne asked.

"Bob's only a captain too. Tell you what, sister, my commanding officer's due in Savannah in a day or so. When I meet him, I'll perform my best coughing fit just for his benefit—and yours."

Eliza Anne embraced Jack again, holding him and holding him until, once more, he began to cough. "Thank you," she said, her eyes standing with tears. "Thank you, dear William. Thank you, dear Jack. And oh, Mama, we all thank you for the dependable, tender way we love each other in this family. I—I just wish I were half the mother you've been to all of us."

"I'll give you a small hint of how to improve, sister mine," Jack said. "Your son Henry needs you to take him a bit more seriously *right now.*"

She started to laugh. "Do you mean his silly puppy love for that child Cliffie Gordon?"

"Stranger things have been known to happen," Jack said.

After a silence, William said, "My Virginia was only three years older than Cliffie when she knew she loved me. Actually, she was just about Henry's age."

Chapter 41

EARLY in March, Lorah Plemmons, her chicken, Easter, on her shoulder, stood at the front window of the Latimer cabin in order to watch Natalie and Burke, arms around each other, as they walked slowly down the path toward the road that led to the almost finished Stiles place. At least, Burke and Sam had managed to get as far as painting the inside of the big middle section of what Mr. Stiles was already calling a mansion. She chuckled to herself. A person would think the size of his house had to do with eternity to hear that man talk. She shrugged. Maybe to him it does, she thought. There's not any two folks on the face of the earth exactly alike. This lifelong conviction had saved Lorah a lot of trouble in her fifty-eight years. Some folks have a time liking another person if they're the least bit different. Lorah had never seen the sense in wasting energy by disapproving just for the sake of disapproving.

Learning to like Missy had been far from easy for her at the start. She'd had trouble because watching anyone dig a deeper and deeper hole for themselves struck her as not very smart. She laughed at herself. Lorah Plemmons had never felt particularly smart, hadn't known many who were, but a person only added to their troubles by acting as though life ought to be ashamed of itself for not treating them better. By demanding their own way. By judging their troubles harder to bear than the troubles of others.

Now, a warm feeling of affection for the pretty red-haired girl flooded her as she saw the happy lovebirds round the curve in the river road and vanish from sight. She certainly liked Natalie Latimer now, loved her, in fact. Would take a skillet to anybody who tried to harm her. She also thought the world and all of Natalie's strapping, gentle, hardworking husband, who went on being so patient with Sam.

Still at the window, Lorah shook her head. Poor Sam . . . good as gold, kindhearted to every living creature. Oh, he did ogle Mary too much, but Lorah had watched many a wounded bird lie perfectly still in Sam's hands, trusting him every inch of the way. Sam had long-fingered, gentle hands and could set a rabbit's broken leg, splint and bind it, so the little feller'd be as good as new once the bone healed. Not once since the day she took him in had Sam said a cross word to her, but he tried Burke Latimer's patience every day of his life because Sam had two faults: he couldn't do any but the simplest kind of carpenter work and he *was* slower than molasses in January. Sam meant nobody any harm, but she'd thought a long time before bringing him along to Cass County with her. Oh, she didn't once think of deserting Sam by leaving him behind, she just weighed even taking the job herself for fear Sam might not fit in. Still, she trusted Sam through and through, as she'd trusted Indian Mary from the first time she'd laid eyes on her.

Lorah's heart bled that Mary tried these days to hold back her deep-down, real Cherokee nature. The girl could imitate a white-throated sparrow so exactly she'd fooled Lorah time and time again. Had caused Lorah to wonder about her own mind when she'd swear she heard the thin, clear repeated call at a time of year when anybody'd know there were no whitethroats around. Mary had finally told her one day that she and her brother, Ben, had used the winter sparrow's call to signal each other in the woods during the time they both lived in a cave over near New Echota, before Burke Latimer took them in to live with him. Mary didn't give that bird whistle much anymore, but Lorah had caught on that usually when she did give it, Mary was whistling up her brother beside his grave in their backyard. The girl kept a bunch of flowers or leaves of some kind on Ben's grave—took them fresh every day, even if the bunch already there in the old jar hadn't wilted yet. She'd go just the same to visit her brother and fix up something fresh and green or still in bud. Except for Natalie and Burke and the Stiles family and Lorah and Sam, Mary had nobody but that fine-looking young Browning feller way off in college in the state of Connecticut.

Lorah shooed Easter off her shoulder and was just about to go back to the kettle of clothes she had soaking out back when she heard Mary's whistle. That she'd been thinking so hard about her and then there she was, came as no surprise at all. All her life, Lorah'd seemed somehow to know up ahead about things, about people coming and all.

Well, most likely Indian Mary would come running around the cabin soon and chide Lorah because she wasn't stirring the wash pot. Oh, Mary chided in good humor. Lorah felt safe and loved by the girl, who only looked Indian about her eyes. "We play a lot, you and me," Mary would say often. They did too. If a person couldn't play at her work, life wasn't worth living.

Lorah headed for the steaming wash pot outside and wished—she supposed for the thousandth time—that she could somehow reach out and protect Mary McDonald's good heart. The girl thought the sun rose and set in Jonathan Browning, who'd finally gone off to visit his rich and powerful parents in Savannah, then sailed on an ocean ship all the way back up North to college. Lorah shook her head, a frown deepening the "thinkin' wrinkle" that never left her forehead anymore. They didn't talk much about him, but Lorah felt she surely must think almost as much about Jonathan as Mary did. Oh, a different kind of thinking, because Mary had suddenly turned from being as scared as a trapped squirrel to a kind of bubbling joy over the young fellow. She was pitiful in her fright when the boy had first left Cass County.

Of course, Natalie took full credit for changing Mary's fear to joy and what she called "high anticipation" for the future.

"Chances are you didn't do our Mary any favor, Missy," Lorah spoke aloud to herself, but directing her words to Natalie. "You took her by the hand up to the top of the mountain all right, but to where a good puff of wind could blow her all the way to the bottom. Rich folks are no different from poor, but they think they are and that's their big trouble. If little Indian Mary likes to eat a chicken leg with her fingers, she oughta be able to do it without some high-and-mighty scolding from you!"

"I'm perfectly aware that sometimes I also eat chicken with my fingers up here on the frontier, Miss Lorah," Natalie would argue, "but at least I know *not* to do it before society people who think it gauche."

Lorah didn't understand the meaning of all Missy's fancy words, but she knew exactly what Missy was saying, and while the way Mary ate chicken was nobody's business, to Lorah eating a chicken leg with her fingers had come to stand for the bad things that must surely be ahead for little Mary if she went to live in Savannah as the wife of what Natalie called the "heir to the Browning fortune." Missy had been spoiled as a girl. Anyone could see that, but Lorah had to love her because anyone could also see that none of that high-and-mighty folderol meant much to her now.

"It does mean plenty yet to Miss Lib, though," Missy would insist. "She loves Uncle W.H. enough to work like a dog up here and do without, but a zebra doesn't change its stripes. Miss Lib may be the kindest, smartest lady ever—but she's a lot like my mother, Miss Lorah. That's why I have to protect Mary and Jonathan. I'm not quite so sure my father couldn't change stripes, but my mother can't and neither can Miss Lib. I'm terribly close to my brother now, because I see plainly that he and I are the only ones in our family who are aware that nothing, *nothing* matters but being in the arms of your loved one!"

Grabbing her wash stick, Lorah began to stir the iron pot full of boiling sheets and to sing snatches of "On Jordan's Stormy Bank I Stand."

Still singing—if that's what you could call it—because she hoped to cheer Mary up from her visit to Ben's grave, she gave the girl a big wave as soon as she saw her heading out to the wash pot.

When the wind caught Lorah's cracked tune and took it to the back of the lot where Mary could hear, the girl joined in as she ran toward her.

"I feel full of hope today, Miss Lorah," she called. "At Ben's grave, I felt sure that today, when Mister Burke and Sam come back from Cassville, they bring me a letter from Jonathan! A letter with—glorious news." She laughed, shaking her head in wonder. "I don't know the news—but it will be good." Taking the wash stick from Lorah, she began to lift out the wet, steaming clothes, to drop them into another pot of clean rinse water. "You have one of your feelings too, Miss Lorah?"

"One of my feelings about whether or not you'll get a letter?"

Mary nodded eagerly.

"No, I'm afraid not, honey, because I happen to know the menfolks won't be riding to Cassville today. Burke's determined to finish up painting the downstairs of Miss Lib's house before dark. Told me so himself."

"Oh," was all Mary said, and Lorah thought she looked as though every bit of that scalding wash water'd been poured over her head. Then with a brave little smile, Mary whispered, "Tomorrow, then. It's good to finish Miss Lib's painting today. But they go tomorrow and then I'll know."

"It's just that Burke wants so bad to finish his own cottage for Missy's sake." Lorah chuckled. "For his own sake, mostly. I haven't heard Missy say a word about wanting to leave their cabin. As long as Burke comes home to her every evening and as long as she can walk over to where he's working and clap eyes on him, that girl's satisfied."

They worked together in silence for a while, transferring the hot laundry into the rinse tub, and then Mary asked, "Do you think I—talk better?"

Giving her a big smile, Lorah Plemmons said in her offhand manner, "Plenty good enough for me. We understand each other, don't we? Isn't that why folks talk at all? To be understood?"

Sometimes when Mary really smiled, Lorah thought she was almost as beautiful as Missy. She knew, of course, about the accident that had robbed Mary of part of her sight in one eye, but except for the scar on her cheek, nothing showed. She didn't seem to squint that eye at all.

"You understand my love for Jonathan?" Mary asked.

"Child, I reckon I understand it as much as the next one. Reach me that wash paddle so's I can stir these things around in the clear water."

"Natalie understands my love for him. She tell—*told* me so. She is on our side."

"Honey, do you think there ought to be sides in love? Did I see you crying so hard right after Mrs. Stiles and the boys left for Savannah because you feel she's *not* on your side?"

Mary nodded. "I don't need to talk good to you. You know already about everything."

"I wish I did, but I did see you cry and I've known all along how partial you are to Mrs. Stiles. She likes you a lot too."

"Until I am Jonathan's wife?"

Lorah grinned. "Maybe. We'll see. Waiting is never easy, Mary, but for some reason known only to the good Lord, it's something we all have to do." They worked a while again in silence, then with a dash and one quick grab, Lorah caught one of Natalie's hens and wrung its neck.

"There," she said, as the dead, but still active, chicken flopped and ran about the yard, then fell over by Burke's extra sawhorses against the fence. "I thought I'd better get that pincie while Missy was over at the job with Burke. She knows we keep pincies and tweedies to eat, but she don't like me for an hour or so after I wring one's neck."

Running toward where the chicken lay, Mary called, "In a minute, I scald it and pick it, Miss Lorah, so you can cook it for dinner."

"Thought I might make some of my dumplings too. That's why I caught that nice fat hen." She laughed just enough to make her little round belly shake. "Too bad it had to be one of Missy's favorites."

Standing together at the rinse kettle again, Mary asked in a puzzled voice, "Did you say 'pincies' and 'tweedies,' Miss Lorah? I never hear those words before!"

"Is that the truth? I'd have thought your mother called hens pincies and roosters tweedies, Mary. I learned both words from my Cherokee friend when I was just a girl. Learned to call a rattlesnake Uncle John from him too."

Mary laughed. "Uncle John?"

"Uncle John. Squirrels are shinnies and little baby calves are tees. Now, I don't see no reason why me and you won't always understand each other, do you?"

On impulse, they embraced. Patting Mary firmly on the back, Lorah chortled, "I reckon nobody anywhere talks better than us!"

Mary smiled at her. "We understand, you and me."

"That's right, child, and we always will."

"You will visit me when I am Mrs. Jonathan Browning in Savannah?"

"Oh, Lord, Mary, I can't promise a thing like that!"

"But we understand each other."

"I know we do, it's just never crossed my mind that I might ever get to Savannah, Georgia!"

"But I did. I visited there. I will never forget the big, fine houses and churches. Everyone must love Jesus Christ very much in Savannah, because the churches are so big for large crowds of people to sit in and pray!"

Lorah grinned. "I guess that's one way of looking at it, Mary."

"You could then meet my friend Mr. William Mackay."

"Mrs. Stiles's brother?"

"Yes, ma'am, but the best thing is that he is—Mister William." She motioned for Lorah to come closer and whispered, "You and Mister William and me, we understand each other."

"Is that a fact?"

"You like his mother, Miss Eliza Mackay, don't you?"

"Felt like I'd known the lady all my life."

Mary smiled again. "Then, you understand Mr. William Mackay." After a sigh, she said, looking off toward the hills behind the cabin, "I'd give almost anything if he would again pay a visit here . . ."

When Sam rode back from Cassville in late afternoon the next day with the mail, both Natalie and Mary leaped up from the new white bench Burke had built at the edge of the cliffs for river watching.

"We thought you'd never get here, Sam," Natalie shouted, running ahead to where he'd reined the horse in the sandy road. "Burke's expecting a bank draft from Savannah. Some money my father loaned Uncle W.H. to pay what he owes Burke. What took you so long? You know Burke needs to buy paint and stuff before you can finish the Stiles house! Give me the mail."

Mary hung back a step behind her, willing, as always, to let Natalie lead. "There is a letter for me?" she asked.

Flipping through the small bundle of letters, Natalie said, "Yes, Mary! And it's just the one you want too. Here. It's from my brother in New Haven. And oh, my—I don't see Burke's bank draft, but look—here's a letter from good old William!"

Mary's eyes shone. "Mr. William Mackay?"

"We don't know any other good old William, do we? It's addressed to Burke and me. I'll open it right now!"

Noticing with some annoyance that Sam was still sitting on Burke's horse, staring at Mary with his dying-calf look, Natalie broke the seal and scanned the first page of William's large, careful script. "Good news, Mary!" she shouted, even though Mary was standing right beside her. "William's coming up here to take care of Etowah Cliffs until Miss Lib and Uncle W.H. get back from Washington sometime in June! And Jack Mackay's coming too, for a visit. Oh, Burke will be so happy! Me too, because everything's always better with good old William around. And Jack always makes me laugh."

"This is strange," Mary said wonderingly.

"What?"

"Only yesterday, I say to Miss Lorah I wish Mr. William Mackay would be here!"

"Well, he's coming—toward the end of next week. We're to be on the lookout for them both about March sixth or seventh. William knows Mr. Milner at Sallie's ford. He'll get someone to bring him and Jack here."

Natalie whirled on Sam and ordered him to stop staring at Mary and take Burke's horse to the stable. After Sam had walked the horse down the road toward where the Stileses' newly built stables stood, gleaming whitewashed and clean, some distance along the river road, Natalie told Mary to run off by herself to read Jonathan's letter alone. "I know you want to and you certainly don't have to be polite with me. You only have to worry about courtesy and good manners when we're having one of our Savannah society lessons."

In response, Mary beamed her delight, and gave Natalie one of the few hugs she'd ever dared give her.

"Anyway," Natalie went on, "I'm going to Miss Lib's new house to tell Burke the news about William and Jack. He'll be so glad he won't know anything else to do but give me a big hug and"—she rolled her eyes as though about to swoon—"and then a long, long kiss!"

Holding Jonathan's letter against her heart, Mary ran all the way to her cabin, and because she took her favorite shortcut and leaped every low bush and drainage ditch, she was gasping for breath from the effort and from her pounding excitement when at last she reached the cabin and slammed shut the door.

"Jonathan," she whispered his name as she broke the simple J.B. seal. "Oh, my Jonathan, you are good!" Her fingers trembled as she unfolded the unusually short note—only one page! A bolt of fear shot through her. Not once had she doubted Jonathan's love, but always, at the back of her mind, "tickling my brain" as Sinai said, was the downright fear that someone might convince him of her unfitness to be his wife. Day after day into week after week, Jonathan lived now at school with Miss Lib's "wellborn whites" and Mary was not white.

" 'My beloved Mary,' " she read aloud, bending over to hold the page flat on the kitchen table because her hands shook too much to read if she stood in the middle of the room holding it. " 'My beloved Mary,' " she read that again, because her need to be his beloved was deeper than the river at any place. " 'My beloved Mary, you may want to smack me for such a short letter, but there is a big surprise up ahead for you and I am trusting you to understand this peculiar letter.' " She spelled out that word: p-e-c-u-l-i-a-r. Jonathan was never peculiar! Not to her. " 'I know my sister, Natalie, is the un-pre-dict-able one in our family, and I do not mean to puzzle you, but my lover's heart cannot resist a surprise! Not many girls could be trusted to allow me to take such a step without further explanation, but I know I can trust you until the last breath of my old age. Now, do you want to smack me? I'll wager you do, since that is all I am going to write today until further ar-range-ments can be made.' " She felt almost happy and too excited to finish the letter, but a little fear was still there. Mostly she felt confused.

"I do trust you, Jonathan, but—I no understand!"

It was all right for her to say "I no understand," because she was alone and no one could hear her mistake in English. Her eyes raced back over the single page to where he'd written that his lover's heart could not resist a *surprise!*

There was a little more, but unable to stand still a second longer even to finish the letter, she began to twirl about the cabin, arms flung wide, kissing and kissing the page because she did love surprises and because Jonathan's dear, square, strong, clean-nailed hands had touched it.

A wild little animal shout of joy escaped her, and then she made herself stop dancing long enough to read the end of the short letter: " 'I will let you hear from me again soon, adorable Mary, so you must go on about your days there by the river and try to be patient with me. This much I will tell you—I will be as quick as possible because my surprise is the best that anything could ever be. Look around you, sweet girl, because spring will be coming this year for us both.' "

As had always been true when her heart seemed about to burst with happiness, Mary's muscles ached to run—to run and leap—outside in the cold, clear, windy March day.

"I trust you," she shouted into the empty cabin, and shouted it again on the tiny porch before she jumped down all three wooden steps and, eyes closed, because the yard was so familiar, ran headlong into Sam's arms.

"Mary! Oh, Mary . . ."

Sam's voice was hoarse and he breathed fast as he held her against his rough woolen work coat. Her own breath stopped. As in a nightmare, she tried to scream. No sound came.

"Don't be scairt, little Mary," he said, struggling to hold on to her. "You know—Sam won't—hurt you. Hey . . . don't fight me! You don't need to fight me, Mary. I—love the—dirt under yore purty feet. Mary, I do!"

Her scream came now, long and full of terror. So piercing that it was not like her own voice at all. She was screaming Burke's name—screaming it again and again, and beating at Sam's chest with her fists until they hurt. When he only tightened his hold on her, she gave the longest, most piercing cry, and as she felt herself begin to faint, she remembered the catamount's scream that had frightened Natalie's horse so long ago in the woods behind Mister Burke's old, burned-down cabin.

Natalie was admiring Burke's mantel in the master bedroom of Miss Lib's new house when they heard Mary's cries. Without a word, Burke helped her down the graceful stairway as fast as Natalie could manage, through the front door, and, still running, they hurried along the river road in the direction of the screams.

Unable to keep up with his long strides, Natalie called, "I know it was Mary, Burke—hurry! Go on ahead. Something terrible's happened to Mary."

"You be careful," he shouted over his shoulder. "Don't fall, but keep coming—I might need you. Where's Miss Lorah?"

"I don't know," she gasped, lagging farther behind in her effort not to trip with their new baby just beginning to show. "She might be out in back of our new cottage, chopping wood scraps."

After a few seconds, Natalie stood still and listened. Plainly, she'd heard a man's short cry of pain, then another . . . then silence, except for the wind moaning in the tall river trees and squawks from Miss Lorah's chickens. The chickens scattered. Then she heard Miss Lorah's angry shout from behind her cabin, followed by the whistle and slash of a long, hard whipping. Natalie had heard that sound only once before, when her beloved Kottie—poor, dead Kottie—had whipped one of the Knightsford Negroes.

Hurrying toward the old cabin where Mary, Sam and Miss Lorah lived, she saw Burke bending over Mary on the tiny porch where he'd laid her limp body.

Before she reached him, Natalie ordered water from the well and knelt beside Mary to wait for Burke to bring it. Mary's lips were parted, her eyes closed, her face drained of color. No matter how hard Natalie tried to rouse her, she lay motionless on the porch floor.

At last Burke ran up slopping a bucket of icy-cold water. Not bothering to hunt for a cloth, Natalie bathed and bathed Mary's white face—splashing with her own hands. The surge of relief she felt when Mary's eyelids began to flutter made her feel almost dizzy.

"She's coming around," Burke whispered. "You did fine, honey. Mary's going to be all right. But did I hear what I thought I heard a minute ago? Did you hear a man shout—and then what sounded like a whipping?"

"Yes," she said. "I heard it. The color's back in her face now," she murmured. "We can ask Mary in a minute. Burke, she was so pale, I thought—I thought for a minute she was—dead!"

She felt Burke studying her. "You really care about Mary now, don't you?" he asked.

"I have changed, Mr. Latimer. Whether you and Miss Lib believe it or not is unimportant."

"I believe it, darling. And I love you for caring about Mary."

She dipped her hand in the bucket again and held it against Mary's forehead. "I want Mary and Jonathan to be just like us." Abruptly she looked up at Burke. "Listen! Is that someone coming through the woods out back?"

Burke hurried to the far end of the porch. "It's Miss Lorah! I thought you said she was behind our cottage chopping wood."

"I can't keep up with everyone every minute, can I?" With him at the other end of the porch now, Natalie called, "She looks so angry! I never, never saw Miss Lorah's face all—dark and twisted like that! Miss Lorah? Miss Lorah!" she cried. "What's the matter?"

"I just hoop-poled Sam like a hound," Miss Lorah said, her voice trembling, as she pounded up to the porch. "Took the wind out of me, but I did it. He deserved it too. How is the poor little thing? Sam didn't hurt Mary, did he?"

"That was—*you* whipping Sam, Miss Lorah?" Burke asked.

"It was. Sam laid hands on her. I was chopping wood behind your new place and heard her scream. Ran here to the front yard and saw it with my own eyes! I figured Sam needed my attention worse than Mary, though. She is coming to, isn't she? She was just—awful scared." Miss Lorah bent over to lift Mary's head and shoulders in one strong arm. Slapping Mary's face, she asked softly, "Hello, child, it's—Miss Lorah. You coming out of it all right?"

"Yes, ma'am," Mary said weakly, looking from one to the other.

"Sam won't bother you no more. I saw to that. He's not a bad boy. Told me after his lickin' how it piled up inside him sleeping in the same cabin with you." Lorah got to her feet. "I reckon we'll have to make some new sleeping space, Mr. Latimer."

Burke sighed so heavily that Natalie turned from Mary to look at him. He didn't exactly seem angry with Sam, but she thought he looked suddenly—exhausted, and for a big, strong man—almost helpless.

"It's taking too long, far too long," he said, "to finish the Stiles place—and ours. I guess Sam will have to sleep in the Stileses' kitchen until I can think of something else. Will he do that?"

"He will if I tell him to," Miss Lorah said. "He's not a bad boy. He's not too smart, but Mary being as pretty as she is and all, he—well, he lost his

head, what there is of it. You're going to be all right now, Mary," she said.
"You know that, don't you?"

"Yes, Miss Lorah, if you say so, I know it," Mary said with a wan, trusting smile.

"Solomon sleeps in Miss Lib's kitchen now," Natalie said. "Would Sam mind sharing the same room with a strange nigra?"

"What's wrong with you, Missy?" Lorah asked in an offhand manner. "Sam and Solomon's not strangers!"

"All I know," Burke said, "is that Mary can't stay with you and Sam, Miss Lorah. Not even tonight. I won't allow it."

"You won't have to," Natalie said. "Your wife's grown up whether you believe it or not. Sam can make a pallet in Miss Lib's kitchen for tonight," she explained, in full charge, "then tomorrow, Mary and I will fix a place for her to sleep *in our cabin.*"

She paused long enough for her words to take effect. Only she and Burke knew how adamantly she'd always opposed Mary's living under their roof. He said nothing, but he stared at her in complete amazement.

"Don't look so stunned, Burke," she went on. "You see, I've just decided that—cabin or new cottage—Mary is going to live right with us until she and Jonathan can get married!"

Chapter 42

WILLIAM and Jack had been up in Cass County for well over three weeks, but only one short letter had come for their mother and sisters back in Savannah.

"There's no point bringing it up every day, Mama," Kate said at breakfast on a sunny early April morning. "We know they got there and William went to run the plantation. He isn't used to hard work like that anymore. He's bound to be too tired at night to write long letters to us."

"More to the point," Sarah said, "William would hate paying postage too often with rates what they are now. I never noticed it in Papa, but William certainly inherited the Mackay Scottish blood when it comes to parting with his money."

"I want you to go to the post office anyway as soon as you're finished with breakfast, Kate. I'm anxious about Jack. There could be a letter from Eliza Anne in Washington City too. Are you through eating?"

"Yes, Mama."

"Then, scoot. I need Sarah to help me hem my new bedroom curtains."

"If there is a letter from Sister," Sarah said, "it had better be addressed to me this time. Her last one was addressed to Kate."

"Sometimes you sound ten years old, Sarah," her mother chided. "I'm going to call you Sallie again if you're not careful. We all know Eliza Anne addresses letters to different ones, but she means them for us all equally. Don't just sit there, Kate. Your bonnet's on the hall tree. I tacked the bow back on yesterday."

"Kate's been gone an hour and a half," Sarah grumbled, tossing aside the summer lace curtain panel she'd been hemming in her mother's room upstairs. "She must have met someone. I hope when she finally gets here, she has some good juicy gossip."

"I hate even the sound of that word," her mother said.

Taking a small rocker by the window to watch for her sister, Sarah began to rock impatiently.

"Do you have to rock so fast? You can't hurry Kate, you know. Oh, dear, am I getting crotchety in my old age?"

Before Sarah could answer, they heard the front door bang and Kate's "Who-o-o" from the hall below. By her rapid footsteps, they knew she did have news of some kind.

"We're upstairs in Mama's room," Sarah called.

A small bundle of mail in her hand and still wearing her cloak and bonnet, Kate rushed into the room. "I'd have been back sooner," she gasped, out of breath, "but I ran into—guess who?"

"Just tell us, Kate," Eliza Mackay said.

"Julia Barnsley!"

"Was she alone?" Sarah asked, all ears.

"She was, and oh, Mama, Julia doesn't look well at all!"

"Young Julia isn't well," Eliza said. "Nor is my old friend her mother, Julia. Is Julia Senior in town too? How is she? The last time she was here in her old home with Charlotte, I sensed that her poor mind was wandering some. Did you ask young Julia about her mother?"

"Of course, Mama. Julia Senior didn't come down this time. She stayed at Woodlands to care for the Barnsley children. Only Julia and Godfrey came, and listen to this—Julia vowed, and you both know she does not exaggerate —that in future when her husband has to come to Savannah on business, *she's* never again going to stay with Charlotte in the old Scarbrough mansion with him!"

Sarah saw her mother's mouth drop open in amazement. "Don't worry, Mama, those two aren't having any trouble. Mr. Barnsley has to be away a lot, but the last time I saw Julia, she told me that while his absences were more and more painful to her, they seemed only to strengthen the strong bond between them."

"You're right, sister," Kate put in. "Julia told me the very same thing just now."

"Then why isn't she coming back to Savannah with Godfrey?"

"I didn't say Julia won't come back to Savannah with him, Mama. I said she will never again stay in the old Scarbrough house—because her sister, Charlotte, is just too unpleasant! I know I'm not as brilliant as Charlotte Taylor, but I certainly hope I'm more grateful. Do you know that sweet Mr. Barnsley has spent hundreds of dollars on repairs on that house—even now that Charlotte has managed through the courts to grab sole ownership? She shows no gratitude whatever, just goes on being cruel to Mr. Barnsley *and* to her own mother! He even pays most of their mother's expenses. Godfrey Barnsley is a good, dear, Christian gentleman and Charlotte Taylor ought to be—"

"That's enough, Kate," their mother said. "You said young Julia didn't look at all well. Is it still that bad cough?"

"Oh, she coughed so much while we were talking," Kate said, "I felt sorry for her. And she was so sure moving to the upcountry would cure her lungs. Julia says she does feel better as long as she's up there, but knows she needs a Savannah doctor, so comes back here, then gets worse every time. I think it's more than our damp climate, though. If you want to know, I think it's her mean sister, Charlotte, treating not only Julia Senior but also both Barnsleys like dirt!"

A sorrowful look came into their mother's eyes, and Sarah knew Mama was about to launch again into her memories of the elegant old days when the young Julia Scarbrough Senior and her handsome, wealthy husband, William, were the social lights of the city.

But all their mother said was: "To see my dear old friend Julia now, one would never think she'd once been the most sought-after hostess in Savannah. And oh, the sorrow she's had to bear. The loss of those little ones years ago, then her adored husband." She shook her head. "It's little wonder Julia is—is confused."

"Well, if you ask me, Julia Senior could outlive her pretty daughter Julia," Kate said.

"Don't even think of such a thing," their mother scolded. "If anything happened to young Julia, I don't know what her poor mother would do! Eliza Anne's heart would be broken too. She hated leaving the upcountry for many reasons, but Julia was certainly one of them. At least, up there, they could visit each other once a month or so. Kate, it's warm here by the fire. Don't you feel a little foolish still sitting there in your cloak and bonnet?"

"Oh, Mama, I forgot. For goodness' sakes, I brought mail too!" She flipped past one or two less important pieces and handed Mama a thick letter from Eliza Anne in Washington City.

"Nothing from William?" their mother asked.

"I'd have given it to you first if there had been. Eliza Anne's letter is addressed to me this time, but you read it aloud to us, Mama. A lot must be happening to Sister up there, the letter's so fat!"

"My spectacles need cleaning. You read it, Kate. But do take off your cloak and bonnet first."

Removing both and tossing them beside her on her mother's bed, Kate began to read: " 'Washington City, 20 March 1844, Monday. William Henry has been begging me, my dear Kate, for several days past to give you an account of the visit Mrs. Tyler paid me.' Oh, my heavens," Kate interrupted herself, "she can't mean the President's wife!"

"Of course not, silly," Sarah said. "Mrs. Tyler's dead! She must mean the President's daughter-in-law, Mrs. Robert Tyler, who's been acting as his hostess at the White House."

"Go on, dear," Eliza Mackay urged.

"All right, Mama. 'It was a most awkward visit, though certainly amusing, and I fear I shall not do it justice on paper. I had just come home to Mrs. Hewitt's boardinghouse, and was sitting in Mrs. Colquitt's room with my pelisse and bonnet on, when a servant came to tell me that a lady in the parlor downstairs wished to see me. So, down I went, and introduced myself to a very sweet-looking little person—not pretty, but with exceedingly pleasant and unpretentious manners—who seemed not to feel it necessary to tell me who she was. Of course, I had not the remotest idea, but she shook my hand warmly, said she was very glad to see me at last, seemed to know all about us, spoke appreciatively of W.H. and how sorry she was that I had not joined him in Washington City sooner. (Remember now, I still had no idea of her identity!) While she was talking, in rushed my son Henry, rudely shouting, "Mother! Mother, come to the door right now and see the President's carriage with four splendid horses! *Now*, Mother—come now!" Well, I tried to pass over his rudeness by whispering to him to leave the room, that I could not go running outside in the midst of a visit. He had no sooner headed toward the parlor door than in came our landlady, Mrs. Hewitt herself, redolent of the kitchen in every way—wearing a soiled cap and an old shawl dragged round her shoulders—looking like destruction itself! I then decided that the charming lady with whom I'd been visiting must be some acquaintance of Mrs. Hewitt's and fell to wondering who occupied the splendid carriage and four horses about which my ill-mannered son had been shouting —fully expecting those in the carriage to be momentarily ushered into the parlor, all the while feeling embarrassed by both my noisy son and the appearance of my landlady. As I was being overcome with humiliation, in dashes Henry again, more determined than before, really imploring me this time—if only for one minute—to come see the splendid horses before they were gone from in front of the boardinghouse! Then, like a bolt of lightning, it struck me that my visitor just *might* be Mrs. Robert Tyler herself! Without shame, because I had no other ideas at hand, I asked her point-blank. Oh, then the beautifully dressed little lady began to apologize to me profusely for not revealing her identity sooner. But you see, she had sent her name by Mrs. Hewitt's stupid servant and naturally assumed he'd told me. It was truly uncomfortable—a thorough mix-up—though actually not unpleasant, and I tried to make amends, but Mrs. Hewitt had other plans. The world, according to Mrs. Hewitt, revolves around Mrs. Hewitt, who then asked my guest if she had come to see *her* on business—if so, Mrs. Hewitt would gladly take her into her private parlor. Poor Mrs. Tyler, completely dumbfounded, politely said no, she did not wish to see Mrs. Hewitt on any form of business. Now, anyone would suppose that our landlady would have had the sense to vanish, but not Mrs. Hewitt! At that clumsy moment (the Haralsons just having moved in), down the stairs came Mrs. Haralson, really dressed like a Georgia cracker. Poor Mrs. Tyler attempted to converse with her reasonably, but vainly, at which point Mrs. Tyler gave up, tried to tell me how deeply she regretted that I'd reached Washington so near the time of her own departure from the city, but insisted that she hoped I would visit her at the White House before she left. Sensing, I'm sure, that there was nothing else plausible to be done, she rose to depart.' "

All through Kate's reading of the awkward "comedy of errors," as Eliza Mackay called it, they had alternated between gasps and laughter.

"Oh, Kate, stop reading while I catch my breath," Sarah laughed. "Poor Sister—what an embarrassing predicament! Is there more to the story?"

"Merciful heavens, I hope not," Eliza Mackay said, wiping her eyes. "No wonder W.H. pestered Eliza Anne to write it up for us!"

"There is more. Listen to this." Kate read on: " 'Mrs. Tyler moved toward the front door, followed by me and seven other women boarders, led by Mrs. Haralson and Mrs. Hewitt in her dirty cap! There, at last, we all viewed the beautiful carriage drawn by the four splendid horses. Two elegantly dressed ladies were seated inside, obviously waiting for Mrs. Tyler to finish her visit with me *and,* as it turned out, with every other lady in the boardinghouse. Mrs. Tyler was dressed well, but quite plainly indeed, and much muffled up. She and her husband, the President's son, are leaving town due to her frail health, but, my dear Kate, you and Mama and Sarah would have been delighted with her gentle and unaffected manners. I will say that Mrs. Haralson's good humor rather rescued me when, after Mrs. Tyler's departure, she asked if I was not ashamed of my cracker friends before such grand company.' ^

"Well, what on earth did Eliza say to that?" their mother wanted to know.

"For pity's sakes, Mama, I can't believe what Sister said! Listen to this: 'Ashamed? I asked in response. Yes, I was ashamed of my cracker friends and cracker son and dirty landlady, *and* of the stupid servant who had called every lady in the boardinghouse! Believe me, all of you, I have entertained guest after guest since with this ridiculous story. Old General Saunders was here to see W.H. and he is a great laugher. You can be sure we had hilarious peal after peal and I can only hope that Mrs. Hewitt, the snooper, was not listening!' "

"Well, we all needed that laugh," their mother said, wiping her eyes again. "Trust your sister to carry off such an awkward affair with what your father would have called 'class.' "

"I'm certainly glad it was Sister and not I who had to carry it off," Sarah said. "Is that the end of her letter, Kate?"

"No. She's quite worried, she writes here, about Julia Barnsley's health. I must write first thing after dinner and tell Eliza Anne that Julia's at least well enough to have come to Savannah this week in spite of how miserable Charlotte makes her. She writes too about how relieved she is that the Barnsley girl, Anna, is with Mary Cowper at the Montpelier school near Macon. She also says Mary Cowper writes to her parents fairly regularly."

"Such an obedient, gentle girl she is," Eliza Mackay said.

"Her mother and father both make it far easier, I'd think, to obey than to disobey," Sarah said, adding that while they were both charming people, Eliza Anne and W.H. were more than strict with the girl. "I don't know where Sister gets her firm discipline. You're the best mother in the world, Mama, but you were never really hard on any of us. And certainly Papa wasn't."

"We're all different, Kate. Eliza Anne is Eliza Anne and she and W.H. alone are responsible for the way they rear their children. Just remember *we* aren't. Have you finished the letter, dear?"

"Just this on the last page: 'For the life of me, I can't understand why Robert Lee has not paid me a visit! I know he's in Washington working daily at the War Department, and I confess I am nonplussed that so far he has ignored me. W.H. seems a bit let down too. At times, I am not altogether sure that my brilliant, gloating husband did not—at least in small part—insist that I come so that he could flaunt me as his adoring wife before my old friend Captain Lee!' "

Genuinely startled, their mother gasped, "Now, why on earth would your sister write such a thing?"

Kate gave her a big smile. "Mama, shame on you! You, of all people, know Sister's sense of humor better than to be shocked by one of her flippant remarks."

"Oh, I suppose I do. You're right. It's just that I'm a little old-fashioned about marriage vows. To me, they're not to be toyed with."

"Sister isn't toying!"

"She accused her husband of it in plain English! Eliza Anne knows perfectly well that W.H. begged her to come to be with him in Washington City because he needs her. Not only as his bosom companion, but she will be an enormous help to him socially and, I daresay, a boon to his political career."

Smiling at their mother, Kate said gently, "Yes, Mama, I daresay too. Promise, though, you won't write anything about 'toying' to Sister. She's having to make a big enough adjustment moving from the quiet and beauty of Etowah Cliffs to a noisy, dirty, muddy city like Washington. I'm sure she longs to see Captain Lee for old times' sake. Sister must need her own close, personal friends in Washington City."

"But you watch," Sarah said, "Eliza Anne will do just fine in the nation's capital. Even if, as she insists, her dresses aren't the very latest style. It does seem to me that W.H. would beg, borrow or steal enough extra money to clothe her in the latest fashions, though, since he was so eager to have her come. You know how vain he is. He'll be taking her everywhere to show her off. Even if Robert Lee chose to marry plain Mary Custis over our sister, Eliza Anne's just got to be the loveliest lady in town."

"Watch your mouth, Sarah," their mother scolded. "No one but Robert Lee knows for certain why he married Mary Custis. I'd think it had to do with close family ties. They were cousins, and heaven knows, Mary adored him from girlhood."

"And don't forget, Sarah," Kate reminded her, "Robert had to bear some of the stigma of being old Light-Horse Harry Lee's son! Remember how snobbish Virginians are too. They always have been. They always will be!"

"We know only one thing for certain," their mother said firmly, "and that is that Robert Lee will visit Eliza Anne the minute he finds out she's in Washington City. They've been friends too long. And no more talk about my being straitlaced and old-fashioned. No more nonsense about my writing the wrong thing to your sister, either."

"Is that the end of the letter, Kate?"

"No, of course not. But since this part has to do with Robert Lee too, I thought perhaps it might upset Mama."

"That's ridiculous and you know it," their mother said. "I love that young man with all my heart! I simply don't want any family meddling and no family speculation. What else did she write about Lee?"

"Only that she's met a Mrs. Thompson, who owns a small cottage at Fort Hamilton, where Jack visited Lee last fall. She wants Eliza Anne to visit her there."

"Ah-ha!" Sarah said.

"Ah-ha what?"

"Never mind, Mama. What else, sister?"

"Oh, Eliza Anne wants me to wash up her good straw bonnet and cut out a coat for Bobby and send all by Mr. Hodgson, who's going as a delegate from our Historical Society to the meeting of the National Institute in Washington City the first Monday in April. She needs a little arrowroot too, since what she can buy there is half flour."

"Does she complain that the dampness bothers her?" their mother wanted to know.

"Just that it rained every day for a week and she had to keep to her rooms and miss church one Sunday. This is the last line, I think: 'If I don't stop writing, W.H. will be furious and you will get nothing done today but read! Your affectionate sister,' and so on. No, wait—here's a postscript. 'The boys are well and send love, as does W.H. And if your kindness stretches far enough, dear Kate, you might put new trim on my bonnet—around the crown only, for the latest Washington fashion.' "

Chapter 43

IN EARLY June, right after the late-spring Moon of Violets and before the first Little Ripening Moon, Mary and Natalie and Burke worked with Miss Lorah and Sam at moving the Stileses' furnishings into the large newly completed part of the Etowah Cliffs house. Always, Mary found only joy in helping Miss Lib, even though she was far away in Washington City.

Living in the Latimer cabin as Mary had done since Sam's assault only strengthened her determination that, if she could help it, there would be no second dead baby for Mister Burke and Natalie to mourn. Natalie, Mary now knew, was her friend—was, as Natalie often said, on the side of Mary and Jonathan forever! There had been other letters from New Haven and in each one Jonathan had made at least one mention of the "surprise" in store for her, but nothing was clear except that whatever Jonathan said or did had to be good and right. As the weeks passed, Mary had begun to laugh at Natalie's fuming about her brother's "keeping them all in suspense." No one hated to write letters more than Natalie, but she had even written to Jonathan herself demanding to know exactly what he planned. In reply, Natalie had received one letter—long and affectionate, filled with how deeply he loved Mary, but still keeping his "surprise" a secret.

They had carried into the large, handsome new wing of the Stiles house only those pieces of furniture which Natalie and Miss Lib's brothers, Captain Jack and Mr. William Mackay, felt their sister would consider nice enough. It had been good to have the Mackay brothers—Captain Jack ill, but always joking and full of laughter, Mister William quiet, hardworking, steady and kind. A week ago, though, Captain Jack's cough grew worse, and although Mister William would be back, he had decided quickly to take his ill brother home to Savannah, where Miss Eliza Mackay and the two spinster sisters could care for him.

On this mid-June morning, bright, early green spreading the trees with the promise of summer, Mary was busy spreading freshly washed linens on Mister William's bed in the master bedroom of the new section of Etowah Cliffs. Her heart sang. This was happy work because Miss Lorah had ironed every wrinkle away from the sheets and bolster cases and also because Mister William was dear to Mary. He would be back soon and having the gentle, pleasant man around caused Ben to seem close again.

Now, before smoothing the woven counterpane over the perfectly made bed, she stopped to listen—almost sure she'd caught the rattle and clank of a wagon coming along the river road below. Maybe, she thought, delighted, Mister William is coming early! At the open window, she found her view of the road hidden by Mister Burke's handsome second-floor porch, so she ran out onto it—and froze. A familiar voice was calling her name!

"*Mary,* where are you? I'm here, Mary—I'm here!"

Jonathan! Her heart cried his name, her voice could not. With all her might, she tried to run back into the house. Her legs were as unmoving and solid as Mister Burke's diamond-design balustrade and white posts. Jonathan's "surprise" was Jonathan himself—standing up now in Mr. Milner's wagon—standing and calling to her and waving his arm high over his dear, beautiful head!

Even in her condition, weighted with the unborn child, Natalie reached her brother first.

"Jonathan, you scamp," she cried when he leaped from the wagon seat to embrace her. "Anyone might expect me to pull a trick like this—but not you! Oh, I'm so glad to see you. Mary and I are close, close friends now. She's living right in our cabin with Burke and me because we're afraid for her to be alone with stupid Sam and—" Catching sight of Mary still rooted at the second-floor railing, Natalie shouted, "Get down here, Mary! Your future husband just arrived."

"The new wing of Miss Lib's house is—is really splendid," Jonathan exclaimed as Burke ran up to join them, beaming, shaking his brother-in-law's hand. "Congratulations! You did a magnificent job, Burke."

"So did you," Burke said, laughing, "pulling off a surprise like this on everybody! Where in the world is Mary, Natalie?"

"She's right up there," Jonathan answered for her, his face beaming. "I think she's too surprised to make her legs move. Stay where you are, Mary," he called, "I'm coming up!" Halfway to the entrance of the big new house, he turned back to Natalie and Burke. "I guess I should tell you. I dropped out of Yale. I've come to get Mary and take her back to Savannah to live as my wife!"

"Jonathan! Does Mama know? Does Papa?" Natalie gasped.

"No," he called from the veranda door. "No one has any inkling except Uncle W.H. I told him last year that I was thinking about quitting college at the end of two years."

"Hurray for you, brother," Natalie cried. "Hurray for you and Mary!"

Upstairs in the doorway off the new porch, Jonathan took Mary in his arms and hugged her and hugged her, both of them laughing and crying at the same time.

"I told you, dearest," he kept saying. "I told you I had a surprise—I meant it. You and I are getting married! And it can't be soon enough for me. Do you think we could get married up here the way Natalie and Burke did?" When she only kept clinging to him, unable to believe he was really there, he repeated, "Mary? I know you want to marry me. We could even have our wedding in the Cassville church, couldn't we? Or the new church Burke and your brother built near Sallie's ford? Darling, say something! I'm here. We're not dreaming. When do you think we can get married? We'd avoid all that fancy-wedding business at home if we just made plans to do it up here, then both go to Savannah—"

"Oh, Jonathan," she interrupted, her voice full of awe, barely a hoarse whisper. "Yes. Yes, I marry you and up here I would like far better, but—"

"But what?" He held her a little away from him in order to peer straight down into her eyes. "*What*, Mary?"

"I no leave up here before Natalie's baby come!"

He frowned. "When is it due?"

"Maybe next month. I cannot go to Savannah with you before that."

"I see." A quick smile replaced the frown. "That's all right, sweet Mary. I'll just have to compose the best letter of my entire life and explain everything to my parents."

"They—they think you are still in school?"

"No, they know my second year's over, but they do expect me in Savannah before the end of this month. You see, I—I haven't written them anything about—any of this. It's the first time in my life I've kept something from them. They just expect me home from Yale any time now for the summer holiday. I hated not telling them, but—" He took her in his arms again. "I couldn't take the chance because, Mary, *no one* is going to stop me from making you my wife—now."

"You say like Natalie—I mean, you *sound* like Natalie. She believe we must let nothing—no one come between us, Jonathan."

"She's right and I don't intend to. When is William Mackay coming back up here. Do you know?"

"Mister William, he be back long before Natalie's baby come."

"Good. I need to talk to William. I'm counting a lot on him with my parents."

"I—I should be scared about—your parents?"

He gave her another hug and his cheerful laugh. "No, you should not be! They'll come around. It may take a while, but I've always been able to count on Mama and Papa when I really need them. Oh, Mary, Mary, Mary," he breathed. "Can you believe we're never going to be apart again as long as we both live?"

William was back at Etowah Cliffs by the first week in July and relieved to find Natalie feeling well and obviously far better prepared, thanks to Lorah Plemmons, than before the birth of her first baby. More worried about Jack than he admitted to anyone but Burke, William still settled with some peace of mind into his summer work of supervising W.H.'s crops. He liked David Holder and his wife, was partial to Eliza, their little girl born soon after Natalie's first child. He knew the whole story about Sam and understood, not only why Burke still missed Ben so much, but that they had been wise to move Mary into the Latimer cabin safely out of harm's way. Deep down, though, William doubted that Sam would ever bother her again. The young man seemed to revere Miss Lorah and, hard as it was to imagine, the woman had given Sam the whipping of his life the day he tried to hug Mary. Maybe that was all Sam meant to do, hug her. Sam talked so little, it was hard to tell exactly what went on in his head.

One thing sure, William had no doubt but that Eliza Anne and W.H. would be mighty pleased with the new brick wing of their house. The bricks, made right on the place from their own clay, were as fine as any he'd ever seen. And Burke had gotten more out of Sam's clumsy fingers than any other man could have done. Natalie certainly had found herself a hard worker. All summer, he had been able to talk Burke into only one day off, for a picnic in the lovely stand of woods behind the big house which they were now calling the Park. The very next day Burke had lit right in finishing the interior of the good cottage he had been trying so long to build for Natalie. He had confided his disappointment that he and Sam had been too slow with the Stiles place for the baby to be born in the new cottage. Burke had a way, though, of settling things down inside himself, then leaving them alone, which had always made William feel comfortable.

As he'd told Miss Lorah on his first day back, William guessed he didn't have a better friend anywhere than Burke Latimer. Her responsive chuckle had somehow confirmed his high opinion of Burke as a man. Miss Lorah Plemmons would be a hard woman to fool and she'd been there to watch Burke go through the throes of his own grief and Natalie's after they'd lost their firstborn. The mountain woman's heart was as big as all outdoors, William knew, but she was so smart along with it, he wondered sometimes how far Miss Lorah might have gone in the world if she'd been born a man with a chance at an education. She'd certainly done wonders for Natalie.

At night, alone in the new Stiles house except for three house servants downstairs, William prayed for them all—for Eliza Anne and W.H. and the boys in Washington City, always thanking the Lord that he, William, didn't have to try to live there in the chaos of an impending presidential election and all that high society; he prayed for little Mary Cowper in school at Montpelier over by Macon away from everyone who loved her; he prayed, of course, for Jonathan and Mary and for poor Jack, thinner and more sallow than ever. He prayed hard for his mother and his sisters, on whom would fall the brunt of Jack's care if he failed to improve. "Mama's had so much heartache, Lord," he pleaded. "Keep her well and strong enough to get through whatever's up ahead with Jack." He never failed to send his love to Virginia and his own two babies right there in heaven with the Lord to whom he prayed. Often, he still longed for Virginia beside him in those lonely moments before sleep. How much help she'd be right now with Natalie expecting her baby any day. Praying for this baby to live had come to be almost as natural for William as breathing. He'd always been partial to Natalie, who'd tried so hard to save his own infant son, and he certainly hoped with all his heart that Burke knew how much he thought of him.

On the evening of July 5, the day following Savannah's gala celebration of Independence Day, Mark and Caroline retired early. Caroline's month-long lung congestion seemed better, Mark thought. At least, she'd given the appearance of enjoying herself all day yesterday during the long, incendiary patriotic speeches and fireworks on the riverfront. But at her insistence, they no longer slept in the same bed at night. "It only makes me more nervous and I cough more," she told him, "if I think I'm keeping you awake, darling." To please her, he'd agreed to sleep in Natalie's room across the hall. He hated being away from her and, try as he did, there was never a single moment free of worry over her health. Dr. Waring had assured them that she was in no serious danger. "She's in no way as ill as Captain Jack Mackay," the doctor said. "I'd be surprised if Mackay lasts more than a few years, but your wife's a strong lady and she doesn't have tuberculosis. You might have to take her to the mountains or up to Newport one of these days, but I do wish you'd stop stewing, Browning."

Wanting so much to be near Natalie when her baby came, and for Caroline to have upcountry air, Mark had tried his best to convince her to make the trip to the Etowah River, but she refused point-blank, insisting that she had no energy for such a long journey.

"I don't like it up there much anyway, darling," she'd admitted. "I know there's plenty of room for us in the new Stiles house now, but don't insist, Mark. Don't make it hard for me, please. I want to be here in our own house resting—with you."

Jonathan's shocking letter telling them of his plans to get married up there, then to bring Mary straight to Savannah, had reached Mark's office on July 3. He'd read and reread it, marveling that what most troubled him was not his son's decision to drop out of Yale, but the near-panic he felt that nothing would ever be the same again at home in Savannah with Jonathan's wife to protect. It never crossed his mind *not* to try to protect Mary, but how this was to be done, he had no firm idea.

After the third or fourth reading, he had reached only one conclusion—he would keep Jonathan's plans from Caroline as long as possible. Mark did long to be near Natalie now, but equally, he wanted to be up there with his son. To talk the boy out of marrying—of cutting short his education? He thought not. As had been true all his own life as Jonathan's father, Mark needed to be with his son, even though it was Jonathan who had brought about the latest crisis.

The decision to keep Caroline in the dark until she felt stronger filled him with guilt, and tonight, as he leaned over her bed to kiss her for the last time until he could crawl in beside her early in the morning and hold her for a few minutes at least before breakfast, he felt like a drowning man—with no secure hold anywhere. They had managed to share a lifetime of large and small crises over Natalie. The looming consequence of Jonathan's decision seemed beyond comprehension.

He'd kept his pact with himself not to mention a word to Caroline yet, but he'd never needed her so much, ever, he thought as he kissed her good night —kissed her forehead, then her mouth—kissed her too hungrily and too long, he knew, because she began to convulse in her effort to hold back the cough.

"I'm sorry. I'm so sorry," he whispered. "Your husband's a very selfish man."

The cough subsiding, she whispered, "I'm the one who should be sorry, Mark. And I am. Oh, darling, I am. It's been such a long time. You, of all men, don't deserve an—ailing wife! Wouldn't you think Dr. Waring could give me something to help this ghastly hacking? It really makes me furious! You know I worry about Natalie too, but she did write that the baby's birth will be easier for her with only Mary and Miss Lorah there. We make our daughter—anxious, Mark. Can't you accept that she doesn't need us until after the baby's born?"

He nodded that yes, he could accept that, but felt dishonest.

"I need you," Caroline whispered. "I need you beside me, though. I need you—in all ways."

He felt his eyes fill with tears and stood up to be sure none fell on her face. "I'm glad you need me, dearest," he said. "I need you too, but most of all, I need you well again, and sleep will do more than any medicine. So, sleep, Caroline . . ."

"Mark—are you disturbed about something besides Natalie? Is something else wrong? Something you're not telling me? You seem—so shut away inside yourself tonight!"

For a moment, he stood there, unable to say a word. She'd always known him better than he knew himself. He was terribly guilty for not telling her about Jonathan's letter. After all, it would be Caroline who would be in the thick of having to teach Indian Mary how to get along in Savannah society, and Caroline was far from well. For an instant, during his first reading of Jonathan's letter, he'd grabbed at the possibility of stopping his son's headlong plans on the plea that his mother was too ill. Jonathan had spiked that in the next paragraph by assuring them that his mother would get well far faster with Mary there to care for her!

"Mark, why are you so shut away from me?" she asked. "You—almost act guilty about something."

"Guilty?" He forced a laugh. "What on earth would make you think such a thing? I never, ever heard of a man feeling guilty for—wanting his own wife!" Desperately longing to leave her on a lighthearted note, he added, "A man might feel—foolishly young, but—not guilty, isn't that so?"

In the dimly lit room, he saw her smile a little. "Yes, darling. Soon, though. I'll be better soon. I promise. Good night. Please sleep well."

"I will," he whispered. "Good night to you, beloved. I'll be right across the hall if you need me. I'll always be very close by, loving you with all my heart . . ."

Chapter 44

ON July 16, a dark, drizzly Tuesday afternoon, William sat with Burke on his cabin steps during the birth of Natalie's second child. From inside, in the back room where Burke and Natalie had conceived the baby and where Natalie now struggled to give it life, they could hear Miss Lorah's encouraging voice—soothing Natalie, giving orders to Mary and to Elizabeth Holder, who had crossed the river again to help.

"Don't see how anyone could keep from believing every word Miss Lorah says, do you, Burke?" William asked after they'd sat for an hour or so in near-silence.

"Uh, no, I don't," Burke answered absently, so worried, William knew, the man couldn't really think. "I don't know how we ever got along without her."

When Jonathan joined them, both scooted over to make room for him on the steps, but aside from assuring Natalie's brother that things were still going all right so far as they knew, there was little to talk about—until they heard Natalie moan, scream and then give what sounded to William like a mingled sob and—laugh.

All three had jumped up at the scream and stood now in the yard, staring at one another.

"I'll go in and find out," Jonathan said.

"Better not yet," William warned.

"William's right, son," Burke agreed, rubbing his forehead hard.

"Your head ache, Burke?" William wanted to know.

"Unmercifully," Burke moaned.

"I don't wonder, but I'm sure the baby's here. Didn't I just hear Mary laugh a little, Jonathan?"

"Yes, sir, that was Mary's laugh."

"I suppose Mary or Miss Lorah will bring the baby out for Burke to see in a little while now," William said, "or maybe call you in to Natalie, Burke."

"I hope so," Burke said, running his tongue around inside his mouth. "That bucket of well water still over there on the corner of the porch? My mouth's as dry as cotton."

William hurried across the narrow porch to bring Burke a gourd filled with cool water, which he drank down in a gulp. "Thanks, friend," he said. "Isn't it—terribly quiet in there?"

Knowing exactly how much trouble Burke was having getting his breath while they all waited for the baby to cry, William put his arm around the big man's shoulders. "Won't be quiet for long now," he said gently. The words were no sooner out of his mouth than two sharp slaps brought the welcome sound of Natalie's baby screaming lustily, while Lorah Plemmons's unmistakable chuckle and Mary's tinkly laughter mingled in wonder-filled relief.

William hugged Burke first. Then Jonathan and William hugged each other. All three rushed into the cabin's main room. There followed a long, long silence—an odd, puzzling silence—from the back room. Then Lorah Plemmons gasped, "Oh, Lord, have mercy!"

Burke's eyes were fixed—staring. William couldn't decipher the expression on Burke's face at all as the three men stood motionless—waiting, waiting.

There came, after what seemed a long time, a snatch of low talk from the bedroom—talk between Mary and Miss Lorah. Then Natalie's weak voice ordered, "You—Mary!"

Still they waited, suspended in time, until Mary appeared in the dimly lit main room, the baby in her arms. Jonathan rushed to her.

"Natalie ask me to take the baby to Mister Burke first, Jonathan," Mary said. "But *she live!* Natalie's daughter, she is—alive!"

Jonathan stepped aside as the girl made her way toward where Burke stood, his face white, dry sobs wracking the tall, muscular frame.

"Mister Burke?" Mary's voice, William thought, sounded almost as though she was praying. "Your daughter, Mister Burke. Natalie say—I bring her to you to see—first, before you go to Natalie. The baby live, but, please, Mister Burke, be strong!"

William saw Burke's hands reach for the infant.

For a reason William couldn't have explained, he and Jonathan slipped out onto the porch and watched through the window while Burke tenderly took the child from Mary. Over his ruggedly handsome face spread what William could only call a holy smile as Burke studied the tiny, even features, examined both pink curled hands a finger at a time, then clasped his daughter against his broad chest. "Oh, Mary, she's perfect! Our daughter is—perfect, isn't she?"

"Mister Burke . . . oh, Mister Burke . . ."

William peered through the window at Mary's agonized face.

"William! Look at Mary's face!" Jonathan whispered. "Something's wrong, isn't it, William?"

"I don't know, son. I can't figure it out."

And then William saw Burke's smile vanish as he grabbed one tiny pink foot and whispered, "My God!"

The toes and arch were turned almost entirely backwards!

"Oh, my God," Burke gasped again. "Mary—her little foot!"

William's own heart felt about to burst as he watched Burke's big hands try ever so gently to turn the crippled foot around.

"No, Mister Burke—*no!*"

"Mary," Burke breathed, "she's—she's—crippled!"

William stopped Jonathan from rushing in to comfort Mary as—weeping now—she stood nodding her head yes.

The little girl was alive all right, and beautiful, but she had been born with a deformed foot—a clubfoot.

Chapter 45

To the surprise of everyone except Lorah Plemmons, it was Natalie who kept all their spirits up during the first two weeks of the new baby's life. Missy's got a whole new grip on herself, Lorah thought as she whipped out newly ironed linens to make up the big bed in the master bedroom of the Stiles place. There was plenty to do in the next day or so, fixing for Miss Lib and the congressman and the two boys to get home for the rest of the summer. Lorah chuckled to herself as she tucked the top sheet in at the foot of the soft feather mattress. Making up the room for the Stileses was the job of one of their house servants, but Missy was so excited that Miss Lib would be home again, nothing would do her but that Lorah tend to it herself.

The day was fine. Certainly fine for early August, thanks to a good breeze off the river. Lorah didn't mind a bit making up an extra bed. She'd do anything—anything for Missy, so brave and cheerful and strong these days. Stronger than her big, strapping husband, to tell the truth. It looked to Lorah as though Mr. Latimer might be having the struggle of his life over that little twisted foot, as though he had failed. But Missy had a way with him. Lorah liked Miss Lib Stiles real well, but making up the bed was a love gift to Missy. Whether Missy knew it or not didn't matter a bit. Lorah felt a deep sense of fulfillment these days. She'd gotten through to Missy about the danger of self-pity and it had freed the girl in a way that seemed to make up for just about everything.

Then there was the pure joy of little Indian Mary and her happy husband of three whole days! The two lovebirds would be leaving first thing tomorrow for Savannah, and Lorah felt that she'd never forget their wedding last Wednesday.

Nothing would do Mary but that she and Mister Jonathan wait for the wedding until they could be sure the baby and Natalie were all right, and Lorah thought that made good sense. Good sense all around, since weddings needed to be happy events. Nothing would do both Mary and Mister Jonathan, either, but that Lorah put on her good flowered dress and stand up with Mary at her wedding in the same plain little church in Cassville where Missy and her man had said their vows some years back.

Lorah was smiling to herself as she folded back and smoothed the top sheet at the head of the bed, because she'd had the time of her life at that wedding ceremony! Missy herself had fixed Lorah's hair just so and made her wear a wide-brimmed straw hat Miss Lib had left behind, and if she did say so, she thought she didn't look too bad when it was time to get in the Stileses' old velvet-lined gentleman's carriage and head for Cassville. Missy wasn't up to the trip, so stayed home with her baby, but ordered her husband to go to give Mary away and, of course, kind Mr. William Mackay went along to be Mister Jonathan's groomsman.

It looked like the whole happy shebang had helped Mister Burke too. He'd talked more on the way back to Etowah Cliffs than Lorah had heard him talk since the day the baby was born. Mister Jonathan kept his arm tight around Mary all the way home, but he showed his pleasure too that Burke entered into the conversation—took it over, Lorah thought, by talking at length about how a really fine carriage like this one was built—of nothing but seasoned hickory, nothing but heat-cured ash in the spokes and hubs and high-quality soft iron to rim the wheels with. Lorah had never thought much about whether a carriage body was slung with four or six heavy leather slings to soak up the jolts. Remembering Burke's words now, she chuckled again to herself. She'd never even thought one way or another about *riding* in a gentleman's carriage! She still didn't care, but she did care that Missy's man seemed picked up in his spirit by the wedding of the half-breed Cherokee girl he'd watched over for so many years.

That Mary was barely able to keep her feet on the ground was plain to anybody who bothered to look. Lorah'd never seen so much joy in any human face as in the young, eager faces of the two young lovers.

"Lord," she whispered, "clear the way of all trouble for them once they're back in Savannah, Georgia. Wrap Mary around and around with Your love and protection should some of those uppity folks take out after her in their sharp, polished ways. And give Mister Jonathan Your own wisdom and sense with his parents. Give his parents Your understanding of how much those two children love one another. And since anybody's likely to worry more if they're not feeling good, give Mister Jonathan's mother her health back."

Yes, Lorah decided, I haven't felt better down deep in my heart in years. She tucked the new counterpane—cool green with blue vines woven together—under new bolsters Sinai had just made out of goose feathers, and even doing that added to her satisfaction. She stepped back to survey her work.

"Looks good enough to pass even Mrs. Stiles's muster," she said aloud to herself in the big, empty master bedroom on the second floor of the fine house Mr. Latimer and Sam had built. "Yes, sir, it looks fine, if I do say so. Missy picked out a mighty pretty counterpane on her first trip to Cassville with her man. In a month or so, I'll start workin' on the baby's crippled foot and—with God's help—we should all have just a *good* summer."

"That's right. Still, the baby is healthy and bright. And Natalie is certainly living up to all I've ever counted on in her. I have counted on Natalie, you know. I've loved her all her life, in spite of occasional confusion about my own judgment. The girl's going to be even more than I'd hoped. We're expecting a fine stay here, William, in great part thanks to my dependable brother."

"When do you and W.H. have to leave again?" he asked.

"The second session of Congress doesn't convene until December second, but if I know my husband, we'll start back in late September. He'll enjoy our time here, but his heart is in the capital. Wild horses couldn't hold him here with the presidential election coming up in November."

"Mama will want to have an idea when to expect you to stop off in Savannah to take your boat North, you know," William reminded her.

"Bless her, yes. So tell her we'll be there at least by early October. Frankly, I've no inclination to miss the pre-election excitement in Washington City either."

PART III

October 1844-January 1849

Chapter 46

BACK IN Washington City in late October 1844 and settled again into Mrs. Hewitt's boardinghouse, Eliza Anne finished a letter to Mary Cowper at the Montpelier school near Macon, then began to dress to meet W.H. Only ten days remained until the presidential election and she could almost feel the capital holding its social breath until the name of the new White House occupant was known.

For this town, she thought, there's a real lull in the social calendar and I find it rather refreshing, because part of me is still beside that dear Etowah River. If W.H. and I had been whisked back into a round of parties and receptions this week, the change would have been too abrupt.

Brushing her thick, wavy black hair, she let her thoughts flow south to her home on the cliffs, to Natalie and Burke and their new child, Callie, and breathed thanks to God that they had Miss Lorah to lean on. Oh, Natalie was spirited and strong and she and W.H. both felt Burke would soon regain his normal manly composure, but it was good that they had Miss Lorah. Good in all ways.

When her thoughts swerved to Indian Mary and Jonathan—man and wife, back in Savannah—she resisted. One thing she'd put off was a long, detailed letter to Mark and Caroline, not only in an attempt to encourage them about Mary's social progress but to brag on Natalie as well.

I'll do that soon, she promised herself, walking deliberately to her high wardrobe to select a small print blue challis dress suitable for the call she and W.H. would make later today on a former First Lady, Mrs. Dolley Madison. W.H. likes me in blue because it accents my dark hair and eyes. Pleasing him is important these days, since the poor darling is so afraid old Henry Clay might be elected President. With such strong Democratic goals in his mind for the upcoming second session of Congress, little could depress him more.

Of course, she hoped and prayed that the Democrat, Polk, would win, in spite of the impression Henry Clay had made upon her as a statesman. At a congressional gathering soon after her arrival in Washington City last winter, Eliza Anne had been presented to Clay and had felt the meeting exciting enough to write at length about him to her family in Savannah and to her ailing best friend, Julia Barnsley, in the upcountry. In spite of his unfortunate

Whig affiliation, for most of her life, it seemed, Henry Clay had served the nation in so many capacities she'd lost count. He'd been nominated back in 1832, right after her marriage to W.H., but overwhelmingly defeated by Andrew Jackson. Still, Clay was a famous man, almost worshipped by his loyal followers, and for years had shared honors in the Senate with Daniel Webster, John C. Calhoun and Thomas Benton. Clay strongly favored a national bank and, of course, to W.H. that made him an adversary. Eliza Anne remembered, though, having heard her old friend Robert Lee praise Clay for the Missouri Compromise, through which Clay had managed to calm the trouble between North and South over the issue of slavery in the new territories.

At her dressing table, she gave herself a wry smile in the looking glass. Except for her dogged loyalty to W.H., she could take no part in the political scene, but unlike many congressional wives, she relished politics and made no bones about it. The smile gave way to a frown as she twisted and pinned the long hair into a bun at the nape of her neck. One man who *would* make a superior President, she thought, is Robert E. Lee—if, like her brother Jack, he weren't so infernally proud of being a soldier. Presidents needed to be thoughtful and levelheaded. At times, Lee had struck her as being almost disgustingly so. She rubbed at the slight wrinkles her frown had left and sighed. It was ridiculous that she and Robert Lee had not yet seen each other alone—even for a waltz—in all this time. In the old days, no one loved dancing and parties more than Bob Lee. Had he changed? Had married life and fatherhood dulled the excitingly handsome young officer who, in her girlhood, was so at home in the Savannah whirl? Oh, she and W.H. had been invited often to Lee's home in Virginia, but she longed to talk with Robert alone, to share memories, really to renew *their* long-standing friendship—to know firsthand about Lee today. Her brother Jack had assured her that Robert was the same brilliant, witty, lovable fellow, but the years did change people, and although she disliked admitting it, she was still hurt that Lee had not called on her. Quite honestly, she did like Lee's plain, but intelligent and artistic wife, Mary Custis. Eliza Anne was still thrilled with the piece of George Washington's Cincinnati china which Mrs. Lee had insisted upon giving her, but the longing for even a short visit alone with Robert lingered. On impulse, she changed brooches from the amethyst she was wearing today to the gold bow pin Lee had given her for her sixteenth birthday.

Tying her three-times-whitened bonnet beneath her chin before walking to the Capitol to meet W.H. in the corridor outside his office, deliberately she turned her attention back to her husband. Last term, W.H. had successfully maneuvered a bill through Congress that appropriated $50,000 for work in the Savannah harbor—an act pleasing both to Jack and to Robert Lee—and because so many representatives had sworn that they'd voted for W.H. the man, even above his bill, she was still bursting with pride. She'd call on Mrs. Madison with him in high spirits today, and do her best to sparkle in conversation, in spite of the fact that Dolley Madison's elegant, but tiny parlor invariably made her feel smothered.

Any notice of Washington City's muggy, often oppressive weather brought longings for the clear, invigorating air at Etowah Cliffs. On her way downstairs at the boardinghouse, she vowed not to give one thought during the walk to the Capitol to anything or anyone outside Washington City! She was too far away today to do anything for Natalie or Burke or their crippled child. Too far from Savannah even to worry about Mary and Jonathan—or Caroline's lingering illness. It was hard, at times even impossible, to keep her two worlds apart, but today she would refuse even one gloomy thought about her beloved friend Julia Barnsley's failing health. Day after day, she had stormed heaven's gates for Julia and maybe she was actually improving. The letter from her that awaited Eliza Anne when she and W.H. got back to Washington City had contained a bit of hopeful news. During Julia's recent visit to Savannah—staying with her friend Mrs. Reid and *not* with her sister, Charlotte—she had at least felt well enough to call on the newly married Andrew Lows. A splendid marriage for Sarah Cecil Hunter, Eliza Anne thought. The impressive Andrew Low was, along with Mark Browning, one of the wealthiest men in Savannah.

It was only one o'clock when she began the leisurely stroll across the pavement on the Capitol grounds, her attention deliberately focused on the color now showing in the trees overhead, their crimson and gold reminding her somewhat wistfully of the Park at Etowah Cliffs. She had no current concerns for the welfare of their fields, thanks to dear William, who had agreed to stay through October, leaving just in time to reach Savannah for election day, November 4. William was still up there today. Reluctantly, she realized, there was no such thing as keeping her mind in the nation's capital. To put an end to the recurring bouts with guilt that she had delayed writing to the Brownings, she vowed to do it this very night. How they must both be suffering at the thought of their first grandchild's affliction!

"You don't really think you'll be allowed to pass me in such a preoccupied manner, now do you, fair lady?"

At the instant she recognized the familiar deep, musical voice, she felt a hand touch her elbow.

"Robert Lee!" she gasped. "Did you drop down from one of those tree branches?"

Falling into step beside her, he laughed. "Not this time, dear Eliza, but it's a wonder I didn't fall all the way down the Capitol steps the moment I saw you coming." They were alone now and he was calling her, as he always had, Eliza—not Eliza Anne. "Where are you going, m'lady?"

They both stopped, Lee looking intently down into her upturned face.

"This minute," she said, "I'm not going anywhere. I'm—inspecting *you.*"

"And how do you find me? Do I pass inspection? Do you truly like my mustache, as you claimed the last time you and your family visited Arlington? Am I getting old and decrepit?"

"You're handsomer than ever, not a bit old, and yes, I do like your mustache. But—" She broke off, frowning slightly, feeling a little too confused for comfort.

"But?" he pressed.

"Why didn't you call on me before your gracious wife was forced to extend the first invitation?"

She had seldom seen Lee at a loss, but his smile was gone as he raised one hand to say, "I swear to you, I did not know you were in town earlier! Look here, Eliza, I shouldn't even have to swear to you. You *know* I had no idea you were here or I'd have been at your door. Not until your congressman began his work late last session on his Savannah harbor bill did I know William Henry Stiles's lovely wife had left her home in the old Cherokee Nation!"

"You've always had a ready answer, Robert. With all my heart, I want to believe you."

He offered her his arm, and they began to mount the long, steep steps toward the entrance to the Capitol. "When I look at you so solemnly, can you doubt me? Can you, Eliza?"

"Personally, I think it was Mrs. Lee who had to persuade you to invite us to Arlington!"

He smiled wryly. "You're still the most beautiful woman in the world— and with the quickest tongue. I confess Mary did learn first that you were here, but I promise that any delay in inviting you would have begun all-out war at what people are now politely calling the Lee-Custis mansion. An all-out war begun by me, had you not been invited immediately. Believe me?"

Still climbing beside him, she looked up into his eyes. "I want to—terribly."

"Oh, Eliza, Eliza . . . how long it's been! I feel as though I'm seeing you again for the first time only this minute, in spite of your pleasant visits at our house, because this is, oh, *this*"—he lifted her gloved hand to kiss it briefly— "this is really like old times back in Savannah when—"

"When what, Robert?"

"When we were young and should have known we were in love!"

"Were—we in love?" she asked shamelessly.

They had reached the top of the long steps. Still gazing down at her, his deep-set brown eyes, at once devilish and kind, were riveted on her face, but he had not answered her question. They stood now at the building entrance as though they were the only people in town, eyes locked. Then, almost sadly, Lee looked away.

"Were we—in love?" He repeated her question slowly, as though deciding, as though in the process only now of making up his mind. Then, abruptly, his quick laughter broke the spell.

"Do you mind sharing the joke?" she asked.

"Will our children—all nine of them—go to their graves in old age wondering if you and I were once, in our lost youths, in love?"

"That's no answer," she said. "No answer at all!"

"I quite agree," he said. "I only know that Jack's letter telling me of your marriage and a later one with the shocking news of the birth of your daughter were like icy water down my back!"

"You married first," she said, not accusingly, merely stating a fact.

"I did, didn't I?" He paused. "Eliza?"

She looked up at him, waiting.

"Does it ever seem to you as though, through all these years in which you and I have been blessed with faithful mates, homes and beloved children, that —we might, in some secret world of our own—still be together? Could we still be together in a way we never were before my marriage? Before yours? Do we, not in your memory—in your very present—still sit sometimes beneath that wide shade tree in the yard of your family home on East Broughton Street? Do we sometimes still sit there, laughing together, Eliza?"

Involuntarily, her hand flew to her brooch. She would have given anything now if she hadn't worn it!

"I noticed the brooch," he said softly. "It was under that wide oak tree that I gave the lover's-knot pin to you. Do you wear it often? Or did you scheme to wear it while walking directly into my path today, lovely vixen?"

For an instant, she felt an odd kind of weakness, then said sharply, "You were nowhere near my thoughts until you called to me just now, sir!" In a moment, because his familiar humor had somehow released her, she smiled up at him. "All right, Robert. I did change brooches before I left the boardinghouse. Now, don't ask me why. I simply changed to this one."

"Still as direct and honest as ever, aren't you?"

"I should hope so."

Inside the spacious rotunda, he led her to a bench, where they sat side by side as Lee plied her with questions about every member of her family and most of their old friends in Savannah. Robert appeared relieved, in fact extremely pleased, that her mother was still reasonably well. Of course, he was "worried half sick" himself over Jack's poor health, but mainly he was concerned that his old friend must be terribly lonely. They spoke of William's tragic loss when the *Pulaski* exploded at sea, and Robert got in a few shots at his favorite target, Congress, because no safety laws for steam travel had yet been passed.

"You might also send along to Jack the delightful news that, thanks to the same illustrious lawmakers, his salary and mine will undoubtedly be cut to sixty dollars a month."

She glanced at her watch. It was time to climb the stair to W.H.'s second-floor office if they were to arrive at Mrs. Madison's on time.

"I'm keeping you," Lee said, rather sadly, she thought.

"Yes. But I—I—"

"You—what, Eliza?"

"I don't know. Robert, I don't know!"

"Have you thought of any plausible answers to even one of my questions you've so successfully ignored?" he asked.

"No. Have you?"

"None. Will your husband run for a second term in Congress?"

She had to smile. Lee hadn't changed. He was still dear and loving and perhaps the most tactful man on earth.

"Perhaps Congressman Stiles is waiting to find out who will occupy the White House before he makes up his mind on a second term. I'm sure he's working for James K. Polk, the Democrat."

"Of course," she said. "So am I."

"Naturally."

"My husband is also talking about trying for an appointment as minister to Havana."

Lee cocked an eyebrow. "Havana? Why Havana? We're not at all likely to run into each other there."

"The post is lucrative. We're under financial pressure still. My husband is building a handsome house on the Etowah River."

"And would you move to Havana?"

"If W.H. were United States minister there, of course."

"Of course." He stood now and reached a hand to help her to her feet. "My regards to your husband," he said.

"And mine to your wife, Mary. Robert, I genuinely like her and hope she and I have established a friendship. One that will last."

"As far as Mary's concerned, you have. Shall I escort you up to Stiles's office?"

"If you don't mind, no. I find I'm quite grateful for our chance meeting— exactly as it's been. Can we just leave it this way?"

For what seemed an eternity to her, he said nothing, but stood looking down at the marble floor of the Capitol rotunda, as though he'd just won a long-postponed battle within himself. There was plainly a kind of relief in his eyes when at last he said, "I see no other choice but to—leave it, to keep it as happy and magical as every moment has really been."

She returned his smile. "Goodbye."

Bowing over her hand, he whispered, "Goodbye, Eliza—beautiful creature . . ."

The Stileses and the Lees met socially again at the Lee home in Arlington shortly after Democrat James K. Polk had defeated Henry Clay in the electoral college. Since the popular vote had been so close, Lee saw it as a sign of too many dangerous divisions among the people. Of course, W.H. was lyrical at the Democratic victory, however it had happened, and Eliza Anne was proud of him as he sounded forth at the Lee dining table on his hopes for the future of the South now that a Southerner—a Democrat—had been elected President. She felt pride in her husband because with all her heart she agreed with his political views, but somewhere within her there lurked a kind of unease because Lee's views were not only far less vehement, they struck Eliza Anne as being not wholly traditional. Mostly Lee sat courteously listening as his guest expounded at length on the value of having as the chief executive a gentleman who cared about the welfare of the South.

"Perhaps most important for the South—and of course, in my opinion, the country as a whole—is Polk's concern for expansion," W.H. went on. "This gentleman means to obtain not only Texas but Oregon as well. One day, Captain Lee, our nation will extend from the Atlantic all the way to the Pacific, thus allowing room for divergent viewpoints North and South."

"Allowing room for new slave states, eh?" Lee asked.

Eliza Anne thought W.H. looked dumbfounded that Lee, a Virginian, would ask such a question.

"Indeed yes, Captain," W.H. replied. "In fact, I daresay that had Clay landed in the White House, we would have fallen into real trouble North and South."

Lee returned W.H.'s gaze, but said only that a military man found himself in foreign territory when he ventured into the complicated realm of politics. "We're both needed, though, Stiles," he added. "You to handle the issues, men like me to fight the battles."

"And there well could be a battle to fight," W.H. forged ahead. "The United States has *every right* to Texas, the Mexicans be hanged! They're a corrupt lot at best. Not only do we need Texas, Oregon and California, the people out there need us. Need our Christian civility. Even strictly military men, sir, must realize that Britain cannot possibly rule the Oregon Territory from three thousand miles away!"

Neither agreeing, Eliza Anne noted, nor disagreeing, Lee said that he did concur that Henry Clay had lost the election in part, at least, because he hesitated to take a firm stand *against* the annexation of Texas. "Clay was in a difficult position," Lee went on. "The President should represent the whole country and there *are* thousands in the North, you know, who don't want another slave state."

W.H. laughed a bit derisively. "Exactly, my good man, and to me those extreme anti-slavery Northerners added a humorous touch to old Clay's defeat."

"Humorous, sir?" Mary Custis Lee asked. "They say Mr. Clay is crushed—truly bitter to have lost out still again for the presidency after such long, distinguished service to the country. I'm told he had his heart set on it."

"He did, Mrs. Lee," W.H. said, "but in my opinion, his heart was not set on protecting the economic needs of slaveholding people like us! I certainly see humor in the results. The northern anti-slavery extremists defeated him!"

"I take it you mean the abolitionists' Liberty Party?" Lee asked.

"I most certainly do, Captain. The so-called Liberty Party's own candidate, James Birney, drew enough votes away from Clay to defeat him. Clay is no abolitionist, but your Mr. Clay—slaveholder though he is—is certainly *not* a states' rights Southerner."

"He isn't *my* Mr. Clay," Lee said, laughing.

"You admit his defeat came, though, because he failed to take a strong stand against annexing Texas. Those rabid abolitionists don't want Texas as a state. They know too well it will come in as a slave state."

Eliza Anne longed to change the subject. W.H. and Lee must not be allowed to argue. The balance she'd always admired in Robert irked her. He is a Virginian, she thought, and a slave owner. Why does he have to cling to that prickly objectivity of his?

"You, Congressman Stiles, are the politician present. As a soldier, *I love the union of all the states.* I've sworn to uphold the *United* States of America, with my life if need be." Smiling warmly, Lee added, "You see, I managed to put in my time at West Point all the way to graduation without a single exchange of blows or words with even one northern man there. They all knew my pride in being a Virginian, but they also knew of my encompassing pride in being an American."

"If Northerners could use even a bit of such candor and fairness, Captain Lee, we'd succeed more quickly in coping with our divergencies," W.H. said, to Eliza Anne's relief.

"Do we have to discuss only politics?" she asked.

"Why not, my dear?" W.H. gave her a slightly withering look. "A presidential election has just taken place at a crucial time in our nation's history! We could easily be at war soon unless President Polk is able to settle the Mexican problem in a peaceful way. Captain Lee's military could be front and center any day, but no one can doubt that for now, the *political* underlies everything."

In the silence that fell around the dining table, Mary Custis Lee passed the fruit bowl again. No one spoke beyond polite refusals. Eliza Anne was watching Lee's handsome, quiet face. He was giving W.H. one of his long, searching looks.

Finally, Lee asked, "Would I be considered a rude host, Congressman, if I said that I agree wholeheartedly that *unfortunately,* yes, the political does underlie—everything?"

To fill another awkward silence, Eliza Anne said, "You sound exactly like my brother Jack, Captain Lee."

"And is that calculated to put me in my place, lovely Eliza?"

Until that moment, he'd called her Mrs. Stiles or Eliza Anne—except on the day they'd met on the Capitol steps. Eliza Anne could think of nothing to say, so only smiled weakly.

An easy expression on his face, Lee got to his feet. "Having been schooled in strategy," he said gently, "this would seem to me to be the strategic time for us to retire to the parlor for more coffee. Will you, Congressman, do me the honor of escorting my good wife?"

Chapter 47

BY THE time the Twenty-eighth Congress adjourned on March 3 of the next year, 1845, Eliza Anne was longing, more than at any other time since the family moved to Washington City, to be back in the quiet beauty of Etowah Cliffs. Yet she found herself deeply dreading to go home. Only last month, word had reached her of the not unexpected, but still scarring death in Savannah of her lifelong friend Julia Barnsley. Grief at her own loss consumed her for days, so that she seemed unable even to pray for poor Godfrey and the Barnsley children—especially Mary Cowper's school friend, Anna, the oldest daughter. It would now fall Anna's lot to try to take her mother's place in the home.

True, the Barnsleys' Woodlands was more than twenty miles from Etowah Cliffs, but an integral, happy part of Eliza Anne's life in the upcountry had been her monthly visits with Julia. Dear old, often confused Julia Senior would never, she supposed, recover from the death of her namesake, especially since there'd already been so much grief in her own troubled life. Eliza Anne's mother felt that Julia Senior had more or less made peace with her mean-spirited daughter, Charlotte, but few expected Charlotte to be of much real comfort. Young Julia had even died in a friend's Savannah house because she was no longer welcome in what had once been the happy Scarbrough family mansion.

Since life would never be the same again for anyone who had loved or been loved by pretty, gentle Julia Scarbrough Barnsley, Eliza Anne, as her closest friend, dreaded returning to her own upcountry home, because Julia would no longer be nearby.

Future days spent beside her river cliffs would never be quite as complete again, Eliza Anne knew, for another important reason. In a highly personal way granted to few women, she herself had become part of national political life. Most days in the capital were too crowded, too busy, and yet she wondered at times, with a kind of sinking feeling, how she would fare back in the near-isolation of Cass County. Would it seem humdrum now? Would she be able somehow to keep the social identity and prestige she'd enjoyed in Washington City with nothing more to occupy her mind than handling servants or trying to keep the peace between Sinai and her fat, often smart-aleck daugh-

ter, Little Sinai? Could she ever settle for one or two visits a week with Burke
and Natalie and their crippled child as a substitute for dinners in Washington
embassies and the White House?

"What time is left in W.H.'s term as congressman should be busy for us
both, since I do all I can to build his reputation socially," Eliza Anne wrote
her mother during the final months of Tyler's presidency, "but the new President, Polk, will not, I'm sure, entertain with the flair to which we're accustomed. I have found it not only easy but enjoyable being quite close to
Tyler's new wife, Julia Gardiner of New York. I flatter myself that she has
needed me, since gossip has been rampant because Tyler, in his fifties, married Julia, a twenty-four-year-old girl. Tongues wag, of course, among those
who feel he married too soon after his first wife's death, because at the time
of the dreadful explosion of that gun aboard the *Princeton* in which people
were killed—including Julia Gardiner's father—it is said that she and President Tyler survived only because they were trysting belowdecks! I hate gossip and in all ways have tried to cultivate a genuine friendship with the new,
young First Lady."

It was certainly true that no one had been invited more often than the
Stileses to Julia Gardiner Tyler's grand receptions at the White House, and as
Eliza Anne wrote her sister Sarah, "I am still thrilled when Julia Tyler re-
ceives seated on a raised platform, acknowledging the formally announced
names of each guest presented to her. It is music to my ears, sister, always, to
hear the names of Congressman and Mrs. W. H. Stiles of Georgia ring out."

W.H. seemed not to find it amusing when she reminded him that at Etowah Cliffs, instead of such flattering formality, it was Eliza Anne herself who
made announcements by whistling on her fingers!

Under new President Polk and his somewhat odd First Lady, there would
be far less entertaining at the White House, but learning to adjust to changing administrations was, Eliza Anne now knew, part of the Washington life
she so enjoyed. There was no doubt in her mind but that she'd find a way to
be friends with the new First Lady, Sarah Polk, because she had an even more
important reason to cultivate her. W.H.'s appointment as minister to Havana
would come or not come at the hand of President Polk. Moving to Havana
was an event Eliza Anne had not yet faced, but W.H. wanted the appointment and for her that was reason enough.

"Things will be vastly different around here, my darling," W.H. had
warned, "with the Polks in the White House. I hope you won't be too bored
for these last few weeks of my term."

"I'm prepared for a change," she'd assured him. "Of course, we enjoyed
the Tylers' grand affairs, but perhaps it's time for something different. I'll go
on cherishing our last Tyler White House function, though—no matter how
rigid the new First Lady turns out to be."

Eliza Anne had seen her young friend Julia Tyler for the last time when, in
the closing days in office, President Tyler signed the bill for the annexation of
Texas and presented the gold pen with which he signed it to his beautiful

bride. Young Julia had solemnly promised Eliza Anne to follow her excellent suggestion of wearing the "immortal pen" suspended from her neck. The Stileses had not seen the Tylers again before they left Washington City, but W.H. had heard that indeed Julia Tyler, on the day they departed, was wearing the pen.

Eliza Anne had made her suggestion at the elaborate White House dinner given by the Tylers in honor of the newly elected southern Democrat, James K. Polk, and his wife, Sarah. Invitations to the affair had been highly coveted and, of course, W.H. took theirs as a sure sign that Polk was seriously considering him as minister to Havana. Whether the appointment came through or whether W.H. decided to run for a second term, Eliza Anne cherished the invitation because she realized that in one way or another the Polks would be important in their lives. Getting to know Sarah Polk was her new goal.

Mrs. Polk was a wellborn Southerner whose marks of breeding were evident at first meeting. To Eliza Anne's relief, the new First Lady was deeply religious—rather extremely so, she and W.H. thought, since Sarah Polk let it be known at once that she would permit no card playing, no dancing and no alcoholic beverages even at public receptions in the White House. A far cry from the warm, somewhat ostentatious style of her young friend Julia Tyler, but one to which they could both certainly adapt. An invitation to the White House remained the sought-after plum. Certainly, she thought, no one could doubt Sarah Polk's devotion to her husband and his political career, and although it caused gossip, Eliza Anne, who had always tried to help W.H., admired Sarah Polk for actually becoming her husband's secretary! She hesitated not at all to let her admiration be known, since she was now sure that, far more than he wanted a second term in Congress, W.H. longed for the Havana appointment. In a way she couldn't quite explain even to W.H., she rather liked the new First Lady even though her liking was a bit guarded.

"I'm not sure why it is," she wrote her mother. "There's much about the woman I honestly admire, but she exerts a strong influence over her husband —a kind of influence that goes beyond the usual wifely support."

By now Eliza Anne also preferred an appointment to Havana over any other because of their continuing financial strain. Havana simply paid more. The final weeks before Congress adjourned were anxious ones. It was no secret to anyone by then how much W.H. wanted the Cuban appointment. Perhaps only Eliza Anne knew the extent to which he was counting on it. As a consequence, one moment on one particular afternoon at a congressional wives' tea at the White House became for her a sharp and painful memory.

Quite casually, she hoped, Eliza Anne had mentioned to Sarah Polk that W.H. anticipated going as her husband's minister to Havana. Fixing her with a direct gaze, Mrs. Polk had stunned her by declaring, "Oh, surely not, Mrs. Stiles! I've given my husband's appointments much thought and there is no doubt in my mind but that you and Congressman Stiles would be far more satisfied in Vienna. The post of chargé d'affaires is open there and I'm sure you'd find Austrian society far preferable to Havana's."

When on that same night, W.H. had broken the news to her of his appointment to Vienna, where the United States had no full minister—merely a chargé d'affaires—she was disappointed to the marrow of her bones, but not totally surprised. The chargé in Vienna would bear a minister's responsibilities, but without quite the prestige and certainly far less money.

"Darling," she asked, as gently as possible, "are you just terribly let down by this?"

When W.H. smiled at her, she felt she might die of love for him. "Yes. Financially, we won't be helped much, Lib, but it well may be that we'll fit in far better with the Hapsburgs than with the court in Havana."

Her relief at the valiant way he took his disappointment lightened whatever sadness she might otherwise have felt at leaving Washington City for the last time. On the boat to Savannah, from where they could now go by train all the way to Cassville, she marveled that her always surprising husband seemed downright buoyant.

"Why wouldn't I be?" he asked as they sat alone on deck with their two sons playing checkers beside them. "Vienna's a challenge, Lib. All of Europe's a challenge right now. I'll rue every hour I have to spend supervising our fields while we're in Cass," he went on, obviously stimulated. "And you may as well get used to my late hours. I intend to spend every night until I leave for Europe in June studying Austrian history." He stretched his legs and eased back into the wooden deck chair. "Do you know I'm even looking forward to our short visit to Savannah? Do you suppose word has gotten there yet of my success with the new bill to build their much-needed customhouse?"

Eliza Anne knew perfectly well that he was as sure as she that all Savannah knew and that his Savannah visit would more than nourish his self-esteem. His final, effective work in Congress had been to obtain ample funds for Savannah's customhouse. The city would receive him gratefully and cordially. Savannah newspapers would run articles on his achievement and good publicity always made him happy. Of course, he was as eager as she too for their reunion in Cass with Mary Cowper. W.H. was proud of both sons, but Mary Cowper, now thirteen, had always been the darling of his heart.

At the end of March, as their steamer moved into the slip on Savannah's waterfront, Eliza Anne's happiness at seeing her family and Savannah friends again clouded a bit as she wondered about Caroline Browning's health. Caroline had been somewhat improved, according to the last letter from home before they left Washington City, but her mother and sisters doubted that Caroline would be well enough to entertain as the Brownings surely would have done for the returning Stileses. Poor Mark, Eliza Anne thought. How hard it must be on him to watch his adored wife's illness linger week after week.

For such an occasion as their triumphal return from the nation's capital, the normal thing would be for all the Brownings and all her family to be right there in the crowd at the waterfront to greet them. As the steamer bumped the dock amidst ringing cheers, whistles and shouts of the gathered throng, Eliza Anne found Mark and William, then both her sisters and her mother—but no Caroline and no Jonathan and no Jack.

"Why the frown, darling?" W.H. asked, giving the crowd his most energetic politician's wave. "Look at the people waiting to welcome us!"

Eliza Anne was waving too, in spite of her concern that her brother Jack was missing, as was Caroline. It was then that she spotted Indian Mary with Mark! "W.H.," she called over the noise, "can you believe Indian Mary's out there big as life—holding Mark's arm? And look how fashionably she's dressed!"

"Why wouldn't Mary be here? She's a member of the Browning family now. She's been our neighbor in the upcountry for years!"

"She isn't waving," she grumbled. "Everyone else is!"

Before W.H. could answer, Mary evidently picked them out in the row of passengers lined up along the ship's railing and began to wave happily—a big smile on her eager face.

"It just took Mary a while to find us. Undoubtedly her bad eye, Lib," W.H. said. "She's certainly giving us a warm wave now, wouldn't you say?"

"There you go again," she said, more sharply than she'd intended.

"There I go—doing what?" he asked.

"Accepting without a hitch! Oh, I'm fond of her too. You know I am, but—" She broke off.

He gave her his most melting smile. "But what, Lib?"

"You didn't even seem very surprised that they got married so abruptly!"

Now his smile turned teasing. "Maybe I wasn't surprised," he said. "Jonathan was plainly smitten with Mary. You knew that too."

"I did, of course," she said grudgingly. "But you might have acted a bit more—well, the way *you* would react to something so shocking."

"Disapproving?"

"At least—restrained. Savannah will crucify Mary and—oh, I can't think how this whole thing must be tormenting Mark and Caroline!"

"Mark looks quite comfortable with her," he said. "Look at them—arms linked. Both smiling."

"No reason why Mary wouldn't look pleased, is there?"

"None. She loves Jonathan as deeply as the young man loves her."

"Let's drop the subject," she said brusquely. "Look, we can get off now. The gangplank's in place. Where are the boys?"

"Ahead of us as usual. Halfway up the wharf. Bobby's already heading for his grandmother."

Eliza Mackay refused her daily nap on their first afternoon back, but did invite Eliza Anne to join her in the big upstairs bedroom for a good talk after dinner.

"You're sure you shouldn't sleep a while, Mama? We'll be here until day after tomorrow."

"I can sleep any time," her mother said, stretching out on the bed where Eliza Anne used to crawl in with both parents after a childhood nightmare in the long-ago years before her father died.

"Don't you want to lie down beside me, dear?" her mother asked. "It will be like old times."

"I think I will," she said, settling herself into the deep, soft feather bed. "I was just remembering all those times I must have annoyed you and Papa when I had those scary nightmares as a little girl."

"Did we act annoyed?"

"Never."

"That's because we weren't. We loved you exactly the way you love Mary Cowper. Will she be at Etowah Cliffs when you get there later this week?"

"She should be. She was coming back from Macon with Anna Barnsley as far as Woodlands for a day or so. Oh, Mama, poor Anna! In Mary Cowper's last letter before we left Washington City, she told me that during the final month of her mother's illness, Anna cried herself to sleep every night. Her grief has quite frightened Mary C., I think. At her age, everything makes such a deep impression and I'll need to do all in my power to assure her that her mother isn't going to die. She's dreading it already and I haven't felt so well in years!"

"Thank heaven," her mother said in the soft, tender voice Eliza Anne had loved from childhood. "I worried a little at times that Washington City's damp climate might worsen your asthma. But you'll be back in the upcountry soon and you're so well up there. Oh, I do wish young Julia might have had access to a doctor at Woodlands. Maybe she'd still be here." She sighed. "Do you suppose Godfrey will ever forgive himself for not being with her at the end?"

"Julia herself persuaded him to go back to Woodlands, Mama. In the last letter I had from her—written from here—she told me she was not going to allow him to stay on in Savannah away from the children. She was quite convinced, I guess, even then, that her own stay here near Dr. Arnold might be a long one." Eliza Anne took a deep, shuddering breath. "We don't—know at all, do we, what might happen each time we have to say goodbye?"

"No, we don't, honey. But God does know."

"Mama, how do people live without faith?"

"I'm sure I can't imagine."

"Young Julia and I spoke of that so often."

"Eliza Anne, your own faith didn't falter in the midst of all that whirl in Washington City, did it?"

Up on her elbow now, looking down into her mother's face, she said wonderingly, "Do you know, Mama, that almost constant round of parties—W.H.'s busy, important schedule there—all seemed somehow to make me even more aware of how much God loves us. I rather marvel, I think, but it's true."

"I'm so glad. But do you know why it's true?"

"Well, I did meet some quite prominent people who seemed only to attend church from habit—who obviously lived only by their own wits. But I think the main reason I seemed to rediscover God's love was W.H. himself."

"W.H.?"

"I know that surprises you, but you know how I've always wondered, prayed—hoped that my wonderful husband would turn a bit more toward God. You've taught me well, though. You taught me a long time ago, maybe because Papa wasn't actually what one could call a spiritually dedicated man, that the way a person lives is the only way we can judge the depth or shallowness of that person's faith."

"Your father lived love. God's love."

"I know he did. And time after time in Washington City, in spite of his heated political biases, in the midst of such taxing work, in the face of the kind of storms the slavery issue invariably raises in Congress, I saw W.H. *do* the Christian thing, have the truly Christian viewpoint. Only once did I think he grew testy and that was one Sunday when he and I were guests of Robert and Mary Lee at Arlington. You know how Robert has always been—an Army man, an engineer from his toes up, not really interested in politics. Actually, Lee was quite diplomatic with W.H. that day, I thought, as he usually is, but do you know, I believe that, in his heart, Lee disapproves of slavery."

"Oh, I think, in his heart, W.H. does too—down deep."

"I won't argue about that either way, but as a politician, he can't let it be known—certainly not as a states' rights southern Democrat!"

"In that respect, at least, Army men have more freedom than politicians to think their own thoughts. Lee thinks the institution of slavery is evil—more destructive even for white people. He told us so himself years ago, dear, when he was still a young man, don't you remember?"

"Vaguely. Anyway, there was one brief moment when he and W.H. could easily have gotten into it. They didn't. Later that night, after we went to bed at Arlington, somehow I was rather overshadowed by the vastness of God's love for all of us—North and South."

"People with white skin and people of color."

"Oh, Mama, if only those dreadful abolitionists up North would stop—"

"Most average northern folk are definitely *not* abolitionists, Eliza Anne!"

"We're *not* 'lords of the lash' down here either and I'm sick of their ranting and raving! There was one eccentric, troublemaking man named Theodore Weld, who wrote the most inflaming, vicious speeches for some of those mean-spirited northern congressmen that anyone ever heard! And would you believe Weld married a Charleston, South Carolina, woman—Angelina Grimké—and she and her sister have had to leave Charleston for espousing Weld's violent hatred of men like my blessed father and dear W.H.?" Her mother surprised her with laughter instead of a sympathetic retort. "I know you're against the spread of slavery, Mama, but I don't see anything so funny about the Grimké sisters!"

"My dear, all citizens of the United States of America have a right to their own opinions and I guess I was mostly amused at Mr. Theodore Weld for picking out a Charleston girl. You have to admit there's a humorous side to the sisters turning abolitionist in such a hotbed of southern fire-eaters as South Carolina!"

"Mama, I don't want to hate anyone over any of this slavery business, but it makes me sick being attacked in such a condescending fashion! We're *not* inferior down here!"

"Lee is right, though. What matters, finally, is the Union."

"For goodness' sake, W.H. believes in the Union too," Eliza Anne flared. "But there has to be at least a measure of fairness, doesn't there? What would both my Sinais or July or Solomon or even your old Hannah and Emphie do without us? How would they live?"

"I don't have an answer to that. No one has. Maybe there isn't one single solution. I just wish slavery had never come about in the first place."

"Mama, people have to live! We have a lot of land now in the upcountry. W.H. says he's forty or fifty hands short as it is. Do you think Henry and Bobby and W.H. could farm all that land alone?"

"As of right now, dear heart, we are switching to another subject. Did you know Mary Browning begged to be on hand with us today when your boat came in? The girl almost idolizes you. Jonathan stayed with his mother so Mary could be there to welcome you home."

"Mama, you've jumped from the frying pan right into the fire, it seems to me. Surely you don't consider poor Mary and Jonathan a happy topic of conversation!"

"I most certainly do. I've never seen happier young people than those two."

"But what's being said here in town over the whole preposterous marriage? Don't you think it's keeping poor Caroline upset when she should be at ease in all ways in order to get over that dreadful bronchitis?"

"I think Mary is only comforting Caroline. Except to meet you today, the girl has almost not left the house since she and Jonathan came back from Cass last year."

"There's been no ugly gossip? No callers to inspect Mary's Indian ways?"

"Of course there has been gossip—and callers. Caroline has visitors when she's up to it. But what I see, my dear, is little Mary slowly, but surely moving deeper into Caroline's heart. Mark's too."

"Oh, Mark has always been kind to anyone!"

"Eliza Anne, listen to me. I'm sure you'll call on Caroline before you leave town and I want you to promise not to criticize Mary in any way. She's Jonathan's wife now, a member of the Browning family."

A rush of guilt caused her to flush. She could feel it. "I know you're right,

Mama, and I was genuinely fond of Mary—until she presumed to marry Jonathan. That's wrong of me. Dead wrong. I stew about W.H.'s Christianity and look at mine! Christians aren't supposed to be snobs. I'm a social snob, Mama. I had no trouble accepting Mary as long as—"

Her mother smiled. "As long as she kept her place?"

"That's ugly of me, isn't it?"

"Perhaps a bit arrogant."

"You know I'm going to need you desperately if Mary Cowper grows up to care about an—unacceptable young man, don't you?"

"You won't need me so much if you listen to God. I can always *only* give all of you children the benefit of my years. The older you get, the more you'll begin to sort out what's really important. Of course, there are going to be awkward times because Jonathan's wife is a half-blood Cherokee. Only the extremely young and foolish would expect otherwise. I'm certain Mary, as young as she is, knows she and Jonathan are in for some heartache. So far, I believe only Bertha Potter has made a point of stirring things up. Would you like my prediction?" she asked.

"Of course."

"I predict that soon Caroline will catch up with Mark, and begin to see Mary as perhaps the most valued friend the family has ever known."

Eliza Anne only sighed.

"While the marriage is far from ideal as we mortals see things," her mother added, "there is nothing in Mary's heart but gratitude."

"I should hope so!"

"That just popped out, didn't it?"

"Yes, Mama, it did. What's in must come out, I guess."

"Give yourself time, Eliza Anne. I'm sixty-seven. You're not yet thirty-seven."

"I understand all that, but why wouldn't a rootless half-breed girl be grateful? She's walked into one of the wealthiest homes in Savannah! Only Andrew Low has as much money as Mark. Mary McDonald owned nothing but the clothes on her back, and those, I have no doubt, Burke and Natalie bought for her. Today at the wharf she was dressed like an heiress!"

She felt her mother's firm, gentle hand on her cheek. "My dear daughter, becoming a Browning is going to be far more difficult for Mary than anyone seems to realize. The fine dresses in which she's undoubtedly quite uncomfortable, the matching slippers which surely cramp her wild little feet, are not the reasons she's grateful. Mary is grateful—for love. With Ben's death, she lost the last living member of her family. She's grateful for more than any of us can comprehend—and have you forgotten? Gratitude is the only human response that never, never blocks God."

After a long silence, Eliza Anne said, "I'll give that some thought, Mama. Now, will you tell me the truth about my brother Jack? Should he be off working on Ossabaw Island now because the Army refused another sick leave? Is he well enough? Don't be careful with me. I'm always too far away to see for myself and I need to know. Is—Jack killing himself because he won't give up the Army?"

"Oh, my dear, that's a dreadful way to put it, but I am being truthful when I tell you that I don't know the answer. I know how he looks—sallow, pale, too thin. I also know how he acts—much of the time—almost like his old self. Your brother Jack could have been a successful Shakespearean actor."

On another sigh, Eliza Anne said, "I know. He wouldn't even have to memorize much. He already knows more Shakespeare than I've even read! I did think he'd make an effort to come to Savannah to see me," she said.

"And you concluded, when he didn't, that he wasn't well enough."

"Yes. I've written him that W.H. is leaving in June for Vienna, that the children and I will be going too, as soon as W.H. can come for us. Vienna is farther away than Washington City. Lots farther. I'm terribly disappointed— and worried that Jack isn't here!"

"Oh, my," her mother said. "I haven't even allowed myself to think how far away Vienna is! I'd so hoped W.H. would get the ministry to Havana. At least, Cuba isn't—"

"I know. Cuba isn't all that far from Savannah. He really wanted Havana. He worked so hard trying for it and he had such splendid recommendations from really important men in Washington. Men such as Cobb, Lumpkin, Colquitt. Our new President, Mr. Polk, is quite peculiar!"

"Peculiar? He's been called a nonentity."

"I know he was a dark horse in the campaign against a famous man like Henry Clay, but he's far from a nonentity. W.H. thinks him one of the hardest-working Presidents. I know Sarah, his wife, works harder than any woman I've met up there. She's actually his personal secretary and I doubt that anyone except Sarah really knows why President Polk wanted to send W.H. to Vienna instead of Havana. The word was that there were just too many men who wanted the Havana ministry."

"Why isn't the Austrian appointment a full ministry?" her mother wanted to know.

"W.H. isn't sure, but it seems that a few years ago, Austria cut back on its representation here. The United States did likewise. W.H.'s goal is to get a full ministry restored. Once he's in Vienna and can convince Polk, I'm sure it will be done." She laughed a little. "Except for his wife, President Polk is definitely his own man. People tend to underestimate him. They shouldn't."

"I'm so proud of you and W.H., Eliza Anne. How I wish your father were here to brag about you both. He would, you know."

She laughed. "I can almost hear it. I still miss Papa. Mark thought so much of him, I think Papa might have convinced Mark to forbid Jonathan his pretty Indian girl."

"Mark did adore your father, but I know Mark better than you know him, my dear. He frets as much as the next parent over both Natalie and Jonathan, but he isn't one to forbid his children the desires—the real desires of their hearts. Jonathan loves Mary and he will always love her. No parent willfully breaks a child's heart."

"Mama, young hearts mend! W.H. and I both feel that a parent's first duty is to insist upon what the parent knows is best for a child."

"Generally, I'd agree," her mother said carefully. "Parents should also realize that having become a parent does not promptly endow them with all wisdom. They still have flaws. Parents are people too."

Chapter 48

I N SPITE of the always fresh magic of spring at Etowah Cliffs, Eliza Anne
was concerned about W.H. From dawn until dark, he worked with their
people and David Holder in the fields, so that by the time he finished his
copious correspondence and study of Austrian history, it was often after midnight when he fell exhausted into bed.

"It's far harder leaving for Vienna than I thought it would be," he said on
a cool evening in May spent with her before a small fire in the still sparsely
furnished new parlor. "I know eventually I'll be back to take you and the
children to live there with me, but, Lib, how will I get through those months
without you?"

"Don't, W.H.," she protested. "I can't even bear to talk about it. We've
been so close here this spring, in spite of the brutally long hours you've spent
working like a common laboring man. We were together so much in Washington City. I felt such a part of your life there . . ."

"You were," he said, giving her the smile that always melted her heart.
"And I'll be just as proud of you in Vienna, my darling. You're the kind of
wife every public man longs for and none has save me. What I don't see is
how I'll even stay sane so far away from your lovely, lovely face—unable to
touch you, to revel in the feel of you. And oh, Lib, I'm ashamed to be leaving
you next month with so much still undone here. I'm leaving you with only
half-finished work and so many problems. So many undelivered new imple-
ments—do you have straight what it is you're to watch out for?"

"I do, sir. Two new John Deere steel plows, one McCormick reaper, a
cotton gin to be set up in the shed below the stables—"

"Dear Lord!" He rubbed both slender hands over his eyes. "But how are
you to pay for all of it? What if my brother Benjamin fails to sell those
Savannah tracts before our orders reach Cassville?"

"He will *have* to sell them," Eliza Anne said. "Your brother knows I can't
go to market with anything of value before late summer and he also
knows—"

"Of course he knows, but will that guarantee the sale he's working toward?
Oh, Lib, Lib . . . you must pray that the President will see fit to reinstate a

full ministry in Vienna. We simply can't exist on my salary as chargé d'affaires."

"I can always sell my brickyard in Savannah. There's another building boom there—you saw for yourself. When you go back down to board your ship for Liverpool, you could advertise the brickyard for sale. It does still have sentimental value to me because your dear father gave it to me, but your peace of mind matters to me now, dearest, far beyond sentiment."

"Lib, do you think John Lumpkin made such an effort to help secure my appointment as minister to Havana because he felt I was the most qualified? Oh, I know he pointed out in his letter to Polk that Georgia had no one in foreign service and that he and I are both from the newly created Fifth District here, that ours is the strongest Democratic district in the entire state, that we are close friends, but—I'm still being considered as a nominee for a second term in Congress. So is Lumpkin. Do you suppose he was merely trying to get his political competition safely out of the way? Or did he think me the one man best suited for either Vienna or Havana?"

"I see no difference," she said. "Either way, the old governor's son paid you a high compliment, didn't he?"

"I suppose so. I've worked hard at learning all I can about Austria. I only hope it's enough."

She reached for his hand. "You do need me with you every minute, don't you?"

"Does anyone doubt that?"

"You seem so sure of yourself always. Cocksure, your political enemies like to believe, but you need me to remind you that you're not only a brilliant attorney, a man of literature and art, you're also a statesman." Pulling his face down, she kissed his nose. "You need a woman of my taste to keep you reminded that you're the one man in all the world I chose to marry."

After giving her a lingering kiss, he whispered, "Don't let plantation problems when I'm gone change your opinion of me, lovely lady. Promise?"

"How could a reaper or a steel plow or the need for a new fence possibly change my heart toward you?"

"But I'll be gone. Gone so far away I can't possibly help you, and such a beautiful lady should not have to struggle with lazy workers and rotting fence posts. Please go on loving me exactly the way you do right now, Lib, even when you find out about all I've left undone here—all the burdens I'm dumping on you for the sake of my own career."

"You haven't said one word about your need to serve our country. You're needed by your family, oh yes—but, darling W.H., your country needs you too. I forbid one more word about this sacrifice we're both making as being only for *your* career. I won't have it, do you hear me?"

He took her in his arms. "Don't change, Lib. Don't ever change . . ."

Chapter 49

ON THE first day of June, W.H. said goodbye to Eliza Anne, the children, all the house servants and field hands, to Burke and Natalie, Lorah Plemmons and Sam, and sailed for Liverpool on June 8, 1845, the same day old President Andrew Jackson died.

His first letter to Eliza Anne, posted in London, told in detail of every British site he visited and, except for his personal page of intimate words for "Lib only," was virtually the same as the series of articles he wrote for both the Savannah *Georgian* and the Cassville *Pioneer* entitled "Extract from the Diary of a Georgian in Europe." Eliza Anne reveled in the new prominence his articles brought. Never mind that he'd made use of his letters to her in the articles. She had become a public person right along with him and nothing anyone said or did diminished her pride in him.

"I'd think Uncle W.H. could write you more personal reactions to all his touring," Natalie declared during the long evening in the Stiles parlor through which Eliza Anne had read and read and read aloud to Natalie and Burke, the Stiles children, Sam and Miss Lorah, all ordered to assemble and listen. Page after closely written page covered, along with lengthy comments and analyses, not only W.H.'s visits in Liverpool, the sights of London and Paris, but details of his arrival at last in Vienna on August 2, fifty-five days after he'd sailed from Savannah.

Everyone present except Burke dozed off at least once. Miss Lorah, sleeping soundly while sitting straight up in a chair, received only an annoyed look from Eliza Anne. To no one's surprise, Sam slept through it all, but regularly she scolded her boys for dropping off and felt secretly pleased that most of the time Mary Cowper appeared to listen attentively.

Burke, who had, she thought, remained quite alert, laughed when W.H. finally recounted the rental of his predecessor's quite elaborate apartment and the bargain purchase of his good furniture.

"I'd say, Miss Lib, that your husband's made a real pleasure trip of it. He's seeing the world and living like a king!"

For a moment, Eliza Anne felt resentful. In a way, the letter did imply that W.H. had left her waiting at home for deliveries of supplies that didn't come, with fields to supervise and people to handle while he enjoyed himself. "As chargé d'affaires, he needs to know the entire picture over there!" she protested. "How else is he to learn it if he doesn't travel?" When she heard Natalie's giggle, Eliza Anne laughed too. "Oh, I know how it sounds," she said, "but the government does pay his travel expenses. They'd better!"

"For Papa to be such an important international diplomat," Henry said, "we sure are poor, Mama!"

"We *surely* are poor, Henry. Watch your grammar."

"But once Papa gets a full ministry," Mary C. said, "I don't think we'll be poor anymore."

"I don't see what difference it makes," Natalie put in, taking Burke's hand. "Miss Lorah's always been poor, and look at her."

At the mention of her name, Lorah Plemmons sat up with a tiny sleep snort, blue eyes bright. "I declare," she said, "I never thought I'd be listening to a letter from such a big man and right from the lips of his very own wife!"

"Well, thank you, Miss Lorah," Eliza Anne said, responding as did everyone to any hint of praise from the wise lady. "You know we're all just plain folk. You should know, you practically live with us."

Miss Lorah, she noted, merely chuckled, but Natalie couldn't let it pass.

"Now, really, Miss Lib, do you—down in your heart—actually *feel* like 'plain folk'?"

"Why, of course I do," Eliza Anne said defensively. "My husband and I both worked hard in Washington City in the service of a true *democracy*. Our Democratic Party believes in the Declaration. We believe 'all men *are* created equal.'"

Burke's smile was engaging as always, but his words went straight home. "All men—except Negroes and Indians, Miss Lib?" he asked.

"I liked old Indian Ben a lot," Bobby Stiles said, "and I really like Mary, but Papa says Negroes are inferior. They're an inferior race. When Mama says all men are created equal, she means all men but Negroes. Some of them are good people, but they're different."

Silence hung over the room so thick and dense, Eliza Anne could only begin to shuffle and reshuffle the pages of W.H.'s long, long letter. All she could think of to say was "That was unnecessary, Bobby. And more than enough. Do you want to hear the remainder of this letter or don't you?"

"I confess what I most wanted to hear was that your husband's all right—feeling well," Miss Lorah said, getting to her feet. "Truth is, if Sam's to have a pair of darned socks to wear to work tomorrow when he helps Burke finish your piazza, Mrs. Stiles, I'd best get back to the cabin and see to my own work. I want to set some dough to rise too."

Sam, Eliza Anne noticed, was already halfway to the front door as she and Miss Lorah wished each other a good night.

"You boys had better get upstairs to bed too," Eliza Anne said. "I promise to read the rest of Papa's letter to you later. You have early chores to do in the morning, so scoot."

Hanging back a little, Henry said, "I'm proud to be Papa's son. I don't think we're plain folk at all. Nothing plain about any of the Mackay family either. Nothing plain about old Godfrey Malbone of Newport. Certainly nothing plain about Grandfather Mackay. After all, he taught Mark Browning all he knows about the mercantile business and Mark's one of the richest men in Savannah!"

"And Cousin Edward Greene Malbone was a famous painter till he died of consumption, and your grandfather, Don Juan McQueen, was close friends with George Washington, General Lafayette, Spanish governors and all," Henry went on. "I'm sorry Miss Lorah's gone, because she'd be glad to know all you and Papa have taught us about *quality* in our family."

"And look how rich our papa's father was! He had one of the best plantations in Savannah at Yamacraw," Bobby said. "Grandfather Joseph Stiles was—"

"That's enough, son," Eliza Anne said sharply. "Bedtime."

When the boys had gone upstairs and only the Latimers and Mary Cowper still sat with Eliza Anne, she began to hunt her place in the letter.

As she searched, Burke said gently, "There's nothing wrong with being proud of your family, Miss Lib. I'm proud that my father was a really good schoolteacher."

"Families are fine, I guess," Natalie said, stifling a yawn. "They just don't matter in the same way after you fall in love."

"Oh, Natalie," Mary Cowper literally gasped. "Thank you, thank you for saying that!"

A look of surprise on her face, Natalie said, "Why, you're welcome, Mary Cowper. I believe it. Look at Jonathan and Mary, how happy they are, and Mary's never going to be a real Savannahian. She's quietly going about the house down there waiting on my ailing mother hand and foot just to make Jonathan happy. Jonathan matters most."

Obviously teasing her, Burke asked, "Mary Cowper, did you have a reason for thanking Natalie so profusely just now? You're moving toward fourteen. You've been away at school. Is there a special young man somewhere?"

"Burke, of course there isn't!" Eliza Anne shot out her words and, instead of apologizing, went directly back to reading W.H.'s account of his twofold duties as chargé d'affaires in Vienna. He was to observe and report on political, economic and military trends inside the Austrian Empire, and he also was the person through whom the United States sent all official communications to the Empire. Ignoring the fact that she'd lost her audience's attention, she read of his meeting with J. G. Schwarz, the American consul in Vienna, the day after he reached the city, and his introduction, when he presented his credentials, to Baron Ottenfils, acting Minister of Foreign Affairs during the temporary absence of the famous Prince Metternich. Even Burke stifled a yawn when she read of her husband's calls on the Papal Nuncio, the Turkish ambassador and other members of the diplomatic corps, but he roused a little, as did Natalie, when she came to W.H.'s own estimates of what he

called "the strange customs" of Europe, of his difficulties in adjusting to
them. For example, in the "definitely superior" United States, a person could
do anything that was not prohibited by law. While in Europe a citizen was
free to do *only* those things permitted by law. Obviously, W.H. was more
convinced than ever that a republic such as the United States enjoyed was in
every way vastly superior to monarchies. He even went so far as to say that in
a republic, virtue was the centerpiece, while in a monarchy, the centerpiece
was fear. Within a few days, he'd learned of countless Austrians who, having
heard about the freedom enjoyed in the United States, were longing to leave
their homeland for our shores.

Throughout W.H.'s reactions to Austrian education and the deplorable
poverty he'd found, Eliza Anne felt her listeners' attention lag again, then
revive when she read of another "strange custom": doors were closed at ten
o'clock at night and all who left or entered after that paid a small fine. W.H.
also deplored the custom of actually preserving the hearts of dead emperors
and empresses.

"Mama, they really cut out and preserve their hearts?" Mary C. asked.

"Evidently," Eliza Anne said. "Your father wouldn't write it if they
didn't."

She felt attention ebb again during W.H.'s criticisms of the Austrian legal
system, but Burke perked up enough to chuckle a little when she read what
even to her seemed a bit extreme—that "Americans were superior intellectu-
ally because of the type of government to which we hold."

"I think W.H. laughed at himself a little at that sweeping statement," she
said, "because he goes on to write that it must be noted that his observations
are based totally on the way he himself has been taught."

"Does that mean Papa thinks his parents taught him that he was superior to
other people?" Mary Cowper asked.

"Oh, I don't think we can go that far, dear. It simply means that your
father's humor took over at that point. He realized and was man enough to
admit that he'd written something a bit extreme."

All Mary Cowper said was "Oh."

"And what does that 'oh' mean?" her mother asked.

"Nothing, Mama. Go on."

"All right, then listen." Eliza Anne was reading again. " 'I fully believe my
background as a southern plantation owner and slaveholder makes me far
more acceptable at the court of the Hapsburgs than had I been a representative of the more common man in the North of our country. Still, I keep my
opinions mainly to myself, not wanting to create delicate diplomatic problems. I also keep my estimates of some of the members of the royal family to
myself, because aside from Archduke Charles and Archduke Louis, whom I
regard as the most intelligent members of the imperial family, my opinion of
the Emperor's brothers, sisters, uncles and aunts is low indeed. Of the Emper-
or's aunts, the Empress Maria Louisa is decidedly the most distinguished, but
her private character is such as to render her an object of censure and disgust.

She has had six children since the Duke of Reichstadt (her only legitimate child!), not only out of wedlock but, 'tis said, each by a different man. She was, of course, Napoleon's wife and the Duke of Reichstadt was his legitimate son by her.' "

Burke chuckled again when she read that W.H. considered Emperor Ferdinand I an " 'idiot and a small man with a very large head and an exceedingly blank and unexpressive face. He does not abound in brain or if so, it is drowned in water so as to render its possessions of no importance. I am told that once I get to know Prince Metternich, I will find him most acceptable. I anticipate this, although I understand that he refuses to converse in English, which unfortunately is the only spoken language I understand.' "

"I'd think Uncle W.H. had better study hard and learn how to speak German and French," Natalie said. "Especially if he expects to get his office elevated and have his salary raised. It still doesn't seem quite fair to me, Miss Lib, to leave you here with all this debt and all those plows and reapers and things coming and no money to pay for them."

"She'll manage," Burke said. "By the way, have you heard from Benjamin Stiles on the sale of those Savannah tracts yet, Miss Lib?"

"Not a word. But on business matters, Benjamin is a firm believer in waiting for tomorrow."

"For goodness' sakes," Natalie spoke casually, "Papa can let you have thousands if you need them!"

"I know he could, Natalie, but as extravagant as W.H. and I are said to be, I don't need thousands. A few hundred will do nicely."

To the obvious relief of everyone, the letter was finished at last. Eliza Anne said good night to Burke and Natalie, then heated some milk for herself and Mary Cowper before they too went up to bed.

"Papa's a very important man now, isn't he, Mama?" Mary C. asked.

"Yes, he is, darling. You'll have much to be proud of when you go back to Montpelier in a month or so. And, Mary C., we must all do everything possible to keep our lives steady and pleasing to Papa while he's away. You realize that, don't you?"

"Oh, yes, I do. How long do you think I'll be able to stay at school, Mama?"

"Why, your father and I have set aside your tuition, darling. There's no question of whether or not you'll be going until you've finished. The boys go to Reverend Howard's school soon too. Your educations are not in question in any way."

"That isn't exactly what I meant," the girl said, not looking at her mother. "I meant, when do you think Papa will come back to take us all to Vienna?"

"Oh, dear, we've only just read his first long letter! I hope and pray not many months will go by before he's back here again, but tonight, I have no idea at all how long you'll be in school at Montpelier."

Mary Cowper said nothing for a time, then asked, "Well, do you suppose we'll be going to Savannah to visit Grandmother anytime?"

"Why, darling?" A bit suspicious of all these questions, Eliza Anne asked carefully, "What's going on in that mind of yours?"

"Oh, I just thought we might take the train down to visit my aunts and grandmother before I have to go back to school. Before Henry and Bobby have to go. I'm sure they'd love a trip to Savannah."

"You know perfectly well that the full responsibility of getting in our crops and taking them to market falls on me this year. I suppose I might try to persuade Natalie to take Callie to visit her parents in Savannah. I'd trust you to go with Natalie. But oh, my, if the idea doesn't strike her just right, there would be no convincing her to leave Burke and he has too much yet to do on our house to leave."

"It doesn't seem right, though, Mama, that the Brownings haven't even *seen* their only grandchild with poor Miss Caroline too ill to travel. Maybe I could help convince Natalie to go!"

"I know you're fond of your aunts and grandmother, Mary Cowper, but I didn't realize you suffered from being away from them."

With a small, nervous laugh, Mary Cowper said, "Oh, I'm not suffering, Mother! I just—I just—"

"You just what, darling?"

"I just thought I'd ask about a Savannah visit."

"Are you terribly restless being at home this summer? Your father and I thought you seemed happy to be back."

Turning her great, deep hazel eyes full on her mother's face, Mary Cowper said, "Mama, I love Etowah Cliffs more than I'll ever love any other spot on earth! Even after we're in Vienna with Papa, no matter how many beautiful foreign places I see, I'll never love any place the way I love it here. I just thought I'd like to—visit in Savannah . . ."

Eliza Anne knew her daughter did love Etowah Cliffs, had watched her riding her horse in its shadowy woods, enjoying countless picnics with her brothers and Natalie on the high river cliffs and surely, her supple young body swam the clear river expertly.

Most girls, she supposed, grew restless at her age. I must expect it of Mary Cowper too, she told herself a few minutes later as she undressed in the lonely master bedroom upstairs.

Settling her weary body between the new sheets Fat Sinai had just hemmed, Eliza Anne longed for Mary Cowper's father more keenly than on any other night since he'd gone away. "Come back for us soon, W.H.," she whispered into the darkened room. "Please don't keep me waiting too much longer. I need you. I not only need your arms around me, I need Mary Cowper's father close by. She's growing up so fast! I don't think I'd realized it until—tonight. She's fond of my mother and sisters, but they aren't the reason she wants to go to Savannah. Oh, my darling, I wish I thought they were the reason!"

Punching her bolster to softness, she turned over, one hand reaching toward his empty side of the bed. "If you were here, dearest, and if you were fretting as I am over our daughter's restlessness, I'd laugh at you and insist your worry was groundless. Well, *mine isn't groundless.* I shan't add to your heavy burdens over there even by hinting at it in a letter, but, W.H., tonight I'm suddenly very concerned about Mary Cowper and I'm ashamed for being. She's as amiable and sweet-tempered as ever—causes no trouble at all, demands nothing of me which I can't easily and gladly give . . . Still, I felt so far away from her downstairs just now. For the first time, beloved, some strange, vast, nameless void is stretching between our daughter and me."

"Forgive me, Lord," she prayed, "for talking more to my absent husband than to You. And please give me peace over whatever is causing my daughter's restlessness!"

Turned on her other side for sleep now—in the exact position she'd always found for W.H. to hold her spoon fashion—she waited for the peace for which she'd prayed.

None came.

Chapter 50

FOR THE first time in her daughter's life, Eliza Anne felt that Mary Cowper was avoiding time alone with her. The feeling was so painful that only today, on this bright early October morning just one week before Mary Cowper was to leave for school, had she admitted it even to herself. Taking the shortcut to Natalie's newly finished cottage, she hurried through the little grove past the Latimer baby's grave—an old grave now, the earth settled and sunken. Natalie had decorated it today, she noticed as she passed, with sprays of the first yellow and crimson autumn leaves.

In every letter to W.H., Eliza Anne invariably urged him to remember to pray and to believe God listens. She was praying a lot these days herself, pouring out her laments to God because Mary Cowper was so obviously spending more time with Natalie than with her own mother. As she so doggedly kept promising W.H., she also told herself that God heard her prayers, but where was the peace for which she begged? "Forgive me, Lord," she murmured as she came in sight of Natalie's freshly painted white cottage, "for not practicing what I preach to my poor husband! Thank You for the sale of the Savannah tracts and that Benjamin asked enough so that I had money to pay for our new machinery, but, Lord, I go right on worrying over Mary Cowper and I don't know why. She hasn't given me a single reason, so why do I feel so far away from her these days? The child is as sweet and docile as ever, but there's a kind of sadness in her lovely eyes when she looks at me, a kind of longing I don't understand at all. In one short week, she'll be gone again. All three of my children will be—gone, Lord, and without W.H., I'm terribly afraid . . ."

Before she reached Burke's perfectly built front steps—not at all sure why she was there—Eliza Anne heard Callie screaming in pain and Miss Lorah's gentle, cheerful voice trying to soothe her. With a shudder, she stopped on the porch, knowing perfectly well that Miss Lorah was at it again, applying scalding wet compresses, then slowly, gently, firmly working at the tiny, twisted foot, determined to do all she could to straighten it enough for the child to be able to walk someday.

For an instant, Eliza Anne thought of turning back, of not even knocking. Natalie, she knew, was as far from the house as possible. Twice before, Eliza

Anne had come upon the scene during what Lorah Plemmons called "the everyday straightening time" and understood so well why Miss Lorah had said that "Missy can't bear to hear her baby cry."

Still standing on the wide front porch, she decided to knock after all—for selfish reasons. I'll need Miss Lorah terribly when my children have all gone. The thought had struck for the first time. It was true. God knows, I'll need her. She knocked lightly and over the child's crying heard the woman call out, "That you, Mrs. Stiles? Come on in! Me an' Callie's just about through for today."

Eliza Anne stepped out of the sunlight into Natalie's cheerful parlor—its walls as yellow as the sun which pointed bright fingers at the twining green grape leaves in the linen Natalie had selected as slipcovers for the furniture which Burke himself had built. There were far more cottages similar to this one in the upcountry than mansions like her own would be someday, but Eliza Anne had never seen any house more livably decorated than Natalie's.

In the kitchen, she found Miss Lorah bending over a pallet on the kitchen table, giving what she called "the last push or two" on the baby's foot.

"Step over here, Mrs. Stiles," the woman said without looking up. "You think that little foot's some straighter than it was? Looks so to me." Speaking in her special Callie voice, Miss Lorah picked up the infant, who stopped crying almost the second she took her in her arms and began rubbing the tiny back. "We're going to dance a jig someday, aren't we, Callie?" she said, the contagious chuckle under her words. "Here, let Mrs. Stiles have a look at that foot. Show her how much better it is."

Eliza Anne dreaded these moments, since for the life of her she could see no change in the deformed foot. She examined it, though, and gave thanks because Miss Lorah's magic with children already had Callie smiling and making happy noises, the pain forgotten.

"If effort and determination will help," she said, "it wouldn't surprise me to see still more improvement, Miss Lorah. You haven't missed a day since she was two weeks old, have you?"

"Missed one," Miss Lorah said. "The morning Missy had a bad cold and couldn't go out in the rain. Missy just has to leave the house when Callie and I work."

"Where is Natalie, do you know?"

"With your pretty daughter somewhere. She bathed the baby, then high-tailed it out of here. Wouldn't surprise me if they went down by the river. Missy said your girl wanted to have a talk with her."

"I see," Eliza Anne said, frowning. "You didn't happen to hear Mary Cowper say *why* she wanted to talk with Natalie, did you?"

Lorah Plemmons was busily heating gruel for the baby, her back turned. "They whispered," she said over her shoulder. "You know how girls are. And I had my mind on Callie. I wouldn't worry if I was you, Mrs. Stiles, not about that daughter of yours. She's not only pretty as a picture, she's a good girl."

"Thank you," she said absently. "I'll certainly miss her when she's gone back to school next week."

"Missy's going to be mighty lonesome without her too, I can tell you." Mixing her Callie talk in with their conversation as she fed the baby, Miss Lorah asked, "Any word about your brother Jack lately? I don't know when I've liked anybody more. Hated to see him go back to Savannah. Poorly as he was, that young man could brighten up midnight."

"He's always been the entertainer in our family, and yes, Mother wrote last week that he's off to Florida again on an Army engineering mission."

"I declare," Miss Lorah said, wiping the baby's mouth with a soft bib. "Just what does that mean, do you reckon?"

"Honestly, this time I have no idea, but he lives and breathes the Army's Department of Engineers. He does everything from harbor surveys to bridge designs to drainage systems when a new fort is needed."

"A lot goes on out there in the world we're shut off from, doesn't it?" Miss Lorah asked with a faraway look in her eyes.

"Too much, I sometimes think. Still, I miss being a part of it as my husband and I were in Washington City. President Polk's wife is such a straitlaced lady, I'm sure social life in the capital has greatly calmed down by now, but it actually seems odd not to know *anything.*"

The easy, soft laughter came. "Might be just as well not to know. Sam was talking around here yesterday about how there might be a war with—was it Mexico?"

"I hope not! But President Polk is determined to keep on adding new western territory. He's trying to get sole possession of Oregon from the British, and Texas was annexed before we left Washington City."

"I reckon I heard something about that too. Even up here in the hills, as little as I ever get to town, a person can't help knowing about all the folks packing up and heading west. I guess there's a lot of empty land out there. But no land's worth shootin' and killin' over. Menfolks are hard to figure. Sam's eyes lit up like candles just hearin' rumor of war! The Lord said there'd always be wars and rumors of wars, though."

Her mind still on Mary Cowper, Eliza Anne changed the subject. "Are you sure you didn't overhear anything Natalie and my daughter might have said, Miss Lorah? Or would you tell me if you did?"

The chuckle underlay her response. "Don't know's I'd tell you or not, but I wouldn't lie to you. If I had heard a word they whispered, I'd just say that I did, and depending on what they said, I'd decide about telling on them."

As they sat side by side on Termination Rock—the stone formation that hung highest and farthest out over the winding Etowah River—Mary Cowper hugged Natalie comfortingly. Once more, she felt grown up and needed, because of Natalie's great sorrow over her crippled baby. Once more Natalie had turned to her for solace, and because of the new, tender experience in her own life, she longed more than ever to be Natalie's friend. Certainly she was able, as she had never been in her younger years, to understand an aching heart. Mary Cowper's own heart ached at every thought of Stewart Elliott, and thoughts of him crowded her mind day and night. While she had done her very best to comfort Natalie, waiting to confide this new ache of her own had not been easy. But her friend had needed to talk first.

As Natalie had rightly said, "No one but you and Burke ever expects me to cry and I *know* you understand me. You also love me just as much after I've cried. It's even better that I shed my tears with you than with Burke because his own dear heart is so broken over Callie's poor little foot."

They could hear the soft plash of the river below, and somewhere behind them in the tall trees that stood around the big new section of the Stiles house, a wren shouted. Natalie blew her nose, then smiled at her.

"Thank you for being you. Most girls your age just wouldn't have any idea what I'm going through. You do pray, don't you, that all the agony Miss Lorah puts her through every morning will help?"

"Oh, yes, yes, I do! And God hears our prayers too. He knows, Mama says, everything that's in our hearts even when we can't put it into words." Mary Cowper sighed. "I'm surely relieved that He does. I—I have a lot in my heart too, Natalie."

And then she began to tell her about the Montpelier tea dance she attended early last spring. It was the biggest affair of the whole year, and young men came from as far away as Roswell and Marietta to dance with the Montpelier girls and spend the night in the homes of various Macon people who had big houses. In detail, she described the new dress she wore. "Mama made up the pattern herself and, Natalie, it was beautiful! She isn't too good at actually cutting and sewing, but Big Sinai is and Mama stood right over her through every stitch. Mama and Aunt Kate bought the material in Savannah at Low's Emporium and you know what beautiful yard goods Andrew Low stocks. Well, because of my dark hair and fair skin, Aunt Kate picked out a clear bottle-green silk twill."

"Oh," Natalie said dreamily, "you must have been beautiful in bottle green."

"Yes, so I was told. And"—she giggled self-consciously—"it was my very first dress-up gown *without* those terrible bundly little-girl pantaloons!"

"Good for you," Natalie said with enthusiasm. "How well I remember when I escaped those things the first time. Come to think about it, I was about your age. Mama agreed to a floor-length blue silk for me—minus pantaloons —but she just barely agreed. You know how mothers are. 'Just not proper, my dear, to go without pantaloons in a floor-length dress until you're at least twelve!' " She shuddered. "I hope I'm never that dreary with Callie when she's old enough to—" Natalie stopped talking and looked out over the river.

"Don't think about that, please," Mary Cowper said in what she believed to be a quite grown-up voice. "Your little Callie's going to be able—to dance someday. Miss Lorah's seeing to that."

"Miss Lorah can do a lot of things," Natalie said slowly, "but that little foot is so twisted, I—I wonder if she'll ever even walk right—without a limp." Quickly lightening her voice, she demanded, "Now, go on, tell me more about this big social event. I can picture you—looking like a dream—but I'm sure there's a far more important part to the story." Peering straight into the young girl's eyes, she asked, "You fell in love that day, didn't you?"

Mary C.'s mouth fell open. "Natalie, how did you know? Does it show? Do I look different? Oh, I feel so different! But I'd die if Mama caught on."

"Why, for goodness' sake? Mothers have to let us grow up eventually, don't they?"

"I suppose so, but—my mother is so, so—"

"Strict? All mothers are. Scold me good if I get that way, will you promise? You see, my Callie's going to be a real beauty. Even if she limps, she'll be so desirable she'll stop men's hearts. Burke says I do. Do you know he still says that about me and I'm an old woman of twenty-five? Who is it, Mary C.? What's the name of this lucky young man with whom you're head over heels in love?"

Mary Cowper took a deep, deep breath and whispered, "Daniel Stewart Elliott!"

"Well, tell me about him. What does he look like? Is he handsome? Where does he live? Will your parents approve his family connections or are you going to have to fight for him the way I had to fight to marry Burke?"

"Oh, my," Mary Cowper gasped, "nothing's been said about getting married, Natalie!"

"Something will be, don't worry. Is he in love with you?"

"He claims to be. And I *should* believe him, shouldn't I? Even though I can't imagine a nineteen-year-old gentleman falling in love with a—mere girl of not quite fourteen!"

"I don't see anything strange about that. Burke's eight years older than I. Years only matter to parents, and when you're truly, truly in love so that you can't breathe without your loved one, Mary C., parents *just don't count!*"

"You—you still think that, Natalie, at twenty-five?"

"I don't just think it, I know it. Where's Daniel from?"

"Oh, he doesn't go by the name of Daniel, people call him Stewart—his middle name. And he's from Roswell. He was born in Liberty County down on the coast near Savannah, but his father, who was a United States senator, died just before Stewart was born. His mother married a Bulloch and moved to Roswell, Georgia, where Stewart grew up."

"How does he earn a living or does he yet?"

"I—don't really know that. He just lives at home, I guess, with his mother and stepfather, Mr. James Stephens Bulloch, who thinks Stewart should leave and begin to earn his own way. From a few things he said to me while we were dancing and once when we had a good talk alone on the school porch, he hinted, laughing of course—he laughs a lot and jokes a lot—but he sort of hinted that one of the reasons he felt drawn to me was that, unlike his stepfather, I seemed to want him around. And I do! Oh, Natalie, I do want Stewart with me all the time. Am I too young to know that?"

"Of course not! Don't forget William Mackay's Virginia knew she was in love with old William when she was only about eleven."

"That's right, isn't it? I'm going to tuck that away to tell Mama if I ever need to—convince her."

"Why should you have to convince her of anything once you're a little older? My advice would be not to tell her even his name for a year or two, but Miss Lib's strong on good family and he's from a good family. His father was a United States senator, wasn't he? Certainly the Bullochs of Savannah are of the elite. Even elite enough for Miss Lib."

"And Stewart was named for his grandfather General Daniel Stewart, who was a Revolutionary War hero!"

"Then you haven't a thing to worry about—providing, that is, that he stays in love with you long enough for you to be marriageable."

"Natalie—there's one thing about him Mama won't like much."

"Won't she think him handsome enough for you?"

"Oh, yes! He's tall and broad-shouldered—and has brown wavy hair and the bluest eyes, but—well, I did notice that he kept excusing himself with two other gentlemen who disappeared with him for just a minute or so behind a screen of potted palms the school put up for decoration and—and—when he rejoined me, he smelled pretty much of what I think was maybe—brandy."

"Did he get actually drunk?"

"No, not drunk. Just more and more fun to be with. Natalie, Stewart is really dashing and entertaining. He's something like Captain Jack Mackay used to be before he got sick."

"Where is Stewart now? Will you see him again, do you think, when school starts again next week?"

"Oh, I hope so! If you promise by crossing your heart not to tell, there is something else."

Natalie crossed her heart. "What?"

"He's written two letters to me this summer. And he sent me the most beautiful oriental lace fan on mother-of-pearl sticks you ever saw in your whole life!"

"Does Miss Lib know that?"

"Oh, no!" She giggled again. "I—I bribed Sam when I first came home this past summer with three of my best Indian arrowheads not to tell a living soul if he found a letter for me when he went for our mail in Cassville. Thank heaven, the bribe was enough to make him slip me both letters and the package from Savannah with the gorgeous fan."

Natalie stared at her in amazement. "You've kept all this only to yourself— *all summer?*"

Mary Cowper nodded. "It was awfully hard, but I had to."

"Did you say the fan was mailed from Savannah?"

"Stewart's been there for almost two months having a great time with old friends, according to his last letter. I tried to get Mama to take my brothers and me to visit Grandmother Mackay, but she had too much to do here to leave. I also thought of asking you to take Callie for a visit with your parents. Mama would have let me go with you. But I soon saw Callie needed Miss Lorah's 'straightening time' every day, so I didn't ask you." Mary Cowper sighed deeply. "Now, of course, it's too late. I have to go back to school. Oh, Natalie, what worries me is that as soon as Papa can get leave from his diplomatic duties in Vienna, he's coming for us, and then I'll be a whole ocean and a continent away from Stewart!"

Natalie, who almost never hugged anyone but Burke and her baby, embraced her. "You're quite grown up, Mary Cowper," she said solemnly. "You really are. I promise you'll grow up even more during the years just ahead when you're so far away from him. I know something about that, believe me. There were times I thought I'd die alone in my bed at night in Savannah before I finally got Papa to take me to find Burke again after the shipwreck. You'll *know* off in Vienna that you're surely going to die. But I promise you won't. Love keeps a woman alive. And if it's any help, don't forget for one minute that I'm here—I'll always be here thinking, thinking of ways to handle your mother and father if, for any reason, they don't approve of Stewart. In the meantime, keep loving him, *keep believing things will work out.* Just as soon as you're back at Montpelier, write and urge him to make the trip from Roswell to Macon again to see you."

"I suppose he will go home to his stepfather's house in Roswell soon," Mary C. said tentatively.

"You'll just have to write to him there and find out. His mother will surely forward your letter to Savannah if he decides to stay there and work."

"I don't think he'll do that," Mary Cowper said with an almost embarrassed smile. "Stewart says there's only one thing he hates more than being away from me and that's the idea of ever going to work!"

Chapter 51

MARY Cowper was far less conscientious about writing home during Eliza Anne's lonely months at the end of 1845 and into 1846 than she had been while she and W.H. were in Washington City. When Eliza Anne mentioned the long silences to Miss Lorah, invariably she was told not to borrow trouble, and so Natalie heard most of her complaints.

"Miss Lib, you're getting forgetful," Natalie scolded one early April morning as the two walked in the Park waiting out Miss Lorah's "straightening time." "I tell you over and over and then you forget that writing is writing whether it's a letter home or a school paper and Mary C. does work hard to keep you happy with her marks."

"I know she does and I know how many times you've said that, Natalie. I'm not after sympathy and I doubt you feel any, since you never wrote to your parents in the old days. You're doing better now, though, aren't you?"

"I'm doing lots better, but so little happens up here that would interest my parents, I find I direct most of my letters to Mary, who misses the upcountry so much. Oh, she and Jonathan are more in love than ever and she's at least getting by, I guess, as a Savannah Browning. But she still writes to me asking if I've made soap yet or found a new stump of fat pine for my fires or how much apple butter I put up—things that really have to do with me now."

"Mark and Caroline want to know all those things too, I'm sure. You do tell them, don't you?"

"Of course I do. What else is there to tell? Making apple butter and soap are important events in my life. But it's usually Mary who answers my letters. Even Papa doesn't write as often as he used to."

"Darling, he's terribly distressed, I know, about your mother. He could have hired someone to nurse her, but my hunch is that Mary is actually relieved to be the one to look after Caroline. It gives her the best possible excuse to stay out of Savannah society and it holds down gossip about her—Indianness. People have little choice but to think her noble to be so devoted to your mother's needs."

Natalie laughed. "Good for Mary, I say!"

Natalie broke off a switch of tender pinkish-green sassafras and handed

Eliza Anne part of it. "Every spring I think new sassafras tastes better than the spring before," she said, chewing and savoring the aromatic leaves.

They walked along for a time in the brisk, cool April sunlight, then Natalie asked, "Miss Lib, can you see that Callie's foot is really improved? Tell me the truth."

Knowing better than to hesitate, Eliza Anne said quickly, "Yes, I'm sure it's changed some. She's certainly trying to stand up alone and Miss Lorah doesn't pamper her. She lets her try."

Natalie was quiet for a long time. "She—she's going to limp. I'm—struggling to reconcile myself to that. Even Miss Lorah says her 'straightening time' won't help much from now on. Callie will be two this summer."

"I know, and that's certainly time for her to be walking on her own, but her little bones and muscles will go right on growing for years. I don't think Miss Lorah means to stop trying to help."

"Of course she doesn't. And Callie's spirit is so sturdy. I know, limping or not, she'll be a far better woman than her mother." Natalie stopped walking to look straight at her. "Miss Lib, how will she ever wear—shoes?" Tears came in a rush and she turned away to add, "Young girls like pretty slippers to match their dresses!"

Eliza Anne embraced her, but Natalie pulled away. "Your mother is awfully pleased that you named your little girl Caroline," she said lamely. "I'm not sure she likes the nickname Callie much, but—"

"Well, I do!"

"So do I," Eliza Anne agreed, her heart reaching toward her young friend.

"Let's change the subject," Natalie said flatly.

"Fine. What would you like to talk about?"

"Do you think there'll be a war with Mexico? Burke's dead set against it and he's terribly wise by instinct—like Miss Lorah. You're married to one, but can you tell me why politicians think war solves *anything?*"

"It solved our need for independence from Great Britain."

"I knew you'd say that! But that's—history. I don't think Burke *can* enlist feeling as strongly as he does that Texas's silly old boundary line can be settled by negotiations. And I know I'd refuse to allow him to. I'd refuse to allow Burke to go to any war!"

Eliza Anne laughed drily. "I doubt even you could manage that. Yes, I think we could go to war with Mexico. We already have troops under General Zachary Taylor encamped at Corpus Christi just waiting for orders. I had a long letter from Robert Lee yesterday. I meant to bring it for you to read."

"I don't care to, thanks. Captain Lee is probably like all the rest—itching to settle things with guns."

"He is not! If there is trouble, he hopes for a promotion so that his small private income can be used for his children's education, leaving his Army pay for their livelihood, but Robert Lee trusts politicians no more than my brother Jack. Of course, Lee will go if he's ordered, but he's not—absolutely *not* in favor of adding any territory through bloodshed. There isn't only

danger of a war with Mexico over the Texas boundary, Natalie, we could get
into another one with Britain over Oregon."

"I don't believe that!"

"You forget W.H. and I know President Polk and he's dead set on acquir-
ing all of California and Oregon."

"I don't like politicians or soldiers." She laughed at herself. "Well, except
Uncle W.H. and Jack Mackay."

"I can see you don't believe me, but Lee isn't the only military man against
a war with Mexico. He vows Colonel Ethan Allen Hitchcock is against it and
so is young Lieutenant Ulysses Grant." She sighed. "It doesn't matter, of
course, whether military men agree or disagree. They go where they're ordered."

"Well, Burke won't!"

"The threat of war doesn't only affect soldiers. Poor W.H. is over in
Vienna trying vainly to get the attention of the President or someone in the
State Department long enough to grant him leave to come home for us. Just
the chance of war affects my darling husband way over there in Austria! It
affects our children—*me*. I can't even make plans. I can't even let the children
know how long they might be able to stay in school."

"At least Uncle W.H. won't have to fight."

"No, he's too important to the nation's European interests. But if there is a
war and the President refuses to grant him leave, he and I could be separated
for an even longer time and—Natalie, I don't think I could bear that . . ."

"If Burke were as far away as Uncle W.H., nothing—*nothing* would keep
me from going to him!" She stopped to look straight at Eliza Anne. "Miss
Lib, why don't you just go to him?"

"I'm afraid to cross the Atlantic without him! I'm not proud of myself but I
can't—I *won't* cross the ocean without my husband." When Natalie went on
looking at her, saying nothing, she added weakly, "I know what you and
Burke went through together on just a flimsy raft, but you were—*together*. I
don't want to die without W.H.!"

"You let him go without you. He's over there, isn't he?"

"I know how foolish I am. I also know you don't understand. Neither does
Mama. Or my sisters. Your parents don't understand either, but I won't go
without W.H.! We'll just have to pray there won't be a war anywhere—for
any reason . . ."

On the overcast, rainy Thursday morning of May 14, Eliza Anne sat at the
well-remembered old family heirloom desk which her mother had just sent to
Etowah Cliffs from Savannah. Her father had prized the superb secretary
built by the famous early American cabinetmaker J. Barry of Philadelphia,
and now, at Mama's insistence, it was hers—the centerpiece of the spacious
parlor. Writing paper, ink and a pen with a new steel nib lay on the handsome
desk before her as she went on staring out her high windows at the steady

silver-gray rain tapping down on the leaves of the newly transplated wild azalea bushes that circled the long veranda.

No words came. She was deeply touched, genuinely pleased that her mother had sent what they'd always called "Papa's desk," but overshadowing her pleasure was the dreadful news she had to write to Mama: W.H.'s request for leave to fetch her and the children to be with him in Vienna had been turned down. "Threat of an imminent war with Mexico precludes any such permission since your watchful eye on public opinion at the court there and throughout Europe will be of the utmost importance to us," the State Department had written to him in early April. W.H had copied the message for her to read word for word and then had come his torrent of pleas for her to take the boys and Mary Cowper out of school and bring them herself to join him. "I cannot face the thought of even this one night alone without you, beloved Lib. I do not command you, but from the depths of my lonely and needy heart, *I beg you* to come to me as soon as you can possibly collect the children and see to things at Etowah Cliffs."

She had known from Robert Lee's latest letter, which had reached her days before the Cassville *Pioneer* carried the story, that on March 28, General Taylor had marched his troops toward the Rio Grande, which the people of Texas, President Polk and all expansionists claimed to be the territory's southern boundary. Eliza Anne herself had been in the gallery of the Hall of Representatives when Congress voted for the annexation of Texas. She knew as well that Mexico had never accepted the claimed boundary as fact and to this day still contended that the Texas boundary was the Nueces River, northeast of the Rio Grande.

Twice, since she and W.H. had left Washington City, President Polk had sent diplomat John Slidell to Mexico to seek agreement on the Texas question and damages claimed by certain American citizens there. The memory of her recent walk in the Park with Natalie brought a sardonic smile. Eliza Anne had known then, of course, of the attempted negotiations by Slidell, but decided against bringing them up since Natalie would only scoff and not believe it. Still, Slidell had gone both times, offering to purchase both California, also a Mexican-owned province, and New Mexico. Twice he had met with failure. So when General Taylor's troops reached the Rio Grande, the Mexicans considered the advance an act of aggression and at the end of last month had sent Mexican troops across the Rio Grande into what Polk claimed to be United States land.

Ironically—irrelevantly, she thought of the day during their final weeks in Washington City when, to everyone's amazement, the first telegraph line had been put in operation between the capital and Baltimore, but on this rainy May morning, she had absolutely no way of finding out what was going on in Washington City, where people's very lives were constantly being juggled about. Undoubtedly, her mother and sisters in Savannah had learned far more than she, stuck away beside her river in the still sparsely settled Georgia upcountry. For all she knew, war might already have been declared!

Well, she thought, taking a deep breath, no matter, I still have to write to
Mama that W.H. can't leave his post in Vienna to come for us. That, in spite
of my vow never to do it, the children and I will be, after all, crossing the
frightening Atlantic without him!

Her terror had not diminished, but she was going. She'd been without
W.H. as long as her heart would allow. Pen in hand again, she began the
letter:

> Dear Mama, Because of the threat of war with Mexico,
> W.H. cannot come for us, and although still deathly afraid, I have
> decided to take the children and go to Vienna to be with him. War
> could have been declared by now, for all I know, but because I must
> wind up my affairs here, collect the children from school and *try* to
> collect monies owed W.H., give long-range instructions to David
> Holder, etc., it will be fall before I can leave. We will visit you in
> Savannah, at present estimate, sometime in September, then on to
> New York to sail for Liverpool, where W.H. will meet us. Oh,
> William, I beg you to escort us *at least as far as New York!* I am
> distraught and would give almost anything for just one hour with
> my beloved Julia Barnsley . . . I still miss her terribly.

For all the rest of May, it rained so steadily that no one was able to ride to
Cassville until Monday, June 1. Sam left that day with Eliza Anne's letter to
Savannah and returned with a letter from her mother with the news that
because of the war now declared with Mexico, Jack had left for an Army
medical examination in New York to find out if he was well enough to fight.
In the same letter, she learned that Dr. and Mrs. Richard Wayne, just back
from a visit with Justice James Moore Wayne in Washington City, had
brought a personal message for Eliza Anne from President Polk himself. The
President, it seemed, was terribly disappointed that she, Eliza Anne, had not
yet joined her husband in Vienna!

"The nerve of the man—President of the United States or not," she flared,
frustrated to be reading her letter alone with no one to share it. What her
mother quoted the President as saying next infuriated her still more: "If you
do not go at the earliest possible time, Mrs. Stiles, I will have to write an
order that you go, since I've been expecting you to be of enormous help to
your husband, whose days are crowded with the gathering and sending of
information to the State Department relevant to our continuing negotiations
with Great Britain over Oregon."

"I'm not his chargé d'affaires in Vienna!" she said aloud. "What right does
he have to order *me*, a private citizen?"

Rushing outside to pace up and down her veranda, she thought of W.H.'s
latest plea for her to come and grew more furious with Polk for overworking
her husband. W.H. contended that his friends in the diplomatic corps as well
as in the court of the Hapsburgs worried over his lack of exercise, due to so
many hours spent at his desk. She had already made her decision—*she was*

going, but not because she intended to contribute to any war effort and certainly not because of Polk's threat of issuing an order! She'd made up her mind to go even before her mother's announcement that, at the President's prodding, war had already been declared on May 12. Certainly, before his prodding of *her*. Did he and Mrs. Polk think she was a miracle worker? Her Virginia-born friend Sarah Polk certainly knew well the enormous responsibilities of operating a large plantation. Did she or her husband think Eliza Anne could just pack up and leave at a moment's notice. And why, she wondered, hadn't W.H. written more about the imminence of war with Mexico?

"Obviously," she told Burke and Natalie when, unable to stand another minute alone, she'd hurried to their cottage, "my dear husband avoided any war news that might further scare me off that ghastly transatlantic voyage. I'm sick and tired being treated like a—a child or a servant!"

"You are going, though, aren't you?" Natalie asked.

"Of course I'm going! But there is simply no way I can leave here before fall—and that's that."

"All right, then," Natalie said in her most mature manner, "do what you can exactly when you can get to it and no more. I've never believed in allowing people to make me feel guilty when they know little or nothing about what my life is like! Burke and I do know, Miss Lib, and we insist that you not let even the President make an old woman out of you by rushing you faster than you can manage. Isn't that right, Burke?"

"Exactly," he said. "Something tells me, Miss Lib, you're also anxious about your brother Captain Jack. Aren't you a little suspicious that maybe your mother, trying to protect you from still more problems, might be concealing just how sick he really is?"

Grateful for their understanding of *her* side of things, she rushed across the cottage parlor and hugged them both. "I am worried half sick about Jack, Burke. But if my own mother isn't telling me the truth, who will?"

"Could you write to your old friend Captain Robert Lee? Won't he be seeing Jack in New York when he goes for that Army medical exam? I think it would help if you knew for a fact that at least your brother won't have to fight."

"Oh, Burke, thank you! Yes. Yes, I'll write to him this evening before I go to bed. But *you're* not going to enlist, are you, Burke? I don't think I could bear it if you did."

"No, he is not," Natalie announced firmly.

With a broad smile, Burke merely nodded toward his wife. "You heard the answer, Miss Lib," he said. "And even if my lovely lady didn't forbid it, I wouldn't enlist. Maybe even Natalie couldn't sway me if I thought the country really needed me. It doesn't. North Georgia's quota of excited, eager enlisted men is already full to overflowing. Only so many go from any one area, you know. Don't fret about your place here. We'll both be on hand and you know we'll do our best to help Holder any way we can."

Her response from Lee to her letter, filled with rage that war had already been declared, came promptly, dated June 15, 1846. It was warm and sympathetic, with news of the birth of his seventh child, but did little to calm her anger over the war. It was Lee's opinion, although he surely intended to obey orders and go to Mexico, that the United States government had bullied Mexico and that Polk had gone barging ahead in order to fulfill a campaign promise to take the vast new western lands. Lee and his wife had traveled to New York to visit Jack in his hotel and had found him "looking ill and feeble." The results of the Army medical examinations were both good and bad. At least her brother would not be fighting in the war, for he had just been given a two-year medical leave from the Army!

Robert Lee would, of course, be leaving soon, but seemed pleased and relieved that on the very date of his letter to Eliza Anne, the treaty by which Britain relinquished its shared hold on Oregon had finally been signed. "Polk got all he wanted in Oregon," Lee wrote, "far more than I expected him to get without a war. One war at a time is more than enough, dear Eliza. We will *not* be fighting again with Great Britain. My own feelings concerning the war with Mexico are mingled with shame for our bullying tactics and some amazement at Polk, who evidently means to take possession of both California and New Mexico. I will, of course, carry out my assigned duties aggressively. En route, I plan to spend a precious few hours in Savannah at 75 East Broughton with your family, who remain so dear to my heart. How different it will be to sleep for even one night in my old room there no longer as a single, carefree young buck, but as an old married man, father of seven, husband of an ailing, but courageous wife—an old man heading for war. If only our ways could cross in that city of so much beauty, but discipline will win over my heart, and long before you arrive on your way to Vienna, I will be gone to Texas to join General John E. Wool, who is organizing a second army to reinforce my fourth cousin, 'Old Rough-and-Ready' Zachary Taylor, and his forces. My heart will lean heavily on your prayers for me, lovely Eliza . . ."

Lee's letter caused her to write her sisters: "This war is a terrible business! I can only be thankful my sons are as yet too young to fight. Already up here in this secluded area, signs abound, Burke says, of what I gather is the foolish national frenzy. Young men who have shot nothing more dangerous than a rabbit are enlisting in droves. I am fond of Sarah Polk, but in this instance, her husband is, in the name of patriotism and sweet reason, mingling the self-righteous wrath of the Old Testament with the enduring patience of the New —and the country is going to embrace his greed for more and more western lands and call it virtue! Were I not so devoted to all of you and my home here, I might only rejoice to be *leaving* the country!"

Chapter 52

IN LATE June the boys returned from Reverend Howard's academy just before it was moved to Charleston to become a girls' school, and Eliza Anne found them both changed. Robert, now nine, resembled his handsome grandfather, Robert Mackay, more than ever and still dreamed of pretty girls, but he'd filled out, as Natalie said, "so sturdily and so tall that except for his dark hair, he might have been Burke's son." Henry was even taller, but slender and blond like his father, and seemed far older than his twelve years. His light blue-gray eyes were even dreamier, his mother thought, than W.H.'s, and although Henry was still quick-tempered, had acquired an almost settled air.

"He's in love," Bobby declared, "with little old Cliffie Gordon and he's going to marry her, Mama—you wait and see. He's dumb to spoil his own fun that way and miss courting all the girls I plan to court before I get married!"

Eliza Anne was far more shocked by young Bobby's cavalier attitude than by his declaration that Henry considered himself still engaged. She dreaded the move to Vienna, but vowed to keep a close watch over both boys until they were safely with their father again. Mary Cowper was making the trip from Lamar Hall at the Montpelier school in the company of her closest friend, Anna Barnsley, who, at nearly seventeen, seemed as fond of Mary Cowper as Mary C. was of her. A teacher would accompany them as far as Woodlands. Anna and her oldest brother, Harold, were then to bring Mary Cowper straight to Etowah Cliffs by the Barnsley carriage.

When three and then four days passed with no sign of her daughter and friends, Eliza Anne, from the habit formed during her months alone, headed for Miss Lorah's cabin as soon as the boys went fishing.

"Looks to me like you're borrowing trouble again, Mrs. Stiles," Lorah Plemmons said, kneading bread dough. "You've got one of the sweetest girls a woman ever had. Your friends at Woodlands might have a lame horse or—"

"Godfrey Barnsley owns more than twenty fine horses," Eliza Anne interrupted. "It's more likely that my mother's longtime friend, the grandmother, Julia Scarbrough, simply didn't get them packed and organized for the trip here. Poor old Mrs. Scarbrough has been just a little off in her mind even before her daughter Julia died. Anna Barnsley wrote that her grandmother seemed almost too controlled when young Julia died. All she appeared to think about was that they must all have proper black mourning clothes. I don't see how Godfrey Barnsley can spend so much time in Liverpool and New Orleans with only his dotty mother-in-law in charge of that enormous estate and the children. Julia Scarbrough's a lovely lady and has certainly had more than her share of grief from deaths in the family, but—"

"That could well be why she didn't have the wherewithal to face losing her own daughter—your best friend. A person can grieve just so much, you know."

"I suppose so. Miss Lorah, do you think Sam could be trusted to ride at least partway over to Woodlands? Then, if he met them en route in the Barnsley carriage, he could ride on back here and put my mind at rest."

Miss Lorah looked up at her, not unpleasantly, just surprised. "Don't you trust your girl, Mrs. Stiles?"

"Oh, yes. Of course I trust her, but—"

"But what?"

"I didn't come here to be questioned," she said crossly. "I came for advice and help! I'm just so exhausted by all I've had to do to try to get us ready to leave, I—I—"

When Lorah Plemmons held out her arms, Eliza Anne fell into them and wept.

"None of my business," Miss Lorah said, leaving white flour streaks on the back of Eliza Anne's dark cotton housedress, "but Missy told me yesterday, I believe it was, that you'd done just fine so far. That you'd even collected some of the money owed your husband, borrowed a little more from her father, that you'd harvested your crops, that your brother William Mackay was aiming to run your brickyard in Savannah and see to its income . . ."

Pulling out of the woman's soothing arms, Eliza Anne dried her eyes and said in no uncertain terms that she did not appreciate even Natalie telling her private business.

When Lorah Plemmons only chuckled, she felt suddenly ashamed. Anyone —anyone could trust this woman with the most personal secret and Eliza Anne knew it well. "I know you don't gossip," she said. "I'm sorry. I'm just so tired. I'm bone tired, Miss Lorah."

"Course you are. You've got a mountain to move and Missy and Burke and I all know it." Smiling a little, she added, "I think even Sam knows it."

"Well, do you think he'd go on horseback to look for—"

A thud of hoofbeats, the unmistakable clatter of carriage wheels, the jangle of harness—young shouts and laughter—stopped her in mid-question.

"No need for Sam to go, I'd say."

"Miss Lorah, do you think that *could* be the Barnsley carriage?"

"Don't know what else it would be this time of day. Now, scoot! Missy and Burke'll beat you out there to meet 'em if you don't get a move on. Burke and Sam's working on your porch. Sounds to me like the team stopped over by your place."

Taking the shortcut through the little grove past the tiny grave, Eliza Anne, her heart pumping with joy at the thought of seeing Mary C. again, heard so much raucous laughter and shouting she wondered who on earth had come with her daughter and the Barnsley brother and sister.

Natalie, probably busy with her child at home, was nowhere in sight, nor was Burke.

Emerging from the grove, she had her first glimpse of Mary Cowper, dressed in light gray travel clothes which Eliza Anne had never before seen. And with her, his arm around her waist, stood a strange young man—head back, laughing uproariously!

Anna Barnsley, taller already than her late mother, was just jumping down from the carriage steps. Her brother Harold, staggering about, ignored her while he jerked at one spirited black horse of the four-spanned team. The young people hadn't yet seen Eliza Anne, but she was close enough to hear the strange young man clutching Mary Cowper shout something about "unfinished business before your old woman sees us." Then, shamelessly, he swept her daughter into his arms and kissed her full on the mouth!

"Mama's not old," she heard Mary C. protest as she pretended to struggle in his arms, glancing toward their house as though she hoped no one was watching. "You'll see, Stewart," the girl said, "Mama's not a bit old—and she's beautiful!"

The word "beautiful" was smothered by another long, passionate kiss, to which her only daughter now responded as though the two were absolutely alone in the whole wide world.

Eliza Anne stopped dead in her tracks and stared. A sudden tightness in her head and heart paralyzed her. She moved only when she heard Natalie call to Mary Cowper as she hurried along the river road, Callie in her arms. Nothing could erase what Eliza Anne had just seen, nothing could ease her pain, but at least she wouldn't be alone when she had to confront her daughter and the brash young man.

"Don't tell me, Mary C.," Natalie called out happily. "Don't tell me—I already know who he is! And I feel as though you don't even need to introduce us, except to be polite."

Natalie and Mary Cowper embraced and then, hidden, she hoped, behind a clump of sassafras trees, Eliza Anne listened as her daughter said, "Mrs. Burke Latimer, may I present my—my friend Mr. Daniel Stewart Elliott of Roswell, Georgia?"

The tall, too darkly handsome young man bowed elaborately over Natalie's hand, then, stumbling slightly, stepped back to encircle Mary Cowper's waist again.

Dear God, Eliza Anne breathed, I do believe he's drinking! What will I do, Lord? What will I say? What *should* I say? He's certainly not welcome here!

For a moment, the young people chatted among themselves, and after Anna whispered something to Mary Cowper that brought on a giggling spell, Eliza Anne knew she'd had enough. More than enough. Not one more minute could she tolerate such brazen conduct in the very yard of her own home. But what should she do? And then, the plan formed as though by decree from heaven: She would slip around through the peach grove, run inside and through her house, then appear as calmly as possible on the downstairs veranda to greet them. As she hurried through the library toward the front hall off the big parlor, she could almost hear Lorah Plemmons—*or* her own mother—remind her that losing her head at a time like this could do only harm.

Tucking a wisp of hair under her house cap, Eliza Anne appeared in what she hoped was a casual fashion on the veranda and waited for her daughter to embrace her, then introduce her to the bold, good-looking young man, who had to be several years Mary Cowper's senior.

With no excessive flourish at all, Steward Elliott bowed over Eliza Anne's hand and, in a rich, low voice showing no sign whatever that he'd been drinking, told her that although he'd expected beauty, he'd never imagined that even Mary Cowper's mother could be quite so lovely.

"But you see, Stewart, where Mary C. gets her beauty, don't you?" Natalie asked as though she and the Elliott boy were old friends.

"Indeed I do, Miss Natalie," he replied, looking about him at the summer-green woods, the winding river sparkling in the sun and the already impressive main house. "I must also say that never in all my nearly twenty years have I seen a more breathtaking spot! May I congratulate you upon your excellent taste, Mrs. Stiles?"

"Of course you may, sir," Eliza Anne said, a bit more coldly than she intended. "I—wasn't expecting an extra house guest, Mr. Elliott, but—you're"—she almost choked on the word—"welcome in our home." Deliberately, she turned to Anna Barnsley. "Your father's abroad, I know, Anna, my dear, but do tell me about your grandmother. Is she fairly well these days?"

Far more mature and poised than Eliza Anne remembered her, Anna said, "Fairly well for Grandmother, thank you. Wearing her dramatic black yet in my mother's memory, of course—being Grandmother—but yes, thank you, she's as well as usual."

"I'm afraid I still miss your mother terribly," Eliza Anne said, addressing both Anna and Harold Barnsley. "But you seem to be holding up beautifully. I—I must say I'm relieved to see you in a gay print dress, Anna, and—evidently quite cheerful." If this was unkind, she'd have to apologize later to Anna, whom she'd always thought sensitive and reserved, but who now dumbfounded her almost as much as the sight of her own daughter in the arms of a strange man whose name she'd only just learned.

"Mama believed in having a good time," Anna said. "You were so close to her, Miss Lib, you know she did. We held a big party in her memory at

Woodlands, which, of course, is why we're late arriving—and why Harold and Stewart and I must start right back home. Grandmother Scarbrough flies to pieces cleaning up after a party—can you believe that? After all the balls and 'Scarbrough blowouts' she and my late grandfather used to be famous for in Savannah!''

Eliza Anne stifled a gasp. "You're—going all the way back to Woodlands today, Anna?''

"It's summer—the days are long. We'll do fine if we can have our horses watered and tended right away, please?''

"Naturally," Eliza Anne said, just as Burke joined the group still standing in the dusty road.

More ill at ease than she'd remembered herself in years, Eliza Anne allowed Natalie proudly to introduce Callie and then her husband. The Barnsleys and Elliott exclaimed at Callie's beauty and ignored or didn't notice her foot. Burke, as always, brought the first comfortable feeling among them by his very naturalness with the three young people, none of whom he'd met before.

"My husband built Miss Lib's handsome house," Natalie said, handing the baby to Burke to hold. "Isn't he wonderful?''

"You actually built it with your own hands?" Stewart Elliott asked in blank amazement.

"With help from my hired hand, Sam, and some of the Stileses' people," Burke answered casually. "It's far from finished, as you can see. An extra brick wing is planned, but a fine house like this takes a lot of time as well as a lot of money.''

Burke whistled sharply on his fingers and turned the horses over to July when he came running from the stables.

"Can't you have a glass of sweet cider while you wait for the horses?" Eliza Anne asked. "Burke has also built quite comfortable porch furniture. Please come in.''

Free of the baby now, Natalie hurried along beside her as the others followed them onto the shaded veranda. "Listen to me, Miss Lib," she warned in a whisper, "you behave yourself! Stop this act of chilly courtesy! You're dragging poor Mary Cowper off to Austria in no time. Don't force her to rebel at the way you're acting with Stewart Elliott. Let her go with lovely memories, do you hear me?''

"But, Natalie, I think he's been drinking—and with my own eyes I saw him kiss her full on the lips!''

"Sh! I'm warning you. Someday when you're terribly, terribly sorry for the way you're behaving, don't say I didn't warn you.''

When the visitors from Woodlands had gone, Eliza Anne stood alone with her daughter on the veranda—in a panic of misery.

"Mama, I've explained it six times already and I'll do it once more because I love you so much. Stewart and Harold were not drinking, they were just still in the mood of the 'get drunk on love' game we'd been playing over the last five miles or so. I—I like Stewart, Mama. Ask Natalie. She knows all about it."

"You told Natalie and not your own mother?"

"I knew I didn't dare," Mary Cowper said, keeping her voice surprisingly steady. "I was barely twelve when I first knew how much he meant to me. Natalie knew—last year. And she understands it too."

"But you say he's nearly twenty years old!"

"Only six years my senior. Burke is eight years older than Natalie and anyway, what difference does age make? He's—he's so gallant and he really likes me, Mama. I know he does."

"The way he kissed you, I'd hope he's not playing another one of his drunken games!"

Tears welled in Mary Cowper's eyes. "He's gone, Mama. I—I don't know when I'll see him again, because we have to drag off to Europe after Papa, so I beg you not to make my heartache worse!"

"We are *not* dragging off to Europe after your father. We're going because we're his family and he needs us all beside him."

Wiping at her eyes with a handkerchief, Mary C. asked, "Are you dying inside to be with Papa again? Have you—died a million deaths here alone—with all of us gone? Especially Papa? Mama, how can you wait to be back in Papa's arms again?"

Her daughter was, overnight, no longer a child. For a long moment, Eliza Anne just stood there on her porch, trying to adjust her own heart, her own perspective. Too exhausted from her labors and anxieties of the past months, she found the adjustment impossible. Not trusting herself to utter one word, she did the only thing her heart commanded—she pulled Mary Cowper to her, sank into one of Burke's sturdy white porch chairs and held her daughter on her lap.

Together, neither knowing quite why the other felt so sad, they wept.

Chapter 53

AFTER spending ten days in Savannah with her family, Eliza Anne and the children, escorted by William, took the steamer *Southerner* for New York, where they all stopped over at the American Hotel until Monday, September 29, the departure date of the sturdy square-rigger that would take them to Liverpool.

Still in the New York harbor, she sat alone in the early afternoon on the sailing ship's broad deck, her mind whirling with images which had formed over the past talk-filled, hectic days since she'd said goodbye to the comparative quiet and beauty of her Etowah Cliffs house.

Goodbye for how long? she wondered, trying to settle herself down inside for the always dangerous voyage so that at least some of her dread of a crossing without W.H. would not distress the children. Dread of so much seemed to permeate her, in spite of her longing to be with her husband. She'd finally admitted to Mama that she deeply dreaded the ordeal of learning how to live in a foreign country—a strange, foreign city—in rooms she'd never even seen. Of course, it helped that W.H. liked Vienna and seemed to be comfortable in the larger new apartment he'd found for them. Certainly knowing that he would be meeting them in Liverpool helped enormously, but it would take several days at sea for her to calm down, to let go of her fear that she might never see her mother and sisters again or poor, ill Jack; that she might never again know the peace and intimacy and pride of ownership of her home on the river cliffs. Might indeed never see Natalie or Burke or Miss Lorah or little Callie again. There were, oh, there were many accidents at sea!

As the tugs began to move the ship slowly away from shore and out toward the open Atlantic, her children stood nearby at the railing, raptly watching the New York skyline grow farther and farther away—waving, along with the other excited passengers aboard, to people on shore whom they didn't know at all.

In the milling crowds along the wharf somewhere did stand her own dear brother William, from whom she'd had great difficulty parting. "I'd be taking you and the children all the way to Liverpool," he'd said, "if Jack weren't so sick. But Mama's expecting Dr. Arnold to prescribe a visit North for him any day. Kate will be along to help. But I'll have to go too."

"You will see that Sarah stays with Mother, won't you?" Eliza Anne had pressed him.

William's good laughter cheered her, since he so seldom really laughed. "No one will have to see that Sarah stays with Mama," he'd said. "She's never yet wanted to take a trip with me along."

"But Sarah really loves you," she'd protested.

"Of course she loves me. She just doesn't like me much."

The thought of an accident at sea had turned her mind to William, who, with the passing of the years, had to Eliza Anne become rather noble. How grateful they should all be that, with Jack so ill, William could continue as the family elder statesman and protector.

The big ship was so near the open sea now, only in her mind's eye could she still see William's tall figure, shoulders a bit more stooped with what she knew was continuing grief. Still, she was taking some of her brother's strength with her into the strange new life abroad.

How time and changing events scattered people who had loved one another for years! Eliza Anne had not seen her old friend Robert Lee in New York, of course, since he'd been fighting in Mexico for some time. But his wife, Mary Custis Lee, in spite of increasing pain from rheumatism had visited her at the American Hotel one afternoon. In an abrupt, rather unladylike gesture, Eliza Anne stretched her own legs out and flexed both arms in mid-air, thanking God that, unlike poor Mrs. Lee, she was in no pain.

"It's dreary, I know," Mary Lee had said, "but I haven't known a day without suffering in so long I've quite mercifully forgotten the pleasure of such a feeling." Eliza Anne was extremely fond of Mary Lee, in spite of what her brother Jack called "Mrs. Lee's rather slapdash appearance"—her careless dress, which to Eliza Anne bordered on slovenliness. One always knew where one stood, though, with Mary Lee. She was outspoken and, at times, sharp of tongue. She was also forgetful. "She will always forget everything that can be forgotten," Lee had laughed the last time they were all together at Arlington, but how he appreciated Mary's courage and kindness. Lee's heart would remain always with his plain, but remarkably artistic Mary, as hers would hold to W.H.'s heart forever. The feeling between Eliza Anne and Lee, which to her was a rare romantic attachment in their youth, now ran far deeper, and to it had been added genuine regard for his adoring wife. No one doubted that Mary Lee did adore her husband and that took a kind of Christian grace and faith, since most other women found Lee irresistible.

Even now, as the mother of seven children, Mary still struck Eliza Anne as being somehow uniquely alone. Lee's Army duties had accustomed her to loneliness through the years, but they had been peacetime years. In spite of her painting, her almost incessant reading and the care of the children, Mary Custis Lee today carried within her a new anxiety because Robert was now at war. *Perhaps because I've been so far from W.H. for so long,* Eliza Anne thought, I'm more aware of lonely anxiety. But at least W.H. was not on the front lines, and if God willed, she'd see him in two weeks or so.

The thought of aloneness turned her darting mind to quiet, aging, but even more appealing Mark Browning, who had been like a brother to her for most of her life. During the Savannah visit, Eliza Anne had made a point of finding time to be with both Mark and Caroline—together, yes, at family gatherings —but she'd seen them separately too. As always, they had both welcomed her straight into their deep, inner hearts. Caroline had not looked well at all. Beautiful as only dark-haired, graceful Caroline could be, Eliza Anne had found her far more frail, more helpless than she'd expected. "But you must believe that I am better," Caroline had insisted. "Eliza Anne, I am *not* going to sicken and die! I am not going to leave Mark alone if it's within my power to go on living."

Head back on the wooden deck chair, she breathed a prayer that Mark would not be left alone. Of course, Indian Mary and Jonathan lived at the Browning mansion on Reynolds Square these days, but— Eliza Anne cut herself off. "I must, I must, I must stop even thinking of Jonathan's wife as *Indian* Mary," she said aloud, hoping no one heard. The deck was not so deserted now that the ship had begun to move swiftly under the power of its wind-filled sails. Other passengers had begun to promenade up and down, past where she sat. The children, nowhere in sight, would join her soon, surely. Mary's always been Indian Mary to me and I'm ashamed of it, she thought, and vowed to try to break the habit now that Mary was Mrs. Jonathan Browning, wife of the Browning heir to more wealth than Eliza Anne could even conceive.

The odd marriage was working out far better than she'd expected, but plainly there had been little serious social embarrassment, no loss of prominent friends, only because Caroline's illness kept Mary at home—kept Caroline and Mark from attending social functions. "Mary should be going out more," Mark had told Eliza Anne, "but she refuses to leave Caroline's side for more than the time it takes her to market or go for short rides with Jonathan. She's helping Caroline in more ways than either of them knows," he declared. "Like you, Eliza Anne," Mark had told her, "Caroline was terrified that Savannah would never accept Mary." When Eliza Anne had asked if Savannah had indeed accepted her, Mark laughed. "Actually, it hasn't been necessary, and people with any fairness at all admire the girl for such devotion to her mother-in-law."

Eliza Anne hadn't said as much to Mark, but a not very Christian thought had crossed her mind: Mary Browning knows how to care for an ill person and doing so enables her to keep her own primitive social skirts clean!

With both Mark and Caroline, she'd found talk of Natalie's child hard. Caroline had characteristically gone straight to the subject—met it head-on: "Before we talk about another thing, Eliza Anne," she'd said, "tell me about little crippled Callie. You can't imagine how dreadfully guilty I am that my illness has kept Mark from seeing our only living grandchild. He won't go up there without me. I've never seen him so stubborn about anything. The child is over two years old and neither of us, thanks to my being so puny, has laid eyes on her!"

"Oh, Caroline, she's without a doubt the most beautiful little girl I've ever seen!"

Caroline stared at her. "More beautiful than your Mary Cowper was? More beautiful than—Natalie as a child?"

"I do believe she is. I honestly do."

"Of course, Mark and I know she has Burke's curly golden hair and that her eyes are now very like Mark's deep gray. But—what I have to know about Callie is—is—"

"Is—what?" Eliza Anne asked, trying to help.

"Does—does the child realize—she's different from other children? Mark longs to know this with all his heart! Now that he's brought it up to me, I also —need to find out."

Eliza Anne still remembered how long she'd waited to answer the poignant question. At last, she'd heard herself say, "Yes, Caroline, in her childlike way, she knows—but only because Burke told her."

"Natalie couldn't bring herself to tell her, could she?"

"Well, it really isn't—Natalie's way, you know. She's always pretended bad things don't happen and hopes everyone else will too."

"That's a polite way of saying that my daughter avoids ugliness when possible."

"But, Caroline, Natalie and Burke—just by being who they are and as they are—do so much for each other. They have so much to give each other. Burke is a real—protector. By explaining to Callie, in words she could grasp, that one of her little feet would always be—different, he protected her from shock in the future. He also protected Natalie against the day Callie would surely have asked her why one of her feet is turned backwards. The child now seems to take it almost for granted."

"Eliza Anne," Caroline whispered. "Is the child's foot—all the way backwards?"

"It was at birth. The forepart of her little foot, toes and all, was—inverted."

"Oh, why? Why?"

"I've asked God that question a hundred times," Eliza Anne had said.

"And you got no answer."

"I—I'm not so sure. Miss Lorah Plemmons has worked wonders. Oh, I think Callie will always limp some—her weight will have to fall mostly on the toes of that foot, but—"

"Talk to me about Miss Lorah, please. We were there such a short time with her. Natalie's tried to tell us in letters. She seems almost too good to be true."

"Where Natalie's needs are concerned, Lorah Plemmons is too good *not* to be true." And then Eliza Anne had talked and talked about Miss Lorah to

Caroline and, later on, to Mark. Both were so delighted with the way the persevering, lovable woman sounded, she wouldn't be at all surprised to learn that Mark had done some outlandishly generous thing in Mrs. Plemmons's behalf. He had asked Eliza Anne what he might do for her. "Anything, anything at all," he'd insisted. "Tell me something we can send Miss Lorah, please! What can I possibly do to let her know even a tiny measure of our gratitude? Money? New dresses? Could I have Burke build a nice cottage for her up there near Natalie?"

Remembering, Eliza Anne smiled a little as she raised her head to look around for the children. She was smiling because she hadn't been able to think of a single thing Lorah Plemmons needed or wanted. Oh, it would please Natalie no end for Burke to have a new house to build, but she honestly doubted that it mattered one way or another to Lorah Plemmons. A gift of money would only make her chuckle, since she'd always raised or made almost everything she had.

Suddenly, now, heading out to sea, she was having second thoughts. A new cottage for Miss Lorah could be just right. Mark might have hit on the one thing that would make those blue Plemmons eyes dance for joy. Miss Lorah loved keeping house.

During her talk alone with Mark, he had pressed Eliza Anne to tell him about Natalie and Callie.

"I can tell you honestly," she'd said, "that your daughter fully expects Callie to be so beautiful when she grows up that young men won't even notice her limp! And, Mark, Miss Lorah's daily 'straightening times,' painful as they've been for everyone, *have* helped. Natalie herself is fine. She's just right with Callie—never overprotects, lets the child try almost everything. And oh, she *is* an incredibly beautiful little girl!"

She smiled again, remembering that about that time in her talk with Mark, Henry and Cliffie Gordon had breezed into the room with the news that they'd just set their wedding date for ten years from that day—September 15, 1856! Eliza Anne had not been the first to know either, because they'd already broken their news to Cliffie's mother, Sarah Gordon. Eliza Anne could picture serious Sarah Gordon stifling a laugh.

She made no effort now to stifle her own at the sight of Henry, Bobby and Mary Cowper hurrying toward her along the wide deck with the news that they were going to have tea in the stateroom of a new shipboard friend.

When the children had gone off again, Mary Cowper occupied her thoughts. As usual, the child had asked, not once, but twice, if her mother would be all right on deck alone for another hour. Her daughter's attentiveness both relieved her and brought fresh pain. She's far too kind and good and sensitive to be allowed to fall in love with a devil-may-care young man like Stewart Elliott, she thought, and a little of her dread of learning to live in a foreign land faded a bit. At least, in Vienna, Mary C. would be safely away from the Elliott boy.

Eliza Anne had questioned a few prominent Savannah folk about Stewart

Elliott and her worst fears had seemed well founded. "He's from a good family," one old friend of the Mackays had told her, "but the boy himself is a wild buck. Charming and quite handsome, but he not only runs up gambling debts here in Savannah, he's been seen often at some of our most questionable taverns—usually drinking far too much!"

Her sigh was deep and she could feel the worry lines form between her eyes. "Stop it," she almost heard Miss Lorah order. "You're borrowing trouble again, Mrs. Stiles." And it was right at that moment that Eliza Anne vowed she would tell W.H. not one word about Mary Cowper's infatuation. W.H. adored his only daughter and heaven knew he had more than enough to worry about with his enormous burden of work for the State Department. He'll have even more work now, she thought, since we're at war with Mexico. Actually, she'd found a direct quotation from W.H. in an article in one of the New York papers in which he'd declared that while most of the European countries were on the side of the United States in its successful effort to obtain the Oregon Territory from Great Britain, almost no nation felt sympathy for America in its bullying of Mexico. She'd be unable to keep up with the progress of the war except through foreign news accounts from now on. Except for his dispatches from the federal government in Washington City, W.H. had only the foreign press to inform him.

The American shore was out of sight now. Only the heaving sea—its vastness fearful and unknown—surrounded her and her children. The big ship, its sails bowed by a good wind, moved her toward total strangeness except that she would be able, if God willed a safe crossing, to see W.H.'s dear face again—and feel, once more, the security of his arms.

Chapter 54

DURING the first months after her daughter and the children reached Vienna, Eliza Mackay felt almost as though she too were living in a foreign land. Oh, they had all seemed to settle in rather well, and considering how much writing Eliza Anne had to do for W.H., she'd done fine keeping her mother and sisters reasonably well informed about life so far away from home. At least every two weeks, a long letter had reached Savannah—at quite a sacrifice, Eliza knew—since her daughter had become W.H.'s right hand. It seemed to be terribly important that the State Department be apprised of European reaction to what had been the sticky Oregon question and, although Eliza Anne's letters scarcely mentioned the Mexican War, she must be writing equally long dispatches on the European reaction to developments in Mexico.

Eliza Mackay had never stopped missing her daughter and grandchildren since the day they'd all left Savannah to live in the upcountry, but having them in a foreign, faraway place like Austria left her with a sense of desolation right in her own home. Her own almost empty, lonely home. In the dreadful heat of last July, William and Kate had taken Jack North in one final effort to help him regain what might be left to him of health. Since then they had dragged the poor boy from pillar to post—from one resort to another, with so many doctors here and there—all, it seemed, holding differing opinions. She marveled at Jack's resilience. She marveled too that Kate seemed to bear up so well and to find time from nursing Jack to keep her informed of every small detail of their travels.

Of course she worried. What mother wouldn't worry? Even about William, who'd stuck by Kate as they all knew he'd do. But what an interruption in the normally steady flow of life the travels must be for William, who, as a rule, kept busy every day in Savannah, seeing to his own investments and to those of the Stileses. Nothing got done, even around the house, it seemed these days, because William wasn't there to see to it. She awoke thanking God, though, that Kate and William had their health, that her own was reasonably good for a woman nearing seventy. She admired her daughter Sarah, who went on trying to keep up with the elderly among their Savannah friends who meant so much to Eliza. She missed not being able to make as many calls as she always had.

Morning, noon and night, she prayed for Jack and took heart each time Kate wrote that he'd seemed to rally a little, that his sense of humor was still lively. But the days of late summer and early fall in the year 1847 dragged terribly. Oh, it helped—how it helped—that Caroline was improving so much. She and Mark were almost like young people again in their shared joy of being able to visit her together. Caroline didn't come every day, but Mark did, as he'd done for so many years, and on this bright, but chilly October morning, Eliza was waiting now for the familiar sound of his steps across her porch. He stayed longer these days because Jonathan was assuming more and more responsibility at his countinghouse. Even on the days when Caroline didn't come with him, Mark felt free to visit because Mary still seemed content to stay at home with Caroline.

The young Brownings had been married and living in Savannah now for nearly three years and the upheaval everyone had expected because Jonathan had married a half-Cherokee girl still only simmered beneath the surface of the city's society. Eliza Mackay felt a little amused by the bittersweet turn of events. She'd hated Caroline Browning's lingering illness, but in a way, God had redeemed it, because not only had Mary been there to care for her, no one had dared criticize the girl for excusing herself from social events.

She looked at her mantel clock, impatient for Mark's visit. It had come to be the bright spot in her long days, and often he brought a letter from Natalie or Kate or William or Eliza Anne. It was nearly 11 A.M. Sarah wouldn't be home from calling before noon. During the year past, minutes had come to matter in a whole new way to Eliza, because the minutes of her life were ticking away far too fast. She'd done what little mending she and Sarah needed done. She'd read the morning paper hours ago. Her eyes tired too quickly for much reading.

And then she heard Mark's steps and hurried to greet him at the door.

"You're looking lovely as always," he said, holding up a letter. "It's from Kate. I came as soon as I could get away. Caroline sends her love."

"She didn't feel well enough to come with you today?" she asked, patting his cheek as he closed the door against the cold wind.

"Yes, she feels remarkably well today," Mark said, seating her in her favorite rocker before the small fire. "So well, in fact, that she and Mary went shopping."

"Oh, Mark, that's glorious news! Dr. Waring must have been right about her anemia. That dreadful-tasting nearly raw liver must have helped."

"Something did. Caroline acts and looks more energetic than she has in years," he said, taking his usual place in Robert Mackay's old armchair across from her. "Here, read your letter from Kate. We both need to know how Jack's doing."

"Thank you, thank you, dear boy. What would I do without you?" she asked, breaking the blob of sealing wax. "Let's see now—Kate wrote this from West Point, New York. I thought they were still on Governors Island, didn't you? I didn't have it straight that they'd go to West Point for Jack's medical examination so soon. Kate wrote this on the fifth of October. 'Dear Mama and Everyone,' " she began to read, " 'We left Governors Island and our kind friends there, who cared for all three of us so sweetly, and were comfortably on board the steamboat before 3 P.M. on Wednesday. We reached West Point by seven. Jack bore the move very well, making jokes about his delight in going from place to place on a litter since he was a lazy man at heart. William hired a pleasant man to help carry Jack. We meet so many kind people everywhere we go up here, and upon our arrival, some Army officers called at once to see Jack and gave him the latest war news from Mexico, which he was eager to receive. Jack was told first of all that his friend Robert E. Lee was safe and well, although, as usual, I am vague about just where Lee is on the front.' "

"Our morning paper reports him at General Winfield Scott's right hand," Mark interrupted, "with our forces moving steadily toward Mexico City. You read that, didn't you, Miss Eliza?"

"Oh, yes. And I'm so proud of Robert, because, if you noticed, Mark, after the account of our dreadful losses, much of the article was taken up with quotations from General Scott in high praise of Lee's poise and genius with the difficult terrain. Lee does like Scott very much too. I guess he's been fond of the general since those early days at Fort Hamilton and in Washington City while Eliza Anne and W.H. were still there." She smiled. "In one of his typically joking letters to me some time ago, Lee wrote that he felt exalted that General Scott, who holds *himself* in such high esteem, should show favors to Robert."

Mark laughed. "The general's fond of luxury as well as himself, I hear. I wonder if his own musicians still move around the battlefields with him in Mexico, along with his grand easy chair. He had both during the Seminole Wars in Florida, you know."

"Oh, I'm sure he hasn't changed, but listen to this, Mark—'Mama, my wonderful brother Jack has just demanded to add the following note of his own: "The Army, my dear mother, is not Kate's forte and so I hasten to tell you (though penning this very slowly) that although he probably won't know of it yet, Lee has, as of 20 August, been brevetted Lieutenant Colonel Robert E. Lee and will, I'm sure, be written of widely as one of the real heroes of the Mexican War, which now looks as promising for our beloved country as my chances for recovery." ' "

Eliza looked up at Mark. "Dear boy, can you believe it? Jack wrote a few lines too! For the first time in weeks. He does seem to go on rallying, doesn't he? Even though"—a small frown came—"he invariably gets weaker again. Oh, pray for *my faith*, Mark! I don't love Jack any more than dear, faithful William, but he's always been the kind of cheerful boy for whom a mother's heart breaks. Will you please pray for—my faith?"

Mark looked at her a moment. "Why, of course, Miss Eliza, but you know I'm in the habit of leaning on your faith!"

"Well, don't," she said. "Don't lean on anyone's faith. I—I think Jack may die. I won't be prepared for it—not at all. Perhaps God is warning me, but whatever happens with Jack—with anyone we love, we dare not depend upon —anyone's faith. Only on God Himself."

Toward the end of Eliza Anne's first year in Vienna, she found a definite kind of satisfaction in her established routine as mother, wife and personal secretary to her husband. "I may know more than any other woman," she wrote her mother, "about the turmoil in the world—both in America and in Europe." Faithfully, she tried to keep her family back home abreast of at least the generalities of her work with W.H.'s dispatches, but she did not mention the fact that long ago she'd noticed her husband's odd lack of interest in the Mexican War. He had dispatched his diplomatic duties nobly during the dangerous days before the settlement of the affair with Great Britain over the Oregon Territory, but had, she felt, been strangely silent about the war with Mexico. In her heart, she felt she knew why. Most of Europe, including the highly respected newspapers, agreed that indeed the United States should end up with Oregon. W.H. had been able to send quite positive dispatches on that subject. Positive dispatches of goodwill toward the United States pleased President Polk and his Secretary of State, James Buchanan. With all his might, W.H. tried to please Washington, since, above all, he still longed to elevate his office as chargé to a full ministry. He could not honestly send encouraging messages concerning the war with Mexico because most European countries felt strongly that the United States was being overly militaristic on that front, and so W.H. had all but ignored the trouble with Mexico.

Finally, though, she noticed a change in her husband's tactics. The whole truth must eventually be told or W.H. would compromise his own integrity, which he considered impeccable. So, by late summer of 1847, he had begun using the word "patriotism" almost as profusely as the United States press was using it, hoping, she sensed, that since Polk loved patriotism, some of the negative tone of the European reaction might be muted. Her sister Sarah had written that Herman Melville, who certainly opposed the Mexican War, accused Americans of using the word "patriotism" far oftener than they understood it.

Eliza Anne and W.H. knew that all Americans did not favor war with Mexico, although most did and lived, it seemed, in a frenzy of patriotism. That Natalie and Burke opposed it she knew well from Natalie's fiery letters —so fiery at times, they brought a smile to Eliza Anne. Copying W.H.'s dispatches, which she went on doing day after day, brought an occasional smile too, but they also tugged at her heart. He was not, in her opinion, being ingenious at all in making frequent use of Polk's favorite word. W.H. was not tricky. Beyond serving his government, everything he did or thought or wrote had one personal goal: security, more luxurious care of her and the children. He was not being cunning in concentrating on what he felt would please President Polk. He was, by his own loftiest standard, merely being prudent.

Finally, late one night, copying a lengthy treatise to the Austrian court, she saw clearly that W.H. had given much detailed thought to the Mexican War in spite of the short shrift he'd given it in his American dispatches. Point by point, he laid out the causes of the successful three-pronged military campaign which the American armies had used. Halfway through the tedious work, she found herself hoping that what she copied would help make clear, at least to the Austrian government, not only that the United States had cause for invasion but that what W.H. had written would ultimately convince Metternich himself and improve the image of the American nation in his eyes. On the whole, she felt, her husband had done more than a reasonable piece of work in declaring that the United States had cause to invade Mexico because it had already annexed Texas. Claims against the Mexican government by Texan American citizens whose persons and properties had been injured during the frequent Mexican revolutions were, therefore, justifiable. Also justifiable was the earnest desire of the United States to acquire and protect California, a Mexican province, because many Americans were now settled there and the land might otherwise fall under British or even French rule.

Natalie and Burke were convinced that efforts to negotiate the entire Mexican problem had not truly been given a chance. Eliza Anne now strongly disagreed and, tired as she was, as she worked late on this November night in 1847, actually enjoyed reminding the Austrian government, in the long dispatch which was keeping her up, that President Polk's efforts toward a negotiated settlement had twice been refused by Mexico.

Eliza Anne's back and hand ached from writing, but her pride in W.H.'s succinct account of the threefold military campaign itself stiffened her spine. W.H. had made the United States actions clear. First, there had been the invasion by General Zachary Taylor to the mouth of the Rio Grand, then in July of last year the occupation of New Mexico and California, under the leadership of Captain John Frémont and Commander John Drake Sloat. Both territories had now declared independence from Mexico and had been declared part of the United States. Still, in spite of American victories, bloody as some had been, and the success of the naval blockade, Mexico refused to acknowledge defeat. Only then did the United States government decide to send an expedition under General Winfield Scott to end the fighting by capturing Mexico City itself.

Finished at last with the long, arduous copying, she undressed for bed feeling extraordinarily proud of her husband, who was still laboring in the next room at his own desk on yet another long dispatch. She had found W.H. at his most appealing early this morning when he'd handed her the long Metternich message to copy, because only then had W.H., in his most disarmingly boyish manner, made his confession: Because he knew Polk wouldn't like negative messages, he'd simply put off the whole issue of the Mexican

War until the last possible moment. As she crawled into bed now, she was smiling. She had seen no point in telling her husband that she'd known of his distaste for the Mexican War for months.

W.H. did revel in popular causes, and although he'd talked at length with her of his own dread of the burgeoning trouble he saw all around them in Europe, she knew he was not reluctant to write to Polk about that, since in no way was it the fault of the United States. He now knew Austrian affairs so well that he honestly feared the disintegration of the Empire should the problems in Vienna and across Europe expand, but being W.H., he'd actually relish his own wordy dispatches on Europe's problems. He was erudite and the dispatches proved it. In writing of European troubles, he had no need to avoid the ticklish subject of Polk's "patriotic" aggression. This was strictly Europe in trouble now. "The floodwaters of liberalism and nationalism have burst their restraining dikes and threaten to inundate most of Europe," he'd already written to Secretary of State Buchanan in mid-1847. Soon after his own arrival in Vienna, W.H. had seen that Metternich's Austria was a hotbed of repression and reaction—both reasons for revolution, but not in any way a slur on Polk policy. Austria was rising up against Metternich policy.

Still, she knew her husband greatly admired the aging, elegant Prince Metternich. While ever the democrat, desiring constitutional government above all else, W.H. found his personal dealings with the Prince pleasant and often said as much in his State Department reports—a fact which Eliza Anne thought might somewhat confuse Buchanan and his aides.

Longing for him to come to bed, she snuggled between the cold linens. Even when her head questioned W.H.'s opinion of events, her heart won because she trusted his final political decisions totally.

No one on the scene in Vienna in late 1847 could possibly doubt his contention that "almost the whole of Southern Europe appears now to be involved in the utmost disquietude." There were plots and counterplots in Italy, in France, in Poland and, of course, in Austria. No one doubted that, as the leading power in both the Holy Alliance and the German Confederation, W.H.'s Austria under Metternich dominated European politics. Certainly, Eliza Anne was not surprised that although he disagreed with Austrian repression, he hoped that Vienna would stay as it was. Diplomacy was a labyrinth!

In the midst of the growing confusion in Europe, Eliza Anne marveled that her husband's interest in all the various nationalities that made up the Austrian Empire remained intense, in spite of his widely divergent views of the various states. He ignored none simply because he happened to disagree, and day in and day out—night in and night out—he studied and mastered their differences.

She felt he kept his work palatable to himself by his adroit comparisons of European ways with American—always to the praise of America. In the Austrian state of Hungary, he found the "pitiable condition of Hungarian peasants," for example, "far, far worse than that of the Negro in the United States, for while the Hungarian peasant has double the labor, he is not so well supplied as the slave under the protection and care of a master whose interest *is* the Negro. Even should that master be a man of little feeling or principle, he will treat his slave with humanity and attention," W.H. wrote. Eliza Anne thought much along these lines too. In fact, she'd given it quite a lot of thought in New York even before they sailed, when she saw with her own eyes some of the dreadful conditions under which northern workers labored. And labor they did, even knowing that when they were too old to work, there was no one anywhere to care for them. Once useless to their employers, the poor folk were left to fend for themselves—quite unlike slaves, who were cared for from the cradle all the way to the grave.

As often happened, her thoughts went to Natalie's hired woman, Lorah Plemmons. She thought of Miss Lorah tonight, though, in a new way. What if Mark Browning hadn't been rich and kind? Probably Eliza Anne's next letter from Natalie would tell her that Burke and Sam had started the new cottage Mark was building for Miss Lorah. But what would Lorah Plemmons have done in her old age without Mark's largess? All the slaves she and W.H. owned would have food and shelter until the day they died. Except for Mark's generosity, Lorah Plemmons would have had to go it alone. Not once had Eliza Anne allowed herself to argue with either Burke or Mark over their stubborn refusal to own people, but they *were* stubborn and had they both been less warmhearted, they could be thought downright cruel.

Chapter 55

EARLY in the new year, 1848, just after Savannahians learned that the Mexican War had ended victoriously with the Treaty of Guadalupe Hidalgo, Eliza Mackay sat alone in her parlor, the pages of a long letter from her daughter in Vienna still on her lap. The letter had roused a nagging worry about W.H.'s love of extravagant things. Goodness knows, he had been born to the wealth of his father, Joseph Stiles, had grown up in plenty, and for years Eliza had kept her counsel on the subject of her son-in-law's continuing debts. Her daughter loved the man with all her heart, and a mother-in-law was required only to love and to be there when needed, not to interfere.

That Eliza Anne and W.H. lived beyond their means was nothing new. Nor was it all W.H.'s fault. From her own grandfather, John McQueen, Eliza Anne had obviously inherited her love of fine clothes, great acreages and costly possessions. If it seemed to Eliza Mackay at times that it was taking an unnecessarily long time to settle the vast estate of Joseph Stiles, she had only to remember how long it took her brother, John McQueen, Jr., to settle their own father's enormous East Florida estate. And, to be frank, once it was settled, Papa had, at the end, left them almost nothing but debts. Joseph Stiles had left both money and property. Evidently, she thought, not enough to satisfy W.H. and her daughter.

The letter from Vienna was certainly full of complaints over a lack of funds. Still, she knew, at least, that they were all well over there, that the children had a splendid tutor, "a pleasant and attractive and talented young man named Von Bohn, who," Eliza Anne wrote, "seems to like our boys and Mary Cowper as much as they like him." In detail, her daughter had given her Von Bohn's busy daily schedule with his charges and Eliza found herself hoping that such rigorous days spent only with youngsters would not overtire the young tutor so that he might resign. Nothing, Eliza knew, would give both her daughter and W.H. such peace of mind in the midst of the growing turmoil in Vienna as a good education for their children, including musical training, at which Von Bohn evidently excelled.

She thought again of her beloved father, called by his Spanish friends Don Juan McQueen—a name her mother hated, but which Eliza, as a girl, secretly loved. Papa had been misunderstood, it seemed, by everyone but his daughter. Were he still alive today, she'd experience the same old delight in playing the McQueen pianoforte for him for hours on end. She glanced now at the old instrument still in the front corner of her parlor and vowed she'd find the strength and limberness of fingers to play as much as he desired for her blessed Jack, who—at William's urging—would be coming home within the month to stay. Perhaps to die.

In her own heart, she had almost settled the inevitability of her once handsome, dashing son's death. She would grieve no less, maybe even the shock would be no less, but as best she could, she'd accepted what now seemed certain. As always, dear, wise William was right to bring Jack home. He and Kate had carried the poor boy about the country from West Point to Newport to New England and back to West Point and were now undoubtedly working at the always difficult arrangements for moving him once more on a litter from shore to ship and, finally, back to shore at home in Savannah.

She breathed a prayer for Jack now—her every breath had become a prayer for Jack—but she also prayed for William and Kate, exhausted, she knew, by their vain efforts to help their brother.

Wiping her eyes, she wondered if indeed Jack could live long enough to reach his beloved Savannah waterfront once more. Fresh tears came, and in order to check them she began to thank God that after all the years of skepticism and refusal to take anyone's beliefs very seriously, Jack had himself been able only last month to write that his own faith was now peacefully in Christ. If anything anywhere could give Eliza Mackay hope and rest from the years of anguish over her elder son, that did.

Shuffling again through the pages of Eliza Anne's letter, she hunted for a cheerful portion and found it in her daughter's colorful description of the peasants' dress as she watched them pass along the street under her apartment window. On another page was the story of an unusually pleasant afternoon spent in the company of Eliza Anne's closest Vienna friend, gentle, charming Baroness Ottilie von Goethe, daughter-in-law of the renowned German poet Goethe. "I went shopping with Baroness von Goethe to buy plates and dishes, etc.," Eliza Anne had written. "She has taken a house near us and I so enjoy her company—except for my heartbreak over her poor son Wolfgang, a young man now, but not at all right in his head and so melancholy that Ottilie cannot even introduce him to me. Still, he has taken a great fancy to Bobby and imagines that he must have looked just as Bobby looks when he, Wolf, was a boy. The Baroness gets misty-eyed when she tells me that poor Wolf begs her to inquire about Bobby's disposition since they look alike and Wolfgang worries that Bobby too will always be unhappy. I'll just say here, though, that my Bobby is the happiest of boys except when his tutor sends him away from the table to wash his dirty hands! Another thing that will interest you, Mama, is that Baroness Ottilie von Goethe herself has forever been fascinated by American Indians and once had a picture taken dressed as a squaw! A friend used to tease her by telling her that she would find an

Indian husband for her if she would only come to America. But that she could not possibly capture a real warrior without a tin kettle and a few trinkets. So armed, however, she could well succeed in being the future mistress of a log cabin or a wigwam. Ottilie's own father once scolded: 'Pray do not read me any more descriptions of log huts and American forests, Ottilie, for I really fear your enthusiasm for savage Indians will carry you there to look at what has been the dream of your young life!' "

Eliza Mackay felt certain that her daughter wasn't making fun of American Indians with her humorous story. At least, she hoped not. She'd always tried to warn all her children about making even careless fun of any of their Negroes or of Indians.

"The Baroness loves my Henry," Eliza Anne's letter went on, "and calls him 'my little ambassador.' Of course, Henry's father blushes, since more than anything poor W.H. still longs to be elevated to what Europeans call ambassadorship. Henry adores Ottilie, speaks rather fluent French with her and waits on her hand and foot. Knowing how you love Goethe's poetry, Mama, I felt you would find it interesting that, even though people have called the great man cold and heartless, Ottilie held him in deep affection and told him all her little girlhood secrets. Every afternoon when dinner was over, Goethe would have a large portfolio of fine paintings placed before him and would point out their beauties to her in tender detail. Ottilie grieves now that he is dead, that she did not show enough interest then because her young head was running with other pleasures. By the way, Mama, the Baroness, who speaks colorful English, vows that I am 'the kindest woman she has ever met.' I think the others could not have been much, but I know her gratitude is excited by my offer to let her poor son Wolfgang have our piano, which is the best in town. You know W.H. would buy only the best! Wolf, poor, sad soul, has no other amusement and is so fond of playing. We can find another quite good enough for practicing. My friend the Baroness is in some distress at not hearing from her other son, due to the growing disturbances all over Austria. She told me this when I went to the seamstress with her today for a lace collar to wear at a ball next week. The lace is point, bought in Paris and cost $130.00! I admired the lace, but what useless expense! I must say that my husband can easily equal it, though. W.H. came home from Innsbruck, alas, with a complete set of new crystal ware with our initials blown right into each piece! Still to arrive, he tells me, are at least two oxcarts filled with elaborate gilded mirrors and fine furniture for Etowah Cliffs. Wherever will we find a way to replace such expenditures?"

Eliza Mackay laid down the letter, not wanting to read again the long list that followed of still more of W.H.'s purchases, most of which would have to be stored in Vienna until the trouble was over and then expensively shipped back to Georgia. She sighed, feeling lonely and helpless. And just as she was wishing quite desperately for Sarah to return from afternoon calls—for someone, anyone to divert her from brooding over either W.H.'s taste or Jack's illness—she heard footsteps on her porch.

She hurried to the door and there stood Mark.

"Good news," he greeted her. "At least to me it is. Burke added a note to Natalie's letter saying that he's done about all he can do on the Stiles house until W.H. returns from Vienna and is now free to work for me. As soon as the ground thaws, he and Sam will lay the foundation for Miss Lorah's new cottage!"

"Dear boy, that is good news," she said, hooking her arm in his as they headed for her parlor. "But tell me, did Natalie give you any idea of Miss Lorah's reaction when she learned that you were building her a house of her own?"

Seating her, then standing with his back to the fire, Mark laughed. "Yes. Natalie said that, for an instant, Miss Lorah looked as though she could have knocked her over with a feather, then the lady began to laugh. When Natalie asked why, Miss Lorah declared that to have a house of her own again would probably turn out to be a good joke on her."

"A joke? Why on earth is it a joke, Mark?"

"Well, it seems that all these years since Miss Lorah's been keeping house for other people, she felt quite free, because it was the other people who had to see to repairs and new paint. Miss Lorah thinks it funny because from now on she'll have to do a lot more than—as she says—'a little sweeping and scrubbing.' "

"If I know you," Eliza said, "you'll see to it that her cottage will be kept in good shape."

He smiled. "So my daughter seems to have convinced her and"—his sensitive face grew solemn—"then, Natalie said, Miss Lorah stopped laughing and wept and wept for joy."

"Mark, how you do help other people! I'm so proud of you."

Ignoring that, he went on. "There's still better news, Miss Eliza. Lorah Plemmons's 'straightening times' with little Callie have worked at least a small miracle. The child can actually walk by herself, with no one holding her hand."

"Oh, you know how happy I am to hear that!"

"She can't really run, but she can walk—at a good clip too, Natalie says."

"I hate to ask, but—with a limp, I suppose?"

His smile faded. "Yes. I guess quite a decided one, but she cuts right along, even through the tangled woods up there, her weight quite well balanced on the toes of that foot. And"—the smile returned—"according to her mother, the child's more beautiful than ever."

"With your deep-set gray eyes and her father's golden curls."

"The beauty has to come from her mother and grandmother, though."

"Tell me, how does Caroline feel today? No bad effects from the small dinner party last night? Mary assured me yesterday that having just the Mercers and Habershams was not going to harm her one bit."

Shaking his head in near-wonder, Mark said softly, "Oh, Miss Eliza, Caroline's so much stronger. I think I can see a big difference every day. Almost no coughing at night anymore. It's—it's so wonderful sharing our bed again!"

"And you're able to sleep through the night now too?"

"Yes. Because she sleeps." He leaned above her rocker to hug her. "My blessed friend, what I wouldn't give if—if Jack could only show some improvement! I'd—give anything, *anything.*"

"I know that, dear boy. I know it so well."

"A letter from Vienna?" he asked, gesturing toward the sheaf of pages on her side table.

"A long one! Would you like to take it home to read to Caroline and Jonathan and Mary?"

"Yes, yes! Thank you," he said, reaching for the letter.

"Oh, wait, Mark. Let me find one place where Eliza Anne wrote somewhat jokingly of—Indians. I'll just point it out to you so that when you read it aloud, you can skip that part. I wouldn't have Mary hurt for anything!" As she searched through the closely written pages, she came upon a P.S. she hadn't noticed before. "Oh, dear," she gasped.

"What is it?"

"I must have missed this earlier. I'll read it to you. 'There is a sale at the palace here in Vienna today of the jewelry of Maria Louisa, and W.H. and Mary Cowper have gone there expecting to purchase some things. Merely as a memento, W.H. insists, of the wife of Napoleon Bonaparte.' Then Eliza Anne adds, 'Needless to say, I fear for our finances, weak enough at best.'" Eliza Mackay tried to smile. It was no use. "I fear for their finances too, Mark. W.H.'s good sense is canceled out so often by his love of beauty." She fell silent a moment. "For months, ever since I learned what my daughter did before she left, I've searched for just the right way to say this to you."

"Don't," he said quickly. "Not a word, Miss Eliza. It was my pleasure to have let Eliza Anne leave Savannah minus those newly discovered debts of W.H.'s at Etowah Cliffs. She was so brave trying to pay them all off herself." He laughed easily. "With the baggage she had in tow, I felt she did not need those debts to burden her too."

Chapter 56

RIDING alone in his new custom-built carriage, its shellacked leather body painted yellow with matching wheels, its lining pale blue English velvet, Mark's mood did not blend either with the cold, sunny late February day or with the beauty of the new carriage. Jupiter, driving proudly up front, had tried to cheer him, and Mark was pleased at Jupiter's pride and his obvious pleasure in the way the well-slung body handled. He was more than satisfied with the carriage itself, the first he'd had made locally by Savannah's Paul Scribbins, who had certainly proven that indeed he did make the finest gentleman's carriage this side of Philadelphia. But the handsome vehicle was not enough to lift Mark's mood today. He was on his way to get Miss Eliza and Sarah to take them to meet Jack's boat from the North for what could only be a sorrowful, emotional reunion. Miss Eliza felt in her bones that her soldier son was coming home to die because William and Kate were both convinced that there was no more hope from any northern doctor, from any more grueling visits to even one more cold-water spa.

The easy ride along Broughton Street did nothing to lift his spirits today for the simple reason that he so dreaded his own first sight of Jack Mackay's emaciated, mortally ill body, and try as he had, he could not conceive how Miss Eliza was going to face her own first glimpse of Jack at the cheerless, windy waterfront. Mark had always marveled at her strength. He counted on it today, no matter how deeply the first sight of her dying son shocked her. And William and Kate . . . both had to be worn to a frazzle after months of hauling poor Jack from one futile treatment to another. They would all need Miss Eliza's strength and certainly she had every right to expect Mark to be strong for her.

I'm not strong, he thought. I know I should be, but I'm not. Each new death of anyone I know—even slightly—brings back my sense of loss over old Sheftall. Didn't I expect the man to die eventually? he asked himself. Wasn't he well into his eighties? Didn't Sheftall live two or three decades longer than most men are allowed to live?

The facts helped not at all. Mark and Jonathan went on—even in the midst of their happiness that Caroline was so improved—missing Sheftall Sheftall. He and his son seemed to feel the old man's death more keenly than anyone else in town. Oh, the people of the city had certainly come out to honor its Revolutionary veteran's final trip along Savannah's shaded streets and squares. Georgia Hussars had escorted Sheftall to the Jewish cemetery and Mark himself had arranged for his own Chatham Light Artillery to fire the final impressive volley over his friend's grave. Sheftall had died in quiet and peace, after a long life, with his faithful Mordecai at his bedside. And right to the end he'd kept his mental agility. The emptiness Mark felt wasn't, he was sure, anything like the kind of grief they would all experience should once handsome, lively, cavalier Jack Mackay die in his early forties.

An unfulfilled life, he thought, cut off in its prime. Oh, Jack had thoroughly enjoyed living in the years when he'd known vigorous good health. No man loved literature more, or theater, or music—or beautiful ladies, but there had been no one lady for Jack to love and no one who loved him in return, so far as Mark knew. So far as anyone knew, for that matter. To Mark, a life without the love of one woman was an unfulfilled life.

Jupiter had begun to slow the carriage now in front of the Mackay house. Caroline had stayed at home today only because Mark insisted. She was well enough to be beside him, offering her strength to Miss Eliza and her children, but he meant to keep her well and Dr. Waring warned about cold wind and missing her regular afternoon nap. Caroline had agreed to stay at home, only to please him, he knew. She had felt fine today when he kissed her goodbye and that's what really mattered. Of course, Mary stayed too, refusing as always to leave Caroline, "just in case she needs me."

Striding up Miss Eliza's familiar brick walkway, Mark smiled to himself. Caroline really preferred to be alone with her new Emily Brontë novel, *Wuthering Heights,* he thought. I've never heard her praise a book the way she's praising this one. Jonathan was keeping to the office, of course, but Mark had tried to persuade him to come along. Just before Miss Eliza herself answered his knock, he admitted to himself that he'd wanted his son with him to bolster his own courage at the difficult reunion.

When Mark, Miss Eliza and Sarah were all settled in the carriage, a strange, unfamiliar silence hung about the three friends—a silence even Miss Eliza seemed unable to fill. Mark sat alone on one seat, facing the two ladies, and for one of the few times in his life, he avoided Miss Eliza's gaze. She kept trying to smile at him, but the sight of her anxious, pain-twisted face was almost more than he could bear.

"Caroline really wanted to come," he said clumsily. "I think she felt up to it too, but Dr. Waring's pretty insistent on that daily nap and—"

"Of course," Miss Eliza said, helping him. "Caroline just must not do one thing to set herself back—not now. Anyway," she added, pulling up the collar of her thick brown cloak, "it's too cold for her to risk having to stand on that—windy river—in case we have to wait for the boat."

Mark had seen the pain on the then younger, unlined features of his friend Eliza Mackay all those years ago when she learned of the death of her beloved husband, but in the long interim between that agonizing day and this, he'd never seen such anguish on her face as now. Miss Eliza was afraid. Afraid, as was Mark, of the first sight of Jack as a dying man. No. She's his mother, he thought. She's more afraid than I could possibly be.

"Caroline told me when I visited her yesterday," Sarah blessedly put in, "that she really hoped Mary would come with you today, Mark, since she's so engrossed in her new Brontë novel."

A small sense of relief pervaded the carriage. Desperately, they all needed the comfort of familiar small talk.

Miss Eliza was looking out the carriage window, but the anguish was still on her face and Mark couldn't quite tell whether tears or watery eyes from the cold, blowy day caused the glisten of moisture on her cheek.

"Well," Sarah went on nervously, "*Wuthering Heights* must be a good novel. Old William wrote that he's reading it too, which means, of course, he's been dull as dishwater for poor Jack and Kate. I know how William is when he sticks his nose in a book. I could clobber him. He just never looks up!"

"The way he looks after all of us, Sarah," Miss Eliza said, her voice firm, "William's the last person any one of us should want to clobber."

"Oh, Mama, I know he looks after everybody!" Sarah's nerves are ragged by now, Mark thought, and he pitied her. People all knew she loved Jack as much as she seemed at times to dislike William. "He looks after us all," Sarah went on, "and revels in every minute of it. Oh, Mama—"

When she broke off in midsentence, Miss Eliza laid a hand on her daughter's arm. "What is it, dear?"

"I—I wish I could stop chopping at William!"

"Then just stop it," her mother ordered softly.

Almost beseeching him, Sarah said, "I've tried, Mark! If Mama can't get it through her head by now, surely you know how I've tried all these years with William. My heart broke for him too when he lost his family, but even before that—when we were only children and you lived with us—there was a gulf between William and me. I'm sure you knew it then. I wish I *could* treat him differently, but he's rebuffed me so often that now if he makes any move to smooth things over, I can't begin to meet him halfway!"

Even if he could have thought of something to say, Mark felt it best to keep quiet. For a long moment, except for the refined rattle of the new carriage and the harness on the span of four, there was silence.

Finally, Miss Eliza said, "It might help, Sarah, if you realize that, in a short time, William could be the only brother you have left . . ."

Sarah almost screamed her protest: "Mama! None of us could bear to see Jack—die!"

"We may all have to—bear it, child."

"How can you even say such a thing?"

"God's grace, Sarah—and some thoughtful preparation by William, who's been right with Jack for all these months of moving him about the North from pillar to post. William's bathed his brother, shaved him, cut his nails, cleaned up after his hemorrhages. William warned me in a letter what to expect."

"I didn't even see that letter!"

"I know. I shared it only with Mark."

"Why?"

"Because I know how you adore Jack. I saw no reason for you to grieve in advance *if* God sees fit to take him. Forgive me, Sarah, if I did the wrong thing."

"God wouldn't do such a cruel thing. Mama, Jack won't be forty-two till June 1!"

"Your father was only forty-four, don't forget."

"But it isn't fair." Sarah was too near tears to do more than whisper now, but her whispers were bitter. "Old Sheftall Sheftall lived to be way up in his eighties! So few people did more than laugh at him and everyone thinks Jack is the most outstanding member of our family . . ."

"My dear child," Miss Eliza said firmly. "We're all heartbroken, but none of our heartbreak has a thing to do with dear old Mr. Sheftall. You must forgive Sarah, Mark. She knows how much you still miss our old friend."

"I know," he said, "I do still miss Sheftall. So does Jonathan—so does Caroline, but I know what Sarah means."

"Oh, Mark, I'm so sorry," Sarah said, only a bit more in control. "Caroline tells me how you all miss Sheftall—almost every time I see her." She straightened her shoulders. "But I've had more than enough of this—talk about people dying! I hate it. It scares me. Besides, Jack isn't dead yet! We're supposed to be on our way to give our sick brother—and poor, exhausted Kate and—*dear* William a real welcome home, aren't we?"

Mark saw Miss Eliza's look of pleased surprise. "Why, Sarah, I don't think I ever heard you call your brother '*dear* William' before."

"That's because I probably never did. Oh, Mama, I am so sorry. I'm going to try to do better. I am. I know you want me to and I know Jack, even though he always teases William and me for—spatting, really has yearned over us for years and years."

"Good girl," Miss Eliza said. "Jack doesn't need anything extra to bother him now."

"Can you forgive me for even bringing it up today?"

"Of course, darling. You're nervous. We all are. You've been honest about how you feel and I think we all need to be honest about this—homecoming. You know we'll all do our best to make it happy for Jack, but—there's no way on earth we won't all be tense and anxious until we've had at least a glimpse of—how he looks. He's lost more than forty pounds!"

Looking straight at her mother, Sarah asked, "Why do I seem more on edge than you and Mark?"

"We're all different. Just as William and Jack are different," Miss Eliza said in a quiet voice, her gaze turned now on the sparkling river, as Jupiter eased the carriage up to the boardwalk that led to the slip where the steamer, in a short while now, would discharge its passengers and baggage.

Obviously determined to conduct herself as normally as possible, Miss Eliza said as Mark helped her down from the carriage, "I'd think that good mountain air would do wonders for Caroline, Mark. Do you think you two will be taking the train up to see your grandchild any time soon?"

"I wouldn't be at all surprised," he answered, now helping Sarah to the street. "We haven't discussed going up yet, but once our travelers are settled in and—I know everyone at your house is all right, it might be a fine idea."

For more than an hour and a half, back in the carriage because of the northwest wind, they waited for the delayed steamer to ease carefully up the Savannah River from the sea, and although Miss Eliza made a valiant effort, conversation never became easy or natural. Mark pleaded with them to allow him to take them home, where they could at least wait in a warm room. Both refused point-blank. For the final, endless half hour or so, Sarah held her mother in her arms for warmth and, he fervently hoped, some small consolation.

Finally, its black smoke filling the blue winter sky, the steamer came in view around the familiar wide bend in the river and nothing would do Miss Eliza but they go back to the wharf—cold wind or no cold wind—just in case Jack might be able to see them in the crowd.

Once the boat had docked amidst the din of shouting stevedores, bells and whistles, the gangplank was put in place, and while the other passengers waited to disembark, Mark caught sight of two men carrying a litter. With them, a few steps behind, unmistakably, he spotted Kate, her bonnet askew, arms loaded with nursing equipment—towels, bottles, boxes.

One of the litter bearers was William, his shoulders more stooped, his lanky frame thinner. A steward, Mark assumed, bore the other end of the litter, although the emaciated form stretched on it under a pile of blankets could not have been heavy. As the litter moved slowly down the gangplank, they saw that only the shock of thick sandy hair in any way resembled Jack Mackay.

When Jack's white bony hand lifted weakly in what was intended to be a cheery salute, Miss Eliza broke into tears in Mark's arms.

After Mark and Jupiter had delivered the Mackays to their home and helped William carry Jack to the downstairs bed Miss Eliza and Sarah had readied for him in one end of the dining room, Mark said goodbye. In the carriage again, he asked Jupiter to take him straight home instead of to his office on Commerce Row. His heart was so heavy for his friends in the old house on Broughton Street, he needed Caroline, who would find a way to comfort him.

Mark had done his best to stay strong for Miss Eliza's sake, for Sarah and

Kate, for the Mackay brothers in their separate torments, but as he mounted the handsomely curving stair to their bedroom, his heart was like a rock.

"Jack's home," he said brokenly from the doorway.

"Thank goodness," she breathed, arms out to him. "I promise not to ask a lot of questions, darling. I can see it's all been terrible for you. Just sit here on the bed beside me and let me hold you."

Sinking into her arms, he murmured, "Caroline, Caroline, how can we ever be thankful enough that you—didn't have Jack's dreadful disease?" Voice breaking, he added with a shudder, "He's—he's no longer Jack! He's a —shadow. Wasted, pale, just skin and bones . . ."

Her hand kept smoothing the back of his head, smoothing it, smoothing it, as she whispered, "William and Kate—oh, I'm sure they're completely worn out from all that hard travel and constant care."

"They are. But in a way, I feel even sorrier for Miss Eliza and Sarah. Kate and William have been with him every day during these ghastly months. They've watched him fail. They said between spells Jack kept rallying, so that their hopes lifted, then—another of those dreadful hemorrhages and the coughing, coughing. But—Miss Eliza and Sarah had—such a shock. I— couldn't believe how—already *dead* he looked!"

"Does he talk? I mean, is there a hint of—the old Jack?"

"That's almost the worst part of it. At least, to me it was. The man tries, oh, how he tries to be—Jack. He even quoted a little Shakespeare when he greeted Sarah. And—" Mark tried to smile. "He seemed quite proud to be the one to tell us before our papers got the word that the great old man John Quincy Adams died the very day the three of them boarded the steamship in New York. Claimed he felt pretty proud to have outlived an old man like Adams." Mark sat up a little, looking down at her. "I hate to think of old Adams being gone, you know."

"I know you do," Caroline teased gently, "and, darling, there's no need to be careful with me about how much you admired Adams. Go ahead, say anything you want to in praise of the old curmudgeon who loathed all slave owners!"

"He *didn't* loathe slave owners!"

"He only loathed *slavery,*" she said along with him, definitely teasing, he now knew, in their familiar way.

"You do feel better, don't you?" he asked, pushing dark curls back from her forehead.

"I've been trying to convince you!"

"Well enough," he ventured, "for me to tell you that the prankster Jack Mackay also smuggled home a copy of the anonymous book old Adams's anti-slavery friend, Theodore Weld, did a few years ago?"

Caroline gasped, *"Slavery As It Is?* That rascal Jack! Army men are not one bit political, are they? Or maybe they can't help starting fights. *I hate that book.* Only Jack would have dared make a joke of it. Everyone in Savannah but you hates that book!"

"I haven't even read it," he said, "and neither have you!"

"I certainly have not, but I know what's in it. Those of us who own our people are even accused of neglecting them in their old age just to be rid of their care and maintenance! And that's a lie."

He touched her cheek. "It's certainly a lie where your people are concerned. But I refuse to turn this into an argument. I told you about the book Jack smuggled into town just to illustrate that—sick as he is—his capacity for fun and controversy still flourishes."

Her smile brought a rush of memories. It was the same bewitching smile she'd always given him when they waltzed as young people across the gleaming floor of the ballroom in the Scarbrough house in the old days. "You—you are—really yourself again, aren't you, dearest?" he asked, tears welling in his eyes. Tears of which he was not one bit ashamed.

"Yes, yes, I am," she said softly, wiping at his eyes. "I'm quite well enough, in fact, for us to visit Natalie almost anytime you say. You've been so patient with me. You haven't even mentioned going to the upcountry in months and months! I know how you long to see our grandchild. So do I. Oh, so do I. We'll be strangers to the child. All because of me. I'm quite well enough to go. Besides, we can take the train all the way to Cassville now. It was those horrid, jolting stages I hated so. Can we go, Mark—soon?"

"You may not believe this, but Miss Eliza asked me just before Jack's boat docked when we were going."

"Doesn't surprise me a bit. Do you know anyone who knows us both as that lady knows us? Now, tell me when to begin packing."

"If Dr. Waring agrees, we'll go as soon as Gerta and Mary can get you ready."

"I've already asked him. The good doctor says—anytime. I've already told Jonathan." Her eyes grew tender. "Mark, Mary—is good enough for Jonathan. She truly—is. Did you ever expect to hear me say that?"

"Yes," he answered simply, "I did."

"I need to confess to you that there were times, while I was so ill, that I thought she was staying so close by me—just in order to avoid Savannah society. Using me as her 'admirable' excuse. How can you love such a suspicious, cynical woman?"

"I had the same thoughts and you still love me."

"You really did?"

"Yes. Not for a long time, though. But I did have them."

"Thank you for telling me." After kissing his hand, she asked, "Won't Mary want to go to the upcountry with us? If Eliza Anne and W.H. in Vienna are so lonely for the river and the hills, think how homesick Mary must be!"

"Well, I see no reason why she can't go too, if Jonathan agrees."

"Do you mean to tell me you really think she'd leave Jonathan for even one night?"

He laughed. "If she wants to go. She'd have to."

"I see, sir."

"What do you see?"

"That the owner of the Browning Company is not going to allow his poor son to leave the 'sacred' business."

"Our son is an equal partner now. I'm not refusing him anything. I just think he would be the first to say that with New Orleans taking so much shipping away from Savannah—so much, in fact, that Godfrey Barnsley moved his offices to New Orleans—Savannah merchants have to stay on their toes."

"You *are* insisting that poor Jonathan not go with us."

"Not insisting—merely explaining." He kissed her forehead. "Ask Jonathan when he comes home for dinner. Whatever our son says, we'll do."

The light knock on the bedroom door made them both smile. "It's Mary," Caroline whispered. "Come to help me dress for dinner. Come in, Mary dear," she called.

Still curtsying in the small-girl way she'd learned at the Moravian school, Mary stepped inside, her smile, Mark thought, more appealing these days than ever. The smile sprang from happiness, he knew, now that she was married to his son and felt more at home with them all.

"Miss Maureen asked me to tell you dinner will be ready in half an hour, Miss Caroline," she said, twirling herself around the room so that the full, long blue-striped skirt stood out around her. "You like my new dress? I put it on to surprise Jonathan."

"I don't think you've stopped surprising him," Caroline said. "And your dress is lovely!"

"You're beautiful," Mark said. "I may have trouble getting my son back to work this afternoon."

Mary laughed. "You know my husband is—is a responsible merchant, Mr. Mark."

Mark still enjoyed Mary's pride when she glibly tossed off a once unfamiliar phrase. She had thoroughly relished "responsible merchant." Amused, he and Caroline watched Mary bustle about the room, selecting a light gray gown for Caroline, matching slippers—a lace-trimmed handkerchief. "You will be beautiful too, Miss Caroline," she murmured as she collected just the right bouffant petticoats for the gown she'd picked out. "Now, you will be a gentleman, Mr. Mark, and leave us while we dress Miss Caroline?"

"Not quite yet," he said. "First, I have a question for you. Your mother-in-law and I are going to the upcountry for a visit. Would you like to leave Jonathan in charge here and go with us?"

Instead of the happy, delighted look they'd both expected, Mary hung her head. "Oh, to see Natalie's little Callie—to see it all again beside the river—would be so good, but no, thank you very much. If Jonathan stays here, I will stay too. I would never, *never* leave him for even one day or night!"

Chapter 57

A T HER mother's desk in their Vienna apartment, Mary Cowper took advantage of time alone to write a letter to Uncle William Mackay, which she hoped to post before her family returned from shopping. "But we need everything, if we're to flee Vienna," her mother had argued at breakfast, "and we should all be along—you, especially, dear—so we don't forget something you might want to take." For once, Mary Cowper had gotten the upper hand over her mother by begging to be left alone to write to Anna Barnsley. So as not to tell an outright lie, she would try, if there was time, to finish at least a short note to her friend back in the Georgia upcountry, but the letter to Uncle William was all-important.

She hoped her handwriting had been improved by the many dispatches copied for Papa lately, giving Mama more time to spend with her friend the Baroness von Goethe before the Stileses left Vienna. Dipping the pen, she figured on at least an hour alone, unless the trouble in the streets was too bad today.

"13 March 1848," she wrote, and began the letter with "My dear uncle . . . What I have to write is a secret just between us. I'm sure Uncle Jack is far too ill to go out and, knowing I can trust you wholly, I have chosen you. Uncle Jack, even were he not dreadfully ill, might think my secret funny and spread it around town, which would break my heart. I know this comes as a surprise, but during my last year at the Montpelier school, I fell in love with a handsome and charming young gentleman named Daniel Stewart Elliott. He also loves me, but beyond that, nothing is as we so want it to be since Mama disliked him on sight, and for the nearly three years we've been in Vienna, has allowed me to receive only two letters from Stewart. He has, I know, sent many more. I'm sure Mama means me only well, but you also know how domineering my otherwise sweet mother can be . . ."

From the street below the window by which she sat, Mary Cowper heard a burst of raucous yelling and so many boots tromping by it sounded like thunder. Papa had sensed there would be a protest of some sort, but he was also certain it would not be violent. "The people may shout a little," he'd said, "and buck the barricades, but there will be Austrian troops at hand and little or no bloodshed." Trembling all over, she prayed her father was right.

Her nervousness, though, was not only because of the yelling in the streets. This was simply a terrible time to be trying to hurry with such an important letter.

"I want to please my parents, Uncle William," she wrote, "but I also know that you, of all people, realize I have to follow my heart. I may never have told you this, but since I was a small child, I have felt a bond between us, a loving bond, and so I am daring to ask a tremendous favor of you now. Stewart Elliott, Anna Barnsley writes, is in Savannah until the end of April. I do not know where he is staying, but Anna says he is often seen at the Savannah Gentlemen's Club gaming room. I know Mama thinks gambling is a terrible sin and I guess I would not be telling you that Stewart goes to the gaming room if I weren't desperate to get word to him. Could you, would you please try to find him and, *in private*, tell him that although our excellent tutor, von Bohn, fell in love with me and wanted to marry me, I have remained true to Stewart, and hope that one good thing, at least, might come from the awful revolt here in Vienna. That good thing would be our return to America so that I might find a way to see Stewart again. I will soon be the age Natalie was when she met Burke, sixteen, and through all the time we've been in Vienna, I have not forgotten Stewart for one minute. Papa says he will soon send us all away. Maybe to Gräfenberg in Austrian Silesia, because things are dangerous here, so please write to me at once about Stewart if you find him. I will be holding my breath until I hear from you. Remember, I trust you not to tell anyone about this letter. My heart pounds at the thought of what I have asked of you, but I can only try to stay calm while I wait.

"Mama grieves and so do I that damage might come to this beautiful city if, as Papa suspects, the Emperor flees the rabble. I do not understand why most of Europe seems to be in revolt, but Papa can explain when he has time to write. The cause seems to be, according to him, nationalism. Of course, we as Americans despise monarchies, but it is so sad to think that there could be killing and also destruction of the beautiful Vienna buildings which we have all come to love. Please keep this letter a secret if you love me. Yr. affectionate niece, Mary Cowper Stiles."

William found the letter from Vienna on his way home from seeing Mark and Caroline off on the Central of Georgia in early April and was relieved after reading it that he'd opened it before he reached the house. He read while standing on the corner of Bull and Bay, and began at once to lay his plans for finding young Elliott. It was too early in the morning to begin looking now, so he'd have to think of an excuse to leave the house again just before dark.

As he turned the corner at Broughton and Abercorn, a dry smile played at the corners of his mouth. He hadn't once thought of *not* keeping Mary C.'s secret! The past months had been so wearing, so tragic watching his brother sicken more and more that her secret romance somehow buoyed him. For the first time in a long time, he felt a little like he'd felt all those years ago when he'd decided to make the trip to north Georgia hoping to find Burke for Natalie. Oh, if Stewart Elliott turned out to be no good, he'd be the first to try to squelch the romance, but in his private thoughts, William had always imagined that his own little daughter, Delia, might have been as beautiful as Mary Cowper. In a way, he guessed, he was going to do his best for his niece, because he would surely have tried to see to little Delia's happiness, if he'd had the chance.

"We'll be a lot more comfortable at Etowah Cliffs in the new Stiles house than we were on our last visit," Mark said as he and Caroline lurched along in the wooden coach bound from Savannah to Marthasville, now being called Atlanta, where they'd change trains tomorrow for Cassville. "Not only will we sleep in the big master bedroom up there, you won't have to take a single jolting stage ride. Cassville's only a few miles by carriage and I've written to have one waiting. Excited?"

"You know I am," she said, "I feel well too. You must be relieved to hear that after all this time."

" 'Relieved' is too mild a word," he said, taking her hand. "I live these days on a kind of roseate cloud because I know you're better, darling. I think of it when I happen to wake up in the night—and first thing every morning. I love you more than I've ever loved you!"

She pressed closer to him on the hard, straight seat. "Do you really? After having only half a wife for so long?"

"I do, I do," he said, looking down into her face, grateful to see color in her cheeks. "Of all men, I'm the most blessed. You're well again, and Natalie is living the life she wanted above all others, no matter what we may think of it. Jonathan and Mary seem to enjoy each other more every day, we have a beautiful granddaughter to look forward to and—"

"Do you suppose Callie's really as beautiful as Natalie thinks she is?"

He laughed. "Our daughter's been known to exaggerate, but to us, the child will be all beauty. Wait and see."

"Oh, Mark," she said after a time, "my heart aches so for William, who will never have a grandchild. Not ever. I ache too for Eliza Anne and W.H., even with their children and his diplomatic successes, they're so far from home in such a dangerous place. Do you ever try to imagine the trouble and chaos all around us in the world?"

"And here we sit side by side—with everything."

"Yes. And I'm so eager to see the progress on Miss Lorah's new cottage. Natalie says the woman can almost not stay away from her house site long enough to get her work done. Miss Lorah must be so happy over what you're doing for her."

"I hope so," he said. "She deserves it."

"I wonder how I happened to marry the best man in the whole wide world?"

"Not the best, the luckiest."

For several minutes, they sat watching the piney woods move by, their darkness brightened here and there by new green of seedling gum trees. Then Mark said, "I hope we aren't selfish to be taking this trip now. I don't see that Jack is one bit improved since he came home. When I was there yesterday to say goodbye, he had another of those terrible hemorrhages. Darling, it was dreadful! I took Miss Eliza and Sarah out of the room, but poor Kate and William simply fell to, held Jack until the coughing and bleeding stopped, then set about rather routinely to clean him up still another time. I think Miss Eliza suffers almost as much for those two, for what they've been going through, as for Jack himself." He touched her hand to his lips. "And here you sit feeling well and looking more beautiful than ever before."

"Even with these black circles under my eyes? And my body skin and bones?"

"Those aren't black circles! They're merely violet beauty shadows, and don't forget, you've already put on nearly nine pounds."

"Will you love me when I'm old and fat?"

He laughed. "Will you love me when I'm old and lame?"

"How's your rheumatism today?" she asked. "You haven't said a word about your knee. Are you just being noble?"

"No, not noble—just glad to be away from the countinghouse and deliriously happy to be with you."

Because of his vow never to allow his mother to help clean up after a hemorrhage, William didn't leave the house for the Savannah Gentlemen's Club until after dark. Even then, he felt ashamed of his flimsy excuse that he needed some fresh air.

"Dear God in heaven," he begged as he headed toward Congress to try to find the Elliott boy, "can't You help us somehow? Can't You stop that coughing and bleeding? I think this was the worst one yet, Lord. How Jack goes on living, I don't know. How Mama stands watching it, only You know!"

As he climbed the steps to the entrance of the Gentlemen's Club, his mind went back to his boyhood when, once or twice, he'd come here with his father. William was not a member, but would have qualified because of family connections, had he cared for such things. He expected no problem getting in, since most of his business associates were members. He could simply identify himself, climb the wide, curving stair and head straight for the poker and pool room on the second floor, where scions of Savannah's prominent families gambled at cards and billiards and—because it seemed the only thing for gentlemen to do when they got together—also emptied glass after glass.

In his room before he left home, he'd glanced again at Mary C.'s pleading letter. Girl-like, she'd failed to give even a hint as to the actual appearance of her young man beyond the fact that he was handsome and charming. Inside the club, William was welcomed downstairs by several friends and acquaintances and, as he'd expected, was free to climb the stair and head for the loudest laughter and the most cigar smoke, the gaming room.

For several minutes, he stood in the doorway, looking from one flushed young face to another. Sons of many old friends stood together at the billiard table or sat around poker hands, smoke hanging so thick in the room that William rubbed his eyes. None of the fashionably dressed participants seemed to notice him and, as usual, he took his time and got his bearings before he went all the way inside.

Lithe, sharp-featured Tom Daniell, son of one of the city's most prominent physicians—ex-mayor Dr. William C. Daniell—stood behind a dark-haired young poker player whose back was to William. Young Tom stood there goading, as both Daniells were known to do. Young bucks such as these, with liquor controlling their tongues, often ended up across the river in South Carolina with dueling pistols pointed at each other the next day—when it was too late to recant. Young Tom Daniell's father, an able doctor, was known not only for his flaming states' rights political views but for prescribing hot pepper tea for bilious fever, and so was also known as "Old Doc Capsicum." He must feed his son Tom hot pepper tea, by the sound of things, William thought with a wry smile.

When the dark-haired player jumped up to admonish young Tom Daniell, William heard someone across the room shout, "Sit back down, Elliott, or you'll be sorry!" At once, William went directly to the fellow and asked his name. The question so surprised the boy that instead of pursuing the argument with Daniell he pulled William away from the table and asked his business.

"I'm not exactly sure," William said. "Is your name Stewart Elliott and do you know a young lady named Mary Cowper Stiles?"

Without a word, the young man took William's arm and led him outside into the corridor, where they could hear each other.

"Yes, I know her, and yes, I'm Stewart Elliott. Do you know Mary Cowper Stiles?"

"I ought to," William said. "She's my sister's child."

A somewhat devilish smile turned the corners of young Elliott's mouth up until his thick brown sideburns almost touched his carefully trimmed mustache. "So you're the bossy lady's brother, eh?"

"I'm William Mackay."

"Whose sister, Mrs. W.H. Stiles, definitely thinks I'm the dregs of the earth because she caught me kissing her lovely daughter. But that was a long time ago. Why are you here tonight, sir? Is Mary Cowper back in the United States?"

"No, her father's still chargé in Vienna. They're all over there—at least they were when the girl wrote her urgent letter to me. I have a message for you from my niece, written, I'd think, under some difficulty due to the insurgency in Austria. She may or may not still be in Vienna by the time I can get a letter back to her. She said if things got worse, her father would be sending the family away for safety reasons."

Laying a surprisingly gentle hand on William's arm, Stewart asked, his voice suddenly earnest, "The message, sir. You said Mary C. sent me a message!"

"She did. I—I'm not at all sure now that I should deliver it, but—"

"Tell me! I have to know! I still love her. Please? *Please*, Mr. Mackay?"

"All right. I do have to admit that your conduct somewhat justifies my sister's opinion of you, Elliott, but Mary Cowper trusts me and what she wants you to know is that she's been true to you and hopes her father might be forced, by the trouble in Europe, to come back to this country soon."

Elliott, William could plainly see, was tipsy, but when he sank back against the wall, the young man also showed enormous relief. "She's—really been true to me?"

"That's what she wrote and Mary Cowper's not one to lie."

"No," the boy said wonderingly. "She's so—so truly good and beautiful, I find I almost can't believe she even remembers me!"

"Well, she does all right. Mary Cowper took the trouble to tell me her parents had been compelled to let a fine tutor go when he fell head over heels in love with her. Because of you, the young tutor seemed to have left her unmoved." William held out his hand. "Well, that's it, Elliott. You have her message. I need to get on home."

Shaking William's hand energetically, Stewart Elliott thanked him again and again, and as though just making the connection, asked, "Your brother is Captain Jack Mackay, sir? The Army officer who's so terribly ill?"

"That's right. I don't like to leave him too long with only my mother and sisters and our aging servants."

"Please believe how sorry I am about Captain Mackay and accept my best wishes for his recovery."

"Thank you," William said, "but I've just about given up hoping for it. Good night to you, Elliott." With a wry grin, William added, "Take things a bit easy for the rest of the evening, all right?"

"Yes, sir! I certainly will. And thank you again. Please tell Miss Mary Cowper that I—love her more than ever and beg her to remain true to me!"

Brushing the crown of his beaver hat, William said he'd be sure to tell her, then couldn't help adding, "By the way, Elliott, my sister, Mrs. Stiles, is a warmhearted, fine lady. Just one word of caution, though—she's also very wise in many ways."

Mid-April found the whole Stiles family still in Vienna in spite of upheaval in the streets. Eliza Anne, in the diary she'd just begun to keep, wrote on April 14, 1848: "The Austrian Empire is experiencing not just one revolution but several in these months following the February revolution in Paris, details of which W.H. has just learned. The causes of our revolts here are so complicated it is doubtful that anyone has a clear understanding of what is actually happening. W.H. and I still feel relatively safe in Vienna, although we may leave at a moment's notice. At times, I feel that my beloved W.H. tends to oversimplify in his dispatches to the State Department, most of which

Mary Cowper and I copy for him. Still (vainly, I fear) hoping to elevate his post to a full ministry, he writes frequently with an authority he simply cannot possess. His own love of liberty and democracy also colors his interpretations of what is now being correctly called a real revolution. Secretary of State Buchanan appears, though, to be quite satisfied with my blessed husband's work. Since I hope to keep this diary private at least until we are once again back at Etowah Cliffs, I will note here that I had to pray hard for forgiveness again when, only today, another letter came for Mary C. from the dreadful young man, Stewart Elliott. Once more, I destroyed it, risking, I know, more heartache for my daughter. W.H. and I are far too busy making judgments about our safety to trouble ourselves over Stewart Elliott. In all this time I have breathed not one word about him to W.H. I write as little as possible to my family in Savannah concerning our revolt here, but I did tell Mama that W.H. took me through the town to see the barricades and the thousands of workmen, peasants and women with axes and long iron pikes over their shoulders. I told her also of our own Vienna citizenry tearing up the paving and piling stones on the barricades, each of which is manned by a student. We saw people actually enter strangers' houses for the purpose of placing stones and broken pieces of iron on windowsills so that residents can throw them down on the troops! Yet, with all the crowds, we sensed a kind of peculiar quiet overall. There were no shouted angry words or screaming, no actual fighting, and these very angry creatures would stand aside for us and twice they helped me over barricades. I felt like shedding tears over the probable destruction of this beautiful place, for I am sure Vienna is doomed. The Hapsburg court has now fled to Innsbruck. The Emperor will never come back to such a lawless city, even if he weren't a coward. W.H. may have to leave his post too, since we cannot afford to set up housekeeping at Innsbruck. It is a mother's grief to watch her impressionable children in such anarchy and I pray the boys will not be influenced to love doing battle themselves. Henry, in particular, and even Robert live in a state of what appears to be enjoyable excitement.

"I would sacrifice almost anything but a member of my family for just one hour on my veranda at Etowah Cliffs by the quiet river."

Even though Mark had written ahead to order a carriage and horses, or at least a buggy, to take them from the train in Cassville to Etowah Cliffs, no conveyance was anywhere in sight when their train pulled in at the tiny station and no one seemed to know of any such advance instructions.

"Oh, darling," Caroline moaned, weary from the long ride, "we should have agreed for Burke to meet us. He wanted to."

"I know. As usual, I was thinking first of Natalie. With the Stileses gone, I hate the thought of her being in that lonely spot without Burke."

"Of course, he's right there now working on Miss Lorah's cottage, but honestly, Mark, do you think he can manage work so nearby forever? You know he can't!" The crestfallen look on Mark's face caused her to change her complaining tone. "Forgive me," she said. "My only excuse for being cross is that I am—dead tired."

"I'll go in the station and see what I can do about renting something to get us there. If I can't"—he gave her his warm smile—"well, you and I have stayed at the States' Rights Hotel before and survived."

"But Natalie's expecting us this afternoon!"

A sturdy wagon and team clattered into sight down at the end of the baggage platform and when they turned to look they both spotted the bright, shining hair of their daughter!

"Mark—look!"

"Yes," he said, beaming. "It's *Natalie*. Who could miss that head? Caroline, she and Burke came for us, after all—in his wagon! And with them—"

"I *see*," she breathed, almost in awe. "They've brought Callie! Our—grandchild! Oh, Mark, I—don't think I can move a muscle! I'm so—happy and I'm—so afraid too . . ."

"Afraid, darling?"

"Yes! I'm shaking like a leaf at the thought of finally seeing that poor little tyke . . ." She swayed unsteadily.

"Here," he said, leading her to a wooden bench. "Sit down. I'll run to meet them and bring them right straight back to you."

Unable to protest—certainly unable to hurry toward Burke's wagon, where Natalie was obviously pulling her child's hair by trying to comb it too fast—Caroline sank onto the bench just as Burke swung Callie down into Mark's uplifted hands.

Without waiting for Burke to help her, Natalie leapt to the ground on the other side of the wagon, raced in a most unladylike fashion around the team and threw her arms around her father—still holding the child. After much hugging and laughing—waving wildly now—Natalie began to run toward her mother on the station platform.

They hugged and hugged while Natalie yelled for Burke to hurry with Callie. "Mama has to have her first look at the most heavenly beautiful little girl in the entire universe! Don't carry her, Papa—put Callie down on the platform. She loves to run!"

"Oh, Natalie," Caroline gasped. "Should she try to—run?"

"Mama, she's going to be four years old in July!"

When Mark let go of Callie's hand, the child headed as fast as she could for the wooden bench where Caroline sat. As long as she kept her eyes on Callie's pretty, eager face and golden curls, Caroline managed not to sob, as her namesake lurched happily toward her—evidently unaware that one side of her little body jerked horribly each time the toe of her left boot struck the platform.

Chapter 58

DAILY, Mark rode Eliza Anne's mare the six miles or so in to Cartersville and back for mail. It was much nearer than Cassville, where the closest post office used to be, but to Caroline, still too far for him to ride every day.

"What you don't understand, Mama, is that he likes to do it," Natalie exclaimed.

To Caroline, a Savannah gentleman could only be worn down with a twelve-mile ride every single day. She was relieved, she supposed, that their daughter had learned how to live in this rough, dreadfully inconvenient part of Georgia, but anyone who *chose* to live away from the coast was at least a little peculiar.

"Honestly, Mother, sometimes you have more coastal arrogance than even I suspected," Natalie laughed as the two climbed the front steps of her quite charming cottage after waving Mark off yet another time. "Now, don't fuss," Natalie went on, "I know you don't mean to be snobbish or coastal and I know you don't feel quite like yourself yet, but—"

"I feel fine," Caroline interrupted, more severely than she meant to be ever again with her grown-up daughter. "I'm aware that your father is an excellent horseman, but you've lived up here in the backwoods so long you've forgotten that successful merchants walk to work, weather permitting, or call for their carriages."

Once inside the cheerful, but oppressively small cottage parlor—more crowded than ever today because an ironing board spanned the backs of two straight chairs—Natalie dove headlong into a basket of Burke's freshly laundered shirts.

"You're perfectly welcome to sit on the porch in the lovely spring sunshine, Mother," Natalie said, "but I put my iron to heat before we went outside to bid Papa farewell on his long, *long* trip to Cartersville and it's just right for doing Burke's shirts now."

"For heaven's sake," Caroline complained, "can't Miss Lorah iron those shirts? They're all work shirts but the one Burke wore to Cassville to the bank, aren't they?"

"Yes, but do you think I love him any less when he's sweating and working than when he's strolling into a bank?" Smoothing a damp cuff just so, Natalie laughed. "Oh, I admit I scorched a few collars at first, but Burke knows it every time anyone else—even Miss Lorah—irons his shirts."

"I must say he doesn't strike me as being quite that fussy."

"He isn't fussy at all," Natalie protested, guiding the hot flat iron carefully around buttons. "He just likes the way I iron."

"I'm sure he does, dear," Caroline said.

"Why not? I iron expertly! Oh, Mama—isn't Callie almost too pretty to believe? I mean, even when you're looking right at that dear little face, you still can't quite believe your own eyes, can you? I think she's the picture of Burke and me both, don't you? Sometimes I feel I can't wait till Miss Lib gets back to see her. And Miss Eliza—oh, I want everyone I know to experience the wonder of just looking at my daughter!"

Laughing a bit, Caroline said, "You talk the way your father always talked about you."

"I know. Papa's always known how beautiful I am."

"Modesty will never be one of your virtues."

"Realizing I'm beautiful has nothing whatever to do with modesty. You and Papa donated my beauty."

"I see."

"You know one of the main reasons Papa rides to Cartersville every day is because he's so hoping the Mackays will forward a letter from Miss Lib or Uncle W.H. Papa and Burke were talking about that horrible Austrian trouble last night. I'm certainly glad Burke's a carpenter, aren't you?"

"If you mean it's better to be up here on the frontier than in the midst of all those warring troops and students and peasants in Vienna, yes, I suppose so."

Natalie looked up from her ironing. "Poor Mama." When Caroline said nothing, she added, "You really have a bad lot, haven't you? Neither of your children turned out the way you'd hoped. Here I am up in Cass County happy as a nummie who just found a sweet flower and there's blissful Jonathan back in Savannah embarrassing you socially with a half-breed Cherokee wife."

Choosing not to pursue either sticky subject, Caroline asked, "What on earth is a *nummie?*"

"A hummingbird! That's Miss Lorah's word. She has all sorts of interesting, made-up words for things. A wren is a ninnie. A rattlesnake is an Uncle John."

"I see. I'm really so glad you have Miss Lorah, Natalie."

"I'd think you would be, but sometimes I wonder. You don't seem to like her much."

"Oh, but I do! It's—it's just that, while I fully appreciate what she's done for Callie's foot and how much she does for you every day, now and then she makes me—quite uncomfortable. Maybe I rather envy her. I think I'd give almost anything to be as—accepting of whatever life offers as that woman seems to be."

Holding up a finished shirt, Natalie laughed. "You don't need to say another word. I know exactly what you mean."

"You do?"

"I most certainly do, because at first she made me furious!"

"I'm relieved to hear that, dear."

"You know how I was before I married Burke. Everything had to please me first. Then, if it happened to please someone else, fine, but me first. I still had a streak of that when Miss Lorah first came over the mountains from Ellijay. She says losing my first baby made the final change in me. I think she made it. And all she had to do was tell me about how tragic her own life had been. She didn't complain when she told me, either."

"I do complain, don't I?"

"Sometimes. But we've always been rich and wellborn and educated. It's rather like being born beautiful. Most people we know inherited their money and the chance at an education and, as Miss Lorah says, their highfalutin ancestors. It's all a matter of luck. She believes what counts is the way we act about whatever life gives us or takes away. I could be devastated by Callie's—foot. I don't think about it, because Burke keeps me reminded that years will pass before Callie's bothered much by it—but, Mama"—Caroline saw her daughter's eyes fill with tears—"Callie will never be able to—*dance!*"

"Oh, Natalie, my poor dear . . ."

"Don't feel sorry for me! For Callie either. Here in the upcountry, there's only an occasional square dance anyway. I know Callie will be much better off here than if she grew up in Savannah."

"You never expect to move back to the city, do you?"

"You know we don't. Burke looked a lot of places before he picked Cass." She scratched a blob of dried starch from the cuff of Burke's good white shirt. "We wouldn't live anywhere else on earth. Callie and her mummy and daddy are here to stay forever!"

Mark and Natalie had tried almost every day to get Caroline to agree for Callie to ride with her grandfather into Cartersville for the mail. Finally, toward the end of the first week in June, they succeeded.

"She'll be fine, Mama. Don't worry at all," Natalie said as they stood in the road beside the mare just brought saddled from the Stiles stables. "Callie's been riding with her daddy since she was two! You're a wonderful horsewoman, aren't you, darling? Tell your grandmother how well you ride."

Swinging excitedly on Caroline's hand, Callie yelled, "Callie rides a horsie better than anybody!"

Mark laughed. "There, dear wife, do you see? Are you ready to go, Callie?"

The child dropped Caroline's hand and ran, lurching toward Mark, shouting one of her made-up rhymes: "Horsie-worsie, me, me, me! Grampa-stampa, me, me, me!"

"That's right," Natalie laughed at her feisty daughter. "You and horsie will get Grandpa all the way to Carters*ville* without a stumble or a *spill*. Isn't that what you said, darling?"

The child whirled to show Natalie her sheer delight in her mother's sing-songy rhyme, then laughed up into Mark's adoring face as he swung into the saddle, motioning for Natalie to lift Callie up in front of him.

"Oh, Natalie, isn't she too heavy for you to lift like that? Burke should have been here to—"

"Mama! I'm a grown woman—a grown *frontier* woman. Won't you ever get that through your head? Anyway, her daddy is way back behind the old cabin hard at work on Miss Lorah's cottage."

Holding Callie securely in one arm, Mark blew kisses to Natalie and Caroline, gave the reins a little flip, and off they trotted. "We'll be back, you two," he called. "And we'll be starved!"

As on a signal, he and Callie let out a joint whoop and, sensing the child's perfect ease in the saddle, Mark urged the mare to a gallop.

For three miles or so, they chattered and laughed and made silly remarks about various rabbits they passed, a redbird and almost every squirrel Callie saw. When she had to "pee-pee," he dismounted, hitched the mare to the gum tree Callie picked out, lifted her down and led her into a grove of pines where the ground was smooth and covered with rich brown needles.

"You don't need to take down my pantalets," she informed him. "Callie do it. Watch!"

Chuckling, he waited as she proceeded with abandon to make a "big river" and then, on her command, brought a handful of sassafras leaves for drying her bottom. All finished, she stood there a moment looking up at the clouds —huge, white, cottony clouds in the bluest sky Mark had seen since his last trip to the upcountry.

"Callie sees a *big* lion up in heaven, Grampa! Look!"

He looked where her chubby finger pointed and sure enough, one cloud did resemble the heavy, thick-maned head of a lion.

"Have you ever seen a lion?" he asked.

"Daddy and me see lions all the time in heaven," she said quite seriously. "First, in a book, we saw lions, then in the clouds. Daddy says my brother, Burkie, is right with those lions in heaven!"

"That's true," Mark said. "You and your daddy have great times together, don't you?"

Her laughter was so quick it startled him. "Now you too!"

"Absolutely! Now you and I are having a great time seeing lions on our horseback trip to Cartersville. An absolutely great time!"

"Absolootely?" She tried the word again. *"Ab-sol-oote-ly.* Ootely, ootely, ootely," she chanted, laughing up at him.

"There, you see? You've learned a new word."

"Ootely, ootely," she repeated, then looked puzzled. "Grampa, how could

Mama lose a baby? I never lose my dolls! Miss Eliza Mackay sent me two dolls."

"She did? You're going to love Miss Eliza," Mark said.

"One doll is leather with red hair like Mama. The other has a china head and hair like yours. Dark. How could Mama lose her first baby before me?"

He thought a minute. "Well, she didn't actually lose it the way you might lose one of your dolls. Your mama got awfully sick, and when the baby was born, it was dead. Gone to heaven, exactly as your daddy said."

"Oh." She thought a second. "Burkie had been sick too?"

"Uh, that's right. Burkie just got so sick he had to go to heaven where everybody is healthy and happy forever."

"You still see that big lion in the clouds, Grampa?"

"Well, I think he's just a little windblown by now, but I still see him. He's moving. Look! Just wait till Miss Lib Stiles gets back from way over in Vienna, Austria, and she'll paint your cloud lion."

"Miss Lib paints clouds?"

"Oh, better than anyone I've ever seen! Many people who paint don't do very good clouds. If she has time to paint at all these days, Miss Lib does, though."

Thinking that they'd better be riding again, he reached for her hand and noticed the frown on her face. "You're frowning, Callie. Is something wrong?"

She said nothing for a long time, still looking hard at the sky. "Grampa, how does Miss Lib get way up there to paint the clouds?"

Laughing, he gave her a big noisy kiss and lifted her into the saddle first this time, then mounted himself, telling her to scoot forward to make room for him. Once more, they headed happily past deep woods, fields of corn and blooming cotton in the direction of Cartersville.

She was quiet for so long he thought she might be napping, until he peered down at her face and saw in it the look of unquenchable thirst for *everything*, the same look he'd seen in Natalie's face almost from the first day of her life. Lightly, he tightened an arm around this precious girl—Natalie's own child— his grandchild. As they rode along, he breathed a prayer for happiness and protection and health for little Callie through all the days of her life.

Caroline stayed on at Natalie's cottage while Mark and Callie were gone, and as she and Natalie hurried down the pine-straw path to meet the returning travelers, Caroline felt as though she couldn't wait to tell Mark of the deeply meaningful time she'd spent with their daughter. They hadn't slipped into one serious spat. Oh, Natalie had lectured her some, but Caroline honestly believed they were friends now and Miss Eliza always said that's all a mother should expect once her child has left the nest.

"Only one letter this time, but it's a fat one," Mark called as he lifted the droopy-eyed Callie down from the horse. "I think it's William's handwriting and it's postmarked Savannah."

"He's probably enclosing Eliza Anne's latest from Vienna," Caroline said, "but I do hope William wrote something himself about poor Jack. Natalie, your daughter is asleep on her feet!"

"We had just that much fun," Mark said proudly. "Actually enough to wear her out, I think."

Mark waited in the road for a Stiles servant to come for the mare, while Caroline went into the house to help Natalie get Callie ready for a nap after her long ride with Grandfather Browning. Thinking of Mark as Grandfather —herself as Grandmother Browning—still seemed strange, but something deep inside her responded to it. The altogether enchanting child seemed a lively symbol of the love she and Mark had felt for each other for nearly thirty years. Instead of feeling old as she'd always supposed a grandparent would feel, Callie made her feel young. Surely, she hadn't seen Mark so full of delight and vitality in years. Oh, at times, he showed similar delight in Jonathan's Mary these days. In fact, Mark shared a kind of special bond with Mary which Caroline had almost envied. Today, she envied no one.

When Callie was sleeping soundly, she and Natalie walked arm in arm through the tiny parlor toward the porch, where Mark waited to read their letter. Natalie gave her mother a heart-stopping smile just before they joined Mark. It was the same heart-stopping smile with which she'd always gotten her way as a young girl, but which raised in Caroline today not one twinge of suspicion that her daughter might be up to something.

When both his beautiful women appeared on the cottage porch, Mark jumped up to escort them to chairs he'd moved into the shade of Natalie's wisteria vine, its purple blossoms replaced now by full, green June leaves.

"Papa," Natalie fussed, "you haven't even broken the seal on William's letter! I thought you'd have it all open and ready to read."

"He's been savoring," Caroline said. "Have you forgotten we do that, Natalie? Your father and I still wait eagerly for letters." She gave Natalie a smile. "Isn't it convenient having us right here so you don't need to write to us?"

"I guess so, Mama, but what you said made me think. Maybe I need to learn to savor more. Now that I have Burke and Callie and live up here by the river, I'm so happy most of the time, I forget to savor." Straightening her long white voile skirt, Natalie settled back in a rocker to listen. "Open it, Papa. We've savored enough."

"All right, let's see what we have here," Mark said, opening the letter. "Well, it seems the top page is a short one from William and the remainder a long letter from Eliza Anne in Vienna. Good."

"I do hope things have begun to calm down over there," Caroline said.

"For Miss Eliza's sake in particular," Mark said, smoothing the wrinkled pages over his knee. "That brave lady has so much to bear worrying about her family in Austria—and Jack."

"Read William's note first, please?" Caroline asked.

"Yes, of course, dear. '30 May 1848, Savannah. Dear Mark and All there, I have the time for only a short note since Jack is very poorly today. Mama insists that I ask for your prayers that his hard hemorrhaging might ease. We slept not at all last night, and as I write this at ten in the morning, the poor fellow has been coughing blood since the sun came up. We do not panic, but I doubt that anyone has faced how changed life would be on East Broughton without Jack's spirit and continuing attempts to encourage us. I enclose the latest from my sister in Vienna. Mama begs your prayers for her and her family too, and that I send love to each of you. Yours, William Mackay.' "

"Oh, Mark," Caroline said, "I do hope you won't feel too guilty not to be there with Miss Eliza if anything terrible happens to Jack!"

"I don't think Papa should feel guilty at all. Sorry, yes, but not guilty," Natalie put in. "Miss Eliza *wanted* him to see his only grandchild. She wrote me that she did."

"That's right, darling," Mark said. "In fact, you almost sound like Miss Eliza, who's always trying to make me see the vast difference between being guilty and being genuinely sorry."

"Oh, there's a big, big difference," Natalie said. "Miss Lorah helped me learn about that when I went on feeling guilty because I—lost Little Burke."

Mark gave her a smile, and in it was all the love and sympathy and pride he felt, but couldn't express. He glanced at Caroline. She was giving Natalie the same kind of smile.

"Jack Mackay's really dying, isn't he?" Natalie asked, almost wonderingly, as though such a drastic change could not be possible.

In the silence that followed, a cardinal began to sing in the tall sycamore, and went right on singing throughout Mark's reading of Eliza Anne's long, troubling letter.

"Eliza Anne dated this," he said, "on 9 May 1848 from Vienna. It seems to be addressed to Sarah. 'Your latest letter, my dearest Sarah, containing one from Anna Barnsley for Mary C. arrived only today. Our mail is just not getting through and those letters which do are delayed. We respected Mary Cowper's desire for privacy with her letter from Anna, but puzzlingly, she begs me to tell her Uncle William that she'd give him a big hug if she were close enough! Why she should want to hug William for a letter from Anna Barnsley, I can't imagine, but even I did not annoy Mary C. with questions. She is growing up, and while I wish she worked harder at her French and German, she does enjoy the new music teacher and likes to play and sing more than I'd dared hope. I am sorry to have to get all three children away from Vienna, but preparations are underway for our departure for Gräfenberg, the resort town in Austrian Silesia where I will take the water-cure treatment of Vincenz Priessnitz for my newly acquired rheumatism and where W.H. feels we will be far safer than in Vienna. There, although not the most comfortable of surroundings, I will also have opportunity to get information for W.H.'s dispatches, as I mix socially with nobility from both German and Italian states. I will do my very best for him. The families of

Prince Lubomirski of Poland, Count Esterházy of Hungary and my beloved friend Ottilie von Goethe are already there for the cure. I am in pain from my rheumatism much of the time, but nothing to add to your worry.

" 'We were disappointed not to hear in your latest that beloved Jack had reached Savannah, but that is the way of letters here these days.' "

"My goodness," Caroline interrupted, "Eliza Anne really isn't getting mail, is she? Things must be dreadful in Vienna!"

"Let Papa read," Natalie said. "Maybe Miss Lib will tell us about the revolution."

"I think she's writing about it right here," Mark said, and returned to reading. " 'W.H.'s first dispatch after his return from Italy summed up his current estimate of the trouble in this way: "I and the other members of the diplomatic corps here have been advised by the Emperor's emissary to leave Vienna, but whatever course may be determined upon, of one thing I am sure, that the fate of Vienna and the Empire now trembles in the balance." Hence, fearing for our safety, we go to Gräfenberg in a few days, where we will take a house by the week so as to move back anytime.

" 'Although she continues to act withdrawn and silent, Mary Cowper helps me so much these days by copying some of her father's dispatches, which she does well. Henry also helps. He has a fancy for writing and loves to copy, but finds it hard to read any handwriting but his own. I detest a governess in the house, but dislike the children having too much free time and Mary C. surely needs to learn French. You will be pleased, I think, to know that I speak it with some fluency and have ever since our arrival in Vienna. Robert is a lively boy and dripping charm.

" 'Today, we are surrounded by troops and barricades, but all seems fairly tranquil at the moment. One walks everywhere since streets are blocked by these barricades mounted with cannon. The German grenadiers deserted and are standing now at the barricades with the students and workmen. I work too hard at preparation for Gräfenberg and at helping W.H. with his work to write to any one at Etowah Cliffs, so I beg you to send my love and tell of my longing to be there once more. Always your affectionate sister, Eliza Anne Stiles.' "

"Oh, Mama, we are so blessed to have husbands not one bit interested in government or politics!" Natalie exclaimed when Mark finished the letter. "Aren't we blessed?"

"We are, darling," Caroline said, reaching her hand to touch Mark's.

With a slightly teasing smile, he said, "I don't think it's quite fair to say that Burke and I aren't one bit interested in politics or government. In fact, I rather think we both amazed each other last night after you two went to bed. Your husband is very knowledgeable, Natalie, about what goes on, not only in Georgia but in Washington City. He and I don't have any desire to take an active part, but we both admire the same men, see almost everything pretty much alike."

"Oh, I know." Natalie grinned. "You're two of a kind, you and Burke. I'm sure you do admire the same men—like 'the godlike Daniel Webster,' Henry Clay, 'the Great Pacificator,' and that *fanatic* evangelist abolitionist named Theodore Weld. I suppose you're still mourning old John Quincy Adams too. Burke is. He hates slavery as much as you do, Papa. And there's some kind of Proviso that didn't get passed in Congress he's still sorry about and I think that was all of two years ago! But at least you're neither one in a dangerous foreign country at the mercy of troops and stone-throwing mobs of common people the way W.H. is. Burke thinks there could be trouble right here in America, but I don't pay any attention to him when he gets started on the North and the South. Only men worry about things like—slaveholding and non-slaveholding states."

"You know I can't agree with that, Natalie," Caroline said stiffly. "I think that unless we get a sensible and wise President this fall there could be *lots* of trouble."

"Foot, Mama."

"'Foot' if you like," Caroline answered. "People have gone crazy expanding the country, and more non-slave states could spoil the balance in Congress between North and South. It would have already if Burke's long-lost Proviso had been passed. Thank heaven it wasn't. Mark, what was that unsavory Northerner's name who tried it? I remember he was a nobody until in ten minutes one day in Congress he tried to set everyone's teeth on edge."

Smiling, but nervous, as he'd always been when the subject of slavery came up in Caroline's presence, Mark said, "His name was David Wilmot, darling, from Pennsylvania."

"Well, I knew he was some wild-eyed northern abolitionist."

"Wrong," Mark said. "Burke and I don't see Wilmot as particularly disliking slavery. His idea left the institution alone where it's already established. It would have prohibited slavery only in the new territories, but not because he thinks slavery's wrong."

"Then why?" Caroline demanded.

"To protect white working people's jobs as they keep pushing west. If slave labor is allowed out there, it would, according to David Wilmot, take jobs from poor whites."

"I've heard enough," Natalie announced, getting up. "We're all having such a happy time. I'm going to nip this dreary discussion right in the bud. I made fresh lemonade and it will now be served."

"Oh, wait, darling," Mark said, peering at what appeared to be a still unread page tucked in at the end of Eliza Anne's letter. "I've just found more from William!"

Scanning the hasty scrawl, he gasped, "Dear God! Listen to this. Brace yourselves, both of you, and listen: 'I began this letter yesterday and had to stop to help with Brother, so was forgetting to mention how well Jonathan handled your Liverpool deal, Mark. Sorry to say my own grief is too deep today to give details here, though. My brother, Jack, died two hours ago. In the agony of her own mourning, Sarah even embraced me. Mourning indeed binds a family together. As I write this hasty scrawl, Mama is helping my sisters bathe Jack and, dressed in his officer's blues, we will bury him tomorrow on his birthday, June 1. Jack died at about the same age our father left us. Sick as he's been for so long, he took the Savannah sun with him. Don't worry about us, but pray that Mama can go on holding up as she is now.' "

For what seemed like several moments, all that could be heard was the raucous cardinal singing in the sycamore tree at the end of Natalie's porch. No one said anything until Caroline murmured to no one in particular, "Anyone would know that Miss Eliza herself bathed Jack."

"Is that all William wrote, Papa?" Natalie wanted to know. "Did you read what's on the back?"

Mark turned the page over. "You're right, Natalie. There is a little more: 'A letter came for Jack an hour ago from his old friend Colonel Robert E. Lee. Since Kate had closed Jack's eyes forever, and wanting to notify Lee, I opened it. Colonel Lee is en route home to Virginia from the war with Mexico by water via New Orleans and Wheeling, thence to Arlington by stage. Lee does not plan to attend the Fourth of July celebration in Washington City, where the cornerstone of the new Washington monument is to be laid and the victory in Mexico celebrated. Robert still reveres his wife's kinsman, our first President, but does not find even a victorious war a thing to celebrate with noise and cheering. Colonel Lee will mourn when his wife shows him my letter about Jack's death, which I am sending to the Lees at Arlington.' "

After another long silence, unbroken now even by cardinal song, Mark said, "Good old William managed to write us quite a lot, didn't he? Considering his own heavy heart."

"He's kind," Natalie whispered. "I—love William."

"We all do, dear," Caroline said.

"I expect writing it down for us to read helped him some," Mark said. "It may have kept us from seeming quite so far away. It probably helped William too when he wrote to Lee. He and Jack were such staunch friends, and in a very real way, I'm sure, the whole Mackay family will value Colonel Lee even more than ever—now."

"Yes," Natalie said. "Every word from him could be almost like a touch—from Jack, couldn't it?"

Chapter 59

JONATHAN took Mary to Etowah Cliffs—their arrival a total surprise—just in time for Callie's birthday party in July. He and Mary came bearing birthday gifts, a new pink dress from the Mackays and a silver spoon with CALLIE engraved on its handle from him and Mary. Natalie had baked a sunshine cake for her bewitching daughter and Jonathan was delighted that Callie received the surprise of all her gifts *and* their visit as occasioned solely by the marvelous fact that she was now four years old.

"The truth is, we came up because we missed you and Mama so much," Jonathan told his father that afternoon on the cottage porch after Callie went in the care of her grandmother for a nap, while Natalie and Mary wandered off for a long walk. "Things were slow at the office after our lengthy Fourth of July celebration, so when I saw how happy my idea made Mary, I hurried right down to the station for our train tickets."

The two exchanged confident smiles.

"Son," his father said, "if you say things were slow enough for you to leave Savannah, I believe it. I can't tell you how glad your mother and I are to see you both. And did you notice how quick Natalie was to get Mary off alone—just the two of them?"

Jonathan laughed. "I certainly did. Does Mama realize how close my sister and wife have stayed even with Mary living in Savannah?"

"Do *you* realize how comfortable your mother feels with Mary now?"

"I hope so."

"Do you doubt it?"

"Not really. Mary loves her, I know, even though she still has a little trouble expressing herself. Papa, sometimes I feel as though I can see all the way to the bottom of Mary's heart. She has only the best intentions toward us all. What surprises me the most, I guess, is that she understands *why* Mama was so—so reluctant about my bringing her to Savannah to live."

"The gossip, most of which we didn't even hear, I suspect, hasn't made Mary feel inferior?"

Jonathan grinned. "I think she really does understand it. She seems to feel nothing but compassion for white people who look down on Cherokees."

"Do you actually believe that, Jonathan?"

"Yes, sir, I do. And I'm sure that if she felt any kind of scorn or—any feeling of superiority left in Mama, she'd *have* to tell me. Being Mary, she couldn't stop herself from telling me. We've always told each other everything. Mary doesn't mind not being invited to take part in Savannah's social life. She seems not to give it a thought."

"You're sure?"

"I'd know that too if she minded. You see, Papa, she's never been a part of a society like ours in coastal Georgia. What you've never known, you don't miss, Miss Eliza says."

"Oh, son, how is my dear old friend Miss Eliza? You've no idea how I've felt not being there. Is she—holding up? Or is she putting on her brave front for the rest of us?"

Jonathan thought a minute. "To me, she seems to be doing awfully well. She spent a lot of time on her letter to you, trying to convince you that even though she's heartbroken at losing Jack the way he used to be, she's so relieved to have him free of his terrible suffering, she can't be anything but thankful."

"I'm sure that's true. I've read and reread that letter. But we're all human. I worry a lot about her, even though I know there is a kind of relief for all of us who cared about Jack."

A broad smile lit Jonathan's face. "Miss Eliza made me promise to try, at least, to tell you—alone, when I could really let you know how proud I am— about a surprise I intended to save to tell everybody together up here."

"If Miss Eliza made you promise, you'd better be true to your word, son. It must be quite a surprise, judging by the look on your face."

"Even if I hadn't promised, I can't wait any longer to tell you. I'll bet Mary's already told Natalie, and if I know Sister, she'll spout it all out at dinner."

"*What*, Jonathan? Tell me."

"Have you and Mama had a letter from the Mercers or Mrs. Scarbrough's daughter, Charlotte Taylor, or the Andersons or the Habershams since you've been up here?"

His father thought briefly. "No, come to think about it, your mother remarked the other night that it seemed curious we hadn't heard a word from Savannah—except from the Mackays, of course. Look here, you've gone quite far enough with your suspense. Should we have had a letter from those people?"

Jonathan looked directly at his father, beaming. "On Wednesday last, Mr. and Mrs. Jonathan Browning entertained in their home on Reynolds Square, and using Mama's best china and her Waterford crystal, my wife presided over one of the most elegant dinners *ever* for twenty of Savannah's elite!"

The look of shock on his father's handsome face pleased Jonathan all the way to his toes. That Papa couldn't think of a word to say for the longest time pleased him still more.

"Son, you really did—all on your own?"

"Yes, sir, we did and it went off like clockwork too. Mary made me bone her up some on which forks to use and when, and she sent me to your cellar to select just the right wines. Maureen and her cousin I hired for the occasion did themselves proud, of course, but, Papa, Mary planned the entire menu herself and carried on a really enlightened dinner-table conversation with all those high-and-mighty folk!"

His father was glowing now. "Son, what on earth did she talk about? Were they impressed?"

Jonathan laughed. "They were terribly, *terribly* impressed, and unless I miss my guess, that's the very reason no one has quite known how to write to tell you and Mama about it!"

"Well, what did Mary talk about? I'd rather have a good conversation with Mary than anyone I know, outside of you or your mother or Miss Eliza, but those are educated, cultured people. I can't imagine what Mary said to them all through two hours or so around that table!"

"One afternoon before Jack died, Miss Eliza read Mary a lot of Miss Lib's letters from Vienna—even some from back in Washington City—and my lovely wife kept our dinner guests highly entertained with her knowledge of W. H. Stiles's role in the United States Congress and in the midst of the chaos of the Vienna insurrection!"

"Son, you're pulling my leg!"

Jonathan laughed. "You know I'm not. Sister might tease like that, but I've never learned the knack of it. Mary talked about Miss Lib's visits to the White House when the second Mrs. Tyler sat on a kind of dais and received guests, then she talked about her close friend in Austria, the Baroness von Goethe, and life in Gräfenberg, where we think Miss Lib and the children are staying because it's still too dangerous in Vienna." His father was laughing so now, Jonathan beamed like a sunrise. "I know what you're thinking, Papa. I couldn't believe my ears and I was right there listening to her! Oh, she did pronounce the poet Goethe's name in a sort of funny way—something like von Gertie—but of course Mrs. Charlotte Scarbrough Taylor corrected her and—"

"I'm sure she did," Mark interjected, still laughing.

"I got a little uneasy when she began to talk about the causes of the revolutions all over Europe, but she came out of it fine. She sounded almost like Uncle W.H. explaining that the poor working people are sick and tired of being stepped on by their monarchies!"

"She's right," Mark interrupted. "That's all true."

"Of course it is, but what really got their attention was when she started telling them about the fine jewelry Uncle W.H. bought at the palace in Vienna—rings and brooches and bracelets that had once belonged to the wife of Napoleon Bonaparte. Now, wait—" Jonathan stopped his father from interrupting again. "She really had their eyes bugging out when she informed them that Uncle W.H. had also had specially made a complete set of crystal with W.H.S. etched into each piece and—"

Jonathan was thoroughly enjoying himself, but his father was laughing almost too hard to listen closely. "Oh, my, oh, my," Papa interrupted, "I can see the fine hand and humor of our beloved Miss Eliza in almost every word Mary had to say!"

"I can too, and funniest yet, to me at least, Mary informed our guests as well of Uncle W.H.'s purchase of enough exquisite Viennese marble so that not only the fireplaces but every downstairs windowsill at Etowah Cliffs will someday be made of it!"

"Miss Eliza McQueen Mackay, shame on you," Mark said, laughing. "Son, did Mary actually use the word 'exquisite'?"

"She certainly did, and it was really sad that Miss Eliza couldn't be there herself to hear Mary pronounce it. Our dinner party was just a little over a month after Jack died. Miss Eliza's still in mourning, of course, but I told her all about it."

"I'm so glad you did!"

"She enjoyed it too, especially when Mary herself—who was with me when I told Miss Eliza—repeated what she'd said about Uncle W.H.'s purchase of all that 'exquisite' Viennese marble. Oh, Papa, I'm here to tell you that no man was ever as proud of his wife as I was that night, and except for stifling two yawns, Mary was just about letter perfect. Of course, Miss Eliza had drilled her on emphasizing the 'ex' in 'exquisite'—and she said it just right."

Wiping laughter tears from his eyes, his father said, "Oh, how I wish your mother and I had been there!"

"No, Papa."

"No?"

"I doubt Mary could have done it if she and I hadn't been giving the dinner—all on our own."

"Well, you're probably right. Tell me, what did Mary say to you about the whole affair that night after you two went to bed?"

"Very little. Mostly she was just worn out. Oh, she did say she wouldn't be half so tired if she'd done a big washing and chopped half a cord of wood."

"She still lives in a foreign environment every day in Savannah, doesn't she?"

Jonathan nodded. "It was that night I decided to bring her up here for a visit. Do you know what she did the minute we got off the train in Cassville? I had my back turned instructing the drayman how to load our bags on the hired wagon, and when I turned around to look for Mary, there she was down on her knees kissing weeds beside the station platform!"

"Poor little thing," Mark said. "Does she talk a lot about her old home up here?"

Jonathan thought a while. "No. Oh, now and then she tells me an old Cherokee legend or wishes for some sassafras tea, but mostly she seems pretty happy. Papa, she loves me."

"I know that! But you two can take one of our boats to Knightsford and dig your own sassafras. Did you forget that?"

"No. It's just that Mary doesn't seem to feel much at home out there somehow."

"It's such a beautiful spot—do you know why she doesn't?"

"Too flat, I think. These hills are her backbone, she says. Mary misses the hills and valleys and rivers up here."

"But the Savannah River runs right past Knightsford."

"She misses river*banks*, she claims. Coastal rivers wind through flat, flat marshland, you know. But don't get me wrong. She doesn't complain." He shook his head wonderingly. "Just don't think I'll ever forget her quietly kissing those weeds. I don't think she even meant for me to see."

"I told Mama we'd only be gone for an hour or so," Natalie said as she and Mary strolled along by the river past the stables and the Stileses' almost finished carriage house—large enough to house four carriages. "I've prattled so much about Burke's fine elevated stable entrance, did I remember to brag about the smokehouse he also built?"

Mary laughed, throwing both arms in the sunlit air. "You did. Twice. Whatever Mister Burke builds is beautiful!"

"But I have been talking too much," Natalie said, "and we've done nothing but poke along. Don't you want to stretch your legs? Aren't you aching for a real run? You must feel terribly penned up staying in the house so much back in Savannah. I think I'd suffocate now if I had to do that."

Beaming, Mary touched Natalie's arm affectionately, then flew off into the woods like a young deer, leaping fallen logs and stands of weeds, arms flung wide as though to embrace the very air circling the tall trees.

Natalie stood alone in the narrow, sandy road, proud in a way that she'd come to understand Mary so well. Relieved, actually, that deep down inside, Mary hadn't changed, that she still loved and belonged to the glorious upcountry.

I belong up here too, Natalie thought. I'm as much at home now as Mary in Burke's blessed land. If I ever have to go back to Savannah again—and I suppose I'll have to when Mama and Papa are too old to travel up here—I know the city will only look bigger to me, not really changed. If I had to, I could still dance on a polished floor and nod properly to the Telfair sisters of a Sunday morning. I wouldn't like any of it, but it would be all right for a visit because I'd always know that I'd be coming back here to our place—Burke's and Callie's and mine. Naturally, I intend to see that Callie's table manners are correct, even though her daddy doesn't like to bother with all those spoons and forks. I'll teach her to speak enough French, I'll watch her grammar, but I also want Callie to be what she really is—an upcountry girl.

Mary's running footsteps were gone now, too far away to hear. She hasn't said one word about hating being cramped up in the city, Natalie thought, and maybe she should complain a little. Who'd have guessed my little brother could have so swept a girl off her feet that she'd up and change cultures! That's exactly what poor Mary had to do. She made a far bigger adjustment than Miss Lib did moving all the way to Vienna. Natalie longed to know exactly how things were for Miss Lib and Uncle W.H. way over in Austria surrounded by an all-out, bloody insurrection. Mary needed this time alone, she decided, so she sat down on a fat pine stump to think a while about her friend Miss Lib, whose latest letter to Natalie had been full of foreign-sounding dishes like *Knödel,* sweet dumplings that made you fat, and lots of gossip about how foolish the Emperor had been to run away when the people really loved him. Of course, Natalie had made no effort to understand what the commotion all over Europe was about beyond Uncle W.H.'s conviction that the people in the Austrian Empire, especially in Hungary, were longing for democracy. Miss Lib, though, seemed far more worried about the interruptions in her children's education every time they had to flee Vienna than about who was fighting any revolution or why.

Oh, once Miss Lib came home, they'd all be caught up endlessly, but in spite of barricades and blood in the streets, Miss Lib had come to love Vienna. So, even with people throwing stones and firing cannons and changing emperors, the Stileses, deep down, had not had to change their ways nearly as much as poor Mary living cooped up in the Browning mansion on Reynolds Square.

It was plain that Miss Lib really did love the beautiful old city of Vienna. She'd written at length about some of its splendid buildings—the imperial residence and the breathtaking Karlskirche built back in the last century and the Kinsky and Schwarzenberg palaces. She'd grown lyrical over the Prater in the spring, when "the flowers looked as flowers in an imperial garden should look." Miss Lib, she supposed, was still in Gräfenberg now, where accommodations weren't too comfortable, but at least her friend the Baroness Ottilie von Goethe was there too and undoubtedly Miss Lib's daily life went on being somewhat the same as it had always been in Savannah. She'd written of shawls and caps and other things she'd made for the Baroness, of their shopping expeditions, of lots of social calls on people with royal-sounding names. Everyone knew that society people, no matter what language they spoke, were about the same everywhere. Curious, suddenly, to know exactly *how* Mary got along with certain Savannah highbrows, on impulse Natalie jumped up off her pine stump and ran after her into the woods.

She found Mary sitting on an old lichen-covered log. The peaceful, faraway look on her pretty, scarred face reminded Natalie of the way Miss Eliza Mackay used to look in church. Hesitating to interrupt Mary's communion with what had once been her people's forest and sky and earth, she stopped a few feet away and waited.

Without looking at Natalie, Mary said softly, "Please, sit down with me. I am just catching my breath. City streets do not keep my legs limber. Here." She brushed some old leaves off the log. "You are welcome to be here."

Natalie felt welcome. Mary and Miss Lorah both had a way of seeming to

be always glad to see her. Maybe, she thought, sitting down, it's because they
both grew up with mountains all around them. There was certainly nothing
prickly in either Miss Lorah or Mary.

"Mister Burke has not changed," Mary said out of the blue. "He still does
not believe even Negroes should belong to another man or woman. Mister
Burke and your beautiful father are full of love."

Evidently Mary had been doing some thinking of her own. "That's right,"
Natalie said, surprised that the always disturbing subject of slavery could be
on Mary's mind when the peaceful look on her face had made Natalie think
of Miss Eliza in church. "Burke hasn't changed," she said, "except to grow
more handsome and more in love with me. And my brother is certainly in
love with you, Mary!" After a moment, she asked, "Do you miss all this too
much sometimes? I thought a lot about that after you leaped off into the
woods just now. Do you get terribly homesick for the upcountry?"

Still looking off into the sun-and-shadow-streaked forest, Mary said softly,
"I stay homesick for the land of my people, but I stay busy and happy. With
all my heart, I love Jonathan. I also revere your sweet mother. She and I were
together so much when she was ill. I have always revered your father because
he is good. I am strange to Savannah people, but I am happy there because I
know at the end of every day I will lie beside Jonathan in his arms. Jonathan is
my life . . ."

Then, with childlike abruptness, Mary began to tell Natalie about the dinner party for Savannah's elite, her soft laughter running under the whole
story. Once past the shock of what Mary and Jonathan had done with Mama
and Papa not even there, Natalie began to laugh too and drew from Mary
tale after tale of how she'd managed to handle each blue blood seated around
the dining-room table that night. By the time Mary covered her singular
explanation of how she regaled them all with the insurrection in Vienna and
the politics of Europe, Natalie was laughing so helplessly she let herself roll
right off the log into the carpet of pine needles!

Mary looked delighted, but also puzzled. "That is—ladylike to roll on the
ground?" she asked.

"No," Natalie whooped. "No, it certainly is not, but who cares? I like it!"

"I make you happy, Natalie?"

Back on the log, upright again, Natalie said, "Yes! You make me happier
than you could ever understand, Mary. I'll wager old Bertha Potter is still
spinning from your erudition."

"I had—erudition?"

"You had far more than that! You not only knew more than anyone at the
table about what's going on in high and low places in Europe, you showed a
kind of cunning to have Miss Eliza bone you up from her stack of Miss Lib's
letters. That kind of cunning makes me happier than I can possibly tell you."

"That was—cunning?"

"Shrewd! And I didn't think you had a shrewd bone in your body. Miss

Eliza must have laughed till the tears flowed when you told her about it. You surely paid her a visit to give her the whole story, didn't you?"

"Oh, yes. Even in her sorrow over Captain Jack, she did laugh."

Natalie thought for a while. "You know, Mary, all those dear society folk thought the world had come to an end when I married Burke and actually learned to keep house. Suddenly, I realize that you and I have—conquered them!"

"Conquered?"

"Yes, indeed! You with your successful dinner party—I with a washboard and scrub bucket! We're both totally victorious!"

"Good."

On her feet, Natalie urged, "Let's go back to my house. I can't wait another minute to tell Mama. And be sure to watch closely when Burke hears about your social success!" Pulling Mary along by the hand as they cut back through the woods toward the road, she added seriously, "You know he's always loved you, Mary. In the right way, of course, but you wait and see— this story is going to make Burke feel victorious too."

"That will be good," Mary said, beaming. "I also have always loved Mister Burke."

Giving Mary a knowing look, Natalie said, "But *not* the way you love Jonathan."

Mary laughed, returning the look. "Oh, no, not the way I love Jonathan!"

Chapter 60

ON A late August afternoon, the day before all the Brownings were to take the train back to Savannah, Burke and Mark found themselves alone in the small parlor of Burke's cottage, while Callie and the three women, with Jonathan helping, were at the Stiles house unpacking an enormous crate of yellow Wedgwood which had just come that morning from Gräfenberg.

"There's enough china in that crate to keep them busy all evening, Burke," Mark said, obviously pleased at the chance to talk with his son-in-law.

"I only hope it doesn't give Natalie big ideas," Burke laughed, pulling up an armchair for Mark, then stretching his tall, muscular frame in another, feet propped on the new footstool which Natalie had just covered in a blue-and-beige cotton print.

"I never thought I'd hear myself say this, but somehow I think my daughter's days of 'big ideas' are a thing of the past," Mark said. "You've made Natalie supremely happy. I now know all her expensive demands as a youngster were a fevered effort to fill the place you occupy in her life."

"She covered another footstool for my easy chair in the bedroom, Mr. Browning. Could I bring it for you?"

"No, thanks, I'm fine. Walking around up here has helped my stiff knee. And, Burke, I'm glad for this chance to be alone with you. Now that my old friend Sheftall is dead, I no longer have a gentleman friend with whom I can discuss either the national or the world scene. Somehow, I feel I can with you —freely."

Mark watched Burke fill his pipe and light it. He took a few puffs, then tossed the match into the fireplace. "Remind me to pick up that burnt match before my wife gets home, sir."

"Is she a finicky housekeeper?"

"No. In all the excitement of the Stileses' china arriving she forgot today, but usually she keeps a big vase of fresh leaves in what she calls her 'summer fireplace.' No burnt matches allowed until winter comes again."

Mark responded with a warm smile.

"And you're right, Mr. Browning. I hope you'll always feel free to speak

your mind with me on—anything. Political or otherwise. We do see eye to
eye, so far as I've been able to gather in the few times we've had a chance to
talk. Actually, I'm relieved that we do. These days a man seldom brings up a
ticklish political subject for fear of starting an argument." He sighed. "At
times, around here—it could be a fistfight. Still, down in Savannah, I'm sure
you have to keep your mouth shut tighter than I. Maybe your merchant
friends don't use their fists so often, but there's one good thing up here—
many men are still strong for the Union."

"Oh, we have strong Unionists in Savannah too," Mark said, vastly relieved that even without mentioning the now almost forbidden word—"slavery"—Burke had brought it front and center. "Actually, I've been lonely
with my political views down on the coast since back when I first chose
Savannah as the one place on earth I wanted to live. Thank God, though, I've
always had Miss Eliza Mackay. I can say anything in the world to that lady—
and do."

Burke looked surprised. "Mrs. Mackay's a slaveholder, isn't she?"

"Yes, she inherited her people, but she's a Free-Soiler at heart."

"She really doesn't want the ugly business extended into our new territories?"

"Indeed she does not! She even went so far as to say once, with the kind of
fervor only Miss Eliza can suddenly whip up, that she wished women could
vote!"

Burke laughed, both interested and amused, Mark could see. "Do you
mean to tell me there's a secret Free-Soiler living in Savannah?"

"Miss Eliza is certainly an anti-expansionist."

"Against the madness to push west? Then she must have been against the
war with Mexico."

"As with many women, she despairs of all wars. She feels the whole country is quite wildly running downhill over the gold they found early this year
in California—over the whole 'manifest destiny'—"

"Madness?"

"Yes. Sometimes I think it is madness, Burke. Do you?"

"I do, although even up here on what is still a frontier, I have to be careful
where I mention the subject."

"Well, we did just finish with one war over it, with Mexico. Oh, I admit I
understand the economic reasons for pushing west. Men don't easily resist
the lure of gold, but I agree with Miss Eliza that we need to solve many deep
problems in the nation before we blithely go on spreading them from coast to
coast."

"Slavery," Burke said. The word had a sweeping, symbolic sound.

"Slavery may be the deepest problem we have. In the land where liberty is
uppermost, even you and I are not free to speak our minds on slavery, Burke.
It's setting Americans against one another. *Are* all people created equal or
not?"

Burke smiled. "You sound a bit like an abolitionist, sir. Natalie tells me your late aunt, for whom she was named, *was* an active early abolitionist. Of course, I hear they're fading a bit, but Miss Eliza Mackay's Free-Soilers are finding followers. Holding steady, not spreading slavery, does seem a fairly safe, reasonable ground." Burke thought a minute. "Mr. Browning, do you mean to tell me that Mrs. Mackay, with her rabid slaveholding, states' rights Democrat son-in-law, wouldn't be a states' rights Democrat if she could vote? That little lady interests me."

"I only know that W. H. Stiles does not particularly influence her thinking."

"Is that so?"

"They get along well, but mainly, I think, because W.H. makes Eliza Anne happy. Also because Miss Eliza knows when to bring up politics and when not to."

"I take it she really believes slavery is wrong."

"More than that, she believes it's evil," Mark said.

"Miss Lib?"

"She will be with W.H., no matter what."

"And when a man says 'no matter what' these days, he could be opening a real can of worms, eh?"

"That's right, Burke. Say, did you ever hear of a New York politician named William Henry Seward?"

"Certainly. Twice governor of the state. May be running for the Senate next year, in 1849."

"That's the man. Was big in the Anti-Masonic Party. He's running as a Whig now."

"Why do you ask? Do you actually know a man with Seward's rabid antislavery beliefs?" Burke questioned with a smile.

Mark grinned a little. "No, I don't know him personally, but Leroy Knight, the attorney who handles my inherited income up North, does know him. Since I've been up here I've had a letter from Knight forwarded from my Savannah office, and although he's only an acquaintance of Seward's, he's a close friend of Seward's powerful personal and political cohort, Thurlow Weed."

"The newspaperman."

"That's right. Weed told Knight that Seward could bring an enormous amount of pressure to bear in the Senate next year by his uncompromising stand *against* slavery. The man's going to say in the campaign this fall that slavery must be completely abolished! I believe Thurlow Weed helped write one speech in which Seward plans to tell the voters, 'Slavery must be abolished and you and I must do it!' When he was running for governor, Seward rather softened his words. Evidently he's finished with hedging. Weed, in fact, is trying to convince Seward to tell those who insist that the Constitution protects the rights of slaveholders to their human property that 'there is a higher law than the Constitution!'"

Burke whistled. "That's really going to start some of old Jefferson's firebells ringing in the night."

"It will indeed—*if* Seward says it."

"Of course, it'll make the Conscience Whigs up North happy. And Seward is running for the Senate from New York."

The two sat quietly for a time, while Burke emptied his cold pipe in a piece of newspaper and picked up the burnt match from the fireplace.

Then Burke asked, only half teasingly, "Could your Miss Eliza Mackay be a secret Conscience Whig?"

Mark's smile showed his deep affection for Miss Eliza. "Bless the lady. More often than I ever have the chance to express, I wish she could vote!"

"Say, Mr. Browning, I'm sure you know our county here is named for General Lewis Cass, born in Ohio, I think, but for years governor of the Michigan Territory. He was President Jackson's Secretary of War back in the thirties. They named the county for him, I'm sure, because Cass strongly favored the removal of the Cherokees."

"I know a fair amount about Cass. Don't forget, I remember the 1812 war with Britain. He was a hero."

"That's the man. The Democrats' nominee for President this fall, of course. I'm sure Mr. Stiles will support him."

"If he's back from Vienna in time, yes," Mark said, "but Lewis Cass doesn't stand a chance against the Whigs' Mexican War hero, 'Old Rough-and-Ready' Zachary Taylor. The Mexican War's the popular war at the moment, don't forget." Mark studied Burke's tanned, rugged face for a moment. "You'll vote this fall, won't you?" he asked.

"Oh, yes, I'll vote. Will you vote for Cass?"

"No," Mark said. "I'm a Whig of sorts—a Conscience Whig, I suppose." He chuckled. "And it's good to be able to admit it safely to someone. Cass opposes slavery, I think. At least, he wants every man to be able to choose for himself, although, so far, he mainly ignores the subject. Actually, Burke, I'd like to think the new Free-Soil Party stands a chance of getting old Van Buren elected in November. I doubt that's possible, though. Right now, I'm not sure who'll get my vote. I only know I will vote. I believe it a duty."

"Do you ever try to sit over in a corner and listen to us, sir? Here we both are—determined to spend our lives in Georgia and neither of us agreeable to Georgia's politics. We are peculiar, I'd say." They exchanged warm looks of understanding. "I'm glad we have each other at least."

A burst of laughter and excited chatter from outside brought their conversation to an abrupt end.

"Do you hear what I hear?" Mark asked. "Could our women folk and Jonathan be upon us so soon? Seems we only started to talk."

Getting to his feet, Burke said, "Let's go out and meet them, shall we? They seem awfully excited about something. I guess women do get that roused over a crate of china."

From the cottage porch, they watched the troop of hugging, exclaiming loved ones hurry up the path. Mark's own smile faded only when he saw Caroline's face. It had been Natalie and Callie and Mary and Jonathan doing all the happy chattering. Caroline was trying hard to smile, but looked as though she'd seen a ghost.

"What's all the commotion?" Burke called as he hurried along the path to meet them.

"Oh, Burke," Natalie caroled, "the best news in the world! Wait till you hear! And, Papa—you're not going to have to fake your happiness the way poor Mama is trying to fake hers. Wait till you hear!"

"Natalie, that's not fair. I'm—I'm genuinely pleased," Caroline said with what Mark could tell was no conviction at all.

"What on earth has happened?" he asked.

"Mary—Mary—Mary!" Callie shouted, her face wreathed in smiles. "Mary and the *baby!*"

"Callie!" Mark gasped. "What did you say?"

"No, Callie," Natalie interrupted, her hand over the child's mouth. "You mustn't tell Mary's secret, dear. It's for Mary to tell. Go on, Mary, before I burst wide open!"

Mark saw Mary look up at Jonathan, a questioning look on her face. "Go on, darling," Jonathan urged. "Tell Papa and Burke the wonderful news."

Mary was smiling, but Mark could see plainly that something also troubled her.

Haltingly, she said, "I—I'm not sure, but I'm—almost sure that on the first night—back up here in my old home, Jonathan and I have—have—loved a child into life!"

Burke and Mark both rushed to hug her. Mary hugged them back, then ran to Caroline. "Please, ma'am," she begged, "please be glad for us! Please do not be—stricken!"

"Why—why, Mary—shame on you! I'm not—*stricken* at all. What a thing to say! You know, just the way you stayed by me when I was ill, I'll stay right by you—if your baby *is* coming."

"Of course she will, Mary," Mark said eagerly. "We both will." He reached for Callie's hand. "We're so happy being Callie's grandparents, when you and Jonathan give us another grandchild, we'll be—twice as happy!"

"Please to be! Oh, I said that wrong. Please *be* happy," Mary almost pleaded. "And—" She turned to Caroline. "Please, Miss Caroline, could you be happy too—if there is a baby for Jonathan and me—that God made the miracle where He also made the miracle of Ben and me—for my mother, Green Willow? Up here in the home of—her people? Please—do I ask too much of you?"

Chapter 61

BACK in Savannah, throughout the unusually hot autumn, Mark worried again about Caroline's health. The intense heat, which lessened little, even at night, robbed her of sleep, and although she was, he knew, doing her best to be glad that Mary *was* carrying Jonathan's child, her struggle showed.

In November, after the country had elected Mexican War hero Zachary Taylor to the presidency, Eliza Mackay, during their daily visit, gave Mark a piece of good advice.

"We can put the election behind us for a time, dear boy, and get back to our personal lives. There's usually a quiet period while the people, like him or not, give a new President time to solve our seemingly unsolvable problems. I know he's a slave owner, but I think President Taylor is rather like dear Jack and Robert Lee where politics go. He's an Army man, not a partisan."

"Well, I voted for Taylor," Mark said, without enthusiasm, "simply because I thought he'd win and, even as a slaveholder, he doesn't want slavery spread into the new lands. Judging by what I hear and read, though, Calhoun will *not* let the matter rest in the Senate—in the country. That man's brilliance and influence scare me."

"All Southerners don't follow John C. Calhoun, Mark. He didn't get his way with nullification years ago because he couldn't convince enough Southerners, if you remember."

"I do, but at the Exchange Coffee House only yesterday, I heard two normally moderate men say quite casually that the South's only way out may be *secession*. Just the word is abhorrent to me. It's been bandied about in South Carolina, I know, for some time, but until now, only by hotheads here in Savannah."

"Don't even speak of secession, Mark! People like to spout. We have to believe it's all spouting."

"It doesn't frighten you?" he asked as she walked with him to the front steps.

"It scares me half to death, if you want to know the truth, but today is— today. Hotheads only cause real trouble if the rest of us allow them room."

He smiled down at her, took her hand. "In all Savannah, you're the one person who allows me to say what I think and feel and you can't even vote!"

"Maybe we can be honest with each other *because* I can't," she said with a twinkle.

"It's more than that."

"I know, but what matters today is that you find out *exactly* what troubles Caroline so much about Mary's being with child. It isn't like Caroline, certainly not after all this time. There's a reason for her to be upset and it's up to you to *find* out and *help* out."

In her fourth month, going right ahead with her daily duties in spite of severe morning sickness, by nightfall Mary was exhausted. Mark had no excuse for not having the all-important talk with Caroline. They had almost every evening alone because Jonathan and Mary went upstairs to bed so early. Still, he dreaded the whole idea of confronting Caroline, of finding out why she so obviously hadn't accepted the news of another grandchild. He had now promised Miss Eliza, though, and that very evening, in the family parlor, he brought it up point-blank.

"I know your heart is broken, darling," he began, "over Callie's crippled foot, but that's no reason to be so downcast that Jonathan and Mary have a baby coming next year. Can't you tell me what's troubling you? Can't you tell me for my sake? I'm so worried over our depressed cotton market, all the cargo I've lost in this new rash of accidents at sea—the drop-off in the Browning Shipping revenues because of the troubles in Europe—I honestly don't think I can bear another cloud. Certainly not between us."

"Oh, Mark, there's no cloud between us! Tell me, had Miss Eliza heard any news from Vienna when you saw her today?"

He answered as patiently as he could, determined not to allow her to change the subject. "Only that Eliza Anne and the children are back in Vienna, which appears oddly deserted. Ominously silent. Barricades still up."

"Just two weeks ago she wrote of mutilated bodies in the streets!"

"I know, but what I don't know is how Miss Eliza keeps her equilibrium. She's still grieving over Jack—now all this uncertainty about the Stiles family."

"Does she have any hope that they might be called home?"

"No. They're all just there, W.H. back from Paris, keeping to their apartment, waiting, it seems, to be starved out. Waiting day after day surrounded by an invasion force of Hungarian troops. Hungary seems determined to become a republic." He paused. "Dearest, there isn't a thing we can do about the trouble over there. Please answer my question. Why is this dread still hanging over you about Mary's child?"

"I'm afraid!"

"Afraid?"

"Yes, and I'm ashamed to tell you why. I loathe my fear, but it's there. An article I read in some periodical of Burke's while we were up there frightened me still more!"

"Caroline, what did you read?"

Struggle showed in every line of her troubled face. "That—even though Mary doesn't look Indian, her child *could*—probably will look like a full-blood Cherokee!" Her eyes filled with tears, her hands were clenched together. "Oh, I can't remember all the piece said, but what would we do if our grandchild—looked like Ben?"

Mark took her quickly in his arms and held her for a long time. "Thank you for telling me. You always end up being fair—and honest. And, beloved, couldn't that just as easily work the other way? Couldn't Mary's baby just as easily look like one of us?" He tried a small, unsuccessful laugh. "Why, he or she might even have Natalie's hair! We've never known where that flaming hair came from . . ."

Clinging to him, Caroline tried to laugh too—at herself. "I must be getting old," she said. "I know Miss Eliza would say I'm borrowing trouble. And she'd be right. But—what would we *do* if Jonathan's son or daughter looked like a full-blood Cherokee? What on earth would we do, Mark? No matter how you and I love Mary, our grandchild *will* have some of that savage blood in its little veins!"

The first Christmas without Jack was made bearable for Eliza Mackay and her family because of a letter from Colonel Robert E. Lee. The letter was written from his home at Arlington a week before the Holy Season and brought this happy news: "Sometime late in January, I will once again be able to run up those front steps at the blessed Mackay house on East Broughton! The Board of Engineers, of which I am now an exalted member, is being sent early in the new year, 1849, to examine lands reserved by the federal government as sites for future fortifications and, of course, this mighty mission cannot be carried out without the old boy to recommend which to keep and which to release. Our party will travel down through Alabama to Mobile, along both 'moskito-riddled' Florida coasts and then triumphantly, for me at least, on up to Savannah, where I will be able to spend two days—one hard at work inspecting federal lands—the other with my beloved Georgia 'family' at 75 East Broughton Street."

Eliza Mackay shared Lee's letter first with Jonathan, who still visited William almost every day. The young man's genuine excitement at the thought of being invited to dinner, with time to listen to the colorful Virginian he'd only met briefly with Jack, pleased her no end.

"Lee's like my own son," she told Jonathan that day, "and it will be so good to hear him speak of Jack. Those two were closer than some brothers. They loved each other so much."

"Lee was closer to Jack than I ever managed," William said, with no hint of jealousy.

"Now, William, that's not true," Miss Eliza said.

"No brothers ever loved each other more than Jack and I," William said quietly, "but he and Lee always had a lot more in common. Literature, the Army, women—the kind of wit and humor I just wasn't blessed with."

"Colonel Lee's a real Mexican War hero now," Jonathan said. "I'll be able to tell my own son—or daughter—that I actually had dinner with him!"

"You certainly will," William said. "We wouldn't think of not having your parents and you and Mary. He was here such a short time the year the Stileses left. Your father knew him long, long ago, but not well. Your parents were married and lived on Reynolds Square by then."

"And only had time for each other," she said. "Oh, they met Lee socially, as another adopted member of our family. I gave him Mark's old room, you know, back when Robert was first ordered to work at Fort Pulaski—some twenty years ago." Remembering, she smiled. "Now that I'm an old woman past seventy, that seems like two lifetimes ago *and* only yesterday."

"I'll do a lot of listening at dinner that night," Jonathan said, still glowing at the prospect. "Colonel Lee and my father will have so many things to talk about. I remember Jack's telling me that Colonel Lee, although he owns slaves, wishes there were a way to end slavery."

"He does," Miss Eliza said firmly. "And I agree with him."

Grinning, William said, "We all know that, Mama. The abolitionists wouldn't believe it, but you and Lee are in the same boat with hundreds of other Southerners there. One thing I'm sure about, though, is Lee's loyalty to Virginia *and* the Union. His life's the Army of the *United* States."

"Oh, yes," Miss Eliza said firmly. "I know he'll have been traveling a lot before he gets here, but my guess is that Lee keeps himself informed on exactly what Congress is up to this month in Washington City—no matter how he pretends to dislike politics. From what I read in the papers, both houses are doing battle right now over what the Constitution really says about spreading slavery into the new territories."

"You're right, Mama. They're wrangling over that, along with the poor old fugitive slave law." William sighed heavily. "One thing I certainly intend to ask Lee is: Are we going to have to go to war North and South!"

"Oh, William, no!" his mother gasped. "I forbid you even to mention such a thing. Our nation is still so young! Why, I'm older than our republic. It's been less than sixty years since George Washington was inaugurated. Don't even think of war!"

"Well, maybe not actual war with guns and bullets, Mama. We'd have to secede from the Union before we could do that, but we fool ourselves that a kind of war isn't already going on in Washington City—in both houses. You haven't read today's *Georgian* yet. Old John C. Calhoun's latest battle plan demands time for what they're calling 'An Address to the South'. They're holding a southern caucus up there right now. Things could get mighty explosive even before 'Old Rough-and-Ready' Taylor gets himself sworn into office next month. The battle lines are already drawn."

"William, stop it!"

"All right, Mama, but don't forget, the North is now so dead set against slavery for a whole variety of reasons, it took sixty-three ballotings and bitter, bitter threats on both sides before W.H.'s friend Howell Cobb of Georgia was chosen Speaker."

"There'll be a way through all this trouble, son," Eliza insisted. "There *has* to be."

"I hope you're right. I'm praying you're right. But it looks to me most of the time these days that the good Lord Himself doesn't see much sense trying to stop hotheads."

Chapter 62

IN THE middle of January of the new year, 1849, Mark, knowing how eager Miss Eliza was for word from Vienna, prepared to leave his office on Commerce Row as soon as he thought the 8:30 A.M. steamer from the North had time to unload its mail. Due to the added stress of work brought on by another cargo loss at sea and the continuing trouble in the cotton market, he'd planned to make his daily visit to the Mackay house later in the day. But in all his nearly thirty-seven years as Eliza Mackay's friend, he'd never been able to ignore even her silent longings. With the revolution in Vienna threatening the very lives of Eliza Anne and her family, his old friend's anxiety was now almost beyond endurance.

Picking up mail at the waterfront was no longer usual, but far quicker than waiting for it to reach the post office. Mark was eager as well for his own mail. Although old Woodrow Woolsey, who, for all Mark's youth, had been attorney for the vast Browning Shipping Company in the North, was long dead, the Philadelphia law firm still carried Woolsey's name. A letter from the firm of Knight and Woolsey would be more than welcome whether it contained word of still more losses due to the trouble in Europe or words of hope for the future. His own uncertainty over the sharp drop in his inherited income was causing increasing anxiety. Once he'd been able to depend upon $75,000 a year. For the past decade the amount had dropped until last year the European problems cut his income to under $10,000. All the more reason to work harder at his own Savannah factorage.

Of course, he thought as he slipped the latest Liverpool cotton market report into a desk drawer, he could always rely on his colleagues, should he, for the first time in his life, be forced into debt. Along with wealthy Scottish Andrew Low, Low's partner, Charles Green, and Savannah River plantation owner James Clack, Mark had, for several years, been a part of a gentlemen's agreement by which was established a safe fund for times of emergency. The safe fund assured Mark and the others that financial needs would be underwritten up to twenty percent, but Mark hated debt. He'd never had to draw on the safe fund. Ample funds had always simply been there. Even in the financial panic of 1837, under Van Buren's presidency, Mark Browning had remained well off, able to come to the rescue of his friends by underwriting their loans. Now, not only did he feel the pressure of the steep loss in inherited income, he could be forced for the first time to borrow money himself in order to have enough for loans to his planter clients when they needed seed for next year's crops.

Andrew Low and Charles Green still appeared more than stable, and although Mark found them both a bit stuffy and pompous, especially Low, he could count on their assistance if worse came to worst. Mark's client James Clack, with inherited wealth, railroad stock and a prosperous plantation, also showed no signs of backing out of the safe fund or of changing factors, in spite of his intense disapproval of Mark's long-held views on slavery. Worse could come to worst, of course, if New Orleans went on steadily depleting business at the port of Savannah. He sighed. At fifty-seven, instead of feeling free to turn over more and more of his factoring business to Jonathan, he was taking on additional burdens.

Still, he thought as he left his office and crossed Factor's Walk on his way to the familiar wooden stair that would take him down to the wharf, he had not been forced for any reason to leave his beloved Savannah. He smiled to himself as he went stiffly and carefully down the steps he once seemed to skim.

Many people younger than I have rheumatism, he reminded himself. I *am* still in Savannah, and Savannah has been kind to me. In spite of my refusal all these years to own slaves, the city has been gracious to me and to my family. If, as Caroline believes, Savannah has been gracious only because I've kept my opinions quiet and retained my wealth, so be it.

For years before Savannah had a post office, he'd picked up mail directly from incoming ships, and he still liked his long-held Savannah habits best, enjoyed the fellowship of the harbor workmen, who invariably went out of their way to find both the Browning and the Mackay mail for him.

In the packet for Mackay, he was relieved to find a thin letter from Eliza Anne, return address still Vienna. News from Europe, to which Savannahians had access, was as muddled as the reasons for the nationalistic revolts which had struck every country over there except Russia and Great Britain. Any direct word from the Stileses would be welcome for many reasons. There were also two letters for William Mackay, obviously of a business nature, since they bore railroad company addresses. William, by now, owned considerable railroad stock.

In his own mail, he was both pleased and puzzled to find the letter he'd hoped for from Leroy Knight, the Browning Company's Philadelphia attorney. The letter puzzled him because it felt thicker than the usual page or so. Sitting on a wharf crate, wanting the fresh, sunny air in spite of its chill, he opened Knight's envelope, skipped the usual headings and began to read the body of the letter: "I am glad to report that your revenues for the year 1848 just past have increased by the sum of $3,000 and a draft will be forthcoming with all necessary reports of the sources of this amount. I do hope your local

Savannah business is improved, as I am aware that the Browning Shipping Company's revenues are still greatly curtailed.

"Under separate cover you will find a package containing a booklet I feel certain will be to your liking, but which could also be extremely dangerous for you in pro-slavery Savannah should it be found in your possession." Mark frowned, wondering what on earth the man could be sending. "I hope that you will open the package personally and in the strictest privacy. You are fully aware of my own anti-slavery sentiments and of my activities up here in behalf of the abolitionist movement. I send a copy of *Slavery As It Is,* which is not signed, due to the author's sincere humility, but if in your isolation there from the important work of abolitionists in the North, you do not know the work of Theodore Weld, your own anti-slavery beliefs will be, I am sure, greatly fortified by his writing. I have known Weld for years and know him to be an authentic Christian, though a bit unusual in his dietary habits, which by many are considered eccentric. One enormous contribution he made was to the late, venerated John Quincy Adams while the old gentleman was still fighting against slavery in the Hall of Representatives in Washington City. Weld was given a desk in the Library of Congress and worked long hours feeding material to the Honorable John Q. Adams for use in his noble effort on the floor of Congress in behalf of our suffering Negro brothers in the South. You may destroy *Slavery As It Is* at your discretion or, if such could be possible in benighted Savannah, Georgia, pass it along for the good of the cause. I have long wanted to send this to you, but hesitated, for obvious reasons, to risk burdening you with the remarkable essay. It was written directly from actual news accounts, slave advertisements and testimonials gleaned by Weld's wife and her sister, both enlightened daughters of a South Carolina slave owner named Grimké. The strife in Congress now between North and South over this hellish issue is rampant. I try to imagine, and fail, what trouble this important essay of Weld's might cause you among your associates who cling to the evil of slavery and I pray the booklet will reach you firsthand and cause only relief that up here, at least, the cause for which your courageous aunt labored so long still flourishes. Not without struggle, though, for those of us who mean to *abolish* slavery, since except for a few brave souls, many who pretend to espouse emancipation merely want to deport our Negroes to Liberia under the insidious banner of what they term 'colonization.' "

Leroy Knight's letter ended with the usual cordial greetings, and Mark heaved a sigh of relief when, hunting through his remaining letters and packets, he found the plainly wrapped booklet from Philadelphia. He was relieved not only because of Knight's strong warnings but also because he knew what trouble such a publication *could* cause him in town were it to become known that it had been sent to Mark personally. He hurried back up the stairs to the privacy of his office to open the package alone.

The sight of his own trembling hands as he opened the essay and scanned the incendiary introduction made him feel oddly ashamed. Writing in a grandiloquent style, the author, Theodore Weld, begged the reader to consider himself a juror and to bring in a verdict on the question: "What is the actual condition of the slaves in the United States?" Quoting from the Bible, Weld also called upon the reader to view the evil institution from God's perspective. Then, from what he called "eyewitness statements and actual newspaper accounts from the southern press," he presented evidence that slaves were "fed poorly, housed in hovels, overworked, scruffily and immodestly clad, sorely neglected in old age and all their lives inhumanly punished."

Mark's mind raced back to his most uncomfortable conversation with Caroline early last year about the very same booklet which he now held in his hands. They had skirted dangerously near an argument, right after the news of John Quincy Adams's death, when Jack Mackay had brought a copy of *Slavery As It Is* home to Savannah as a prank.

As he flipped now through the pages, Mark's heart pounded with a new, nameless fear. The deplorable conditions described by Weld certainly did exist on many plantations in many parts of the South, he was sure. Even, he supposed, on some Savannah River plantations near Caroline's Knightsford. But Miss Eliza owned her house servants, William still owned nine people, and although William seemed to have no guilt at owning slaves, he was not, could never be, what abolitionists were calling a "lord of the lash."

Mark felt surprisingly disturbed by what he'd just read, almost confused. True, he had risked much by refusing to own another human being, by hiring Jupiter Taylor, a free person of color, by hiring a German nurse for the children and an Irish cook, but he had never felt free to press Caroline to sell Knightsford, where she'd grown up. He had even avoided the subject of Knightsford slaves. In fact, except with Miss Eliza and Burke, he'd avoided the subject altogether. But had he ever—before this moment—felt actual fear over it? Today, if he were honest, he did. Here he sat in his own office, at his own desk, holding a booklet that could, if his business associates knew he had it, be downright dangerous. Dangerous? What kind of danger? Being ostracized in town? He gave a mirthless laugh. In a very real way the Brownings were partially ostracized now because Jonathan had married a sweet half-breed Cherokee girl who meant no one an ounce of harm.

Disgusted with himself at the unaccustomed fear, he grabbed the Mackay mail, tossed the abolitionist essay aside and, as best he could with his stiff knee, hurried all the way to East Broughton Street.

Half an hour later, he had been quieted as always by even a short visit with Miss Eliza and William. There was vast relief also that Eliza Anne had written that W.H. was at last asking to be freed of his duties as chargé d'affaires in Austria and that after some sightseeing the family would be sailing for home in the fall of this year. The news made Miss Eliza so happy he couldn't bring himself even to mention his panic at receiving the incendiary booklet from the North. How could he be blamed anyway for an unsolicited gift from a man he knew only by correspondence—on a purely business basis?

He forced himself to stroll slowly back to Commerce Row, trying hard not to face some tormenting questions: Would he feel so threatened if he weren't in temporary financial straits? Had his sense of security in Savannah all these years been because of his wealth and prominence after all?

Inside his countinghouse, just around the corner of the short corridor that led off the entrance hall and into his private office, he heard plainly guarded voices. Men's voices, agitated, but barely audible.

"You expect him back soon, then?" Andrew Low's Scottish burr was unmistakable.

"Oh, yes, sir," Mark's clerk Jeremy Tread whispered back. "The way Mr. Browning left his mail spread on his desk, I'm sure he only went to the Mackay house for a brief visit. He's most orderly where his desk is concerned."

"And is it your custom, young man, to look at private mail on Browning's desk?" Charles Green's British accent was also plainly recognizable.

"Yes, Jeremy Tread," the raspy voice of James Clack asked, "are you regularly such a snoop?"

"No, Mr. Green, Mr. Clack," the young man said nervously, "but it is my custom to be a loyal citizen of Savannah! Gentlemen, I beg you to look at *this!*"

Charles Green, Andrew Low and James Clack, fellow members of the safe fund, were the last three men in town Mark wanted to face today. He stood there gripped by such panic that he struggled to slow his own breathing. His rabidly pro-slavery head clerk had surely seen the abolitionist essay from the North which Mark himself had stupidly left on his desk in plain view, and although he couldn't see into his office, Mark knew Jeremy was exposing him. He'd mistrusted the new head clerk from the start, but had allowed Jonathan to convince him to give the young man a trial.

Unable to stand there another moment shaken by the possible crisis ahead if his clerk *was* showing the radical booklet to the three men whose financial support he might still need, Mark coughed to let his presence be known and strode into his office.

"Gentlemen," he said, "I'm honored by your presence." Of his clerk, he asked, "Did you need something, Jeremy?"

"Oh, no, sir. I—I was just taking care of these gentlemen until you returned."

"Then you may go about your work."

When Jeremy left, Mark seated his three safe-fund colleagues in the roomy office, himself behind the desk. "A pleasant day for January," he remarked. When no one responded beyond a nod, he added, "I've just returned from Miss Eliza Mackay's house. You'll be interested to know, I'm sure, that there was good news from Vienna in the letter I delivered. At least, good news for all of us who think so highly of the Stiles family. W.H. has asked to be relieved of his duties and evidently they plan to return sometime this fall."

"That is splendid news," Andrew Low said. "The Stileses have had a difficult time over there. No one knows that better than you, Browning, with the losses you've sustained from your world shipping income. Are those losses continuing?"

Resenting Low's curiosity, but realizing that, as a member of the safe fund, Low had every right to ask, Mark replied merely that he had learned in the same mail that there had been a slight increase in Browning shipping.

Mark then broke an awkward silence by offering cigars, which were refused. "Did you gentlemen have particular business with me today?"

"Far more urgent business than any of us knew until we arrived," heavy-shouldered James Clack said in a cold, almost threatening voice. "Actually, we have a demand to make. We demand to know, Browning, exactly what troublemaking plans you—"

"Now, hold on a minute," Charles Green interrupted. "I strongly advise caution, Clack. The four of us have enjoyed too fine a business relationship to risk bad feelings among us, so I urge that—"

"Bad feelings over—what, sir?" Mark wanted to know.

"Intelligent gentlemen can always discuss their way around any thorny issue, it seems to me," Green said a bit uncertainly, "and with strong business ties affecting us all, both here and in Liverpool, I see no reason to jeopardize—"

"It is because of those strong business connections that I feel we must be honest and aboveboard," Andrew Low broke in, his voice at its most authoritative. "Your head clerk appears to have your best interests at heart, Browning. I hope you're aware of that."

Mark now had no doubt. Jeremy Tread turned out to be the hothead Mark had feared all along. Even Jonathan had admitted that since the Browning fortunes had suffered during the past year, Jeremy was eager to work for either Low or Green, hoping for a higher income. Mark had honestly not expected the connivance to go this far. He could conclude only that Jeremy Tread had shown the dangerous abolitionist work of Theodore Weld to the three men in the hopes of building his own stock with them.

The painful silence lengthened until Mark could bear it no longer. He looked first at Low. The slightly heavy, but handsome face was closed, stern, and appeared far older than his thirty-six years. James Clack, somewhat Mark's senior, was openly sneering. For all the years they'd been slaveholding client and factor, Mark and James Clack had both avoided the subject of Mark's anti-slavery views, but neither strongly held opinion was a secret to the other. At this moment, Clack appeared ready to explode, his bulbous face —as Jack Mackay would have said—was as discolored as though he'd taken an emetic. Only Green seemed fairly composed, as always, seeking the diplomatic way out.

"I'm quite certain of what happened just before I walked back into this office, gentlemen," Mark said as calmly as possible, reaching as he spoke for the booklet still on his desk. "Should we take care of whatever business brought you here before we discuss this publication which my head clerk has taken the liberty to show you?"

With a toss of his shock of thick, dark red hair, Andrew Low said, "Our business, when we came, was purely philanthropic, sir, and compared to that potentially damaging book you hold in your hands, of relative unimportance. We came for your Union Society pledge for Bethesda Orphanage. Even now, we are not here to make trouble among us. None of us doubts the mutuality of our business need for one another, especially until Savannah's economy improves."

"As you know, Browning," Charles Green said, "every prominent man in town is aware of your northern political opinions on the treacherous subject set forth in that ill-advised publication called *Slavery As It Is*. Regardless of our individual views on the topic, we've all held to an unspoken agreement to keep the peace among us. This has been true across the city, in fact. I feel you'd have to say that, in the main, you've been left alone with your— somewhat singular convictions."

"True," Mark said. "I've been grateful for that." His heart was thumping as though he were a schoolboy in trouble, and it angered him, shamed him, muddled his thinking. He knew, though, that the less he said the better, that he must try to stay calm.

"Southerners, *true* Southerners," Clack said in a voice so arrogant and insulting that he might have given Mark a glove across the face, "truly *loyal* Savannahians, Browning, are not in the habit of taking serpents to their breasts! You *should* be grateful. Grateful, indeed, that we have accepted you for your commercial power and otherwise positive influence in the community. But if those damnyankee abolitionists are secret allies of yours—"

"I don't believe I said that I *should* be grateful," Mark broke into the tirade, anger mounting. "I said I *am* grateful. I know my refusal to own slaves has made my wealth and standing in the community absolute necessities to me through the years. Without my prosperity, nothing would have made it possible for me to live here, no matter how deeply I love the city. I could wish that—" He could feel his voice about to break with emotion, so he cleared his throat before he went on. "I could wish that my—obvious devotion to the city might have been enough to merit your friendship. I know better now. Perhaps I've always known better. But I—pray you not to allow the sight of this booklet—to affect your attitudes toward my son, Jonathan, who is in no way to blame for my owning it."

As on a signal, the three men got to their feet.

"Your son is quite acceptable to us so far," Andrew Low said. "We have all tried to show only kindness to his Indian wife and certainly the young man cannot be blamed for his father's unfortunate views."

Mark was standing too, but silent. He simply stood there, scarcely aware that he still held the abolitionist booklet in his hand.

"We will assume your usual generous contribution to Bethesda Orphanage, Browning," Charles Green said, once more the diplomat. "So perhaps in order to avoid trouble in the business community, you should consider our brief visit today mainly as a strong warning."

A fleeting frown furrowed Mark's brow, then vanished. "A—warning, Mr. Green?"

"I'll clarify that, sir," Clack said sharply. "You will continue to keep your traitorous pro-northern views *and* that lying book to yourself or our safe-fund agreement with you is a thing of the past! Is that plain enough, Browning?"

"Spoken like a true South Carolinian, sir," Mark snapped, and hated himself for having sunk to Clack's level. Coastal South Carolinians *were* in the main red-hot fire-eaters where slavery was concerned and Clack had been born in South Carolina on a plantation outside Charleston. "I apologize for adopting your—insulting tactics, Mr. Clack, but—"

Andrew Low's quick grab of Clack's doubled fist barely saved Mark a blow on the chin. During the scuffle, as Green helped restrain James Clack, Jonathan rushed in to stand beside his father.

"Is there trouble, gentlemen?" Jonathan asked.

"Only because of your father's indiscretion, young man," Green said evenly. Motioning toward the book, which Mark still held, he added, "It seems some of us are too well read. As British citizens, neither Low nor I need to allow ourselves to become embroiled in the growing dissension between North and South, but as cotton merchants, we *are* involved. For now, in order to end this unpleasantness, we are taking our leave. The warning holds, Browning. Your son is our witness. If you come out of your present business difficulties, you'll come out on your own—unless you destroy that incendiary publication you're holding in your misguided hand."

"I echo Mr. Green's words, of course," Andrew Low said. "The uninformed of the city still go about their shallow days as though real trouble is not brewing in the Congress of the United States at this very instant." He shook his finger at Mark. "Trouble *is* brewing. If we whose interests lie with the South are to put an end to acts of northern aggression against our southern economy, those of us with sound business judgment must find a way to control *some* among us with little or no judgment." He took Clack's arm and propelled him toward the door. "I believe, Mr. Clack, that we have made our point well and should bring this unfortunate interview to an end."

Mark and Jonathan, still standing side by side behind the desk, said nothing beyond a cold, polite murmur of "Gentlemen." Neither nodded nor bowed.

At the open door, Clack whirled around, shook his fist and said in a voice that could be heard all over the offices, "Watch the papers, Browning, if you think you can go on ad infinitum with your traitorous conduct in the city you claim to love! Watch the papers for developing news. Even the lamebrains who pretend the Union can go on forever will find out the truth—and sooner than most think. Don't you forget it!"

When the callers had gone, Jonathan went to close the door softly. He stood there in front of the desk for a long time before he said, "Papa, we're—all right so far. We'll go on being all right."

"Yes, son. Yes."

"Between your views on slavery and my marriage to a Cherokee, we do make it hard on Savannahians."

The boy's disarming smile, more warming than the pale January sun on this cold morning, brought a half smile to Mark's face. It brought genuine warmth to his heart.

"Thanks, Jonathan," he said. "We just have to stay proud that we are—Savannahians too."

Chapter 63

ON THE late January day the Mackays' cherished friend Colonel Robert E.
Lee was expected for dinner, Caroline busied herself about the Browning mansion with unusual energy. In fact, during the past two weeks, for
Mark's sake, she'd been taking full responsibility for running the household.
Seeing her up and in charge seemed to make him act a little more like
himself. For days he hadn't been Mark at all. Oh, he wasn't cross, but withdrawn, indulging in long, unexplained silences, unnaturally moody. Caroline
worried and with reason, because for so many years she'd depended upon his
gentle cheerfulness, his even disposition. Only Natalie, in the old days, had
seemed capable of destroying his good humor. Something was terribly wrong
now. Caroline knew her husband, knew him so well she had actually felt his
pain even more keenly than her own at their first sight of Natalie's child
limping toward them.

No one, *nothing* should ever hurt this good man, she'd thought again and
again through the years, but he was hurt now, deeply hurt. Until he was free
to tell her about it, she was doing what she'd always meant to do—relieve
him of the burden of even one family decision or concern.

Knowing how eagerly the Mackays looked forward to the visit of Colonel
Lee, Caroline had made the decision that the Brownings would not arrive at
the Mackay house until just before dinner.

"Dinner won't be served," Caroline told Mary as they mounted the stairs
together to dress, "until four. The Mackays need a good visit with Colonel
Lee before we get there. So don't let Jonathan rush you. He's so eager to be
with Colonel Lee again, you may have to be firm with him. We aren't arriving
until almost time to sit down at the table."

"It will help Miss Eliza to talk to Captain Jack's good friend," Mary said,
"but I am almost afraid to meet such a splendid officer—a hero to Jonathan."
With a sly grin, she added, "I promise to keep still except when spoken to. I
want you to be proud of me—not ashamed."

"Oh, Mary, Mary," Caroline said, "I'm never ashamed of you. And you
mustn't be at all conscious that your baby is several months along."

In the upstairs hall, Mary asked, "You are sure? Big stomachs are to be
hidden in public."

"Not with friends as close as the Mackays and on such a special occasion. We'll all only be—proud of you."

"I hope *you* will be."

Ashamed of herself for not being able to show proper joy and anticipation over the little one on its way into all their lives, Caroline reached for Mary's hand. "Believe me, whatever troubles you about me, even the tiniest bit, is my fault, not yours. And we're *not* waiting until the last minute to arrive because of you at all. I simply think the Mackays and Colonel Lee need time alone to speak of Jack, who meant so much to each one of them."

"Yes, ma'am," Mary said thoughtfully. "I will be careful to talk right since Colonel Lee is so beautiful with the words he writes. I will never forget what he wrote after he learned of his friend's death, that always his 'heart will bear the scar of Jack's death and the joy of his life.' I long also to be beautiful with words!"

Giving Mary a hug, Caroline said, "I didn't realize you even saw that letter from the Colonel! I'm impressed. You do seem to remember—what matters. And regardless of how I act at times, please remember also that I not only love you, I trust you with—keeping all our hearts safe." She glanced toward the master bedroom, where Mark was dressing. "Especially my poor husband right now."

"He is troubled, I know."

After Mary went to her room, Caroline stood a moment outside their bedroom door. Bless Mary, she thought, for not asking questions about Mark's strange, depressed mood, because I certainly have no answers.

Even before Mark rattled his familiar tattoo with the old knocker on the Mackays' front door, they heard happy voices and laughter from inside. As they waited on the porch, Mark couldn't help feeling relieved that Colonel Lee was doing what Jack always said he did best—making the most of any bad time. It could, he knew, have been a distressing, sorrowful event, this first meeting of the Mackays and Lee just a few months after Jack's death.

Miss Eliza and the girls still wore black mourning dresses, but the house was ablaze with both candles and new oil lamps and the Brownings were greeted all around with embraces, handshakes and smiles. The gracious, handsomely uniformed Lee was right there at the door with the welcoming family and in seconds Mark had forgotten the last vestige of the boyish jealousy he'd carried through the years. Years in which he'd wonderd at times if the adored Robert Lee might have been first in the Mackay hearts—above Mark—because Lee was a native Southerner.

After Miss Eliza proudly introduced Mary as Jonathan's wife, Colonel Lee bowed to Mary, then clasping Mark's hand, said, "So we meet again, sir. Do you know I always remember you as the gentleman whose very own Mackay bed I slept in upstairs at the end of the hall? Browning, for all this time, I've felt ridiculously envious of you. But I ask you, did a man ever sleep so well or enjoy such marvelous dreams as in that room—in that bed?"

"Never," Mark said, his heart going out to the striking, warmhearted younger gentleman.

"Of course, it's been a long time," Lee went on easily, "but somehow I feel you'll agree, Browning, that whatever is admirable about us both is due to the Mackay influence—and," he added with a chuckle, "their taking in a couple of homeless strays like us."

Mark could tell that Caroline liked Lee enormously too and felt a little of the tightness around his own heart loosen as the cheerful Virginian seemed almost to blot out the ugly second meeting in his office today with Andrew Low. Mark knew that he would now never waver in his own hatred of slavery, but he had, since today's encounter, felt weak and apprehensive. Andrew Low, in spite of his tendency to be gruff and a little overbearing, had, Mark thought, always been a friend. Oh, Low had come alone today, he vowed, because of that friendship—merely to underline the warning of the earlier unpleasant confrontation with Green and Clack. "I pray you will not fall on further reverses, Browning," Andrew Low had said today, his eyes cold, narrowed with anger. "The cloddish folk in our town seem not even to be aware that if some preventive measure isn't found in Washington City, the country could well be torn apart. Men of our intellects *are* at last aware of that danger. Your abolitionist colleagues at the North will not be permitted to make the South a further victim of their aggression into our personal affairs! Slavery *is* our personal affair. I came again today merely to warn you. I cannot —will not—move a finger to help you financially unless and until you—recant."

Mark had not recanted. Blessedly, he needed no financial help now. Another brief letter from Leroy Knight in Philadelphia had informed him that the first income report from the Browning Shipping Company had been erroneous in Mark's favor, by nearly $4,000. He could, of course, make no further investments, nor could they take a trip North when Savannah's stifling heat came again, but most likely he would not now need help from even one stiff-necked Savannah gentleman. He and Jonathan were going to be able to care for their wives and go on living almost as well as ever. Low's unpleasant visit still rankled, though. Still hurt. Most painful of all, the enmity shown him by his safe-fund colleagues caused him to feel alien to Savannah itself!

Seated now with the others around the large, familiar Mackay dining table, Mark smiled at Miss Eliza, who sat beside him. "I do like your Colonel Lee more than ever," he whispered. "And whatever the source of his charm, he has already given my sagging spirits an enormous lift."

She did not respond at once, but laid one small, age-spotted hand over his. "You're still worried about something, aren't you?" she asked softly. "I wish you felt free to tell me. I'm imagining all sorts of things."

He patted her hand. "Don't do that," he said. "You know I'll tell you eventually. And I do thank you for wanting us here this evening. Being with Colonel Lee is a rare privilege."

* * *

The guest of honor was extraordinarily kind to Mary, Mark thought, and felt grateful to the man, although Robert Lee did strike him as someone who would readily recognize Mary's real value. Jonathan hung on Lee's every word and beamed his pleasure each time the Colonel made a point of including Mary. Even William laughed more than usual as the excellent meal progressed. Each course was lovingly served by plodding old Hannah and the still sprightly Emphie, each smiling every time she pushed through the door from the kitchen with another bowl of carrots or stewed apples or fluffy chicken dumplings. The meal was evidently a favorite of Colonel Lee's from the happy, fun-filled times spent at the Mackays' in the old days.

Years ago, Bob Lee had first come to Savannah as a young lieutenant to work on the foundations and drainage of the now massive federal Fort Pulaski, but Hannah and Emphie treated him as though he'd been their treasured guest only a few days back. Mary, who'd known Jack Mackay so briefly and not as a healthy, young prankster at all, laughed at every West Point escapade Lee recounted from days when he and Jack had been classmates. Maybe, Mark thought, seeing Mary in this company, observing the gallant attentions paid her by Colonel Lee, would help settle some of Caroline's fears that the new baby might *look* Cherokee. He smiled to himself—*at* himself. I must really believe Colonel Robert E. Lee is a magician!

By the time Hannah lumbered in with the crystal stand bearing what she called "Lootenant Lee's *most* favorite"—a five-layered devil's food cake—they had not only laughed and laughed but twice had been near tears at something touching Lee had remembered about Jack. The contrasts—both tears and laughter—made still more poignant the Colonel's own sense of loss because his old friend was no longer there.

No one bothered to correct Hannah's "Lootenant Lee," because he'd been only a lieutenant when she'd served and adored him as a young man. The merriment around the table lightened Mark's own dejected heart to the extent that at every lull in the good talk, he stopped letting his mind rush back to the unvarnished antagonism Andrew Low had displayed earlier today. Outside this brightly lighted, love-filled home lay brewing a dark, dark trouble which could wound them all, he knew, but tonight at least, if possible, he meant to try to put it aside.

Especially, he longed to put completely out of his mind a new, terrifying realization that had shadowed his entire day—had so depressed him that he'd even thought of begging off Miss Eliza's cherished dinner party with Lee. Miss Eliza had tried so hard to teach him through the years that worry over something that had not yet happened was "borrowing trouble." The terrifying new realization had to do with Jonathan. Should there be real trouble ahead for the country, Jonathan, at nearly twenty-three, would be the perfect military age! Should today's *Georgian* editorial be right about the "very real threat of war with the North unless Congress comes to its senses," Jonathan would surely be conscripted. Mark had hidden the paper from Caroline, and as Emphie set down before him a plate of scrumptious cake, he breathed a prayer that William wouldn't bring up the alarming editorial, that no one would even mention the latest news of Calhoun's hotheaded address to the slaveholding members of Congress.

The prayer had no sooner formed in Mark's mind than William said, "We know you've been away from Washington City for a few weeks inspecting federal lands, Robert, but I always got the impression that Army officers managed to keep up on the foolishness back at the capital. How do things look to you now that old Calhoun's shot off his mouth to Southerners? You think the old man's right that we don't have any choice but to secede if it turns out we're outnumbered by congressmen from a new free state of California?"

A deathlike silence filled the candlelit room. After only one bite of Hannah's cake, Mark laid down his fork. He glanced first at Jonathan, whose eyes were riveted on Lee's face, then at Caroline and Mary. They were both puzzled, frowning. Caroline, he was sure, because she knew too well what William's question meant. Mary, he supposed, because she didn't quite understand.

William pressed his question. "Have you had time today, Colonel, to read the newspaper?"

"Uh—not in detail," Lee said quietly, his voice cautious. "I was on horseback until noon. Then I rode straight here, if you remember, still covered with your good old black marsh mud." Lee looked at Miss Eliza for a moment, then added, "But your alert mother brought the *Georgian* upstairs to me the minute she knew I'd bathed and dressed. I did read that jarring editorial your friend Bulloch wrote about what he's calling 'the very real threat of war,' William. I remember Bulloch. He's an intelligent man and I do value our free press, even when it gives the Army short shrift, but—" Now Lee laid down his fork too and looked straight at William, his voice no longer cautious. "I am also a firm believer that Americans, North and South, are not foolish enough to dwell for long on anything so insane as—breaking up our hard-won Union. Thinking men know, of course, that the kind of fire-eating going on in Congress now could lead to—an act of sheer insanity." Lee paused. "I still mean, though, to cling fast to the absolute fact that we *must* stay together. No matter how fine our Army, how advanced our armaments, in the Union only is our strength!"

"Lootenant Lee?" Hannah interrupted in a loud whisper from the kitchen doorway. "Lootenant Lee—you don't like devil's cake no more?"

"What?" Lee, seeing he'd hurt Hannah by putting his fork aside, got up to bow to her. "I love it more than ever, Hannah! I just don't want to spoil my pure joy in every delicious bite by having to—think or speak of unpleasant subjects!"

"Yes, sir," Hannah said, somewhat relieved. "Just so you still like it the best of any cake you ever ate."

"I do, because, Hannah—it *is* the best. The very, very best!" Taking his place again at the table, Lee held up a hand to silence any more questions from William and devoured every crumb of the huge slab of rich cake. A glance at the door showed Hannah, smiling and satisfied, on her way back to the kitchen.

"Now, William," Lee said, wiping his mustache with a linen napkin, "I'd hoped the topic wouldn't come up, but I quite understand your wanting to know, since I am here inspecting federal lands for new fortifications, if I happen to have any inside information. The answer is no. Army officers are the last to learn about any new madness going on among our exalted politicians in Washington City—except, of course, that it's usually a good guess that Congress has turned down an important appropriation we really need to defend the nation."

William smiled briefly at the familiar Army jab at Congress, then grew solemn. "Well," he said, "what Bulloch quoted right from Calhoun's so-called Southern Address sounded pretty dangerous to me."

"It sounded so because it *is* dangerous," Lee said, nodding thanks to Emphie for refilling his coffee cup.

"We've all heard talk of secession, but this is the first time I recall seeing it in print and—"

"William, hush! Not another word about any of this," Sarah Mackay scolded. Actually, this was the first Mark had heard from Sarah throughout the meal, except to laugh and cry at Lee's reminiscences about her brother Jack. "Look what you've done, William! You've forced Robert to gulp down his favorite cake by your stupid, bad-mannered question!"

Miss Eliza straightened regally in her chair. "Sarah, William asked a difficult question, but in my opinion it was neither stupid nor bad-mannered. I, for one, want to hear—I *need* to hear what Robert has to say about that frightening speech of Calhoun's. I read it too."

Smiling at Miss Eliza, Lee said, "If I were a member of Congress, God forbid, I'd stand up to give at least one woman the vote, Mrs. Mackay. That one woman, of course, would be you. So help me, I'd trust *your* judgment above that of any gentleman picking his teeth from any seat in the entire House or Senate!"

"Flattery is enjoyable," she said, her voice oddly unsteady, "but you'll be gone tomorrow, Robert, and we *need* to hear what you have to say. Please, *please* tell us exactly what you're thinking!"

Mark looked at Miss Eliza beside him. Her hands were clenched together so tightly the thin, aging skin over her knuckles was white and shiny. Lee's half-joking flattery had not made her smile. Silence again filled the room. The only sounds came from the kitchen, and Mark thought even they were unusually subdued. Everyone was looking at Lee, waiting for what he might say next.

"Please, Robert," Miss Eliza begged again.

"All right." And then Lee began to speak softly, looking directly at no one, almost as though thinking aloud. "A green, new representative from Pennsylvania named David Wilmot some time ago seems to have opened a Pandora's box—and in that box, in my opinion, were knots and knots of writhing, poisonous snakes. Oh, his proposal was defeated, but the troubling slavery issue was shoved front and center. Both sides grew more daring—Southerners *and* abolitionists. Wilmot himself freely admitted that his Proviso, *prohibiting* the spread of slavery into the new territories, was not conceived from any long-held sympathy for the bondage of the Negro. His reason behind it was simple, really, and had to do only with politics and the economy. Should slave owners be allowed to take their people into the new lands, Wilmot's own laboring-class white constituents from Pennsylvania would be deprived of work because slaves would be there to do it."

Lee stopped, one finger idly toying with an unused spoon on the table beside his empty cake plate. For a few seconds, Mark noticed, even the kitchen was quiet. Emphie and Hannah were listening too. Why not? he thought. Both are Mackay slaves.

Caroline's sudden, hard coughing spell broke the silence. Mark ached for her, because breaking into a spell in public still embarrassed her terribly.

"Please forgive me, Colonel Lee," she said, after a sip of water.

"Not at all, Mrs. Browning. I'm sorry to be hogging the conversation in such a manner, but—"

"It's my fault, Robert," Miss Eliza put in. "And I want you to go right on, if you will, please."

Lee smiled warmly at his hostess and said, "Now you're flattering me, dear friend, but my own ego, Jack always said, is as outsized as that of any congressman. I revel in all this attention. Army officers are seldom listened to for any length of time." Leaning back in his chair, he chuckled. "The difference between congressmen and Army officers is that congressmen don't admit their conceits. We do, merely by dressing up in these elaborate uniforms." He gestured toward his blue jacket and ticked a gold button. "Actually, I'm glad that as an officer in the United States Army, I'm expected to do little more than ride over and pass an opinion on federal lands. Politicians, on the other hand, take unto themselves the awesome task of passing or rejecting actual laws—laws that bless or rip at people's daily lives." He paused a moment, then, his voice full and strong, almost fervent, he said, looking at Mary and Caroline, "Miss Mary, Mrs. Browning, you two charming ladies may be the only two around this table who haven't heard that I consider slavery an outright evil. Somehow, I feel that you, Browning, and your son have heard it often either from Mrs. Mackay or from William—or Jack."

Jonathan, at the far end of the table from the guest of honor, addressed him directly for the first time. "Yes, sir, William and Miss Eliza have both told me, but I'd certainly like to hear it straight from you because I—I know that any talk of secession *could* lead to—war." Jonathan looked around the table. Everyone watched his face, especially his parents. "You see, Colonel Lee," he went on, "I'm the only one here who would, in case of war, be called upon to —fight. Except you, sir, of course."

"Of course," Lee said. "And how would you—respond to such a call, Jonathan?"

"I'm not sure. That's why I wish you'd go on. I've never had any particular thought of a military life." He smiled slightly. "Except for joining my father's Chatham Artillery Regiment here, of course. Whatever I do, though, I like to have the facts straight. To know the truth. I may not get another chance to listen to you. I—admire you more, I'm sure, than you have any idea."

The look Lee gave Jonathan both pleased and troubled Mark. It pleased him because in the look was genuine admiration for his son. It troubled him because, quite evidently, Lee had been thinking far more deeply on the dark issue of secession than he'd led them all to believe.

After a short silence, Lee said, "Well, young Browning, the country needs thinkers like you, men who aren't afraid to weigh things, to accept—truth, if they're fortunate enough to discover it. In this enlightened age, I like to think there are many—even in the South—who *do* consider slavery an evil institution. Our Declaration of Independence plainly states that 'all men are created equal.' I loathe having ownership of my people on my conscience!"

Mark glanced at Caroline. She was staring at Lee.

"Materially," Lee went on, "I'm a poor man with a wife and seven children to care for. I live in a fine house inherited by my wife from her family. There are, of course, many slaves attending it. I, personally, own one woman named Nancy and her children. When I left for the Mexican War, I made a will in which I simply could *not* include Nancy and her little family as *my property,* since I do regard slavery as a moral evil. In that will, which still stands, they will all be liberated as soon as it can be done to their advantage. That said, I must add that hundreds of other slaveholding Southerners are in the same boat with me—including our Mrs. Mackay, who thoroughly agrees with me on the troubling subject."

Mark fidgeted in his chair, not daring now to look at Caroline, who probably didn't even know how many Knightsford people she owned. For all the years of their married life, they'd skirted the painful issue.

When he could bear it no longer, Mark did look at his wife, seated directly across the lighted table. Suddenly, she seemed so distant, so closed off, so alone, he longed to rush to her and hold her, counting, as they'd done so often, on the power of nearness to push aside the ugly problem.

Caroline's eyes were fixed on her partially eaten dessert. She was looking at no one.

"Do you feel, Robert," William asked after a time, "that Northerners are, as Calhoun declared, 'committing actual acts of aggression against us down here'?"

"I can't answer that, William," Lee said. "I can speak only of my own convictions. While I wish always to do what is right, I am also unwilling to do what is wrong—whether at the bidding of the North or at the bidding of the South. Don't forget, my friend, I'm an officer in the *United* States Army. I'm sure we all—around this table and across the country—hope, in our own ways even pray, for eventual emancipation." Rather abruptly, he turned to Mark. "Browning, I understand that you are more or less unique in Savannah—that you refuse to own anyone."

Again Miss Eliza touched Mark's hand. "I told him," she said simply.

"You're correct, Colonel," Mark said, his heart pounding as the hateful scenes in his office rushed back. This time, though, it was mainly Caroline, his own adored wife, who was causing his heart to pound. He could not hurry to her, take her into his arms at the dinner table! He could only hope that in the ongoing silence, no one could hear his own struggle even to draw his breath.

"I assume you, Mrs. Browning, are in agreement with your husband on the hated subject?"

Mark caught Jonathan's eye. The boy was as agitated as he. Even Mary leaned forward in her chair, half turned to Caroline seated beside her. Mary's every muscle and nerve were taut—ready, Mark was sure, to spring to Caroline's rescue.

Instead of a direct answer, which anyone who knew Caroline would have expected of her, she looked coldly at Lee for a moment, then asked, "Sir, you're a Virginian, a Southerner—*is* there another solution to this—despicable state of affairs—beyond the South's separating itself from northern aggression?"

"There is prayer, Caroline, my dear!" To Mark, Miss Eliza's quick words were far more than a helpless reminder. They were a *plea.*

Shoulders straight, chin lifted high, face a mask, Caroline demanded, "And for what do we pray, Miss Eliza? For *what* do we pray, Colonel Lee? Do we pray for God to change *us* or *them?* Is God really concerned with the wording of the Constitution of the United States? Slave owners are *protected* by the Constitution, you know, no matter how—some may choose to interpret one sentence from the Declaration of Independence from Britain!"

Mark watched Caroline's every reaction—flashing eyes, color flushing her throat—hands out of sight in her lap, but, he knew, trembling. Mark felt surprisingly touched by the look of genuine compassion on Lee's handsome face.

No one spoke.

Mark was still looking at Lee when Caroline's sudden helpless gasp—a half sob—ripped into the silence. Fighting a kind of panic he'd never known, Mark stared at her, unable to move. Along with the helplessness, her gasp was full of anger, and when Caroline's straight, stiff shoulders began to heave, he leaped to his feet and rushed around the table, but stopped short of where she sat weeping—for once in her life—totally out of control.

Jonathan and Mary were on their feet too, white as ghosts and clinging to each other. It was his place to do something, Mark knew, but the very inaction of Jonathan and Mary, both of whom would normally be trying to help, held him motionless a step or two short of where his wife sat sobbing.

Lee was standing too, as was Miss Eliza, William and both sisters. Mark heard the kitchen door creak. Emphie and Hannah were surely listening—staring, wide-eyed, through the crack.

"My deep apologies, Mrs. Browning," Lee said at last, his tone one of tenderness. "If what I said caused this—pain, I am truly sorry. Mrs. Mackay is right, though. We must all pray and leave the results in God's hands, to whom a thousand years are but a day . . . We dare not—panic, any of us—whatever opinion we hold!"

Still rooted where he stood, unable even to touch her, Mark did the only thing he could do at this—awful moment. He prayed—wordlessly—for the sobbing woman he loved more than he loved his own life.

After an agonizingly long time, he sensed more than saw Miss Eliza slip around the table to where he stood.

"Take her home at once, Mark," she said firmly. "For Caroline's sake—take her right home. She needs to be away from all our staring faces—at home. With you."

Outside, Mark had only a moment on the porch alone with Miss Eliza while Jonathan, William and Colonel Lee helped Caroline down the familiar front steps of the Mackay house just as Jupiter appeared running from the back door toward the Browning carriage. Evidently Jupiter had overheard too, from the kitchen, where he'd eaten his own dinner.

"I'm more sorry, Miss Eliza," Mark whispered, "than I can ever tell you! I know Caroline will be—devastated tomorrow at what she said—and did." Irrelevantly, foolishly, he added, "She hates—bad manners above everything."

"I'm ashamed of you, Mark, for even thinking such a thing!"

He grasped her hand. "So am I," he whispered.

"Take her home and hold her in your arms—all night. And pray—oh, how we must pray for God's light to shine all the way across our—poor young nation! Into every heart. Into every mind . . ."

"I'm—truly afraid," he said hoarsely.

"So am I, dear boy. We have reason to be, because—without light in every heart, such a darkness could fall over this land that no one of us alive now may ever be able to see things whole again . . ."

Afterword

THANKS to a series of resolutions by Henry Clay which we now know as the Compromise of 1850, the darkness Eliza Mackay prophesied did not fall for a little more than a decade, but the Union was indeed hurtling—even that night—toward darkness. Robert E. Lee did have dinner in the old Mackay house on East Broughton in Savannah in late January of 1849 and what he said to his friends about his dislike of slavery and his love of the Union was carefully extracted from his own words.

I must here emphasize my indebtedness to Margaret Sanborn, author of *Robert E. Lee* (Volumes I and II, published in 1966 by the J. B. Lippincott Company and expertly edited by Carolyn Blakemore, my own editor now at Doubleday). Ms. Sanborn's excellent research and writing did much to help me draw the character of the younger Lee and doubly confirmed his close relationship with the Mackay family of Savannah. Some of Lee's own words on slavery and the Mexican War came also from *The Gray Fox* by Burke Davis (the Fairfax Press edition published in 1981).

Again, I must try to express my appreciation of the Georgia Historical Society, for years, my second home in Savannah. There I had access to many of Lee's own letters to Jack Mackay and Eliza Anne Mackay Stiles and to as much of the extensive Central of Georgia Railroad Collection as had been indexed as I worked. Along with Barbara Bennett, to whom this book is dedicated, I am grateful to Karen Osvald, Anne Smith, Tracy Bearden, Randy Rippey and at the very end of my research on *Before the Darkness Falls,* Dr. Lewis Bellardo, now director of the Society, and Stuart Bogue. Also in the Society's vast collections, I had access on microfilm to a diary kept by Eliza Anne Stiles during her husband's diplomatic service in Vienna. It was from this diary that I learned of her intimate friendship with the Baroness Ottilie von Goethe and of the complexity of the Austrian Revolution.

During the writing of *Savannah,* the first in the Savannah Quartet of novels, I was blessed to have found Bobby Bennett willing, in the midst of a busy schedule, to sign on with me as my principal researcher. Her expertise, her knowledge of the huge Society collections and her loyalty to me have, through the years, transformed a highly satisfactory working relationship into a deep friendship which I not only cherish but mean never to lose. The very least I could do to show a small part of my gratitude, Bobby, was to dedicate *Before the Darkness Falls* to you. With your keen intellect, creative imagination and delicious humor, you not only keep me on track in the highly complicated research, you keep me encouraged and delighted with our every contact. You already know I thank you and that I love you.

To See Your Face Again, the second novel in the Savannah Quartet, was dedicated to Marion Hemperley, deputy surveyor general of the state of Georgia, who not only made possible the material for the upcountry sequences in *To See Your Face Again* but stayed with me through this one as well. Marion and his lovely wife, Martha, are also now my real friends.

The truth is that many among my really interesting friends have come to me as a result of historical research. Certainly Fred and Sara Bentley of Kennesaw, Georgia, are high on my list. They not only help me with research but know exactly how to spark me—to keep me going. Fred swears that his Sara is "exactly like" my character Natalie. Sara has the kind of humor that allows her to enjoy the whole idea that I no longer call her Sara. Together, "Natalie" and Fred Bentley climbed around the ruins of Etowah Cliffs taking photographs and even sent a Savannah gray brick from its foundation which I keep right beside my desk. Fred also drew floor plans of the old house, which he'd studied in detail years ago before it burned. Needless to say, I made daily use of the pictures and of Fred's drawings and will go on doing so in the next novel. Fred and "Natalie," you are both deep in my heart.

Through my longtime research helpers, and kindred spirits, Scott and Frances Smith of Old Fort Jackson in Savannah, I met the gentleman who came to be central to me in the difficult task of attempting to untangle the complex national history of the 1840s. His name is Dr. Perry Cochran, history professor at Georgia Southern College in Statesboro. To Perry, the men on the political scene in my period are still alive! He is not only politically compatible with me today, he knows how to reach me with the humanity of the gentlemen who, until I met Perry and his brainy, attractive wife, Linda, were rather trapped in the pages of dusty history books. I thank them both from my heart. Perry and Linda, we are far from finished!

Hugh Golson of Savannah, history teacher and descendant of the Stiles family, along with Elizabeth Layton of De Land, Florida, both continue to contribute far more than either realizes to the books I write about their interesting ancestors. Without the warm interest of both Hugh and Elizabeth, I might not have dared expand what began as two novels to four, freely using their distinguished, but very human ancestors' own lives. And now, but in time for novel number four in the quartet, into my life flew a delightful letter from another direct descendant, Élise Stiles Heald of Kirkwood, Missouri. Not only does she like what I am doing with the novels but she also promised that, as had her sister, Elizabeth Layton, she would gladly send pictures of her pieces of the treasured Stiles furniture which once stood in the Etowah Cliffs house. I wish I thought I were writer enough to do justice to the Stiles and Mackay families, because judging by their descendants, they were a discerning, tasteful, fascinating and very human clan. In a singular way, the enthusiasm of the descendants has unique meaning to this novelist. I wouldn't have experienced the pleasure of Élise Heald's surprise letter had I not already known and loved Mr. and Mrs. Frederick Knight III (Fred and Julia) of Malbone and his parents, Mr. and Mrs. Frederick Knight II of Cartersville, Georgia. My deep and lasting gratitude to all the Knights, not only for their charm and warmth one December night at dinner in the old Malbone dining room, but for their ongoing enthusiasm for what I try to do with the story of their remarkable family. I hope they all know that I mean every ancestor only well and fully appreciate their trust in me. Since the Stiles, Mackay and Gordon families are so interrelated, I feel this is the place to thank Stephen Bohlin-Davis of the Juliette Gordon Low Birthplace on Bull Street in Savannah. I've yet to meet him, but because Stephen and the entire staff have become dear to my closest friend, Joyce Blackburn, as she works on her biography of Juliette Gordon Low, it seems almost foolish that we haven't met. Via Joyce, Stephen has helped me immeasurably with visualizing the 1840s interior of the Gordon house.

To each warmhearted, interested person who stood in line so long at the excellent Public Library in Cartersville, Georgia, when *To See Your Face Again* was first published, my everlasting thanks. I remind all of you—Lee Howington, director of the library, each student who took part in a TV show with me, the officials of the local government and the Art Center who honored me, and every single area reader—that more than ever we still belong to one another. In a very real sense, although I live on the Georgia coast, I'm also an upcountry woman. My thanks to my special Cartersville friends, Elizabeth Clark, Marjorie Jolley, Robert E. White and a bright young man named Jeff Abernathy of Adairsville, who is refreshingly involved with the history of the Stileses' friends the Godfrey Barnsleys. I must also show continuing gratitude to Frances Adair, whose fascinating book, *A Little Leaven* (her gift to me), taught me many upcountry customs, including the way Natalie made soap.

Once again, I'm indebted to Dr. Linda McCurdy of Chapel Hill, North Carolina, for her superb work with the University of North Carolina's vast Stiles Collection. Thanks to Linda, the Washington letter to her Savannah family from Eliza Anne in which she recounted the mix-up when President Tyler's daughter-in-law visited her, is mainly in Eliza Anne's own words. Linda also found a letter from Eliza Mackay clearly showing her views against the spread of slavery. I am indebted as well to Brenda Williams of Augusta, Georgia, for her excellent chronology of happenings in nineteenth-century Savannah, which I'm still using. I remain grateful, as always, to my beloved friend, Savannah's "famous" historian, Lilla M. Hawes; and to the late Dr. Richard Harwell for his doctoral thesis on W. H. Stiles. At the Brunswick Library across the marshes and salt creeks from the island where I live, Marcia Hodges and Anna Yando, along with Jim Darby, director, were again on hand to find the answer to my every question.

Two of my closest island friends, Sarah Plemmons and Frances Burns, made a special research trip for me to Ellijay, Georgia, where Sarah's magnificent mother, Lorah Plemmons, once lived. In fact, in 1919, when Sarah and her twin sister, Mary, were three, Anna Gould Dodge of St. Simons Island made the then difficult trip to Ellijay to bring the widowed Lorah and her girls to the coast. As housekeeper and true mother to the children at the Dodge Home, Lorah remained until the Home closed in the late 1950s. Anyone who knows me knows how dearly I loved and admired Lorah Plemmons, who died a few years ago at the age of nearly 102. In 1961, when we first found St. Simons Island, my friend Joyce Blackburn and I met Lorah, then in her late eighties—out in the garage behind her little house at Frederica—trapped behind some heavy lime sacks from which she intended to "lime her flowers." We found her alone and trapped *and* laughing at herself until the tears rolled down her cheeks! From that moment until we buried her in Christ Churchyard in 1977, Joyce and Lorah and I shared a friendship so steady, so deep, so filled with fun and laughter and (her) wisdom, that we have never stopped missing her. For many years I've wanted to write her into a novel, and although I fictionalized her early life in these pages and although she wasn't born until just after the Civil War, she was an upcountry lady from Ellijay and this book seemed the right place to do it. I wish I thought I had wholly captured her. I doubt that anyone could. Her mind was too facile, too bright, too wise, and her spirit too many-faceted for captivity. My loving gratitude to Mary and Sarah Plemmons for wanting me to write about their mother and for trusting me to try. My thanks also to Ruth M. Hamrick for so freely helping Sarah Plemmons and Frances Burns in Ellijay at the Gilmer County Library. Of course, I thank Sarah and Frances too.

Except for a few stiff muscles at the end of a long day's work, I don't feel seventy, but I am. Yet I can honestly say that I have liked *no other* period in my life half as much as now. For me, everything has changed for the better because Eileen Humphlett, who had expertly handled typescript for *Margaret's Story* and the first two novels in the Savannah Quartet, now works full-time for Joyce and me. No longer do I have to return (or answer) all telephone calls or mail; no longer do I handle (or mishandle) my business. I am, for the first time in my long writing life, at the conclusion of a big novel—not tired. Eileen helps me with cheer, skill, common sense, great sensitivity and an enduring sense of humor. She knows me like a book, anticipates both my needs and my eccentricities. Having never done any historical research, she flew to Washington, D.C., and returned with exactly the kind of material I needed for the sequence when Eliza Anne and W. H. Stiles lived in what was then called Washington City. Joyce and I call Eileen our Overqualified Keeper and she has humor and perception enough to know that we both do indeed need a Keeper. More than that, she comes replete with three delightful offspring, Beth, Jay and Mark, and her handsome husband, Jimmy (Dr. James Humphlett), who helped with the Washington, D.C., research. I am curbing myself when I settle for saying from my heart—thank you, Eileen— mostly for being as you are. For helping Eileen so graciously in her Washington research, we both thank Larry Baume, curator, and Josephine Wyman of the Columbia Historical Society and, at the Library of Congress, Virginia Wood and Sandra Lawson. Through them, we were also helped by D.C. archivist Dorothy Provine.

Happily for me, as with *Savannah* and *To See Your Face Again,* Carolyn Blakemore, senior editor at Doubleday & Company, is my editor for this book. Carolyn has been my friend for far longer than we've worked together professionally. I so wholly respect her talent and expertise in my behalf, I can only hope that we can remain author and editor as long as I know we will remain friends. Carolyn has also given Eileen and me the high-caliber friendship and help of her talented assistant, Howard Kaplan. Thank you, Howard, for so much, and my thanks also to my careful copy editor, Jack Lynch, to art director Alex Gotfryd, book designer Beverley Gallegos, jacket artist Stanislaw Fernandes and everyone at Doubleday who worked through the long and complex process of making this book. I only know my southeastern sales representative, Ed Waters of Atlanta, personally, but if the other Doubleday reps are anything like Ed, I am indeed fortunate. By the way, one of Ed's main attractions to this author is his delightful wife, Ruthie, who, although a Little, Brown sales representative herself, has hauled around more than her share of Price novels and manages, during the busiest autographing parties, to keep both Ed and me—and my readers—in line.

To my hardworking agent, Lila Karpf of New York, with whom I share so much of meaning and who does so much for my self-esteem, once more, my heart-deep thanks. Lila is one of God's choice gifts to me. I wouldn't have Lila were it not for my longtime and much loved friend Faith Brunson, buyer for Rich's superb book sections. For more than twenty years, Faith and I have stuck together through whatever happens to be annoying or delighting us. I can always count on her knowledgeable advice and loyalty, without which I'd be lost. Faith, for many reasons known only to you, thank you.

To my close, close friends Nancy and Mary Jane Goshorn of my hometown, Charleston, West Virginia—know my heart and never forget how much I treasure you both—not only for all the love-motivated work you do for me on my cumbersome announcement list and for the love you showed my late mother, but for what you are within yourselves. The truth might as well come out: Though we live almost a thousand miles apart, Nance still does most of my clothes shopping! And successfully, because we share many of the same eccentricities.

More than one Eugenia worked on *Before the Darkness Falls.* Eileen's bright and delightful sister, Eugenia Hunter of Marietta, Georgia, not only did a marvelous job of proofreading as the writing progressed; she liked the book, which helped keep the other Eugenia going. Thanks, Jeanie Hunter. There are countless others—supportive, important in their separate ways—where my writing is concerned. My friend and sister-in-law, Mildred Price of Nashville, Tennessee, her daughter, my niece, Cindy Price Birdsong, of Memphis, who had the good taste to marry Mike Birdsong, a part Cherokee Indian jewel, so that she could have that beautiful last name—and their bewitching little brave, Michael Andrew. There is my best critic and real friend, Frances Pitts of Duluth, Minnesota; enthusiasts Mary Wheeler and Genon Neblett of Nashville, Tennessee; my junior high school Latin teacher, Ethel Jones of Henderson, North Carolina; my high school Spanish teacher, Mary Ann Hark of Rome, Georgia; and the patient soul who tried to teach me arithmetic, Helen Blackwood of my home state of West Virginia. There is also my forever friend, Easter Straker of Lima, Ohio, to whom I dedicated *Savannah*, and her pal, Mary Porter, now also mine; my beloved friend, Reba Spann of Sumter, South Carolina; spirited Mary Harty of Savannah; and generous and fun Jimmie Harnsberger of Macon, Georgia. Close at hand on St. Simons Island is my bright encourager, Gene Greneker, whose interest means more than she suspects. There is my essential friend, Sarah Bell Edmond; also Ruby Wilson, Emma Gibson, Freddie Wright, Ann Parker and, slowing my aging process by handling my often wild finances, there is beautiful Gwen Davis.

By now, I've run out of adequate ways to communicate what my dearest friend, Joyce Blackburn, means to me, what she does for me, how she stimulates and comforts me. From the start of our rare friendship, many years before things worked out so we could share a home, she has kept me believing in myself. Joyce has watched me more closely than anyone on earth from age thirty-three to seventy. Her intellect and taste are so superior, I marvel that she seems not to have tired of the watching. As always, she went through *Before the Darkness Falls* line by line, finding overused words, better words, writing notes in the margins of many drafts that both encouraged me and brought me up short. Once more, she has done all this, and once more, words grow stubborn when I try to thank her. Again, I've done it inadequately, but as usual, she will ride out this inadequacy too.

My eternal thanks go to my readers who bother to let me know that they go on, when the novels are ended, still thinking of the people I write about, and that they are "waiting impatiently for the next novel" in the Savannah Quartet. After a short rest, so am I. Each person I've thanked here has given me some special gift. None means more than the enduring loyalty of my readers.

Eugenia Price
St. Simons Island, November 1986

CHRISTIAN HERALD
People Making A Difference

Christian Herald is a family of dedicated, Christ-centered ministries that reaches out to deprived children in need, and to homeless men who are lost in alcoholism and drug addiction. Christian Herald also offers the finest in family and evangelical literature through its book clubs and publishes a popular, dynamic magazine for today's Christians.

Our Ministries

Family Bookshelf and **Christian Bookshelf** provide a wide selection of inspirational reading and Christian literature written by best-selling authors. All books are recommended by an Advisory Board of distinguished writers and editors.

Christian Herald magazine is contemporary, a dynamic publication that addresses the vital concerns of today's Christian. Each monthly issue contains a sharing of true personal stories written by people who have found in Christ the strength to make a difference in the world around them.

Christian Herald Children. The door of God's grace opens wide to give impoverished youngsters a breath of fresh air, away from the evils of the streets. Every summer, hundreds of youngsters are welcomed at the Christian Herald Mont Lawn Camp located in the Poconos at Bushkill, Pennsylvania. Year-round assistance is also provided, including teen programs, tutoring in reading and writing, family counseling, career guidance and college scholarship programs.

The Bowery Mission. Located in New York City, the Bowery Mission offers hope and Gospel strength to the downtrodden and homeless. Here, the men of Skid Row are fed, clothed, ministered to. Many voluntarily enter a 6-month discipleship program of spiritual guidance, nutrition therapy and Bible study.

Our Father's House. Located in rural Pennsylvania, Our Father's House is a discipleship and job training center. Alcoholics and drug addicts are given an opportunity to recover, away from the temptations of city streets.

Christian Herald ministries, founded in 1878, are supported by the voluntary contributions of individuals and by legacies and bequests. Contributions are tax deductible. Checks should be made out to Christian Herald Children, The Bowery Mission, or to Christian Herald Association.

Administrative Office: 40 Overlook Drive, Chappaqua, New York 10514
Telephone: (914) 769-9000

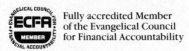 Fully accredited Member of the Evangelical Council for Financial Accountability